To Hemlock Run

James Boyle

Scribe Memnon Press

ISBN 10: 0692830235
ISBN 13: 978-0692830239

One

The green and white highway sign said they were eight miles from Bosque, thirty-seven from Genoa, and a hundred-forty from Aberdeen.

They were almost there.

“This really is the middle of nowhere,” Lisa murmured, peering out the passenger window. “Isn’t it?”

“Pretty much.”

They had climbed out of the Puget Sound Basin about an hour ago and were now driving through the heavily-forested southern foothills of the Olympic Mountains. Gone were the shopping malls, the housing developments, and the maddening traffic. Now they followed a narrow two-lane highway as it wound between dark masses of cedar and hemlock that threatened to swallow the patched asphalt. Even the occasional farm or ranch house seemed to be slowly losing its fight with the forest.

There was hardly any traffic. Most travelers to the coast took Hwy 12 farther south.

"You sure you want to do this?" Jason asked.

"We've already talked about this."

Something appeared ahead on the side of the road. Jason slowed, eased left to go around the body of a doe lying halfway into the right lane.

Someone had tied a Mylar balloon to one of its feet. It read "Get Well Soon!"

♦

Bosque, like many small towns in the timber lands of western Washington, was dying. It was slowly and steadily starving to death as its young people moved to the cities to find work and stayed there and their parents and grandparents grew old and died. There had been a time when Bosque's businesses thrived, when traffic flowed thick on Main Street, but now only some of its older residents remembered those days. They had ended with the demise of the timber industry in the early 1980's.

A carved wooden sign at the city limits called it "Gateway to The Olympics" in faded, peeling paint. Behind it, like a single tombstone, an old rusted wigwam burner was all that remained of an abandoned mill.

Jason slowed down to the posted speed limit and eased into town. He didn't think a speed limit was even necessary. There wasn't any traffic to speak of.

They passed through an area of mixed residential homes, some older, slightly worn frame houses, along with a few newer manufactured homes. The lots all seemed to be large. Chain-link fence was a common motif.

The business district was just sad. Three blocks of crumbling, red-brick buildings faced each other over the street, like monuments of a lost civilization. Nearly half the windows were soaped up, old signs fading away in the elements. Jason saw one for "Bosque Antiques," another simply "Quiltshop."

Weeds grew tall along the edges of vacant buildings.

"Nice place," Lisa said, mostly to herself.

Jason couldn't think of a worthwhile response.

A few businesses had hung on. They passed a small bank, a co-op grocery, a hardware store, and a saw shop. None seemed terribly busy for a Saturday afternoon.

A tavern called *The Bent Nickel* had a handful of cars parked in front and a neon *Bud* sign burning bright red in a dark window.

Midway down the next block a sign hung over the sidewalk on their left: *City Center Café.*

"There it is," Lisa said.

"Good thing, too. We were about to run out of town."

Lisa smiled.

Jason pulled a U-turn at the next intersection and parked at the curb in front of the café. A late model Camry was parked in front of them. Beyond that, was a battered blue Ford F150.

They were the only cars parked on the block.

"Check out the window," Lisa said.

One of the café's two bay windows had been replaced with a sheet of plywood. The patch wasn't brand new, but hadn't been there long enough to weather. It was a week old, maybe two.

"Coincidence?" she asked.

He shrugged. It was possible, he supposed.

"How do you want to play this?" he asked as he shut the engine off.

Lisa frowned at him. "What do you mean?"

"What if she isn't okay? What happens if something is very wrong?"

"Then we try to help her."

"If we can."

She nodded.

"Well, let's do it then," Jason said and climbed out of the car.

Jason walked around to meet Lisa on the sidewalk in front of the café. It was pleasantly warm in the sunshine, a slight breeze stirring the air. The Olympic Mountains loomed ghostly blue over the buildings across the street.

Jason held the door for Lisa, followed her into the café.

His first impression was surprise. For a town so obviously in decline, the interior was remarkably clean and modern. Booths upholstered in denim and blond wood lined the walls to either side, with framed historic photos spaced above. At the far end, he could see a stainless steel pass-through into the kitchen.

The air smelled of fried onions and bacon. Country music played softly in the background.

It was the middle of the afternoon, after lunch, but before dinner. Only two tables in the restaurant were occupied. A man in jeans and work boots read a paper at the table to the left of the door, under the remaining bay window. An elderly couple shared a slice of pie in a booth against the wall to the right.

"Hi." A dark-haired young woman in jeans and tee shirt slid out of the booth nearest the kitchen. "Pick a place. Like some coffee?"

"Sure," Jason said.

Helen clearly hadn't recognized them. After all, they were probably the last people she'd expected to see today.

Neither he nor Lisa moved toward a booth. Lisa wouldn't take her eyes off the young woman as she gathered menus, cups and a pot of coffee. Jason had only met Helen a few times, but this was clearly her. She was the same slender young woman with long, dark hair, who'd come over to Lisa's for coffee or help on a paper.

He'd always thought she looked like a soccer player.

The man to their left noisily folded his newspaper.

Helen turned back to them. "Anyplace is fine—."

The look on her face was the nearest thing to terror Jason had ever seen.

"Hi, Helen," Lisa said.

"What are you doing here?"

Jason shrugged, smiled. "Road trip."

"Yeah," Lisa agreed. "I wanted to see how you were."

"I'm okay," Helen said. Her eyes darted to the man with the newspaper, then back. "Please, sit down."

She directed them toward one of the booths closest to the kitchen—and farthest from the other customers—and urged them again to sit down. They did. It seemed important to her. Lisa took the side facing the kitchen; Jason slid in facing the door. The man with the newspaper was talking into a cell phone now.

Helen poured each of them a cup of coffee.

"It's sweet of you to worry about me, but really I'm fine. I just need to help my parents for a while. I'll probably be back next semester."

"It was so sudden," Lisa said.

"It was a quick decision." Again, she glanced toward the man with the newspaper.

Jason did too. The man had put away his cell and again seemed intent on his newspaper.

"Friend of yours?" Jason asked.

Helen made a face. "I'd better warm up some coffees. Be right back."

She left, tending to the elderly pie-eaters first.

"Something's wrong," Lisa whispered to Jason.

Jason nodded and made a show of picking up and examining his menu. Yeah, something was definitely wrong in Helen's world, unless she was normally terrified at the sight of visiting friends. He watched now as she exchanged a few words with the newspaper guy as she filled his coffee.

Her body language was—strained.

"What do we do?" Lisa asked.

He didn't know. They could hardly help someone who didn't want their help. Or was too afraid to ask for it.

A few moments later, Helen returned to their table, sliding a ticket book out of her apron. "Decide on something? Mom makes the best burgers in town."

Jason refrained from pointing out that they were probably the only burgers in town.

"We'd like to split a club sandwich," Lisa told her.

Helen jotted this down.

Jason turned to glance back at the kitchen. He couldn't see anyone beyond the narrow pass-through window. "Your folks do all the cooking?"

Helen all but winced. "Dad did until he broke his arm. It's why I needed to come back. Mom needed help until he can cook again."

"What happened to your dad?" Lisa asked. "Is he okay?"

"Yeah, but he's—"

The street door opened and a man in the tan and brown uniform of a sheriff's deputy stepped into the café and slid his sunglasses off. He was tall and built like a pro linebacker, with a powerful chest and biceps that strained the short sleeves of his uniform shirt.

Helen's eyes dropped to her ticket book. "I'll get Mom working on this."

Without looking at the deputy, she turned, walked over to the pass-through and hung the ticket on the cook's wheel. "Order up!"

The deputy didn't seem to notice. He exchanged a few words with the newspaper guy as he passed, then the pie-eating couple, who looked up at him with smiles. The friendly neighborhood cop.

He nodded at Jason too as he slid into the booth across from them. He wasn't smiling. "Passing through?"

Jason smiled. "What gave us away?"

"Don't get many strangers in these parts. Not this time of year."

Jason sipped his coffee. There didn't seem to be anything to say in reply to that. Lisa was pointedly staring straight ahead.

Helen brought a cup to the deputy and poured him some coffee. She was so tense, Jason thought she'd pull a muscle. The deputy said something but was too quiet to hear.

"It's nothing," Helen told him. "I promise."

He grabbed her arm at the wrist. Helen tried to pull her arm away, but there wasn't much of an effort there, not that she'd be able to overpower him anyway. He outweighed her by probably a hundred pounds, all of it muscle. Again, he said something to her too quietly to be heard, but the tone made the hair on Jason's neck stand on end.

Lisa looked at Jason like she thought he should be doing something.

Like what, Jason wondered, challenge him to a duel?

Stoneware clattered in the pass-through and a bell pierced the air.

Helen pulled away from the deputy, avoided Jason and Lisa's gaze altogether, and hurried to pick up the sandwich. She set the platter down between them, along with a caddy of ketchup and mustard. The scent of hot French fries welled up between them.

"Can I get you anything else?"

Jason shook his head. "I think we're good."

Lisa was going to say something, but the pleading expression on Helen's face stopped her. Instead, she just shook her head.

♦

They ate their sandwich in silence. There wasn't a lot to say, particularly with Deputy Friendly sitting in the next booth, lingering over his coffee. Helen busied herself, wiping off counters, filling backups, and tending to her customers' coffee cups. Occasionally, she'd exchange a few quiet words through the pass-through with the woman cooking—her mother.

There was no sign of her father.

"It doesn't feel right," Lisa whispered to Jason. "Leaving her like this." Her eyes flicked sideways toward the deputy.

Jason knew what she meant. But what could they do?

As they were about halfway through the sandwich, the elderly couple finished their pie and tottered over to the cash register. Helen met them there. She took their money, chatted a little, and then held the door for them as they left.

"What brings you to Bosque?" the deputy asked Jason. "It's not exactly a tourist hotspot."

"Just exploring," Jason smiled. "We like to see the real country, not just the tourist one."

"Well, it's real here, that's for sure. It can get very real here."

Jason and Lisa exchanged a look. What did that mean?

"You ought to go over to Genoa though. That's the next town south of here. It's got the County museum and a real nice boardwalk down by the marina. There ain't much to see around here."

"Thanks," Jason said. "We'll probably do that."

Lisa was mesmerized by the process of dipping a French fry into a pool of ketchup.

♦

Nothing more was said until the sandwich was reduced to crumbs and they were getting ready to go.

"Let me get it," Lisa told Jason as she dug her wallet out of her purse. She spoke quietly enough to not be overheard. "It will give me a chance to talk to her."

"What are you going to say?"

"I don't know," she said. "'Call me. Let me help.' Something like that."

He nodded.

Across the way, the deputy had spread some paperwork across his table. He seemed to be ignoring them. But he hadn't left.

An idea struck her. Jason clearly saw it move across her face.

"Do you have any business cards on you?"

Silly question. He was a reporter; he always carried business cards. She knew that.

"Sure."

"Give me one."

Jason did and watched Lisa scribble a short note on the back, along with her cell number. She then slipped the card between a ten and five dollar bill and set them on the lunch ticket. The sandwich and drinks came to just over twelve dollars. Helen would have to see the card when she made change.

"Nice," Jason told her.

Lisa smiled.

When Helen met them at the cash register, Lisa merely handed her the entire package. "The change is for you."

Helen paused, barely met their eyes. "You don't have to do that."

"Just don't share it with anyone else," Lisa told her.

Jason smiled and followed Lisa out the door.

♦

The nearest decent motels were in Genoa, the next town south on Highway 101. Genoa was larger than Bosque—at least twice as large—and seemed to have weathered the changing economy better than its neighbor. The fact that it was the county seat and home to the courthouse and sheriff's department probably helped.

There were actually more than two motels in Genoa, as well as a handful of competing restaurants, one a dinner house advertising "Steaks!" and several gas stations. They rented a room at a little place just off the highway on the south side of town called the Twilight Inn. It was clean and quiet and that was about it.

But it was a place to rest and wait.

"Do you think she'll call?" Jason asked once they were settled in their motel room. He was stretched out on the motel's queen-sized bed trying to find something worth watching on the television. Lisa sat cross-legged at the small table beside the bed, her shoes kicked off on the floor below her, her cell phone within easy reach on the table.

"I hope so."

"I don't think there's much we can do, if she doesn't."

Lisa didn't bother to respond. She knew the situation as well as he did. It had been Lisa who had been the driving force behind this road trip. Lisa, who had been absolutely positive something had been seriously wrong when Helen abruptly withdrew from the university and moved out of her apartment next door to Lisa's.

"Kids withdraw from school all the time," Jason pointed out. "What makes you think this is different?"

She shook her head. "I don't know, Jason. Helen makes it different."

He waited.

"You don't know her that well," Lisa finally told him.

That was true. For most of the previous year, he and Lisa hadn't been spending much time together. They were "cooling off." In other words, a couple of near-death experiences in the San Juan Islands had forced Lisa to take a hard look at what she wanted from her love life.

The result was a weird hybrid. Neither was involved with anyone else, but they weren't boyfriend/girlfriend either. They were very, very, good friends who sometimes had sex with each other.

"You should have seen her, Jason," Lisa said. "You know she was in my History 111 section this term?"

Jason knew that. It was one of the reasons Lisa and Helen had become such good friends so fast. Helen hadn't known anyone in Seattle when she'd moved into the apartment next to Lisa in August. Neighborly small talk had quickly revealed that Helen was majoring in history, which was also Lisa's field. Then, once classes began, it turned out Helen was taking a class in which Lisa led the discussion group.

The rest, as they say, was history.

"She aced everything I threw at her, loved it, and wanted more. She was amazing. Most freshmen are either too lazy or too overwhelmed with what work they already have. She was different."

Jason had found a college football game on television. He watched Stanford complete a short pass against Colorado with the sound off. Stanford was leading by fourteen points.

"It was like she was—"

"Blooming."

"Yeah," Lisa smiled, but sadly, like at a wake. "She was blooming. That's why it was so strange when she suddenly dropped out."

"And wouldn't return your calls."

She shook her head.

Even stranger—and this was what had piqued Jason's curiosity—when she moved out of her apartment, it had been a group of young men packing the U-Haul. Helen and her parents had been nowhere to be seen. Why hadn't she helped move her own things, her private stuff?

So now they sat in a Genoa motel room, waiting for the phone to ring.

"It has to have something to do with that cop," Lisa said. "Was he creepy, or what?"

Jason agreed the deputy was creepy, in an abusive husband/town bully way. And it was quite a coincidence that he should show up right after they'd arrive. It was almost like someone had been watching and intervened to keep Helen from talking to them.

The next question would be why?

♦

They waited for the phone to ring.

And they waited.

They watched Stanford win the football game on the room's television, two full episodes of *Law and Order*, then switched to the improbable end of an even more improbable action movie that had something blowing up every sixty seconds while men shot up a major American city. In real life, Jason thought, any city subject to that level of violence would have the National Guard patrolling the streets within hours.

But it passed the time.

When the producers finally ran out of blanks and the movie ended, Jason sat up on the edge of the bed and faced Lisa. "You hungry?"

Outside, daylight was rapidly fading below the hills, growing deep shadows among the trees and in the corners of the motel room. Some of those shadows had crept onto Lisa's face to fight the reflected glow of the television.

"She isn't going to call, is she?" Lisa said.

"I don't know." He didn't. He didn't know much about this situation at all, other than that Helen seemed to be afraid of something. That something could be the deputy. It could be something else. He just didn't know. "Maybe she can't safely call until the restaurant's closed. Maybe she needs to wait until she gets home."

Lisa nodded, but didn't look encouraged.

"Come on; let's find some place to eat. Bring your cell. We won't do her any good by starving."

Lisa checked her cell phone's screen one more time before grabbing her purse.

♦

They found a restaurant within a few blocks of the motel that seemed to be doing a decent business among the locals, even at the tail end of the dinner hour. *Darcy's* was almost twice the size of Helen's family's café and kind of a generic American diner. The booths were of blue vinyl and wood-grained Formica. The walls held mediocre prints of wildlife and the floor was an industrial carpet of an odd orange color that reminded Jason of a government office. Jason half-expected the waitresses to be wearing polyester dresses with white aprons, but the two women taking orders wore blue jeans and tee shirts with *Darcy's* written across the bust.

"Hi," the younger of the waitresses approached them, grabbing two menus from the rack behind the register. She looked young enough to still be in high school. "Two tonight?"

Jason agreed.

She asked them to follow her.

Jason let Lisa step ahead and then followed them both across the restaurant to an empty booth where the waitress set their menus. As he walked, he was aware that many conversations had paused as they came into view. Curious eyes followed them. Jason made eye contact with one man in his early sixties. Jason smiled and nodded greetings. The man returned his nod, but didn't smile.

Lisa slid into the booth and set her cell phone on the table just to her right. Jason sat opposite her.

"Something to drink to start with?" the waitress asked.

Both elected to have water.

The waitress—her name was Callie—left them to look over the menu.

"Nice place," Lisa said without looking up from her menu.

"Noticed that, huh? You'd think they didn't get many visitors around here."

Lisa smiled.

They quickly decided to play it safe and order cheeseburgers. Unless the cook was a complete imbecile, he could make a serviceable cheeseburger. And if the cheeseburger wasn't anything to write home about, odds were that anything more complicated would be disastrous.

When the waitress returned, they told her what they'd decided. Lisa stuck with fries as her side, but Jason decided to take a chance on the potato salad.

"Good choice," Callie said as she gathered their menus. "It's kind of our specialty."

"Their specialty is potato salad?" Lisa asked when they were alone again.

He shrugged. "That's what she said."

"Did you know that potato salad is believed responsible for something like half of all cases of food poisoning?"

"It's probably because it wasn't kept cold enough."

Lisa nodded. "It's the eggs."

"Of course."

"You'll probably die tonight."

"Probably," he admitted. "You'd look great in black, you know."

"Would I? Thank you."

Lisa picked up her cell phone and looked at the screen.

"Battery dead?" he asked.

"The battery's fine." She set the phone down again.

"If this is domestic abuse and she's not ready and willing to leave him, he could take any interference from us out on her. You know how it works."

She shrugged. "And if she never calls?"

"You can't help someone who doesn't want the help."

♦

Their burgers came and weren't bad at all. They were actually juicy, and flavorful, with real lettuce, tomatoes, and crisp onions. Even the potato salad was pretty good.

Jason paid for their meals. The remaining restaurant patrons paid them no attention.

Helen still hadn't called. It was almost 9:00 now. It was looking less and less like they were going to hear from her.

Jason let a very quiet Lisa into the passenger seat of the car and walked around toward the driver's door. As he stepped out into the street, he noticed a police car parked at the curb about a block down the street behind them. It was probably a coincidence, but the hair stood on the back of his neck.

He didn't believe in coincidence.

Jason climbed behind the wheel and started the engine. Should he tell Lisa about the cop? He decided against it. She was already upset and it was probably nothing anyway.

Jason switched on the headlights and pulled away from the curb.

Another car pulled out into the road behind him.

Jason was getting a bad feeling about this.

The car pulled up closer behind them. Now Jason could clearly see the light bar on the roof. The emergency lights weren't flashing, but they were there.

"Don't look now," he told Lisa. "But I think we're about to be pulled over."

"What? Why?"

"I don't know."

The car behind them still hadn't initiated a stop. He was probably checking the license plates for warrants. It would come up empty, but was standard procedure and took some time. Cops liked to have some idea who they would be dealing with before actual contact.

"What can we do?" Lisa asked.

"Nothing." Certainly nothing sudden, or easily misinterpreted.

He continued toward the motel, driving just a hair under the speed limit. There was no other traffic.

They were a block from the motel when the flashing lights lit up the night behind them.

"Shit. Here we go," Jason said and pulled over to the curb. He shut his engine off, set his hands on the steering wheel, and waited.

The police car swung over to the curb behind them.

"Jason?" Lisa's voice was strained, tight.

"Relax. We haven't done anything."

An officer stepped up to Jason's window and showed his flash over them. "License, registration, and proof of insurance?"

Jason removed his driver's license from his wallet and the registration and insurance cards from their spot above his visor and handed them to the officer.

The cop spent a full minute examining the documents. He appeared to be a city cop, judging by his navy blue uniform, not a sheriff's deputy like the guy harassing Helen.

That was something.

He turned the flashlight on Jason and Lisa again. "What are you folks up to tonight?"

"We just had dinner," Jason told him, blinking into the brightness of the flashlight. "We're heading back to the motel now."

He pointed toward the motel building, less than a block down the road.

"You didn't go anywhere else?"

"No, sir."

"I pulled you over because a car matching your description was spotted tonight at a known narcotics location."

In Genoa? Genoa, Washington? The cop made it sound like someone was moving pounds of heroin and cocaine, like it was Miami, or something.

"The restaurant and the motel are the only places we've been," he said.

"It's a mistake," Lisa added. "It must be someone else."

The cop asked for Lisa's identification. She removed it from her purse and handed it to him.

"Anybody have any narcotics on them?"

"No, sir."

"Anything in the car?"

"Nothing."

He peered at them for another minute, while Jason made a mental note of his nameplate: Schmidt. Officer Schmidt.

"Sit tight," Schmidt said and walked back to his car.

"What's going on?" Lisa's asked.

"I don't know."

Maybe it was an honest case of mistaken identity.

Maybe.

A few seconds later, a second squad car pulled in behind the first. The second officer got out and walked up to the lead car. The Officer Schmidt stepped out and the two shook hands. As Jason watched in his side mirror, the two cops talked for a while. They looked like old friends.

With a sinking feeling in his stomach, Jason recognized the second cop as the muscular bully from Helen's restaurant.

So much for an honest mistake.

. "What's he doing?" Lisa whispered.

Jason checked his side mirror. "He's talking to another cop who just got here."

As soon as he said it, the meeting behind them broke up. The deputy walked up to Jason's window and handed him their identification. He made no attempt to hide his identity as he leaned over to look through the window at them. "You're free to go, Mr. Reynolds. Miss Martin. This was obviously a case of mistaken identity."

Jason handed the documents to Lisa to stow in her purse.

The deputy--his nameplate read Wilcox—smiled at him. "Have a good evening. And a safe trip back to Seattle."

Jason said they would.

"Oh, and get that tail light fixed."

"What's wrong with—" He knew before the words even left his mouth.

Lisa jumped as the city cop smashed the driver's side tail light with his baton.

"Be careful," Deputy Wilcox said, "It's a dangerous world out there," and returned to his car.

A second later, the flashing lights shut down and first one, then the other police car pulled away from the curb and roared into the night.

Jason sat in the car for another moment before starting it up.

"What was that all about?" Lisa asked.

"Fair warning." He finally started the car and put it in gear. "He knows who we are and where we live."

Two

The village of Santa Teresa was a haphazard collection of small homes scattered along a sandy slice of the tropical Pacific. A few more substantial buildings of stucco stood a bit inland around a traditional square. A single road, the only real connection to what passed for western civilization, ended in the public square where a well, a Catholic church, and the occasional market were the highlights of village society.

In addition to the Indian fishermen and farmers, there was also a small colony of ex-pats—mostly Americans—who called this village home. It was one of the unwritten rules that no one asked the Americans why they were here. If they wanted to tell you, they would tell you. Otherwise assume it was because of the tropical climate and the warm, clear Pacific.

It was a very small town and not on any tourist itinerary. Everybody knew everyone else by name. Any stranger in town could not help but be noticed.

On an autumn Tuesday, just before midday, the man once known as Taylor Smith pushed open the mosquito screen and stepped into the town's only tavern, just off the central plaza.

The interior of the tavern was about what you'd expect. No expense had been wasted on décor. Bare stucco walls stained by years of tobacco smoke and dust. A packed earth floor. The bar itself and the tables were painted plywood. There was no air conditioning, so every door and window had been propped open to try and catch a breeze. It was still uncomfortably hot.

The only other customer was another ex-pat, named just David, who practically lived here. Just David didn't even look up from his beer.

“Morning, John,” the newcomer greeted the bartender.

“Morning,” John was younger—in his mid-twenties—and looked like a surfer, which was exactly what he was. Santa Teresa was a temporary funding stop in his worldwide search for the perfect wave.

“The usual.”

John already had it poured and set the glass of amber alcohol before his customer. There were no ice cubes. There were never any ice cubes.

“Listen.” John’s voice dropped to a husky whisper. “Two dudes were in here yesterday. Two strangers.”

“Yeah?”

The bartender nodded. “They had a picture of you. Wrong name, but the picture was yours.”

Mr. Smith swallowed some of his scotch. “Anglos?”

“Naw, Salvadoran, but not from around here. They were dressed for the city. Know what I mean? Real sharp.”

He did. “What did you tell them?”

“That I'd never seen you before. Of course.”

Smith thanked the bartender. To show his appreciation, he slipped him an American ten dollar bill.

He downed the rest of his scotch. “They still in town?”

“I don’t know.” The bartender shrugged. “I haven't seen them.”

♦

It had to be one of the cartels, Smith decided. Only the cartels had the finances and will to send two men out to this little village with the sole purpose of finding him. The Federal Police could do it, but there was no extradition with the United States and he had been careful to do nothing to draw their attention.

Besides, the cartels had better intelligence, finances, and man power.

Most cartel members would also kill their own mothers for the $100,000 Joseph Mullens had put on his head a year ago.

Smith crouched behind the trunk of a palm and peered at the little cottage he'd called home for the last few months. It looked dark and deserted, as it should. No one was supposed to be there. He lived alone and he'd spent last night with a female friend in the next village. His modest car remained exactly where he'd parked it, in the narrow space between the cottage's south wall and the beginning of the forest.

He hadn't seen a strange car anywhere, but the killers could have hidden it somewhere.

The cottage was the perfect location to set up an ambush. Sit a couple of men in the darkened house with suppressed .22's and shoot him as soon as he stepped through the door. The neighbors wouldn't hear a thing.

It's how he would do it.

The big question though was what now? Smith was armed. He'd retrieved a 9mm Baretta from the lockbox he'd hidden in the woods. He always had weapons and money in more than one location. It was his standard insurance policy. Just in case.

That wasn't the issue.

The issue was what did he do with the gun? Did he kill the assassins? He didn't doubt he could, but he wasn't sure that was such a good idea. The cartel leadership took a dim view of people killing their soldiers. Retribution was harsh, bloody, and not necessarily confined to the actual offenders. If they could not find him, they'd settle for killing every citizen of the village, just to send a message.

Then, of course, they'd pursue him for the rest of his life. The profit motive would no longer be relevant. It would be a matter of honor. They would probably issue their own contract and the payoff would be as large as Mullen's.

Many, many people would happily kill him for a quarter of a million dollars.

No, as much as he'd enjoy ending his assassins, the best thing to do was disappear again. Move to some new out-of-the-way location and hope no one tracked him down again.

But that was growing tiresome.

Smith turned away from the cottage and went back to his emergency lockbox hidden in the forest. This time, he removed a fairly large sum of cash and a set of identity papers.

He reburied the box, disguised the evidence of his work, and returned to the path leading to his girlfriend's house in the next village.

As he walked through the forest, he found himself thinking that this needed to stop, this having to flee every few months because someone got it in their head to collect the contract on him. He was getting too old to be continuously looking over his shoulder.

Something needed to be done.

Three

The shrill ringtone of Lisa's cell jolted Jason out of a fitful sleep. Before he could even comprehend what was going on, Lisa had leapt from the bed and was fumbling with the phone.

It was 1:13 in the morning.

Jason sat up on the bed. He was still wearing street clothes. So was Lisa. The bedside light was still burning. The television flashed some kind of advertising. The last thing he remembered was convincing Lisa to stretch out beside him and watch a movie. They had just about given up on Helen ever calling, but were too stressed to sleep. Or so he'd thought.

Lisa finally managed to accept the call and put the cell to her ear. "Hello, Helen?"

She listened for a bit. "I'm so glad you called. Let me put you on speaker, so Jason can hear too."

She punched the appropriate button and set the phone on the table. Jason walked over to the window, peeked around the blind into the parking lot, looking for any sign of the local police. There was nothing. Nothing he could see anyway. He dropped the blind and took the second chair beside Lisa.

"Okay," Lisa told Helen. "Tell us what's going on."

"I shouldn't even be calling. If Travis finds out…"

"Travis is the cop that came in to the restaurant?" Jason asked.

"Yeah, Travis Wilcox. He's a deputy sheriff. Look, it was very nice of you to come all the way to check on me, but there's nothing you can do. Really. I'll be okay."

"Helen, we aren't blind." Lisa said. "Anyone could see you're terrified. Is he hurting you?"

"No. No, he's never hurt me."

Something occurred to Jason, a flash of epiphany. "Did he hurt your dad?"

A pause. When her voice returned, it sounded smaller, diminished.

"Please. You're only going to make things worse."

"Helen," Jason told her. "I'm a reporter for the *Seattle News*. A reporter. Shining bright lights on the bad guys is what I do best."

They were answered with silence. Lisa and Jason exchanged a glance.

"Please. Just go home. I'll be okay."

The line went dead.

♦

"I could call her back," Lisa suggested, though her tone of voice suggested even she didn't think it was a good idea.

Jason got up and walked over to the motel room's window and peered out into the parking lot again. Again, he saw nothing out of the ordinary, just like the ten times before.

He had the uncomfortable feeling that they had just walked in on a game already in progress, where they didn't know the players or the rules. The last time he'd felt this way had been in Port Salish almost a year ago. The game then had killed people.

He touched the circular scar between the thumb and forefinger of his right hand. It was a reminder of a bullet wound. Everyone who'd been shot didn't have scars though. Some were dead.

"Someone out there?"

He hadn't heard Lisa come up beside him.

"No," he told her and let the blind fall back into place. "Nothing at all. There isn't even any traffic."

Jason turned back to Lisa. She looked exhausted, her face pale and drawn, dark patches forming beneath her eyes.

"So what now?" she asked.

"Get some sleep. Tomorrow go home."

"So that's it?"

"Nope. We just don't do it from here."

He was already making a mental list of phone calls to make.

♦

Despite his best efforts, Jason could not get back to sleep. His mind refused to let go of the day's events, refused to accept that there was nothing he could do at this time of the morning, so far from all his resources. Lisa didn't seem to have the same problem. She'd fallen asleep within minutes of stretching out on the bed.

He lay there for a few minutes, listening to the steady rhythm of her breathing.

For a moment, he longed for the routine of waking to the comforting warmth of her presence beside him in bed. Until Port Salish, it had been almost a daily occurrence. They had been drifting toward marriage, almost unthinkingly. Then Lundgren's hired guns had made it clear that they would kill all of them. They had nearly succeeded and that had profoundly affected Lisa.

Jason finally eased out of the bed and tiptoed over to the little table in front of the window. He resisted the urge to glance out at the parking lot again. He'd been under surveillance the entire time he'd been in Port Salish and hadn't spotted them once. Why did he think it would be different this time?

Because this felt different. It felt more like an extreme case of bullying than organized crime.

If a bully was watching them, they'd have no problem being visible, being intimidating. That was the point. This was about the exercise of power, not just gathering information.

He looked up at the closed drapes for a few seconds.

"Well, crap," he finally whispered, then eased over to peek around the curtain into the parking lot. Once again, he could see nothing out of the ordinary.

Jason sighed, returned to the little table and fired up his cell. One of the nice things about being a reporter—and they were few and far between these days—was that nearly every tool you needed was an app on your smart phone. He opened one of those applications now and began writing notes: what he knew about Helen's situation, what else he needed to know, and where he could possibly find the information.

A file-sharing program in the cloud would automatically copy the notes onto his laptop and his pc at the newspaper. One of the marvels of modern technology.

He knew, through Lisa, that Helen had been having trouble with a boyfriend, who was controlling and possibly abusive. This boyfriend was a deputy sheriff named Travis Wilcox. Deputy Wilcox, based on his behavior today, certainly seemed the abusive type. The fact that Deputy Wilcox was able to enlist a Genoa city cop in a barely-legal roust last night indicated he also had more power than the average bully, even the average bully cop. He certainly hadn't seemed worried about getting caught, or about any complaints he and Lisa might have lodged with the department.

For some reason, Travis Wilcox seemed to think he was untouchable. Was he untouchable? If so, who was protecting him and why?

They needed to answer that question before they made another move.

♦

Jason woke Lisa just as dawn was lightening the skies above the ridges to the east. They took turns showering and changed into clean clothes, then repacked and loaded their things into Jason's car. It was Sunday morning and the entire world seemed to be holding its breath. Even in the transient world of the motel parking lot, no one was moving. No headlights gleamed on the deserted street.

They stopped just long enough to drop the room key at the office, then got on the highway, headed for home.

They didn't even stop for breakfast until they were out of Dunham County, in a one-room diner in a tiny village called Dexter, just across the Thurston County border.

"It feels like we're sneaking out," Lisa told him over a plate of scrambled eggs and hash browns. "With our tails between our legs."

"I know." Jason nodded and sipped his coffee. Blessed coffee, he could have gone all day without eating, but without coffee? It wasn't going to happen. "But it's the smart thing to do."

"How do you figure?"

He glanced quickly at the diners around them. The place was about half full; it was still relatively early. In a small town, he assumed the big rush would come around midday, when all the church-goers were released from Sunday services.

No one seemed to be paying any attention to them.

"If it looks like we ran scared, Wilcox will think he's won. He'll relax, maybe not punish Helen for involving us."

Lisa shrugged, chewing hash browns.

"You do have to promise me one thing though," he told her.

"What's that?"

"You don't contact Helen. You don't call or text her. You don't message her on social media. No contact at all. Nothing. Promise?"

"Why?"

"If Travis should see anything from you, he could take it out on her. He could see it as disobedience from Helen and punish her."

Her eyes dropped and she nodded. "What if she contacts me?"

"That's different. You just don't initiate anything, okay? It's too dangerous. We don't know the situation."

"So what are you going to do?"

"I'm an investigative reporter," he smiled. "I'm going to investigate."

Lisa smiled.

♦♦♦♦♦

The seventh hole at the Thurston Hills Country Club was a 425 yard par four, with just enough of a dogleg to the right to hide the green behind the thicket of cedar lining the fairway. A slight breeze—barely strong enough to muss hair—moved from their left to right. The warm autumn air smelled of evergreens and fresh-cut grass.

Judge Alan Barton finished his practice swings and set up over his ball in the tee box.

State Senator Morris Barton—the Judge's big brother—stood beside the golf bags, his arms crossed as he watched his brother tee off. Though no one was officially keeping score, he was leading by two strokes after six holes.

Alan swung with a fluid motion and impressive follow-through. The ball arched into the distance before curling slightly to the right at the end and bouncing to a stop on the right edge of the fairway. It lay about thirty yards short of Morris' ball.

"Nice shot," Morris said. It would have been better if it had been more to the left, to get the angle on the green around the dogleg, but he wasn't going to tell his brother that.

"Someday I'm going to fix that slice," Alan said and slid his driver into the golf bag.

"You'll make it up on the green."

The truth was Alan had sliced since he'd first picked up a driver more than forty years ago. If he was going to correct his swing, he would have done so by now.

The two men began walking down the gently sloping fairway toward their balls. Though both were well into their sixties, they'd been blessed with the good health and strong constitutions that seemed to run in the men of their family. Both their father and grandfather had lived long, productive lives. Their grandfather had still been falling trees in his seventies.

"So tell me about this new piece of legislation you're working on," Alan said as they walked.

"I think you'll like it," Morris said. "John Jones and I are going to introduce it in a couple of weeks, if everything goes well. We're calling it the Local Control Restoration Act."

"Interesting title."

Judge Alan Barton, like nearly all Bartons, was a conservative Republican. He had been quick to support Morris' run for sheriff and then state senate, donating funds generously. Though his position as Judge meant he had to appear non-partisan, he had his fingers in many political pies, but behind the scenes.

"If we can push it through and convince the governor to sign it," Morris told his brother. "It will mean Olympia will decide how much logging and mining is done on public lands in Washington State, not D.C. It will be a lifesaver to some of the struggling communities out there."

"Not to mention the lumber and mining companies."

"Of course." Morris smiled. "Jobs, jobs, jobs."

"So how are you going to get a Democratic governor to sign the bill?" he asked. "He's basically a Sierra Club member."

"Leave it to me. I can be very persuasive."

The Judge's eyebrows went up. "The Governor?"

"Why not? He likes to hunt and fish."

"Won't he be expecting a trap?"

Morris looked shocked. "From me?"

The brothers' laughter echoed across the fairways and greens of the golf course.

♦♦♦♦♦

"What do I do if she calls me?" Lisa asked. They were beginning the descent out of the Olympic foothills into the Puget Sound basin. The cities that clustered around the Sound were less than an hour ahead of them. Traffic had grown denser, the roads straighter. Civilization beckoned.

Both of them had visibly relaxed.

"Try to get as much information as you can," he told her. "Take notes, specific notes. What, exactly, is going on? What has Travis done to her? What can we do to help? That sort of thing."

She looked over at him. "I should just have her call you."

"You could, but you're her friend; I'm just an acquaintance. I'm also male—sympathetic—but still male. She may not be as open with me. She might not want to talk to me at all."

Lisa sighed heavily and watched the forest and scattered farms pass outside her window.

"Besides, I'm got to be in Port Salish Tuesday, remember? I'm not going to be in the best position to help for a few days."

"What's Tuesday?"

"Timothy Marks' trial."

"I thought that was still a couple of weeks away."

"Nope. It's Tuesday. Well, the trial starts Tuesday morning, but I'll be going up tomorrow night."

Timothy Marks was the first to go on trial in the aftermath of the Port Salish crime spree the year before. It was a symptom of the current overwhelmed justice system. More than seven people killed in one small town and almost a year later the courts were only now beginning to get around to holding someone accountable.

"Surprised he didn't take a plea bargain," Lisa said.

Jason doubted the prosecutors had offered Marks much of plea bargain. Marks had been a lieutenant in the San Juan County Sheriff's Department and the Patrol Division commander. He had also been on the payroll of the Lundgren Corporation. It had been on behalf of Lundgren that he had been sabotaging investigations for years. He had also appropriated some methamphetamine from the evidence locker in order to frame a fellow deputy who had been helping Jason. The criminal justice system didn't show much mercy to a dirty cop.

But Marks hadn't been one of the actual killers, just corrupt and greedy.

"Are you going to have to testify?"

Jason shrugged. "The D.A. says she doesn't plan to use me, but wants me there in case things change. Besides—"

"—It's your story."

He smiled. "It's my story."

And it was a good story. Both he and the newspaper had won a Pulitzer because of it. The Lundgren story had also made him into an occasional commentator on CNN, a minor celebrity among his fellow journalists across the Northwest, and landed him an agent who was shopping a book about the case to a handful of publishers.

In short, the story had changed his life.

"How long will the trial last?" Lisa asked.

"It's scheduled for three days," he told her. That's what the District Attorney had told him last week when they'd talked on the phone. But that could change without notice. Trials were like that.

"So you're not going to be able to do anything until next weekend?"

It sounded like an accusation.

"I don't have to leave until tomorrow evening. Until then, I will be asking questions."

She stared out her window.

Four

The newsroom of the *Seattle News* was buzzing with Monday morning energy as Jason wove through the cubicles and to his own desk. At a quarter to 9:00 in the morning, all the day shift reporters were there, catching up on respective weekends, telling stories. The jumbled conversations formed a mid-level background hum, punctuated by the occasional laugh. In just a few minutes, it would be all business as everyone got their assignments.

Jason set his briefcase and laptop on the floor and settled into the desk chair.

"Good morning," Debbie French said from her desk immediately to his right.

He returned her greeting and pushed the button that powered up his computer. The hard drive whirred as it began booting up.

"How was your weekend?" She asked. Today she wore a teal-colored Hensley shirt with creased khaki slacks and deck shoes. Her dark hair was gathered into a loose pony at the nape of her neck and clipped there with a tortoise shell barrette.

She looked like she should be in a Psych 101 class.

"Interesting," he told her. "Yours?"

"Uninteresting. Not interesting at all. The opposite of interesting."

Jason smiled. "Sorry."

"So it goes." She shrugged. "Tell me about your interesting weekend."

Jason spent a few minutes sketching out the events of his trip to Bosque with Lisa, their brief visit with Helen, and the encounter with Deputy Wilcox in Genoa.

"Wow," she said when he finished. "Did she ever call back?"

"Nope. Didn't really expect her to."

Debbie nodded. ""How's Lisa doing?"

"Frustrated. Depressed. Helpless."

"I would be too."

Jason agreed.

"Are you guys back together? You spent the night in a motel room?"

"No. Yes, and it was purely platonic."

The computer beeped and Jason logged in to the paper's network. So did every other reporter in the newsroom. An intraoffice email message contained his assignment for the day. It could be anything, the results of whatever the Editorial Board decided the paper needed for the next edition, and assigned by his editor, Miles. To his relief, he saw that his schedule had been left open other than a notation: Lundgren trial. His day was free.

Beside him, Debbie groaned.

"Lose the Lottery?" he asked. They called the morning story assignments "The Lottery" because there never seemed to be any pattern to who got what. It seemed perfectly random.

"I'm supposed to write up something about the closing of Merril's Department Store. Another fucking fluff piece."

Barely five feet tall and maybe a hundred pounds in a winter coat, Debbie looked the sweet, innocent girl next door. Every man who met her felt an instinctive need to protect her. That included the editors at the *News*. But that innocent smile masked a mind as kind and gentle as a white shark's. She wanted red meat, the bloodier the better.

More than one person had underestimated her and paid the price.

She began to gather her things. "I guess I'd better head down and see if I can wring some decent interviews from the loyal workers and shit."

"Maybe it won't be quite as fluffy as you think."

She made a face. "What'd you get?"

"Nothing."

"Nothing?"

He nodded. "I've got to head up to Friday Harbor today."

"That's right. The trial. What about that other thing? That cop down state?"

He looked at her. "What about it?"

"You're not going to drop it, are you?"

"Excuse me. Have we met?"

She smiled. "Atta boy."

♦♦♦♦♦

Sheriff Michael Barton looked up as Deputy Wilcox stuck his head into his office. "You wanted to see me?"

"Yeah. Have a seat."

He leaned back in his chair and watched as the young deputy stepped over to the client chair and sat down. Wilcox didn't look particularly concerned with being called into the boss's office, but Michael had known the young deputy his entire life and couldn't recall him ever looking concerned about anything. He was big and strong and confident and few people had ever challenged him. Michael wasn't sure whether that was a good thing, or not.

But Wilcox was also his kid sister's boy, so what could you do?

"Did you issue a BOLO Saturday night for a maroon Toyota Camry?" he asked.

The Be On the Look Out notice, or BOLO, asked all law enforcement to help find a particular vehicle or person.

"Oh yeah." Deputy Wilcox smiled. "Yes, sir, I did."

The Sheriff peered at his deputy. "'Seen at a known narcotics location?'"

"Well, yeah. Something like that."

"What known narcotics location? Is there something going on I don't know about?"

Wilcox smiled again. Even looked a little embarrassed, if that was possible. "Naw. Just some city folks sticking their noses where they don't belong. I wanted to give them a little scare."

The Sheriff peered at him. "Is this about the Miller girl?"

Wilcox nodded.

Sheriff Barton wanted to ask his nephew whether this girl was worth all the trouble, but thought better of it. He knew what the answer would be.

"Next time you want to use this department's resources to deal with a personal problem, you talk to me. Understood?"

"Yes, sir," Wilcox said, but paused significantly, like he had something else to say.

"What?"

"Scott likes having her available. I thought keeping her in line *was* Department business."

"I don't give a damn what Scott tells you. I run this department. Understood? You run it by me first."

"Yes, sir. It won't happen again."

The Sheriff waved him away. "Go arrest some criminals."

Wilcox didn't need to be told twice.

The Sheriff watched him leave, then shook his head and returned to the paperwork he'd been working on. "Dumbass."

♦♦♦♦♦

Jason's first call was to an extension at the Attorney General's Office at the State office building. It was on his contact list, though he hadn't used it often.

"Criminal Investigations," the male voice answered. "Brandon Donovan."

"Hey, Donovan. It's Jason, from the *News*. Got any plans for lunch?"

A pause. "You buying?"

"Absolutely." Well, the paper was buying.

"What do you want?"

♦

Le Bistrot was a small, relatively expensive restaurant on the east side of downtown near the complex of buildings that held the city and state brain trusts. The food was good and the location excellent. At lunch, there was usually a waiting list of various government cogs trying to get in. Sometimes the wait was longer than the average employee's lunch hour.

Jason, however, was not your average paper-pusher. He was flexible. He'd arrived early and secured a table well before the rush began. He was nursing his second expense account cappuccino when Brandon Donovan appeared at the other side of the table, complete with dark suit, power tie, and brief case.

He looked like an overworked government attorney.

"Reynolds, you degenerate," Donovan said as he set his case on the floor and pulled out the chair opposite Jason. "Do you ever do any actual work?"

"Not if I can help it."

A server appeared at their side. Brandon ordered a latte with an extra shot and the server left to retrieve it.

"You eat here often?" Jason asked. While waiting for Brandon arrive, he'd had a glance at the menu and the prices. It was a tad on the expensive side.

"Me? You kidding?" Brandon shook his head. "Only when someone else is paying for it. Since you *are* paying for it, I'll have the meatball sandwich."

Jason decided to just have a bowl of clam chowder. He didn't need the heartburn, either from the meatballs, or the credit card bill he was going to get. The paper would reimburse him for the meal—probably—but only when they got around to it. In the meantime, it would be his bill.

The server returned with Brandon's coffee, took their food order, and disappeared again.

"You still going out with Lisa?" Brandon asked.

Jason shrugged. "It's complicated."

"Okay," Brandon paused. "You want to talk about it?"

"There's nothing to talk about. We just decided things were getting too intense, too fast."

Brandon nodded as if he'd suspected as much.

"What happened up at Port Salish didn't help either."

"Oh, that's right. I heard it was pretty hairy up there. Congrats on the Pulitzer, by the way."

Jason smiled. "Something about almost dying makes people reassess their priorities."

Jason had known Brandon since they'd been freshmen in the same dorm at the University of Washington, each of them small town kids on their own in the big city. By pure coincidence, they'd also both enrolled in the same freshman comp section and from then on their friendship had only grown. Through four years of undergrad studies, several girlfriends, graduation and a career for Jason, law school for Brandon. Now Brandon was a real lawyer, working for the State and married to Jessica; Jason was a reporter with a Pulitzer.

It was remarkable that their friendship had continued strong as ever.

"You need to come over to the house, Lisa, or not," Brandon told him. "We could barbeque, or something."

Jason thought that was a good idea and they made tentative plans, subject to spousal approval, of course.

"So," Brandon looked at him over the rim of his espresso. "How did you manage to get tangled up with the Dunham County Sheriff's Department?"

Jason told him about the trip he and Lisa had taken over the weekend, paying particular attention to the two encounters with Deputy Wilcox.

"Really? He broke your tail light?"

"Well, it was actually the city cop who broke it. But yeah."

Brandon shook his head. "I thought that only happened in bad movies."

"It felt like a bad movie." Jason didn't think he had slept more than fifteen minutes that whole night.

"Well, the bad news is that questionable police behavior isn't within our jurisdiction."

Jason frowned. "But you're the Attorney General's Office."

It had been the first call he'd made.

Brandon shrugged and leaned over to dig something out of his briefcase. "What can I say? The law's the law. It doesn't have to make sense. Unless it's a case of consumer fraud or misconduct by a state official, we have no jurisdiction unless invited in by the local prosecutor."

"What about corruption? What if the cop is dirty?"

"Go to the local police chief or county sheriff. If that doesn't solve the problem, go to the respective city council or county commission."

"And if that doesn't work?"

Brandon thought about it for a moment, his eyes finding something on the ceiling, then shrugged. "I don't know. Move?"

Jason didn't reply. He was still trying to get his head around the idea that there was no state oversight of local policing. He'd always assumed the feds monitored the state, the state monitored the counties, and the counties oversaw the cities. But he'd been wrong. In effect, a crooked law enforcement agency could do whatever they wanted. The people wouldn't be able to do a thing about it.

"It isn't all bad news," Brandon set a manila file folder on the table between them. It looked empty. "I guess someone had enough to open an investigation into misappropriation of State funds by the Dunham County Sheriff's Department."

Jason perked up.

"I thought you might like that."

"What happened?"

"There were allegations that the Sheriff's deputies were using Search and Rescue vehicles—bought with State grants—as personal toys. You know, ATV's, boats and personal watercraft. That kind of thing."

"Okay, cool." He pulled the file closer and opened it. "What did they find?"

"Nothing at all." Brandon shook his head. "The investigation went nowhere."

"The Blue Wall of Silence?"

"Of course. But there's more than that. I get the impression, reading between the lines mind you, that the investigator wasn't exactly welcomed in the community."

"That's interesting."

Jason scanned the brief report as the waitress returned with Brandon's sandwich and his chowder. He wasn't surprised that the cops wouldn't cooperate. He wouldn't expect them to, not when fellow cops are the subject of the investigation. Cops normally close ranks against an outsider. It was a tribal reaction, us against them. But considering the bullying he'd seen in Bosque and Genoa, he would have thought the civilian population would have jumped at the chance to take them down.

Apparently, he was wrong.

The waitress asked if she could get them anything else. Both men shook their heads and thanked her. She went away.

"See what I mean?" Brandon asked when Jason looked up from the report.

"Yeah, I do." Basically, all the report said was that the investigator not only could find no corroboration of the original complaint, he couldn't find anybody willing to talk about the sheriff's department at all. No one. At all.

"So, what are the chances I can talk to the guy who ran the investigation?" Jason asked.

Brandon had just taken a bite of his sandwich. He held up a hand for time while he chewed furiously. A drop of marinara clung to the corner of his mouth. "Thing is…" He swallowed. "She resigned not too long after the report. I hear she's a partner in a private firm now."

Jason raised his eyebrows. "How long after?"

Brandon shrugged. "Above my pay grade, but not long."

"Interesting."

Brandon just smiled.

"So are you going to give me the lawyer's name, or what?"

"Have I ever let you down?"

♦

Melanie Epperson, like many prosecutors before her, had become a defense lawyer when she'd moved to private practice. Jason supposed it was a matter of two sides of the same coin. Or maybe there was an advantage in knowing how the other side thinks. Whatever the reason, the former staff attorney with the

A.G.'s Office was now a junior partner with the firm of Soreno, Kraft, and Thomas, which specialized in criminal defense and corporate liability.

A sign out front said so.

Jason pushed through the glass doors of the modern-style office building on the corner of SW 6th and Washington.

He was in a reception area that whispered money. The furnishings were upholstered in leather the color of milk chocolate, the coffee and end tables were of dark glass and darker wood. An abstract oil hung on one wall and mellow jazz murmured from overhead speakers.

A young blonde woman sat at the reception desk, waiting for him to notice her. She looked like a Fox News anchor.

"May I help you?" she asked when they'd made eye contact.

"I hope so," he told her and presented his card. "I need to speak to Melanie Epperson."

When he'd first started as a reporter, he'd probably have added "if she has a few moments." Now he knew better than to offer an easy way out. When faced with a reporter, most people in power did not "have a few moments" to spare. If they wanted to duck him, so be it. But he wouldn't make it easy for them.

The receptionist glanced at the card, back up at him. "Do you have an appointment?"

Of course he didn't.

"I think she'll want to talk to me," he told her. "Tell her it's about the Dunham County Sheriff."

The receptionist picked up a phone, still peering at his card, and punched in a number.

Jason wandered over toward the sofa dominating the waiting room, mainly to avoid looking too anxious. Like many things in life, people are more willing to grant you something if it doesn't seem terribly important to you.

"Mr. Reynolds?"

He turned back to the receptionist. "Yes?"

"Ms. Epperson will be right out."

"Thank you."

He turned back and sat on the sofa. What kind of magazines populate the waiting room at a law office? *Harvard*

Law Review? Supreme Court Quarterly? He looked through the reading material on the coffee table in front of him. *Architectural Digest*, *Golf*, and *National Geographic* dominated the titles. Interesting. Not a *Readers Digest* in sight.

About five minutes later, a door swung open behind the reception desk and a brunette woman strode into the waiting room. She wore a navy pinstriped skirt with matching blazer over an ivory silk blouse. An overcoat was draped over one arm. The other hand held a thick leather briefcase.

"Mr. Reynolds?"

He rose to his feet. "Thanks for seeing me."

"A reporter asking about Dunham County? How could I refuse?" She smiled. "But I have court in forty-five minutes. If you want to talk, you're going to have to walk with me."

"So let's walk."

He followed her out onto the sidewalk, where she turned left, heading toward the courthouse. She paused to let him catch up. They continued side-by-side.

"You always walk to court?" he asked.

"It's easier than trying to find a place to park," she said. "What makes you interested in Dunham County?"

"You ran an investigation into the Sheriff's office down there, right?"

Melanie glanced at him. "That isn't common knowledge."

"I have sources."

"I guess." They walked for a moment or two in silence. "Yeah, I investigated the Dunham County Sheriff. Not that it did much good."

"That's what I understand. Your people couldn't find anyone willing to testify against the Sheriff's Department."

"We couldn't find anyone willing to talk, period."

He looked over at her. "Care to tell me what really happened?"

They stopped at the corner of 6th and Alabama, waiting for the light to change. Melanie set her briefcase on the ground and turned to face him. "Have you actually been to Dunham County?"

"I was there this last weekend. It was—interesting."

She peered at him. “You had a run-in with the Sheriff?”

“One of his deputies,” he told her. “He decided to give us a message. Not only was it not friendly, but he didn’t even bother to hide it. In fact, he got a city cop to help him. That piqued my curiosity.”

“What did you do?”

He shrugged. “Pissed someone off, obviously.”

The light turned green and they moved with the crowd across Alabama Street, then continued North on SW 6th.

“Sheriff Michael Barton is not someone you want to piss off,” she told him.

“I gather that. Any Sheriff is not someone you want to piss off, but this smells different. Know what I mean?”

She nodded, but did not add anything. The courthouse loomed two blocks ahead of them.

He was running out of time.

“What’s going on in Dunham County?”

Melanie glanced over at him. “You really don’t know, do you?”

“No, I really don’t. That’s why I’m talking to you.”

She glanced at him again, then stopped to switch her briefcase from her right to left hand. It looked pretty heavy.

“Could I carry that for you?”

She gave Jason a look he could only describe as incredulous. “Let’s see, should I, a defense attorney on her way to her client’s trial, let a newspaper reporter carry my briefcase for me? Um, thanks anyway.”

“Just trying to help.”

“Like I said, I’ve got it.”

He smiled and shook his head.

“Back to your problem. Ever hear of Morris Barton?”

It took him a moment. “Republican State Senator?”

“State Senator, multi-millionaire businessman, and the patriarch of the Barton clan of Dunham County.”

“Okay.”

“The Barton clan, headed by Morris Barton and his son, Sheriff Michael Barton, run Dunham County like a medieval fief. Nothing happens there without their okay. No one crosses them without paying a price.”

Jason took this in. “Like a Mafia family.”

“Kind of,” Melanie shrugged. “I don’t know how much actual crime they’re involved in because we couldn’t get anyone to talk. Not a single soul. My investigator thought everyone was too scared to say anything.”

“Physically scared?”

“I don’t know.” She shrugged. “He couldn’t get anyone to talk even off the record. No one would say anything, good or bad. Not a word.”

That was telling. There were a lot of people who wouldn’t testify against someone. Either they were afraid of retribution, public opinion, or just didn’t want to make the commitment. But most of those same people would give all sorts of information if assured that their name would be kept out of it.

That no one was willing to talk even off the record meant the Barton tentacles ran deep.

They caught the light at Utah Street and crossed over to the block leading up to the courthouse. Suddenly, the people around them all wore black suits and conservative dresses.

“So you just called off the investigation?” he asked.

“Not exactly,” she said.

“What happened?”

“Senator Barton had a meeting with the Attorney General.”

“The Attorney General himself?”

She nodded. “The top of the pecking order. A few days later, I was called into my supervisor’s office and advised that it would be a good career move to find a position in private practice.”

“He had you fired?”

She shook her head. “It was much more subtle than that. I could have stayed on at the AG’s office, but I would never advance. My career would go nowhere.”

“Spend the rest of your life chasing penny ante frauds.”

“Exactly.”

They’d arrived at the wide flight of stairs leading up to the courthouse doors. Dozens of people were climbing up and down around them. Some were obviously lawyers going about their business. Others grouped together appeared to be the families of victims or defendants. Their faces spoke of lives teetering on the edge.

"It wasn't much, I know." Melanie turned to him. "But I hope I've helped."

"You have. Thanks." He handed her one of his cards. "Give me a call if you think of anything else that can help."

"I'd love to talk some more, but I have a client to defend." And she started up the steps.

"One more thing," he stopped her. "The name of the original complainant was not in the file. I'd like to talk to him."

Melanie was shaking her head. "You can't. She's dead."

"You're kidding."

"Nope. She was murdered a couple of weeks after we dropped her case."

"Murdered?" He was so surprised all he could do was repeat her words.

She held his gaze. "Her name was Elizabeth Jensen and the case is still open."

He quickly memorized the name.

♦

It was after 2:30 when Jason returned to the newsroom. The work area was quiet and mostly deserted with most other reporters off working their stories. The few who were at their desks chatted quietly on their phones, or typed on word processors. Nobody noticed Jason walk by; no one waved.

Debbie wasn't there. She was probably still working the department store story.

He settled down behind his desk and paused a moment to organize his thoughts.

Jason pulled his cell phone from his pocket and checked his messages. There was nothing important; nothing from Lisa. He toyed with the idea of calling her but decided against it. If Helen had called, he would certainly have heard about it. There was no other point in calling. He hadn't learned anything substantial yet, nothing he wanted to tell Lisa, anyway.

He would check in just before he headed to Anacortes, in a couple of hours.

Jason set his cell aside and woke up his computer. As soon as the screen saver went away, he logged in to the paper's internal network and called up its search engine. As soon as it loaded, he plugged in the terms "Jensen, Elizabeth" and pressed enter. If the paper had run a story about her, the engine would find it.

Five seconds later, the engine returned the results of his search. Sure enough, the first story was from the Metro section two years ago. It read, *Woman Dies in House Fire*.

He clicked on the link.

It was a digest article, one of the little sketches they used to give quick summaries of minor or developing stories, usually along the edge of the page.

Woman Dies in House Fire

A Renton woman died early this morning in a house fire. Elizabeth Jensen, 32, was pronounced dead at the scene by EMT's. Fire fighters responded at 3:18am to a 911 call reporting a house fire at 43090 SW Madison St. They found the duplex fully engaged and worked to limit damage to neighboring structures. Ms Jensen was the only resident and was not found until the fire had been extinguished. Investigation into the fire and the victim's death is ongoing.

Nothing remarkable there. It was a tragedy, sure, but tragedies happened every day, car accidents, plane crashes, drownings, heart attacks. There was nothing suspicious about it. Not on its own.

He returned to the search results screen and clicked on the next article. It was dated three days after the first.

City Employee Dies in Suspicious Fire

Elizabeth Jensen, 32, Assistant Director of Human Resources for the city of Renton died Saturday in a fire investigators have termed suspicious.

According to Renton arson investigator Len Freeney, the fire at 43090 SW Madison St. early Saturday morning bore all the hallmarks of a deliberately set fire. Authorities will not know for sure until chemical tests are completed. The autopsy on Ms. Jensen is scheduled for the end of the week.

Ms. Jensen had worked for the City of Renton for nearly six months. Co-workers expressed shock, calling her quiet and unassuming, a consummate professional. She had previously been the city manager for Bosque, in Dunham County and an assistant city manager for the city of Sheridan, Oregon. She is survived by her parents, a brother and a sister.

Jason quickly wrote some notes on a legal pad beside his keyboard, questions he'd like answered. Such as, what were her parents' names and would they like to talk to someone? Had the detectives on the case looked into the Dunham County connection? Would the detectives be willing to talk to him? Would her divorce attorney?

Another thought occurred to him. He pulled his briefcase into his lap and found the file Brandon had given him. He quickly flipped through to the last page, the page that listed the date the Attorney General's case was officially closed.

Then checked the date of the fire.

They were almost exactly a week apart. The fire was set six days after the case was officially closed.

Jason wondered when Senator Barton had forced Melanie out of the Attorney General's office. He jotted a note to call her and find out. She would still be in court now. He probably wouldn't be able to get a hold of her until the morning.

And in the morning he would be in Friday Harbor.

Five

Gerry Peterson, editor-in-chief and publisher of the *Bosque Examiner*, pushed himself away from the computer screen and rubbed his tired eyes. He was getting too old for this. That thought was beginning to assert itself more and more into his life lately, which in itself was a sign of aging. Like forgetting things. He saved his work and closed down the program.

Wednesday's edition was ready for press. They would accept classified ads until five o'clock. Other than that, it was done.

He stood up and stretched his back.

Gerry was alone in the office this afternoon. He'd sent Allison home at lunch because there wasn't much for her to do the rest of the day. Just be there in case someone came in or called wanting to place a last-minute classified.

He grabbed his empty coffee mug and walked back to the break room to get some more.

Allison had left the radio on, tuned to the little AM station down in Genoa. Katy Perry was singing her latest hit and that was the only sound in the office other than the background hum of hard drives.

Allison had made a fresh pot of coffee before she left, bless her heart. He poured himself a cup and wandered back to the outer office.

It was in quiet times like this, just waiting to put the paper to bed that he wondered how his life had led him here. He had always wanted to be a newspaper reporter. At least since he'd gotten his first taste of it in high school. Like most journalism students his age, he had dreamed of becoming the new Woodward and Bernstein, but then he'd gone off to college where he'd learned the bitter truth: print journalism was in trouble.

Newspapers across the country (indeed across the modern world) were closing on a daily basis, victims of changing demographics and new technologies. Only one niche was holding its own, even thriving. Local weeklies.

One of his professors had said it outright: "If you want a real career in newspapers, find a local paper that's for sale and buy it. As long as you don't piss off the local grocery stores, you're guaranteed a steady income."

So that's what he did. He'd worked for a while at some of the bigger dailies around the region until he had some money saved up and the *Examiner* came up for sale. The rest was history.

He'd owned the *Examiner* for twenty-five years now and she had provided him with a comfortable living. He wasn't exactly growing rich, but he had no debt to speak of and a sizeable retirement account. Business had been good, because he'd never forgotten the first rule of small newspapers: don't piss off the advertisers.

Local papers were bought mainly by locals for the weekly grocery sales.

So you don't piss off the advertisers. You avoid controversy. You play it safe. And you make money, decent money.

But Woodward and Bernstein hadn't stayed away from controversy. They hadn't played it safe when they were investigating the Watergate cover-up. They didn't care whether any advertisers were pissed off. They risked everything in their pursuit of justice.

The front door opened and an elderly woman stepped in and approached the front counter. Gerry grabbed a classified ad form and went to meet her.

♦♦♦♦♦

Debbie announced her arrival with a thump as her bag hit the ground and a heavy sigh as she collapsed into her chair.

"How was shopping?" Jason asked without looking up.

"Fuck off, Jason," she said, then cocked her head to one side. "Actually, they had some pretty good closeout deals. No…very good."

She paused to think about it.

"It wasn't as bad as you thought?"

"It's the same old story." She shrugged. "A big business buys a smaller one and starts downsizing, leaving a lot of employees with no future."

Jason had heard the story more than a few times in the last few years. It seemed to be the modern way of doing business. It made the stockholders a lot of money and the upper management big bonuses.

"A lot of middle-aged salespeople aren't very happy right now," Debbie said as she turned to her computer.

"Can't blame them."

"No, of course not. I just don't know how to help them. This sort of thing has become so commonplace that people don't even pay attention anymore."

Jason agreed. "Or they're so worried the same thing could happen to them they just keep their heads down and walk on by."

"Exactly."

Neither said anything for a beat or two. The subject wasn't entirely foreign to them. The *Seattle News* was in better shape than many papers, but there were rumors. Both knew their jobs could disappear at any moment.

"Any suggestions as to how I should approach this?" Debbie finally asked.

"About all you can do is put a human face on it," he told her. "Let the reader know that these are real people going through this. That it's someone's mother, brother, etcetera."

She groaned and turned to her computer.

♦

While Debbie worked on putting her story together, Jason finished going through the paper's coverage of Elizabeth Jensen's death. Within a week of the fire, the autopsy results came in and the case was officially termed a homicide. There was one follow-up story, asking the public for help, and then nothing. The case disappeared from the news, supplanted by new, fresher outrages. Elizabeth Jensen, murder victim, was forgotten.

Jason glanced over to Debbie. She was frowning at the screen of her monitor, her lower lip pinched under her teeth. She often did this while she was concentrating. It made her look even younger, if possible.

She glanced over at him. "What?"

"How's the story going?"

Her eyes narrowed. "What do you want?"

"What makes you think I want anything? I'm a caring guy." He made a show of being hurt. "Maybe I just wanted to know if you were having trouble with a tough story."

"Oh, okay. A caring guy."

"That's right. Sensitive."

"Sensitive."

"Yep."

"I'm almost done. Thanks for caring."

He smiled. "It's who I am, a caring guy."

"So you said." She shook her head. "Do you need something, Jason?"

"Now that you mention it, I could use help with some legwork while I'm stuck in Friday Harbor."

"Is this the cop thing last weekend?"

He nodded.

"What do you want?"

♦

Jason texted Lisa before he left the office. A text was better than a call. If she were in the middle of a class, or something, it would be much less of an interruption.

Getting ready to leave. Call me.

He hung around the office for a few minutes until it was clear she wouldn't be calling him immediately, gathered his briefcase and laptop and headed for the stairwell.

"Give them hell," Debbie told him. Despite the grumpiness, she was overjoyed to be helping Jason on a story that might actually have some meat to it.

"I will. Let me know what you find."

She promised she would.

He was waiting for the light to cross John Street when Lisa returned his call. He fumbled in a coat pocket, found the phone and accepted the call on the third ring.

"Sorry it took so long," she told him. "I was in class."

"I figured it was something like that. How are you doing?"

"Okay. I didn't sleep very well last night."

He thought she might not. She'd still been pretty upset when he'd dropped her at her apartment last night. A year ago, he probably would have spent the night, but things had changed. Last night he hadn't asked and she hadn't offered.

"I assume you haven't heard anything," he said and joined the flow of pedestrians across the street. His car was parked in a structure about two blocks away.

"No. Nothing. Have you been able to find out anything?"

"Nothing substantial. Nothing that can help us," he told her. "But I've got some feelers out and Debbie's going to work on a couple of things while I'm gone. I don't have anything solid, but something definitely smells."

He had decided to keep the death of Elizabeth Jensen to himself for now. Telling Lisa would only increase her stress needlessly. At this point, he wasn't even sure it was related to Helen's problem.

"That's something, I guess. I wish you didn't have to go to Friday Harbor."

He couldn't think of anything to say to that. He turned into the parking structure. Almost at once reception on the cell grew worse.

"I feel like I'll be helpless while you're gone."

"You aren't helpless," he told her. "In fact, there's a couple of things you can look into for me."

"What?" She sounded almost eager. Research was her specialty. Almost. Her specialty was Pacific Northwest history.

"Find out everything you can about the history of Dunham County." He told her how to spell it. "Then find out everything you can about State Senator Morris Barton and the Barton family."

"How is he involved?"

"I don't know that he is. It's one of the things I want to find out."

Her research skills had been instrumental in taking down Lundren Corporation last year. He hoped she'd find something crucial this time too.

Jason arrived at the parking structure's elevator, but waited to press the call button. He had no illusions about the cell phone reception inside a metal box within a concrete building. Instead, he waited outside while he finished talking to Lisa. The few other people seeking their cars simply stepped around him.

"You want me to call when I've found something?" Lisa asked.

"Text or email would probably be better. I have no idea what my schedule is going to be and I doubt cell phones are allowed in court."

"Okay."

"Look, I'd better be going. I'm in the parking garage and I'm going to lose service. I'll text you when I get there and when I know what's going on."

"Say hi to Danny for me."

He told her he would and ended the call.

♦

If you flew a private plane, Friday Harbor was about forty-five minutes northwest of Seattle, in the San Juan Islands.

Jason, however, didn't have access to a private plane, so like most people, he drove the eighty miles to Anacortes and caught the state ferry to the islands. Washington's ferry service is considered part of their highway system and is just as dependable. It is also the only public way on or off any of the islands in the San Juan Chain.

The ferry took a couple of hours to make the trip because it stopped at every island on the way, but they were nice hours. It was late September and the afternoon sun was warm over the water, with a gentle breeze to keep the temperature reasonable. The Sound was peaceful around them, deep blue with only gentle swells distorting the surface. A handful of fishing boats tried to scare up a salmon, but it was getting late and most fishermen had already headed to port for their dinners.

The islands were beautiful. They drifted to either side of the ferry, dark with forest down to the waterline and smelling of cedar. Gulls wheeled overhead. Most of the islands were uninhabited, the rest showed just a few scattered buildings.

Jason spent the first hour at the rail watching the scenery and the late season tourists, but grew tired and returned to the cabin for a cup of coffee and a comfortable seat.

Since school was in session, most of the people in the cabin were older—retirees—taking advantage of the lack of children to enjoy the scenery in peace. He thought the average age in the ferry cabin was probably sixty.

Jason pulled out his cell and checked his messages. Debbie had not yet contacted him. Neither had Lisa, which meant Helen still hadn't called her.

He wasn't sure whether that was good or not.

For want of anything better to do, he typed a text message and sent it to Danny. *You working?*

Danny was Sgt. Danielle Hayden of the San Juan County Sheriff's Department. Last year, she had been his partner in exposing Lundgren Corporation's crimes. She would also be one of the key witnesses against Timothy Marks, former Lieutenant in the same department. He had been her boss.

Marks had also tried to frame her for distributing methamphetamine.

Danny texted back within moments. *Naw. Meeting w DA all day. Just hanging now.*

On ferry. About an hour out.

k. waiting.

I'll give you a buzz.

k. Dinner?

Dinner.

He smiled, slipped his phone back into his pocket, and sipped his coffee.

♦

About twenty minutes later, Jason was on the point of falling asleep when his cell chirped again. This one was from Debbie. Quickly alert, he opened the message.

Detectives on the murder are Stefanie Kim and George Pieczinski. Still on Renton force. Want me to grill them?

Jason smiled at the image of Debbie grilling two police detectives. Not that she couldn't do it. In fact, the detectives would do well to not underestimate her. It was just such an unusual image, her little girl next door up against two hardened cops.

He considered her question a bit longer. His instinct was to say no, he wanted to do it himself, but that meant delaying the interview until at least Friday, more probably sometime next week. And there was no particular reason—other than ego—that he had to be the one doing the interview. It wasn't like he was looking for anything in particular and Debbie knew most of the background. The interview would just be about gathering as much general information as possible.

He opened his keyboard and typed in a text. *Go for it. Tell them you're trying to refresh the public's interest in the case. Pick their brains. I want everything they have.*

The reply came within seconds. *We'll know what they know.*

Jason smiled again. He could almost see her licking her chops. "Sic em, Debbie."

♦♦♦♦♦

Dunham County District Attorney Patrick Barton looked up from the brief he was working on. His Assistant D.A. Jon Fielding hovered in the doorway. He had knocked on the half-open door a second ago.

"You got a second?" the ADA asked.

Patrick took one look at the distressed expression on his best prosecutor, saved his document, and minimized it on his monitor. "Sure. Come in. What can I do for you?"

Jon took a seat in one of the client chairs. "It's the Miller case."

"Okay. What's the problem?"

Jon looked like he was being tortured. "Have you looked at it?"

"Not in depth," Patrick shook his head and eased back into his chair. "Tell me about it."

"Thomas Miller, the owner of the City Center Café in Bosque, is alleged to have attacked Deputy Sheriff Travis Wilcox on September 20 in the parking lot of the First Federal Bank in Bosque. He has been charged with assaulting a law enforcement officer and resisting arrest." Jon met his boss' eyes. "Apparently Deputy Wilcox is the boyfriend of Mr. Miller's daughter."

Patrick nodded. "Father doesn't like how the boyfriend treats his daughter. Ugly, but it happens."

"I know," Jon said. "But the story doesn't track."

"What do you mean?"

"The defendant admits he went to the bank that morning to deposit the previous day's receipts. The bank confirms he routinely did so. He has no criminal history, no history of violence. Suddenly he decides to attack his daughter's boyfriend, a deputy sheriff, while that boyfriend's in uniform, in public, and heavily armed?"

"What does Miller say happened?"

"In his statement, Miller says Deputy Wilcox attacked him without reason, breaking his arm with the baton, then handcuffed him and charged him with resisting arrest."

"Have you talked to Deputy Wilcox?" Patrick asked, but only because it was expected of him at this point. Wilcox was his nephew and he had no illusions about the deputy's character.

Wilcox probably thought he had a good reason for going after Mr. Miller—not necessarily legal, but good in his opinion—but he might just as well have simply been bored.

Jon shrugged. "He's sticking to his story."

"Of course."

"When I asked Deputy Wilcox why he was in the bank parking lot in the first place—he doesn't bank there, I checked—he just said he was on patrol. He said he doesn't need any other reason to be anywhere in the county."

Patrick lowered his head to rub his brow. This job was tough enough without having to deal with his idiotic family. He was getting sick of it, to tell the truth.

"What do you want me to do?"

Patrick considered his options. No matter what he did, problems would have to be dealt with, either with his staff, his conscience, or his family. Which did he want to face?

"Who's the defense attorney?" he finally asked.

"Jim Swanson."

Jim Swanson had been a defense attorney longer than Patrick had been alive. He was nearing sixty-five years old and still worked fifty hour weeks and was as sharp as a new razor. There was no way Patrick or his assistant would be able to sell him on a reduced charge with a case as weak as this. He would laugh in their face.

"Dismiss the charges," he finally said. "Without prejudice."

"Deputy Wilcox isn't going to be happy."

"I'll deal with the deputy."

♦♦♦♦♦

The San Juan County District Attorney's Office had arranged a motel room for Jason for the length of the trial. It was standard procedure for out of town witnesses. The District Attorney could not require witnesses to make themselves available for the length of a trial and expect them to absorb all the costs, too. They'd never get anyone to testify.

Jason's motel was the Harbor Inn, across the street and a convenient two blocks away from the courthouse. He would be able to walk over easily. The District Attorney's Office probably had a standing contract with the motel.

As soon as the ferry docked in Friday Harbor, Jason drove to the motel and checked in at the office. He'd decided it would be better to be settled in his room before he called Danny.

The clerk behind the desk found his reservation, accepted his paperwork, and handed him the key to room 214, on the second floor looking in the general direction of the harbor. Jason parked his car and started carrying his luggage up to the room. It was a two trip operation. He had a suitcase and a garment bag. Then there was his laptop, his camera, and his briefcase. All for three or four days away from home.

He set his briefcase down by the desk.

The room was nice, with a queen-sized bed, and an actual armchair in front of a flat screen television, in addition to the usual small table and chair.

It was nicer than anything he'd ever rented on his own.

Jason walked over to glance in the bathroom. It was as big as his apartment's kitchen. "I may never leave this place," he murmured.

He jumped when a knock sounded on his door, then frowned. No one knew he was here but the motel staff. Did they have instructions to let the D.A. know when he checked in? If so, he'd expect a phone call rather than a personal visit.

Jason opened the door.

"Hi," Danny stood there, a wise-guy grin on her face. "Are you ready? I'm about to faint from hunger."

Six

Sylvester's Steakhouse wasn't the type of restaurant Jason was used to visiting with Danny. The entire time he'd been in Port Salish last year, the only place they'd eaten out was a burger place called *Mary Lou's*. It was a good burger place, but a burger place nonetheless. It catered to a certain section of the populace and its décor reflected this, everything from the framed photos on the walls to the country music on the sound system.

Sylvester's had some sort of chamber music drifting from hidden speakers. Lots of strings and woodwinds, the type of music Jason always associated with Public Radio. It also had real cloth tablecloths and cloth napkins and heavy crystal water glasses. There were as many waiters as waitresses and the customers wore suits and dresses, not jeans and tee shirts.

And *Sylvester's* had real wine in glass bottles.

It was nice and just a handful of blocks from the motel.

Jason sipped the merlot they'd selected and looked across at his friend. "You've grown your hair out. I like it."

"Really?" Danny stroked a strand between two fingers and her thumb then tossed it back over her shoulder. "It hasn't been this long since high school."

"It makes you look," he searched for the right word. "Softer."

"Softer? Thanks." She smiled and looked down at her wine. "It helps not being in uniform all the time. I don't have to put it up. Putting up long hair is a pain."

"They've let you stay in street clothes?"

"Yeah," Danny smiled and her eyes met his. "They decided to make me a detective, covering the south county."

"Congratulations. You deserve it. I figured they'd offer you Marks' old job."

"Naw," She shook her head. "It's still too much of an old boy's club to make a woman a commander. They didn't even offer me the job."

He was stunned. "After everything you'd done? That's ridiculous."

"I wouldn't have taken it anyway. I didn't want to move up here and I didn't want to sit behind a desk all day doing paperwork." She shook her head. "That would have bored me out of my skull."

The waiter arrived at their table with a dinner salad for each, refilled their wine glasses and disappeared again, never said a word.

"How's your mother doing?" Jason asked.

Danny speared a clump of lettuce with her fork. "Oh, she's fine. All healed up good as new and something of a celebrity." She smiled. "All her friends think she's some kind of crime-fighter."

Jason laughed. "She sounds like a trooper."

He'd never actually met Danny's mother. Things had been happening too fast last year and he'd had to go back to Seattle right away.

"Oh, yeah. Takes more than a car wreck to keep my mother down."

"I can believe that. I know her daughter."

Danny rolled her eyes and chewed her salad. "You two would get along just fine."

Jason smiled and tried his own salad. He wasn't a huge fan of salads in general, but this one was good, full of an assortment of textures and flavors. For a few moments, he concentrated on that.

The waiter appeared to remove their salad plates as soon as they finished and replace them with platters holding sizzling steaks, baked potatoes and steamed Brussel sprouts. He refilled their wine and water glasses and disappeared again.

He hadn't said a word since they'd placed their orders.

"I could get used to living like this," Jason told Danny.

"Yeah. But it would be a shame to have all this," her eyes made a circle of their surroundings, "become routine. Wouldn't it?"

"When you put it that way."

She smiled and sliced off a dainty corner of her steak. "So how's Lisa?"

"Good. She told me to tell you 'hi'."

"Hi, Lisa."

He peered at her. "You expect me to believe you two haven't talked over the past year?"

"Me and Lisa?" Danny raised her eyebrows. "We might have chatted now and then."

"Yeah, whatever. You probably know more than I do."

Danny just smiled and chewed her steak.

"Just tell me this, have you two already decided my future, or do I still have some say in it?"

"Oh, no. Your name hardly came up."

He looked at her, a piece of his steak paused halfway to his mouth. "Really? 'Hardly came up?'"

She laughed. "Well, okay, you came up. But we didn't decide anything. We didn't even try to decide anything. We just talked."

"Maybe I should be asking you how Lisa's doing."

"Oh, I couldn't tell you anything you don't already know." She smiled at him like she was in on the joke and he wasn't.

"Like that Lisa wants more from me than I can give her right now?"

"That pretty much sums it up."

♦

They finished their dinners. As soon as they'd set their forks down the waiter appeared again to remove their plates and to ask if they'd like to see the dessert menu. Jason was amazed. How did he do it? Hide around the corner and watch them? He was half-tempted to look for surveillance cameras.

"Have you tried our cheesecake?" the waiter prompted them. "Your choice of chocolate or salted caramel?"

"Oh, god," Danny groaned. "Cheesecake's the last thing I need."

But her eyes said she wanted it. Wanted it badly.

Jason was pretty much satiated by the meal, but he was willing to sacrifice himself to make her happy. "Would it be possible to share a slice?"

"Absolutely. Would you like the chocolate or caramel?"

Jason and Danny exchanged a glance. He looked back up at the waiter. "Caramel."

"Coming right up." He disappeared.

"I'm going to regret this in the morning," Danny murmured. "And the afternoon."

Jason could almost see her salivating.

He decided he was buzzing a bit from the wine.

"It's a special occasion."

"It is a special occasion," she agreed. "The reunion of the Hayden-Reynolds detective team, the team that single-handedly brought the Lundgren Corporation to justice."

"Yeah, we make a pretty good team, don't we?"

"Damn good."

He thought she might be buzzed on the wine, too.

The waiter returned with their cheesecake and set it carefully between them on the table, then disappeared again. Jason noticed now that the crowd in the restaurant had thinned considerably. Only two tables besides their own still had guests eating.

"What time does this place close?" he asked Danny.

"I have no idea. What time is it?"

"Almost 11:00."

"We could ask someone."

"When he comes to pick up the dessert plate."

That settled, they set upon their dessert. It was everything advertised, creamy and sweet and completely decadent. For a few moments, they did nothing but wallow in that decadence.

"So," Jason sat back, away from the dessert, leaving the rest for Danny. "Is Marks actually going on trial tomorrow?"

Danny shrugged without looking up from the cheesecake. "As far as I know."

"The case against him seemed bulletproof. You wouldn't think he'd want to go in front of a jury."

"He hasn't yet," she told him. "I wouldn't be surprised if they announced a deal when court convenes tomorrow. I guarantee the phone lines between the lawyers are burning up right now."

"You think the D.A. will deal with him?"

She looked up at him. "She'll let him plead guilty."

"You think he will?"

"I do. Like you said, he doesn't want to go in front of a jury and his lawyer certainly doesn't. Juries don't like dirty cops. They're just holding out for the best deal they can get."

"Which will be a sentencing recommendation?"

She smiled. "He might have a chance of getting out before he needs a walker."

♦

They weren't quite the last customers to leave the restaurant, but they were close. One other group of four was still laughing over the last of their wine as Jason and Danny made their way to the cashier's stand. Jason put the meal on his credit card, included a nice tip for their amazing waiter, then joined Danny for the walk to the parking lot. It was a little past 11:30.

"You alright to drive?" he asked.

They had taken Danny's car since she'd known where they were going. It was a brand new Jeep Grand Cherokee in a lustrous black that was all but invisible in the shadowy parking lot. Her previous ride, a Subaru wagon, had been a casualty of the Lundgren case.

"I think I can make it three blocks safely."

"Wouldn't want you to get a DUI," he said. "Though it would be ironic, considering what we're doing tomorrow."

"Yeah, that'd be a riot. Get in the car."

He did as he was told.

Danny started up the engine and pulled out of the parking lot, heading back toward the motel. "Thanks for dinner. I enjoyed myself."

"Me too."

It was only three blocks to the motel and there was no traffic this time of night so it took just a couple of minutes to make the trip. Danny pulled into a vacant spot in the lot next to his car and switched off her engine. "The D.A. wants us at the courthouse by 8:00 in the morning."

"I suppose we should be getting some sleep then."

Neither moved.

"You want to meet up for breakfast tomorrow," he asked. "Before court?"

"Sure. Want to meet at my room or yours?"

He looked at her.

"I'm two rooms down from you."

He smiled. "Of course you are. Yours then."

They climbed the stairs together, complaining about their overfull bellies, said good night and parted in front of his room.

♦

The San Juan County courthouse was not your stereotypical courthouse. It had none of the usual cues that this was a dignified institution where matters of life and death were decided, no elegant columns or grand staircases, no wise inscription above the entrance. It was just red brick and glass windows. It could have been just another office building. It could have been a school.

At fifteen minutes to eight Tuesday morning, Jason followed Danny into the red brick building.

"We'll be on the second floor," Danny told him and led him to the stairs. "Courtroom two."

"Lead the way."

Danny was wearing creased black slacks and a black blazer over a white cotton blouse. Her hair was clipped at the nape of her neck in a loose pony. The only jewelry she wore was a pair of small gold hoops in her ears.

Jason wore his black suit with a white shirt. At the last minute, he'd decided against a tie. He wasn't on trial and he didn't want to be mistaken for another lawyer. God help him.

"If you need to do anything on your phone, do it now," Danny told him. "They don't allow cells while court is in session."

"I'm good."

He'd already exchanged texts with Debbie, who had an appointment with the detectives on the Jensen case this afternoon. He'd given her a couple of questions to ask. Otherwise, he trusted her instincts.

An Assistant D.A. waited for them outside the courtroom.

"Good. You're both here." She shook hands all around. "Andrea wants to speak to you."

"There've been developments?" Danny asked.

"You could say that. But I'll let Andrea tell you."

They followed her down a short corridor and through a secure door into the cramped offices of the District Attorney. It looked much like a police squad room, with battered metal desks pushed back to back against each other while Assistant D.A.'s worked phones and their computers. Files and file boxes were stacked everywhere. No one even looked up as they passed.

Andrea Meade's office was in the corner and only slightly less overwhelmed with paper. Files lay piled and spread across her desk, while file boxes were stacked three high along one entire wall. The wall behind her desk held bound copies of the Washington Statutes.

The District Attorney was in her late forties and looked permanently tired. She smiled, stood, and shook hands with each of them. "Please, sit down."

Jason and Danny each took a client chair.

"As you might have guessed," the D.A. said, a smile making up for the dark smudges under her eyes. "Timothy Marks agreed to plead guilty to a set of reduced charges and a sentencing recommendation."

“I hope you didn’t reduce the charges much,” Jason said.

“We didn’t. He’s pleading to two felonies and will do a minimum of ten years in the state pen. He’ll be collecting social security by the time he’s a free man again.”

Danny gave a satisfied nod. “I hear his wife has filed for divorce too.”

“I’ve heard the same.” Andrea smiled. “His life is pretty much destroyed.”

“Couldn’t have happened to a more deserving person,” Jason said. Though most of Marks’ actions had been directed at Danny, he’d had to watch her deal with it. That had been hard. He might have actually wanted revenge more than she did.

He was kind of disappointed he wouldn't be able to watch Marks’ face as the guilty verdicts were handed down.

“What, exactly, did Marks plead to?' he asked. “I need to know the details. I have a story to write.”

“Of course.” The D.A. smiled and handed him a sheet of paper from one of the stacks on her desk. “This is the press release we'll send out this afternoon. Naturally, I thought you'd like an early look.”

He smiled and accepted the paper. “Very thoughtful.”

“The former Lieutenant Timothy Marks,” Andrea continued, “has agreed to plead guilty to two counts of perjury, two of rendering criminal assistance and one of official misconduct. Each count is worth ten years in prison. We have agreed to drop conspiracy to murder, theft, and obstructing justice charges and are recommending a minimum of fifteen years before parole.”

Jason had been scanning the press release. It said pretty much what the D.A. had told him, absent some of the detail. He looked up now, from Danny to the D.A. “How's the judge?”

Andrea smiled. “Not a fan of dirty cops. Marks will be in prison a while.”

♦

“One down, two to go,” Jason told Danny as they descended the stairs from the D.A.'s office.

“Only two?” Danny glanced at him, frowning. “You going soft on me all of a sudden?”

He smiled and shook his head. “I'm not counting the little guys, Smith's soldiers. They're just fall guys, pawns. I want to see Taylor Smith and his boss, Director Mullens, on their way to prison. That's when I will feel we've won.”

“You do realize no one knows where Smith is, right?”

“He'll turn up. Sooner, or later.”

“Not if he has any sense, he won't,” Danny said. “He should just stay in whichever tropical paradise he's in and live that life of luxury.”

“Providing Lundgren's people will leave him alone.”

Danny looked at him. “You don't think Lundgren has enough legal troubles to keep them busy without worrying about Smith?”

He looked over at her. “You think they'd just let it go?”

The Sheriff answered his private line on the second ring. “Sheriff Barton.” He sounded distracted, like he was in the middle of reading a good Louis L’Amour and hadn’t completely shifted his focus to the phone call.

“Good afternoon, Mike. This is Patrick over at the courthouse.”

“Hey, Pat. How’s Molly and the kids? Haven’t seen them in a while.”

“They’re good. The kids are growing like weeds. We’ll have to get together sometime before the holidays.” Patrick knew this would never happen and so did the Sheriff. Molly despised most of his family and only withstood the big family gatherings because it was her duty. She would never voluntarily go just to socialize.

“What can I do for you today?” the Sheriff asked.

“I’m calling to personally let you know that we’ve decided to dismiss the charges against Thomas Miller.”

“Miller, Miller…”

“Assault on a Law Enforcement Officer, resisting arrest?” Pat prompted him. “Wilcox was the arresting officer?”

"Okay. Yeah, I remember. In the bank parking lot up to Bosque."

"That's the one."

"What are you doing again?"

"I'm dismissing the charges, without prejudice."

A pause. "Why would you do that?"

"Because Travis' story stinks, Mike. No one with half a brain cell is going to believe it happened the way he says it did."

"Since when did it matter? Wilcox is a Barton."

"Wilcox is a hot-headed idiot, is what he is. We've got to give the folks on the jury enough evidence to be able to pretend they believe us. Travis basically flipped off the whole system this time."

The Sheriff was silent.

"I've left the door open to re-file charges," Pat told him. "Bring me some witnesses, some new evidence, give me something I can present to a jury with a straight face and I will re-file the charges."

Again, the Sheriff was silent for a beat. "Anything else?"

"That will do it. Have a nice afternoon."

Patrick Barton disconnected. His hands were shaking.

It was Danny's turn to buy and she had picked a little deli within walking distance of the courthouse. They sat now amid the early lunch crowd over sandwiches and open bags of chips, a diet Coke for Danny, root beer for Jason. "I've got the rest of the week off for court duty."

Jason smiled. "Me too. Wonder how long the County will keep paying for our motel rooms?"

By her sudden frown, Jason guessed she hadn't thought of that.

"Hold on a second," she told him and quickly punched a text into her cell phone. "I'll find out."

Jason took a bite of his sandwich. It was good, pastrami and Swiss on marbled rye. Tasty, and for all the wrong reasons, health-wise.

Danny's cell buzzed. She read the text and looked up at him. "They'll pay for tonight, then we're on our own."

He shrugged. "That seems reasonable."

"So much for vacation," she said. "I don't think I can swing that motel much more than a day."

Jason probably could—he had come into a fair bit of money during the last year, between his dad's estate and the profits from the story—but wasn't sure how to do it without making it sound like a pass. "I thought you detectives made the big bucks."

"Oh, yeah." Danny laughed. "It's more than I was making before. But I just had to buy a new car; my old one was totaled, remember?"

"Insurance?"

"Oh yeah, they paid," she said. "Replacement value for a ten year old Suzuki wagon. I had to come up with the rest."

"Considering the circumstances, the County should have kicked you some extra money."

"The County," She snorted. "The County doesn't have any money. After the Deception Island mess, they had to take out loans just to keep the lights on."

"Sorry."

"It's all good. Just a bump in the road," she said. "I'll be caught up again in a couple of months."

"Listen, I did pretty good financially from our little adventure," he told her. "If there's anything I can do to help, just ask."

Danny smiled and reached over to squeeze his hand. "How about you just buy me a movie tonight and we'll call it good?"

♦

They were almost back to the car when Jason's cell chirped an incoming text.

"Hold on," he said as he fished it out of his pants pocket. "It's from Lisa. I'd better see what this is about."

Danny nodded and paused to gaze at a dress through a shop window. It was one of those rare, beautiful days in the islands. Warm, sunny, and nearly windless. Nearly everyone who didn't absolutely have to be inside was out walking or sitting in the park. Cars drove with windows and sunroofs open.

Jason stepped over beside Danny, out of the traffic flow, and opened the text.

You're probably still in court. Finished report on Dunham County and Barton family. Basically the same. Emailed it to you. Call me later.

Nothing catastrophic. Nothing from Helen.

"Everything okay?" Danny asked.

"Yeah," he said. "She's finished some research for me."

"Oh?" her eyebrows shot up. "Another hot story?"

"That's what I'm trying to find out. Something smells, but I'm not sure what it is."

"Tell me about it."

Jason told her about Lisa's friendship with Helen; Helen's sudden withdrawal from school, and the events of his and Lisa's weekend trip to Dunham County. As he talked, they strolled along the sidewalks of downtown Friday Harbor in the direction of the courthouse. It was nice. Comfortable in street clothes, without the traffic noise and clouds of exhaust the same walk would have encountered in Seattle.

"What do you think's going on?" Danny asked.

"I don't know," he admitted. "Other than my impression that Helen was afraid of the deputy, Wilcox." He shrugged.

"But you smell a story?"

"Yeah," he nodded. "I smell a story. Something hinky's going on down there."

She peered at him. "*Hinky*?"

"It's a technical term."

"Oh. Well, maybe it's an abusive relationship, that's all. They can be very bad, but they're pretty common, unfortunately."

"It's certainly possible."

"But?"

"It didn't feel like just another abusive relationship. It felt like the tip of an iceberg. I can't explain it."

They were approaching the courthouse now. Their motel was across the street and a block further down.

"You know anything about the Dunham County Sheriff?" he asked.

She looked up at him. "Only that there is one. I haven't worked with them."

"Is there any way to find some information about them?"

"Maybe," she said. "But we'd be breaking a handful of rules to do it."

Jason smiled. "Just like old times."

Seven

The San Juan County Sheriff's Office occupied a gray wood-framed building directly across Second Street from the courthouse. It looked more like a real estate office than the headquarters of a law enforcement agency, but that seemed to be the pattern in San Juan County. Danny's office in Port Salish looked like a dental practice and the courthouse looked like a school.

Jason followed Danny onto the porch and through the station's front door. They stepped into an entryway fronted by a Plexiglas front desk and a secure door to the squad room. The beige walls were covered with public safety posters and photos of fugitives. Molded plastic chairs in the same godawful orange all government offices seemed to prefer lined the walls under the posters.

Danny pulled her credentials from a pocket and showed them to the desk sergeant. "I need to borrow a desk and computer for a few minutes."

"Detective." The desk officer said and touched a button somewhere. The door clicked open.

Danny pointed toward Jason. "He's with me."

The Sergeant glanced up at Jason.

Jason flashed his most harmless-looking smile.

"Make sure he stays with you, Detective."

Jason clipped a visitor card to his jacket lapel, followed Danny through the secure door and across the squad room to the first unoccupied desk. He pulled over a nearby chair and watched as Danny logged in to the desktop computer.

"Okay, what are we looking for?" she asked.

"How about anything about the Dunham County Sheriff?"

"It doesn't work that way," she shook her head. "We can only run checks on individuals and it will only show arrests and convictions. It won't tell us someone beats up their girlfriend, for instance, if the police were never involved."

It figured. Nothing was ever as easy as it should be.

"Try Travis Wilcox."

She typed the name into the proper field. "Middle name?"

"No idea."

"This the boyfriend?"

He told her it was. And the cop who'd accosted him and Lisa in Genoa.

The computer beeped as the results screen appeared.

"Oh, this is an interesting guy."

Jason leaned in to peer over her shoulder. The screen displayed a standard web site. The subject's name, social security number, and address in Bosque, Washington were displayed at the top. Below that, a highlighted line said he was currently a corporal with the Dunham County Sheriff's Office. On the right side, a color photograph, borrowed from DMV or his department identification.

Below that was listed each of Wilcox's run-ins with the law.

"Can you print that out?"

"Sure." She hit a couple of keys and a printer somewhere began to whirr.

"Minor In Possession," Danny read aloud. "Assault, assault, criminal mischief, another MIP, another assault."

"Somebody likes to party. And fight."

"I guess." She said and pointed at a column. "Get this: the charges were dropped. Every one of them. These are all just arrests; he has no criminal record."

Jason frowned. "Seems awfully lucky."

"Seems more like a guardian angel."

"'Guardian angel?'"

"Yeah, guardian angel, rabbi, mentor. There are different names for it," she said. "Friends in high places who make problems like this go away. How much you want to bet he has a family member somewhere in local law enforcement?"

"Not a dime," he told her. "Not a dime. Notice that there's also nothing at all in the last three years? I wonder if that's when he joined the force."

"Let's see if we can find out."

Danny hit another series of keys and a new screen popped up, a familiar blue and white one.

"Facebook?"

She smiled. "Us cops use social media too. It's a great source of information. Let's see whether Deputy Wilcox has a Facebook page."

She typed the deputy's name in the search box. A few seconds later a list of possible candidates appeared, along with their profile pictures.

"There," Jason pointed to the third entry in the list. "That's him."

Danny clicked on the name and called up Deputy Wilcox's Facebook page. The background photo showed him posing with a buck deer, obviously his kill. The timeline showed much of the usual meaningless drivel one found on Facebook.

Danny clicked on the "Work and Education" link.

"There you go," Danny said.

The page said that Travis Wilcox had graduated from Bosque Consolidated High School in 2013, graduated from the Washington State Police Academy that same year, and immediately joined the Dunham County Sheriff's office as a patrol deputy.

That explained the sudden absence of recent arrests. No matter how much Wilcox liked to drink and fight, his fellow cops weren't going to arrest him. Even if he beat up and terrified his girlfriend, they would look the other way, make excuses. Cops didn't arrest fellow cops, unless they had no choice. It was the brotherhood of blue.

"Let's see who his daddy is," Danny clicked on the "friends and family" link. Facebook only showed the family he both admitted to and had Facebook accounts, so Jason sincerely hoped he was close to his family. Especially his guardian angel.

"Wow," Danny said when the results displayed.

Dozens of thumbnails filled the screen. Wilcox had one heck of an extended family. Jason saw cousin after cousin, a couple of brothers, a sister, aunts and uncles. But what drew his attention was the very first profile.

"I think I've found Wilcox's guardian angel." He pointed to the profile.

It was State Senator Morris Barton. He was listed as grandfather.

"Maybe," Danny said and pointed at another profile. "Or maybe this one."

She pointed at another profile. It was Sheriff Michael Barton. The Sheriff was his uncle.

"No wonder your girl was afraid," Danny said. "This guy is connected. Very connected."

♦

"So what now?" Danny asked. They were camped in Jason's motel room, having decided they wouldn't be able to find out anything else at the sheriff's office they couldn't find in the civilian world. Strictly speaking, it was illegal to use department tools for private purposes. After the events in Port Salish, they both had a certain amount of capital within the department; but it wouldn't be wise to push it. They'd left before somebody got curious and asked what they were doing.

Jason set two cans of vending machine Coke on the table and took a seat across from her. Danny thanked him. "So, again, what are you going to do now you know who you're up against?"

"I don't know. I need to read the email Lisa sent me, see if she uncovered some gems in her research. Maybe when I get back to Seattle I can run down some people who used to live there."

He was also dying to hear what Debbie had learned from the Renton detectives.

Danny stifled a yawn and popped the tab on her Coke.

"So tell me, Detective Hayden," he peered at her as he opened his own Coke. He thought she looked weary. "How does one take down a department that's corrupt from top to bottom?"

"I don't know." She thought about it for a few seconds. "The easiest way is probably to bring in an outside agency, like the State or Feds."

Jason was already shaking his head. "I've already talked to a contact with the Attorney General's Office. They can't do anything unless they're invited in by the locals. He said the ultimate authority rests with the individual city and county councils."

"Really?"

He nodded. "I didn't know that either. I always thought the State Police supervised the County, which supervised the City. That sort of thing."

"Learn something new every day," she shrugged.

"So it begs the question, who polices the police?"

"Like you said: the city and county councils. And the sheriff and district attorney in most counties are elected offices. If they are corrupt, vote in someone else."

"That's how it's supposed to work anyway. The reality is often different."

"I know. If law enforcement is that corrupt, odds are the political system is too." She smiled briefly, sadly. "Your best bet is probably to do what you do best: write the story. Maybe when it's made public, it will generate enough pressure that they'll have no choice but to crack down."

"That reminds me." He groaned. "I still need to write a story about Marks' trial today or my editor will have my head."

Danny stifled another yawn. Naturally, Jason immediately had to yawn too. Then Danny yawned again.

"Sorry," she said. "I guess I was more stressed about this trial than I thought. I feel like I haven't slept in a week."

Jason checked the time. It was just after 3:00 in the afternoon. "We have a couple of hours before dinner. Why don't you crash while I whip up a story for Miles? Power nap?"

"Good idea." she pushed herself away from the table. "Text me when you're ready for dinner."

"Why don't you just stretch out here? I promise I'll be quiet."

She hesitated, glancing at the bed. "You sure?"

"I'm not afraid," he said as he pulled his laptop from its case, "if you're not."

♦

It took Jason nearly two full hours to cobble together a story that he felt comfortable sending to his editor. The problem was the trial itself was anti-climactic. The plea deal meant he had none of the high drama a trial usually provided. With no drama coming out of the trial, it took nearly all his writing skill to infuse some into the story.

While he struggled on the word processor, Danny slept on the bed five feet to his left, her legs drawn up into a fetal position, her hands tucked under her head. She looked peaceful. Her chest slowly rising and falling, her hair spread in a dark halo over the pillow, lips slightly parted.

Jason could clearly see what she'd looked like as a child.

His awareness of her sleeping right next to him may have contributed just a bit to the difficulty he had with his story.

At exactly 5:12 he logged on to the newspaper's network, uploaded his story and sent it to Miles, his editor. He hoped they'd be able to pair it with a file photo. Or they could run it without a photo; they would do what they wanted.

It wasn't a headline story. But it was a story.

He glanced over at Danny, wondering whether he should try and wake her. If they were going to do the dinner and movie thing tonight, they didn't have a whole lot of time to waste.

The decision was made for him. His cell chirped an incoming text. He slid it out of his pants pocket and checked the display. It was from Debbie. He opened it.

Talked to your detectives. Too much to text. Call me.

Jason glanced at Danny, who was still sleeping soundly, then tiptoed out of the motel room, easing the door closed behind him. He took a few steps down the walkway and dialed Debbie's cell.

"Hey, Jason," Debbie answered before the first ring ended. "I hear your big trial was kind of a bust."

"Yeah, but it all ended up in the same place. He's going to jail for a long time."

"Would have been nice to see his face when those guilty verdicts came down."

"Yeah, but I'll still take it," he told her. "You said you had something from the detectives?"

"They were happy to talk," she said. "It's still an open case, but if they don't get something to work on soon it will officially go cold."

"Do they have any suspects? Persons of interest?"

"Not really. There's an ex-husband, but he's got a rock-solid alibi. He's a sheriff's deputy and was on duty the night she died. In fact, he was writing a speeding ticket at the exact time of her death."

"That's about as good as an alibi gets. Let me guess, he's with the Dunham County Sheriff's Department?"

"Just a minute," Jason could hear her paging through her notes. "And we have a winner. That important?"

"Could be. Was he the only suspect?"

"The only real one. She didn't seem to have any other enemies. All her co-workers and neighbors liked her. They couldn't find anyone else with a motive. And this was a vicious crime, Jason. They tied her up, raped her, doused her with lighter fluid, and burned her alive."

"Jesus…"

"Yeah."

"You said 'they.'"

"That's right. They don't think one person could have overpowered her like that."

"Any witnesses? Forensic evidence?"

"No. The closest neighbor—in the other half of the duplex—was out of town. No one else noticed anything before the fire. And the fire destroyed most of the forensic evidence.

The autopsy couldn't even tell for sure whether she was raped, though they're assuming she was."

"Because?"

"They didn't want to say, but she was naked when she was tied to the four bed posts and set on fire." Debbie said. "Whoever this was, they're animals."

"And they've gotten away with it."

Debbie made a sound that sounded like a growl.

"How far did they look into the Dunham County connection?" he asked.

"They looked into it. They went over there and asked questions. The problem is there is no evidence and their best suspect has an air-tight alibi. They can't even get a search warrant. Unless some new evidence shows up, there's nothing they can do."

Jason groaned.

"And there's something else. According to her ex, she was emotionally unstable, extremely vindictive."

"Yeah, but that's her ex," Jason said.

"But get this, apparently she claimed to have been gang raped just before she'd moved to Renton, supposedly by her ex-husband and some of his friends. The investigation could find no witnesses, no evidence and was eventually closed as without basis."

"Who did the investigation?"

"The Dunham County Sheriff," she told him. "The alleged crime took place in their jurisdiction."

"So we basically had the ex-husband's buddies investigating themselves and finding themselves innocent."

"Pretty much," Debbie said. "Even the Renton detectives said it's like a banana republic over there."

"So they think it was the ex-husband and his friends?"

"They wouldn't say that, but I get the impression that's what they think. They just don't have enough evidence."

"The Blue Wall of Silence."

"Yeah," she said. "Anyway, I hope this helps."

"It does. Thanks. You going to do a story for the detectives?"

"As soon as I hang up."

"Do me a favor? Email a copy to me?"

"Done."

They disconnected.

Jason turned back toward the motel room. Danny stood right behind him, her arms wrapped around herself. Her eyes were puffy slits against the daylight and her hair tousled.

He had to fight the sudden urge to cuddle her.

"What's going on?" she asked.

"I didn't want to wake you," he told her. "One of my colleagues just interviewed the detectives who investigated the death of the Attorney General's complaining witness. She was just briefing me on what she'd learned."

She shrugged. "Which was?"

"The Dunham County Sheriff's Department appears to be dirty. Pigsty dirty."

♦♦♦♦♦

State Senator Morris Barton poured three fingers of bourbon into a glass, added a couple of ice cubes, and carried it back to his desk. "You sure you don't want some? It's fourteen years old, smooth as silk."

His grandson smiled but shook his head. "Not tonight. I want my judgment clear for a while."

"Are you saying my judgment isn't clear?"

"Not at all." Scott shook his head. "But you've had a lot more practice than I have."

"Now that's true." He smiled and sipped his bourbon.

Morris pulled a chair over beside his grandson and executive assistant and sat where he could have a clear view of the computer monitor. The screen showed a photograph, a still image from the video Scott was about to begin editing. The screen showed a darkened bedroom, one of the guest rooms from the hunting lodge.

Placing the micro cameras around the lodge had been Scott's idea. The Barton men had been holding parties out at the lodge for generations, either drunken blowouts with friends and hunting buddies, or as a little something extra for clients. It was simply good business, a fringe benefit of being a friend of the

Barton family. Anything that could be embarrassing never left the lodge.

Then Scott pointed out the obvious. Each of those potentially embarrassing incidents could be used as leverage. Each of them was potentially invaluable. It was the ultimate currency: power.

"Remember J. Edgar Hoover?" Scott had asked. "How do you think he managed to stay Director of the FBI for more than thirty years? No matter who was president?"

Morris didn't know that he'd given it much thought. He'd always found history boring.

"Hoover had files on everyone. Files full of dirt and potential embarrassment. Everyone, including presidents, had to know that any move they made against Hoover, any attempt to cross him, would mean the contents of that file would be made public."

Morris could see the possibilities.

"Most of the time, Hoover's files never had to be used. It was enough that everyone knew they existed."

It had been a brilliant idea, and it had served Morris well, both in business and in the halls of the State capitol.

Scott started playing the video. After a few seconds, the image of the bedroom came to life as the door swung open and a young woman in a short party dress stepped in, followed by a middle-aged man with a half-unbuttoned dress shirt.

"Hello, Congressman," Morris said.

Danny insisted she needed to freshen up before dinner. Jason recognized that any argument would be useless, so he followed her back to her room and settled at the little table while she carried her makeup kit into the bathroom and flipped on the lights.

"Tell me what you found out about the murder."

Jason told her what Debbie had learned from the Homicide detectives, from the circumstances of Elizabeth Jensen's death, to their inquiries in Dunham County. She was particularly interested in the divorce and her accusations of rape.

"In other words she might be a vindictive kook," Danny said.

"Possibly," he admitted. He could see Danny's reflection in the bathroom mirror. She was carefully lining her eyes. "Except that you'd think she'd have shown some sign of it to her neighbors and coworkers. It's hard to hide that level of vindictiveness. But they all had nothing but good to say about her."

"Yeah. It's more likely her ex and his friends decided to shut her up for good."

"And send a message to anyone else who might be thinking about causing them trouble," he added. "Doing so could be bad for your health."

"Exactly."

"But we have the same problem the detectives do," he said. "We have no idea who 'they' are."

"Sure you do. They're members of the sheriff's department."

"Yeah, but which ones?"

"That's what you need to figure out," she said.

"That, and find enough evidence to prove it."

And he needed to do it before Helen became another victim.

♦

They were trying to find some place to eat. Jason was going through the restaurant section of the phone book, courtesy of the motel. Neither of them was familiar enough with Friday Harbor to have any real preferences, other than the steak house they'd gone to the night before. And that had been too rich and too expensive to be a regular thing.

"What do you feel like?" he asked.

"I don't know…something light. No more steaks and cheesecake for a while, I think." She patted her hips pointedly. Jason thought her hips looked fine. And the rest of her smelled just fine after her efforts in the bathroom.

"How about some seafood? A nice snapper filet maybe."

He looked up at her. "You like seafood?"

"Yeah. Shouldn't I?"

"No. That's great. Let's do seafood."

Lisa hated seafood. She couldn't even stomach the smell of it. It didn't matter what shape or form it came in. She'd disliked clam chowder just as much as salmon; shrimp just as much as calamari. Needless to say, as a couple, Jason and Lisa had never set foot in a seafood restaurant. Though Jason liked seafood on occasion, he had sacrificed it on the altar of their relationship.

They found a restaurant that was aptly named *Chinook* down on the harbor. It had huge picture windows offering views of the harbor and marina. The interior walls were covered with netting, ship's wheels, and glass floats. The air was heavily scented with the smell of the Sound.

Jason imagined that during the height of tourist season, he and Danny would have had to wait an hour or more for a table. Tonight though, the dining room was about half full and they were shown immediately to a nice table, overlooking the harbor. When the waitress asked whether they'd like a cocktail to begin, they exchanged a look. Jason ordered a Widmer's Hefeweisen; Danny said she'd have the same thing.

"Their chowder is world famous.," Jason said, when the waitress had gone for their drinks and they were looking over the menu. "It says so right here on the menu."

"Every restaurant along the coast has world famous chowder. Didn't you know that?"

When the waitress returned with two glasses of beer, they were ready to order. Danny chose a baked snapper filet with a baked potato. Jason went with the halibut steak, also with a baked potato. Instead of salads, they had to try the world famous chowder.

The waitress left to get their meals started.

Jason lifted his beer glass. "To stopping the bad guys."

"Stopping the bad guys." Danny lifted her glass to clink against his.

They both drank.

The beer was good: fresh, hoppy, and ice cold.

"Speaking of bad guys," Danny looked up at him. "What's your plan?"

"My plan?"

"What are you going to do about those guys in Dunham County?"

"I don't know. I don't have one yet."

"Well, that's a first," she smiled. "You always have a plan."

"I'm working on it."

Danny peered at him over her beer. "It's not like you to shy away from a murderer."

"This one's complicated. What if my asking pointed questions puts Helen in more danger? What if they assume she brought me in and retaliate? What if my trying to get justice for one murdered woman ends up causing another?"

"Good point."

Jason took another swallow of beer. It didn't help.

"However, doing nothing isn't likely to help her much either," Danny said. "Whatever she's tangled up in is likely to get worse before it gets better. That's how these things go. Abusers never stop abusing. Not voluntarily."

Jason was aware of that. "It would be so much easier if she just asked for help."

"There's something else you have to think of."

"What's that?"

"There's got to be ten or twelve thousand people in Dunham County. Helen Miller is probably not the only one in danger."

♦

The "world famous" chowder the restaurant advertised on its menu was good, creamy, with plenty of chunks of potato and clam. Jason liked it. He polished off the entire cup. Danny did the same with hers. However, neither could see a reason for it to be "world famous."

"Maybe they got a good review from a foreign tourist," Jason offered.

"I think every restaurant on the coast is required to say it. The Tourism Board says so, or something."

He laughed.

The waitress cleared away their chowder cups and returned a few moments later with their entrees. They smelled fabulous.

"I can't believe I gave this up for so long," Jason said, a flaky chunk of halibut balanced on his fork.

Danny smiled. He'd told her about Lisa's aversion to seafood. "I'm kind of surprised Lisa asked you to get involved in this thing with Helen, considering what happened last time."

What happened last time was that someone had tried to shoot Jason to stop his investigation. To be more accurate, they had successfully shot him, but failed to kill him and failed to derail his investigation. He had the scars to prove it, one on his bicep and one in the webbing between the thumb and forefinger on his right hand.

Then they'd tried to burn them all to death.

Lisa had not taken it well. Not well at all.

"I don't think she'd thought it through that far," he said. "She just wanted to help her friend. I was her best way of doing that."

Danny thought about it and took a sip of her beer. "What do you think she would say if she knew a murder was in the mix this time? A very brutal murder?"

"I don't know." Jason thought about it for a minute. "I don't know. The situation isn't the same. We aren't the same people. Our relationship isn't the same."

Danny speared a green bean with her fork.

♦

"I don't think I ever told you how much I admired you that weekend," Danny said. Their dinner plates had been cleared away. Now they were nursing their second beers and chatting.

It was nice.

"What for?"

"You'd been shot, yet you were the only one calm enough to keep us from running to the emergency room. It probably saved our lives. You had to have been scared to death and in serious pain, but you kept your head. Not many people could do that."

Jason could feel his face growing warm. "I think I was in shock more than brave, or anything. But thanks."

"Still," she smiled. "It had to hurt like hell."

"It did, but mostly later that night and it wasn't life-threatening."

"Let me see." She grabbed his hand and pulled it across the table. Her fingers carefully traced the pencil-diameter-sized scar between his thumb and forefinger. "Does it still hurt?"

"Not much. My arm gets stiff sometimes, but not my hand."

She did not release his hand.

Jason turned his hand over and grasped hers. Her hand felt warm and dry and strong.

She smiled and squeezed his hand.

"So," he managed to say. "Want to get out of here?"

♦

The ringing woke Jason from a dead sleep. He reached over to the nightstand to turn off the alarm, but couldn't find it. His bedroom was still pitch black. It was so dark he couldn't even find the face of the alarm clock. He flailed away across the surface of the nightstand. Nothing. The ringing continued like a bad dream.

"What is it?" Danny mumbled in the dark beside him.

Jason sat up, abruptly aware he wasn't at home. He was in a motel room. And it wasn't his alarm ringing. It was his cell phone.

The phone rang again. After the fourth ring, it went to voicemail.

Beside him, Danny rose on one elbow. "That your phone?"

"I think so." He'd put the phone on the charger last night. It was across the room.

It rang again. Jason lunged out of bed and got to the phone just as the second ring started. He glimpsed Lisa's name as he accepted the call. "I'm here."

"Sorry I woke you, but I got a call a few minutes ago."

He glanced at the time. It was barely 6:00 in the morning. "Helen?"

Jason wasn't half asleep anymore.

He turned toward the bed. Danny had switched on the bedside light and was sitting up, the bedclothes clutched over her breasts, watching him. A part of him remarked how weird this was. He was on the phone, talking to Lisa, with Danny lying naked in his bed, watching him.

"No," Lisa said. "It was Helen's mom. Helen's missing."

Eight

Almost an hour after full dark, the fishing boat cruised past the breakwater and into a small port on the coast of Oaxaca, Mexico. It moved sedately through the calm night, accompanied by the muted putt-putt of its ancient diesel engine. The crew did little but watch the lights go by. Their work was behind them, setting and retrieving nets during the daylight hours, trying to fill their hold for the morning fish market.

The skipper expertly maneuvered the boat into the little commercial marina and eased it into a vacant slip. Two crew members—wiry men in faded tank tops and jeans—leapt from the boat and tied off the bow and stern lines. A second later, the diesel coughed twice and went silent.

The crew tied and latched doors and covers with the efficiency of people who have done the same thing every day for many years. As they worked, they spoke in lightning-fast exchanges of Spanish.

"Hey, Juan!" a man called over from a nearby boat. "Do any good today?"

The captain, Juan, chuckled. "A little bit. I paid for my fuel anyway."

His friend laughed. "Sometimes that's a good day."

"You speak the truth, my friend. You speak the truth. Goodnight, Cesar. I need to get home before my children forget what their daddy looks like."

"Goodnight. Tomorrow is another day."

With the boat secure, Juan and his crew gathered their personal belongings, thermoses, battered lunch pails, overshirts for the cool mornings, and climbed down onto the dock and started the trudge home.

If anyone noticed that there was one more person in the crew than there had been when the boat left that morning, they knew better than to mention it.

Once in town, Taylor Smith thanked his new friends in Spanish and parted company. While the fishermen went home to their families, he walked in the direction of a nearby hotel.

Tomorrow, after a good night's sleep, he would begin the process of getting into the States without raising any red flags.

Nine

"What do you mean 'missing'?" Jason asked.

"They can't find her. They don't know where she is," Lisa told him. "She went out last night and never came home. She's never done that before. She wouldn't do that."

"Do they know where she went? Who she was with?"

"Her mother said it was that deputy she was seeing," Lisa said. "Jason, she said they called him, but he said he didn't know where she was. He told them she ran away."

"Ran away? Really?"

"I know." Lisa was on the point of tears, herself. "She doesn't know what to do."

Jason couldn't blame the mother, considering what he knew about the Dunham County Sheriff's Department. Mrs. Miller certainly couldn't trust them to help her. Sure, it was possible that Helen had grown fed up with her situation and decided to make a fresh start somewhere else. She clearly hadn't been happy. But Jason's impression had been that the only reason she had gone back home in the first place was to help her family. That need hadn't changed. It seemed out of character to abandon them now.

Motion across the room caught his eye. He looked over in time to see Danny gather her clothes and scurry into the bathroom. A second later, the shower started up.

"How'd she get your number?" he asked Lisa.

"She was looking through Helen's things and found the business card we left with her."

"So Helen kept it," Jason said. "That's good."

"I told her I'd talk to you and call her back. What do you want me to tell her?"

Jason paused a moment to consider his answer.

"Tell her she and her husband need to go about their normal routine. Open the restaurant like usual. It won't be easy, but they need to be where they usually are in case Helen tries to get a hold of them."

"You think she's okay?"

"I hope so, but if she is, she may not have her cell phone. They need to be in a place she can reach them on a landline."

"Okay," Lisa said. "What are you going to do?"

"I'm not sure. I'll probably head down there, but not until later this afternoon or evening. There's some people I want to talk to first."

"What do you want me to do?"

"Stay there, near the phone," he told her. "You're their contact person. Helen's probably talked about you. You're familiar. They'll feel more comfortable talking with you."

Lisa agreed.

"Have them call you if they hear from Helen, or if there are any other developments. You can let me know. My cell is fully charged. I'll always have it nearby."

Lisa accepted this. "You'll let me know what happens?"

"Of course. Now call Helen's mother back and tell her I'm working on it."

"Okay. Be careful, okay? Promise me."

"I promise."

"Danny too."

She disconnected before he could react.

♦

Danny emerged from the bathroom a few minutes after Lisa's call. Her hair was wrapped like a turban in a white towel and she wore the same slacks and blouse she'd worn yesterday. Any change of clothes she had was still in her own motel room.

She walked over to kiss him on the cheek. She smelled clean and soapy.

"What's going on?"

"Helen's gone missing," he told her. "Her mother called Lisa."

"I figured it was something like that," she said, removed her turban, and sat on the edge of the bed to begin toweling her hair. "So what's next?"

"Go down there, I guess. See if I can help."

She nodded. She was drying her hair by rubbing lengths of it between two parts of the towel. It looked like a ritual.

"You want to come with me?"

She stopped her drying motions, looked up at him.

"Like you said, we make a good team. And you're not scheduled to work the rest of the week anyway."

"I was scheduled for court duty. That's no longer necessary and the boss knows it," she told him. Then, after a moment. "But I could ask to take it as personal time."

"Would you?"

"Understand, I have no jurisdiction in Dunham County. No official status at all. I would be there as a private citizen."

"I'd rather have you helping me as a private citizen than a dozen FBI agents."

"You're sweet," She smiled and resumed drying her hair. "What do you think we'll be able to do down there?"

"Like a wise person once said, write about it. Make it such a spectacle that the public forces someone to crack down."

"And the folks who burned that woman to death are just going to let us do this?"

"Probably not," he told her. "But we're smarter than they are. And I have a feeling they're not used to resistance. They're certainly not expecting it."

She tossed the towel to the side and stood. "I'm going to change clothes and make that phone call."

"Okay."

He stepped over to her and they embraced.

"We're going to need to stop at a drugstore at some point too," Danny said.

"We are?"

"Unless you want to be a daddy." She smiled. "I'm not on birth control."

Joseph Mullens was not accustomed to being kept waiting. Important people did not wait. Powerful people did not wait. Until a year ago, he had been one of them, an important, powerful man. No one made Lundgren Corporation's Director of Security wait for a meeting, not if they knew what was good for them. No one.

Technically, he still was Director of Security. He was just on administrative leave until the indictments hanging over his head went away.

Which was why Mullens was sitting in the posh waiting area at the law firm of Beckham, Hopkins, Cullen, and Thomas, trying to not look at his watch. He didn't want the bimbo behind the reception desk to have the satisfaction.

Finally, almost twenty minutes after the scheduled appointment, Fredrick Beckham strode through an oak door and into the waiting room, his hand extended. "Joseph. Sorry to keep you waiting, but I was on a conference call for another client."

Mullen had risen to his feet and accepted the attorney's handshake. "No apologies necessary. Such things happen."

Neither of them believed a word they were saying, but it was part of the dance.

"Come back to my office," Beckham told him. "We can talk there."

Mullens followed the attorney through a door and down a long carpeted corridor to a nicely furnished corner office. It was only fitting, since Beckham was the senior partner in the firm. It was also fitting that the senior partner was personally handling his case.

"Can I get you some coffee?" Beckham asked as he ushered Mullens into his office. "Or something stronger? Bourbon? Scotch?"

"I'm fine. This isn't a social call."

"No, it isn't, is it?"

Beckham stepped around his desk and lowered himself into a black leather desk chair. "You've heard that Timothy Marks agreed to plead guilty to reduced charges?"

"I heard." Mullens selected one of the client chairs and sat facing his attorney. "Marks was a useful idiot. He was always expendable."

Beckham adjusted a legal pad on his desk, straightening it. "He will probably testify against you."

"Not if he knows what's good for him. Has there been any other progress?"

"The District Attorney is confident of her case. She wants you to do serious jail time."

"That's unacceptable."

"I know," Beckham shrugged. "But that's where we are right now."

"So we beat her at trial."

"That might be easier said than done."

Mullens met his eyes. "Are you saying you can't win this case?"

"I'm saying the District Attorney is confident for a reason. She has a very strong case. She has you on tape, for God's sake. You think a jury is going to ignore that?"

Mullens didn't care about the difficulties; he cared about results.

"So how do we make sure the jury never hears those tapes?" he asked.

"We've filed a motion to have the entire group of files Smith turned over to Reynolds thrown out," Beckham told him. "We're arguing that since the contents were illegally obtained, they should not be admitted as evidence. The prosecution will argue that it wasn't a government agent that obtained them, so they should. The judge will decide."

"The judge will decide what? For us, or against us?"

Fredrick shrugged. "If I had to predict, I think she will rule against us. Neither Smith nor Reynolds *were* agents of the government, legally."

"Can we get a different judge?"

"Not with a guarantee that the outcome will be different."

Mullens nodded, calculating. Beckham was a good attorney. He trusted his judgment—as much as he trusted anyone—but he was an attorney. He was used to thinking within certain legal parameters. Mullens was used to working in whole dimensions Beckham had never considered. And never would.

"I'm assuming you have a Plan B?"

"Of course." Beckham said. "We attack the chain of custody, try to make it look like someone altered the contents before the police received it. Someone who might have a motive to act against you."

That struck Mullens as a more fruitful possibility. "Like Smith?"

"Smith," Fredrick agreed. "Or Reynolds and his friends. They're the only ones who can link this stuff to you. They say Smith gave it to them, but Smith is unavailable. If we can throw doubt on their credibility…"

"It all goes away."

"Possibly."

Joseph Mullens smiled. He was beginning to see all sorts of possibilities.

Jason showered, shaved, changed into fresh clothes and was packing his things when Danny rapped on his door. He let her in, they exchanged a quick kiss and he returned to gathering his things.

"Did you call your boss?"

She nodded. "He wasn't terribly happy about it, but I have the rest of the week. Have you talked to yours?"

"Not yet. But as long as I'm working a story, Miles will be fine with it," he told her. "Besides, I have a Pulitzer. For a while, I'm golden."

"Must be nice."

"It has its perks."

She let that remark go. "We need to talk some specifics before we go."

He turned to her. "Such as?"

Such as logistics. They had two cars and two sets of luggage sitting in Friday Harbor, on an island in Puget Sound, which wasn't home to either of them. They were heading to Dunham County which lay on the Pacific coast 150 miles southeast of them as the crow flies. Unfortunately, that crow flew over the roadless Olympic Mountains National Park to make the journey in 150 miles. Jason and Danny would have to drive around the mountains, either to the north, or the south, making their journey closer to 300 miles and six hours travel time.

There was no point in bringing both cars. They decided to take Danny's new Jeep because it was so cool and Jason's car was already in the Dunham system, courtesy of Deputy Wilcox.

After some discussion they decided to leave Jason's car in the long-term parking at the Port Townsend ferry terminal. It made sense. From there, they would skirt around the southern edge of the Olympics by heading west on Highway 10.

They loaded all their luggage into Danny's Jeep, checked out of their motel rooms and went for breakfast. While waiting for their food, Jason called the newspaper and let Miles know what he was up to. As he'd expected, Miles was fine with it. As long as there was a story.

He also called Lisa, to see whether there had been any new developments. There hadn't been.

"Was there anything useful in the profile I sent you?" Lisa asked.

Jason had to admit he hadn't had a chance to read it yet. "But I will read before I get there tonight."

"Okay." He wasn't sure whether she sounded hurt, or not.

A Brief History of Dunham County

Dunham County is rural and sparsely populated, with more than eighty percent of the land area covered by thick forest, steep terrain, usually both. The largest community is the county seat of Genoa at 4892. Only two other communities have populations over 1000: Bosque, at 2378; and Donald, at 1020. Olympic Mountains and Pacific beaches-related tourism is the largest employer during the summer months. Forest products, fishing, and government services are significant occupations.

Dunham County was founded in 1890, when citizens successfully petitioned the new Washington State Legislature to split off the western half of Jefferson County to form a new county. They argued that their interests were being ignored by a county government centered on the far side of the Olympic Peninsula in Port Townsend.

One of the leading petitioners was the owner of a sawmill and logging company in the town of Bosque named Hiram Barton. Hiram was the current Senator Barton's great-grandfather. He was also an aggressive and ambitious businessman who realized that having the county government closer to home would make it much easier to influence.

Barton Lumber was successful. By Hiram's death in 1921, it was the largest employer in the county. His oldest son, Jonas, took over, investing in the new technology of logging trucks and automated equipment, which boosted profits even more.

Jonas Barton lost big in the stock market crash of 1929 and committed suicide. He was unmarried and childless.

Jonas' younger brother, Samuel, took over what remained of the company. But Barton Lumber was not Samuel's only—or even primary—job. He worked as a deputy sheriff, becoming sheriff himself in 1931, when the previous sheriff was murdered. (That murder was never solved, by the way). So as the Depression hit, he had a good steady income from the County, separate from the mill.

Before long, Samuel Barton began taking advantage of the Depression by buying up foreclosed properties for pennies on the dollar throughout the County, much of it timberland and commercial properties. By the beginning of WWII, he owned more than a third of all private land in Dunham County, including virtually the entire town of Bosque and a quarter of Genoa, the County seat.

As demand for lumber increased because of the war, he began building new mills.

By the end of the war, Barton Lumber was perfectly positioned to exploit the post war boom. It had six lumber mills running at full capacity and several logging crews supplying those mills with his own timber. Samuel Barton was making millions.

Plus, he was still bringing in paychecks as Dunham County Sheriff.

Samuel retired due to health concerns in 1970 and turned the business over to his oldest son, the future State Senator Morris Barton. In 1975, Morris began selling the mills, even though they were incredibly successful. By 1979 all but one of the Barton mills had been sold and the money reinvested, mostly in commercial property in the Seattle area.

Then, in 1980, the bottom fell out of the lumber market. Mills closed down throughout the Pacific Northwest. Of all the lumber companies in western Washington, only Barton Industries escaped relatively unscathed. The Barton family was now one of the wealthiest in the state and one of the largest private landowners.

The most recent estimate has Morris Barton's net worth at $450,000,000.

In 1982, Morris Barton ran for and won the office of County Sheriff, the same office his father had held twenty years before and his grandfather before him. By all accounts, his tenure was successful and he was re-elected several times. In 2000, he turned that and his business success into a successful run for the State Senate as a Republican and has been re-elected twice. His oldest son, Michael Barton, took over as sheriff when Morris went to the Senate. His grandson, Scott Barton, served as campaign manager for his most recent campaign and continues as executive assistant.

Other than twenty years between 1962 and 1982, a Barton has been County Sheriff since 1931.

Another son, Patrick, is District Attorney. His daughter, Marcia Barton-Wilcox, and son-in-law run the businesses, though Morris remains as Chairman of the Board. The Mayor of Genoa is a cousin; so is the Police Chief and nearly half the deputies in the sheriff's department, and three out of five County Commissioners. One of the local judges is Morris's brother.

In other words, in many ways, Dunham County and the Barton family are the same entities.

P.S. Near as I can tell, a Barton has never been convicted of a crime in Dunham County.

Just something to keep in mind.

Lisa

Ten

"So let me see if I've got this right," Danny said as she guided the car around a tight turn. She was behind the steering wheel, while Jason sat in the passenger seat. He had just finished reading Lisa's report to her. They were still a couple of hours from Bosque. "We're going to be taking on basically the entire County government?"

Jason shrugged. "It sounds that way, doesn't it?"

They were heading east on Hwy 10, a two lane road that served as the northernmost east-west route across the peninsula, not the best. Hwy 12, farther south was a better, wider road, but out of the way if you were coming from Port Townsend.

Right now, they were stuck behind a Budweiser truck going forty-five around the curves and there was no good spot to pass it.

"I'm assuming you have a plan for this," Danny said.

"Of course."

She concentrated for a few moments on following the beer truck through a series of ess curves through the low, forested hills.

"Were you going to share it with me at some point?"

“Sure.” He smiled. “We’re going to blow them away with the power of the press.”

“Oh, okay. Thanks, I feel better now. I was obviously worrying over nothing.”

“What I thought,” he told her. “Is that, after getting all the info we can from Helen’s parents, we make no secret of who I am and why I’m there: a fairly high-profile reporter with a major daily newspaper behind us.”

“You think that will scare them?”

“I don’t think the head of the Barton clan got to be a state Senator by being stupid. My status will at least get him to play it cool. Doing anything to me would draw too much attention.”

She braked again as the beer truck slowed for a tight turn. “You’re assuming he has tight control over everyone in his family.”

Jason glanced over at her. “You think he got to this point by running a sloppy organization?”

Danny considered this for a minute, her eyes never leaving the road and the grimy rear end of the beer truck. “But, from what Lisa said, it sounds like his dad is the one who actually built it. And face it, if you control the entire legal system, you can get away with anything. Do that long enough and human nature says you start getting sloppy.”

“Which means you make mistakes,” he told her. “And you make a lot of enemies. People who are just waiting to get their chance at revenge. I’m hoping I will provide them that chance.”

She nodded.

“How are you on your history?”

“I suck,” she told him. “Always have.”

“Okay,” he said. “Have you heard about the Aztec Empire and how they were conquered by Hernan Cortez and five hundred Spaniards?”

“I remember something about that.”

“Well, it wasn’t that simple.”

“Nothing ever is.”

“The Aztecs had a wide-ranging empire across central Mexico, but they only directly ruled part of it. The rest were vassal states, who decided to ally with them and pay tribute rather than risk being conquered. But the vassals did not like or respect the Aztec; they feared them. So when the Spanish soldiers came with their horses and firearms, all these vassal states defected to the Spanish. They saw their chance to get rid of their hated Aztec overlords and they took it."

"Probably not the best decision, looking back now."

Jason shrugged. "They couldn't know that. They saw the Spanish as liberators."

A sign said a passing lane was coming in a half mile.

"Finally," Danny muttered.

Jason smiled.

"So you're going to be Cortez to Senator Barton's Montezuma?"

"That's the idea."

♦

Jason and Danny pulled into Bosque just after 7:00 Wednesday evening. It wasn't full dark yet, but it was getting there. The sun had dropped behind the western hills, throwing the Chumash River valley into deep shadow while leaving the sky above bright and almost white. The shadows were even deeper in the town itself, which had already all but shut down for the day. Most businesses had closed hours ago, their staff already home eating dinner or camped in front of the television with a cold beer.

The Pacific Ocean, about ten miles further west, lent a salty tang to the air.

"This place is even worse than Port Salish," Danny said. "Dead as a doornail."

Jason had taken over the driving duty about an hour ago. He kept a steady pace now, just below the posted speed limit, as they cruised into the older business district.

"Where are we going?" Danny asked him.

"I told Lisa to have Helen's parents meet us at the restaurant," he told her. "But I kind of want to get the lay of the land first."

"Okay."

Jason pointed out the Miller's restaurant on the left as they passed. It was the only place on the block with lights on, but seemed to be largely empty this late on a Wednesday evening. Only one vehicle was parked at the curb, a newer model pickup.

He could see no police or sheriff's cruisers anywhere. But that didn't mean anything.

"What are we looking for?" Danny asked. "Exactly."

"The Sheriff's people," he told her. "Keeping eyes on her parents. Last time, when Lisa and I came here, the deputy showed up about five minutes after we did. Someone called him."

Danny peered out her window as they continued through town. Not that there was a whole lot to see. Everything was locked down, dark and deserted. Only a couple of other cars moved on the streets and the sidewalks were empty. The only lights besides the streetlights were the yellow glow of windows in houses sitting in the blocks behind the main street.

No one seemed to be watching the restaurant.

A couple of blocks beyond the restaurant the town opened up and the buildings were newer and farther apart. Shortly after, they approached a new gas station with a minimart attached. It was lit up like a beacon and several cars were parked in the lot, a group of teens gathered near one of the cars.

"So now we know where the young people hang out," Danny said.

"And we can assume the cops aren't anywhere nearby."

"Buzz kills."

Jason pulled in to the station and parked beside the other cars. The teens ignored him.

"What are you doing?" Danny asked.

"Following a hunch. Helen wasn't that much older than these kids and it's a small town."

He shut the engine down and released his seat belt.

"Want any help?" Danny asked.

"No, I don't think so. I don't want to come across as intimidating. And you look like a cop."

"I look like a cop?"

Jason grabbed some business cards and stepped out of the car. The teens ignored him. Three boys and two girls, laughing at something as they stood between a tricked out Acura coupe, complete with a spoiler and custom paint job, and a lifted 4X4 Ford pickup with oversized tires and chrome roll bar. There wasn't a spot of dust on either paint job.

Jason smiled and strolled over toward them, trying to appear as non-threatening as he could manage. The conversation among the teens abruptly stopped, laughter cut off. He was an adult. The enemy was present.

"Hey guys," he said, smiling all the way. "Sorry to bother you, but I hope you can help me with something."

"What you need?" one of the boys said. He was clearly the alpha male, leaning on the Acura like he'd built it from scratch himself. He wore a tank top, cargo shorts, and a baseball cap turned backwards.

Jason handed each of them a business card. "Do any of you know Helen Miller?"

"Yeah," one of the girls said.

"What's it to you?" the alpha said and shot the girl a stifling look. Jason could see her wilt.

"She's gone missing. I'm helping her parents look for her. Maybe you guys could help point me in the right direction."

"She's missing?" The girl who knew Helen asked. She was tall, with dark hair hanging loose on the shoulders of a flannel shirt, worn open over a white tee and skinny jeans. Silver rings flashed on every finger. She was probably seventeen, but could have been a few years older or younger.

"No one's seen her since last night. You know who she hung out with, who her enemies were? Who should I be talking to?"

"Maybe she just took off," the alpha male said, "Got the hell out of this town."

"It's possible," Jason shrugged. "But would she do that without telling anyone?"

A series of shrugs all around.

"Who would you say is her best friend? Who did she hang around with?"

"Probably Jennifer Wilson," the second girl said. "That's who she hung out with in high school the most. I don't know how much they still do."

Jason repeated the name to make sure he had it right, thanked her.

"Wasn't she going out with Wilcox?" one of the boys said to no one in particular. Both girls agreed this was true.

The alpha male was shaking his head. "You don't want to screw with Wilcox."

"Why not?" Jason asked.

"Cause he don't take shit from anyone, that's why."

There comes a point in any interview where you've received all the information you're going to get. Jason had reached that point in this discussion. He politely thanked them all and urged them to call his cell should they think of anything that might help.

"Do you think she's okay?" the dark-haired girl asked.

"I don't know. I hope so."

Jason thought she was going to say something else, but she finally just wished him good luck.

He thanked them again and returned to the car.

"Did you learn anything?" Danny asked.

"Her best friend is named Jennifer Wilson. And everyone is afraid of Deputy Wilcox."

♦

Jason turned back on to the highway, heading east, back the way they'd just come. They were heading to the Miller's restaurant.

"How are you going to handle this?" Danny asked. "It's been almost twenty-four hours since they've seen their daughter. They're going to be beside themselves."

"I know. I'm accepting suggestions."

"Be calm, sympathetic. You don't know what they're going through; you can't even imagine what they're going through. Just tell them you're going to do everything in your power to find their daughter."

"The voice of experience?"

"Once or twice. Just don't promise anything you might not be able to deliver. They're clutching at straws and if you promise to bring her home safely and she ends up dead, they will never forgive you."

He nodded. "I don't know that I'd forgive myself."

He pulled in to the curb in front of the *City Center Café* and shut down the engine. The café was still lit, but looked completely empty. The sheet of plywood that had been covering one window last weekend was gone, replaced by new glass. The same truck was parked at the curb as when they'd passed earlier. They were parked directly behind it. The rest of the block was empty and dark. Several vehicles were parked in front of the tavern on the next block.

"One more thing," she stopped him with a touch on his arm as he released his seat belt. "What do you want my role to be?"

Jason smiled at her. "My partner."

"Besides that."

"You're advising me on law enforcement issues," he told her. "And keeping everyone honest. Including me."

♦

The *City Center Café* wasn't completely empty. One man sat alone in the first booth to their left as they walked in. He looked to be in his sixties, wore faded flannel and work jeans. A filthy ball cap rested on the table next to his platter of chicken fried steak and mashed potatoes. He glanced up as Jason and Danny stepped in, went back to his dinner.

Another man, who looked to be somewhere in his fifties stood up from the booth nearest the kitchen. He wore jeans, a loose gray cook's shirt and a yellow fiberglass cast over most of his right arm and elbow. "Welcome to the Café. Sit anywhere you'd like. Can I start you off with some coffee?"

"Coffee would be great," Jason said and ushered Danny to the booth opposite the one the man had just come from, which, judging from the coffee cups and mangled newspapers, was the break table for the staff. Danny slid into the side facing the kitchen. Jason slid in across from her, facing the door.

It was the same booth he and Lisa had sat in last weekend. He was in the exact same position.

The man—Mr. Miller, Jason assumed—placed two mugs of coffee in front of them, along with two menus. "Our special tonight is spaghetti with meatballs and garlic bread."

Jason glanced at Danny. They hadn't eaten anything but snack food since lunch. She shrugged and nodded.

"We'll take two specials," he said and handed the man the menus. On top, he'd placed one of his cards. "And we'd like a word with the owners, when they can."

Something passed over the man's face, almost a flinch. "We close in fifteen minutes. You'll probably be our last customers."

Jason nodded. They would still be eating when the front door was locked. It was perfectly normal. Restaurants did it all the time. The employees weren't often terribly happy about it, but it wasn't unusual.

Helen's father left to submit their order to the kitchen. He kept Jason's card.

"Wonderful," Danny muttered under her breath. "Spaghetti. And I'm hungry."

"You don't like spaghetti?" He thought she'd agreed to it. Now he felt bad.

"Oh, I love spaghetti with a good red sauce. But have you ever tried to carry on a serious conversation while eating spaghetti?"

He'd never thought about it. But now that she'd mentioned it, he could see how one's dignity could be in jeopardy. Only a cop would have a "do not eat" list for witness interviews.

"Dibs on the garlic bread," she said.

"You can have it all," he said. "Maybe we can even get some extra."

Helen's father stepped up to their table with a coffee pot in his left hand and wordlessly refilled their coffees. When he was finished, he walked down to the chicken fried steak guy and refilled his. They didn't exchange any small talk either.

Jason and Danny waited until he'd passed their booth and headed back into the kitchen to speak again.

"He doesn't seem to be beside himself with worry," Jason said when he was out of earshot.

"No, he doesn't, does he?"

"He doesn't seem to be much of anything," Jason said. "He's certainly not the jolly innkeeper."

"Did you see his forearm?" Danny asked. "The one not in a cast?"

Jason shook his head.

"Lots of little scars. Splatter burns, like from hot oil. I think he's normally the cook and his wife or Helen dealt with the customers. That broken arm changed things."

"That's what brought Helen back in the first place. They needed her help."

"He's probably feeling responsible for what's happening to his daughter. Probably feeling pretty guilty too."

"He's not showing it."

"Maybe that's how he deals with things," Danny said. "By shutting down, going inside. It's how my dad used to deal with problems. You could always tell when something was bothering him by how quiet and distant he was."

Jason stopped and peered at her. "I think that's the first time I've heard you mention your dad."

Danny shrugged. "He never came up before."

She looked up as the man approached carrying a single pasta bowl in his good left hand. A woman, also in her fifties and wearing a soiled white apron, followed with the second bowl and a side plate with their garlic bread. Jason could see just how inefficient being one-handed was in the restaurant business.

They set the food in front of Jason and Danny.

"Any word?" Jason asked quietly.

Mrs. Miller gave her head a tight shake.

"Enjoy your dinner," she said quietly. "We'll close soon and talk then. That would be for the best."

Helen's parents left to attend to their duties.

Jason and Danny ate their spaghetti quietly and quickly, working against a deadline. The chicken-fried steak guy finished his dinner and ordered a slice of pie. Of course. Helen's parents busied themselves with restocking and cleaning their work areas to prepare for closing. It made for kind of a weird atmosphere, like everyone was trying to stay busy as a dreaded medical procedure approached.

Finally, the old guy finished his dessert and slid out of his booth. Helen's father took his money, ushered him out the front door, and locked it behind him. He flipped the "open" sign to "closed" and switched off the outside lights.

The restaurant was officially closed. Jason had seen no sign of Deputy Wilcox or any other law enforcement.

Jason and Danny each took one more bite of their dinners and pushed the plates toward the edge of the table.

"It might be easier if we're on the same side of the table," Danny suggested. "You know, let them relax in their body space, team up."

That made sense. Danny slid out of the booth and moved over next to Jason, where they could see the door.

They sipped their coffee and waited.

A minute or so later, the Millers walked out of the kitchen, as a couple, holding hands. Mrs. Miller walked just slightly in the lead. As they approached the booth, Mrs. Miller dropped her husband's hand and grabbed Jason and Danny's soiled pasta bowls.

"Tom," she said as she moved them to the table directly across the aisle, the break table. "I thought you'd brought back all the dirty dishes?"

"All but those."

She shot him a dirty look, then slid into the booth beside him. Jason ended up facing Helen's father across the table; Danny sat across from his wife.

Jason started by introducing himself. "I don't know how much Lisa told you, but I'm an investigative reporter with the *Seattle News*."

Helen's father—Tom—nodded. "You're the one who found those graves up in the San Juans last year."

Jason glanced at Danny, who just smiled. "It was actually several people—including my friend Danny here—but yes, I wrote the story."

"None of us would even have bothered to look at Lundgren Corporation if it hadn't been for Jason. Once he gets onto a story," Danny said. "He's relentless."

"And from what I've already been able to find out about these people, I think our best weapon is to make everything as public as possible. I can put them on the front page of the *News*."

Mrs. Miller nodded. Her husband just frowned.

Jason opened his recorder app and set his cell on the table between them. "I'm going to record this just to make sure I get everything right. I've learned to not completely trust my memory."

Neither objected, or seemed bothered by the idea.

"Tell me about the last time you saw Helen."

"It was last night, just after closing," Mrs. Miller said. "Almost twenty-four hours ago."

Jason waited. He sensed, rather than saw, the couple grasping hands under the table, giving each other strength.

"We closed and cleaned up like usual," she continued. "Then went upstairs. We have a two bedroom apartment on the second floor."

Jason had not been aware of that. It made sense though now that he'd heard it.

"So Helen showered and changed and told us she was going out with Travis."

"That's Travis Wilcox?" Danny asked. "The deputy sheriff?"

"Yeah, Travis Wilcox."

"He's a son of a bitch," her husband said.

Jason thought that pretty much summed it up.

"Were they going somewhere together, or was she just going to hang out at his place?"

Mrs. Miller shook her head. "She didn't say and I didn't ask."

"Maybe we should have," Tom Miller muttered.

"Tom, she's nineteen, a grown woman. We can't treat her like a child."

Jason didn't want this conversation to degenerate into a marital quarrel. It would do none of them—particularly Helen—any good. In fact, the couple could shut down completely and miss telling them some critical detail. He couldn't let that happen.

"How did she seem, emotionally?" he asked. "Did she seem upset or worried, or anything?"

"No, nothing like that. Nothing unusual."

"When did you start worrying about her?"

They exchanged a look, seemed to agree on something.

"When she didn't show up in time for work," Mrs. Miller said. "She's never done that before. Not without calling. She just wasn't here."

Danny spoke for the first time. "Helen has a cell phone?"

"Yes. We tried calling, but it just goes to voicemail."

"You mind if I try?"

Mrs. Miller told Danny Helen's cell phone number. Danny tapped it into her cell and put the phone to her ear. A moment later, she shook her head. "Inbox is full."

She shut down her phone again.

"Did you talk to Deputy Wilcox?" Jason asked. "Ask him if he knew where she was?"

Tom Miller blew air through his lips.

"We called him, of course." His wife said. "He said he hadn't seen her since two in the morning. That's when he says he dropped her off here."

"She rode with him?"

"She doesn't have a car," Mrs. Miller said. "She always rode with him or one of her other friends. If she wasn't going to be gone long, she borrowed ours."

Tom sighed. "All her savings were supposed to be for college. He even managed to ruin that."

"How did he do that?"

Mr. Miller lifted his right arm, encased in bright new fiberglass from his hand past his elbow. "He gave me this. A couple of blows with a baton and suddenly I'm not much of a cook anymore, am I?"

Jason could see how that would be a problem.

"Helen never admitted it, but I know that he broke my arm to get her to come back. He knew we wouldn't be able to run the café without her help. Not like this."

"Tom isn't much of a people person," Mrs. Miller said. "He's not very good at things like small talk and being cheery, so he isn't the best waiter. But he's a tremendous cook."

"Wait a minute." Danny was frowning. "He just walked up to you and broke your arm? Just like that?"

"Just like that." Tom nodded. "And then charged me with resisting arrest. I'm out on bail now."

"Were there witnesses? People who saw what happened?"

"Sure. It happened right in the parking lot of the bank here in town. Not that any of them would testify against Wilcox. It wouldn't be good for their health, if you know what I mean. His uncle's the Sheriff."

Jason knew perfectly well what he meant.

"They don't need to testify. They just need to be willing to tell me what they saw," he told them. "I'd like you to write out a list of people who might have seen what Wilcox did. I will try to talk to them."

"I can do that."

Jason turned his attention to Mrs. Miller. "I want you to write out a list too. I need to know every friend Helen has. Every girlfriend, every male friend. Every person she might conceivably have confided in about her worries and fears. As much as we love our parents, there are some subjects we just don't feel comfortable discussing with them."

"Okay," Mrs. Miller said. "I can come up with most of them, I think."

"Now, have you filed a missing person's report?" Jason asked.

"What's the point?" Tom snarled. "They going to arrest themselves?"

"I meant with the City Police."

"There is no Bosque Police Department," Mrs. Miller told them. "The Sheriff's Department handles all calls outside Genoa. It will be the Sheriff's Department we'd be dealing with."

That made things a bit more complicated.

"You still need to call 911 and report Helen missing," Danny told them.

"Again, what's the point?" Tom objected. "They aren't going to do anything."

“It creates a paper trail,” she said. “State law requires all 911 calls to be recorded and stored. If you call and they don’t do anything, the 911 call is evidence.”

“And if they just erase it?”

“That, in itself, is also a crime,” she told him. “And it raises the obvious question of why would they want to erase the tape? What are they hiding?”

“She’s right,” Jason agreed. “We need to force their hand, make them make a mistake.”

Jason had no illusion that filing a report would accomplish anything in a concrete sense. The Dunham County Sheriff’s Department wouldn’t seriously do anything that might hurt one of its own. But it was important to get them on the record. Even if—as he suspected—they just opened a file, then closed it immediately, it established a record. And it established that they didn’t act on it.

That fact could come back to bite them.

“This is important,” he told the Millers.

Mrs. Miller nodded. “I’ll make the call.”

Her husband still didn’t seem convinced.

♦

Filing the missing person’s report was the ultimate in anticlimax. The deputy who arrived ten minutes after Barbara Miller made the call was young, sympathetic, and completely professional. He asked all the right questions—many, in fact, of the same questions Jason and Danny had asked—and scribbled the answers in his notebook. He’d asked Jason and Danny who they were when he’d first arrived. They told him they were friends of the family. Otherwise, the deputy paid no attention to them.

After about twenty minutes of question and answer, he sat back in his booth. “I think I’ve got all the information I need for now. We’ll send an alert to all our patrol deputies to keep an eye out for her as soon as I get it in the computer. A detective may contact you tomorrow if he needs more information.”

“Thank you,” Barbara Miller shook his hand as he rose from the booth.

"She'll probably show up on her own in the morning," he said. "It happens more than you think with girls her age."

"Girls her age," Jason thought to himself, were just about the young deputy's age. He couldn't have been much more than twenty himself.

Throughout the interview, Tom had volunteered nothing, only answering direct questions and then only with one-word answers. His eyes never left the table top. If the young deputy had picked up on the hostility, it didn't seem to bother him.

"I can show myself out." The deputy met Jason's eyes, turned and walked out the front door, already talking on his shoulder radio.

"Well," Danny murmured beside Jason. "Now they know we're here."

"Yep."

Barbara Miller got up and locked the door behind the deputy. She turned back to the rest of them. "Now what?"

Jason patted the lists in his pocket. "Nothing more tonight. We should all get some rest. The fun will start tomorrow."

Eleven

After collecting the Millers' lists and exchanging cell phone numbers all around, Jason and Danny left to find a motel room. Just like last time, when he and Lisa had come down, they had to travel the thirty miles to Genoa to find a decent motel. They ended up renting a room in the same motel he and Lisa had stayed in. It was clean, quiet and located close to the highway and business district.

He'd rented one room under the names Mr. and Mrs. Jason Reynolds.

During the drive over, Jason had paid close attention to his rearview mirror, but had seen no sign of anyone following them. In some stretches, there had been no lights behind them at all.

So far, so good.

"You think we should hide the car?" Danny asked as they headed toward their room.

"I don't think there's much point yet. If they want to find us, it won't be hard. There aren't that many motels around."

The motel was laid out in a horseshoe shape around a central parking area and a small, kidney-shaped pool. Their room was on the second tier on the short wing farthest from the street and the office. The parking area was about a third full. It would probably be packed during tourist season.

Or not. He didn't know how many tourists made it out to this remote corner of the state.

"Dibs on the bathroom," Danny said as they entered the room. "I've had to pee for an hour."

"Go for it," he set their suitcases on the luggage stand provided and arranged his laptop and briefcase on the small desk. The other bags he left on the floor beside the bed. He pulled out the lists the Millers had written out for them and sat at the desk to look them over.

The first was the list of possible witnesses Tom Miller had written out. Actually, he'd written the first name in an awkward, shaky hand because of the cast, then his wife had taken over and written out the names as he provided them. There were three names; two men and one woman. He had also noted where they worked, or could be found, and how likely they'd be to help. None of them rated five stars for prospective helpfulness.

Jason switched to the other list, the list of Helen's friends. Three women, two lived in Bosque and one lived here in Genoa. Her name was Jennifer Wilson, the same name the girl at the gas station had given him. They would start with Ms. Jennifer Wilson in the morning. The Bosque friends would come later.

Last on the list was a Bosque address and phone number for Travis Wilcox.

He heard Danny come out of the bathroom behind him.

"Feel better?" he asked.

"Starting to," she said, her breath hot in his right ear. Her arms snaked down over his shoulders to hug his chest. "Want to help?"

He dropped the lists on the desktop.

♦

"You thirsty?" Danny murmured later, lying beside him, her head on his bare chest, her fingers playing with the hair surrounding his navel.

"You want me to get you something?"

"Yeah," she said. "Something fizzy, like a Sprite or 7Up."

Jason had seen a number of vending machines in an alcove near the motel office when they'd checked in.

He slid out from under her and found his pants. "You want anything to snack on? I'm thinking chocolate myself."

Danny was sitting up in the bed now, one hand pinning the sheet over her breasts. "Chocolate is good."

He buttoned up his shirt and slid his feet, sockless, into his shoes. "Anything else?"

"Nothing you can get from a vending machine."

"Hold that thought." Jason checked his pockets for money, found a room key and slipped that in another pocket. "I'll be right back."

She smiled. "I'll be here."

Jason stepped outside. The motel courtyard was dark and deserted under sodium vapor lights. About two thirds of the parking slots held cars and trucks, but there was no one moving on any of the walkways and only a few lights burned behind the windows.

And it was cold. Despite the bright, sunny days, it was almost October and the nights got cold. He shoved his hands into his pants pockets and started walking down the catwalk toward the stairs.

It was kind of spooky, being the sole person moving in the entire visible town. His footsteps on the concrete seemed unnaturally loud, his very presence out of place.

As he descended the stairs, movement out on the street caught his attention. He looked over as headlights swept across the parking area and a car turned on to the street in front of the motel. It was a city police car.

Jason hesitated for just a moment, then continued down the stairwell, trying to appear nonchalant.

The police car moved down the street sedately, cruising at an even speed. From what he could see, it didn't seem to pay any particular attention to him, or to the motel itself. It appeared to be on routine patrol.

Still, he kept his head down until the car had moved out of sight, bought two Sprites from one vending machine and a couple of Hershey's bars from another and headed back to the room.

He didn't see the police car again.

But his heart was beating a hundred miles an hour when he stepped back into the motel room and locked the door behind him.

Danny was sitting up on the bed. She had put on a tee shirt and pair of pajama bottoms and gathered her hair into a ponytail while he'd been out. The television was on and she was flicking through channels with the remote.

Talk about a mood shift.

"What's up?" Jason handed her one of the cans and set the candy on the bed beside her.

"Your cell phone rang while you were gone."

He hadn't bothered to bring it with him. It was sitting on the charger next to the television. "Did you answer it?"

"Of course not. I just looked at the screen in case it was the Millers. It was Lisa."

Naturally. Nothing quite broke a romantic mood like a phone call from the other, on again, off again, ex-girlfriend.

"Crap," he said. "Sorry, I forgot to call her. I said I'd let her know when we got here. She's probably worried."

Danny shrugged.

He leaned over to kiss her on the forehead. She accepted it, brushed his hand with her own.

"I should call her."

"You going to tell her about us?"

"I don't think so," Jason said. "Not yet, anyway."

She smiled. "Waiting to see if it works out?"

"No, of course not. I just don't think telling her serves any purpose right now. We'll just be hurting her."

Danny shrugged, nodded.

"You disagree?"

"No. You're right."

She wasn't exactly filling him with confidence about this. But he saw no point in telling Lisa anything yet. He wasn't even sure what he and Danny were. Were they boyfriend and girlfriend? Lovers? Friends with benefits? Or were they just scratching each other's itch for a few days? It was too soon to tell. They hadn't even talked about it, hadn't told each other where they thought it might go. They hadn't even talked about what they each wanted.

"You need to let her know you're alive before she completely melts down," Danny told him. "I'm going to take a shower."

She climbed across the bed to kiss him. "Be gentle. You know how she worries."

He told her he would and watched as she padded into the bathroom.

A few seconds later the shower started.

Feeling like things were spinning just a bit out of control, Jason sat at the motel room's little desk, pulled his cell phone off the charger, and called Lisa.

She answered on the first ring. "Dammit, Jason! I was just about to call the police!"

That wouldn't have been very productive, given the situation. He didn't tell her that though. He wasn't stupid.

"I'm sorry. We got busy talking with Helen's parents and then had to find a place to stay," he told her. "I should have called when we first got to town."

"Well, I'm glad you're okay. How are they doing? Helen's parents?"

"As well as can be expected. They're in a tough situation."

"I can't even imagine. Do you think you'll be able to help them?"

"I hope so. It will depend on whether I can get anyone to talk to me," he told her. "We'll find that out tomorrow."

"Please, let me know what's going on. I feel like I'm on another continent over here."

"I will. I promise," he told her. "Sorry I worried you today."

"Find Helen."

They disconnected.

Danny emerged from the bathroom a short time later. She was wearing a Washington Huskies blue tee shirt now over the pajama bottoms. Her hair lay dark and wet on a towel across her shoulders.

"Everything okay?" she asked.

"Yeah. She was just worried."

"Good. Because we need to discuss our strategy for tomorrow."

♦

They talked the situation over for a couple of hours, going over every scenario and strategy they could think of, looking for weaknesses, vulnerabilities. What they wanted was the quickest way to the information they needed—Helen's location—while not exposing themselves to any more danger than necessary. For there was danger. There was no getting around that. Neither of them had any illusions about the local Sheriff's Department being any kind of force for good. And if the Sheriff didn't already know he and Danny were here, snooping around, he would by the end of the next morning.

The important question then was what would Sheriff Barton do about it?

"If I were running the show—" Danny started.

"—you would have canned and arrested these guys long before it got this far."

"So sweet." She flashed a smiled. "Yeah, besides that. I would have the deputies stay nearby, watching, but leave us alone. Don't hide; show everyone our presence, but don't actively interfere. It would intimidate everybody enough that we will have no more luck getting people to talk to us than the AG's investigator did. Other than that, they wouldn't have to do anything at all."

Jason nodded. It was how he would do it too. It was how any reasonable bad guy would do it. But it remained to be seen whether these guys would be reasonable.

"These guys don't have anything to worry about though," he said. "That's what concerns me. It's not like they're risking getting arrested or thrown in prison, or anything. That might make them reckless."

"Or overconfident."

"Or overconfident." He shrugged.

That was the problem they were facing. The sheriff's office was almost completely unpredictable. In Port Salish, the

Lundgren goons they'd been facing had been just as interested in avoiding police attention as they'd been on stopping Jason. It had been a weakness, another tool Jason and Danny had been able to use to their benefit.

Here, law enforcement would be a tool used only against them.

Even more frightening, Elizabeth Jensen had no longer been a threat to the Bartons when she'd been murdered. She'd moved away and the A.G.'s case had been squashed. She hadn't been killed in some desperate act of self-preservation; it had been revenge in its most brutal form. They had punished her for crossing them.

He and Danny had only one advantage over the Bartons right now, Jason realized. But it wouldn't last long.

"They don't know who we are," he told her. "Or where we are. That's our advantage."

Danny frowned.

"Unless they got your license plate number outside the restaurant tonight, which I don't think they did."

Danny shook her head. "But there are only a few places for strangers to stay."

"Which means we need to be out of here before they come looking for us."

"Now?"

"No. The morning should be soon enough." Jason said. "But we need to try and get some sleep."

♦♦♦♦♦

Detective David Barton poured himself a cup of coffee and settled down behind his desk to start the day. It was just after 9:00 Thursday morning. While his computer booted up, he paged through the reports generated by the overnight patrols. Most were routine: traffic violations, one DUI, a handful of domestic and neighborhood disputes. He saw pretty much the same thing every morning. The only differences were in volume. There were usually many more calls on the weekends than during the work week and during the summer than the winter.

One report this morning though, wasn't routine. He read through it. Read through it a second time, then picked up his desk phone and punched in a number.

"Morning, Dave," Sheriff Barton said. "What can I do for you?"

He seemed to be in a good mood.

"I've got a missing person's report here, filed last night. It was filed by the parents of Helen Miller. I thought you'd want to know."

"Yeah, I do. The Millers? That's interesting."

"What do you want me to do with it?" Interesting, or not, he had a report here. Normal procedure would be to assign it to a detective for further investigation. But the situation here wasn't normal.

Travis Wilcox was known to be seeing the Miller girl and Travis was the Sheriff's nephew, David's cousin. Despite his last name, he was a Barton. The rules were different for the Barton family.

The Sheriff thought about the question for a minute. "Have someone go through the motions," he finally said. "But don't waste any time on it, if you know what I mean. She's probably just run off with some boyfriend anyway, right?"

"Right. I'll get on it."

"Take your time. Take your time," the Sheriff told him. "Are you coming out to Hemlock Run this weekend? It will be a good time, I promise."

"I don't think I'll be able to get away, not this weekend. Eddy has a little league game and Pam a recital. I'm pretty well booked."

"Your loss."

Detective Sergeant Barton smiled and disconnected. Maybe twenty years ago, he'd have been excited at the prospect of a Hemlock Run weekend. Now he had a family and that was enough for him.

♦♦♦♦♦

By 7:00 the next morning, Jason and Danny had showered, shaved, repacked their things and checked out of the motel. For good measure, Jason had played the eager tourist and asked the desk clerk how long it took to drive to Astoria, to the south, just in case. There was no sign of any police presence outside the motel. No one seemed to be following them as they drove away.

They ate breakfast at a perfectly ordinary pancake house, then punched the address of their first witness—Jennifer Wilson—into the navigation system of Danny's Jeep and let it do the work.

Just after 9:00 in the morning, Jason led Danny up the walk toward a small and old, but clean, cottage in a neighborhood of similar homes. A ten-year-old white Civic, dirty with road grime and sporting a child safety seat in back, was parked on gravel to their right. A space beside it was empty, but a fresh oil stain on the gravel told of another vehicle that often parked there, probably at work now.

The yard was as much dandelions as grass, but neatly cut. Tangled nasturtiums hid the foundation.

"Starter home," Danny said as they approached the front door.

Jason agreed. It wasn't fancy by anyone's standards, but it was the Wilsons' and they were taking care of it. As much as the budget allowed.

As Jason rapped on the door, he heard the squall of a young baby. He glanced at Danny to see if she had heard it.

Danny had.

A new baby meant whoever was home would probably be sleep-deprived and stressed.

Just as he was about to knock again, the door opened and a pudgy young woman appeared, gently rocking a tiny baby in one arm. Wisps of limp, dark hair escaped a ponytail to hang in her face and dark smudges hung under her eyes. She wore a Mickey Mouse tee over gray sweat pants. Neither looked particularly clean.

The baby was maybe a month old, maybe less. It looked lost in a pink onesie.

Jennifer smiled wearily at them. "Sorry, we can't afford to buy anything right now."

"We're not selling anything." Jason identified himself as a reporter for the *News* and Danny as a consultant working with him. "Sorry to bother you, but we're investigating the disappearance of Helen Miller. We hoped you'd be able to help us out by answering a few questions?"

"Helen?" She frowned. The weariness in her eyes gave way to alarm. "What do you mean? Helen's disappeared?"

"No one has seen or heard from her since Tuesday night."

"It's Thursday now," Danny added.

Jason had called the Millers this morning from the pancake house and confirmed there'd been no new contact. Helen's parents had been in the process of designing and printing "missing" posters to hang around town. The Millers had also not heard anything from the Sheriff's Department. Yet.

"Oh, God. I hadn't heard anything. I've been out of the loop for a while," she said and backed away from the door. "Please come in. What can I do to help?"

"Just give us some information," Jason repeated, as he and Danny stepped into the house.

It was small, reasonably clean, and smelled of baby powder and sour diapers. To their right was a kitchen, dishes piled in the rack dryer, mostly clear baby bottles. To their left, the living room was carpeted and held a small sofa and a matching recliner facing a flat screen television. Fresh diapers, wipes, and a coffee mug sat on the coffee table. The television was tuned to one of the morning talk shows.

Jennifer hit a button on the remote and shut the program down.

"Sorry about the mess," Jennifer said. "I haven't had time to tidy up yet."

"That's perfectly okay." Jason took a seat on the couch. "You've got your hands full."

"Yeah. You should see my place." Danny sat beside him.

Jennifer smiled and settled into the armchair, her baby safely in her arms. Despite the crying they'd heard earlier, the infant was asleep now.

"How old is she?" Danny asked. Her voice had taken on that soft tone peculiar to women when babies are the subject of discussion.

"She'll be three weeks on Saturday." Jennifer smiled down at her daughter. The smile was so deep and genuine, it erased all the fatigue from her face. In that moment she was beautiful. In that moment, she glowed. "Her name's Leah. Leah Marie Wilson."

"She's beautiful."

"Thank you." Her smile faded as she looked up at them. "What's going on with Helen?"

"We don't know," Jason told her. "Her parents say she went out Tuesday evening and no one has heard from her since. She won't answer her cell and her mailbox is full."

"Oh, God. Have you talked to Travis? Travis Wilcox?"

"Not yet." He shook his head. "You're the first person we've talked to, other than her parents."

Jason activated the voice recorder app on his cell phone and set it between them, explaining it to Jennifer as he did. She was fine with the idea.

"Do you think Deputy Wilcox could have done something to her?" Danny asked.

"Travis Wilcox is a sadistic bastard. He never loved Helen. He just loves running her life."

Jason glanced at Danny. She raised her eyebrows.

"I thought he was her boyfriend?" he asked.

"The only reason she was anywhere near him was because he'd hurt her parents if she didn't."

"She told you this?"

"Not in so many words," she told them. "But it doesn't take a genius."

"We heard Wilcox broke her dad's arm to get her to come back to him?"

"I hadn't heard that. But it isn't a surprise. It worked, didn't it?"

"Yeah, it did." Jason sighed. "And he can get away with this?"

"It's Dunham County," she told them. "And Travis is related to the Bartons, who run everything. One uncle's the Sheriff. Another's the D.A."

"So if someone filed a complaint against him?"

"Bad things happen."

"Do you know a woman named Elizabeth Jensen?" Danny asked.

Jennifer shook her head. That was a dead end.

"Back to Wilcox," Jason said. "How well do you know him?"

"Well enough. More than I want to. He was two years ahead of me and Helen in school and I watched him hurt my best friend for years. He's a bully and a pig."

The baby stirred in her arms. She cooed a little and gently rocked her back to sleep.

Jason and Danny waited, unwilling to do anything to disturb the baby.

"Actually," Jennifer looked up at them. "I'm kind of surprised no one's blown his head off yet. My Sammy sure wanted to."

Jason and Danny exchanged a surprised glance.

"Sammy's your husband?"

She nodded. Her eyes shone.

"Why did your husband want to kill Wilcox?"

Jennifer stared down at her baby, gently rocking asleep in her arms.

Danny's voice was soft when she asked the next question. "Did Deputy Wilcox rape you?"

"Yeah." Jennifer said, her voice even softer. "He raped me."

♦

Jennifer wasn't enthused about reliving her rape. That was understandable. Neither Jason nor Danny relished making her relive it either, but they needed to know Wilcox's tactics. Most people continued to use whatever methods worked well until they are forced to change. Wilcox would be no different. If they were going to bring him to justice, they needed to be able to anticipate any moves he might try against them.

Without so much as a glance between them, Jason ceded the role of lead to Danny and Danny took it.

As gently as possible, she drew the basic facts of the attack from Jennifer.

Jennifer's assault had begun very similarly to Jason's encounter with the deputy. He'd come at her when she'd been driving alone, after dark, on a rural road near her parents' home outside Bosque. She'd been running to the store to rent a movie for the evening. Wilcox had pulled up behind her and turned on his emergency lights.

Jennifer had been sixteen, only had her license for a few weeks and had never been pulled over before. As soon as she saw the lights, she'd slowed and pulled off the road into a gravel wayside. It had been a convenient spot. The area was dark and deserted, the nearest houses scattered hundreds of feet away, their residents closeted behind closed blinds and darkness. The road was not especially well-traveled. But it was Bosque. It was small-town America. And it was the cops. She hadn't been unusually worried or scared. She was just nervous because she'd never been pulled over before.

Wilcox had walked up, opened her door, and dragged her out of the car. She hadn't had time to react. Before she could even process what was happening, he had pinned her down over the hood of her car, pulled down her shorts and underwear and raped her.

No one noticed a thing. She could have been on the dark side of the moon as far as the rest of the world was concerned.

When he was finished, Wilcox simply zipped up, returned to his squad car, and drove away.

He never said a word.

♦

For a moment, Jennifer was quiet, just looking down at her baby, blinking back tears. Jason didn't know what to say. He felt guilty for being male.

"What did you do?" Danny asked, her voice gentle, almost a whisper.

"Nothing." Jennifer shrugged. "I went home and took about five showers."

"You didn't tell anyone?"

"Not for a long time," Jennifer said. "Eventually I told Sammy. He knew something had happened and made me tell him. I thought he was going to kill Wilcox, he was so mad."

Jason sighed. "I wouldn't have blamed him."

"But it wouldn't have changed anything," Jennifer said. "Except that Sammy'd be dead or in prison. I finally convinced him to move us down here and never have anything to do with Travis Wilcox again."

"Did it work?" Danny asked.

"I guess." Jennifer shrugged. "I haven't seen Travis since."

"Good," Jason said. "It looks like you're building a nice life here."

She smiled, kind of sadly.

"Have other women been assaulted like you?" Danny asked.

"I don't know. Probably. It's not something you talk about over coffee. But he's always thought girls were just his playthings."

Danny frowned. "What do you mean?"

"You know the type. He was the guy in school who thought it was fun to grab girls' butts and boobs in the hall between classes. The guy who thinks taking a girl to a movie means she owes him sex and doesn't take "no" for an answer." She looked directly at Danny. "Know what I mean?"

"Yeah. I know the type."

"So, no, I don't think I'm the only victim," she said. "But I couldn't give you a list, or anything."

Danny just nodded, but Jason could tell that inside she was livid.

"He sounds like a pig," Jason said. "So why in the world was Helen going out with him?"

Danny answered that question "Because he was the alpha male. The big man on campus."

"Exactly," Jennifer said.

"Going out with him made her the top girl, socially. And by the time she figured out her mistake, she'd lost control."

"And you don't cross Travis Wilcox," Jennifer said. "You just don't."

The baby, who'd been asleep during their entire conversation, began to fuss.

"She's probably hungry," Jennifer said, shifting the baby in her arms.

"We've taken enough of your time," Jason said, rising to his feet. "Thank you very much for talking with us. We know how hard it must be."

Danny too rose to her feet.

"Look," Jennifer said, "Can you leave my name out of it? We've got a baby now…"

Jason and Danny both assured her they would never reveal her identity without her express permission. That seemed to ease her mind a little. He also left a business card with her in case she thought of something else that might be important.

"I just remembered something." Jennifer said at the front door. "You know what the girls used to call condom packets in high school?"

"No, what?"

"Get out of jail free cards. Is that screwed up or what?"

♦

"It's perfect," Danny said when they were back in the car. "He turns on his flashers; people pull over. It's automatic, even for a woman alone at night."

Jason agreed. "And if they don't, they can be charged with attempting to elude a police officer."

"I guarantee Jennifer is not his only victim."

"No, she's not. The question is whether we can find the others and, if we do, will they be willing to tell their stories?"

"I know."

Jason sat behind the wheel, driving them back toward Bosque. They had left Jennifer with their thanks and another promise that her name would never be divulged without her permission. Though Jason fully intended to use her experience in his story, she would appear disguised as an anonymous source.

It would be enough. They weren't dealing with a court of law and its rules of evidence. The public had a much lower threshold.

Danny was staring out the passenger window as the forested hills passed, broken by the occasional creek or ranch house. "Do you think they know about us yet?"

"I don't know." He hoped not.

Trouble was he had no way of judging how effective the local grapevine was. Every small town had one but the effectiveness varied. Much of it had to do with the popularity of the subject. If something bad happened to a popular girl in high school, for instance, the odds were the entire school (and half the town) would know within hours.

Jason didn't know the social structure of the area, or the places where gossip was most often exchanged.

What he did know was who knew about them and what they were doing. There were the teens they'd talked to last night, but he wasn't counting on that getting far. As a general rule, teens didn't talk to adults unless they absolutely had to. The Millers knew what they were doing, as did Jennifer. How much they would talk about it was a different matter. They wouldn't do anything to sabotage the case, but they might confide in friends that someone was here and was trying to help. Would word eventually, somewhere down the line, get to the sheriff's office? Almost certainly. The question he couldn't answer was when that might happen.

"I think we should assume they will know about us by the end of the day," Danny told him. "For our own safety."

"Okay. Any suggestions?"

"Mainly keep our eyes open. I don't think they will actually do anything, not yet. I think it will mainly be a show of force, intimidation. They will try to scare us off."

"Or scare the witnesses."

"Yeah. Or that."

Danny turned to him. "But I could be wrong. What if Wilcox decides he wants to take us out? Right now?"

"Let's hope we don't have to answer that."

"I don't know. I'd kind of like a chance to tangle with Travis Wilcox."

♦

Highway 101 turned right and headed northeast along the south bank of the Chumash River for the last ten miles before Bosque. Barely a mile before the city limits, it topped a ridge and began to descend the north side. The buildings that marked the beginning of the town clustered in the distance.

Halfway down, the posted speed limit dropped from 55 to 45. And then, a hundred yards later, to 30.

A classic speed trap.

"Jason…"

"I see it."

Parked on the shoulder on their side of the road, was a brown over white Dunham County Sheriff's car.

Jason touched the brake just a bit. He was already within the speed limit, but he wanted to be sure. He wanted to do absolutely nothing to attract any attention. If the deputies didn't know what car they were driving, he wasn't going to help them find out.

Neither of them breathed as they followed the black minivan ahead of them down the hill, gradually slowing as they approached the squad car.

"How are we supposed to act if we're innocent?" he asked. "Look at the car, or ignore it?"

He thought he'd read something about that, somewhere.

"If you're innocent, you don't have to act at all."

They approached the squad car, passed it. Nothing happened. No emergency lights lit up. The car didn't move out onto the road.

Jason resisted the urge to watch the sheriff's car in his rearview mirror. That would be counter-productive and dangerous. As it was, he glanced up every few seconds until the squad car was out of sight. It never moved.

"Could he have just missed us?" Jason asked.

Danny shrugged beside him. "Not if they were my people. Not if they were looking for us."

"I'll take that as a 'no'."

Twelve

Danny punched the address of their next witness—another friend of Helen's, according to her parents—into the navigation and followed the displayed directions. The satellite led them four blocks off Main Street, heading south on Franklin past the old downtown and into a neighborhood of solidly middle class ranch homes.

21456 Franklin Street stood on their left, halfway down the block, a well-maintained blue ranch with white trim. The lawn was thick and green. Planters along the foundation contained lush looking irises and dahlias.

A two-year-old red Accord was parked in the drive.

According to the Millers' list, this was the home of Sophie Mangold, one of Helen's friends.

Jason pulled in to the curb and switched the engine off. "Pretty nice place for a nineteen year old."

"Parents' place. Bet you anything."

Jason was not about to take that bet.

They climbed out of the car and followed a concrete walk up to the front door.

Jason checked the street in both directions. No one appeared to be watching them. No one seemed to be around at all. The neighborhood was very quiet.

Jason pressed the doorbell. Muffled chimes sounded inside.

"How are we going to do this?" Danny asked.

Jason shrugged. "Same as last time?"

"Just wondering." She murmured. "I hope it's not another rape case."

"Me too."

He pressed the doorbell again. Footsteps thudded inside and a few moments later, the door opened about four inches and a young woman's face appeared. "Yeah?"

Jason gave the same pitch he'd given Jennifer earlier that morning. He was a reporter for the *Seattle News* and he was looking into the disappearance of Helen. He was helping her parents, not the cops.

"Helen's mother said you're one of her best friends," he said and handed her one of his cards. "I'm hoping you can help us find her."

She glanced down at the card, backed up. "I can't help you."

She pushed the door closed, but Jason wedged his shoe in the jamb. "Please. It will only take a minute."

"Your name will never come up," Danny added behind him. "We just need some information."

"I don't know anything."

"Do you know where Helen is?"

"Move your foot. Please." Her eyes were shining. "I can't say anything."

Jason carefully met her gaze. "We're going to make Travis Wilcox pay for his crimes, but we can't do it alone. We need your help."

She swallowed hard, but shook her head. "I can't."

Jason sighed, but pulled his foot back. "If you change your mind, call me."

"I'm sorry."

The door closed with a solid thud. A second later, a lock snicked home.

"Well, that went well," Jason said as he turned back to Danny.

"She was terrified."

"Yes, she was."

They walked back down the path toward the car. There still was no sign of the sheriff's department. That, at least, was good news.

"I wonder," Danny started to say as they reached the car and climbed in.

"What?"

"If Wilcox raped her too?"

That was a good possibility, judging from her reaction. She'd been very much afraid, more afraid than could be explained solely by them asking questions. In fact, she was acting like she'd been attacked recently. Or threatened with attack.

He told Danny this as she programmed the next address into the navigation system.

"We may never know," she said.

"Oh, I think we will. Sooner or later."

"Why's that?"

"She kept my business card."

♦

The third name on the list Mrs. Miller had given them had an address on the east end of town, about ten blocks from Sophie Mangold's. This was a less solidly middle class neighborhood. The houses were older, smaller, and in poorer condition.

An abandoned metal swing set rusted amid knee-high grass behind the witness's house. The hollow carcass of a washing machine decayed beside the empty drive.

Jason and Danny walked up a cracked and weather-shifted walkway to the front door and knocked. Jason would use the same spiel he had before.

There was no response to his knock. No muted activity from inside.

Jason knocked again.

"It's the middle of the day," Danny said. "She could be at work or school."

He nodded. It was actually remarkable that they'd been able to contact the first two in the middle of the day. Most people spent their daylight hours either at school or work, trying to pay for the house they could sleep in at night.

He tried knocking one more time.

There was still no sign of life inside. No muffled sounds of television; no rhythmic thumps of feet on hardwood floors.

No one was there.

Or someone had called ahead and warned them that he and Danny would be coming by with uncomfortable questions.

They returned to the car.

While Danny found the addresses of the witnesses provided by Bob Miller, Jason watched the windows of the house. The half-drawn curtains never budged. No shadowy face appeared to peek out at them. It was human nature to check and see if the danger had passed. If someone had been in the house they would have looked.

No one was there.

Danny finished plugging the next witness's address into the navigation system, waited for the computer and satellites to make their calculations. "You need to turn around. Head back to Main Street."

Jason did and followed the system's directions to Main Street and a small office building on the east end, a handful of blocks on the Seattle side of the Millers' café. A sign above the door and across plate glass windows announced it as the Adams' Insurance Agency. The person they were looking for was Vern Adams, the agent himself.

Vern Adams, however, wasn't pleased to see them, once he realized they weren't shopping for insurance.

"I'm sorry, you've wasted your time," he told them and returned to the seat behind his desk. "I can't help you."

"You didn't see what happened?" Jason pressed.

"I can't help you. Now, if you don't mind, I have work to do."

Adams picked up a pen and returned to the form he'd been working on.

Jason glanced over at Danny. She shrugged. What were you going to do? You couldn't force someone to tell you what they saw.

They left without another word.

The second witness was much the same as the first. Her name was Shirley Nelson and she worked at the hardware store one block south of Main. She was in her late fifties, with graying hair cut short, wearing jeans and a red flannel shirt.

She was shaking her head, before Jason had finished introducing himself. "You're wasting your time. I didn't see nothing."

"We haven't told you what we're talking about yet," Danny objected.

"Don't matter. I didn't see nothing about nothing."

There didn't seem to be anything more to say.

♦

"Now I know how big city cops feel in the projects," Danny said when they were back in the car. "No one wants to talk."

"Nope."

It reminded him of stories he'd heard from reporters who'd covered police states behind the old Iron Curtain. It wasn't as though the locals liked how they were living, or didn't believe you wanted to help. They didn't believe you could. And the possibility of help alone wasn't worth risking the punishment for speaking out.

"Like Jennifer said, bad things happen when you go against the Bartons. The locals know that."

"And they have to live here. Long after we leave."

"I know." Jason agreed. "You can't blame them."

"But it makes our job harder." Danny returned to the list Mr. Miller had given them. "Do we even bother checking with the others?"

"I don't know."

The odds said everyone else they talked to would have the same response, especially in Bosque. The Bartons had trained everyone well. Keep your head down and your mouth shut; mind your own business and you'll be fine. Interfere and you pay a price.

"I think we need to show the people of Bosque that we can hurt the Bartons and their sheriff's department," he said. "Until we prove that, until we prove they aren't all-powerful, I don't think we're going to get much cooperation."

Danny agreed.

"I have enough to write a story about what's going on down here, but it's one-sided. I guarantee that my editor won't run it like that."

"What do you need?"

"I need to talk to Travis Wilcox," he told her. "I need to give him a chance to explain."

"You sure?" Danny peered at him. "We'll lose any advantage we might have."

"I don't think we can avoid it."

♦

Deputy Travis Wilcox lived in a neighborhood of nice homes in the hills east of Bosque. The lots here seemed to be laid out in ten acre parcels, including pasture and forest land. Nearly everyone had a travel trailer or RV parked somewhere near the house. Most had sizeable barns or shop buildings. Boats hid under fitted tarps. ATV's loitered near the shops. Horses grazed in nearby pastures.

Wilcox's place was a two story farmhouse with a fresh coat of yellow paint, set off by chocolate brown trim. A matching metal outbuilding to the left was probably a shop or garage, judging by two closed bay doors. A boat was parked on a trailer between the two buildings. No other vehicles were parked on the concrete drive.

The lawn had been mowed recently, but not raked. Cut grass formed lines three feet apart across the space. No mower was in sight.

"Love the smell of fresh-cut grass," Danny said when she'd climbed out of the car.

"Pretty nice place for a deputy sheriff."

"He's a Barton, remember."

"I remember."

Up close, the property wasn't quite as impressive. The planters along the house's foundation were a tangled mess of weeds and shrubs, and the windows were covered with a layer of dust and dirt.

"Check this out," Danny pointed to something on the walk directly in front of the door. A half-dozen irregular splotches of yellow paint formed a loose line across the concrete, parallel to the house. "Someone was sloppy."

"Or didn't care."

Jason stopped in front of the door and waited a moment, just listening. He heard nothing from inside the house, no television or stereo, no voices. A horse in the near distance blew, a crow called twice and a second answered in their hoarse language. The wind wandered around the cedars.

"I don't think anyone's home."

"Let's find out," Danny said and reached past him to press the doorbell.

Chimes sounded inside.

No response.

He knocked on the door. The raps sounded odd and felt even odder. He touched the door again with his fingertips, then by laying his hand flat on its surface.

"What?" Danny asked.

"The door is metal, not wood."

"Curious."

"That means something to you?"

"Fortified." She shrugged. "Steel doors are harder to break through than wood ones. Drug dealers sometimes use them."

That was curious indeed. Why would a deputy sheriff have a fortified front door? Why would he want one? Or had it been installed by a previous owner? They'd have to ask Wilcox sometime, because he wasn't here right now.

Jason rang the doorbell one more time, but it was more for show than anything else. No one was home.

He was wondering what the odds were that Helen was being held just a few feet from them right now, but bound and gagged so she couldn't call out. Or maybe she was far enough away she couldn't hear them. Like maybe in the shop.

"Helen! Can you hear me?"

Danny glanced at him then began shouting too.

"Helen!" Jason moved slowly toward the shop building to their left. "Helen!"

The building was huge. There would be plenty of room to hide a person, if you were into that sort of thing. In fact, anyone with a basic construction background could build a genuine lockable cell in there and no one would be aware of it.

"Helen!" he yelled. "Helen! Can you hear me?"

Danny grabbed his arm to stop him at the end of the house. "Jason, don't!"

"What?"

"You can't go over there."

"Why not?"

"It's private property. We'd be trespassing..." she told him. "We'd turn Wilcox into a victim."

"What if Helen's in there?"

"Is there any evidence she is?"

He had to admit there wasn't any. There had been no response to any of their calls. They had no concrete reason to believe Helen was anywhere on the property.

"Let's just go. Before we get in trouble."

"Okay," he told her.

They turned away and walked back to the car.

"What now?" Danny asked.

"We go see the Millers."

♦

Jason parked the car at the curb across the street from the *City Center Café* and switched the engine off. There was no sign of the Sheriff's Department, or any other police agency. In fact, they had not seen a sheriff's car since the speed trap at the south end of town this morning.

They got out, hurried across the street between passing cars, and stepped into the Millers' café. It was just before 11:00 in the morning.

Lunch had not yet begun, so the restaurant wasn't busy. Only one booth had customers—a young couple—and they were already eating when Jason and Danny stepped in.

Tom Miller had started up from his seat in the far booth with the opening of the door. He recognized them, waved them over, and returned to his seat.

They walked up the aisle between the booths toward the Millers. They were sitting together on the side of the booth facing the door. A man sat on the other side of the booth. He was middle-aged, with graying brown hair and a matching brush mustache. He wore a tan corduroy jacket over an open dress shirt and faded jeans.

"This is Gerry Peterson," Tom Miller told them. "He runs the local paper, the *Bosque Examiner*."

Jason shook Gerry's hand. So did Danny.

"Gerry's going to do a story on Helen's disappearance," Barbara Miller told them.

"That will be a big help," Jason said. "Getting the word out."

"Well, not as much as I'd like," Gerry said. "This week's edition just came out today, so this story won't make it into print until next Thursday, but I will put something on our website tonight. I try to keep that as up to date as I can. It's also linked to Facebook."

"It will still be a big help," Jason said.

"I hope it works," Barbara said. "It's been almost two days. I saw somewhere that the first twenty-four hours are the most important."

"Mrs. Miller—," Danny started.

"Barbara, please."

"Barbara, that's television, and even on television, the twenty-four rule only applies to child abductions. This is something different."

"She's right," Jason added. "There's no reason to think anything's happened to her."

Barbara Miller looked up at him, her eyes shining. "Did you find something?"

"That's what we're telling you," Jason said. "We didn't find anything to say she isn't okay."

The door opened and an older couple walked in, laughing about something. Tom Miller heaved himself to his feet and moved to greet the couple. Barbara excused herself and hurried into the kitchen. After stepping aside, to allow them to get to work, Jason and Danny sat across the table from Peterson.

"I have to say," Peterson said. "It's an honor to meet you, Mr. Reynolds."

"It is?"

"Sure. We don't get a Pulitzer Prize winner in Bosque very often."

"Thanks." Jason shrugged. "You've got an interesting community out here."

Peterson smiled, but let the remark go without comment. "What's your connection to the Millers?"

"Are you writing a story on me?"

"Maybe. It would make a good general interest feature." Peterson searched his eyes for a moment, nodded. "Rumor has it you've been around, asking questions."

"I'm an investigative journalist. Asking questions is what I do."

Peterson smiled. "Finding any answers?"

"Some. Mostly just more questions."

"Dunham County can be like that. Folks don't like to talk to outsiders much"

"So we've discovered," Danny murmured.

Peterson closed his notebook. "You know, I wanted to be an investigative reporter when I was younger, fresh out of journalism school. Woodward and Bernstein were my heroes."

Jason smiled. "I keep a copy on my desk in the newsroom."

"Me too. The ultimate underdog story."

"Speaking truth to power," Jason added.

"So how did you end up running the paper in Bosque?" Danny asked.

"It's a long story. Let's just say it was a great business move, but a lousy journalistic one."

"Why's that?"

He shrugged. "Too many compromises over the years, I guess."

"Mind if I ask you a question, or two?" Jason asked. "I'm sure you have sources I will never get to even if I spent a month here."

Peterson smiled. "If you'll sit down for an interview with a poor, local newspaper."

"Deal."

"What do you want to know?"

"How about Travis Wilcox? What can you tell me about him?"

"Honestly? He's a sociopath. No conscience whatsoever. And he's backed by the most powerful family in the county."

"We've kind of figured that out."

"So if you're looking to go after him, I'd make sure you have plenty of ammunition and expect some return fire."

Jason nodded. "We figured that out too."

"Do you think Wilcox is involved in Helen's disappearance?" Danny asked.

"I don't know," Peterson said, "but I wouldn't put it past him."

♦

The customers who'd pulled the Millers away were quickly followed by another, then even more as the day edged toward lunch time. Gerry Peterson and Jason exchanged business cards and promised to get together sometime over the weekend to do an interview, then Peterson said he needed to get back to "the shop" and left.

A short while later a handful of young women came in carrying boxes bearing the logo of a print shop. They were family friends, back with flyers to distribute.

"That's good," Jason told Danny. "Hanging flyers will help."

Danny frowned. "You think that will help find Helen?"

"It will help them feel like they're doing something."

Danny nodded.

Something occurred to him. He stopped Tom Miller as he passed on the way to the kitchen. "We've got to be going, but I have a question for you."

"Okay."

"Have you seen or heard from Travis Wilcox since Helen went missing?"

Danny watched, frowning.

Miller shook his head. "Nope. Probably a good thing too."

"But you talked to him?"

"On the phone."

"Was it a cell phone or a land line?" Jason told him.

Tom thought about it for a second. "His cell phone, I think. It was a number Helen had left with us. What's going on?"

"Just a thought," Jason assured him. "Nothing to worry about. We'll be in touch later."

Tom Miller looked a bit confused, but hurried toward the kitchen,

Danny had slipped out of the booth to stand beside him. "Want to clue me in?"

He led her toward the door. "We may have been looking at this thing all wrong."

"Oh?"

♦

"How were we looking at this the wrong way?" Danny asked when they were back in the car, "Or is it a secret?"

"It's not a secret," he told her as he pulled out into the lunchtime traffic, heading west, toward Genoa. He still hadn't seen a sheriff's cruiser. "There's also no guarantee it's right."

"So tell me."

"Well, we've been operating under the theory that Travis Wilcox did something to Helen, right? Either kidnapping, hurting, or killing her."

"Yeah." She said. "Okay."

"So we've been investigating *him*, trying to build a case. But what if Wilcox isn't exactly the primary suspect in what's happened? What if they're both missing?"

She turned to peer at him. "You mean Wilcox is a victim too?"

"No, not a victim, so much as following orders. What if this whole thing has nothing to do with Wilcox's bullying, or sexual predations? Or only tangentially. What if he's holed up with Helen somewhere because somebody higher in the food chain wants her out of circulation for a while? He's just the person charged with keeping her that way?"

Danny didn't say anything, thinking about it. She turned to look out her window. "You know what that means? If you're right?"

Jason wasn't sure. He hoped he did.

"It means we don't have to just worry about Wilcox lashing out against us."

"We have to worry about the entire organization. We have to worry about everybody."

Thirteen

Jésus Sifuentes looked up from Paco's tricky neckline as his front door opened and a tall American stepped in. It wasn't terribly unusual to have an American in his barber shop, since it was only a block or two from Mexico City's tourist district, but few tourists looked like this guy. His hair was shoulder-length and streaked with gray, his beard untrimmed and more gray than brown. He looked like he'd gotten lost in 1972 and just made it back.

Except for his clothes. He wore blue jeans, a navy polo shirt, and hiking boots. All were brand new and perfectly clean.

"*Buenas dias,*" Jésus told him. "*Uno momento.*"

The man smiled and sat in one of the chairs in the waiting area. He found a newspaper and began to read. In Spanish, Jésus noted.

Jésus returned to the haircut he was working on and finished it in a few quiet minutes. The lively conversation they'd been having seemed to have been suffocated by the stranger's presence. He finished up, accepted Paco's money, and watched him pass through the door into the bright afternoon.

"Let me clean up a bit first," Jésus told the stranger in Spanish. "I don't want you walking out with hair all over your shoes."

"There's no hurry, my friend," the man replied, also in Spanish, but with a bit of an accent suggesting Nicaragua or El Salvador. "A job worth doing is worth doing well."

Jésus paused in the process of sweeping cut hair into an out-of-the-way pile. "My father used to say the same thing."

"Sounds like a wise man."

"Yes, sir, he was." Jésus said and crossed himself, then returned to cleaning the floor around the barber chair.

When the area was clean, the stranger took his place in the chair and Jésus spread the apron over his clothes. "What would you like me to do today?"

The stranger grinned. "I have a meeting tomorrow with a bank manager. I need to look respectable again, like a business man."

Jésus whistled softly through his teeth. "What about the beard?"

"Maybe leave a goatee, but trim it close."

The barber agreed, selected a pair of scissors and began cutting his hair. "You must have been on holiday. You are very tanned."

"I was, but business won't leave me alone."

"Tell me about it," Jésus said as hair fell away before the scissors. "I can hardly take a day off myself. I have too many kids to feed."

"Some things never change, do they?"

Jésus continued working, gradually hacking back the jungle of his customer's hair. But he kept glancing up at the man's reflection in the mirror, more and more frequently as he worked. The man looked familiar, but Jésus couldn't place him. Had he been a customer before? It hadn't been recently. No one had cut this hair for at least nine months.

The man watched him, smiling with amusement.

"Do I know you from somewhere?" Jésus finally asked. "You look so familiar."

The man's smiled deepened. "U.S. Marines, Camp Pendleton."

It took a moment, but Jésus' eyes grew wide. "*Señor* Smith? Taylor Smith?"

"Good disguise?" Taylor Smith smiled.

"I've never seen you with hair! I can't believe it! I had no idea it was you!"

Smith just smiled.

"Mama will be so happy to see you!"

Smith's smile faltered. "I'm afraid I cannot stay. It is too dangerous. Men are looking for me, cartel men. I don't want them to find you or your family."

Jésus crossed himself. He understood. Everyone in Mexico understood. The entire country had been living in fear of the drug cartels for a generation.

"Remember the package I left with you?"

"Of course. It's in a safe place."

Smith smiled as Jésus went back to work.

Perfect.

Fourteen

Scott Barton, Executive Assistant to Senator Barton, was sitting at his desk in the senate office building, studying staff reports on various pending legislative bills. Like it or not, it was how the process worked. No congressman had the time to read and form an intelligent opinion on every bill submitted. Some of them ran to thousands of words. So they hired staffers to read the bills, reduce them to concise summaries, and make recommendations.

One of Scott's jobs was to review the summaries, highlight the parts he thought most important or most insightful and make his own recommendations to the honorable Senator, his grandfather.

As Executive Assistant, nothing got to the Senator without his approval. Nothing. He was like the President's Chief of Staff. The Senator was one of the most powerful men in the state; he, as the gatekeeper, was therefore also one of the most powerful. And he truly loved it.

He was creating a powerful network of movers and shakers throughout the government and the state at large. He was on a first name basis with the Governor, the previous governor, and most senators of both parties. He was acquainted with Washington's two U.S. senators—both Democrats—and all the

Representatives. He had IOU's sitting in virtually every office in the State capitol.

It was all part of his strategy.

In two years, at the end of the Senator's current term, he would resign his position and file the paperwork to run for the House seat representing his adopted home in suburban Olympia. The current holder of that seat was an aging Democrat who would be vulnerable to an energetic, but experienced, young man with fresh ideas.

Scott had no doubt whatsoever that he would win that election. After a few years in the House, he would either join his grandfather in the Senate, or, depending on the political winds, run for Governor. From there, he would set his sights on the other, bigger, Washington.

His desk phone rang.

He answered it without a thought. He scarcely had ten minutes without a phone call on any given day. "Yes?"

Allison, the receptionist with the breathy voice and tight little ass, answered him. "Your father, the Sheriff, is on line one. He says it's important he talks to the Senator."

"The Senator is in a committee meeting, Have him leave a message."

"I told him that, but he insisted he talk to you," she told him. "He says it's urgent."

Scott fought off irritation. It was one of the skills he was working on, the ability to let nothing fluster him. To always appear calm and collected.

Sheriff Barton, his dear father, was testing him, though. What could possibly be happening in Dunham County that was so damn important?

"Okay," he finally said. "I've got it."

He disconnected the line with Allison and sat there for a moment watching the little "hold" light blinking for line one. Making the Sheriff wait a few seconds more would just reinforce how busy the men he was bothering were.

Scott finally pressed the button and picked up the call. "Sheriff. Dad. Allison says you have something urgent for the Senator."

"Yeah, we got a reporter down here from one of the Seattle papers, looking into this Miller girl thing. Gerry Peterson, down at the *Examiner*, says this guy is the real deal. He's dangerous."

"What's this reporter's name?"

"Just a second." The Sheriff seemed to be searching for something. "His name is Jason Reynolds."

Scott knew that name. Jason Reynolds…Jason Reynolds… After a moment he had it. Jason Reynolds. He had been the one who brought the Lundgren Corporation to its knees last year over a seventy-year-old crime. Having him turning over rocks in Dunham County could be very bad, or it could be nothing. He needed more information.

"How much does this reporter know?"

"I have no idea. He might not know anything."

"Are you willing to bet your life on it?"

Sheriff Barton had no answer for that.

Scott made a quick decision. Another skill he was working on. "Listen, I cannot stress how important this weekend is. We think the Governor will be coming. We cannot afford to have any disruptions right now."

"What do you want us to do? Take the reporter out of the mix?"

Scott hesitated to make a decision like this without running it by the Senator, but the older man actually was in a committee meeting and didn't want to be disturbed for anything short of a death in the family. Scott had been training for exactly this situation his whole life. He had no qualms with making an executive decision.

"Okay, here's what you do," he told the Sheriff. "Find this reporter and keep an eye on him. Try to find out what he knows. If he tries to go to Hemlock Run, or shows any interest in it at all, he might need to have an accident. Otherwise, just watch him and leave him alone. Make sense?"

The Sheriff agreed it did.

"Do you know where he is now?"

"We're working on it."

"*Working on it*?"

"There are only a few motels in the county," the Sheriff told him. "We'll find him."

"Do that. And let me know if there are any changes." Scott disconnected without waiting for a reply, father or not.

♦♦♦♦♦

Jason and Danny worked out a basic defense strategy as they drove, bouncing ideas off each other, using her strengths to complement his and vice versa. It was like a year ago when they were working to take down Lundgren. It felt good. It felt like a get-together with your old college buddies. It felt right.

"Other than surprise," Danny said when they were on Hwy 101, heading south, only a mile or two from Genoa. "The best thing in our favor is the fact that they don't know where we are. We need to keep it that way."

He agreed. It would be all but suicidal to give Dunham County a chance to locate them. Only if the Sheriff and his people didn't know where they were would Jason and Danny be able to do any damage.

In military terms, they were going to stage a guerilla war.

♦

Jason and Danny implemented the plan they'd devised on the way to Genoa. That meant driving south the hour-and-a-half from Genoa to Aberdeen, in Grays Harbor County, and the small, regional airport. There, Jason rented a nondescript midnight blue Toyota Camry. There were two reasons to rent a car: he wanted something no one had seen them driving and Danny was going to have to go back to work at the end of the week. He needed independent transportation.

He also withdrew as much cash as the ATM would allow.

Jason rented a room at a mid-range chain motel near Hwy 101 as Mr. and Mrs. Jason Reynolds again and used Danny's Jeep on the registration. Any serious law enforcement search would quickly find his credit card use and be outside their room in a matter of minutes. They were betting any search Dunham County mounted wouldn't cross county lines.

Not yet.

And if they did find the room later on, it would have them searching for Danny's Jeep.

They had picked up some fast food—one of the questionable benefits of a larger town—and eaten in their room, listening to the local news on the television as they did. There was no mention of either of them. There was no news out of Dunham County at all.

Even the slot devoted to election coverage didn't mention Dunham County.

"How do you think they'll react to your story?" Danny asked as she stuffed the empty wrappers in a trash can. The room smelled like French fries and tacos.

"Hopefully, they'll run around in circles trying to figure out what we know and what we'll do next. Best case would be they start turning on each other."

She climbed up on the bed and sat cross-legged, her back against the headboard. "Do you think they'll lash out at the people we talked to?"

"How would they know who we'd talked to?" he asked as he pulled his laptop from its case and set it up on the motel room's desk. "They haven't been following us."

"Word gets around." Danny shrugged. "People talk. You know that."

"I know."

He needed to write his story. The quicker he had it put together and submitted it to Miles, the better. It would give him more time to execute the inevitable changes his editor would want. And they needed to get in tomorrow's paper. They needed to keep the pressure on the Sheriff's Department.

But Danny's question now had him worried about retaliation against the people they'd talked to, especially the Millers. They were the most vulnerable. A deputy had actually seen the Millers with Jason and Danny when he'd taken their missing person's report. He couldn't see how the Sheriff's people would know they'd talked to Jennifer.

"You think I should give the Millers a call?" he asked Danny. "Let them know what's going on?"

"I think we should warn them. Things are about to get interesting and they might be caught in the middle."

It was approaching 5:00. The Millers would be gearing up for the dinner rush, if not actually hip-deep already. It was not a good time to call and he didn't see that much of a rush. The story wouldn't hit the newsstands until the morning.

Jason turned to his laptop and began writing his story.

♦

Jason wrote the story in the form of a simple narrative.

He started with a young woman he called Mary, driving alone to the grocery store one night in a small town in Dunham County, Washington.

Police emergency lights flashed behind her and, like any good citizen, she pulled off the road as soon as it was safe, which happened to be an isolated gravel wayside. Deputy Sheriff Travis Wilcox dragged her out of her car, bent her over the hood and raped her.

Mary never filed charges against Deputy Wilcox.

She probably wasn't Deputy Wilcox's first rape. She probably wasn't his last. Forcible rapists seldom stop with one victim, especially when they get away with their crime. And Deputy Wilcox has never been charged with rape.

No one has ever filed charges against Deputy Wilcox and for a good reason. Bad things seem to happen to people who cross Deputy Wilcox and his friends at the Dunham County Sheriff's Department.

Ask Elizabeth Jensen.

A year before Mary's rape, in Travis Wilcox's rookie year with the Dunham County Sheriff's Department, Elizabeth Jensen filed for divorce from her husband of eleven years, Randy Jensen. Randy Jensen is also a deputy with the

Sheriff's Office and, coincidentally, was Deputy Wilcox's training officer and close friend.

The divorce was contentious, very contentious. Accusations were made by both camps, suggestions of abuse and infidelity; neither side was willing to compromise on anything, from pets to money, but especially money. This dragged on for several months, until Elizabeth told her attorney that she had proof her husband had been having sex with underage girls.

Her attorney went to his counterpart with a new offer, using the information as leverage.

Two days later, four masked men were waiting in her house when she got home from work. She didn't have a chance. They quickly overpowered her and spent several hours beating, raping, and sodomizing her. When they left the next morning, Elizabeth managed to drive herself the thirty miles to the nearest hospital in the County seat. She was treated by the emergency room staff and a rape kit collected. The police were called.

But her attack had occurred outside the jurisdiction of the City Police. The rape kit, photographs, and all other evidence was turned over to the agency with jurisdiction over the crime, the Dunham County Sheriff's Department.

Nothing happened.

No one from the Sheriff's Department ever took a statement from her; no one came to process her house for evidence. The Sheriff released a statement to the local paper stating that she was involved in a bitter divorce and that the charges were a ploy to gain advantage in court.

A day after the official statement, Elizabeth Jenson gathered her things and moved to Renton, a suburb of Seattle, leaving everything else to her estranged husband. Shortly after, Elizabeth Jensen filed a complaint with the

Washington Attorney General's Office alleging misappropriation of state funds in the Dunham County Sheriff's Office. An investigation was opened and investigators were sent to Dunham County, but were unable to find any corroborating evidence and the case was closed.

Within a week, Elizabeth Jensen was dead. Someone raped and killed her and set her apartment on fire. The murder case is still open.

Enter Helen Miller. She had been Travis Wilcox's girlfriend through high school but, like Elizabeth Jensen with Randy Jensen, broke up with him just before going off to college in Seattle. According to friends, she had grown tired of his abuse and infidelity and was more than happy to begin a new life in the big city.

Travis, however, did not like anyone—especially a woman—telling him "no." When persuasion and threats didn't work, he broke her father's arm and charged him with "resisting arrest."

With a severely broken arm her father could no longer do the cooking at the family restaurant. Helen had to return to help her parents. Within weeks, she had relented and started seeing Wilcox again. Now, Helen Miller has disappeared. The last person known to have seen her? Deputy Sheriff Travis Wilcox.

So why is the one person all these cases have in common—Travis Wilcox—still walking free? Not only that, but why is he still carrying a badge and a gun? Part of it can be attributed to the "Thin Blue Line," the tendency for law enforcement officers to rally around and protect their own. It happens everywhere. But Dunham County is a special case because Dunham County has the Barton family, the wealthiest and most powerful family in the area, and Deputy Wilcox is part of the Barton family.

Why has nothing been done to bring Travis Wilcox and his like to justice? Because in Dunham County, the Barton family is the justice system. The County Sheriff is Wilcox's uncle. Another uncle is the District Attorney. As many as half of the deputies on the sheriff's payroll are cousins. Why is nothing being done? Because the law enforcement authorities are protecting their family.

In effect, the Dunham County Sheriff's Department is a private army that can do anything they want without repercussion. That is a recipe for creating monsters. Travis Wilson appears to be a monster.

(At the end, he inserted a statement saying the Dunham County Sheriff was unavailable to comment before this article went to press.)

He sent a copy to his editor, one to Lisa, one to Debbie, one to the Dunham County Sheriff's Department, one to the Dunham County District Attorney, and one to the *Bosque Examiner*.

♦

Within minutes, Jason's phone started going crazy with text messages.

The first was from his editor, Miles, *I'm assuming you can back up every accusation.*

Jason smiled and replied. *Of course.*

You better. This is dynamite.

That was kind of the point, wasn't it? To blow the case open. At least he was hoping it would.

Front page? He asked.

Probably. Or front of Metro.

Any word from Dunham County?

Not yet. Will let you know.

The front of the *Metro* section would work. It was where most of the city and state news went and the second most popular interior section, after sports. It was good placement.

The next text came from Lisa. *Tomorrow?*

Yep.

Give them hell. No other word?

No, but sometimes nothing is good.

Hope so.

He did too. He hoped no news was good news and that Helen's body wasn't lying somewhere out in the woods right now.

"Is it like this every time you write a story?" Danny asked.

"God, no." He shook his head. "This one is special."

"It'll be in tomorrow's paper?"

"For the whole world to see."

She nodded. "So we need to be ready for the fallout."

♦

The call Jason had been expecting came just after 11:30. The caller was Miles, his editor. He told Danny who it was and picked up the call.

"We've heard from Dunham County," his editor said. "They say—and I quote—'The Dunham County Sheriff's Office refuses to comment on the allegations made in Mr. Reynolds' story without more time to study the situations described.' They also said something about it being irresponsible of us to print unsubstantiated, blah, blah, blah."

"So, exactly what we expected?"

"Yeah. We'll insert a 'refused to comment' line in the story."

"That should keep the lawyers happy."

"Nothing makes lawyers happy; they're like editors. Now get me a follow-up. Tomorrow."

"Of course."

Jason disconnected.

Danny looked up from her position propped up on pillows against the headboard. She was ready for bed, in just a tank top and panties. Jason was in his boxers.

"News?" she asked.

"The Sheriff will not comment."

"Interesting." She frowned. "Isn't that pretty much what Lundgren said after your story last year?"

"Pretty much. It's the standard response, especially if you're not completely innocent."

"So now what?"

He thought about it for a minute. "We go back to Bosque and see how they reacted to the story. See if they're freaked out enough to make some kind of mistake."

Danny remained quiet, distracted.

"What? Something's bothering you."

She thought about it for another minute, or maybe she was choosing her words. "I'm still worried they'll retaliate against the Millers."

"It's a calculated risk," Jason admitted. "I don't think the Barton's will act while the world is watching them. They aren't stupid."

"No. But they've never had to pay for a mistake either. What we would consider reckless, is perfectly normal to them."

He took a moment, considering her worries. It made a certain amount of sense.

"We already warned the Millers. They're going to be careful."

"I'm just not comfortable putting innocent civilians at risk. They didn't ask for any of this."

"No, they didn't."

"If something happens—"

"I know." He reached over and drew her next to him, nestled in the crook of his shoulder. "Me too."

As their breathing grew deeper and they slipped away into sleep, Jason's thoughts remained with a young woman with unwashed hair and exhausted eyes and the intensity of the love she had for her tiny daughter. And another young woman, sleeping beside him now, her scent filling his world, who had offhandedly told him they'd had unprotected sex a couple of nights before.

Fifteen

Jason was awake early Friday morning. While Danny was in the shower, he threw on yesterday's jeans and a sweatshirt and walked down to the motel's office. It was before 7:00 and still dark. Aberdeen was just beginning to stir for the day. A light rain fell from the darkness, pushed by an occasional gust. The air felt colder than it had yesterday.

The motel offered a free continental breakfast and coffee for its guests. Jason selected two bear claws and poured two cups of coffee. He then stopped at the desk and bought a copy of the *News*. His story had made the front page. It was below the fold, but on the front page.

Good. Let as many people see it as possible. It was also featured on the paper's web site for those who no longer read actual papers for their news.

He carried everything back to the motel room, where Danny was out of the shower and drying her hair. She was dressed in jeans and a WSU sweatshirt.

"I'm running out of clean clothes," she told him.

Jason was too. When he'd packed his suitcase he had been expecting to spend three days in court in Friday Harbor, not running around Western Washington for who knows how long.

He imagined Danny was in the same situation, though maybe more so, being a woman and all.

"Maybe we can find a motel with laundry facilities tonight."

She nodded.

"I'd better get cleaned up," he said. "We need to get on the road."

He handed her the paper, his article displayed on top.

♦

They were checked out of the motel and on the road before 8:00. Jason drove the new rental car in the lead, with Danny following in her Jeep. The idea was to drive straight through the hour-and-a-half to Genoa, check on Jennifer's well-being and stop at a diner somewhere in town for an early lunch and to get a feel for how the community was reacting to the story. Only then would they continue on to Bosque and the Millers.

Jason had the beginnings of an idea for when they got to Bosque too, but he hadn't told Danny yet. He didn't think she would like it very much.

If the local news talk radio programs were any indication, his story was a major topic of conversation this morning, behind only the Huskies mediocre football season and the latest farce in the Capitol. The callers who talked about the issue were evenly split between law-and-order types who thought law enforcement could do no wrong and people who absolutely detested anything and everything having to do with Dunham County.

There seemed to be no middle ground.

One woman caller put it this way. "It wouldn't surprise me. Those are some of the meanest, most in-bred people you'd ever want to meet. It's like stepping back into old Mississippi up there."

Jason had to raise his eyebrows at that. From his reaction, so did the radio host. Of course, the radio station was out of Aberdeen, in Gray's Harbor County, not Dunham County. There could have been just a bit of tribalism working against the neighboring county.

But more than a few people applauding the story identified themselves as having relocated from Dunham County at some point.

That was interesting. He had an idea those still living in the county might be a bit more careful voicing their opinions.

♦♦♦♦♦

Patrick Barton was the last to arrive. He'd had to finish writing a brief that positively had to be filed with the judge this morning. No excuses would be accepted and he hated to trust it to one of his associates. They were smart and as dedicated as anyone, but green as the hemlocks blanketing the Olympics. Most were only months out of law school and were here to gain experience, not because they were dedicated to the justice system in Dunham County.

So it was well after 10:00 before he let his secretary know he would be in the Sheriff's office, and climbed down the two flights of stairs separating the District Attorney's office and the Sheriff's Department. He pushed through the doors and waved at the desk sergeant, who opened the secure door for him.

He was the District Attorney. His job brought him to the sheriff's department on a fairly frequent basis, so his face was well-known. He never had to show ID.

His cell chirped an incoming text. It was the Sheriff. *What's the holdup?*

I'm here, he replied. Keep your shirt on.

He slipped the phone back into his coat pocket, and strode through the empty squad room toward the Sheriff's office on the other side. Most of the deputies were out on patrol somewhere. Only Randy Jensen sat at a desk, slowly typing information into a computer with his index fingers.

When the deputy looked up at him Patrick pointed toward the Sheriff's office. Jensen nodded.

The Sheriff's office door was closed. It was one of those doors you found in older buildings like courthouses and schools, where the lower half was painted wood and the upper half pebbled glass. "Michael Barton, Dunham County Sheriff" was painted in gold across the glass.

He knocked on the glass.

"Come in."

Patrick opened the door and stepped into his brother's office. Everyone else was already there: Judge Alan Barton, his uncle; Marcia Barton-Wilcox, his sister, who ran Barton Industries; and Michael's son, Scott, who must have driven over from Olympia this morning. Scott was, no doubt, representing the Senator.

"Glad you could join us," Scott said as Patrick unbuttoned his jacket and took one of the vacant chairs.

Patrick ignored him. Scott was two years out of law school, quite impressed with himself, and thought he had the world by the ears.

"Something to drink?" Michael asked, already at the mini bar against the wall to the right of his desk.

"No, thanks. It's a little early in the day for me."

Michael shrugged and returned to his chair behind the desk.

"Okay," the Judge said. "Everyone's here. Can we get started? I have court to prepare for."

Judge Barton—Patrick's uncle—was the senior of two judges in the county. The brief Patrick had been working on was for the other one, Judge Stewart Hoffman, which was why he'd been working so hard. Hoffman wasn't family. He wouldn't automatically rule in Patrick's favor.

Michael started. "Well, we all know about this reporter and his damn story. The question is: what are we going to do about it?"

For a few moments, no one said anything.

The Judge finally broke the silence. "I don't know that we have to do anything. It's not like anyone's going to come roaring in to arrest us, is it?"

This caused a few chuckles.

"In a week, everyone will have forgotten about it." Scott agreed. "As long as we don't feed the news cycle."

"If there are no more follow-up stories," Patrick agreed.

"If no one talks there will be no follow-up stories."

"If," Marcia said. She was three years younger than Michael, a year older than Patrick, and had taken over the Barton business interests when the Senator retired to run for office. "But in the meantime, our reputation will still be taking a beating. Much of business is built on reputation. Even if this blows over quickly, it could still cost us millions."

"People put that much faith in some lousy newspaper?" the Sheriff asked.

Marcia smiled without humor. "Business people—investors especially—are very allergic to risk. At even the hint of something bad, they grab their money and run for their burrows. And this Reynolds isn't just any reporter. He brought the Lundgrens to their knees last year. People pay attention to what he says."

"People also have short attention spans," Scott, said. He was the youngest person there, but everyone listened for two reasons: he actually was possibly the smartest one in the room and—more important—he spoke for the old man, the Senator. "It's an axiom in politics that you don't feed a bad story. The quicker it moves off the front page, the better. To do that, we don't comment in any way and we keep Reynolds from writing any follow-up stories."

"How do you propose we do that?" Sheriff Michael asked. "I gather you're not suggesting we kill him?"

"Not yet." Scott smiled, but shook his head. "That would only draw more attention our way. As you all know, we have an important event up at Hemlock Run this weekend, an important political event. Nothing can be allowed to interfere with that. And if investors are skittish around a scandal, politicians are absolutely paranoid."

Nods all around. Everyone was aware of the situation.

"I think the best action would be to dry up his sources. Starve him out of the story."

They thought about this for a few moments.

"And if that doesn't work?" the Sheriff asked.

"Discredit him, if we can," Scott said.

The Judge cleared his throat. "The festivities up to Hemlock Run begin tonight?"

Scott nodded.

"The guests begin arriving this evening," the Sheriff added.

"Then I don't see how we'll be able to tell whether the reporter's written any follow up stories in time to do anything," the Judge said. "His next story wouldn't come out until the morning either way."

"He's right," Patrick said. He was uncomfortable with the entire subject. It seemed to be as far from upholding the law as a person could get without actually doing something illegal. There was room for debate on even that.

"Have you got eyes on him yet?" Scott asked the Sheriff.

"Not yet." Michael shook his head. "He wasn't at any motel in Bosque or Genoa last night, but we have every unit looking. We'll find him."

"Maybe he goes back to Seattle every night," Marcia suggested.

"Maybe. But if he comes back to Bosque, one of our people will see him."

"I hope you're right," Scott said. "We can't have him writing another story."

The Sheriff smiled. "I may have an idea of how to disarm Reynolds, if it comes to that. Take away his thunder."

All eyes were firmly on him now.

"I think you'll like it."

♦♦♦♦♦

About a mile south of Genoa, Jason signaled to Danny behind him and pulled off the highway into a gravel lot edging a small strip mall. It seemed to be a sort of park-and-ride location. More than a half-dozen cars and SUV's were lined up across the gravel, dark and locked up tight. Maybe a group commuted to Aberdeen every day and took turns driving.

Whatever. It was just what they needed.

Danny parked, locked her Jeep, and climbed into the passenger seat of Jason's rental. Unless the Sheriff had been tracking his credit card activity, they would not be looking for a dark blue Camry. It would give them a bit of an edge. He hoped.

Danny leaned over to kiss him on the cheek, rain drops beaded in her hair. "You drive like my grandma."

"Your grandma was a wise woman," he replied. "The cops had no idea she even existed."

"Whatever." She buckled herself in and flipped her hair back over her shoulder. "And Grandma is very much alive, thank you. The women in my family are long-lived; the men, not so much."

The rain had been falling steadily all morning. Now it seemed to thicken, bordering on a downpour from an opaque layer of featureless, dark cloud. The rainy season had officially begun and here, in rain forest country, it probably wouldn't stop for more than a day or two until June.

"We should have packed raincoats," he said as he pulled back on to the highway.

"Speak for yourself," Danny said. "Mine's in my garment bag."

Which was in the rental's trunk. Right on top, if he remembered correctly.

It was raining hard, but with little wind, and this was coastal Washington, so people were used to driving in rain. They were used to rain, period. Other than the rhythmic motion of wiper blades and more headlights than usual, you wouldn't have been able to tell that the weather had turned bad. Traffic moved them easily the last few miles toward Genoa and then into the outskirts.

"Do you remember how to get there?" Danny asked.

"I think so." He'd always had a pretty good memory for directions, landmarks, and the like.

Danny reached over and punched an address into the car's built-in navigation system from a scrap of paper. "Now you don't have to."

He looked over at her and smiled. "Thanks."

"No problem."

The navigation system led him through a series of turns and back streets Jason never would have managed on his own. He had no idea whether it saved them any time or distance, but it brought them to Jennifer's house. They were approaching from the opposite direction than last time, but they were there.

"Looks quiet," Danny said.

Jason agreed.

The whole street was deserted. At this time on a Friday morning, most of its residents would be either at work or school, the rest kept inside by the downpour. All the houses looked dark and buttoned up. Jennifer's was no different. In fact, it looked much like it had the last time they'd been here, down to the grimy Civic squatting in the drive.

Jason pulled in to the curb, two houses from Jennifer's and across the street, slipped the transmission into "Park" and switched the engine off.

They sat there for a moment in silence, just watching as nothing moved in or near Jennifer's house.

At least there was no sign of the Sheriff's Department nearby.

"She could be lying dead in there," Danny said.

"Or she could be perfectly fine."

Danny didn't react. Her eyes never strayed from the house.

Still there was no sign of life. No sign of Jennifer, her baby, or her husband. Nothing.

An idea struck him.

"Where's her husband?"

Danny frowned at him. "I don't know. At work?"

"Exactly. He's at work, just like he was yesterday. Just like every weekday of their lives."

"Okay." She wasn't following his reasoning.

"If Wilcox and his buddies were going to lash out at her, would they have waited this long to do it? They got a copy of the story last night."

Danny frowned again, shook her head. "Wilcox doesn't have that much self-control. I don't know about the others."

Jason agreed. "None of them have ever had to have any self-control. They take what they want when they want it. Why wouldn't they? No one has ever stopped them."

Jason could see her visibly relax. "You think she's okay."

"I think she's just fine."

She continued to gaze at the house.

"She's probably just trying to get some sleep. New baby and all."

"You're probably right." Danny admitted, but continued watching the house. "I'd feel better if I could see her."

Jason didn't think that was a good idea. "The absolutely last thing she needs right now is to be seen talking to either of us."

"I know that. I'd still feel better if I could see her."

Jason was starting to get nervous. They'd been sitting at the curb now for a while. It was a quiet residential street in a small town. People here would know their neighbors, at least well enough to recognize them and their cars. How long before someone noticed the strange car parked outside their house? How long before someone noticed two people sitting in that car? How long before someone called the police?

"We can't stay here much longer," he said.

"I know."

His cell phone chirped.

They both jumped like they'd been shocked.

Jason pulled the phone from his coat pocket and looked at the display just as it chirped again.

It was Lisa.

"Who is it?" Danny asked.

He told her, opened the text. *I'm coming over after school tonight. Where are you staying?*

"Shit."

Danny looked over at him. "What?"

He showed her the text.

Her face remained neutral as she turned her gaze back to Jennifer's house.

We're kind of floating, he texted back. *Let us know when you're close.*

"What did you tell her?"

"To let us know when she gets here."

Danny nodded.

His phone chirped. *K. Be careful.*

K.

He started the car and pulled out into the street, headed west, back toward Hwy. 101. Danny didn't protest. As they passed the Wilson house, it remained dark and quiet, as though deserted.

♦

"We need to discuss this," Jason said after a couple of quiet minutes. "Don't you think?"

Danny shrugged. "I don't know."

He forced himself to wait. He didn't want to provoke a fight. He didn't want to fight at all. They couldn't afford it. All their energy needed to be focused on the Bartons; Lisa showing up tonight was a distraction. And a distraction with all sorts of emotional baggage.

That, of course, made the issue even more important.

"Maybe I should just go home," she finally said. "I need to be back to work Monday anyway. That would solve the whole situation."

"No, it would just avoid the problem," he told her. "Besides, I don't want you to go. I like having you around."

"Thanks."

He stopped with traffic at the light at the intersection with Hwy. 101. A powder blue minivan was ahead of them. It was Friday and traffic was relatively heavy, even in a small town on the coast.

"It would make it easier though, wouldn't it?"

"No, it wouldn't."

They sat there in silence for a minute.

"Okay, let's say I don't go." Danny looked at him. "What do we do when she gets here? Pretend nothing happened? Rent separate motel rooms?"

"Why should we? We've got nothing to be ashamed about. Do we?"

"No, I guess not."

The light ahead of them switched to green. The minivan moved straight through the intersection, heading toward the harbor. Jason switched on his turn signal and turned right on to 101, heading north toward Bosque.

"If we're not doing anything wrong, why are we feeling so guilty about this?" Danny asked, as much to herself as to him.

"Because Lisa's our friend. We don't want to hurt her."

Danny nodded.

"But she's also very smart. She'll figure it out quickly, if she hasn't already. Trying to pretend something else will just insult her."

Danny agreed. "How do you think she'll handle it?"

That was the thing: he wasn't sure. She would be hurt. She would probably feel betrayed by both of them, but especially by Jason. They weren't technically going out anymore, weren't still boyfriend and girlfriend, but neither of them had gone on more than a few casual outside dates. This would be the first real relationship for either and it was with a mutual friend. Yes, she would be hurt. How bad and whether she'd be able to get past it, he had no idea.

"Maybe we should call her before she leaves Seattle and let her know," Danny said. "If the situation were reversed, I think I would want to be told up front."

He assumed that when she said "we should call," she meant him.

♦♦♦♦♦

Deputy David Howell had spent the morning fruitlessly patrolling the southern stretches of Hwy 101 in hopes of spotting the reporter. Personally, he figured Reynolds had holed up back in Seattle last night and only spent his days causing mischief over here. It wasn't that long a drive and the reporter, like most people, probably felt safer on his own turf.

If they found him, it would either be on Route 12 or 10, farther north.

But David was nothing if not a good soldier, so he would patrol his assigned sector until he received orders telling him otherwise. The paycheck would appreciate the overtime involved too. He had his eye on a certain fishing boat.

By mid-morning, his patrol had taken him north into Genoa. The city itself wasn't part of his area, but he continued north anyway, figuring he would use the Harbor Way loop to turn around and head south again. It was convenient.

As he approached the intersection in fairly heavy traffic, he moved into the left turn lane and braked as the traffic control light turned yellow, then red. One car was ahead of him in line.

The police radio crackled as the other patrols across the county reported just as much progress as he was having. Zero. Every single patrol car was out today. All hands on deck. Not a surprise considering the story Reynolds had published this morning.

He was only on the periphery of the Barton clan, but even he had felt the urgency behind the search.

David looked down to the copy of two photographs clipped to his dashboard. One was taken from Reynolds' driver's license; the other from the *News*' website. Both showed a young man in his late twenties, with dark brown hair, cut a bit long, and intelligent eyes.

He looked up again just as a dark Toyota sedan turned right onto 101 from across the intersection, heading north. A glimpse of the driver drew his attention.

David sat up in his seat. Had that been Reynolds? Leaving Genoa, of all places? Why would he be in Genoa? Where would he have been in Genoa? They'd checked all the motels without finding him. Nothing suggested he had friends in the area willing to put him up for the night. Still, something had struck him as familiar.

He immediately ruled out following the car. It would mean trying to cross traffic illegally from the left turn lane. The only safe way to do that would be with lights and siren. That would let Reynolds know—if it actually was him—that he'd been discovered.

David picked up the radio microphone, but stopped.

Had he actually seen Reynolds? After all, it was just a glimpse across a multi-lane intersection through a downpour. His own windshield wipers had been going, and the Toyota's side window had been covered with raindrops and grime.

If he called in and everyone converged on 101 between Bosque and Genoa, and it turned out to not be the reporter, their entire effort could be ruined. Reynolds could drive in from Portland on another route and no one would know.

David Howell replaced the microphone on its clip. When the turn signal turned green, he turned left on Harbor Way and continued on his patrol.

♦♦♦♦♦

"I assume you have a plan of some sort."

Jason didn't understand the question. He'd spent the last few minutes trying to come up with a scenario where telling Lisa that he and Danny were sleeping together didn't end up with one or more people in tears and never speaking to the others again. He wasn't having much luck with it. How do you do that? Do you just blurt it out? "Hi, Lisa. I thought you should know that I'm screwing Danny. Have been for a week and we both really like it." That seemed a tad cruel. Or, "You need to know, I've met someone and we're sleeping together. Yeah, you know her."

He was at a loss.

"A plan," she said. "Like where are we going and what we're going to do when we get there?"

"I thought we were going by the Millers to make sure nobody lashed out at them?"

Danny nodded, but seemed dissatisfied.

"What?"

"What if Wilcox or his buddies are watching the café?"

"Crap…" He eased off the gas. "I wasn't thinking."

"Not about this anyway."

He didn't feel it wise to comment on that, one way, or the other.

"What about giving them a call?" Danny asked. "Maybe they've had a visit today from the Sheriff's Department."

"Good idea," he said. "Why don't you do that?"

Danny muttered something, but punched the number into her cell phone. A second later: "Hi, Mrs. Miller—Barbara—this is Danny Hayden. I'm helping Jason Reynolds?" She listened for a while. "No, we haven't. We just wanted to check in and make sure you guys are okay." She listened for a while. "Good. No one from the Sheriff's Department has stopped by to see you?"

Danny caught Jason's eye and shook her head.

He relaxed a little.

"We probably won't stop by unless something new develops. It's too dangerous for everyone, but we're still working. Don't give up hope. We haven't."

She disconnected.

"Everything okay?"

Danny shrugged. "Depends on your definition, I guess. They haven't seen anyone from the Department."

"But?"

"But they're slowly going crazy. The waiting, the helplessness, the not knowing is tearing them to pieces."

Jason could only imagine the hell they were going through. Had been going through for nearly three days now. In reality, he probably couldn't even imagine it. He didn't know what it was like to have a child, much less have her go missing.

"She's worried about Tom," Danny said. "She thinks he's about to snap."

"That's the last thing we need."

Danny nodded. "It's the last thing Helen needs too. Or her mother."

If Tom Miller lost it and decided to try to get some sort of personal justice by attacking Wilcox, it would accomplish nothing constructive, certainly not with his right arm in a cast. At best, Wilcox would just subdue and arrest him. If Wilcox wasn't feeling charitable, Tom Miller could end up dead, and legally.

"I'm open to suggestions."

But Danny had nothing either. She just shook her head and turned to gaze out her window.

They were getting close to the area where they'd seen the speed trap the other day. They were climbing the hill now; the trap had been set up on the downgrade on the other side, heading into town. He had no reason to think the Sheriff wouldn't have some of his people there today. Why wouldn't he? Highway 101 was the main traffic corridor between Bosque and Genoa and parts south. If they wanted to find Jason and Danny, it was the perfect southern bottleneck.

He eased up on the gas.

The loss of momentum caught Danny's attention. Her gaze snapped to the road in front of them, then to him.

"Find a map of Bosque," he told her. "See if there's a back way in that avoids the speed trap on the south end of town."

She pulled out her phone and began tapping keys.

"Hurry," he told her. He could only go so slow before he started attracting as much attention as if he were racing through traffic. And they were running out of road.

"Got it," she said, reading the display of her smart phone. "Take a right on Heritage Way. It should be coming right up."

He spotted the road up ahead, approaching fast. He braked, turned on his signal, and made the turn without it looking too much like a sudden decision. Or he hoped so. At least the cars behind him didn't honk, or anything.

"What now?"

The road they were on seemed more like a country lane than a city street. All he could see to either side was second and third growth cedar forest, with a generous mix of willow and alder, their leaves already turning yellow. He could see no houses at all.

"From what I can see," Danny said. "Every cross street to the left eventually ends up in town. But we've got a mile, or so, before the first one."

As far ahead as he could see, the road ran straight, up and down the gentle hills, with nothing to either side but forest and brush, thick cedar punctuated with fern thickets and leafless willow in the low spots. He couldn't see another vehicle on the road.

An idea popped into his head.

"What?" Danny asked as if she'd seen it happen.

"What if we had Lisa stay with the Millers? They know her. She could be comforting. Maybe she could even keep Tom from going off the rails. Or at least give us some warning if he does."

"Yeah." Danny was nodding. "And it would avoid the whole 'who's sleeping with whom' question."

"That too."

Danny didn't say anything for a few moments. Then groaned and shook her head. "Look at us. We're such cowards."

"Because we don't want to hurt our friend?"

"Because we'd do backflips to avoid a confrontation."

"I'm thinking it's less avoiding it than postponing it."

"Semantics."

"Maybe." He shrugged, nodded. "But you have to admit, it would be one less thing we'd have to deal with. And we can't afford to be distracted going up against the Bartons."

"You're right. We don't need the distraction. But it feels wrong, like we're sneaking around."

"I know—"

His cell phone rang. Jason managed to pull it out of his pocket and glanced at the screen just as it rang a second time. It was Gerry Peterson, the publisher of the Bosque newspaper.

"I'd better take this," he said and pulled off onto the shoulder.

"Who is it?" Danny asked.

He told her as he accepted the call. She turned to look at the forest out her window.

"Mr. Peterson."

"Gerry, please. You don't pull your punches, do you? Word is the Barton family held an emergency summit this morning. I don't think I've ever seen them this rattled."

"Good." Jason smiled. "I hope none of them get any sleep for a while."

Peterson chuckled. "I think we should get together for that interview, don't you?"

"I think that could be interesting."

"How about in an hour?"

Jason blocked the microphone and turned to Danny. "He wants to meet in an hour."

She shrugged. "Okay."

He returned to Peterson. "Okay. We'll see you in an hour. Where do you want to meet?"

"I don't think my office would be a good idea."

Jason agreed.

"In fact, I don't think anywhere in Bosque is a good idea. Do you know where Donald is?"

"No. Sorry."

"It's the next town north of Bosque on 101. Just a wide place in the road. Main industry is selling booze to the folks on the reservation."

"Okay. I can find it."

"There's a place down on the beach called *Crazy Larry's*. I'll meet you there."

"*Crazy Larry's*," Jason repeated. "In about an hour."

They disconnected.

Danny was peering at him. "*Crazy Larry's*?"

Jason shrugged and put the car in gear.

Sixteen

"Welcome home, Mr. Smithson," the customs clerk said and handed the passport back to the man in the business suit.

Terrance Smithson thanked the young woman, picked up his briefcase and strode from customs into the arrivals terminal at Chicago's O'Hare airport. It was late in the morning local time, but the terminal was still caught up in its chaotic dance of moving humanity. There didn't seem to be a square foot without someone standing or walking through it.

Mr. Smithson wove his way through the crowd in the direction of the United Airlines ticket counter. He had more than an hour, but he never took anything for granted. He would get where he was going and then relax.

He felt at ease in the crowds, completely invisible. He had always felt the best way to get lost was to plant yourself in the largest group of people you could find and then blend in. Here, it was perfect. He was one tanned, Caucasian businessman in an Armani suit among ten thousand Caucasian businessmen in Armani suits.

Halfway between terminals, he walked right by a pair of Chicago's finest. The officers never noticed him.

When he finally reached the United Airlines terminal, he found an empty set of chairs, sat in one and set his briefcase in the chair beside it. He opened the briefcase, pulled out a baseball cap with the Chicago Cubs' logo on the front, and dropped it on the floor in front of his feet. He made a show of looking through files and notebooks for something.

"I think you dropped this," a male voice sounded.

Terrance glanced at the hat, then up to the man speaking. He wore a dark brown, hipster beard and black leather coat over a polo shirt.

"Thanks."

Smithson took the cap from the Good Samaritan, then picked up his briefcase and moved it to his lap, freeing up the chair next to him.

The Samaritan sat in the vacant space. "Heck of a time to be going to Toronto, isn't it?"

"It's still early," Terrance replied with the second half of the password. "It might get cold at night, but the days should still be nice and warm."

The Samaritan drew a thick manila envelope from his inner coat pocket and passed it over to Terrance.

Terrance opened the envelope and peered at its contents. The passport was obvious. The rest, not so much. He looked up at the other man. "A wallet?"

"It seemed more secure than letting everything rattle around loose."

Terrance shrugged. He opened the wallet enough to double check that everything he'd requested was there.

He pulled a business envelope from the briefcase and handed it to the Samaritan, who slipped it into his coat pocket without looking at it. Terrance took the wallet from his own coat, removed the cash and slipped the money into the new wallet, tossed the old wallet into the briefcase, slipped the new one into his coat pocket.

"Anything else?" the Samaritan asked.

"No. We're finished. Thank you."

"You have my number."

The Samaritan rose, quickly merged into the passing foot traffic and disappeared.

Terrance waited long enough to make it less obvious that the two men were connected, then closed his briefcase and walked up to the United Airlines ticket counter. When his turn came, he stepped up to the clerk and handed her his new passport.

"What can we do for you, Mr. Sanford?"

"I'd like a one way ticket to Vancouver, British Columbia. First class, if you have a seat available."

She tapped a few keys on her computer. "We do have a seat by the window, leaving at 2:30."

"Perfect," he said and handed her a Visa card for payment.

So, while a man known as Terrance Smithson disappeared into the metropolis of Chicago, one Trevor Sandford prepared to travel from Chicago to Vancouver, BC., returning to the airport he'd left a year ago.

Trevor Sandford—or Taylor Smith as he was sometimes called—was returning to the Great Pacific Northwest.

Seventeen

Patrol Sergeant Randy Jensen wasn't actually disobeying his orders; he was interpreting them loosely. He'd been assigned to watch the intersection where WA-10 joined US 101 in western Bosque in case Reynolds went through there, which seemed reasonable. Anyone trying to move from the north or east part of the county to the south or vice versa would go through that intersection, especially if they didn't live here and weren't familiar with the back roads. It was a decent plan. Maybe it was even a good one.

But Jensen wasn't at the intersection of 10 and 101. He was almost five miles from the intersection, sitting in his unmarked car in a parking lot just off Deane Street. He had been here now for a good hour and had no intentions of moving unless the Sheriff himself walked up and ordered him to move his ass.

Sgt. Jensen had a hunch and he was running with it.

He took a sip of cold coffee from the disposable cup he'd picked up earlier and shifted in his seat. Sometimes the equipment belt was a pain in the ass, literally.

A car drove by in the parking lot, but the driver didn't pay any attention to him. Generally speaking, he didn't care whether they noticed him or not. He was the law; he didn't worry about what ordinary people thought. But today he was trying to stay in the shadows. He didn't want the man he was watching to get a warning call.

Ever since the paper came out this morning with all those allegations against him and Wilcox and the Sheriff's Department, Jensen had been wondering where Reynolds got so much information, especially about his wife. It had to be someone local and someone with a lot of local knowledge.

Someone who was willing to talk about it.

Who fit that description better than a fellow newspaper reporter, a member of the brotherhood, the man who ran the local paper?

So he was sitting in the parking lot of Dunham Drugs, watching the office of the *Bosque Examiner* across the street. From here, he could see both the paper's front door and Peterson's ratty old Chevy pickup in the parking lot. If Reynolds was somewhere in town, Jensen would bet his paycheck that sooner or later Peterson would be meeting him.

Jensen intended to crash that little party.

Thing was, he had more to lose than the Bartons. He was not wealthy. His dad had run off when Randy was twelve and never looked back. There hadn't been child support, much less trust funds for anybody. Everything Jensen had, he'd earned himself. He hadn't allowed that bitch of a wife to take his stuff and he wasn't about to let anyone else do it either.

If this Reynolds crashed and burned the Sheriff's Department, the Bartons would survive just fine. They'd still be rich as hell. He, meanwhile, would be left virtually penniless. And he had no intention of ever being penniless again, ever.

So far, nothing at all had been happening at the sorry little office, other than a few old ladies going in to place ads, or something. It was incredibly boring. He had already spent nearly more than an hour watching.

Jensen took another sip of cold coffee.

He sat up as the front door to the newspaper office swung open and Peterson strode out carrying a brief case. He slid it into the cab of the pickup, glanced around nervously, then climbed in behind the wheel. A few seconds later, the pickup backed out of its spot and moved to the parking lot entrance.

Jensen cranked up his unmarked's engine and coasted over to the entrance of the drugstore's lot. He took his time. It wouldn't be the smartest thing to be facing each other across the street while waiting for traffic.

It wasn't an issue. Peterson's pickup pulled out into the street, heading west toward Hwy 101 well before Jensen reached his own entrance. Jensen signaled and turned onto the street almost a block behind Peterson.

"Let's see where you're going, asshole," Jensen muttered.

♦♦♦♦♦

"It looks deserted," Jason said as he pulled the car to a stop in Wilcox's empty drive.

Danny nodded, peering through her window at the rain-streaked house.

They had decided they had enough time to swing back by the deputy's house before the meeting with Peterson. Jason, especially, wanted to know whether the deputy had been simply out on patrol when they'd come around yesterday, or whether he had disappeared when Helen had. He didn't know how significant that would be, but it would change the complexion of the investigation. It could mean something had happened to both of them, or it could mean he was actively holding her prisoner somewhere.

It would pretty much rule out the possibility that he was an innocent bystander.

Now, sitting here out front, the house looked exactly as it had the day before, dark, neglected. The rows of grass cuttings still marking the lawn were soggy and losing their rich green. The wind ruffled the plantings along the foundation.

"Hang on a sec," Danny said and climbed out of the car.

Jason had no idea what she was doing. He watched as she pulled her hood up over her head and scurried through the rain up the walkway to the front door. Was she going to knock and see if he'd answer? That seemed unlikely. Not alone.

A few moments later, Danny hurried back and climbed into the car. "No one's been here since yesterday."

"How do you know?"

"An old cop trick." She showed him her open hand. A small pebble, no bigger than a grain of rice, lay on her palm. "I left it on the doorknob yesterday. No one has turned the knob since then."

"I think I saw that in a movie once."

"Funny."

"So Wilcox hasn't been home for at least two days. Where is he?"

"Same place as Helen?"

"Maybe," he said. "Let's hope that isn't a ditch somewhere."

Danny nodded.

His cell chirped.

Danny glanced over as he retrieved the phone from the console where he'd left it earlier. "Lisa again?"

He glanced at the display. It wasn't Lisa. He didn't recognize the number. "I don't know who it is."

Jason accepted the text.

check hemlock run.

What the hell did that mean?

"What?" Danny asked.

"I have no idea." He showed the message screen to her.

She shook her head. "Maybe Peterson knows."

♦♦♦♦♦

Gerry Peterson was having something of a personal crisis. He was well over fifty years old now, never married, and hadn't had a real romantic attachment in at least ten years. In truth, he had been married to the paper for most of his adult life. It had been struggling when he purchased it years ago and he had coddled and nurtured it, enticed advertisers, and persuaded local organizations to use the *Examiner* to promote their projects. After a couple of lean years, the paper had steadily grown in circulation and revenue until virtually every household in the northern county subscribed and he was making more money than he'd ever imagined.

Financially, he didn't need to work another day in his life.

By most measures, he was a business success.

But, as a wise man once said, there is more to life than money.

Now, as he drove north on Hwy 101, he was wondering what his financial success meant.

Thing was, more than thirty years ago when he'd graduated from journalism school, money was one of the last things on his mind. True, he wanted to make a living working at a newspaper and he had student loans to repay, but he hadn't imagined this life. He hadn't imagined living to avoid offending an advertiser. He hadn't imagined studiously walking a neutral line between any and all controversies.

What he'd imagined was being an investigative reporter like his heroes, Bob Woodward and Carl Bernstein. He'd imagined himself wielding the power of his pen to ferret out corruption and abuse and make it right. He'd imagined himself making a real difference. He'd imagined himself helping to create a better world.

He'd imagined himself doing exactly what Jason Reynolds was doing right now.

Reading Reynolds' story in the paper this morning had hit him like a punch to the gut. It had been a hard-hitting glimpse into the corruption Gerry had been pretending didn't exist for years. It was the story he should have written.

Instead, he'd collected his profits and looked the other way.

A log truck heading south sprayed dirty rainwater over his windshield and he turned the wipers up a notch. The drizzle of the morning had turned into a fairly steady rain. Traffic was light, especially heading north. Most were probably older folks heading up to the reservation casino for a little recreational gambling. Personally, he'd never seen the attraction in losing your hard-earned money at a slot machine, but that was the root of his problem, wasn't it? He didn't gamble. He had made his career by playing it safe, by doing nothing to irritate the Bartons.

That didn't mean he hadn't been aware of what they were doing.

He actually had considered writing about their activities over the years. He'd even gone as far as actually writing the stories. He'd never printed any of them, but he hadn't trashed them either. A file containing them and some of his research and documentation was hidden in his briefcase right now. It would help Reynolds fill in some blanks and background.

Peterson hadn't been courageous enough to print anything about the Bartons, but Reynolds had no such qualms. Reynolds would publish the story.

So he would help Reynolds write his story.

The Bartons and their friends had been running Dunham County like a Mafia family for too long. Too many crimes had gone unpunished. Too many good people had been hurt. It was time to seek justice. He'd thought about writing the story himself, to hell with the consequences, but felt in his gut that it was too late for him. He had missed his chance.

No, it was too late for him to change his tune now. But it wasn't too late to do what he could to help Reynolds.

He turned up the car's heater against the damp chill and tried to relax the muscles in his neck and shoulders.

♦♦♦♦♦

"We should tell Lisa what we want her to do," Danny said, "And why."

They were on Hwy 101, heading north. Somehow, they had managed to get through Bosque without being discovered. They'd seen sheriff's squad cars twice in different parts of town, but each time the car had been a block or more away. Unless the Sheriff had somehow traced Jason's credit card purchases, there was no way to identify them without a good look at their faces. Still, there was a noticeably heavy police presence today.

"Give her a call," he told Danny. "Or text her. A text would be better. She's probably in class."

"Okay," Danny said, but made no move to get her phone.

Jason turned up the windshield wipers against the thickening rain and glanced over at her. She was staring out her window at the thick wall of salal and cedar lining the road. The rain seemed to make the greens darker and richer.

"Are you upset?" he asked.

"What?"

"Are you upset because of the Lisa thing?"

"No." She shook her head. "No. I'm just thinking."

Jason watched the wet blacktop ahead of them. It sure felt like she was upset with him.

Traffic was light as the road followed the gentle hills toward the coast itself. It wasn't far away now. Jason could smell the salt in the air, just like back home in Seattle. If he wasn't mistaken, the little town of Donald was right on the beach.

Danny stirred in the passenger seat. "What if it's a trap?"

"The meeting with Peterson?"

"Yeah. Hasn't it struck you as quite a coincidence that he wants to meet today, just after you published your story?"

"But he brought the idea up yesterday when we met him at the Millers'."

"I know. But who else has approached us in all this?"

She had a point. With the exception of the Millers, no one had volunteered anything in Dunham County. He and Danny had always sought them, not the other way around. And most of the time, even those people had refused to talk to them.

"Okay, I see your point," he told her. "I assumed it was just a little journalistic envy, or the Cortez effect I told you about. Maybe he has other motives."

"We don't even know for a fact that he's even the sole owner of the Bosque paper. The Bartons could be his business partners. We don't know anything about him."

He had to agree with her. They didn't know a lot. They didn't know Peterson and didn't know what his motives were. For instance, why were they traveling so far out of Bosque to meet? Jason had assumed it was meant to avoid any Barton spies, but there could be a different reason.

Maybe the Bartons had better control over the residents of Donald than Bosque. Maybe since it was smaller there were be fewer potential witnesses to worry about.

"Peterson's been running his paper for years. Why now? Why suddenly move against the Bartons?" Danny said. "What changed?"

"I don't know."

"Me either. I'm just asking questions."

"Okay." Jason had slowly reduced his speed until he was traveling a full five miles under the speed limit. So far, no vehicles behind him had caught up to protest, but that wouldn't last long. "How do we deal with this?"

"My professional opinion?"

"Of course."

She smiled. "Well, we should go nowhere near the meeting site—what was it called?"

"*Crazy Larry's.*"

"We should go nowhere near *Crazy Larry's* until we've thoroughly scouted the area. If the Sheriff is hoping to take us into custody, they will have at least four officers—maybe more—assigned to the job. They will have to have transportation. We should be able to spot the cars parked nearby."

Jason nodded. She was making sense, as usual.

"Other than that, we're going to have to wing it."

That's what he was afraid of.

♦

Jason and Danny entered the southern outskirts of Donald almost thirty minutes before they were scheduled to meet with Peterson. The southern outskirts weren't much—a thrift store, an auto body shop, and two vacant buildings with faded, peeling paint—but Donald wasn't much of a town, either. It was the smallest incorporated city in Dunham County, according to the Wikipedia article Danny had found, with just over a thousand citizens, and stretched for a little more than a mile along either side of 101.

"This might be harder than I thought," Danny said, peering out her window at the passing buildings.

Jason knew what she meant. The problem was the way the town had been developed. It was laid out as a strip along 101 with the businesses along the highway and the dwellings on side streets behind the businesses. It had the random look of a town that had grown without direction of any kind.

That meant that most of the businesses fronting 101 had been built with parking lots large enough for a small convention, sitting empty most of the time. It would be very hard to have a strange vehicle go unnoticed. Jason had to assume everyone in Donald knew exactly what everyone else was driving.

And their car would obviously not be local.

"Lots of bars," Danny said, halfway to herself.

She was right. There were the usual businesses one expected to find in any small town: a small grocery; a branch of a regional bank; a hardware store; and a diner-type restaurant. Every other business was either a discount liquor store, or some sort of bar or tavern.

"It's the reservation," Jason said. They were just a few miles south of the Kwamamish Reservation, which was probably dry. Most reservations were. "Can't buy alcohol on the rez, so the profiteers crowd the edges."

Danny nodded.

"There's the place," Jason said, pointing to a small cement block bar and grill to their left, on the ocean side of the highway, between a closed tee shirt shop and another liquor store. A sign in red neon script labeled it *Crazy Larry's*. A handful of cars crowded against the side of the building.

"Keep going," Danny told him.

He did.

They continued to the north end of town, where he pulled over to the side of the road. "Now what?"

"Turn around. Head back through town."

He made the turn and started back through Donald, heading south. "What am I doing?"

"Looking for police cars, probably unmarked ones," Danny said, peering intently through her side window. "They'll probably be Dodge Chargers, most departments use them now. But there's an outside chance they'll be in old Crown Vic's, or even private cars. Look for someone sitting in the driver's seat, watching the bar."

They retraced their path, heading south through town, Jason studying every car on his side of the road, while Danny did the same on her side. Neither of them spoke. They were concentrating. Their lives depended on getting this right.

And about a block south of *Crazy Larry's*, it paid off when Jason spotted a dark colored car that could have been a Dodge Charger parked beside a closed liquor store. It was so new Jason could see rain beading on its hood.

A single person was sitting inside.

"Keep going," Danny told him. "We can't let him know we've made him."

She never even glanced over.

Jason continued south to the end of town, but neither of them saw any other suspicious vehicles. That presented a new wrinkle.

"If this is a trap," Jason said. "They should have more than one officer on scene, shouldn't they? You said four."

"Usually," Danny agreed. "At a minimum, we want to have at least two officers for every suspect. More, if possible. Overwhelming force. It makes it easier to keep them under control. I assume they'd be trained the same."

"So it isn't a trap?"

She shrugged. "We don't know for sure. It could be that they have a tactical team waiting somewhere else for a signal to move in. The guy we saw could be a spotter."

Jason nodded. "Or Peterson is on the level and they're watching him for some other reason."

"Heck of a coincidence."

"We don't know enough about Peterson or the situation to make that judgement."

At this point almost anything could be possible. It could be a trap. It could be nothing. Jason wasn't even certain now that the car he'd seen had even been a cop. He wasn't sure of anything.

It was a paralyzing feeling.

They were parked in a lot for a real estate agent on the south end of town. The engine and wipers were running, but the transmission was in park.

"Maybe we should just call the whole thing off," Danny suggested.

Jason was already shaking his head. "No. Peterson knows too much about the Bartons to let him walk away."

"But if he's baiting a trap?"

"I didn't get that vibe from him on the phone. He seemed excited by what we'd done in this morning's paper."

Danny sighed. "You have something in mind?"

He did.

♦

The idea wasn't complicated, but it took a little persuasion on Jason's part to convince Danny to go along with it, mainly because it involved them splitting up. It was based on the idea that if any sheriff's officers were lying in wait, they would be expecting him to drive up and park right in front, like a normal person.

So, he wouldn't do that.

Instead, Jason and Danny switched positions in the car, so Danny could drive and she lent him her yellow raincoat. It was small in the shoulder and arms, but he didn't think anyone would notice in the rain. Everyone outside was wearing some sort of raincoat and paying little attention to anyone else.

When they were situated, Danny shifted into "drive" and drove through town past *Crazy Larry's*, and then pulled into the gravel lot of another bar a few buildings to the north. They didn't see any police cars other than the Charger waiting by the liquor store.

"I still don't like the idea of splitting up," Danny said.

"There's no other way of keeping an eye out for the Sheriff," he told her. "You're my early warning system."

"I know. I still don't like it."

He could live with that. He hoped so anyway. "Can you see the place from here?"

Danny turned to look to her left. "Yep."

"Okay. Cells ready?"

She nodded. They had set up a warning message on her cell phone and left it up onscreen. All she'd need to do if trouble showed up was hit "send" and Jason would receive the warning.

"Here goes nothing. Keep an eye out." Jason raised the hood of the raincoat and opened the car door.

"Jason?"

He stopped and looked at her.

She leaned over and kissed him on the lips. "Be careful."

Jason smiled and stepped out into the rain.

Eighteen

Jason walked across the potholed parking lots, doing his best impression of a local alcoholic trudging head down through the rain to his favorite watering hole. He even stumbled a couple of times for authenticity. It took every fiber of his self-control. The entire time he felt like a target was taped to his back, crosshairs zooming in from some hidden rifle.

He safely reached the front door, glanced once at Danny, then pulled opened the door and stepped inside.

The interior of *Crazy Larry's* was the absolute opposite of what he'd been expecting. Between the name and the general rundown feel of the entire town, he'd been expecting a gloomy dive with neon lighting, nicotine-stained walls, and a fog of stale cigarette smoke.

Instead, he walked into what could best be described as a bistro. It wasn't large, but the area was bright and open with polished hardwood floors, rain-spotted floor-to-ceiling windows overlooking the beach, and original watercolors on the walls. A modest, but well-equipped bar stood to his left, where a lone man studiously nursed a beer while a bartender in his forties sliced lemons. Small tables had been lined up beside the windows, with a handful gathered in a space to his left. Three were occupied by middle-aged couples. A fourth table, farthest away in the corner by the window, held Gerry Peterson.

A young woman in a black polo shirt and white apron approached. "Good afternoon. Pick any table you'd like."

"I'm actually meeting the gentleman at that table." He gestured toward Peterson.

She seemed genuinely pleased with the news. "Would you like some coffee to start with?"

"Absolutely. Is there somewhere I can hang my raincoat? Hate to drip all over your beautiful floor."

She showed him to a coat tree in a corner. He hung his raincoat, using that movement to examine the other patrons in the room. None of them looked the least bit suspicious, nor did anyone seem interested in him, or Gerry Peterson.

He saw nothing that looked like a concealed gun.

Satisfied as he could be, Jason walked across the room and sat down at the table across from Peterson.

"You're late," Peterson said.

Jason shrugged and set his cell phone on the table. "Couldn't be helped. These are dangerous times."

"Yeah." Peterson's nod was either sad or weary. "They are."

The waitress arrived with Jason's coffee and a menu. She vanished before he could tell her it would be a minute or two.

Peterson also had a mug of coffee sitting between his hands, the menu lying unread to the side.

"You're taking a pretty big risk yourself," Jason said. "Meeting with me."

Peterson shrugged.

Jason turned his gaze to the soggy beach outside the window. It was empty as far as he could see. The foam of the surf line laid almost a hundred yards away over a featureless expanse of wet and windblown sand. Not even the most dedicated beachcomber was out today.

"Mr. Reynolds," Peterson said.

Jason turned back to the older man.

"I actually didn't ask you here to interview you for my paper."

Jason sipped his coffee, smiled. "I had a feeling…"

Peterson held his coffee cup between his hands, like he needed the heat to warm them. "I was impressed with your story this morning."

Jason thanked him, but wished he would get on with it. He had a terrible feeling they were working on borrowed time. Unseen tentacles were closing in.

"Reading your story awoke something in me," Peterson continued, "the ghosts of Woodward and Bernstein, I guess."

Jason smiled at the name check.

"Anyway, you wrote the story I should have written years ago, but didn't. And now it's too late for me to grow a conscience."

"But you can help me take them down."

Peterson nodded. "Everything you printed in your story was true, as far as it goes, but it only scratched the surface of what's going on in Dunham County."

Jason waited. Peterson wouldn't have brought him this far unless he had something valuable for him.

Peterson studied him for another minute, as though trying to judge some aspect of his character. Or maybe he was trying to make a decision about himself. After a few seconds, he pulled his briefcase on to his lap.

♦♦♦♦♦

Danny sat sideways in the driver's seat of the rental, trying as hard as she could to simultaneously watch both the front of *Crazy Larry's* and the suspicious car parked across the road from the bar, all while remaining inconspicuous to any curious citizen who happened by. The compact field glasses she'd removed from her purse didn't help. It was hard to look innocent with field glasses pressed to your eyes. If she managed to pull this off, she thought to herself, she was going to deserve a serious reward, like a pint of chocolate mint ice cream.

She shifted a little in an attempt at comfort and raised her field glasses again to scan her two targets. Nothing had changed. Basically nothing had happened while she'd been watching other than the rain thickening some. All the potholes scattered across the parking lots splashed with muddy brown water.

She lowered the binoculars again and glanced at the cell phone in her left hand. For at least the tenth time, she woke it up and glanced at the warning message they had composed. All she would have to do if things went south was hit "send."

Providing she didn't drain the battery by constantly waking it up.

As if in response to her thought, something caught her attention out on the street. She raised the field glasses just as a sheriff's department squad car pulled off the highway and stopped directly beside the car she'd been watching.

Danny almost hit the panic button right then, but stopped herself. Perhaps the second car had just been passing by and stopped to chat. It happened all the time. Patrol could be terribly boring and lonely work, especially in a rural area. Sometimes it was just nice to chat for a bit.

So she watched as the cars idled beside each other, the occupants apparently talking for several minutes.

"Come on," she whispered, "get on with your patrol. Go get some lunch. Get some coffee."

But they didn't go anywhere. They continued talking.

Planning? Were they organizing something, like a takedown?

Just when her patience and survival instincts were stretched to the breaking point, a second sheriff's squad car pulled off the highway next to the others.

Danny didn't hesitate this time. Jason needed to get out of there. She hit the "Send" button on her cell phone.

♦♦♦♦♦

Peterson pulled a thick and worn manila file folder from his briefcase and set it on the table between them. Jason noticed that the folder had several stains that looked like coffee rings, and the spine at the lower end had been worn down to the base fibers. A thick rubber band held the contents in the inch-thick folder.

Jason's curiosity had tightened into excitement now. He was practically quivering.

Peterson closed his briefcase and returned it to the floor beside his chair. "Under the circumstances, I don't think it's a good idea for the two of us to spend much time together. There are just too many prying eyes around, if you know what I mean?"

Jason understood. He was having trouble keeping his hands under control. They wanted to open the file and page through the documents in there, but he needed to be patient. Peterson hadn't actually given the file to him yet.

As if reading his mind, Peterson placed a hand flat on top of the file. "Since we don't have time for the question and answer conversation you probably need to have, the best I can do his hand over every bit of information I have on the Dunham County Sheriff's Department and the Barton family. That way you can go through it and narrow your questions down a bit."

"That's all information on the Bartons?"

"And the Sheriff's Department." Peterson said. "I may have been afraid to kill the golden goose, but that didn't mean I wasn't paying attention to what it was doing."

"May I?"

"Of course," Peterson said and pushed the file across the table to him. "It might take you a while to get through it. It's more than twenty years' worth, in roughly chronological order."

Jason removed the rubber band and opened the file to the first page. It was basically a short summary of two unnamed witnesses saying the sheriff's department wasn't cracking down on the methamphetamine traffic because they were behind it.

He looked up at Peterson. "Meth? Really?"

He shrugged. "Hearsay, as the lawyers would say, but that was the rumor. That was also twenty years ago, when I'd just moved here and hadn't learned yet what questions not to ask."

Jason's cell phone chirped notice of a text. Both men jumped as though it had been a gunshot.

"Crap!" Jason glanced at the display to confirm it was Danny.

It was. "We've got to go. The Sheriff's people are outside."

Peterson's face went pale.

Jason was already on his feet, wrapping the rubber band back around the file, slipping his cell into a pants pocket, wondering whether he had time to get his raincoat. “Is there a back door here? Beach access maybe?”

“Yeah.” Peterson pointed to a doorway near the bar. “A deck opens onto the beach. What do I do?”

Jason tossed a five onto the table for his coffee. “Wait five minutes after I leave, then leave yourself. Go home. As long as they don’t catch us together, you should be okay.”

Peterson didn’t look terribly assured.

“I’m taking this,” Jason showed him the file folder.

“It’s yours.”

“I’ll be in touch,” Jason told him, grabbed his raincoat and slipped out the door Peterson had pointed out. It opened onto a modest wooden deck, slick and gray with the rain. From there, a flight of wooden stairs led down to the deserted beach.

Jason shrugged into the raincoat as he walked and tucked the file under the protective rubber. At the top of the stairs, he glanced one more time toward Peterson, who still sat at the table where Jason had left him. No cops of any kind were in sight.

Jason gave the newspaper man a salute and hurried down the stairs.

♦♦♦♦♦

Gerry Peterson waited until a full seven minutes had passed since Jason Reynolds had disappeared onto the beach. It was the longest seven minutes of his life. Every instinct screamed that he needed to flee and he needed to do it right now. But Reynolds had been right. If sheriff’s deputies were waiting for them outside, the best thing would be to not act guilty and not be caught together.

If nothing else, it would give them plausible deniability. It would also help his personal safety that he no longer had the file on the Bartons. He could say he just came here for a little peace and quiet. He came up here every week or two for just that purpose. The employees at *Crazy Larry’s* could verify that.

When he felt he'd waited long enough, he got up, grabbed his briefcase and left his own five beside Reynolds' on the table for his coffee and walked to the front door.

He had to pause and take a couple of deep breaths before pushing open the door and stepping outside into the rainy day.

Nothing happened.

Peterson fought the sudden urge to pee his pants, and hurried through the rain to his truck. He tried to avoid looking around, but couldn't help himself. He could see no sheriff's squad cars anywhere. Maybe Reynolds' partner had panicked over nothing. Maybe the whole thing had been a false alarm.

He unlocked his truck, tossed the briefcase into the passenger seat, and climbed behind the wheel. Still, nothing happened. His hands were shaking so bad, it took two tries to get the key in the ignition, but he did and the engine started right up.

So far, nothing unusual had happened. He might just have gotten away with this thing.

He backed out of the parking space, signaled, and pulled out on to Hwy 101, heading south toward Bosque. His CD player picked up where it had stopped when he'd arrived, part way through Steely Dan's *Aja*. He turned up the volume on *Deacon Blues* and actually began to relax a little.

Then he saw the police lights.

♦♦♦♦♦

Randy Jensen smiled as he pulled to a stop immediately behind Peterson's pickup and slipped the transmission into "park." Sometimes it was just too easy. Turn on your emergency flashers and all the good citizens pull over and stop, praying that the law wasn't actually looking at them. But sometimes the law *was* looking at them and they cowered in their pretty cars and pleaded and cried and bargained and begged for mercy.

From him.

The radio crackled to life and Sean came on. "Want backup?"

Randy sighed. They'd talked about this already. How many times did you have to explain something? He keyed the microphone. "Negative. Keep an eye on that bar and see if that damn reporter comes out. If he does, follow him and let me know his 40."

Got it now?

"10-4."

Randy reached over to the kit he had on his passenger seat and pulled out a battered Hi-Point .40 he'd taken from a meth head last year. Somehow, he'd neglected to mention it in his report.

Oops.

He checked that the pistol was loaded and cocked, shoved it into his coat pocket and stepped out of his car.

Randy could see Peterson's reflection in the side mirror. The newspaper man looked worried. Good. He should be worried. He should be scared shitless.

♦♦♦♦♦

Jason had to summon every ounce of will to keep from running away from *Crazy Larry's*. Every instinct told him to get away as fast as he could, but he had to ignore that instinct. Nothing would draw exactly the attention he didn't want more than the sight of him in his bright yellow raincoat running down the beach. It also didn't help that no one else was out today, because of the rain. There was no crowd to disappear into.

At least the wind was at his back, pattering the rain into the back of his raincoat, not his face.

He glanced up as he walked, trying to judge just how far away Danny had parked from the bar. Unfortunately, he hadn't paid that much attention to how many buildings he'd passed on his way in. He'd been more concerned with the sheriff's car across the road.

Jason also had to resist glancing behind him. Innocent people stumbling through the soft sand along the top of the beach didn't glance back to see if they were being pursued. He just kept his head down and walked.

He passed the third building north from *Crazy Larry's*, hesitated, then decided to climb up a wooden staircase between it and the next building. From there, he should be fairly close to

Danny. He could at least see where she was and adjust his route accordingly.

He hurried up the stairs, then followed a narrow concrete walk between the buildings and to the edge of the parking lot.

Danny sat in the car maybe thirty feet to his left.

She spotted him and waved him over.

Again, Jason had to force himself to walk calmly over to the car and slip into the passenger seat. "What's going on?" He tossed the raincoat hood back, away from his face.

Danny glanced at him. "Peterson just left. The black Charger followed him. Another car is still watching the bar."

Jason looked for himself. A single sheriff's squad car was now sitting pretty much where the black car had been when they'd arrived.

"There was a third sheriff's car when I sent the text," she told him. "It went north."

It had probably been sent to cut off any escape in that direction.

"We'd better get out of here," he said.

♦♦♦♦♦

Randy Jensen approached Gerry Peterson's car in the standard position, at the driver's eight o'clock, not because he was worried about his safety—he figured Peterson was as dangerous as a piece of soggy toast—but out of habit. Peterson sat there obediently, his hands on the steering wheel at two and ten o'clock. He was doing everything the experts recommended. He was the poster child of cooperation.

"Sir," Jensen asked. "Could you turn the vehicle off?"

Peterson slowly reached down and switched his engine off. Now there was no sound but the patter of rain on sheet metal and the occasional hiss of cars passing on 101 behind Jensen.

"Do you know why I've pulled you over today?"

"No, sir." Peterson shook his head. Where Jensen was standing—behind and to the side—it was awkward for Peterson to make eye contact. He had to look back over his left shoulder.

"I pulled you over because you haven't been minding your own fuckin business."

The newspaperman's face went pale. Jensen pulled the Hi-Point out of his jacket pocket, took two steps to the left and fired twice into Peterson's head. The .40 bullets punched right through the man's skull, spraying blood and brains across the cab of the truck and shattering the passenger window across the cab. Peterson slumped forward against the shoulder restraint.

♦♦♦♦♦

Two concussive bangs sounded through the rain. Danny and Jason ducked down in their seats. Neither had to ask what the noise had been. They were clearly gunshots.

"Go!" Jason yelled.

Danny already had the car moving, its tires churning up gravel as it headed toward the parking lot entrance and Hwy 101.

"Which way?" Danny asked. They would either have to turn right or left, south or north, toward Bosque or away from it. The reasonable choice would be to head north, away from Bosque, and away from the imminent danger. But the Bartons could be anticipating that move too and be waiting for them.

"Which way?" Danny repeated.

To the right, Jason could see the flashing red and blue emergency lights.

"Go right," he said. "Go back to Bosque."

Danny glanced at him, then executed the turn onto 101, heading toward the flashing lights, ahead on their right. It appeared to be just off the highway, like a standard traffic stop.

The marked squad car pulled out about a block ahead of them, beacons flashing, travelled a couple of blocks, and pulled off the road behind the unmarked black one. Backup had arrived.

Traffic had slowed, as drivers moved carefully around the emergency lights and gave in to their morbid urge to view someone else's bad day. The public always found other people's mistakes and tragedies fascinating.

"Crap," Danny said as the three cars ahead of them slowed to a crawl as they approached the scene. "Just drive, people. You don't need to see everything."

The absolute last thing they needed now, was to be sitting in a car moving at walking speed right beside the sheriff's cars.

"Any ideas?" Danny asked.

He didn't have one, not a good one. They could turn inland and try to find a back road that would take them past the police activity, but that would be more obvious than just going through like everyone else. "Just try to blend in," he told her. "Try to avoid eye contact with the cops."

"You think? You're going to be closest. Keep your head down."

Jason brought out his cell phone and made an obvious show of reading something on the screen. It would at least keep his face turned away from the police as they passed. The Sheriff's people didn't seem to know the vehicle they were driving; if they had, he and Danny would already have been in trouble.

If they played it cool, they might just get out of here in one piece.

"Oh, God."

Jason looked up at her, followed her gaze over to the side of the road.

He was just in time to glimpse Gerry Peterson's bloody head through the window as they passed by. All the air seemed to have been sucked from Jason's lungs. He had just been talking with Peterson, not ten minutes ago. He had just been talking to him.

Danny accelerated away from the bloody truck, her face pale.

♦♦♦♦♦

Sgt. Jensen returned to his car and slid in behind the wheel. He tossed the Hi-Point back into the kit bag on his passenger seat. That would come in handy later, when they finally caught up with that damned reporter. As luck would have it, he knew of a pawn shop owner who could be persuaded to testify that he'd sold that very gun to Jason Reynolds.

Until then, he needed to set some wheels in motion.

He picked up his radio microphone, called into central dispatch, and identified himself. "Requesting a homicide detective at my location. The victim is Gerald Peterson, the owner of the *Bosque Examiner*. The suspect is Jason Reynolds." He read the description straight from the bulletin he'd been given this morning. "Suspect was observed arguing with the victim prior to the shooting."

After he answered the dispatcher's follow-up questions, Jensen returned to Peterson's car, removed the newsman's briefcase and put it in his car's trunk.

Now the gears of the legal system were in motion, grinding steadily toward Reynolds and they wouldn't stop until he was just a grease spot.

Nineteen

Sheriff Mike Barton looked down at the note his deputy handed him. His face grew red, then even more red, like a boiler about to explode. Scott Barton could see his father struggling to keep his temper under control and watched the process with a clinical interest. It was amusing.

The deputy stood awkwardly off to one side. He seemed to be expecting either some orders to come out of the message the Sheriff was reading, or a physical attack.

"That stupid son-of-a-bitch!" the Sheriff finally looked up at Scott. "Christ!"

"What?"

They had been discussing final preparations for the weekend at the lodge. Scott would be heading up there shortly. He wanted to make sure everyone was on the same page before he traveled somewhere with spotty cell coverage.

Now something even more interesting had turned up.

The Sheriff looked up at the deputy as if surprised to see him. "Get Jensen on the horn. Now. Buzz me in here when you've got him."

"Yes, sir." The deputy fled the office.

"What's going on?" Scott asked again.

"Gerry Peterson is dead, shot in the head. "

"The local newspaper guy?"

"Yeah." Sheriff Barton said. "I've known him for years. He was absolutely harmless. Now someone's blown his brains out."

"Someone?"

"Sgt. Jensen says this reporter, Jason Reynolds, killed him."

Scott watched his father, trying to read the subtext. "Wasn't Jensen named in Reynolds' story this morning?"

"Hell of a coincidence, ain't it?"

Scott nodded, trying to think this through. "So much for 'low profile.'"

"No shit."

Scott's mind was already racing. The prospect of the Governor spending the weekend at the lodge was probably out of the question now. As soon as the politician got wind of this latest development down here, he would do everything short of defecting to be nowhere near Dunham County. Everyone in the political world knew that scandal was contagious.

But there were others who would still be willing to come for a weekend of freedom at the Bartons'. Several senior senators and congressmen from both sides of the aisle would be there, scandal or no scandal. Not having the Governor lowered the stakes quite a bit, but there would be other opportunities.

There were always other opportunities. Always.

Scott peered at his father. "What are the odds he actually killed Peterson?"

"Reynolds?" Sheriff Barton shook his head. "Why would Reynolds kill Gerry Peterson? No, this is Jensen, trying to throw the winning touchdown pass."

"Well, this does kind of pull Reynolds off our back, doesn't it?

Scott smiled to himself. Jensen sounded like a self-starter. For, if nothing else, this would certainly keep Reynolds from screwing up any more of their life for a while. Nothing was more effective at disarming your enemy than legitimately threatening his life.

The Sheriff's phone rang. He had the receiver to his ear before the sound of the ring had faded away. "Jensen? What the hell is going on up there?"

♦♦♦♦♦

When a murder investigation is initiated, it soon takes on a momentum all its own.

Once authorities determine that a homicide has taken place, a case file is created. Every piece of evidence, every witness statement, and every report from every officer working on the case will be included in the file. Detectives interview witnesses and friends of the victim to establish a suspect. When a suspect has been identified, but his/her location unknown, the system has created a protocol and a series of tools to help locate that suspect.

The investigating department will issue a BOLO (be on the lookout) to all patrol units, providing each with the suspect's name, photograph, vehicle description, as well as home and work addresses. This enlists the eyes and ears of every officer in the effort to locate and arrest the suspect.

Similar notices will be sent to any nearby agencies or jurisdictions which the suspect may be hiding in, or traveling through on the way somewhere else. A notice will also be sent to the State Highway Patrol, who will look throughout the state.

A separate notice will be sent to the Department of Motor Vehicles, who will place a "flag" on the suspect's driver's license.

The system was designed so that, in short order, as many people as possible across the state—and eventually the nation—would be enlisted in the search for the suspect.

And so it was that a rookie reporter for the *Seattle News* named Mackenzie Rossiter, working the police beat, happened to recognize a name on a notice sent by Dunham County. She checked the name twice, to make sure it wasn't a mistake, then pulled out her cell phone and dialed the *News* office.

♦♦♦♦♦

Danny and Jason drove for fifteen minutes in silence after seeing Peterson's mangled head on the side of the road in Donald. They were both in shock. Jason had known there was a certain amount of danger involved in what they were doing—you can't keep tweaking the dragon's nose and be surprised when you get burned—but he had not prepared himself for such gratuitous violence. And it was gratuitous. Gerry Peterson had not been a threat to anyone. There was no reason to kill him.

Except, of course, as a way to silence one Jason Reynolds.

The first few minutes had been terrible, as they both processed the violence and expected to see sheriff's squad cars roaring up from behind at any moment. Even when nothing materialized, it didn't seem to ease the tension.

Then, maybe five minutes later, three squad cars and an ambulance passed heading north with emergency beacons blazing. A mile later, a State Police car passed, also heading north.

"Enough of this," Danny finally said and pulled over in one of the roadside viewing areas scattered along the coast.

Jason just now remembered he still had Peterson's file tucked against his side under the raincoat. His mind was moving so slowly, it felt like he'd been drugged.

"They killed him," Danny continued. "They shot him like he was a rat, or something. And they did it right out in public, where anyone could see. In front of witnesses."

"I know." Jason agreed. "They don't care who sees them. Why should they? What is a witness going to do?"

"We can't afford to be winging it anymore. We can't be making it up as we go, or more people are going to end up dead. We're going to end up dead. We need a strategy, a concrete strategy."

Jason agreed. The problem was that they didn't have enough information yet to create that strategy. The last few days had all been about gathering information, trying to assemble enough rope to hang somebody. And it had pissed someone off. He had written the story last night as a way of prodding the monster, get it to react.

It had reacted all right. Now Gerry Peterson was dead, his brains blown all over the inside of his truck. And it was Jason's fault.

No, he hadn't pulled the trigger, but there was no way of getting around the fact that if Jason hadn't written his story, Peterson probably wouldn't have met with him, and he would still be alive. He, Jason, was at least partially responsible.

The knowledge lay like a sandbag across his chest.

Even worse, they still didn't have enough rope to hang anybody.

For a few moments, they sat in silence as the rain pattered on the car and the waves thundered to foam against the beach below them. Other than them, the viewing area was empty.

"Jason?"

"I don't know." He pulled the file out from under the raincoat. "But we need to find some place safe to hole up while we go through this. We owe it to Peterson."

"What is it?"

Jason told her about his conversation with Peterson about the file.

She seemed duly impressed. "It's everything he's collected about them?"

"That's what he said." Jason shrugged. "I didn't have time to look at it before we had to get out of there."

The file Peterson had died getting to them.

Again, he felt that sandbag across his chest.

"So we need to find someplace safe to hole up for a while," Danny said. "Which rules out anywhere in Dunham County."

Jason agreed. The first obvious problem was that to get to any motel outside of Dunham County, they would have to drive through most of the County. To get to Aberdeen, would involve driving south through both Bosque and Genoa; to get out of the county to the east, would mean driving through Bosque. The only other possibility would be to turn around and head north, but that would also mean driving right by Peterson's body again and the gathering of sheriff's deputies.

There was risk in every choice.

"South," he finally said. "We go to Aberdeen. That way we can also pick up your car."

"And from now on, your credit card stays in your wallet," Danny said. "We should get rid of this car too. It wouldn't take a genius to subpoena your charge history and figure out exactly what we've been doing."

Jason agreed.

♦

The first text message came just as they were leaving the southern edges of Bosque, heading toward Genoa. When his phone chirped, he and Danny exchanged a glance. Now who could that be? He pulled his cell phone out of his pocket and checked the display. The message was from Miles, his editor.

Warrant out for you for murder. Anything you want to tell me?

"Crap."

Danny glanced at him. "What?"

He read the message to her.

"They're pinning Peterson's murder on you."

That was how it looked.

He composed a reply to Miles, typed it out and sent it. *Just trying to stop me. Innocent.*

Keep in touch.

"You need to shut off your phone," Danny told him. "Shut it off and take out the battery, just like Port Salish. They can track cell phones, remember?"

He did. Jason had given a similar speech to Danny last year in Port Salish when Lundgren had tried to frame her. At least then most of her fellow deputies had never really believed the charges. They had nothing like that here.

Every law enforcement officer in the region was going to be gunning for them.

Jason powered down his cell phone, then flipped it over and removed the battery.

♦♦♦♦♦

Scott Barton, Executive Assistant to State Senator Morris Barton, pulled his Mercedes off the highway just behind the Sheriff and just within the city limits of Donald. He waited while the Sheriff decided on a parking spot, then pulled in immediately behind him and switched the engine off. The rain was steady, beating a tattoo on the roof of his car and running in minor tributaries down the windows.

Scott sighed as he turned up the collar of his raincoat. The least they could have done is wait for better weather. But no. He was going to have to get wet.

Outside, it looked like the typical law enforcement clusterfuck. A minimum of six squad cars were parked on both sides of 101, along with an ambulance and two fire trucks. Nearly a dozen men in uniform milled around in scattered knots amid the flashing lights. Most of them had absolutely nothing to do and no reason to be here, other than wanting to be part of the excitement.

Yellow crime scene tape had been wrapped around a blue full-sized pickup parked just off the west side of the highway. Scott could make out what looked like blood sprayed across the pickup's windshield.

No one had bothered to cover the victim.

Two deputies had to keep the curious motorists moving or traffic would have come to a complete halt.

Scott waited for the Sheriff, then followed him across the highway toward the biggest knot of officers.

"Where's Jensen?" Sheriff Barton demanded.

"Right here, sir." An officer in the center of the knot of men stepped forward. Randy Jensen didn't appear the least bit intimidated by the attention of his boss. He was in the tail end of his thirties, with strawberry blond hair buzzed short and a ruddy complexion.

By the size of the deputy's shoulders, legs, and arms, Scott surmised he was no stranger to anabolic steroids either. Several of the deputies looked that way.

"What the hell happened here, Sergeant?"

Without being asked, the other officers found something they needed to do somewhere else. It was a social instinct. Don't hang around when it looks like one of your colleagues is about to be chewed out. You didn't want to risk becoming collateral damage. It was self-preservation, pure and simple.

"He was like this when I drove up. No one was around. He was just dead," Jensen said. "But it had to be Jason Reynolds. Peterson came up here to meet him at a bar called *Crazy Larry's*. They must have argued over something."

"You saw them meet up?"

"Why else would he drive all way up here? It's Donald. Even the people who live here don't want to be here."

The Sheriff wasn't amused.

"The way I see it," Jensen continued. "This will solve all our problems. Reynolds will be too busy trying to save his own ass to stick his nose in our business. And maybe he gets killed in a shoot-out when he is caught."

Sheriff Barton planted his hands on his hips. He looked more tired now than pissed off. "You sound like you have it all figured out."

The deputy smiled. "I have an idea that if we search the place he's been staying, we'll probably find the murder weapon. Maybe even Peterson's missing briefcase."

The Sheriff rubbed a hand along his jaw. "Do we know where he's been staying?"

Jensen smiled. "It doesn't really matter, does it?"

Scott smiled to himself. He decided he liked Sergeant Jensen.

♦♦♦♦♦

The next text came fifteen minutes later, as they were just beginning to approach the northern edges of Genoa. They still hadn't seen much of a police presence, just one more squad car heading north with emergency lights blazing. In a way, the lack of cops actively searching for them was a relief. It meant they weren't in a full flight for their lives. But after a few minutes of relief, Jason began to worry that they weren't seeing enough of a police presence.

As in what were the Sheriff and his people up to?

When the cell went off, they both jumped about four inches. Danny turned to him. "I thought you turned your cell off?"

"I did. It's not my phone." It wasn't even one of his ringtones.

"Oh crap." She handed him her purse without taking her eyes from the road. "Could you see who it is?"

"Sure."

He found her cell phone in the main compartment, between a brown leather wallet and a holster containing a small pistol. He did not doubt for a second that it was loaded, either. She was a professional.

Jason pulled out her cell and woke up the display.

One unread message waited for her attention.

"Want me to open it?"

She glanced at him, back to the road. "Please."

It took a little experimenting because she had a different model phone, but he finally opened the message.

"It's from Andrea Meade, the District Attorney."

"I know who she is. What's she want?"

"*My star witness wanted for murder? What's going on?*"

Danny blew air through her lips. "Crap."

"Bad news travels fast."

She didn't say anything. Were her eyes glistening?

He waited a couple of beats. "Do you want to say something back to her?"

"I'm thinking," Danny murmured.

Jason waited, watched the sodden landscape sliding by his window. It had only been raining for a day and already the ditches were full of standing water.

"Okay. I think I've got it." She glanced over at him. "Ready?"

"Shoot."

"It's like Marks, but everybody."

Jason typed her words into the phone. "Send it?"

She nodded.

He pressed "send."

Danny stared straight ahead through the windshield.

"You okay?" Jason asked.

"Oh, sure."

Her cell rang again. It was another text from Andrea. He opened the text without bothering to ask and read it aloud.

"*Call me ASAP. 911*"

"Great. Just great."

"Talk to me, Danny," Jason said. "What's going on?"

She hit the brakes, slowed down and pulled over into an empty gravel lot surrounding an abandoned cinderblock building. Judging from the rusted canopy projecting toward the road, the property had once been a gas station, though the pumps were long gone.

Danny stopped the car and unfastened her seat belt. "You drive for a while."

Jason unfastened his seat belt and they quickly traded places. Jason slipped behind the wheel, while Danny took the passenger seat, arranging her purse on the floor by her feet. Jason shifted into "drive," but kept his foot on the brake.

"You going to tell me what got you so upset about Andrea's text?"

She sighed. "It means the San Juan Sheriff's Department has received the 'wanted' notice on you. They were probably who brought it to Andrea's attention."

That made sense. But it didn't explain her emotional response.

"I'm a sworn law enforcement officer," she said. "Now that my bosses know what's going on, they expect me to do my duty. You're a fugitive; I have to arrest you."

Jason didn't know what to say.

"I don't have any choice, not if I want to keep my job," she said. "And stay out of jail."

"Why?"

"Because I'm an officer of the court. I swore an oath to enforce the law and all actions of the courts. It's my duty."

"But we both know this is a false accusation. You're my alibi."

"You don't get it." Danny was already shaking her head. "It doesn't matter. We can't have thousands of cops all over the country each deciding which warrants to enforce and which to ignore. It would be chaos."

Jason could see the logic to this. He didn't like it, but he could see the logic.

"The only way the system has a chance of working is if every officer enforces every warrant equally. The job of deciding which ones are legitimate has to fall to the courts."

"What happens when doing that could lead to someone being harmed, or killed?" Jason asked. "Like me?"

"I don't know. I'm still working on that."

He nodded, still holding the car in place with the brake.

"I need to talk to some people back home," Danny said, as much to herself as to him. "Maybe we can figure something out."

"And in the meantime?"

"Consider yourself under arrest."

♦

They entered the northern part of Genoa and all conversation between Jason and Danny died out. This was probably the most dangerous stretch of their journey today. It was an urban area, so traffic was denser and slower. Genoa had its own city police force, which would have received the bulletin and have all their patrols looking for Jason, the murder suspect. It was also the County Seat, which meant it housed the Sheriff's headquarters and jail, as well as the courts, and probably a State Police barracks, so there would normally be higher police traffic in the area.

Altogether, Genoa seemed a likely place to get caught.

They both concentrated on watching their surroundings. Jason didn't have a clue what they'd do if someone spotted him. Try to lose them, he guessed. If that was even possible. But they would need as much notice as they could get. So they watched.

"Jason…"

He saw it as soon as she tensed in the seat beside him.

A Genoa city police car sat on the cross street to their right, waiting for a break in traffic. Or maybe it was just a convenient place to watch the passing cars.

Traffic was heavy—it was Friday afternoon—and Jason's choices were limited. Anything too erratic would just attract the cop's attention. He toyed with turning off somewhere, but just as quickly ruled it out. He didn't think he could make it look like anything but a sudden, panicked decision.

"What are you doing?" Danny hissed.

"We're just a normal couple heading downtown for dinner and a show. Nothing to see here."

Danny nodded.

At least the rain was still falling, pushing windshield wipers to work harder and flooding the lowest margins of the street.

Traffic pushed them past the cop at thirty miles an hour.

"Shit." Two cars behind them, the police car pulled into the street and followed. "He's a couple of cars behind us."

Somehow, Danny resisted the urge to look behind her. "How far back?"

"A couple of cars."

"No lights?"

Jason shook his head. Not yet anyway.

Traffic stopped with a red light at the intersection with Harbor Way. The cop stopped with the rest of traffic, still two cars behind them.

"It could be a coincidence," Danny told him. "It probably is."

Jason's shoulders were beginning to ache with tension. He tried to force himself to relax but he wasn't kidding anyone, particularly his muscles.

"What exactly is the protocol for this sort of thing?"

"What thing?" Danny looked at him.

"Pulling over a murder suspect."

The light turned green and traffic edged forward. The Honda immediately behind them turned right on to Harbor Way, leaving a middle-aged Ford between them and the police car. It continued to follow, sedately, without emergency lights.

How long was this going to go on? If he just decided to follow them all the way through town, Jason thought his heart would give out.

"I'm definitely not cut out to be a fugitive," he said.

Danny glanced at him, laid a hand on his thigh. “You’re doing fine. Just a normal couple, remember?”

Two more blocks passed before another red light stopped them behind a lifted 4x4 Chevy pickup. The cop still sat behind them, on the far side of the battered Ford.

The driver of the Chevy gunned his engine; the mufflers roared like rockets.

“He should ticket this joker for excessive noise,” Danny muttered. “Those tires look wide too.”

Jason glanced at her.

Danny shrugged. “Positive vibes.”

“Okay.”

The light turned green ahead of them. The 4x4 pickup gunned his engine again and pulled out into the intersection. Jason followed at a more leisurely pace, as did the Ford and the squad car.

Was he waiting for backup? Or was it truly just coincidence?

A right turn lane appeared in the roadway, just in time for a sign directing traffic to turn right for the Barton Memorial Hospital.

The squad car signaled, then pulled into the turn lane and slowed down for the right turn.

“He’s going to the hospital,” Jason said, smiling like an idiot.

Danny released a great sigh and gave his thigh a squeeze.

He didn’t think he’d ever felt so wonderful in his life.

The Seattle Opera Association had rented the ballroom of the downtown Marriott for the evening. An assortment of delicacies covered a linen-draped table along one wall, from chilled prawns to lox, sashimi, and caviar spread over dainty crackers. A glossy mahogany bar on the opposite wall did a brisk business, white-jacketed bartenders smiling as they mixed drink after drink without pause. More men and women in white jackets roamed through the crowd with flutes of champagne and trays of appetizers.

The reception was honoring baritone Simon Heinlein, visiting from the New York Metropolitan Opera. It was a chance for the city's wealthy and powerful to be seen supporting the opera and a chance for the opera to hit them up for money. All the men wore black evening wear, the women, gowns. Serious jewelry glittered on fingers and deep in cleavages, competing with the skyline out the ballroom's vast windows.

Senator Morris Barton sipped his martini and scanned the crowd from his spot near the bar. This was not his favorite way to spend an evening; he was much more comfortable with a handful of friends at his club, but it came with the job. Despite what the voters back home might think or hope, most of the government's real business was conducted at events just like this. He'd already had conversations with a handful of local CEO's and two of his fellow Senators.

A distinctive laugh drew his attention to a small group of women across the room. He smiled as he watched his wife giggling with her friends, one hand unconsciously covering her mouth like it always did when she laughed. It was a girlish mannerism and every time he saw it, he was reminded of the young girl he'd persuaded to spend her life with him. That made him smile. Even if it wasn't part of his job, he would probably come anyway just because Lynn enjoyed these affairs so much.

He'd just returned to scanning the room when motion to his right caught his eye. He turned as Joseph Mullens stepped up beside him, two caviar-covered crackers and several prawns balanced on a plate in one hand.

"Joseph!" the Senator said. "It's been a long time. How are you doing?"

"I'm doing well, Senator. How are the rusted wheels of government treating you?"

"Frustrates the hell out of me, but I can't complain, can I?"

"No," Mullens chuckled. "I suppose not."

They paused for a moment to exchange greetings with a couple heading for the bar. Stanley Crawford was in his late seventies, spry and wiry for his age, but with the pasty gray complexion of a man with heart troubles. Word was that Stanley was worth about three hundred million dollars. The attractive woman on his arm—his third wife—was thirty-three and what the Senator's friends back home would call a first-place trophy wife.

"Surprised she hasn't already screwed him to death," Mullens muttered.

"Guess he's tougher than he looks."

Actually—and Sen. Barton knew this from personal experience—the sexy Mrs. Jessica Crawford didn't really like sex very much. Oh, she would spread her legs if persuaded, but she didn't enjoy it. She didn't like getting all sweaty, or her hair messed up, not to mention the other messier parts of the experience. She did it because it was expected of her.

For her, a sexless marriage for money was just fine.

"I'm glad we ran into each other tonight," the Senator switched the subject. "Because I think we've developed a common problem."

Mullens smiled. "What would that be?"

"Jason Reynolds. I believe he is much of the cause of your recent legal problems?"

"Ah, yes. The article in the paper this morning. He didn't paint a flattering picture of your family operation."

The Senator smiled and swallowed the rest of his martini. "Let me buy you a drink. I think I may have a way to make both of our problems go away."

Twenty

There is an art to passing through the world unnoticed and few people have mastered that art. Most people expend all their energy in the other direction. Starting in late childhood, but especially the preteens onward, everyone strives to be "noticed," to be "outstanding," to be "a head above their peers." Everything from the music they listen to, to the clothes they wear, to their hair styles, to their choice of car and choice of occupation is in the service of making themselves stand out in a crowd.

But sometimes circumstance dictates that you needed to avoid being noticed. Sometimes, you need to travel through the world with as few ripples as you can manage. For most people, it is almost an impossible task. Their skill set is in ways to get noticed, not in ways to be invisible.

It's why almost all fugitives get caught within a few weeks.

So how do you become invisible?

The secret is moderation. Moderation is ordinary, humdrum. Moderation is normal and entirely forgettable. The moderate man dresses ordinarily. In the business district, he wears a dark suit and conservative tie, nothing flashy. In a farm town, he wears jeans, work boots, and a flannel shirt.

He wears what everyone else is wearing.

He is polite, but not overly so. At a restaurant, he never returns the food, no matter how bad. Waitresses remember difficult customers. They also remember extravagant tips and the people who don't tip at all. He tips precisely 15% and as soon as the waitress clears and resets his table, she forgets about him.

People only have room for a limited amount of memorable people in their lives; he doesn't allow himself to be one of them.

The most effective assassin he had ever known looked nothing like the assassins in the movies. He wasn't James Bond. He wasn't Jason Bourne. He was a balding man with the beginnings of a potbelly, who stood barely five-foot-six in shoes and wore glasses. If he wore a suit, he looked like an accountant; if he wore work clothes he looked like a janitor. He was absolutely nondescript. That was his genius.

Even highly-trained operatives often looked at him once and immediately dismissed him as nonthreatening. That was their last mistake.

The invisible man pays cash whenever possible, but doesn't flash a wad. That too, is memorable. He doesn't flirt or make friends and he never makes enemies.

And when you have to share an aluminum tube with two hundred people for a four-and-a-half hour flight from Chicago to Vancouver, you are friendly, but keep to yourself.

When the nice woman in the seat beside you smiles and asks, "Why are you going to Vancouver? Business?"

"My mother passed away." You smile sadly and shake your head. "I'm going back for the funeral."

The lady gasps. "I'm so sorry."

You smile, accept her apology, and turn to face the window as the jet taxis toward the runway. Americans are uncomfortable with the subject of death. It's a cultural thing. The nice lady will secretly thank you if you never speak with her again.

And as soon as the plane lands in Vancouver, she will march off and continue her life with no further thought of the poor man she sat next to on the flight.

The passenger known as Trevor Sandford smiled as the plane gathered speed.

Twenty-one

The first thing Jason and Lisa did once they'd escaped Genoa was stop and switch into Danny's car. They left the rental locked and empty in the park-and-ride lot. With luck, it would take the locals a couple of days to figure out something was wrong and call it in.

Jason would undoubtedly be charged up the wazoo for that, but his budget was not his biggest concern right now.

The rest of the trip went smoothly and they arrived in Hoquiam, just north of Aberdeen, just as darkness was beginning to gather under the unrelenting rain. By that time, they had come up with a strategy for the rest of the day. It was largely practical, dealing primarily with their safety and security. They needed a place to hide from the police, get some sleep and something to eat, and they needed a safe way to communicate with the outside world.

They cruised carefully through Hoquiam and into Aberdeen proper, where they stopped at a busy Walmart. It brought back memories of last year when Jason, Danny, and Lisa had sought refuge in a grocery store parking lot much like this. It had even been raining just as hard. They had also been running from false charges then and in need of some rest.

"I'll be back in a minute," Danny told him as she pulled her hood up over her head. "Keep your head down."

He told her he would and tried to make himself as small as possible as she ran in to the store. Her mission was to find some food and drink so they wouldn't have to leave their motel room and, if possible, a pair of pre-paid—and untraceable—cell phones.

They'd had to do the same thing in Port Salish a year ago, and for the same reason. Cell phones could be tracked. Most of the smart phones now even had built-in GPS locators. All it would take was a subpoena to the service provider and Dunham County would know precisely where he was.

Fifteen minutes later, Danny appeared scurrying head down through the rain. She dumped two bags into the back seat and climbed in beside Jason.

"Any luck?"

She nodded, pushing her raincoat hood back off her head. "Yeah. I got some food, a six pack of iced tea, and two disposable cells."

"Anyone seem suspicious?"

She shook her head. "And no one was talking about it. It wasn't any kind of big thing around here. Not yet anyway."

"Good," he said and started the car.

They found a motel several blocks away. It was part of a mid-level national chain, nice, but not terribly expensive. It was also Friday night and the desk clerks were busy checking people in. They scarcely noticed as Danny rented the room under her name, double occupancy, with her credit card and her ID and license number. Jason didn't even go in with her.

"Piece of cakc," Danny told him when she returned to the car with the room keys and directions to the room. "Hope you don't mind the second floor. It's a bit more secure."

Jason trusted her on the subject. She was a cop; she'd been on the other side of manhunts and knew what the police disliked the most—like having to try and sneak a swat team up a set of exterior motel stairs without giving themselves away.

♦

They carried what they needed in from the car, unpacked, and locked themselves in the motel room. The idea was to stay holed up in the room and out of sight until they left tomorrow. Sometime between now and then, they would have to decide exactly what they were going to do and where they were going to go when they did leave. But for now, they were just hiding.

"What time is it?" Danny asked. She had the television remote in her hand.

Jason didn't know for sure. He usually used his cell to keep track of the time. "Check your cell. Why?"

"I want to catch the local news," she told him. "See just how bad our situation really is."

He returned to spreading the food across the room's little table. Danny had bought bottled iced tea, two ham and cheese sandwiches, and two small tubs of potato salad, She'd also purchased a package of Danish. Probably for tomorrow's breakfast.

Danny found a local station. The news would begin in about ten minutes. She dropped the remote on the foot of the bed and walked over to sit across the table from Jason.

He cracked a bottle of iced tea and handed it to her, then opened one for himself.

"What happens if we're on the news?" Jason asked.

"It makes things a lot more complicated," Danny told him. "Especially if they place me with you. The media will turn every civilian watching it into extra eyes for the police. Then, we risk being identified everywhere and every time we show our faces."

He unwrapped his sandwich. That would make things much more difficult, especially for Danny. She couldn't afford to be caught in the company of a fugitive.

"Maybe you should go home. Get away from me before you ruin your career."

Danny had just taken a bite of her sandwich; her mouth was full, but she shook her head adamantly.

Jason took a bite of his own sandwich, waited for her to shoot down his idea.

"I'm not going to cut and run on you," she finally said. "You're a fugitive. There's almost nothing you can do to protect yourself from the Bartons on your own. Hell, if I left, you wouldn't even have a car."

He shrugged. "The car thing would certainly cramp my style."

"It's not going to happen."

"One man is dead because of me," he told her. "I don't want to add your career to my conscience."

She caught his eyes, held his gaze. "It's not going to happen. We're wasting time talking about it."

Jason had to accept that.

The fanfare and lead-in for the local news program started. It billed itself as "Channel 7, Your Newschoice for Aberdeen and the Gray's Harbor Community." The music stopped and a young woman with brown, shoulder-length hair and perfect teeth smiled into the camera.

Jason and Danny watched with the intensity of people whose lives depended on what they were about to see.

"In today's top story," the anchorwoman said, "Dunham County authorities are requesting your help in locating a suspect wanted in connection with a murder in the small town of Donald."

Jason and Danny exchanged a glance.

"According to Dunham County Sheriff Michael Barton, a man was shot to death early this afternoon while sitting in his car beside Hwy 101 in Donald. Witnesses identified Jason Reynolds, a reporter for the *Seattle News*, as seen arguing with the victim just before the shooting and is the only suspect."

A photograph of Jason appeared on the screen over the woman's left shoulder. Jason recognized the DMV photo from his driver's license. It was a couple of years old now, but close enough. Anyone seeing the news tonight would easily recognize him on the street.

It was a strange surreal feeling, surprisingly like the experience of winning the Pulitzer last year. He had gone through the whole thing, ceremony and all, like it wasn't real. It was a dream he would awaken from at any moment.

Now the dream had turned dark.

"Sheriff Barton warns the public that Jason Reynolds is to be considered armed and dangerous and should not be approached. Anyone with information about this man or his whereabouts is urged to contact your local police or the Dunham County Sheriff's Department."

A phone number appeared on the screen.

"Well, there's no mention of you," Jason said as the newscast moved on to the activities of the city council. "That's something."

"Yes, it is. Quite a bit, actually."

He raised his eyebrows and took another bite of his sandwich.

"It means I can still walk around without having to be constantly looking over my shoulder. Something you're not going to be able to do for a while. There may be hope yet."

"What about the whole 'Officer of the Court' thing?"

"I'm still working on that."

♦♦♦♦♦

Lisa Martin had left Seattle just a bit before five o'clock, so she missed the local news broadcasts, but she wasn't much of a television viewer anyway. Being a graduate student and student teacher didn't leave much time for sitting in front of the television and cable was expensive. She got most of what news she needed from newspapers and web sites she could access with her cell phone or computer.

She was still about an hour east of Bosque when her phone signaled a text had arrived. With a practiced efficiency that used to drive Jason insane, she opened the message from Suzie, her best friend, while steering with the other hand.

Have you seen the news?

Nope, she replied.

She continued for a few moments, waiting for the reply she knew was coming. "Just spit it out, Suze."

Jason is wanted for murder.

Lisa dropped her phone and almost ran off the road as she tried to catch it. She slammed on the brakes, just barely avoided the ditch on the right and straightened out in her own lane.

Her heart was pounding like she'd run a mile.

The people in the car following her quickly doubled the distance between their cars. They probably thought she was drunk.

She took a deep breath to try and chase away the disorientation. Jason accused of murder? It was impossible. She couldn't wrap her head around the idea. Jason didn't own a gun. He didn't like guns. Even during the mess last year in Port Salish she didn't think he ever fired a shot. Even when the bad guys were shooting at them, he still hadn't fired a shot. Danny had, but not Jason. She just couldn't picture him killing anybody, certainly not in cold blood, certainly not murder.

Lisa tried to find her phone by reaching down between her thighs, but couldn't feel it anywhere. It must have slid under the seat. She would have to pull off the road, get out, and do a thorough search.

Unfortunately Route 12 in this stretch was narrow and winding through a thick forest without a single turnout or even sizeable shoulders. It was like driving through a tunnel. She had no choice but to drive on, alone with her thoughts. With nothing but fear to drive her imagination.

♦♦♦♦♦

"I think the best thing we can do," Danny said when they'd finished eating, "is go back to San Juan County. If I take you into custody there, at least you'll be safe."

Jason wasn't thrilled with the idea. He might be *safer* in the San Juan County jail than in the Dunham County one, but he would still be in jail. Not only was jail the complete absence of fun, but he would be powerless to do anything to stop the Bartons while he was locked up. He would be a prisoner. Prisoners couldn't do anything without the jail's permission. And he wasn't absolutely sure the Bartons wouldn't be able to reach him, even in the San Juan jail.

"Legally, won't San Juan County have to send me back to Dunham?"

"I'm not sure how that works," Danny said. "That's the sticky part. I need to convince the Sheriff and the District

Attorney to go along with us on this. I'm hoping we can at least lose the paperwork for a while."

"But how will I be able to do anything if I'm in jail?"

"If Dunham County catches you first, you may not even make it to jail."

Peterson's death today had made that perfectly clear. The people they were working against had no compunction about killing people. None at all.

"What about Helen?" he asked.

"This is about keeping you alive, Jason," she insisted. "We need to worry about your safety right now, not Helen's."

"I can't agree to this." Jason was already shaking his head. "It's as good as telling the Bartons they've won, I surrender. It's exactly what they want me to do. It's why they're framing me."

"I know. I know."

For a moment, they sat alone with their thoughts.

Jason was thinking about Helen Miller, alone and scared wherever the Bartons might be holding her. He didn't think she was dead, not yet. But if he were arrested and jailed in San Juan County—even if he were protected from the Bartons—it would mean Helen was on her own, totally alone.

Her parents were possibly in even a worse position. Their daughter was in danger and their best hope for help would be locked up hundreds of miles away.

He couldn't leave them like that.

Danny reached over and took his right hand.

"Has it ever occurred to you that you can't win every battle?" she asked him.

"Yeah, it has," he told her. "And it scares the hell out of me."

"Why?"

He took a moment to frame his answer. "Because it means either evil became too strong for good to defeat it; or I got scared for my own skin and walked away rather than fight the evil." He looked up at her. "Know what I mean? I don't want to live with the knowledge that I could have done something and didn't."

"Even if it means you could lose your own life?"

Jason shrugged.

Danny squeezed his hand.

"Remember how obsessed you were with Deception Island?"

He remembered. Both Lisa and Danny had been dead set against it from the beginning as too dangerous. "It was where the answer was."

"I know."

For a few moments, neither spoke.

Jason gave her hand a squeeze. She returned the squeeze. "You sure you don't want to just go home, where it's peaceful and quiet and most police are the good guys?"

Danny looked away, blinking rapidly.

"Let's go through the file Peterson gave me. Maybe he gave us enough rope to hang the Bartons."

"I still need to call Andrea back. I need to tell her something."

"Tell her as much of the truth as you can. The charges are an attempt to shut me up. I'm in danger from the Dunham County Sheriff and his deputies and that you don't know where I am. I can contact you by phone, not the other way around." He smiled. "You might even tell her you're trying to talk me into turning myself in."

♦♦♦♦♦

Andrea Meade, District Attorney for San Juan County, set her glasses on her desk and stretched her back. It was after 6:00 and she'd been working since 7:00 this morning. Most of her prosecutors and clerical staff had already gone home to start the weekend. She took her duties seriously and expected the same from the people who worked for her, but she also insisted they take their scheduled time off. In this job, you needed to decompress, recharge the batteries. You needed to take your weekends.

If possible.

She would be home with her girls now herself, were she not waiting for Hayden to call.

Andrea slipped her glasses back on and found the notice of the Dunham County "want" for Jason Reynolds. The notice contained little information. Just Reynold's name and vitals, the legal justification for the "want," and the originating agency.

It wasn't unusual. The Sheriff got notices like that every day. The difference here, was that not only did she know Jason Reynolds personally, but he was the key witness in the biggest case of her career. Without him and his testimony, she didn't think she could convict Mullens or any of the other key people from Lundgren Corporation. And having Jason sitting in jail on a murder charge would put a serious dent in his credibility, to say the least.

A suspicion flared in her mind. From what she had learned as she'd built her case, it would not be out of the question for Mullens to arrange the charges for the sole purpose of ruining her witness's credibility.

The problem would be proving it.

Her cell phone rang. In the silent, mostly empty office, the trill sounded like an air raid siren.

Andrea picked up the phone and checked the display. It showed a telephone number only, no name. She didn't recognize the number.

She frowned. The thing was, she didn't give just anyone her private cell phone number.

She was expecting a call, but not from this number.

It rang again. Two more and it would go to her voice mail.

She usually didn't answer calls from numbers she didn't recognize. She was too busy to deal with misdials and telemarketers.

But something was different this time.

She accepted the call just as the third ring began. "Hello?"

"Andrea?" a woman's voice said, "This Danny, Danny Hayden."

"Danny? Where are you? You said you'd call me back hours ago."

"It's complicated. I'm playing it safe and using a disposable phone."

That explained the unfamiliar number. "So tell me what's going on with these murder charges."

"They're fabricated," she said. "He was with me when that poor man was killed. We both heard the shots."

"Okay. So you both go in, give the detectives sworn statements. They realize their mistake and release him. Problem solved." Hayden knew all this. She was a detective with the sheriff's department; Andrea shouldn't have to tell her how the system worked.

"It isn't that simple."

"Why not?"

"Because the Sheriff's Department here are the ones framing Jason."

Andrea rubbed the bony flat between her eyes. She felt a headache coming.

"Why would they do that?"

"Because he's investigating the Sheriff's Department. It's dirty, corrupt. We think it was a sheriff's deputy who killed this man for the sole purpose of framing Jason. What better way to shut him up?"

Andrea was skeptical. "The entire Sheriff's Department?"

"Everyone in a leadership position anyway," Danny said. "I'm serious, Andrea. It's bad down here. It's like a third world dictatorship, or something. A police state. As bad as Lundgren was, they had nothing on what's going on over here."

Andrea picked up the "want" notification again from her desk top and looked at the originating agency. It was the Dunham County Sheriff's Department, signed by Sheriff Michael Barton. She knew next to nothing about them. The two counties hadn't had a lot of contact.

"Andrea? You still there?"

"I'm still here." She was trying to process this.

"Jason is afraid that if Dunham County gets a hold of him, he's going to have an unfortunate accident, either during the arrest or once he's in the jail."

"What do you think?"

"He's right. Dunham County will kill him if they can."

Andrea was still having trouble believing an entire sheriff's department could be that dirty. In her state. In the 21st century.

"Is Jason with you now?"

"No." Danny didn't hesitate. "I don't know where he is. We thought it best to separate for now. He has my cell number and said he'll check in."

"He needs to turn himself in."

"I know, but he's not going to walk in to his own murder. I can't blame him."

"We both know that the longer he's on the run, the higher the chance some trigger-happy patrolman is going to shoot him. The best way to stay alive is to voluntarily surrender."

"I know. That's why I wanted to talk to you. I might be able to get him to turn himself in to San Juan—us—if you can promise him protective custody."

"Protective custody?"

"I know it's a longshot, but there must be a way to keep him out of Dunham County's hands. Is there some precedent where a suspect who's in real danger in one jurisdiction, can be held in a second one for his own safety?"

Andrea frowned. "Protective custody from another law enforcement agency? I'm not familiar with anything like that."

"But it's not impossible."

"No, but I'd have to look into it—"

"Please, do it; look into it then. Otherwise, Jason is as good as dead. Okay?"

Andrea was impressed by the urgency in Danny's voice. That urgency was the biggest factor in her decision.

"Okay," Andrea sighed. "I'll look into it. But I'm not promising anything. The best course for Jason is still to turn himself in and prove his innocence in court."

"Normally, I'd agree with you. But not this time."

"Okay. I get it. I'll see what I can find out."

"Thank you. How about I call you again tomorrow?"

Andrea sighed. So much for her weekend. "Okay. Call me tomorrow."

"Thank you," Danny said and disconnected.

Andrea Meade set her phone down and looked at the "want" document again. "Well, crap."

♦♦♦♦♦

Lisa couldn't find a place to pull off the road until she reached the tiny crossroads community of Cedar Mill nearly thirty minutes after she'd dropped her phone. It had been a long thirty minutes. She could hear the tones as texts kept coming in, but could do nothing about them. She felt horribly impotent. Finally, she pulled into the parking lot of the Cedar Mill Market, which also served as the Post Office and City Hall and who knew what else, parked her car and climbed out into the drizzle.

Her cell phone was pretty much right where she thought it would be, nestled under the driver's seat along with a crushed paper coffee cup and a forgotten Hershey's chocolate bar. She retrieved the phone and climbed back behind the wheel.

As expected, she had missed texts and calls. They were all from Suzie, who was probably freaked because Lisa had gone dark.

She immediately called Suzie.

Suzie answered before the first ring finished. "What the hell happened? You just stopped answering."

"I'm sorry. I dropped my phone and it slid under the seat."

"Thank God you're okay."

"Tell me more about this news story. Jason is wanted for *murder*?"

"That's what they said. They said he shot someone in some town called Donald."

There it was again, Jason and murder in the same sentence. "I don't believe it."

"I know," Suzie said. "It's beyond bizarre. Have you heard from him?"

"Not since I told him I was coming over a few hours ago."

She'd assumed she hadn't heard from him because he was busy investigating Helen's disappearance. Besides, they weren't going out anymore. Neither of them checked in with the other like they used to and weren't expected to. But now the silence took on a more ominous tone.

Suzie paused for just a second. "What are you going to do?"

"I'm going to try and get a hold of him right now," Lisa told her. "I'll let you know if I learn anything."

"Okay. Be careful."

Lisa disconnected and immediately called Jason's cell phone. It went to voicemail without ringing. At the beep, she left a message: "Jason, it's Lisa. Please call me. Or call the Millers. I'll be there in about an hour."

She wanted to say more, but didn't. There was no telling who might be listening in to his voicemail. Instead, she texted him once, pretty much the same message, and then sent Suzie a text explaining how she hadn't been able to reach him. Her communication finished, she slipped her phone into the caddy between the seats.

Lisa backed out of her parking spot, and pulled back on to the highway.

♦♦♦♦♦

Molly Barton walked in and sat beside her husband on their living room sofa. "They're finally asleep."

Patrick glanced at his watch. "Only thirty minutes. That must be some kind of record."

"Swimming lessons tire them out."

Patrick smiled and reached over to squeeze her thigh just above her knee. "They also have a very persuasive mom."

She smiled, pulled her hair back and lifted it off her shoulders. "Is that your new case?"

"Yeah." He sighed, glancing down at the thin file folder spread across his lap. He often reviewed his cases at home. It was an old compromise, a way to spend time with his family and still get necessary work done. "It's the new one."

"Is it true?" She asked. "That reporter killed someone?"

"That's what Michael says."

"And we both know your brother always tells the truth."

Patrick sighed. This was an old and unresolved battle.

"So how much evidence do they have?"

"Some." he said. "They have the murder weapon. A few circumstantial witnesses."

"Fingerprints?"

He smiled at her. "You know, you would have made one hell of a defense attorney."

"I decided to marry the love of my life and have kids instead. It's not as stressful and you didn't answer my question."

"See what I mean?" he said, smiling. "And no, there are no fingerprints on the weapon. Everything else is circumstantial: a witness who saw them arguing, the victim's briefcase at the suspect's supposed rental, along with the gun. And that's about it."

Molly frowned. "He rented a place in Donald?"

"No. In Bosque."

"Okay, but why would he rent a place? He was just here to research some newspaper articles. Wouldn't it make more sense to just get a motel room?"

"I know." Patrick could only shrug. "Interesting, isn't it?"

"And why would he leave all that evidence in his place? Wouldn't a killer get rid of the gun? Or at least keep it with him?"

Patrick just shook his head.

"You can file murder charges with this?"

"It's Dunham County. I can file murder charges with a roll of toilet paper."

"Ew. In other words, you're rubber stamping whatever shenanigans your brother and dad are up to," she said. "Again."

"I don't want to argue about this tonight."

"I don't want to argue either," She told him, laying slim fingers on his arm to emphasize her point. "It's just hard to sit here and watch your family use you like this. You're the smartest, kindest, person I've ever known and you're one hell of an attorney. You deserve to be treated better."

Patrick hesitated. "It's complicated. You know that."

"Families always are. Have you met mine?"

"Oh, yes." He smiled. "They're lovely people."

"Nobody likes a funny prosecutor. Do you have any idea how hard it is to watch you waste your talents like this?"

Oh, he knew. Or he could imagine.

"Imagine if you were District Attorney and your family wasn't an issue. Think of the things you could accomplish. Think of the difference you'd make."

"I know."

"Enough." She kissed him on the cheek, gave him a one-armed hug around the shoulders. "I do love you, you know."

"I love you too," he told her. "You keep me grounded."

"Speaking of dirt. I think I'm going to draw myself a bath. Maybe you could join me in a little bit?"

He smiled and returned her kiss. "If you're lucky."

"We'll see who's lucky." She stood and sauntered from the room.

A few seconds later, he heard her climbing up the stairs. The water started in the master bath.

Patrick stretched his neck and looked down at the file on his lap again.

After a couple of minutes, he closed the folder and tossed it aside.

Twenty-two

While Danny stepped into the bathroom with her cell phones, both disposable and regular, to return the call from Andrea Meade in privacy, Jason set about reading through the file Gerry Peterson had given him. Giving the file to Jason had been the last voluntary action of Peterson's life.

That made opening the battered file folder feel ceremonial, solemn.

Jason set up on the motel's dinner table, with a legal pad from his briefcase next to it, ready for any notes he might need to take. He also had his second bottle of iced tea. The television was playing a rerun of an old *Law and Order* episode, but the volume was set low enough that it was background noise, not a distraction.

And he began to read.

The first thing he noticed was that it read more like a personal journal than a news article or even a reporter's notebook. Peterson seemed to write down each rumor or incident as he heard it, with the date and often the time noted. The entries were then arranged chronologically in the folder. It painted a picture of a man growing increasingly aware of something rotten going on around him.

The first entry was the one he'd seen at *Crazy Larry's*. It was more of an anecdote than an actual news story. From the sound of it, Peterson—new in town—had noticed the meth problem in the area and wondered aloud why local law enforcement wasn't doing more to combat it. In answer, someone told him "Why would they arrest their customers?"

When he asked his assistant at the paper about it, she told him that was just a rumor. But they didn't arrest many druggies, did they?

At the time, the Sheriff had been Morris Barton, the current State Senator. Michael Barton had been a captain.

♦♦♦♦♦

Danny closed the disposable cell phone and, feeling more guilty than she probably needed to, stepped out of the bathroom.

Jason looked up from his spot at the little table, a pen poised in his hand. "Everything okay?"

She nodded and crawled onto the bed, settling against the headboard and crossing her legs, Indian-style. "Andrea's going to look into some legal issues. I'll call her back tomorrow."

"I still don't want to go to jail. Not even in Friday Harbor."

"I know," Danny told him. "She's exploring our options."

Jason returned to his file.

Danny turned up the volume on the television. She had little else to do, other than worry. While Jason was busy reading the file he'd gotten from Peterson, she was just sitting there, trying to ignore the net methodically closing around them.

She had been on the other side of a manhunt. They never ended well for the fugitive because the police had everything going for them and the fugitive almost nothing. The police had thousands of trained observers spread out across the state, actively looking for them. They had technology. They could track a fugitive's cell phone, banking and credit card activity. If the vehicle was equipped with GPS, they could track that. And now that the media was involved, they potentially had hundreds of thousands of ordinary citizens who could recognize the fugitive at any moment.

Unless you had access to an underground network and a serious supply of cash, it was only a matter of time before the police found you. She and Jason didn't have any such network and they didn't have much cash.

Her cell phone signaled a new text, her private cell, not the disposable one.

Jason looked up.

Danny checked the display. "It's Lisa."

"You'd better answer her. She's probably half-crazy with worry."

"I know."

She opened the text. *Where are you? Are you okay? Please answer. Jason isn't.*

I'm okay. Jason is fine. Where are you?

With the Millers. What can I do?

Danny read each message to Jason. He nodded approval. "I think she should stay there. Keep the Millers from flipping out and make sure the Sheriff doesn't come after them."

"Just like we talked about before."

"Exactly."

Danny typed in the message, then added, *Tell the Millers we're still working.*

Please be careful. Let me know what's going on.

We will.

She set her phone aside, then, on second thought, powered it down and removed the battery just as Jason had done. At this point, the Dunham County people didn't know of her involvement, but that could change at any moment. She didn't want the first notice of that change to be a SWAT team bursting through the door.

♦♦♦♦♦

It was nearly 10:00 by the time Jason finished reading Peterson's file on the Bartons. It had been fascinating. Fascinating, like photographs of car accidents and crime scenes can be fascinating. It was a blow-by-blow chronicle of the Barton's reign of terror. And Jason didn't use the term "reign of terror" lightly. He doubted there were stretches of more than two or three months at a time when Peterson had heard of no crime to note.

He closed the file folder and groaned as he stretched his back.

Danny was reclined on the bed, two pillows behind her as she watched a movie on television. Now, though, she looked over at him. “Did you find the solution to all our problems?”

“Well,” he said. “I don’t know if I’d go that far.”

“But you found something?”

“Oh, yeah. I found lots of somethings. Gerry Peterson was thorough, if nothing else.” Jason picked up the legal pad with his notes and walked over to sit on the bed beside her. “Where do you want me to start?”

“What’s got you most interested?”

“That’s easy: the Kwamamish Indians.”

Danny frowned at him. “An Indian tribe?”

“They’re the ones who have their reservation on the coast north of Dunham County. Donald, the little town where Peterson was killed, is just a few miles from the reservation border.”

“Okay.”

He smiled. “It seems the Kwamamish Nation and the Bartons aren’t the friendliest of neighbors.”

“What? You mean the Bartons aren’t good neighbors?”

“Shocking, isn’t it?” He flipped through to the second page of the legal pad. “In this case, the first signs of trouble were when some logging equipment belonging to Barton Forestry was vandalized in the spring of 2011. Peterson included a copy of the article the paper wrote. It was believed to be the work of radical environmentalists.”

“But it wasn’t.”

“Nope. The following week, more equipment was vandalized—rice in radiators, sugar in gas tanks, tires shredded—but this time messages were left in spray paint: ‘Get off our land!’”

“I think I remember hearing something about this on the news. It got pretty ugly as I recall.”

“Yeah, it did. The Kwamamish claimed Barton Forestry was illegally logging on Reservation land. The Bartons said they owned the timber land and the Indians were illegally sabotaging their equipment and operations. There was more vandalism and sabotage, human chains blocking access roads, protests at Barton Forestry headquarters and the county courthouse. Barton enlisted the sheriff's department to break up the demonstrations and they turned into riots. Shots were even exchanged, though no one was hurt."

Danny nodded. "I remember."

"Anyway, the leaders of the Kwamamish protesters were two brothers Joe and Eddie Winston, and Joe's wife, Angela. About 4:00 in the morning of September 9th, a group of as many as eight men, dressed like SWAT, broke into the home where the Winstons were sleeping and abducted them. Before anyone—including their neighbors—could even figure out what was going on, the activists were loaded into a waiting van and whisked away.

"Let me guess," Danny said. "The Bartons."

"The Sheriff issued a press release stating that Joseph and Angela Winston had been arrested on outstanding warrants and were lodged in the Dunham County Jail. Eddie, Joe's younger brother, had somehow escaped and was still at large."

"That must have made the Indians happy."

"Oh, yeah. And it gets better. Within two days, both Joe and Angela Winston were dead. Angela hung herself in her cell, and the next day, Joe, her husband, was killed as he attacked some corrections deputies.

"According to the rumors Peterson heard around town—and especially from friends on the Kwamamish Reservation—the Sheriff's deputies had done much more than go out of their jurisdiction to arrest the Winstons. According to these rumors, they had gang-raped Angela while forcing her husband to watch, then killed him."

Danny murmured something under her breath. The muscles of her jaw were clenched tight. She pulled her hips back under her so she was sitting upright.

"At this point, the Kwamamish were preparing for an all-out war. That's when the Governor intervened. He sent in State Police to separate the two sides and asked the FBI and the Bureau of Indian Affairs to investigate the various claims on both sides." He looked up at Danny to make sure he had her attention.

"The Federal investigation determined that the Kwamamish were right. The Bartons had been illegally logging on Kwamamish land. A Federal judge ordered them to remove all equipment and personnel from the area immediately, plus they had to pay the Tribe the cash equivalent value of all timber removed from the area, as well as punitive damages."

"Good for them," Danny said.

"But here's what I found truly interesting," he told her. "It seems the Bartons have a hunting lodge that was also illegally on Kwamamish land. It had been there for at least three generations and the Bartons were able to negotiate a lease deal so they could keep the lodge."

Danny shrugged. "The Court shouldn't have let the bastards keep that. They should have taken everything and given it back to the Indians. And then made the Bartons give the Kwamamish some of the Bartons' land for good measure."

Jason nodded. "You'll never guess what they named their hunting lodge."

"You're right. I'll never guess it. You'd better just tell me."

"They call it 'Hemlock Run.'"

Danny frowned at him. "'Hemlock Run?' Where have I heard that before?"

"It was texted to my cell phone. Remember?"

By the quick change in her expression, she did.

"I think we'll find the key to this whole thing at the Bartons' hunting lodge. We need to get up to Hemlock Run."

♦♦♦♦♦

One of the perks of being wealthy was that you got nicer toys than everyone else. Some men bought luxury sports cars, others yachts, still others magnificent mansions. The wealth allows you to indulge whatever interest you have. It also allows you to firmly establish your status as head and shoulders above all the average working stiffs around you.

Currently, Senator Morris Barton's favorite toy was a six million dollar helicopter, an AgustaWestland AW-109, capable of carrying six passengers at a speed of two hundred fifty miles an hour. He kept it based at Olympia Regional Airport while the Legislature was in session. With the AW-109, the three-plus hour drive back to Dunham County and his home outside Bosque only took forty-five minutes.

And face it. People looked at you differently after you've stepped out of your own helicopter. They looked at you with awe.

The Senator climbed into the seat beside his pilot, buckled his safety harness, and slipped the headset over his ears. The rotor was idling. In a few minutes though, the turbine was going to crank up and the noise was going to get bad, too bad to talk over and bad enough to damage a person's hearing.

He turned to look at the four men in the seats behind him. "Buckle up, gentlemen, and put on your headsets. It's going to get loud."

The men did as he suggested. They were relying on his experience, since most of them had never been on a helicopter before. Morris smiled to himself. If the press could only see this: the Democratic and Republican leadership from both Houses of Congress, together for a weekend getaway in the hopes of working through the partisanship and toward a more effective government.

This was how it was supposed to work.

That was the public story anyway.

"Everyone ready?" the pilot asked.

Morris nodded to him. "Take her up."

The whine of the turbine intensified and the rotor picked up speed, the familiar *chop, chop* coming faster and faster.

Morris turned back to the windscreen. "Let the games begin."

♦♦♦♦♦

Danny peered at him. "Do you hear yourself?"

Jason hesitated. He had the overwhelming feeling this was a trick question.

"You're using the exact same tone of voice you used last year. In fact, you could just trade 'Deception Island' for 'Hemlock Run.'"

Jason shrugged. "It's kind of a similar situation. Isn't it?"

"Oh, yeah, it's similar. It's a similar chance of you getting your ass shot off."

"I'm wanted for murder, Danny. There's a good chance my ass will get shot off period."

"I know." She grabbed a pillow from beside her and clutched it to her chest. "You're probably tagged 'armed and dangerous' too. A lot of cops—maybe most—will shoot first, ask questions later."

Jason couldn't dispute that. In Dunham County especially, they probably had a story of a desperate gunfight ready to go, like a document template. Suspect killed resisting arrest. There would be no attempt to arrest him. They couldn't afford a public trial.

"So. You going to walk right up to the door? Peek in a window to see what they're doing?"

"It would be nice if it were that easy. We'll have to figure out how to approach it when we see what the situation is."

"We don't even know for sure where it is, or how to get there."

"True. But I guarantee folks on the reservation do," he told her. "And I'd bet anything they know exactly what the Bartons are doing up there."

"What you're betting is your life. And maybe mine."

"And Helen's. Don't forget Helen in all this. She's already at risk. She may already be there."

Danny nodded, but was anything but enthused.

Jason carefully took the pillow from her grasp and tossed it aside. She didn't resist, looked puzzled. He scooted up beside her against the headboard, slipped an arm around her. She responded by shifting her body against his until they meshed. It felt good. They had not spent enough time just holding each other the last few days.

For a few minutes that's exactly what they did.

♦

Holding each other was enough for a while, maybe half an hour, then just holding each other was no longer enough. It was nothing planned, certainly not by either of them. The evening hadn't even been romantic. Cold sandwiches and bottled iced tea in a modest motel room? Please. Sometimes, that was simply how things worked. Sometimes, Nature was bigger than you and swept you away. Again.

"You know," Jason murmured when they lay spent in each other's arms, the sweat slowly cooling their skin. "Studies say that when people face threats to their lives, instinct creates powerful urges to continue the species."

"Do they?" She sounded half-asleep, her head lying on his chest, directly above his heart. Jason could smell the shampoo in her hair, the earthiness of her sweat.

"That's what they say."

"So what we just did was instinct?"

"Something like that."

"So it has nothing to do with me? Any nearby woman would do?"

Jason hesitated long enough for her to raise her head and look at him.

"If that were true," he smiled. "I certainly wouldn't be stupid enough to admit it."

She laughed, laid down against him again.

"Seriously though," she said. "We need to talk about this thing."

"This *thing*?"

"Going out to the Barton's hunting lodge. Do you think it's a good idea to drive all the way through Dunham County again?"

That wasn't the *thing* he'd thought she'd wanted to talk about.

"We could go around it, I suppose," he said, "but that would mean spending an extra hour or two exposed on the roads."

Danny nodded. She was tracing a little circle with her finger just below his navel. It wasn't helping his concentration.

"And wouldn't they be concentrating their search farther away by tomorrow? Isn't it normal to move the dragnet farther out with the passage of time?"

"No one says 'dragnet' anymore."

"Whatever. Wouldn't the last place they'd be looking be right in the middle of their own county, their home turf?"

"It depends," she told him. "It depends whether they believe we've actually fled the area, or just holed up somewhere. Besides, the only place they *can* search is within the county. They have no jurisdiction anywhere else."

"And they don't know what vehicle we'll be driving."

"Provided they haven't figured out who I am yet."

"How would they do that?"

She shrugged. "We're known associates and we were seen together."

"Let's hope they haven't made that connection yet."

"There's one more thing."

"What's that?"

She propped herself up on an elbow. "What makes you think the Indians will even talk to you? They don't have much reason to trust any white person, certainly not a stranger."

Jason had to acknowledge the truth of this. It was a handicap and a large one. It could be insurmountable, but they would never know unless they tried. And he hoped he was holding a wild card.

"I'm counting on one of the oldest truths of human nature."

"Do unto others…?"

"Nope." He shook his head. "The enemy of my enemy is my friend."

♦

Jason opened his laptop, turned it on and waited for it to boot up. Danny was in the shower, cleaning up. In between the lovemaking, they had hammered out a compromise on the trip up to Indian country. They had agreed that if they had not found out what was going on at the Bartons' hunting lodge by Sunday afternoon—and neither of them had been arrested or killed—they would continue around the Olympic Mountains and east to Port Townsend. There, they would pick up Jason's car and head back to Port Salish. In Port Salish, Danny could return to work and they would decide whether Jason would turn himself in, or not.

Jason still had no intention of turning himself in, but Danny had not given up, either. It remained to be seen who would last longer.

In the meantime, Jason had some things he wanted to do. He wasn't sure how safe it was to use his laptop. He knew law enforcement had the ability to trace any computer through the internet, but his instinct said that was a sophisticated operation, beyond the abilities of a rural police department.

He was betting his life on it.

When the computer had finished booting, he used the motel's Wi-Fi to access the internet and then logged into the *Seattle News'* network.

If someone was watching such things, they would know he had logged on. To be safe, he needed to do his business as quick as he could.

Jason clicked on the icon to access his email.

Seconds later, he was there. Dozens of unread emails had piled up over the past few days. Most of them were mundane. Just normal correspondence from his day-to-day life. The last few, though, were different. He had emergency requests from Debbie, Miles, and Lisa, wanting to know what was going on. There were actually two from Debbie and three from Lisa.

He jotted a quick note to Debbie. "I'm going to be sending you a new story tonight (Friday). Kind of "interview with the fugitive" thing. Work your magic, then run it by Miles. P.S. I'm innocent."

He immediately logged out of the network.

Danny stepped up behind him, smelling of soap and skin lotion. Jason hadn't even heard the shower shut off.

"What are you doing?" She leaned her hip against him. She was wearing only pink panties and a tank top.

"What I do best," he told her. "Writing a story."

She looked skeptical.

"What? You doubt my powers?"

"Not at all. Of course not. But do you think they'll actually print it? You're wanted for murder."

"Of course they'll print it." Jason smiled. "It's a great story." He held up his hands as if framing a headline. "'Fugitive

Reporter Speaks.' My editor will be drooling as soon as he hears about it."

"He sounds like a prince."

"You have to know him. Miles is a newspaper man of the old school. He comes across as a hard-ass, but he's actually a teddy bear inside. As long as you don't get between him and the paper."

Danny went stiff against him, sucked in her breath.

"What?"

He followed her gaze to the drapes covering the motel's window. Blue and red lights flashed on the other side of the drapes. His heart skipped a beat. The muscles across his shoulders tightened.

Maybe he'd been wrong about their ability to trace his computer.

"Crap . . ."

Both moved wordlessly. Danny retreated back toward the bed, found a pair of jeans and began getting dressed. Jason went to the window, edging over to peek past the blinds. He fully expected to find a SWAT team gathered outside their motel door.

The walkway outside their room was empty. No policemen were out there at all, SWAT or otherwise.

The flashing police beacons were down in the parking lot where two squad cars had boxed in a battered-looking Japanese sedan. One officer was in the process of searching the car while the other watched the car's occupants. Two bearded men and a woman leaned against one of the squad cars and studied the ground. No one seemed phased by the steady drizzle.

Jason felt the relief go over him like a warm, tropical wave. "They aren't after us."

Danny stepped up to his side. "What's going on?"

"Looks like a drug bust."

She took a peek at the activity. "A good one too. Meth probably. Aberdeen has a serious meth problem."

The officer searching the vehicle had placed a couple of small plastic bags on the roof of the Toyota.

Jason didn't care what was in the bags. He was just glad the police were occupied with someone else. He let the drapes fall to their natural hang and returned to his computer. As Danny stretched out on the bed, he opened his word processor and began to write.

Twenty-three

The Kwamamish Indian Reservation, home of the federally recognized Kwamamish Nation, occupied three hundred-fifty square smiles along the Pacific coast of Washington State, directly north of Dunham County. It was poor and sparsely populated. Its largest community, Dualip—home of the tribal government—held only 750 people, all but a handful Kwamamish. The reservation was bordered on the east by Olympic National Park and home to much of the only remaining undisturbed temperate rainforest in the lower forty-eight states.

Logging and lumber products, fishing, and a Casino near Donald were the largest employers. The average annual income was about twenty-five thousand dollars.

The Kwamamish Nation was governed by a council elected by the adult Kwamamish members. The Council selected a President and other Officers.

Like many Native Reservations across the country, the Kwamamish Nation occupied a unique position in the law enforcement world. In theory, it was a separate, sovereign state, with its own constitution, police force, and judiciary, separate from the Federal government, the State of Washington and the counties surrounding it. In practice, they didn't have the infrastructure to imprison anyone for periods of more than a year. For serious, violent crimes on reservation land, they relied on investigators from the FBI and prosecutors from the U.S. Attorney's Office.

The arrangement was not always welcomed in either the reservation or the communities surrounding it.

♦♦♦♦♦

Jason and Danny were awake, cleaned up, and out of the motel by 6:00 Saturday morning. The idea was to sneak through both Genoa and Bosque by blending in with the Saturday morning traffic rush. That meant being on the road, heading north by 6:30. They bought gas and coffee at a gas station mini-mart and headed north out of Aberdeen. Jason was driving.

"Would you hate me if I slept for a while?" Danny asked from the passenger seat.

"Of course not."

It had been a short night for both of them. He thought he might have slept for three hours, maybe. Danny hadn't slept much more than that.

As she settled deeper into her seat, Jason turned up the heater and found a news channel on the radio. He doubted the Sheriff would have given a whole lot of new information to the local news folk, but it would give him a general idea of their situation.

Right now though, the radio hosts were discussing a local city council race. He'd have to wait for the next news cycle.

At this time of the day, they had the road almost to themselves. It was still dark and Highway 101 had maybe a half dozen cars moving, scattered over its four lanes. The rain from yesterday continued this morning but had eased to a heavy drizzle, just enough to need the wipers.

Last night he had written a story for the newspaper, part rebuttal to the murder charges and part profile of the information Peterson had given him. Debbie had been excited about it, so had Miles, but it was too late to make it into Saturday's paper. Debbie said it would probably be run as a feature in Sunday's edition.

That was almost better. The Sunday edition had the largest circulation and therefore the most readers. Sunday features were read widely and then talked about around the water cooler Monday.

It was also reassuring that his colleagues at the paper were not buying into the Jason Reynolds-as-killer storyline.

"Dunham County Sheriff's officials are requesting the public's help in locating a murder suspect," the radio's news reader said, his rich baritone adding gravity to the words. "Jason Reynolds is wanted for questioning in Friday's shooting death of Gerald Peterson, the owner and publisher of the *Bosque Examiner*. Mr. Peterson was found shot to death in his car in the small town of Donald, north of Bosque. The victim and suspect were observed in a heated exchange shortly before the shooting. Police think Reynolds may have fled to the Seattle metro area."

Danny stirred. "Guess I'm still not on the radar."

"I thought you were asleep."

"Not yet. I can relax a bit more now."

He smiled. "Me too."

It meant no one was looking for her Jeep. They were all but invisible.

♦♦♦♦♦

District Attorney for San Juan County, Andrea Meade hadn't slept much either. She had spent last evening doing research in her own collection of legal volumes as well as several online resources. She'd finally called it a night at about two in the morning and collapsed into bed beside her husband. Her ever-patient husband. Her husband, who had never questioned her drive or ambition. Never doubted that the hours spent with her law books and legal pads were necessary, or that her time could be better spent.

All he did was roll over toward her, take her in his arms and whisper in her ear, his voice coarse with sleep, "Fix it?"

"I don't know," she'd admitted.

"Tomorrow. Fresh eyes."

Within seconds, he'd slipped back into sleep.

Andrea had slept too, just not well and not nearly long enough.

Wrapped in a cozy bathrobe, she stumbled out into the kitchen and put together the makings of a pot of coffee. While the machine gurgled up its magic broth, she walked to the front door and brought in both morning papers before they were soaked by the persistent drizzle. As a public official and a legal one, she felt it was part of her job to keep up with what was happening in her state and country.

She closed the door again and glanced over the front page of each paper.

The *Times*' front page was almost entirely devoted to covering the various state and national elections, which was pretty much a rehash of every other day. The names just changed. Thank god she wasn't up for re-election until next year. She dreaded the entire process.

The front page of the *News* was just like the *Times* above the fold, concentrating on election coverage, but below the fold, they went a different direction. There was a color headshot of Jason Reynolds, next to a headline that read, "Profile of a Killer??" The byline was assigned to Deborah French.

"Well, that's interesting," she murmured and carried the papers back into the kitchen.

She laid the *News* out on the counter and read the story about Reynolds. It was basically a review of his history and background. The argument was a common one in legal defense: "Look at all the good things he's done over his lifetime. He couldn't possibly be capable of murdering someone." Andrea had put several people in jail despite just such a defense. As a prosecutor, she knew that everyone was capable of the most brutal crimes, if the situation was right.

She just couldn't see what the circumstances would be that would turn Jason Reynolds into a killer. By all accounts, he hadn't even returned fire when Lundgren's hit squad had him and his friends pinned in the vacation home last year. He'd had a gun in his hand the entire time and he'd never fired a shot. Forensics had proven that.

Andrea had been a prosecutor for years. Just like a cop, she had developed an instinct for such things, a gut feeling. Her gut told her that Jason Reynolds had nothing to do with that man's murder. The problem she was trying to figure out was what she could do legally to help him.

She had come up with an idea last night, but it was risky.

The coffee maker finished its brew with an asthmatic gasp. Andrea turned away from the paper and opened a cabinet in search of a coffee mug.

♦♦♦♦♦

Shortly before ten in the morning, Jason passed a wooden sign saying, "Welcome to the Kwamamish Reservation" painted in bright red and black over a white background. Almost immediately, the scenery changed. The road had more potholes and the shoulders were more overgrown. The scattered buildings he could see seemed older, more neglected, though there were several that had been freshly painted, with simple, but immaculate lawns.

Water stood in the ditches to either side of the road. The rain had thickened again, pounding now in unrelenting waves on car and road alike.

Danny stirred and sat up beside him, eyes puffy with sleep. "Where are we?"

"The Reservation."

"Oh." She rubbed her eyes.

The drive had been absolutely uneventful. Other than one City Police car headed the other direction in Genoa, Jason had actually not even seen a cop car. It was kind of weird. The Dunham County Sheriff's Department was supposedly in the midst of a manhunt. He'd expected to see a sizable presence on the roads. Instead, it was like all the patrol officers had been given the day off.

He was kind of worried about that. He always worried when an enemy wasn't doing what he'd expected. It made him wonder what they were up to.

"Do you have any idea where you're going?" Danny asked.

"The main town," he told her. "It's where the tribal government is located. I thought that would be a good place to start."

She looked at him. "You do realize it's Saturday. Government offices won't be open."

Jason smiled. "But the council members probably live nearby. And everyone in town will know who they are and where they live."

A sign appeared along the road, announcing that the town of Dualip was twenty-five miles away. Another sign directed drivers to stop at the Salmon Spirit Casino a mile ahead for a guaranteed good time.

"Maybe we should stop at the casino?" Danny asked. "Ask around there?"

Jason was shaking his head. "Already thought about that. Casinos tend to attract the criminal element, right?"

"Okay."

"So what are the odds that the Bartons have kept their hands off this? I'm not going to bet our lives that none of the casino employees are on the Barton payroll."

"Good point, but that's true everywhere."

He shrugged. "It's about the odds."

"Stop at the casino anyway," she told him. "I need to pee. I need to call Andrea too. I promised I'd call her today."

Jason agreed. He could use a bathroom break himself.

The Salmon Spirit Casino appeared on the right, inland side, of the highway. It was a large, square, three story building that looked more like a warehouse or hanger than a casino. Or it would have were it not for the bright paint and neon lights. It was smaller than most of the casinos Jason was familiar with in the Puget Sound area, but that was probably as much a matter of population density as anything else.

The parking area around the building was less than half full, which was still pretty good for fairly early on a rainy Saturday. All the slots nearest the building were full, with pickups and SUV's outnumbering cars by about two to one. Few were new and many were marred by rust and splotches of primer. They thinned out with distance from the casino's doors.

Jason pulled into a vacant slot and switched the car off. “Okay, we stick together; find the rest rooms, do our business and get out.”

Danny smiled. “Aye, aye, sir.”

♦♦♦♦♦

It was nearly 11:00 when Andrea Meade’s cell phone rang. She was sitting at her desk in the study, trying to be patient. Her husband, who owned a real estate agency was off manning an open house. She picked up the phone before it could ring again. The display showed the same number Danny had used yesterday.

She accepted the call.

“Danny?”

“Hi, Andrea. What can you tell me?”

“First, are you okay? Have you talked to Jason?”

“We’re both fine. That’s all I’m going to tell you.”

Andrea smiled. “Fair enough. So here’s what I’ve figured out. The good news is that the D.A. in Dunham County has not yet filed murder charges against Jason. That means technically he’s only wanted for questioning. You get him over here and I will tell Dunham County that they are welcome to come question him in my office.”

Danny seemed excited by the idea. “Sheriff Schneider agreed to this?”

“Absolutely. I’ve already cleared it with him.”

“Thank you, Andrea. Thank you so much.”

“You’re welcome. Just get him here as quickly as you can. And remember, we have no control over any law enforcement outside San Juan County, so you’re still going to have to be careful.”

“I know.”

“One more thing,” she said before Danny could end the call, “I tried calling the Dunham County Sheriff to get some clarification on the case, but it seems the entire command structure has taken the weekend off and can’t be reached.”

“In the middle of a murder investigation?”

"That's what I was told. I thought you might find that interesting."

"I do. Thanks, thanks for everything."

Danny ended the call.

Twenty-four

The man known now as Trevor Sanford pulled his Acura sedan up to the window at the border crossing south of Vancouver and handed his passport to the Border Patrol Agent. The crossing was busy. At least a dozen cars waited in line behind Sanford.

"Good morning, Mr. Sanford," the Agent said, quickly tapping on his keyboard. "What brings you into the States?"

"Business meetings in Seattle." Sanford smiled. "Trying to pick up some new accounts, you know."

The Border Agent nodded. It was a common enough reason. Vancouver was the largest city in western Canada; Seattle was the largest city in the American Pacific Northwest. A lot of goods and services flowed between the two.

The Agent could see a sample case in the backseat of the Acura. Two spare suits hung from the clips above the rear windows.

The Agent read his computer screen and handed the passport back to Sanford. "Have a nice stay."

"Thank you," Sanford said and pulled away from the kiosk.

It was that easy.

So much for heightened border security.

Trevor Sanford, also known as Taylor Smith, set the cruise control and headed south for Seattle.

Twenty-five

The town of Dualip was actually little more than a village strung out along either side of the highway, where 101 crossed the Quinault River. The residential areas seemed to be an even mix of older clapboard cottages and trailer houses. Some were in good repair, freshly painted with neatly tended yards, but a lot of others were clearly showing the effects of time and neglect. Many had derelict cars and trucks rusting in front yards. Some walls had been patched with raw plywood. Some roofs with faded plastic tarps.

The overall impression was a community struggling valiantly against poverty. And, as in every struggle, sometimes you lost.

Neither Jason nor Danny said much as they drove through the little town. There wasn't a whole lot to say. It was sad and it had been sad a long time. Jason couldn't help feeling a little pang of guilt, not so much because he was white, but because he was relatively wealthy and managed to forget communities like this existed not far from his own home.

The Kwamamish Reservation wasn't even terribly unusual. Most reservations were centers of poverty, substance abuse, and hopelessness.

Like most people, he just managed to keep this out of his daily consciousness.

They moved into the business section of town which seemed to be even more run down than the residential areas.

"I'm going to start crying soon," Danny said.

A few businesses were open and apparently profitable. They passed a grocer, a discount cigarette store, and a couple of clothing resellers. Almost incongruous was a satellite television dealer and another selling cell phones. A hardware store seemed to be doing okay as did a saw shop.

A sign told them the tribal offices were two blocks to the left, as was the library.

"They'll be closed," Danny told him. "Except maybe the library."

Something else had caught Jason's attention. "There." He pointed down the street ahead of them. "That's what I was looking for."

A slightly tattered vinyl banner featuring black print on a white background advertised a "Farmer's and Crafters Market."

"A farmer's market?" Danny asked.

"I guarantee that's where all the tribal elders—not the politicians, but the power behind the politicians—gather every Saturday. More issues are probably decided there than any council chamber."

Danny shrugged. "In the rain?"

"It's rainforest country. If they were to let rain stop them they'd never leave their houses."

He turned at the sign and followed the street down to a small waterfront district facing the river and a small marina berthing a dozen or so fishing boats. The Farmers Market was set up across the street from the marina.

"See?" Jason said.

A painted plywood canopy had been built over what amounted to a vacant lot. A dozen or more vendors had set up tables under the canopy. Several shoppers were browsing the offerings. Most of them were Kwamamish, but Jason spotted at least one young white couple.

He parked and switched off the engine, turned to Danny. "Ready to make contact?"

"Sure. I don't know what we're doing exactly."

"I believe it's what you cops call playing your gut."

She shook her head. "Whatever."

They climbed out of the car and hurried through the rain into the shelter of the market. The tables were arranged in a rough "U" shape, with the opening facing the street. They moved toward the first table on their left.

"Hello," the man behind the table said. He wore a heavy down jacket and knit cap despite the space heater glowing behind him. "How you guys doing?"

"We're doing well," Jason said. "Thanks."

"It's our first trip out here," Danny added.

The man had stacks of small mason jars on either side of the table, framing him in the middle. Half were hand-labeled as tuna, the other half, salmon. Vacuum-packed packages of smoked salmon laid flat on the table between the jars. They all looked good and the prices were well below anything Jason would find anywhere in Seattle.

"These are good prices," Danny whispered to him. "Real good."

Jason looked up at the man. "You make all these yourself?"

"Yeah." The man smiled. "And my wife and kids, my mother and sisters. It's a family thing."

"Cool."

Jason told him they were going to look around a bit, but would probably be back to pick up something.

"I love smoked salmon," he said.

"This is smoked in the old way," the man told him. "Over a cedar fire in a handmade smokehouse.

"We'll be back."

They wandered over toward the next table.

"What exactly are we looking for?" Danny asked softly enough to not be overheard.

"The boss."

"The boss?"

He nodded. "I'll know him when I see him."

The next table featured handmade knives with handles of carved antler and bone. Impressive workmanship, but not really

Jason's thing. Danny seemed a little more impressed, but not enough to spend her money.

They worked their way through the market, pausing to look at each vendor's wares, chatting a little here, examining a craft there. In short, they acted like tourists, people with time and money to kill, enjoying a rainy Saturday on the coast. In addition to the canned fish and knives, they saw beautiful embroidery, weaving, and woodworking, even miniature totem poles. The vendors were for the most part friendly, as befitted business people trying to coax them out of their money.

Near the end of the market they came to a table covered with little Ziploc bags of what looked like herbs. Some seemed to be dried leaves, others roots, some were ground so fine it was impossible to tell what they'd originally been. Two women sat behind the table, bundled up in winter coats and scarves, but with their heads uncovered. One had salt-and-pepper graying hair braided down her back. The other woman had pure white hair divided into two braids.

They looked up and smiled as Jason and Danny stepped up to their table. "You're a long way from home," the younger of the two said.

"Just a bit," Jason smiled.

"What are these?" Danny asked, picking up one of the envelopes and sniffing it. "Teas?"

The older woman laughed.

"Yes and no." The younger woman chuckled too. "Not like Liptons. They are medicine. Traditional medicine. You're holding red willow bark, which will cure headache."

"You're healers," Jason said.

"She is a healer." The younger woman pointed to the one with white hair. "I'm just her student."

Jason smiled. "We're all just students, aren't we?"

"That we are, young man," the older woman said. "That we are."

Danny had picked up another bag and was examining the contents, a green, flaky substance.

"That's dried raspberry leaf," the younger woman said. "Steep it in boiling water to make a tea. It will help with cramps during that time of the month."

Danny blushed and set the bag down again.

"But you didn't travel all this way because of menstrual cramps, did you?"

Jason froze in position. Danny did the same beside him.

"You look like deer in headlights," the younger woman laughed and pulled a newspaper from the floor beside her chair. It was the morning's edition of the *News*. Jason's photo was prominent next to the article below the fold. "Relax. I recognized you as soon as you walked in. If I was going to turn you in, you'd have been in handcuffs by now."

Jason relaxed, but just a little. It had never occurred to him that he would be recognized on the reservation. He had thought of it as kind of a safe zone.

"So are you just passing through, or did you really think you could hide out in a town that's ninety percent Indian? In case you hadn't noticed, you two don't exactly blend in."

"I think there is no love lost between the Kwamamish people and the Dunham County Sheriff."

The older woman turned and spat on the ground.

He took that as a "yes."

"Actually," Jason dropped his voice a little. "I came here hoping someone would be able and willing to help us."

"Help you do what?"

"Help us get out to the Hemlock Run Lodge."

"Why would you want to go out there?"

"Because I think something at Hemlock Run holds the key to making the Bartons pay for all the crimes they've committed. I'm going to find it and I'm going to be the one who makes them face justice."

"You're the one?"

"Yes."

The woman watched him for a few seconds, like she was measuring him, then turned to Danny. "What do you think? Can he do what he says? A lot of good people have failed before him."

"If anyone can, it's him," Danny said. "He's relentless."

The woman turned back to Jason. "Relentless, huh?"

"Some people call it driven."

"Or pig-headed," Danny added.

The woman—the younger of the two sitting behind the table—smiled. "My name's Gloria. If you really want to go to Hemlock Run, I might be able to help."

"We have to," Jason said.

♦

A half hour later, Jason and Danny sat by the window in a small diner on the edge of Dualip, about a mile and a half north of the Farmers Market. It's where Gloria had suggested they wait.

Carmen's Café occupied the repurposed ground floor of an old farmhouse on the north bank of the river. It was a good idea, but one that had never quite come to fruition. In reality, it seemed like the owners had simply removed all their personal furnishings from the living and dining rooms and brought in second-hand tables for their customers. The wooden floor was scuffed and splintered in places and the wallpaper out of style. But while the atmosphere was nothing to write home about, the staff was friendly and the soup was good. Jason was trying the mussel stew; Danny had chickened out and ordered a bowl of clam chowder.

"They're orange!" Danny said, shaking her head. "It looks like they're glowing."

"They taste good." Jason shrugged. "A little chewy, but good."

This was his first experience with mussels, and truthfully, it had taken a few moments to get over the odd optics, but they tasted like clams or oysters, earthy, a little bit nutty. And they were almost pure protein. The Indians along the coast had lived off them for thousands of years.

Every few seconds he glanced over at his new, disposable cell phone sitting on the table. Their new friend, Gloria, had promised to call if she could find someone to show them how to get out to the lodge.

But first, she'd made absolutely sure that they really wanted to go there. The implication was strong that it was not someplace you traveled to lightly.

Jason had assured her they were serious.

The cell phone rang. It's ringtone sounded like an old fashioned bell alarm. Jason picked it up.

"Mr. Reynolds?"

"Yes."

"My son, Jimmy, gets off work in fifteen minutes," Gloria told him. "He won't take you to the lodge; it's too dangerous. But he will get you close and show you how to get there."

"Thank you. That's perfect. We don't want to put anyone in more danger than we have to. How old is your son?"

"Oh, he's nineteen," she laughed. "I'm not sending you out with a kid. Jimmy can take care of himself."

"We'll make sure he gets home safely."

"Like I said, Jimmy can take care of himself. You two concentrate on keeping yourselves alive. You're walking into a den of snakes."

He assured her they'd be careful and ended the call then told Danny what Gloria had told him.

"Her son?"

He shrugged. "Apparently, he knows how to get there."

She looked skeptical.

"You okay with this?" he asked, lifting a spoonful of squash-colored soup to his mouth.

"Sure, I guess. I don't know what you're expecting to find, or what we can do about it, but I agree we need to know."

"Excuse me?"

They looked up at a slim young man with long, dark hair tied back in a ponytail standing beside their table. He wore a white button up shirt over black cargo pants and sneakers. "My mom said you needed some help?"

"You cook here?" Jason asked.

The young man frowned. "Yeah? Is that a problem?"

"No, not at all. Your mother just didn't tell us that," Jason said. "She just said to wait here."

He shrugged as if there was no explaining his mother's thinking sometimes. "You have a car? We'd better get going while there's still daylight."

Twenty-six

Hemlock Run Lodge was built on the shores of Black Creek, named either for the dark volcanic rock which formed its bed, or because for much of its length the creek ran between ridges so steep and so high that sunshine seldom penetrated down to the water's surface.

The Lodge itself was the brainchild of Ezekiel Barton, grandfather of the current patriarch of the family, State Senator Morris Barton. In 1919, shortly after the end of the Great War, Zeke Barton decided he wanted some place to get away from both his business interests and his family responsibilities. He settled on remote Black Creek in the foothills of the Olympics as the perfect place. There was plenty of game in the area—deer, elk, and bear—as well as trout in the creek.

Zeke Barton built a rough log cabin out of the native hemlock and carved out a horse trail to reach it. Zeke's cabin served him and his extended family well for years.

After Ezekiel passed away and his oldest son Hiram took over the family business, Hiram spent most of his time acquiring timber land and growing the business. While he did that, the cabin gradually decayed and the forest re-absorbed the trail his father had carved out of the wilderness.

But as he entered middle age, Hiram began to look at other things besides business. One of these was the cabin he'd spent so much time in as a child. It was little more than overgrown ruins by that time, but Hiram had never quit just because a project wasn't easy. He destroyed the the old cabin, then built a small dam across the creek. It created a narrow, deep lake which provided perfect habitat for monster lake trout.

With the heavy equipment which was just becoming widely available, he carved a road out of his father's old horse trail and then leveled a hill just above the new lake's high water mark. Here he built the new lodge and named it Hemlock Run. It was constructed of peeled and varnished logs and roofed with cedar shingles manufactured in the Barton plant in Bosque. Hemlock Run had a great room, a dining room, kitchen, baths, a master bedroom and six smaller bedrooms for his children and guests.

His business instincts being what they were, the lodge became more of a retreat for himself and his business cronies, than a family vacation spot.

When Morris took over after his father's death, he added an outbuilding with another full kitchen, sitting room and six more bedrooms. It could serve as servants' quarters or extra guest space. He also built another outbuilding, inland from the lake, housing a diesel generator, which provided electricity to the lodge. A satellite gave them television.

He also carved a helicopter landing pad out of the forest a short distance away.

Several ATV's provided transportation around the grounds.

It was a private slice of paradise out in the middle of nowhere.

♦♦♦♦♦

"Turn left up here," Jimmy told Jason from the back seat. "Just before the building with the mossy roof."

Jason made the turn, emerging onto yet another gravel and packed dirt road, heading east, toward the towering ridges of the Olympics. The rain had tapered off to a persistent drizzle, just enough to make wipers necessary. They had decided to take Danny's Jeep because their guide had a fifteen-year-old Nissan pickup. As Jimmy put it, they didn't know each other well enough to crowd into the cab of his truck.

Besides, the Jeep had four-wheel-drive.

The road quickly took them out of the town's residential areas. Small ranches and scattered farmhouses took over, with occasional goats and horses grazing peacefully in rain-soaked pastures surrounded by forest. Each of the ranches looked like they could be overrun by the forest at any time.

Then it was just forest, growing thick and lushly green right up to the edge of the narrow road.

"What happens if we meet someone else coming the other way?" Danny asked.

"Squeeze over as far as you can. He'll do the same thing. But there isn't much traffic out here this time of year," Jimmy told them. "Just some mushroom hunters."

"And people heading to the Bartons' lodge."

Jimmy didn't reply.

For an undeveloped road out in the forest on an Indian Reservation, the driving surface was in remarkably good shape. There were a few places washed out by the rain, but it wasn't an issue.

Jason wondered whether the Bartons maintained it to facilitate travel to the lodge.

About five or six miles from town, they approached a fork in the road.

"Bear to the left," Jimmy told them. "The road to the right leads off the Rez in a few miles. It's how the Bartons and most of their guests get up here. The rest come in by helicopter."

"Helicopter?"

"Oh yeah. The Bartons are rich. Hadn't you heard?"

Jason had.

"How far is it?" Danny asked.

"The lodge? About ten miles as the crow flies. Maybe fifteen by road," Jimmy said. "But we're not going to the lodge; we're just going to get close."

Jason glanced up at the young man in the rearview. "Because?"

"It wouldn't be good for your health, or mine. There's a steel gate across the road, manned by deputy sheriffs. They're usually not too friendly."

♦

"Have you ever been there?" Danny asked. "To the lodge?"

Jimmy hesitated a moment. "Once or twice. Me and my friends."

Jason glanced at him in the rearview mirror. "Why?"

"Because our folks told us not to. You know how it is. We called it 'counting coup.'" The young man laughed. "Counting coup isn't even a Kwamamish cultural thing. It's Plains culture. We stole it from the movies."

Danny looked perplexed. "What's 'counting coup'?"

Jimmy smiled. "It's the idea that it takes more courage to touch the living enemy and escape, than to just kill him. We would sneak onto the lodge grounds and steal some trinket to prove we'd been there."

"You could have gotten killed," Danny told him.

"That was kind of the point."

Danny shook her head. "Men."

"I didn't say it was the smartest thing we ever did."

"No, you didn't." Jason smiled. "Besides, I think it's part of being a teen. I don't care what culture you come from."

"Counting coup?"

"Or something similar."

Jimmy pointed ahead of them, where the overgrown remnants of a road opened on the left. "Pull in here and park. We'll walk the rest of the way."

Jason did, thanking Danny's foresight in buying a Jeep which would have no trouble surviving the weed-ridden track. Its four wheel drive also meant not having to worry about getting stuck. He pulled in far enough that the Jeep would not be visible to a casual traveler on the road and killed the engine.

He was immediately struck by the quiet. The ticking of the engine as it cooled sounded like a snare drum.

"The gate is around the next bend," Jimmy said. "I think we have a better chance of not being seen if we walk from here."

Jason thought that sounded like an excellent idea.

When they were all out of the Jeep, Jimmy led them across the road and then in a low, crouching walk along the tree-lined shoulder. After about a hundred yards, Jimmy stopped. The others did the same. Jason was right behind him. Danny brought up the rear.

Just beyond them, the gravel road bent to the right, out of sight.

Jimmy peered around the corner for a minute, then moved back to Jason. "Take a look," he whispered. "The guard is sitting in a car just behind the left pillar."

Jason crept up to the turn. It was just as Jimmy had described. A black fence that could be wrought iron hung between two brick pillars. It looked strong enough to stop a tank. A sheriff's cruiser was parked behind the pillar on the left.

An ornate sign in wrought iron hung on one of the pillars announcing the property as *Hemlock Run.* Another sign, in normal black on white lettering announced that it was private property, and that everyone should keep out or face trespassing charges.

Jason returned to the others and Danny moved up to take a look.

When she had returned to the group, they retraced their steps back toward the Jeep. It was so quiet, Jason thought they sounded like a heard of elephants, kicking gravel and brushing against branches, but that was probably just nerves. They were prowling around the Bartons' deepest, darkest hideaway. The Bartons were probably violently sensitive about that.

The Bartons weren't, however, superhuman.

Yet he still found himself whispering. "Is that gate always guarded?"

"I have no idea," Jimmy said. He wasn't whispering, but his voice was low. "I haven't been up here in a couple of years. It isn't one of my usual hangouts."

Danny caught Jason's eye. "We're not going to get past that guard."

"No," he agreed. "We're going to have to find another way in. I wonder how far the fence runs."

Jimmy looked at each of them in turn. "You're serious about this? You want to sneak into the Bartons' lodge?"

They had arrived at the Jeep again by this time and stood there in the misty rain.

"Absolutely," Jason told him.

Jimmy turned to Danny, who nodded. "We need to know what's going on up there. And we need to get proof."

"Clear, undeniable proof," Jason added. "Something that will take the Bartons down for good."

Again, Jimmy peered at each of them. "You want to take the Bartons down?"

"I think it's about time someone does, don't you?"

"No one's ever been able to do it. People have died trying."

Jason smiled. "That just means it's hard, not impossible."

"The people around here have put up with their crap long enough," Danny said. "Every one of the Bartons needs to spend the next thirty years in prison."

Jimmy shoved his hands into his pants pockets. "Do you have guns?"

"I do," Danny said.

"Why?" Jason wanted to know.

"Because if they catch us, there won't be any arrests. They will kill us just like they've killed everyone else who stood up to them. We will just disappear." He looked up at them again. "Are you ready to kill someone to save your life?"

"I'm hoping it doesn't come to that," Jason said.

"Of course. But we've got to be ready. Our lives—all our lives—could depend on it."

"Wait a minute." Danny frowned. "What's with the 'we' all of a sudden?"

"Well, I'm not sending you in there alone. You guys don't know the area and I bet neither of you has spent much time hiking in the woods, have you?"

They admitted they hadn't.

"You need a guide and I'm here and willing."

Jason looked to Danny. He thought Jimmy's arguments were pretty strong. They weren't experienced at moving through the forest, especially after dark, and in unfamiliar terrain. It would be next to impossible for the two of them to quietly approach Hemlock Run. If they could even find it in the dark.

The odds would move significantly in their favor with a guide.

Danny seemed to have reached the same conclusion. She gave a small nod.

"Good," Jimmy said. "Now let's get out of here before someone drives by and starts asking questions."

♦♦♦♦♦

Lisa Martin checked her cell phone one more time and set it on the table in front of her. There was still nothing, no word from Jason or Danny. They could be dead for all she knew. She felt helpless and was beginning to have a deeper and broader appreciation for what Helen's parents had been going through for the past four days. She wondered how they'd managed to keep themselves together as well as they had.

She looked up now as Barbara Miller slid into other side of the booth. Dark circles hung under her eyes and the lines beside her mouth had deepened noticeably since a week ago.

"Thanks for all the help today," Barbara told her. "It's made a lot of difference, especially for Tom. He's been so frustrated, between his bum arm and Helen."

Lisa smiled. They had just finished cleaning up after the lunch rush. She had acted as Tom's scribe—writing out the orders as the customers gave them—and then his extra hands when it came time to deliver food. The system had worked pretty smoothly, better than anyone could have predicted.

And it had given her something concrete to do.

Tom was in back now, updating the restaurant books.

"No word from your friends?"

Lisa shook her head.

"That may not be a bad thing," Barbara said. "Sometimes no news really is good news. Your friend Jason taught me that one. It's the only thing that's been keeping us going. As long as no one has found a body, we have to believe Helen's alive. No news is good news."

Lisa nodded. "I know."

"Besides, I think your friends are both very smart and very brave. They've already accomplished more than anyone could expect. They might actually be a match for the Bartons."

"I hope so."

Jason and Danny tried to talk their new friend out of taking them back to his house to wait for dark. They used the "harboring a fugitive" argument, the "you hardly know us," and the "really, we'll be fine" arguments, but he was steadfast. He just sat there in the back seat of Danny's car, smiling to himself and refusing to bend before their reasoning.

"You need a place to rest and figure out how to do this," he insisted. "Besides, hospitality—unlike counting coup—really is a Kwamamish tradition."

They finally relented and followed his directions to the south side of town and a small ranch-style home with faded cedar shake siding and white smoke curling out of a chimney. Jason parked behind an older blue Camry and shut off the engine.

"Better grab some warm clothes," he told them before getting out. "It gets cold when the sun goes down. Boots, if you have some."

Jason agreed.

"You have a real camera? Not your phone?"

"Yeah, telephoto lens, flash, and everything."

"Is it charged? It might be a good idea to bring it and a charger inside too. It would suck if you got all the way out there and the battery went dead."

Jimmy left them, disappearing through the front door of the house to announce the arrival of company.

"You get the feeling we've lost control of this operation?" Danny asked as they sorted through their luggage.

"Only a little bit."

They gathered their warm clothes, Jason's camera and laptop and followed Jimmy into the house.

Jason stepped into a foyer-type entry way. Shoes and boots lined the base of a wall under metal hooks supporting coats and raincoats of multiple sizes and descriptions. The air smelled of wood smoke and a fascinating stew of herbs and spices. It reminded him of walking into an old fashioned tea shop.

Danny raised her eyebrows to Jason's glance.

"This way," Jimmy found them and led the way further into the house.

They emerged in a small, but nicely decorated living room. Gloria was sitting on a sofa facing a television tuned to a game show. A wood stove in the far corner hissed and clicked as it pumped heat into the room. The walls were decorated with family pictures and nature paintings.

"Well?" Gloria asked. "Did you find what you were looking for?"

Jason shrugged. "Maybe. We don't know yet."

"I'm going to take them back up after dark," Jimmy told them. "Less chance of being discovered that way."

Gloria caught Jason's eye. "You do know what you're dealing with up there, don't you?"

"Oh, yeah. We're quite familiar with what the Bartons are capable of."

"Good. Because if you go creeping into a wolf 's den, be prepared for the wolf to defend himself."

Danny assured her they were ready. "Believe it or not, we've been in this situation before. We're here. The bad guys are not."

Gloria rose to her feet. "Well, you're going to need to eat something first. I hope tacos are okay."

Jason opened his mouth to protest when Jimmy stopped him.

"Don't waste your breath. 'Hospitality,' remember?"

"Tacos will be wonderful," Danny said. "Let me help you."

♦

"So, forgive me for asking," Gloria said when dinner was winding down. "But what, exactly, do you intend to do when you get up there? You have a plan, right?"

"We do," Jason said.

"Go in guns blazing like John Wayne?"

"No," Danny was shaking her head. "Absolutely not."

"Not that they don't deserve it," Jimmy said.

"No, they don't deserve it," Jason said.

Everyone stopped to look at him.

"Killing them would turn the Bartons into victims. They aren't victims; they're predators. They deserve to be paraded in public with their hands cuffed and ankles shackled. They deserve to have their crimes read aloud into the official record and then their fate decided by a jury of fellow citizens. They deserve to have every one of their victims sitting in the gallery as they're sentenced to decades in prison," he said. "Shooting them is too easy."

"Okay." Jimmy nodded. "What he said. Killing them is too easy."

"Besides," Danny said. "Legally, we'd be in the wrong."

Gloria looked distressed. "*We'd* be wrong?"

"We'd be trespassing. In Washington, they have the legal right to defend their property from trespassers. The Castle Doctrine."

"That's bull," Jimmy said. "Do you know what they do up there?"

"No, not exactly," Jason said. "Do you?"

Jimmy grew silent, shrugged. "There's been rumors."

"What kind of rumors?"

"You know, wild parties. Lots of alcohol, drugs, hookers. That sort of thing."

Gloria began to gather the plates from the table. "Some of the ladies might not have volunteered too, if you know what I mean."

He did.

Gloria deposited the dirty dishes in the kitchen and returned for another load. Danny was already on her feet, stacking more dishes.

"So what do you hope to do tonight?" Gloria asked.

"Sneak in there with a camera," he gestured toward the camera sitting on its charging chord. "Get solid evidence of what they're doing on film and use that to take apart their whole organization."

"That will only work," Danny picked up a stack of plates and carried it toward the kitchen. "If we can also get the photographs out."

The doorbell rang.

Everybody stopped in mid-motion.

"Are we expecting visitors?" Gloria asked the room.

"I am. I called Tony." Jimmy stood and started for the door. "Sit tight. I'll be right back."

Gloria slipped into the kitchen and began running water in the sink for dishes. Danny pulled her pistol from her belt holster and held it down by her thigh. Jason moved off to the side. He could hear Jimmy talking quietly and the muffled sound of an answering voice. A man's voice.

Seconds later, the front door closed again and Jimmy returned to the room with a brown paper grocery bag.

He looked at Jason, then Danny. "Relax guys. It was a friend of mine."

He set the bag on the table with an ominous thump, reached in and pulled out one, then a second semi-automatic pistol.

"What are those for?" Jason asked.

"Protection," Jimmy said. "None of us are going unless every one of us is able to protect the others. The Bartons will not hesitate to shoot us. We have to be willing to shoot back. Deal?"

Jason stared at the ugly blue metal.

"He's right," Danny said. "We have to be able to defend each other."

"But our object is still to get in and out without anyone knowing. We're not looking for a gunfight."

Danny and Jimmy agreed.

Jason took one of the pistols, surprised by how heavy it felt.

♦

The sun set at 6:07 pm that Saturday. By 6:30, they agreed it was dark enough to start up toward the lodge. They didn't want to get there too early while light made them more visible, or too late when the headlights of the car would be noticeable for miles against the darkness of the forest.

"If you're not out there a lot," Jimmy told them. "You don't realize just how dark it gets at night. In the woods, artificial light stands out like red neon."

All three of them were bundled up in layers of sweaters, sweat shirts and heavy socks. Though the rain had finally stopped, the sky remained covered by an opaque layer of cloud and a moist chill filled the air. More important, everything was wet.

Once they left the edges of town, there was no ambient light at all. It was as dark as the inside of a tomb.

Jason drove Lisa's Jeep up the same road he had earlier this afternoon, but now it was full dark and following the play of the headlights was much like driving through a dark tunnel. He could see absolutely nothing that wasn't directly in front of them.

The pistol was a cold weight pressing against his side. He was carrying it in an old fanny pack Jimmy found for him. His camera hung from a strap around his neck.

Danny and Jimmy each carried a set of field glasses in addition to their pistols. Everyone's cell phone was turned off.

"Okay. Better cut the headlights," Jimmy told him. "We're getting close."

Jason did and was immediately blind. He stopped the car until his eyes could adjust to the sudden change of light.

"You okay?" Jimmy asked.

"Driving while blind. Yeah, I'm fine."

"We'll pull off the road pretty quick," he told Jason. "Look for an opening like the one yesterday on your left side. It's about a hundred yards ahead."

Jason's eyesight gradually came back, but Jimmy had been right, there was no darkness like the darkness of a forest without moon or starlight. Everything was differing shades of gray and black, with the road the lightest shade.

Danny spotted the opening Jimmy had been talking about. Jason turned in and pulled far enough in to keep the car out of sight from the road and shut the engine off.

A deep, primeval silence took over.

"The creek is about a hundred, hundred fifty yards ahead of us," Jimmy told them. "There's a game trail just this side of the creek that leads up to the dam. That's how we'll get to the lodge."

Jason thought it sounded like a decent plan.

"Who has the best night vision?"

Danny didn't hesitate. She pointed to Jason. "He does."

"Okay. I'll go first because I know the way. Danny you follow me; Jason brings up the rear. Voices carry out here, so we need to try and avoid talking if we can. Just take our time, keep together, and try not to break any legs. Any questions?"

"Are there going to be snakes?" Danny asked.

"No," Jimmy laughed. "It's too cold for snakes. But there might be bears and cougars."

He opened his door and climbed out into the darkness.

"Bears? Cougars?" Danny asked. "Really?"

"He's kidding," Jason told her and opened his own door. He hoped he'd been kidding.

♦

It wasn't actually raining, but everything—every stem, every branch, and leaf—was covered with water. Within fifteen minutes, Jason's feet were wet, but he refused to let that distract him. Instead, he concentrated on simply following Danny's shadowy figure in front of him. The entire world was opaque darkness around them, alien and threatening. Occasionally, something small would scurry through the brush. Other than that nothing other than them moved. Nothing else made a sound.

Not for the first time in his life, Jason realized just how much of a civilized, city-dweller he had become. He didn't have the skills needed to survive out here.

The idea that he and Danny could have snuck up on the lodge on their own now seemed as unrealistic as them taking a stroll on the moon.

About forty-five minutes later, Jimmy brought them to a stop. They had reached the game trail that ran along the creek. They needed to make a turn to the right.

"How much farther is it?" Jason asked, his voice lowered to just above a whisper.

"A couple of miles. But we'll be in forest. We'll have to go slower or someone's going to get an eye poked out or leg broken. It's going to take a while."

Jason nodded.

"Ready?"

Jason said he was.

Danny said she was.

"Let's go." Jimmy ducked between two trees and disappeared into the dark.

Danny followed him.

Jason followed Danny.

♦

The average adult human walks at a speed of about three miles an hour over relatively level ground with good footing and visibility. Jason didn't know exactly why, maybe it was the lack of visual stimuli, but a part of his brain started trying to figure out exactly how slowly they were moving. Because they were moving slowly. As Jimmy had warned them, the trail presented more dangers than the overgrown road had.

It was a game trail, not a hiking trail, which meant it wasn't created by or designed for humans walking upright. Random branches often crossed the trail at inconvenient heights. Either they had to crawl under them, or bend them out of the way, then hold them so the person behind wouldn't get whipped across the face.

Twice, a tree had fallen across the trail and all progress stopped while they figured out how to climb over or go around the tree and then had to wait while Jimmy tried to find the trail again on the other side.

Once, they had to splash across a smaller creek that crossed the trail on its way to Black Creek. None of their boots were waterproof. There was so much moisture on the foliage that they were all wet anyway, but it was still cold and miserable.

And once, they froze in silent fear as something unseen ahead of them on the trail snorted. They'd waited in silence for another noise, but there was nothing. Then a branch snapped. It sounded like a bone breaking in the darkness.

Jason slowly unzipped the fanny pack and grabbed his pistol.

It snorted again. This time something hit the ground with it, almost simultaneous.

Jason felt, rather than saw, Jimmy relax.

"Find another way, little sister," Jimmy whispered.

"What the hell?" Danny asked, also whispering.

Another snort, this time followed by the sounds of something crashing away through the forest. From the noise, Jason thought it could have been a tank, or maybe an elephant.

"Just a doe. Nothing to worry about," Jimmy said.

Jason re-zipped his fanny pack again. "That was a doe?"

"Yeah. Just a doe."

They continued walking. Jason had no idea how long. They just walked.

"Listen," Jimmy finally stopped them. "Hear that?"

Jason listened. All he could hear was the claustrophobic quiet of the forest. It almost seemed as though the hemlock and cedar crowding around were so quiet the silence drowned out all other sounds. Only the occasional scatter of small feet across fallen needles somewhere in the dark. That, and the distant murmur of a stream.

Of course.

"The creek?"

"The spillway off the dam," Jimmy said. "We're almost there."

Without another word, they started down the trail again.

It took at least another half hour of picking their way through the brush and grabbing branches, but finally a shadowy mass emerged from the darkness on their left—the dam the Bartons had built across the creek. The splashing rush of the spillway was the only sound Jason could hear. It was loud enough to even drown out their whispered voices.

Jimmy led them up a final steep slope to a flat area about the width of a single lane road and completely free of shrubs and trees. Directly ahead lay the dark mass of the artificial lake. It smelled of cold water and quietly lapped in the stillness.

A quarter mile to their right, the lodge was lit up like a cruise ship in the middle of a nighttime sea.

Twenty-seven

"Wow," Danny murmured.

Jason agreed. The lodge was truly a magnificent sight. Yellow light glowed from every single window and door and spilled out on to a flagstone terrace running to the edge of the lake. More light painted the trees yellow behind the building. In fact, the entire building seemed to glow like gold against the darkness surrounding it.

Jason could see no other light of any kind. Anywhere.

Multiple figures moved behind the windows, but at this distance, no details could be seen. Jason pulled his camera out of its case and hurried to attach the telephoto lens. Beside him both Danny and Jimmy had binoculars to their eyes.

"See anything?" he asked.

"It looks like a party," Danny said.

Jimmy agreed.

Jason finished attaching the lens to his camera, powered it up and directed it at the house. Even cranked up to its full 200mm telephoto range, the figures were still too small, too far away to make out facial features or exactly what they were doing. He snapped a couple of reference pictures anyway, just because.

It did look like a party of some sort.

He lowered the camera again. “I need to get closer.”

“Careful.” Danny whispered. “Stay beyond the light spill.”

“I will.” Jason pushed himself to his feet, cradling the camera against his midsection. He figured that in order to get the kind of shots he needed to nail the Bartons, he needed to get within about fifty yards of the building. Closer would be even better.

He could feel it. He could feel the jaws of the trap closing on Dunham County. He just had to take some photographs. The memory card in his camera had three gigabytes of storage. He intended to fill the whole thing.

“Hold on.” Jimmy stopped him. “What about guards or security systems?”

“Shit. You’re right.” Jason dropped down with the others. He would have walked right into it.

“I don’t think they’ll have a security system,” Danny said. “Most of them require a constant power source and a hardwired phone line. I don’t see an electric or phone company building a line all the way out here for just one building, even if it is the Bartons.”

Jimmy pointed at the lit up beacon of the lodge. “They seem to have plenty of power.”

“A generator,” Jason said. “Run it when they’re here. Turn it off when they leave. Danny’s right, a passive system doesn’t make sense. But guards do.”

Jimmy admitted the logic of this.

The question was how vulnerable did the Bartons feel out here? They were in an obviously remote location, which was a layer of security in itself. They also had not faced any serious opposition in a decade or more. Even during the height of the conflict with the Kwamamish, Hemlock Run had never been involved. The conflict had been further south, near the Dunham County border. They shouldn’t be feeling terribly vulnerable. If you weren’t feeling vulnerable, you’d probably think the guard at the gate was all the protection you’d need.

“I think they’re too arrogant to be worried about security,” he said. “Who would they be guarding against?”

"Us?" Danny offered.

"We're in Seattle hiding from the law." He smiled. "I'm going to try to get closer."

"Be careful."

Before they could talk him out of it again, Jason rose to his feet and followed the edge of the tree line toward the building. He moved as quietly as possible, always keeping an eye on the lodge in case someone came out. So far no one had, but all he needed was someone to step outside to grab a cigarette and spot him skulking around in the dark.

Sound from behind startled him. Jason stopped and crouched down, only to discover Danny and Jimmy coming up from behind.

"You scared me," he hissed at them.

"Sorry. Couldn't just sit there while you wandered around," Danny said.

Jason tried to slow his racing heartbeat.

A quick glance at the lodge revealed a problem. As he'd followed the shoreline of the lake, the angle he had on the windows grew more and more shallow. In effect, the closer he got to the lodge, the more it appeared to turn sideways. By the time he got within good photographic range, he would have no view of the windows at all.

Jason explained the situation to the others.

"Circle around to the back?" Jimmy offered.

That was one option.

"The farther we go in," Danny pointed out. "The farther we have to get out. And the more chance of being spotted."

"I'm not walking out of here without the evidence we came for."

Jimmy nodded. "Just stay back in the trees as long as we can. Their night vision is going to be zero after being in there. We should be fine."

"Let's hope."

♦

Forty-five minutes later they had completed a wide arc through the woods, using the yellow glow of the lodge as a guide. It was like a lighthouse in a sea of darkness. Unless they had badly miscalculated, they were now directly behind the building. The most nerve-wracking part of the journey had been crossing the driveway, the packed gravel road that led down to the front gate. One-by-one they'd darted across the open ground between the forest at each edge. Thankfully, no one had decided to go down and check on the gate guard at that exact time.

Now Jason led the way as they turned toward the building.

A few minutes later, Jason edged around the massive trunk of a red cedar and looked down at Hemlock Run. Danny edged up beside him on his right. Jimmy slipped around the other side of the tree.

They were on a slight rise that put them about five feet above the floor of the lodge and about twenty-five yards away. The height difference put Jason in a perfect position to look directly through the windows, one on either side of a closed wooden door. And there was plenty to see.

Three older men—somewhere in their sixties, he guessed—sat in a cluster of armchairs. They wore sport shirts and jeans, seemed completely relaxed, laughing often, glasses of amber liquid in their hands. Jason guessed they were either drunk or well on their way.

More telling were the young women with them. They sat on the men's laps, or on the arms of their chairs. They wore only the flimsiest of lingerie. One was topless.

"Jesus," Jimmy murmured off to Jason's left. "Looks like one hell of a party."

Jason was snapping photos as quick as he could.

"How old are those girls?" Danny asked. She was watching through her binoculars, seeing the same thing Jason was.

"I don't know," he said. He was horrible as guessing women's ages. "But they're not very old."

One of the men reached up and caressed the topless girl's bare breasts, first one, then the other. It looked like he was testing fruit for ripeness.

"Bullshit, 'they're not very old,'" Danny insisted. "They're teenagers. They're just teenagers."

Jason caught his breath. One of the men, the one farthest to the right, had turned Jason's direction and Jason recognized him just before the man nuzzled the neck of the girl on his lap. He was Anthony Mason, the Democratic leader of the State Assembly.

"What the hell?" Jimmy asked. "The guy is old enough to be her grandpa."

"I don't think any of the women are here because this is how they wanted to spend their weekend," Jason told him. "Those guys are all politicians from Olympia. They see this as one of the perks of the job."

"They're whores?"

"Something like that." Though he doubted the Bartons actually paid them. The Bartons seemed to consider women their playthings by birthright.

Jason continued to snap photos, trying to get as many images as he possibly could. In the other window, he found the current Sheriff of Dunham County, leaning back on a sofa, his arms spread along the top. A blond head bobbed over his lap.

Danny was muttering beside him. It took a moment for him to figure out what she was saying. She was repeating "You motherfuckers," over and over.

♦

A door opened in a smaller building to their right, spilling more yellow light into the night. Instinctively, Jason drew back into the tree line. Danny did the same beside him.

"I don't give a damn. Get your ass moving." The voice was male and faintly familiar to Jason.

Jason turned his camera to the new subject and started shooting. A tall, muscular man was escorting a much smaller woman toward the main house. She wore an extremely short and form-fitting black dress.

Because of the darkness Jason could not make out either face. But he could clearly see that her arms were crossed over her breasts.

He continued to shoot photos.

"Move it." The man pushed her with a hand between her shoulder blades. The woman rocked forward, stepping rapidly a few feet before she could regain her balance.

Danny made a frustrated sound beside him. He imagined she was using all her self-control to keep from intervening. He glanced over to make sure her weapon wasn't out of its holster.

The couple opened the wooden door and yellow light spilled out over them.

"Jesus," he said. He quickly snapped more photos before the couple disappeared inside.

"What?"

"That was Helen Miller," he said.

Danny lowered her binoculars and turned to him. "You're kidding."

He shook his head. "Nope, and the man pushing her around was Travis Wilcox."

♦

"I want to put a bullet in the head of every man in there."

Jason felt much the same and he wasn't a woman. The Bartons had targeted every person in the county with working ovaries, solely because they had ovaries. That was bad enough, but the fact that the victims couldn't do anything to stop the attacks or get justice against the attackers made it even worse.

However, good as it might feel, fantasies of revenge were useless right now.

Jason and the others had retreated back into the safety of the woods to figure out what they should do next. The facts on the ground had changed. The original idea was to come here, gather the evidence they could, and get away safely to do their real damage later.

Now Helen was here and they knew it. They couldn't just leave without her. Could they?

"She's probably been here the entire time she's been missing," Jason told the others. "Travis was probably told to hold her here for some reason. Maybe she got cold feet, or something."

"Maybe she doesn't enjoy being forced into prostitution," Danny said.

He nodded. Or that.

"Do you think all the girls are forced?" Jimmy asked. "Into doing that?"

"Yeah." Danny said. "I do."

"Think about it," Jason told him. "You're a dirty cop. You pull over some sixteen, seventeen year old girl, still in high school. You make a show of finding some meth, or a gun in their car. Just like that, their future is destroyed. Unless they agree to do something for you."

Jimmy shook his head. "Bastards."

"Yeah, we all agree they're bastards," Jason told them. "The question is what do we do about it? Right now? Do we try to get out of here and get help? Or do we somehow try to intervene?"

"There's only three of us." Jimmy said quietly. "And a lot of them."

Jason had to agree. "And there are probably lots of weapons around. At least three of them, counting the guard at the gate are with the sheriff's department and it's a hunting lodge. We have to assume we'll be outnumbered and outgunned."

Danny made a frustrated sound. "We've got to do something."

"I know."

"It would take a SWAT team to take down everyone in there," Jimmy told them. "Even if we didn't get shot to hell, most of those bastards would scatter and get away. Or they'd take the girls hostage. Then what?"

Even Danny had to admit he made sense.

"Much as I hate to admit it," Jason said. "Our best bet may be our original plan."

"Leave them there?"

"For now," he said. "We get as much evidence as we can and hand it over to someone who can actually do something about it."

"Such as?" Danny asked. "We both know the D.A. in Dunham County won't do anything and no one else has jurisdiction."

"Who do you know at the FBI?"

It was too dark to see her frown, but he could feel it. "I know a couple of agents. But why would the Feds intervene? It isn't their jurisdiction either."

"But it is their jurisdiction. This lodge is on Kwamamish land," Jason told them. "It's leased, but legally it's still Reservation land, which means it falls under Federal jurisdiction."

Thank you, Gerry Peterson.

♦

They also decided they needed to get as many photos as possible. If nothing else, Jason wanted to make sure he had documentary evidence of every man who participated in the sexual festivities, as well as every young woman who was being victimized. He wanted to be able to identify everyone involved. The camera was the best tool for that.

Jason returned to his post beside the cedar tree and continued to take photographs of the activity in the lodge. Danny sat with him for a little while, but finally could no longer watch what was going on.

"It makes me sick to my stomach."

Jason couldn't blame her. As the night wore on, the men in the lodge lost whatever inhibitions they may have had and were now having a full-fledged orgy. It was a sickening sight. He hoped it would generate the same response with Danny's FBI friends, not to mention the good voters of the State of Washington.

♦

Whether it was the alcohol—because a lot of alcohol had been consumed—or the advanced ages of all the men participating, the party began to die down earlier than Jason would have imagined. One-by-one, the men either passed out where they sat, or grabbed the nearest girl and staggered off toward the interior of the house. Jason assumed the bedrooms were back there.

Before long, no one was moving at all in the main room, though it remained lit up as bright as ever. It looked like the aftermath of a frat party.

Jason lowered his camera and crawled back to where the others waited under a giant hemlock probably older than all of them put together.

“The party seems to be over.”

“Good.” Danny was visibly trembling.

“You okay?”

She nodded. “Just getting cold.”

“I think we’ve got just about everything we’re going to get,” he told them. “I want to get a couple of shots of the party favors.”

He had seen what looked like drug use a few times. He would truly love to get some photos of drugs or paraphernalia to add to his collection.

“Why don’t you guys start back?” he suggested. “I’ll get a couple more pictures and be right behind you.”

Jason returned to his spot. Unfortunately, though his spot had been great for shooting the partiers, it wasn’t as good for what he wanted now. The angle was wrong. He couldn’t see the tops of the tables. That would be where any leftover drug evidence would be laying.

He needed to get closer.

Jason watched for another few minutes, but nothing moved. It looked like everyone was asleep, or otherwise occupied.

He thought he should be able to get down to the window, take some quick photos and get away without anyone being the wiser.

Jason crept down the slope until he was next to the building, right beside the window. From where he stood, he could hear nothing from within the building. Nothing at all. Somewhere in the woods an owl hooted. Another answered.

He ducked his head to the corner of the window. Just a quick peek. Nothing alarming stood out in the room. It was empty. Even the drunk passed out across the love seat was no longer there, somehow making it back to his bedroom.

Jason told himself all he needed was a handful of quick shots of the furniture groupings, maybe three or four photos. Then he would get out of here.

He raised the camera and stepped out in front of the window.

Just as he suspected, a plastic bag of marijuana and a glass pipe lay on the end table between two armchairs, along with a half-empty bottle of Jim Beam and a pair of pink panties. An empty liquor bottle lay on the floor.

He snapped a couple of shots of the end table, then switched to the glass coffee table in front of the sofa across the room. A bag of white powder lay on the table top along with what could have been a residue. Cocaine, would be his guess. These guys were too rich and too smart to be using meth or heroin, but all sorts of smart people got sucked into using coke. In some circles, you weren't considered successful until you developed a coke habit.

He snapped several more photos of the package on the coffee table.

Movement caught his eye.

A man about Jason's age stepped around a corner, wearing only boxers and a white tee shirt. He scanned the room with a disgusted expression and reached for the light switch. He looked up and their eyes locked.

♦♦♦♦♦

Scott Barton woke and lay in bed for a moment, orienting himself. Judging by the dead silence in the rest of the house, he guessed the party had burned itself out. All those tough-as-nails politicians—the leaders of the State—were actually just horny old men who couldn't hold their liquor. Some things never changed.

The knowledge that the party was over, made the bright glow seeping under his bedroom door even more annoying. Some people had no sense of courtesy or waste. When you were the last person to leave a room, you turned off the lights. Most annoying of all, was the knowledge that he'd never be able to go back to sleep while those lights were still on. It was unfinished business and he simply couldn't ignore that.

"I swear," he sat up on the edge of the bed. "It's like I'm babysitting four-year-olds."

The young woman asleep beside him groaned and mumbled something.

"Forget it. Go back to sleep."

Helen already had. Alcohol and physical exertion made sleep easier.

Scott stood, walked out of the bedroom and out to the lodge's great room, shielding his eyes against the bright light. He groaned as he took in the mess the guests had left behind. No, he wasn't babysitting four-year-olds; he was babysitting fraternity boys. Overgrown fraternity boys. The mess would be dealt with tomorrow.

As he reached for the light switch, something drew his eyes to the window.

A man stood there, a camera in his hands.

Jason didn't run, he fled. He didn't even consider the tree line he'd come from. He ran as fast as he could straight down the length of the lodge, about five feet from the wall. It was instinct and adrenaline. Besides, there was a better chance there of not running headlong into a tree trunk or being clotheslined by an unseen branch.

He wasn't even zig-zagging. He was in a headlong sprint aimed in the general direction of the forest beyond the end of the building, his camera crashing into his chest in perfect time with his footsteps.

Though he kept expecting the blow of a bullet between his shoulder blades, it never came. He never heard a gunshot. He never even heard a shout. Just his footsteps pounding on the ground and the raspy sound of his breathing.

Finally, after what seemed forever—but was probably only a few seconds—he crashed through the edge of the forest and stopped himself by hooking a passing trunk. His momentum spun him around to face the lodge again. Sweat poured down his face; his thighs and lungs burned; his breath moving in pants. Jason crouched on his knees below the branches and waited.

He was surprised no one had given chase, but then again, the guy hadn't been dressed either.

There was no doubt Jason had been discovered, but he had a couple of minutes.

Jason quickly pulled the memory card from his camera and stashed it inside the ankle band of his right sock. It wouldn't stand up to a serious search, but if someone just took the camera, he would be okay. That done, he returned the camera and lens to the padded case. Safer for the camera and a hell of a lot more comfortable should he need to run again.

The next question was: where were Danny and Jimmy?

Scott Barton didn't chase after the guy with the camera. He wasn't dressed and he wasn't really the chasing type. He hired people to do the chasing for him.

As soon as the man, who he had the sinking suspicion was the reporter Reynolds, fled, Scott picked up the nearest house phone and dialed the gate. It rang twice before the deputy answered.

"Wake up you worthless piece of crap! There's an intruder on the property! He had to walk right by you!" He interrupted as the deputy began his excuses. "Sit tight and wait for orders from Wilcox. Don't let anyone off the property!"

He disconnected and dialed the number of one of the bedrooms, praying the musclebound idiot wasn't too drunk to be useful.

"Yeah?"

He sounded fine, sleepy maybe.

"This is Scott. I just saw someone with a camera looking in one of the windows."

"Crap."

"Yeah. Take care of it. The idiot at the gate is waiting for orders."

"Okay."

Scott disconnected again and set about deciding what the next step needed to be.

He turned and walked back to his room to get dressed.

Jason crouched in the shelter of a massive hemlock trunk and carefully watched the area. The fact that no search party had immediately come after him was reassuring. Maybe the guy in the boxers hadn't seen him. Looking through a window from a bright room into darkness usually made windows act like mirrors.

But Jason hadn't been mistaken about the eye contact. There was no mistaking eye contact. The guy had seen him.

Right now though, his biggest worry was about Danny and Jimmy. He had no idea where they were, whether they knew the Bartons were on to them, and no way to contact them other than face to face.

Worse, the last thing he'd told them was that he would follow right behind them, just as soon as he finished the photos. If he didn't show up, would they head back to look for him? Would they walk right into a search party?

He didn't know what to do.

A door thudded closed somewhere in the lodge. A few seconds later, what sounded like a motorcycle engine started up.

Jason wondered what that was all about.

He got his answer a few seconds later when two headlights switched on and swung in his direction. Jason ducked behind the tree trunk and hid there until the lights moved on. He looked out just as someone on a four-wheeled ATV roared by, heading toward the gate.

So someone *was* looking for him. He wasn't sure whether that was a good thing or not.

Where were Danny and Jimmy? Were they holed up somewhere waiting for him? Or were they trying to get away themselves, hoping to meet up somewhere along the way? If it was the latter, where would they wait?

The most obvious answer to that question was at the base of the dam, where the deer trail ended. It was the route they'd used to get in. It was the logical route out. And it was the best place to meet up if they became separated.

He turned that direction and began picking his way through the dark undergrowth.

Twenty-eight

Scott Barton emerged from his bedroom fully dressed and carrying both his briefcase and overnight bag. As he was gathering his things, he'd done what he did best. He made a decision. The fact that he heard no raised voices, no sounds of scuffles, or gunshots only reinforced his decision. The idiot deputies were not going to find the camera man. They probably had trouble finding their own butts with toilet paper.

He set his bags on the floor, found the house phone, and dialed the front gate. "Anything?"

"No," the deputy said. "We haven't seen anything moving since you called, not even a deer."

It figured. He was getting a bad feeling about this.

"Is Wilcox there?"

"He just left on the ATV to look around over by the dam."

Scott hung up.

Wilcox was checking up toward the dam. That was the most sensible statement he'd heard so far. As he remembered it, the camera guy had run off in that general direction. He had assumed it was to head back down the drive, but he could have just as easily turned to go to the dam.

Why he would do that was beyond him, but people sometimes thought in strange ways.

Scott turned and walked to the sliding glass door, opened it, and stepped out onto the flagstone terrace.

From here, the dam was just a short walk along the edge of the lake.

As if mirroring his thoughts, the headlights of the ATV swept along the tree line beyond the building and continued over to the edge of the dam. It stopped there and the engine switched off. A figure climbed off the vehicle and began examining the woods with the beam of a flashlight.

Scott walked over. “Wilcox!”

The deputy stood just within the tree line, shining the flash farther into the shadowy forest. He turned at the sound of his name.

“Anything?”

“Naw, not yet. He could be ten feet out there and we wouldn’t see him,” Wilcox said. “Not if he stays down.”

Scott sighed. Wilcox had a valid point. The woods around the lodge were impenetrable, the definition of wilderness. He hated it.

“If you don’t find him in five minutes, set up a roadblock down by the ‘Y.’ It’s still the only road out if here. I doubt he hiked all the way from Bosque.”

Wilcox told him he would.

“And take that idiot at the gate to help you.”

Jason decided the hardest thing he’d ever tried to do was to hurry through a forest in the dark and do it quietly. After a few yards, he determined it was impossible. He could go fast, or could move safely and quietly. If he tried to keep up his pace, he would sound like an elephant crashing through the brush. And he would either knock himself cold against a tree trunk, or take a false step and break an ankle.

He had just decided to slow down and was leaning against another tree trunk, trying again to catch his breath, when the sound of the ATV grew from the direction of the gate. He dropped to his knees just as the headlights flashed across the lodge, then turned toward the dam.

The ATV stopped just a few feet up the bank from him. The engine switched off.

Jason laid flat on the carpet of dead needles.

A figure climbed off the ATV and switched on a flash. He began playing the light across the vegetation over Jason's head.

Jason flattened against the ground. He didn't know what else to do. If he tried to run, the man with the flashlight would certainly hear him. Yet he didn't want to show up in the flash's light. All he could think of was to try and make himself as small as possible. Other than that, it would be a matter of luck.

The man with the flash took a couple of steps farther into the trees, a couple of steps closer to Jason.

Jason closed his eyes. It was all he could do.

"Wilcox!" a new voice called. "Find anything?"

"Naw." Wilcox turned to face the second man, standing up by the ATV. "He could be ten feet away out here and I wouldn't see him. Not if he stays down."

The second voice seemed to weigh his words carefully.

"If you don't find anything in five minutes," the second man said, "set up a roadblock down by the 'Y.' It's still the only road in and out of here."

Wilcox said he would.

The second man walked away.

Wilcox played the flash over the forest again a few more times, but it felt token. The deputy turned, walked back to the ATV, started it up and drove off the way he'd come.

Jason released his breath, surprised he'd been holding it.

♦

Jason waited another ten minutes before he dared to move. It was fear, he readily admitted. He was afraid. He was afraid Wilcox would double back, or that the entire conversation with the other man had been some convoluted ruse to get him overconfident. He feared that as soon as he took a few steps, the flashlight would come back on and he'd be standing there like a spot-lit deer.

But that was fear speaking, and often, left to its own devices, fear was paralyzing.

He might have stayed right there, safely lying on the ground until daylight were it not for the thought of Danny and Jimmy out there somewhere, either waiting for him to show up, or actively looking for him.

That tipped the balance.

Jason was able to force himself to his knees beside the tree, then fully up to his feet. Nothing happened. He took a few tentative steps. There were no shouts, no blazing spotlight to pin him. Slowly, deliberately, he began to move toward the dam. Now he concentrated more on moving quietly than quickly. The searchers could come back at any time. If they did, he didn't want to make their job any easier.

He still had heard and seen nothing of Danny and Jimmy. They could be anywhere. All he could do was get himself to the dam and hope they'd avoided Wilcox on the ATV.

Within a few minutes, he could hear the water rushing over the dam's spillway. He was getting close.

He stepped on a branch and broke it. In the stillness, it sounded like a pistol going off.

Jason froze, mentally cursing his sloppiness.

The stillness only seemed to grow deeper. Only the rushing of the water over the dam broke the quiet. There seemed to be no reaction to his mistake.

Jason took a few more steps. Still no reaction, no pursuit.

He edged around a large cedar trunk, feet sinking into the spongy needle debris on the floor. A kind of whicker sound caught his attention just before he was struck across the face.

Jason's vision went red, then black, and he fell.

Scott Barton loaded his overnight bag into the trunk of his Mercedes, parked behind the lodge, tossed his briefcase into the passenger seat and climbed behind the wheel. He was not panicked. Panic was counter-productive. It was a fight-or-flight response mechanism and forced your mind into simplified, black and white, choices. Without panic, the reasonable mind understood there were always a multitude of options. There were always shades of gray.

He started his car, glanced to see that all the gauges were reading "normal," then backed out around the lodge, shifted gears and headed down the road toward the gate.

Scott wasn't worried about what the guy with the camera had photographed, not personally. He always made a point during these weekends of making the necessary introductions, then leaving. He was a facilitator, not a participant. Granted, he never slept alone, but that was different. Helen was different, not like the other whores around here, and it was always just them, in private. Scott was sure his face was not included in any compromising photographs.

The biggest threat to him, personally, was the all-too-real factor of guilt by association. If the cameraman had the proper connections, every one of the men currently sleeping off their drunks in the lodge was about to find himself in the center of a public nightmare. Many would end up divorced from their wives. Most, if not all of them, would be forced to resign their elected office, or face recall. They certainly could kiss any chance of re-election goodbye.

Scott's first priority right now was to establish as much distance as possible between himself and those men. That meant leaving, and leaving right now.

He could be back in Olympia before day break. With the right pressure, he could convince one or two women to swear publicly he had been there all weekend.

If it came to that.

His headlights showed the gate coming up quickly. It was closed, but unmanned.

Good, he thought, they were taking his suggestion and had set up a roadblock farther down the road.

He pushed the button on a remote and waited for the gate to roll out of the way, then eased the car through.

If either of the deputies at the roadblock asked what he was doing, he had a reason already laid out. He was heading for the office to begin damage control. Just in case the cameraman escaped.

Scott smiled to himself at the idea of putting the blame back on the deputies. It's all on you, boys. You redneck, emotionally-stunted, idiots.

♦♦♦♦♦

Jason didn't think he'd ever felt such pain, not even when he'd been shot last fall. This was a whole new level. Whoever had hit him had managed to not only hurt his nose, but both his eyes as well. He'd immediately collapsed to the forest floor, his vision gone to an opaque, angry red, while his nose screamed and both eyes burned like they were melting. He was absolutely helpless.

A part of him heard the sound of someone beside him, but he didn't care. They could put a bullet in his brain and he wouldn't fight. He couldn't. All he wanted was the pain to stop.

Another part of his brain wondered whether that is what had happened. Had he been shot in the face? He hadn't heard the discharge, but it seemed he'd read somewhere that you never hear the shot that hit you. When he'd been shot in Port Salish last year, he hadn't known it until Lisa had pointed it out to him. Oh, he'd known something was wrong with his arm; he just hadn't known the problem had been caused by a bullet.

"Jesus! It's Jason!" Someone said nearby.

Somebody else was gathering him in their arms.

Naturally, his instinct was to fight.

"Jason! It's me, Danny," she said. "Are you okay? We thought you were a sheriff's guy, following us."

"Sorry dude," Jimmy said. "I booby-trapped you."

Jason relaxed a little. "My eyes. I can't see."

His entire face seemed to be wet. He couldn't tell whether the moisture was blood, tears, or what it was. He wasn't sure he wanted to know.

"Come on," Danny tried to lift him to his feet. "Let's get him to the dam. We need to get him some cold water."

With Danny and Jimmy on either side, they managed to stumble to the dam. The sound of the falling water was almost loud enough now to drown out their voices. It had begun to rain again too. Jason could feel scattered drops hitting his head and shoulders.

His friends settled him on to what felt like an old fallen log. It had the consistency of a boulder-sized sponge.

"Man, I'm so sorry," Jimmy said again. "I didn't know it was you. We didn't know where you were."

"I'm going to get some water from the creek," Danny said and hurried away.

Jason groaned. "What did you hit me with?"

"A snap back," Jimmy said. "A springy branch I bent around the tree. When you were close, I let it go."

"Effective," Jason told him.

"Old Indian trick."

Danny returned and had him lay sideways on the fallen log while she poured cold water over his eyes. "Open your eyes a little," she told him. "Let it wash away any garbage. The cold will help keep any swelling down too."

Jason took her word for it.

And after the initial shock of the cold water, it did sooth the burning.

When the water was gone, she had him sit up and gently dried his face. "How does it feel?"

"Better," he told her. And his eyes did feel a little better. A little.

Then the most important question of the day. "How's your vision?"

He carefully opened his eyes. The world around him was a mix of varying grays and blacks. It might have been a little blurry—it was too dark to tell—and his eyes still burned, but he could see.

He told them.

The tension physically drained from the others.

♦

While Jason recovered from Jimmy's low tech booby trap, they caught each other up on all that had happened since they'd split up. Primarily, it was Jason.

He told them about taking the damning photos of the drugs and then being spotted by the man in boxers through the window, causing his headlong flight toward the tree line. Danny told him they'd heard someone running, just the footfalls, but they'd had no idea what was going on. That was why they hadn't waited or gone back for him when he hadn't shown up.

"But it was weird," she said. "There was no shouting and it sounded like just one person running."

"It was. Just me."

"He didn't chase you?" she asked.

"No. No one did. Of course, I didn't know that until I had stopped in the trees."

"What about the guy on the ATV?" Jimmy asked. "He was looking for something."

"Wilcox."

"It was Wilcox?" Danny started.

"Almost positive. I think the guy who saw me got Wilcox out of bed to search, along with the guard down at the gate."

"And now they're blocking the road?" Jimmy asked.

"That's what the guy told Wilcox to do just before they left."

"Oh, hell," Jimmy said.

"Please tell me there's another road out of here," Danny asked.

"Sure," Jimmy said. "There are all sorts of old, overgrown logging roads out here."

Danny sighed.

"Trouble is, even the Jeep won't survive most of them. We'd have to walk."

No one said anything.

"Does anybody have any ideas?" she finally asked.

Silence.

Jason blinked his eyes quickly, trying to get his vision to return to normal. "I think we figure that out when we get to the Jeep and see what the situation looks like."

He pushed himself to his feet.

"You sure you can do this?" Jimmy asked.

What choice did he have?

"I'll just follow you guys."

♦♦♦♦♦

Travis Wilcox was bored. There was absolutely nothing he hated more than guard duty. It meant sitting in the front seat of a squad car that smelled of corn chips watching nothing come down the road from the lodge while Metcalf dozed beside him. And doing it for hours. He'd already woken the other deputy twice in the hour since Scott Barton had passed through.

Scott Barton was a whole different story, the pansy-ass. "I'm headed to the office to start damage control," he'd told them.

Damage control, my ass, Wilcox thought. The bastard was getting out of Dodge to protect his own butt and that was all. He had as much honor and loyalty as a trout. Well, Travis was cut from a different material, real Barton material. His last name might be Wilcox, but he was a Barton through and through.

Metcalf started snoring beside him.

"Christ, Metcalf." He elbowed the other deputy in the ribs.

Metcalf jumped, looked around wildly. "You see something?"

"No, I didn't see nothing," he told him. "But I 'm getting tired of babysitting your sorry ass."

Metcalf groaned. "I can't help it. There isn't even radio to listen to out here."

"You're getting paid good money for being out here. The least you could do is stay awake. If that guy gets by us, the gravy train will come to a quick end."

"I know. I know. Maybe some fresh air will wake me up."

"Good idea. I could use some myself."

Travis climbed out and closed the passenger door behind him, just seconds after Metcalf had done the same on the driver's side. The night was as dark as the inside of a stomach. Dawn was still a couple of hours away and the overcast spit a constant drizzle down through the darkness to make everything thoroughly miserable.

Travis wondered whether the guy with the camera was sitting somewhere out in the woods right now, soaking wet, just waiting to get away. Or had the guy planned for this whole outing? Did he have a tent and a warm sleeping bag? Was he sleeping even now, ready to make his escape come daylight, long after the excitement and search had died down?

Scott had told them to maintain the roadblock until daylight, but Travis was having his doubts.

"I'm going to walk down a ways," Metcalf said. "See what's going on."

"Knock yourself out."

"Fuck off, Wilcox."

Travis laughed. Metcalf could walk until his feet fell off and there still would be nothing going on. They were wasting their time.

Metcalf pulled the flash from his equipment belt and began strolling across the gravel, playing the flash over the brush and trees beside him as he walked.

"Let me know if you find Bigfoot."

"Ha, ha."

♦♦♦♦♦

Even feeling their way through the rain-dripping forest along a barely visible deer trail, the trip back to the car seemed to pass quicker than the trip to the lodge. Someday, when things were a bit more relaxed, Jason thought he'd need to do a story on that. A human interest story. Why does the trip out seem to take so much longer than the trip back? No matter what the circumstances.

Jason had followed Danny the entire way, much of the time by keeping one hand on her shoulder. His vision was better, but still wasn't good. Of most concern, his eyes felt swollen.

He hadn't dared touch them since they'd left the dam.

It seemed like they'd only been walking an hour or so when Jimmy stopped them and crouched down. "This is where we leave the trail."

Jason saw Danny nod ahead of him.

"The car is about a hundred, maybe a hundred-fifty, yards away," Jimmy continued. "We need to decide what we're going to do about the road block."

"We have to be ready in case they have already discovered the car," Danny added. "We didn't hide it."

No, they hadn't. They'd just pulled far enough off the gravel road to keep it from the casual passerby. If someone were actually looking, they could find it fairly quickly.

"Suggestions anyone?"

"Well, first, we need to find out whether the car is safe, or not," Danny offered.

"She's right," Jason said. "One step at a time. We need to assume they've found the car and are using it to bait us, until we find otherwise."

"So we approach it carefully and quietly. Expect a trap until there isn't one," Danny said. She turned to Jimmy, then Jason. "Are you willing to use your gun to defend yourself?"

"Against those bastards?" Jimmy said. "Just try me."

She turned to Jason.

He unzipped the fanny pack and pulled out the pistol. "They're not going to get their hands on you. Wilcox definitely isn't. Not while I'm breathing."

"Can you see well enough to shoot?"

"Let's hope we don't have to find out."

♦♦♦♦♦

"Hey!" Metcalf yelled. His right hand went for his holster, scrambling to get his gun out. "Wilcox! I saw someone."

Wilcox drew his own Glock from its holster and strode up to where Metcalf stood. The other deputy trained his sidearm and flash on the opening where an overgrown track left the road and disappeared into the scrub.

"What?" Wilcox asked.

"I saw something," Metcalf said. His hands were trembling, causing the flash to jump all over the place. "A man. I saw his face, like he was peeking around the bush to see where we were."

"You sure?"

"What?" Metcalf glanced at him. "Of course I'm sure. It was a white guy, brown hair. As soon as I spotted him, he ducked back behind the bush. It sounded like he was running through the brush."

Metcalf was lazy and a sad excuse for a lawman, but he wasn't stupid and he wasn't prone to seeing things. And what he described is exactly how Wilcox would expect the cameraman to act. He would want to scope out the roadblock to see what he was up against. How many deputies there were, how they were armed. He would want to know what he needed to do next.

"Listen," he told Metcalf. "We're going to end this right now, okay?"

"Good by me."

"We go in side-by-side, behind our flashes. He's probably got his car stashed back there. We find it. We find him."

"Right."

"One more thing," Wilcox said. "The only friendlies out here are me and you. You see anyone else—anyone—you take them down. Got it?"

"Got it." Metcalf switched off his weapon's safety.

"Let's go. One step at a time." Wilcox took a step into the track on the right side, his Glock held up in front of him, the flash held up by his left ear, just like they trained in the academy. Five feet to his left, Metcalf moved in a similar stance. Together, they followed the twin grooves in the overgrown grass.

"Something's been through here recently," Metcalf said.

"Shut up."

It was true though. Something had gone through here. Much of the grass had been pushed over by something big and heavy and hadn't had enough time to straighten out yet. But he didn't want their voices to give the cameraman notice they were coming.

In the quiet, voices carried forever.

They advanced a few more careful steps, with nothing to show for it but soaked trouser cuffs and cold feet. All the lights showed were thigh-tall grass and overgrown shrubs at the edge of thicker forest. Someone could be hiding five feet away and be all but invisible.

Something flashed red in the darkness ahead of them.

"You see that?" Metcalf hissed.

"I see it."

They were the tail lights of a late model SUV.

Had someone just hit the brakes?

"Easy," Wilcox said as he advanced slowly, methodically, his flash sweeping between the trees to either side of the car. The car itself appeared to be empty and wasn't running. The flash of red had been the lens' reflectors, not the tail lights themselves.

The deputies stopped about five feet behind the car. There had been no movement anywhere around them and no sound of someone fleeing through the brush. The cameraman had gone to ground.

"It will be better for you if you give yourself up," Wilcox said into the darkness. "If we have to root you out, it might not be in one piece."

"More deputies are on their way," Metcalf added. "There's no way out. Might as well surrender peacefully."

"Come out with your hands up where we can see them."

They advanced another step. There was still no sound or movement ahead. The car was cold and dead, moisture beading up on its surfaces.

"I'm running out of patience," Wilcox said.

"Okay, okay," a male voice drifted out of the darkness ahead of them. "I'm not armed. Don't shoot me."

Wilcox directed his flash toward the voice, somewhere on the other side of the car, but he could see nothing. Metcalf was having the same trouble, judging by the way his flash kept sliding side to side.

"Step forward into the light where we can see you. Hands up by your head."

"Okay. Don't shoot."

Wilcox took another step forward, his eye line right over the sights of his pistol. He had no intention of letting this bastard go anywhere. He just needed him to step into the light. Just one step.

Something cold and hard thudded against the base of his skull.

"Just give me an excuse," someone hissed. "I'll blow your brains out right now."

◆◆◆◆◆

The trap worked just like Jimmy said it would.

"It's human nature," he told them. "They're looking for a single white guy. When they see a single white guy, it won't even occur to them that he might not be alone."

Jason was the decoy, because he was precisely the guy the deputies were looking for. While Danny and Jimmy hid themselves in the shrubs and trees to either side of Danny's Jeep, Jason walked down to the gravel road to show himself to his pursuers.

It had been just a bit nerve-wracking. What if they immediately shot him?

Then it became frustrating, because he couldn't get their attention. He poked his head around the shrub right beside the track entrance, but nothing happened. The deputies seemed to be sitting in their car. He couldn't tell whether they were even awake.

He even took a few steps out into the road, praying the entire time he would survive, with no reaction from the deputies.

Just as he was beginning to wonder whether they needed to come up with another plan, the doors to the squad car opened and the deputies climbed out. From there, it was just a matter of showing his face.

"Hey!" a deputy had yelled.

But Jason had already been hurrying back, past his friends lying in wait, past the car, and into the darkness beyond. He stepped into the forest and waited.

Any doubts that the deputies had taken his bait were dispelled by the flashlights advancing steadily toward him. As soon as the deputies had progressed far enough, Danny and Jimmy had sprung the trap.

It had been flawless. A good ambush, executed perfectly.

Jason heard Danny's voice and saw the flashlights move off target.

"Everything good, guys?" he asked.

"Good for us," Jimmy said. "These guys, not so much."

He hurried past the car to where the four people stood as if frozen. Danny and Jimmy held their pistols to the heads of the deputies. The deputies stood with their arms extended, still holding their pistols and flashlights. They were probably afraid to move a muscle and with good reason.

Jason walked up to Wilcox and took hold of the pistol. "I'll take this."

Wilcox made only token resistance. He didn't resist at all when Jason took his flashlight.

Jason stepped over beside Danny. "You okay?"

"I haven't killed him yet," she said. "Have I?"

No she hadn't. Not yet, anyway. But the muzzle of her pistol had never strayed from the base of Wilcox's skull.

She handed something to Jason with her left hand. Handcuffs. "Do the honors?"

"Hands behind your back," he told Wilcox. "You know how this works."

Wilcox didn't move. It was like he was calculating his odds of overpowering them without getting his head blown off. Jason was afraid he might actually have enough of a hyper-opinion of himself to try something.

Jason needed to stop that quickly.

"My friend here has a particular hatred for guys who abuse women," he told Wilcox. "When she says she hasn't killed you *yet*, I'd take that seriously. All she needs is an excuse."

Wilcox seemed to deflate a little and moved his hands to the small of his back. "You're dead. All three of you are dead."

"Stop. You're scaring me." Jason snapped the handcuffs around his wrists and turned Wilcox around to face him.

"Let me," Danny said and stepped up to Wilcox. "This is for Helen and all the others."

She drove her knee into Wilcox's groin. He made a strangled groan deep in his throat. His knees folded and he went down.

"Not such a big man now, huh?"

Twenty-nine

They disarmed the second deputy and handcuffed him, just like they had Wilcox, but didn't hurt him. They didn't have to. Deputy Metcalf was quite eager to cooperate. Or maybe he was eager to avoid ending up a crumpled ball amid the over grown grass. Jason confiscated the deputies' weapons, cell phones, and their portable radios.

"These could come in handy," he told Danny, showing her the radios.

She shrugged. "Until they figure out we have them."

Once Wilcox was able to stand on his own again, Danny and Jason marched them back down the track and to their squad car, while Jimmy followed in her Jeep.

At the squad car, Jason opened the car's back door. "Get inside."

Metcalf immediately climbed in the back, scooted across to the far door.

Wilcox hesitated outside. "Those doors don't open from the inside. We'll be trapped in there."

"Consider it a favor. We could handcuff you to a tree. At least here you'll be warm and dry."

Wilcox locked eyes with Jason. "I'm going to enjoy watching you beg for your life. Maybe I'll make you watch your lady friend beg first."

"Get in the car." Jason held his stare. "While you still can."

Wilcox smirked, but slid into the back seat next to Metcalf.

Jason slammed the door closed before he did something he might regret later.

Jimmy jumped behind the wheel of the cruiser and pulled it over to the side of the road, out of the way. He then shut the engine off and threw the keys as far as he could into the woods. No one would ever find them.

Jimmy got into the passenger seat of the Jeep, beside Danny at the wheel; Jason climbed in the back and pulled his laptop out of its case. He dug the memory card out of his sock and waited for the computer to boot up.

He needed to start putting the evidence together.

♦♦♦♦♦

"So what now?" Metcalf said.

"I don't know. Maybe we could take a nap."

"Fuck you, Wilcox. I was just asking."

Wilcox took a moment to try and control the rage burning inside. He wanted to save that rage for the next time he met Reynolds and his bitch of a girlfriend. He would put it to good use then.

Just the thought caused him to break into a smile.

"Wait until we see someone leaving the lodge," he told Metcalf. "We can signal them."

The sun was just beginning to lighten the skies to the east.

♦♦♦♦♦

Jason began downloading the photos from the camera as soon as his laptop finished booting up. There were a lot of photos. He had taken multiple shots of every subject in keeping with the old photographers' rule that the more shots you had the better the chances that one will be usable. But it meant he was copying a lot of data. It would take some time and a sizeable chunk of what little battery power his laptop had left.

"How long before somebody finds those guys?" Danny asked.

Jason looked up from the computer and out the window. He was sitting in the back seat directly behind Jimmy, the laptop in his lap. Outside, it was just becoming full light—gray, rainy, depressing—but daylight nonetheless.

"I'd expect the partygoers to start leaving around mid-morning. That's when someone will see them. Maybe even a bit earlier."

"And when they do," Danny added, "they'll come looking for us."

Jimmy glanced over at her. "You think they know who we are?"

"No," Jason said. "But they know this car. It's just a matter of time before they figure out who Danny is."

"And they already know Jason," Danny added.

Jimmy nodded.

"We can't be anywhere near you or your family when they come looking."

The young man turned to look at Jason. "You need to have your eyes looked at. And both of you could use some sleep."

"We'll sleep when we can be sure everybody is as safe as possible," Danny said.

"You should let my mom have a look at those eyes."

Danny turned to look over her shoulder at Jason. "He's right. Your eyes don't look so good."

They didn't feel so good either. Now they itched as well as burned and felt swollen like he was having a major allergic reaction.

His computer beeped a warning. His battery was almost drained. The operating system was giving him a chance to close the program before he lost any unsaved data.

Jason stopped the download from the memory card.

Crap. “Well, I need to charge my laptop battery. I guess stopping for an hour won’t be too dangerous.”

Jimmy smiled into the rear view mirror. “Mom would kill me if I let you leave looking like that.”

♦

Thirty minutes later, Jason lay stretched out on the sofa, an aromatic bundle of soggy herbs cooling slowly over his eyes. Gloria, Jimmy’s mother, had been awake when they’d pulled around to the back of the house to hide the Jeep. After giving her son a gigantic, heartfelt hug, she took a quick look at Jason’s face and ushered him over to the sofa.

“What happened?”

Jimmy briefed her on the booby trap he’d unleashed on Jason. “We thought he was a bad guy.”

“What kind of tree was it?” she asked.

“That important?” Danny asked. She had been tasked with getting the laptop plugged into an outlet so the battery could recharge.

“It could be. Some plants have irritants in their bark and foliage. Some are downright poisonous.”

“Cedar,” Jimmy said. “I think it was a plain old red cedar.”

“Good. Cedar is good.” Gloria said she’d be right back and went away, Jason assumed to gather and prepare ingredients.

“Okay,” Jimmy said now. “What should we be doing?”

“You’ve done enough,” Danny told him. “We don’t want to put you or your family in any more danger.”

“Honestly, she’s right,” Jason told him. “We already owe you. We couldn’t have done this on our own. But I couldn’t live with myself if something happened to you or your mom because of us.”

Danny agreed. “This isn’t your fight.”

“I need to show you something.” Jason heard the young man walk across the room, then back again. “Here. Check this out.”

“What’s going on?” Jason asked, frustrated by his blindness.

"It's a family portrait," Danny told him. "Black and white, showing two little boys and a girl posing on a picnic table, I think. The oldest boy looks about ten. The youngest, the girl, might be four or five."

"It's my mom and her brothers, Joe and Eddie."

Jason frowned. Those names sounded familiar. He just couldn't place where he'd heard them.

Gloria returned and laid a warm wet cloth across the poultice. "You should let this work overnight to be most effective."

Jason ignored her. "Winston. Is your last name Winston?"

"It is."

"So Joe and Eddie, the leaders of the protests against Barton's logging on Kwamamish land, were your uncles?" He touched Gloria. "Your brothers?"

"They were," she said, her voice still soothing, but with a tinge of something else, like sorrow. "They were my brothers. Now relax and concentrate on the herbs, on your eyes healing. As it is, we're going to have to rush it."

He did as he was told.

"So you see, you're wrong about it not being our fight," Jimmy said. "It is our fight. The Bartons killed our family."

♦♦♦♦♦

Senator Morris Barton woke, as usual, within an hour of daylight. He had always been an early riser. It had served him well over the years, but could be annoying as hell. Sometimes you just wanted to sleep in and instead you lay there, wide awake, thinking about all the things you should be doing. Even more annoying was the soft snoring of the sex kitten lying next to him.

After lying there vainly for ten more minutes, he finally resigned himself to the inevitable and got out of bed, slipping into a silk dressing gown and slippers before heading out of his bedroom in search of coffee.

It was almost 7:30, Sunday morning.

He walked out into the great room, where the bulk of last night's party had taken place. It was quiet. A single Indian woman—part of the staff—was softly humming to herself as she straightened up the room.

She looked up and smiled shyly, her arms full of empty liquor bottles. "Good morning, sir."

"Good morning." He made no offer to help with her load of bottles. "Coffee in the kitchen?"

"Yes, sir."

He continued in to the kitchen. Mary was working there, amid the scents of fresh chopped onion, bell pepper, and coffee. She looked up at him. "Ready for breakfast? Denver omelets are today's special."

"I'll wait until our guests are awake."

He found a ceramic mug and filled it from the air pot set up on a sideboard, immediately sipped the hot liquid and replaced what he'd just swallowed. He turned, removed a copy of the morning paper from the stack the staff had brought in this morning. The headline was of yet another terrorist attack in Iraq, the latest episode in the war that would never end.

He was heading back out of the kitchen, reading the article, when Mary stopped him.

"Yes?" He turned back to the Indian woman. He thought she might be the cleaning girl's mother, or something.

"It may be none of my business, but there was no guard on the gate when we came through this morning," she said. "We had to let ourselves in."

He frowned. "You didn't see one anywhere?"

"Well, a car—one of the sheriff's cars, you know—was parked on the side of the road just this side of the 'Y'."

"Okay, thanks."

Morris forgot about the terrorist attack for the moment and went to the house phone in the great room. He quickly dialed the gate.

It rang seven times before he hung up.

The guard may have been taking a leak or something when the cleaning staff came in this morning. But the odds he would be taking another one now weren't good.

He dialed the gate again. This time he waited while it rang five times before he hung up. By that time he had seen the headline and photograph below the fold of the front page. It read: "Journalist Wanted In Dunham Murder Refutes Charges."

"Oh, crap."

♦♦♦♦♦

"What is this stuff?" Jason asked, his eyes shut tightly against the poultice Gloria had placed over his eyes and the bridge of his nose. If felt kind of like warm mud, but had an earthy scent he thought he should recognize.

"Mostly oatmeal," Gloria said. "Some arnica oil, a few other things."

"This will help?" Danny asked.

"It will reduce the swelling and bruising and keep it from getting infected," she said. "To be most effective, we should keep it on until the oatmeal completely dries out, but it's better than nothing. Of course, you should still get him to a doctor as soon as you can."

"We will," Danny told her. The voice of authority.

"I can't just lie here until this stuff dries," Jason said. "I don't have the time. We don't have the time. We still need to finish downloading the photos, decide which ones to use, write some captions, write a note for the Feds."

"Jason." Danny stopped him. "I can download the pictures. I can even start sorting them."

He had to admit she could do those tasks just fine. She might not be able to identify all the politicians involved, but she would certainly be able to sort them all by the main subject.

Jimmy volunteered to help as much as he could. But he would have to go to work at 9:00. Anything else would seem suspicious.

Everyone agreed he needed to go to work.

"It's going to be a long day," Danny said.

"I'm nineteen. It won't be the first time I've worked without any sleep. At least I'm not hungover." A second later: "Sorry, Mom."

"I have another question for you," Jason said blindly into the darkness. "For you and your mother."

"What's that?"

"We're going to send the evidence from the lodge to the FBI. Should we give it to the Tribal Police too? Or maybe the Tribal Government? Do you trust them?"

Neither answered for a couple of moments.

Gloria was the first to react. "It was the Tribal Council that agreed to lease the land that lodge is on to the Bartons. Many people—"

"Most," Jimmy corrected.

"Many people preferred the Bartons not set foot on Kwamamish land again."

"Including you?"

"Including me. The Bartons killed my brothers and sister-in-law. Not only did they walk away without paying legally for their deaths, but now we're going to let them keep their little playground? No, I was not happy."

"Jimmy?"

"What Mom said."

"Why did they do it?" Danny asked. "They had the Bartons in court, in the wrong. Why let them keep that lodge?"

"Money," Gloria said. "They thought they could soak the Bartons with that lease and have a steady source of income. And they thought it was best they let the Bartons keep something, like a peace offering, saving face. That's what they told us anyway."

"But a lot of members weren't happy about it?"

"Nope."

That seemed to rule out the Tribal leadership.

"What about the Tribal Police? Do you trust them?"

"They're mostly okay," Jimmy said. "I mean the individual cops are mostly just guys, know what I mean?"

Jason did.

"They're okay," Gloria agreed with her son. "But the Chief answers to the council." She left it at that.

"So what do you suggest?" he asked. "I don't want to leave the tribe out of this."

No one spoke for a minute. They seemed to be considering the options.

"I think the FBI is the right idea," Gloria said. "You might also send it to the BIA office in Aberdeen. Let the Feds inform the council."

"You're going to write about it in your paper too?" Jimmy asked. "Right?"

"Absolutely. I'll start writing as soon as I get this thing off my eyes."

Gloria patted him on the hand. "It's waited this long, it will wait another hour."

He felt the couch shift as she rose to her feet. "I'm going to fix some breakfast. I bet none of you thought to bring anything to snack on last night, did you?"

Of course not.

Senator Morris Barton read the entire article standing there beside the phone, his coffee slowly growing cold in his fist. For the most part, it was a standard "I'm being framed" argument, which was to be expected and could be dismissed. Two things made this one different: Jason Reynolds was an exceptional and compelling writer and the story he'd put together was just as compelling. The second issue was the evidence Reynolds cited. He made a pretty strong case that he had no motive to kill Gerry Peterson; he'd only met him a couple of times, the last time just before the killing and the gist of that meeting was that Peterson wanted to help Reynolds expose the Dunham County Sheriff.

But what caught Morris' eye was Reynolds' statement that he was with another law enforcement agent—one from an outside agency—when they both heard the shots that killed Peterson. He didn't identify this agent, but stated that the agent would have no problem testifying in Reynolds' behalf.

That was about as good an alibi as you could get.

What worried Morris was this agent from an outside law enforcement agency. This was the first he'd heard of this. An outside agency? Which one? The FBI? The Attorney General's Office? The State Police?

He picked up the house phone again and dialed Scott's number. It was still early, but he didn't care. His grandson was used to calls from him at odd hours. It was part of the job description.

Someone picked up on the third ring. "Yeah?"

It was a woman's voice, probably that Miller bitch that Scott liked so much. His infatuation with her had been the cause of most of their recent problems.

"Where's Scott?"

"Um, he's not here," the sleepy woman said, her words slurring. "He left a while ago."

"Where did he go?"

"How should I know?"

Morris hung up and went back into his bedroom to get dressed.

A few minutes later, dressed in jeans, sneakers and a raincoat, Morris slid behind the wheel of a Dunham County Sheriff's cruiser parked behind the lodge and started the engine. He executed a quick three-point-turn before heading down the gravel road toward the gate.

Morris was not armed, but the cruiser came with a twelve-gauge clipped to the console between the front seats and the onboard computer.

As Mary had said, there was no guard on duty at the gate. There was supposed to be one whenever they had VIP guests. That was the protocol.

He got out to open the gate and noticed, off to the side of the road, one of the lodge's ATV's. He walked over for a closer look. The seat had rainwater pooled on the vinyl seat and the engine was cold. It had been here for hours.

Now he was worried.

Morris returned to the car and continued down the road, this time with one hand on the twelve-gauge.

It wasn't long before he spotted the squad car, pulled over against the brush on the left side of the road. He thought he saw movement in the back seat.

Morris parked, climbed out into the rain, shotgun in hand, and slowly approached the other car. There was no one in the front seat. The back seat windows were steamed up, but he definitely saw something moving in there.

He hesitated, then decided the bad guys wouldn't be locked in the back of a police car. At least, if they were, they wouldn't be a threat.

He opened the back door.

"About time," Travis Wilcox said. "Get us out of here. I need to take a piss."

♦♦♦♦♦

It took a less than thirty minutes to finish downloading the photos from his camera's memory card. Danny supervised the operation and did most of the work. Jason was still trapped on his back while the poultice over his eyes slowly dried. It had cooled off a while ago.

"Can I take this off yet?" he asked.

"Not 'til Mom says so," Jimmy said. "The longer it stays on the better."

"Lord," Danny said from across the room. "Do you know how many pictures you took last night?"

"I don't know." He didn't. He'd just been taking photos, as many as he could. "A lot."

"Well, you took almost three hundred. Do you know how long it's going to take to go through all of these?"

"Most will be duplicates. Several shots just to make sure one comes out usable."

"It's still going to take a while."

"That's it," he said and sat up on the couch. A slightly damp cloth fell into his lap. "I need to get this stuff off so I can get to work."

"Mom!" Jimmy called into the back of the house. "We need you out here!"

"Jimmy?" Jason asked.

"Yeah, I'm right here."

"Do you have internet access?"

"Sorry. The nearest place I know of is the Tribal Offices, or the library."

"What are you thinking?" Danny asked.

"That we should get out of this house and out of this town. The longer we're here, the more danger Jimmy and Gloria are in. We should find a motel somewhere with internet access, hole up there and put our package together."

Gloria entered the room. "Is the patient losing patience?"

"I need to be working."

"Well, let's get this stuff off you; see how you're doing."

She began peeling and scraping the poultice off Jason's eyes. "Did I hear you say you were going to leave us?"

Jason sat still, afraid to move with her working so close to his eyes. "I think we've pushed our luck here. The Bartons or their people will come looking for us. We don't want you caught in the crossfire."

"I appreciate your concern, but we aren't exactly helpless."

"I'd just feel better," he said. "I don't know what Danny thinks."

"Danny thinks Jason's right," she said. "We're going to need an internet connection anyway, might as well get everyone as safe as we can."

"Sounds like it's been decided then," she said and wiped his eyes with a warm, wet cloth. "Okay," Gloria said when she was finished. "Open your eyes slowly. It's going to be bright, but the swelling and inflammation is better."

Jason opened his eyes, squinting against the sudden brightness. He could see just fine, but more importantly, his eyes felt better. The burning and itching were gone.

Thirty

Taylor Smith pulled his car over onto the shoulder about a block east of the main gate of Redwood Estates and pulled out his cell phone. One of the benefits of modern technology was that no one thought twice about someone sitting on the side of the road, as long as they had a cellular phone stuck to their ear. What was suspicious behavior on the surface, suddenly became mundane.

With the dead cell phone against his ear, Taylor watched the activity across the street. It wasn't terribly encouraging. Not only were there two guards manning the booth at the gate, but they had access to a vehicle parked to the side. That meant they had immediate chase ability. If someone suspicious got by them, they had the means to actually do something about it besides make a call.

And both of the guards were armed.

But that wasn't unexpected. Redwood Estates was an exclusive community and was home to people with enough money and enemies to take their security seriously. So they had a private firm in charge of their safety, Advance Security. He knew Advance by reputation. That reputation was very good.

Though every security scheme had holes and blind spots, he doubted Advance would have many and none of them would be large or easy.

It would be suicide to get to anyone living in Redwood Estates by going through the front gate. Even if he managed to get through the security perimeter and to the target, he would never make it out unscathed. Not without a full strike team.

At night, he could probably jump a wall, but that would leave him on foot, with even less of a chance to escape.

Naturally, Joseph Mullens, suspended Director of Security for Lundgren Corporation, lived in a lovely home in Redwood Estates, near the golf course. It made a certain amount of sense. As someone who made a good living by devising and ordering quasi-legal dirty tricks, he would be concerned about others attempting to do the same to him.

He would also undoubtedly have his own high-end passive security system on his house.

Taylor Smith lowered the cell phone and pulled his car back out onto the street, passing the gate without bothering to look that direction. He was just another citizen, peacefully passing by.

He was already working out the problem he now faced: how to arrange a friendly face-to-face with his former employer during one of Mullens' excursions outside the security perimeter. Since Mullens was on house arrest while he waited for his trial, those excursions were probably minimal.

But, at a minimum, he would need to meet with his attorney from time to time and possibly a parole officer. Both offered a lot of possibilities, but required more information.

In the meantime, Smith had grown intrigued by the new adventure the young reporter Reynolds seemed to have embroiled himself in. Part of Smith's research as he'd traveled was to read every newspaper and magazine article he could find about Mullens and his legal troubles. Tangential to that, of course, was Reynolds, the guy who had brought him to justice.

Taylor had grown to admire the journalist last year, even though they'd been on opposite sides of that fight in Port Salish. Reynolds had proved himself resourceful and not easily scared away. And, he had to admit, Reynolds had been true to his word.

Taylor always respected a man who was true to his word.

He wondered now whether he might be able even the odds up a bit in Reynolds' current problem while he waited for Mullens to poke his head out. It would be fun and help pass the time.

Thirty-one

Travis Wilcox had worked himself into a rage. As soon as Morris had managed to unlock the handcuffs and the deputy had relieved himself against the shrubs at the edge of the road, he had wanted nothing but to jump in the functional squad car and go after the people who had humiliated him.

Morris wouldn't let him. "They're long gone. You'll just waste time."

"Bullshit. One of them was Indian. They're holed up on the Rez somewhere."

Morris wasn't relenting or intimidated. "You think you're going to accomplish anything on the reservation? You're wearing a Dunham County Sheriff's uniform, and driving a Dunham County squad car, you dumbass. You're out of your jurisdiction and everyone on that reservation knows it. Nobody will give you the time of day. Nobody."

"They'll talk plenty after I get through with them."

"You just don't get it, do you?" Morris said. "The Kwamamish don't like us. At all. They will shoot you, or beat you to death with baseball bats and no jury in the world will convict them. They probably wouldn't even be arrested."

Metcalf had been standing awkwardly to the side up to now. “He’s right, Travis. Besides, they could be anywhere by now.”

“Fuck!”

“We’ll go back to the lodge, wake up the Sheriff, and figure out what to do,” Morris told him. “Something that might actually do us some good.”

Travis stared off into the distance for a while, his chest heaving, his hands curled tightly into fists at his side. “That fucking bitch kicked me in the balls. I’m going to make her pay for that. I’m going to make her pay hard for that.”

“If we do this right,” Morris said. “You’ll get your chance. But we can’t be running in a thousand different directions. We need to be smart.”

Travis nodded. “Okay. Let’s go make a damn plan.”

♦♦♦♦♦

Lisa Martin was busy helping the Millers get prepped for business. Over the last few days she had become something of an amateur restauranteur. At first, she had been annoyed with Jason for shunting her off to something safely on the side, while he and Danny chased bad guys, but she’d gradually changed her mind. She genuinely liked the Millers and grew to like the work more than she thought she would.

What was more important, she thought her presence here—if not her actual physical help—had kept Tom and Barbara from going crazy with the not knowing. To a certain extent, the Millers and the physical labor had done the same for her.

She didn’t think she would have survived just sitting somewhere wondering whether Jason was alive or dead.

The ring of her cell phone startled her. She jumped and knocked a container of sliced tomatoes to the floor, where they splattered in a juicy, red mess.

She picked up the phone. The display was a number she didn’t recognize, which could mean anything. She accepted the call. “Hello?”

“Lisa. It’s Jason.”

Her heart seemed to leap into her throat. “Jason. We’ve been so worried about you.”

“I’m fine. Danny’s fine. I can’t talk too long in case they try to trace the call, but I wanted to tell you Helen is alive. I’ve seen her.”

“She is? Oh, thank God! The Millers will be so happy.”

“Well, we don’t have her yet, so don’t get too excited, but she is alive,” he said. “I’ve got to go. Watch the news the next couple of days.”

“Jason?”

But he had already disconnected.

“Barbara! Tom?”

She went to spread the good news, tracking tomato juice as she ran.

♦♦♦♦♦

“You think that was a good idea?” Danny asked.

“I needed to give them something. This all started over their daughter and until today, all they had was hope.”

She nodded without taking her eyes off the road. They were somewhere north of the reservation, following Hwy 101 through the wilderness that was the western edge of the Olympic Mountains. For most of their journey the road had been the only evidence that civilization had ever ventured this far out. They had most of the road to themselves.

“I just don’t want to give them false hope,” she said. “We don’t have Helen. And after tonight, the Bartons could start cleaning up witnesses. It would be horrible if she showed up dead now.”

He admitted she had a point. It was too late now, though.

Jason sighed and returned to his laptop. He was sorting photographs and identifying the men in them when possible. It was a long and tedious process, but it needed to be done or it would take the Feds weeks to just figure out what they had.

Neither he or Danny, nor those girls, had weeks.

He was also running out of battery life again.

"So let's see if I've got this straight," Sheriff Mike Barton rubbed his eyes. He was wearing pajama bottoms and a bathrobe, nothing else. He looked like he'd just been dragged from bed, which was the truth. "Two of my own sworn deputies got overpowered and disarmed by some guy with a camera?"

Travis Wilcox looked insulted. "There were three of them and we were ambushed. We're lucky we weren't killed."

Metcalf nodded, his face pale like he hadn't thought of that possibility before.

"You're alive because they didn't want to kill you," the Sheriff said. "Please tell me you at least got the plate number of the vehicle."

Both deputies studied the floor.

"Jesus Christ. You're supposed to be trained observers."

Travis muttered something. Metcalf looked ready to pass out.

"Your sidearms? Tazers? Radios?"

They didn't bother answering.

"Jesus Christ."

"The important question is: what do we do now?" the Senator said, bringing them back on subject. "It looks like somebody snuck in, took some pictures—of what, we don't exactly know—and managed to outwit our security detail before escaping."

Travis visibly colored. Metcalf just stared at the floor like a kid resigned to the whipping he saw coming.

The Sheriff wouldn't even look at them.

"We need to decide what to do," Morris insisted.

The Sheriff ran a hand over his scalp, as if trying to smooth down some unruly part of his crew cut. "Well, the first thing is to get back to civilization where we can at least communicate. I can't figure what they think they'll do with those photos. We're on private property. It's embarrassing, that's all."

"It could destroy a few marriages," Morris told him. "Do the same to a few political careers. Any photographs would have a certain value as leverage, but that's about it, as long as none of the girls get out of line."

Travis snorted. “Those bitches know better than to say one word we don’t want them to say.”

“Make sure it stays that way,” the Sheriff told him.

“What about this Miller girl?” Morris asked. “She’s the one who started this whole shitstorm.”

“I can put the fear of God into her, too,” Travis said.

“Okay. And don’t send her back with the others,” the Sheriff said. “She might still be useful.”

Travis nodded.

“Go down to the dorms,” Morris told him. “Get the girls who are there up and ready to go. I’ll wake the VIPs in a bit and send the rest of the girls down.”

“Okay.”

“Let’s have them ready to load by noon.”

Travis nodded, rose to his feet, and walked from the room.

“What do you want me to do?” Metcalf asked.

Sheriff Barton turned to him. “Get your ass back down to the gate and make damn sure no one else gets past you.”

Metcalf scurried out of the room.

The Sheriff looked up at the Senator. “If they want to use the photos for leverage, they’re going to have to contact us.”

“And we need to have something to trade.”

♦♦♦♦♦

By mid-afternoon, Jason and Danny had reached a tiny community on the north coast of the Olympic Peninsula called Neah Bay and checked in to a motel with both Wi-Fi and a parking lot somewhat hidden from Hwy 101. It was the off-season, so the rate was about half of what it had been three months before, and it was mostly vacant.

It was perfect.

They were exhausted, from being up for thirty straight hours and the unaccustomed nighttime hike through the forest. Jason was certainly feeling it. His thighs and shoulders ached and would not stop. In fact, a bunch of other muscles he wasn’t even aware of joined them.

That was in addition to his damaged eyes.

In Neah Bay, they grabbed a couple of burgers from a place near the motel, stocked up on soft drinks from the vending machine and locked themselves in the room. Jason was still wanted for murder and the Bartons had seen Danny's Jeep. It was best to show their faces as little as possible.

Jason had managed to sort a lot of the photos during the drive, but his eyes tired quickly and there were still a lot to go through. The first step was to delete any pictures that were blurry, or didn't capture anyone's features enough to identify them. That weeded out one group of photographs. That still left well over a hundred to work with. Next, they needed to delete all those that were merely duplicates of other photos.

It was slow, tedious work.

"You know what we need?" Jason asked as he opened another Coke, wishing it were coffee, and took a drink. Several hours of peering at photographs tended to make his eyes cross under the best of circumstances, Jason's damaged eyes tired even quicker, so he took a lot of short breaks. "We need to identify these guys."

Danny gave a little shrug, nodded. "It would certainly save the Feds from spending time doing the same thing. How do you propose to do it?"

He'd recognized a couple of the men because he worked for a newspaper and they were politicians. It was like osmosis. The rest were either familiar but unknown, or total strangers to him. Danny hadn't known any of them for certain, but a few had seemed familiar.

"I think if we get on the State Congressional web sites, we'll find most of these guys, smiling for the camera."

She raised an eyebrow. "Wow. You're good."

"I am, aren't I?" He spent a few moments logging on to the motel's Wi-Fi. "We'll see if you think the same thing after we try this."

"Yeah, I might just lose faith in you."

Jason smiled and opened the Washington State Legislative web site. One of the features was an alphabetical listing of the Senators and Representatives, complete with a professional, smiling, headshot.

Unfortunately, it only allowed them to view one photograph at a time.

"This is going to take forever," Danny said over his shoulder.

"But there is a bright side," he said as he called up the next photo. "There's only a hundred forty-seven congress people and some of them are women."

Danny groaned and slumped in her chair.

♦♦♦♦♦

The helicopter with Morris Barton and his guests lifted off late that Sunday morning, turned and headed east toward Olympia. Sheriff Michael Barton gave them one last wave and headed back down the walkway toward the lodge. The girls—all except the Miller girl—had been loaded into an extended van a few minutes ago and driven off. Within a few hours they would all be back home in Bosque and Genoa. The Sheriff wasn't worried that they'd end up as liabilities. Travis said he'd make them see that zipping their lips was in their best interests. Travis was a liability in many ways, but no one could put the fear of God into women more effectively than Travis Wilcox.

Travis himself had left just a few minutes before, Helen Miller firmly ensconced in the back of his squad car. She hadn't looked particularly happy.

The Sheriff didn't care. He had given his orders.

He slipped into the passenger seat of his car and buckled his safety belt. "Go," he told his driver.

The deputy shifted into drive and moved down the graveled drive toward the gate.

Sheriff Barton sat back in his seat and began to think about his next move.

♦♦♦♦♦

Naturally, the VIP guests were concerned when Morris told them about the security breach. Which is what he wanted. Fear was a great motivator and he wanted them fully motivated to get their crap together and be ready to go within an hour.

Everyone needed to be out of Hemlock Run as quickly as possible.

Almost to a man they asked with panicky eyes what kind of security breach it had been. Morris had assured them that someone had penetrated their perimeter, but that was all. It could have been just a nature lover, a mushroom hunter, or someone looking to poach an elk. It was probably nothing, but he wanted to play it safe.

Every one of them appreciated that and hurried to get ready for the helicopter.

Once on the helicopter, of course, meaningful conversation was all but impossible, which prevented him from having to give any more detailed answers, answers he didn't have. Not yet. Not until he talked to Scott.

As the skyline of Olympia began to appear in the windscreen, Morris pulled his cell phone from a pocket and checked the signal. It was good.

He typed out a text and sent it to Scott. *Coming into airport. Where are you?*

The reply came within a minute.

At office. Writing press releases.

Well, that was something. At least he wasn't hiding somewhere. Morris still wanted an explanation for why Scott left everyone sleeping at Hemlock Run and fled back to the city, but it was something.

I'll be there soon. Wait for me.

He sent the text and slipped the phone back into his pocket. Now that he'd made contact with Scott he felt a little less like the wheels were coming off.

Morris sat back in his seat and tried to relax.

By early evening, Jason and Danny had identified all the men they could in the photographs and separated the photographs into files for each of them. They had clearly identified Senators William Congreave and Bruce McKean, as well as State Representatives Anthony Mason and Daniel O'Hara—all of them members of the legislative and party leadership—as well as Senator Morris Barton, Sheriff Michael Barton, and everyone's favorite, Travis Wilcox. There were a few other men they couldn't identify.

Though a couple of the girls looked familiar to Jason and Danny—one, Jason was almost positive was one of the girls he talked to at the convenience store when he and Danny had first arrived—the only one they had been able to firmly identify was Helen Miller.

"I hope that isn't going to be a problem," Jason said when they were finally finished.

"Just because we can't identify them doesn't mean they can't be identified," Danny told him. "The Feds have all sorts of resources we don't."

"Oh, that's not what I'm worried about. I'm worried that without identification the Feds won't take this seriously enough. It's a political scandal. It's disgusting, but is it a crime?"

Danny frowned. "It's pretty obvious that it's prostitution. Last time I checked, that's still a crime, doubly so if the prostitute is under age, or coerced. And it's pretty obvious that Helen isn't doing anything of her own free will."

"Yeah. I know. I would still feel better if we could give them the names and ages of the girls, direct evidence that some of them were underage. Something to get them moving quickly."

"So would I, but there is no such thing as a perfect case. You work with the evidence you have and I think this will get their attention."

"I hope so."

"Especially after you work your magic with the email explanation we'll send with it."

"Yeah, about that." Jason groaned and stretched, suddenly weary. "Law enforcement-wise, what do we need to tell them? What's most important?"

Danny thought about the question for a few moments, drank from her Coke. She looked tired, too. "First, we identify ourselves—mostly you, since you took the pictures—and the time and location the photos were taken. Probably mention the specs of your camera too, so the experts can judge the reliability of the photos."

“To make sure they weren’t Photoshopped, or something?”

“Exactly. And location is important to prove that the crimes were committed in their jurisdiction.”

“The Reservation.”

“Yes. Next, we make the case that a crime is being committed. We tie in the drugs, the coercion we observed and our belief that the girls were underage. We identify those we can and then let the photos do the work.”

Jason’s brain was already beginning to test out phrases and structure, searching for a hook.

Jason closed the photo files and opened the word processor.

It was time to start writing.

♦♦♦♦♦

They had just left the southern edge of Donald, heading toward Bosque when the idea hit Sheriff Barton, like it was a rock kicked up by a passing truck. He snapped up in his seat, alert, and grabbed the microphone off the squad car’s console.

Deputy Metcalf glanced over, but returned his eyes to the road. He didn’t say anything.

Sheriff Barton called directly to Wilcox, in his car somewhere on the road in front of them.

When Wilcox responded, the Sheriff asked where he was.

“Just passed milepost 321,” Wilcox told him. “About fifteen miles north of Bosque.”

“Change of plans. Get a hold of Jensen and the others, have them assemble in Bosque. I’ll be there in half an hour.”

Wilcox acknowledged the order. “We gonna have some fun?”

“We’re going to end this shit, once and for all.”

♦♦♦♦♦

Jason wrote pretty fast. He could spill a lot of words on to a page, especially if he was knowledgeable or passionate about the subject,. They weren’t always terribly good words, but they were words. Writing was like breathing, he could create a page without even trying. The work came in revising what he had written, polishing. Most stories were completely re-written at least three times before his editor ever saw them.

Then Miles would usually want at least one change before it went to print.

The email letter to the FBI and Bureau of Indian Affairs was no different. He was now working on the second version, trying to incorporate suggestions from Danny and fixing phrasings he himself didn't like.

This letter, more than possibly anything else he'd ever written, had to be perfect. If done right, it would galvanize numerous Federal and State agencies to take immediate action against both the Dunham County Sheriff's Department and the Barton family behind it. If done wrong, the Feds could either walk away, or take so long to move as to be effectively the same thing.

It was important that he strike the right balance of urgency and legal impartiality.

Danny helped as much as she could, but her eyes quickly glazed over like most people's did when confronted with the grunt work of writing.

When his cell phone rang, both of them jumped.

It was his disposable cell. No one had the number.

"Wrong number?" Danny suggested.

She stood and walked over to peer around the curtain into the parking lot.

The phone rang again. He checked the display. After a moment, he realized it was Lisa's number. He had called it to let the Millers know Helen had been seen.

Danny turned from the window and shook her head.

"I think it's Lisa," he said and picked up the call.

"Jason? I'm sorry. There was nothing we could do."

Her voice cut off as someone took the phone away.

"Lisa?" He stood. As if he could do anything to physically help from here.

Danny watched with alarm.

"Reynolds? You're a hard man to find."

"Who is this?"

"I have something you want. You have something I want. Let's make a deal."

Thirty-two

Lisa Martin grabbed the final bus tub and lugged it back to the dishwashing station behind the kitchen and began sorting and rinsing the dirty dishes. It wasn't a particularly pleasant job, but someone had to do it and one-handed Tom clearly couldn't. She had decided to put off returning to Seattle and tomorrow's classes until later this evening so she could help the Millers get through the weekend. It seemed the kind thing to do.

At least they'd heard some good news. And the effect had been astonishing. Neither of the Millers had seen or spoken to their daughter yet and didn't actually know where she was, but she was alive. They knew that now. Jason's call had brought energy back into their steps, smiles back to their faces.

She placed the last plate in the rack, rinsed it and rinsed out the plastic tub, turned and carried it back out to the dining room.

The Sunday lunch rush was all but over, with less than half the tables occupied now, mostly by older men and women dressed in suits and dresses. It was an old tradition to go out for lunch after church on Sunday.

She set the plastic tub on its cart just as Tom arrived with a stack of dirty dishes balanced between his good hand and hip.

"Let me get that." She took the plates with both hands and placed them in the tub.

Tom was shaking his hand, like it hurt. "Almost didn't make it."

"You know, no one's going to complain if you make two trips."

"Yeah, but—"

The front door burst open and a half-dozen men with assault rifles burst into the dining room.

"Police! Don't move!"

"Stay where you are!"

"Police!"

"Don't move!"

Women screamed. Men tried to duck under tables. Boots pounded on the floor. Two of the men aimed their assault rifles right at Lisa.

Lisa didn't move. She was afraid to even breathe.

One of the men approached, his rifle aimed straight at her. "Hands up! Hands where I can see them!"

There was so much shouting, it was hard to hear.

But the rifle was aimed right at her head. Lisa raised her hands, terrified that any sudden motion would make the man shoot her. But also terrified she might not obey fast enough. Beside her, Tom had also raised his hands, best he could. A second man stared down a black assault rifle at him.

"On your knees!" the man screamed at her. "Get down on your knees!"

Lisa did as she was told, her eyes never leaving the black circle at the end of the rifle's barrel.

"Don't move!"

Someone jerked her hands down behind her back, snapped handcuffs over her wrists and cinched them tight.

"Ow!"

No one paid attention.

"Get them out of here!"

Someone jerked her to her feet and pushed her toward the door.

She'd never felt so weak and so humiliated in her life. Every customer watched as she passed. There was nowhere to hide. She couldn't even walk at her own pace. The hand wrapped around her right arm just above the elbow propelled her forward, not quite fast enough to make her fall, but fast enough she couldn't quite get her feet under her.

Outside, Lisa practically fell across the sidewalk and into the side of a sheriff's squad car.

She looked over as Tom and Barbara Miller ended up in similar positions against another squad car to her left.

"I've got this one," a familiar man's voice said behind her. "She looks like she might have contraband hidden on her person."

Someone laughed. More men's voices.

Lisa glanced back long enough to recognize Travis Wilcox.

"Against the car!" Wilcox pushed her down against the wet surface. "Anything in your pockets that might hurt me?"

"No."

Lisa felt him lean against her; his breath hot in her ear. "How about your bra, honey? Anything in your bra I should know about?"

He grabbed her right breast, gave it a squeeze.

All Lisa could do was close her eyes.

♦♦♦♦♦

"Who is this?" Jason asked, mostly to stall while he looked for the speakerphone feature on the phone. He had a pretty good idea who he was talking to.

Danny had returned from checking the view from the window and sat in the chair beside Jason, her eyes never leaving the phone.

"Oh, I think you know who this is," the man said.

"Actually, I don't have a clue. Who is this?"

Jason found the speakerphone and activated it.

"This is Michael Barton, Sheriff of Dunham County."

"Okay then, Mr. Barton, let's talk."

The Sheriff paused as if deciding whether to correct Jason.

"Let's not waste any more time. If you ever want to see any of the Millers, or your sweet girlfriend alive again, you will bring the memory card and every copy of every picture you took at Hemlock Run last night to the Sheriff's substation in Bosque in one hour. It will be an even trade, the pictures for your friends."

Danny was frowning and emphatically shaking her head.

"I'm afraid your timing is bad," Jason said, thinking fast. He'd already rejected the idea of playing ignorant. "I'm not in Dunham County anymore, or anywhere nearby. I couldn't physically get there for at least three or four hours even if I wanted to. And there's no way we're doing this exchange in the middle of the night on your turf. It just isn't happening."

The Sheriff chuckled. "Fair enough. What time would you like to make the exchange?"

"Broad daylight. How about high noon?"

"Just like in the Duke's old movies, huh?"

"Always been more of an Eastwood fan myself, but sure, just like John Wayne. And we do the exchange at the Millers' restaurant. I assume there hasn't been an accidental fire?"

"The exchange happens at the Bosque substation; that's non-negotiable. Your friends are inmates there. The pictures are their bail. They stay in cages until you bail them out. If you want them to enjoy our hospitality until noon tomorrow, that's fine by me."

Danny was again furiously shaking her head. To be sure she was making her point, she drew a finger across her throat.

Jason ignored her. "We do the exchange in the parking lot outside the building. I never set foot inside."

"I can do that. Noon, tomorrow?"

"Noon, tomorrow."

"Don't be late. Some of my deputies can get kind of rambunctious around a looker like your girlfriend. I'm going to have my hands full keeping them in line until noon. After that there are no guarantees."

Danny was glaring at the phone. The Sheriff was fortunate she wasn't telepathic.

Jason struggled to keep his own anger in check. "Let me talk to Lisa."

"Sorry. The fee for that is the pictures. See you tomorrow."

The Sheriff ended the call.

"Damn it!"

"You're not going down there." Danny protested.

"I don't have a choice. The Millers and Lisa are as good as dead, if I don't."

"It's a trap, Jason. They will kill you, then kill everyone else and say it was all part of some prison break attempt, or something. You know that. They have no intention of letting any of you walk away from this."

"I know," he told her. "But I have to do something."

Danny released a sigh. "I don't believe this."

"What do you want me to do? Just not show up? Sorry, guys…"

"No, of course not. But there has to be another way."

"Believe me, I have no intention of walking into my own execution," he told her. "So we have until noon tomorrow to come up with a plan."

♦

They talked the situation over for more than an hour. What it came down to was the same problem they'd had the entire time: the Bartons held all the cards in Dunham County. As long as the exchange was to take place there, Jason and Danny would always be at a disadvantage.

"Maybe I could get a rifle and set up as a sniper somewhere," Danny suggested.

Jason shook his head halfheartedly. It was actually the best idea they'd come up with to this point, but it still had glaring holes. Where would she get the rifle with no notice? How would she get into position near the Sheriff's station without being discovered? What if there was no vantage point suitable for a sniper? Would and could she shoot and possibly kill someone under those circumstances—especially a fellow cop—knowing she'd be acting outside the law? How would they survive the firefight sure to follow?

"Also, you're supposed to be at work in Port Salish tomorrow morning," he pointed out. "You can't hardly ask for more time off so you can go shoot some deputies in another county."

"Definitely not in those words."

Jason shook his head. "You coming along wouldn't help enough to make a difference. We'd still be outgunned and out-manned."

Danny brought her fingertips to her temples, like she had a headache. She probably did. Jason was getting one. "You can't expect me to just wave goodbye as you drive off to certain death."

"I know."

"I also promised Andrea that I'd bring you in."

"But that was before they got a hold of Lisa and the Millers. It's a major change in the circumstances."

They sat there for a few moments, each racking their imaginations for some way out of the corner they were boxed into. Unfortunately, there didn't seem to be any easy answers.

Jason looked down at the email they'd been crafting for the FBI.

"You know," he said. "What I need is real back-up. Real, professional, organized backup with legal authority and serious firepower."

"Yeah, that would be great." Danny smiled. "Any idea how to get it?"

Jason looked over at her. "Got any good contacts at the Bureau?"

"Sure. I guess." Danny shrugged. "I don't know how good they are. I worked with a couple of agents during the Lundgren case."

"Did you work close enough to have cell phone numbers? Email addresses?"

"Maybe. Where are you going with this?"

"The FBI. This is a kidnapping, isn't it?"

"Dunham County won't bill it that way, of course," she said. "But yeah, it is."

“False imprisonment, whatever. The FBI handles kidnappings, right? It’s one of their specialties. We send the file just like we were going to, but now you raise the ante with a phone call, reporting a kidnapping.”

Her mouth opened, as if to protest, closed again.

“You tell them the situation and the time and location of the exchange,” he told her. “With a little luck, and some prodding from you, the Feds will swoop in and save the day.”

Danny was frowning now, considering it. “So you’re not going to bring ‘every’ copy of the photographs to the exchange?”

“Of course not. I never was. I want those bastards to go down, no matter what. I’m sending them to everyone we talked about and maybe a few others just for good measure.”

“What others?”

“The U.S. Attorney, the Washington State Attorney General, maybe even Andrea. And the newspaper, of course. I want so many people to know what is going on that there’s no way the Bartons will be able to skate.”

Danny pulled out her phone.

“What are you doing?”

“Going through my contacts,” she told him. “I might not have the information on here. I might have to get back to my office.”

“You’re going back there anyway.”

Danny shot him a look and went back to her contacts list.

Scott Barton watched his grandfather’s face, reading his reaction. They had just ended the call from Scott’s father, the Dunham County Sheriff, describing his plan to—as he put it—“end this crap once and for all.” Now he waited to see how the Senator would react. That would largely determine how he, Scott, would react himself.

They were in the Senator’s office, Morris sitting behind his desk, still wearing the jeans and sport shirt he’d put on this morning at the lodge. He’d driven here straight from the airport. Scott had changed into business attire as soon as he’d reached the city and been waiting in the office when the Senator had arrived.

He'd even had a couple of sample press releases ready for the Senator to go over. Each, with slightly different wording, said any photos of the Senator were the products of Photoshopping and were a blatant attempt by his political enemies to sabotage his work on behalf of his constituents.

Then the Sheriff had called.

Morris focused on him now. "What do you think?"

"It could work," he shrugged. "If Reynolds is stupid enough to believe the Sheriff will honor the agreement."

The Senator frowned. "Reynolds doesn't strike me as a stupid man."

"No, he doesn't."

"But I don't think you give your old man enough credit either."

Scott smiled. He had always thought that if his father hadn't been born the son of Morris Barton, he would be driving a tow truck now, rather than Sheriff. Michael Barton was ruthless, but he wasn't a thinker. He'd gotten where he was by birthright.

He certainly wasn't going to say that, not out loud.

"From what I've learned about this Reynolds guy, he doesn't seem the type to walk away while 'innocents' are in danger."

Scott shrugged. "But he has no real hope of freeing them. Unless he has something up his sleeve we don't know about."

Morris smiled, like he knew something Scott didn't. "What could he have that would overpower the entire Sheriff's Department?"

Scott didn't have an answer for that, other than the photographs, but he couldn't see how they'd help Reynolds out of this situation.

"All that being said," Morris peered at him. "What do you suggest we do?"

"Keep our distance, maintain plausible deniability."

"Just in case it blows up?"

"Just in case."

The Senator smiled wryly. "You would actually throw your own father to the wolves, wouldn't you?"

"If needs be," Scott said. "To save your political future."

And his own.

♦♦♦♦♦

Drew Parsons, in jeans, a tee shirt, and stocking feet, didn't look like an FBI agent, but that was kind of the point. It was Sunday. On Sunday he wasn't an agent, or even a cop. On Sunday, he was a husband and father. On Sunday, he was just a guy relaxing in front of a Sunday Night Football game. Jenny sat beside him, her nose in a mystery novel. The kids were in their rooms, doing their homework.

A normal Sunday evening at the Parsons' house. Drew wouldn't change a thing.

"No..." he groaned as the Cowboys' quarterback was swallowed by two defensive lineman. Romo held on to the ball, but it was a seven yard loss and now fourth down. Time to punt. Again. The Cowboys had done a lot of punting today. Not much scoring. The scoring had all been done by the Saints.

His cell phone rang. By the ring tone it was a call, not a text.

Jenny looked up from her book.

The display said Danielle Hayden. The name was familiar, but only faintly. He couldn't place it. He obviously knew her, or her name wouldn't be in his phone's contact list.

"Who is it?" Jenny asked as it rang again.

"I'm not sure." He accepted the call.

"Drew? I don't know if you remember me. Danielle Hayden, a deputy sheriff out of San Juan County? We worked together on the Lundgren case last year?"

And like that, Drew remembered her. "Oh, yeah, of course. What can I do for you?"

He remembered her, but had no clue why she would be calling him at home on a Sunday evening. He communicated that to his curious wife, by shrugging and shaking his head.

"Sorry to bother you, but this is kind of an emergency. There isn't time to go through regular channels."

"What's going on?"

"There's been a kidnapping. The exchange is supposed to be tomorrow at noon, but it's complicated."

Drew forgot about the football game. He stood and walked out of the living room and into the spare room he used as an office and sat at his desk. A pen and scratch paper were right in front of him. So was his computer,

"How is it complicated?"

"For one thing, the kidnappers are law enforcement officers."

Drew thought he'd misheard her. "Say that again?"

"It's a long story, but the kidnappers are Michael Barton, the Sheriff of Dunham County, and his deputies."

"I think you'd better tell me that story."

The cells at the Bosque sheriff's substation were never meant to house prisoners for long. They'd been designed to hold them only until they could be transported to the main County Jail in Genoa. They didn't have beds or toilets. Their only feature was a twelve inch wide varnished wood bench bolted to the floor along the three walls opposite the door. The walls were steel, painted gray, except for the front, where the door was. That wall was gray steel up to waist level, shatterproof Plexiglas above that. The door was made of the same gray-painted steel, with a Plexiglas window in the upper half.

They were designed for the deputies to have visibility of all prisoners at all times.

The station had two cells, so women and men could be held separately. Prisoners could not see from one cell into the other.

Lisa Martin and Barbara Miller had been sitting in their cell for nearly six hours now. Bob Miller was next door. Or Lisa hoped he was. She hadn't actually seen the deputies put him in the cell.

She shifted on the hard wooden bench, trying to find a comfortable position, and looked over at Barbara. The older woman looked exhausted, defeated. Like she was resigned to the next indignity.

Lisa was terrified, but she was not defeated. Not yet.

"How are you doing?" she asked.

Barbara shrugged. "What are they waiting for? Why don't they just do what they're going to do and get it over with?"

"I don't know." Which was a bit of a white lie. She didn't know for certain, of course, but she suspected the deputies had taken them as hostages against Jason. He had hurt them somehow. Maybe with the stories over the last couple of days. But they'd been stung and had panicked enough to pick up the Millers as insurance.

Lisa suspected they hadn't even known she'd be there. She had been a bonus.

Both women looked up at the sound of voices in the corridor. Lisa's heart jumped into overdrive, trying to beat its way out of her chest.

Deputies arrived at the door to their cell. A key scratched home and the lock snicked open.

Lisa reached for Barbara's hand without knowing she was doing it. Barbara grasped her hand, squeezed it.

The door swung open and Travis Wilcox led two muscular deputies into the cell. He walked straight up to Lisa as the other two covered his sides.

"On your feet, beautiful," Wilcox said. "We need to ask you a few questions."

"Like, do you spit or swallow?" Another, older deputy said.

All the deputies thought this was pretty funny.

Lisa's mouth had gone completely dry, so dry her tongue was stuck to the roof of her mouth. She felt paralyzed.

"Now this is going to happen, one way or another, honey," Wilcox told her. "So how about we don't make it difficult?"

Lisa could not take her eyes off Wilcox, his powerful arms and shoulders, his cold, hard eyes, his cruel smile. Her mind kept repeating the same word over and over in her head. Please, please, please, please.

"Okay. Have it your way." Wilcox stepped forward and grabbed the hair on the top of her head, pulling her to her feet.

Lisa could do nothing but cry out and grab his wrist. It was like grabbing a tree branch.

"Leave her alone!" Barbara cried, but was silenced by a blow from the older deputy.

"You want to do this the hard way," Wilcox said. "We can do this the hard way."

Lisa couldn't fight him, couldn't overpower him, couldn't escape. He dragged her toward the cell door and out into the corridor.

One of the other deputies relocked the cell. He was laughing.

"When we're finished," Wilcox whispered in her ear. "You'll be able to tell your boyfriend what it's like to be with a real man."

♦♦♦♦♦

Miles Condiff was also watching the Sunday Night Football game. The City Editor for the *Seattle News* sat in the living room of his apartment sipping a beer and watching the Saints dismantle the Cowboys. He always enjoyed watching the Cowboys lose. He didn't even mind all that much that he was enjoying the show alone.

His second marriage had ended with a whimper two years ago. His children were basically grown, both of them off at college now—Derek a senior at Portland State and Abbie a sophomore at Washington State—and he was not seeing anyone socially. Hadn't for a couple of months now.

The companionship was nice, so was the sex, but he was no longer sure he was willing to pay the price that usually went with it. Besides, his ex-wives had always maintained he was married to his job. They were probably right.

His cell signaled a new text.

Miles grabbed it from the coffee table, saw the display and sat up straight. It was from his wayward reporter, Jason Reynolds. He must have just switched his cell on because Miles had been trying to reach him for days, without success.

He opened the text.

Check ur email.

Jason Reynolds was not the kind of reporter to waste time with fluff or false alarms. His heart sped up as he walked over to the computer desk on the other side of the room, logged into his email service and opened the email Jason had sent him.

"Holy shit," was his only reaction as he read. "Holy shit…"

♦♦♦♦♦

Senator Morris Barton walked down the underground corridor that linked the Senate office building with the parking structure next door. Normally the corridor was busy as legislators, staffers, lobbyists, and constituents moved constantly between the two buildings. But on this Sunday evening, he had the entire corridor to himself and it was an odd feeling, like walking through an empty school.

He shuddered as the spooky feeling ran down his spine. He shoved his hands deeper into his coat pockets and picked up his pace.

There wasn't any real danger. The State Police ran security for all Capital facilities. He was sure there were too many patrols and too much video to make it a good target for muggers.

Still, he glanced behind him as he walked. And when he reached the fire door that led into the parking structure, he paused to look through the little window before he stepped through.

As though any muggers would just be standing there in the open, waiting for him.

Morris walked into the garage and hurried toward his Cadillac, parked about a hundred feet away. No other vehicles were nearby. The entire parking level seemed empty.

His heels echoed across the stained concrete as he walked.

Morris had his keys in his hand as he rounded the tail end of his car. He unlocked the car with the remote and pulled open the driver's door.

His chest exploded with pain. Pain like he'd never known before. It was like every muscle in his body had cramped at the same time. He didn't remember falling, but was suddenly lying on his back, staring up at the concrete beams supporting the garage's next level.

He was having a heart attack. It was the only explanation. All the stress…

"Don't worry Senator." A man's bearded face appeared in his field of vision. "It's just a Taser. Hurts like hell though, doesn't it?"

♦♦♦♦♦

In addition to the FBI, Jason had emailed copies of the letter and photographs to the United States Attorney in Seattle; the Law Enforcement Division of The Bureau of Indian Affairs, in Aberdeen; and the headquarters of the State Police in Olympia. Jason had also spent several hours writing an article for the newspaper. He'd sent that, along with the photos and a brief explanation of what they were doing directly to his editor's private email.

Now they just waited. The proof of whether this worked or not would be in what happened at noon tomorrow.

It had not been an easy decision. Even now that it was done, neither Jason nor Danny were resting easy.

"What happens if the newspaper runs your story tomorrow?"

He'd thought about that, but didn't think it was an issue. "Not going to happen. That would mean stopping production in its tracks and completely redesigning the entire layout of the paper. I don't see them doing that. Not unless the President's been assassinated."

Danny nodded.

"Besides, Miles isn't even working tonight. He'd have to convince everyone else to do it."

"I hope you're right. I wouldn't want to guess what the Bartons would do if they found out those photographs are floating around already."

Jason had thought of that too. Even just sending the photographs to law enforcement agencies was taking the chance that someone out there was in the Bartons' pocket. If they found out that Jason had never had any attention of turning all the photos over, there was no telling what they would do to their hostages.

No. He knew exactly what they would do. They would do what they'd intended to do all along. Kill them all. They'd just do it quicker.

"Does it ever bother you that you're playing chicken with other people's lives?" Danny asked.

"Of course. And I wouldn't do it this way, if I could figure out another, better, way."

They had both spent a lot of time trying to come up with an alternate strategy this evening and had not been able to come up with anything that wasn't much, much, worse. Which just showed how vulnerable their situation actually was.

"I know," she said. "But I'm cop. I should be protecting people, you know, not putting them at risk."

"The Millers have been at risk ever since Helen first dated Travis Wilcox."

"Yeah." Danny said. "But we brought it to a head. We pushed it."

"Yes, we did."

They were lying in the motel bed, trying to rest before they needed to get on the road again. Danny had to be to work in the morning in Port Salish. The only way to do that was to catch the ferry at Port Townsend at 6:30, which was more than two hours away by car.

Unfortunately, neither of them was finding rest easy to come by, despite both being physically and mentally exhausted.

"We couldn't come up with a better option," he told her. "And we tried."

"So why do I feel so awfully responsible for this?"

"Because it's who you are. It's who we are. We're champions."

"Champions?" She chuckled. "Champions of what? Ineptitude?"

"Not that kind of champion," he told her. "Champion as in 'knight in shining armor' champion. Champion, as David was champion of the Israelites when he defeated Goliath, champion of the Philistines."

"Oh. That 'champion.' A hero."

"Yeah, a hero, but with no superpowers other than a serious commitment to protecting those that can't protect themselves. Every good soldier is a champion. The best cops, journalists, and firefighters are champions because they are willing to sacrifice their own lives for the good of others."

Danny made depreciating sounds. "Danielle Hayden, champion of the people?"

"Don't sell yourself short. No one else has stood up to the Bartons. And most people won't. They don't want to take the chance of losing. They want someone else to stop the bad guys."

Danny agreed. "Or they hope if they keep their heads down the bad guys won't notice them."

"But you—the champion—can't walk away. You—the champion—know that, unless someone stops the Bartons, they most certainly will victimize someone else."

"Evil never stops on its own."

"No, it doesn't," Jason admitted. "So it falls to the champions—people like you and me—to stop it."

"So, am I your sidekick? Or are you mine?"

Jason thought about it for a minute. "Co-champions, I'd say. Partners."

♦

At 6:30 Monday morning, Jason and Danny joined the crowd of other early birds, waiting to board the morning ferry. Danny's luggage was stacked at her feet, at least the luggage she was going to take with her. The important things.

They each had large cups of coffee clutched in their hands, the steam warming their faces.

The ferry had docked a few minutes ago. Cars were streaming off the motor deck now, while a handful of foot passengers moved down the gangplank. Transportation Department employees monitored the operation. Seagulls bickered overhead. The air smelled rich with the odors of the Sound.

Within a few minutes, boarding would begin.

“I still don’t like this,” Danny said. “I should be going with you.”

“I know. But I need you to keep the heat on the Feds. I need you to light a fire under the cavalry.”

Danny ignored him, sipped her coffee.

“Besides, you need to keep your job and keep Andrea from putting us both in jail. She’s probably going to be upset when I don’t show up.”

“You think? She went out on a limb for us.”

“Imagine if neither of us showed up.”

“I know, but it still sucks. You need someone to watch your back.”

Jason didn’t answer. They’d spent most of the night arguing about this. This was the compromise they’d settled on. Like most compromises, it left neither of them happy or satisfied, Danny least of all.

The P.A. system announced that boarding was beginning.

“Here,” Danny quickly shoved something into his coat pocket.

“What—“

His hand found the heavy object and immediately recognized her pistol.

“You need to be able to protect yourself,” Danny said.

“Danny.”

“Don’t argue.” She kissed him, picked up her luggage and started toward the gangplank.

He watched her go, one hand on her pistol in his pocket.

At the top, she turned once and waved. Jason waved back, hoping it wouldn’t be the last time he saw her.

Thirty-three

Shortly before 11:00 pm, a middle-aged man with a neat goatee and a perfect tan checked into a Holiday Inn near the hospital in Genoa. He rented a double-occupancy room on the ground floor to make access easier on his father, who suffered from multiple health issues, including Alzheimer's, and was waiting in the car. The man, his driver's license identified him as Trevor Sanford, of Seattle, even stepped over to a window a couple of times during the rental process to check on him.

The clerk was impressed with his caring demeanor. The guy truly loved his dad. It was admirable. You didn't see it that often in men.

Mr. Sanford paid for the room with a Visa card, thanked her, and returned to his car.

The room was on the ground floor, mid-way down the nearest wing, and he was able to park directly in front of the room's door.

No one heard from Sanford or his father the rest of the night.

Thirty-four

Danny carried her luggage into the Port Salish sheriff's substation just before 9:00 Monday morning. To be more precise, she carried one bag in, and Deputy Sullivan the other two. She'd had to get a ride in from the ferry terminal. Jason had put her on the ferry at Port Townsend this morning, then borrowed her car for the long drive back to Bosque and his noon appointment with Sheriff Barton.

His car had either been impounded or stolen from the ferry parking lot.

It hadn't been an easy moment for either of them.

"Moving in?" someone asked as she passed.

"Yeah. I live and breathe this stuff, you know."

She asked Sullivan to set her luggage in a corner of her office and thanked him. He smiled and went out to his own desk.

Once she'd caught up a bit on the pile of messages on her desk and touched base with Drew, she'd check out a county car and take her stuff back to her house. She could use the county car until Jason returned with her own.

She would also need to check out a Department Glock to replace the one she'd given Jason.

It would only be a day or two. Right?

High on her priority list was a shower and clean clothing. She had packed enough for three days in court, not a week tromping all over the Olympic Peninsula. Her choices for work this morning had not been optimal.

She very much needed to clean up.

But first things first.

While her computer booted up, she went through the pile of pink message slips that had been left for her. There were dozens of them. About half were inquiries regarding several routine cases she was working on: a couple of burglaries, a few drug distributions, a domestic violence issue. None of them were terribly urgent. Another handful were from Andrea's assistant prosecutors, who obviously hadn't heard she had not returned to her regular duties immediately after Marks' trial.

One message though immediately drew her attention. The duty officer last night had taken it—she recognized his scribble and the time stamp—and it was short and blunt.

"In town and thought you might want some help—your tailor, Smith." A cell phone number was scribbled in the contact spot.

Danny eased back into her desk chair, her shower completely forgotten. She only knew one tailor named Smith. And he wasn't a tailor, he was a Taylor. Taylor Smith, the security manager for Lundgren who had given them so much trouble last year. Until Travis Wilcox, he had been the most ruthless man she'd ever known. He was also one of the most complicated men she'd ever known. He had ordered the assassination attempt on Jason that had left him wounded and another woman dead. He had ordered Lt. Marks to frame her for distribution of meth. But he had also been the one who had given them all the evidence they'd needed to bring charges against Lundgren Corporation and its hoods.

Last she'd heard Taylor Smith had fled the country.

Apparently, he was back.

She pulled her cell phone from her pocket and called Jason.

♦♦♦♦♦

Jason was in a small rural version of a convenience store, grabbing some more coffee, when he received Danny's call. He'd hit the wall about thirty minutes ago and finally had to pull over before he fell asleep and killed someone. He hadn't had any meaningful sleep since Friday morning and much of that time awake had been spent hiking through rain forest. He thought every single muscle fiber in his body ached and got downright mean if he tried to use it. His legs were the worst, but his arms, back, and neck were also involved.

And of course, his eyes were still sore, a lingering reminder of Jimmy's booby trap.

He bought a large, strong coffee, along with a bottle of aspirin and swallowed four tablets just before his cell rang.

He listened as Danny read the message to him, jotted down the number as she gave it to him. "You think it's really Taylor Smith? Our Taylor Smith?"

"You know," Danny said. "I think it is. The night officer who took the message said he was very specific: he was Smith, my tailor, like a code."

"Only a few people would understand, like you and me."

"That's what I thought. So why would Taylor Smith resurface after a year in hiding? And why would he want to help us?"

"That's a good question."

"Are you going to call him?"

Jason didn't know yet. There were other things to take into account, such as it being some kind of trick by the Bartons. He also didn't have a lot of time to waste. But then he remembered something that changed his mind, something that made his heartrate speed up.

"Did you catch the news this morning?" he asked.

"No. It was playing on the ferry, but I was dozing, so I didn't pay attention. What's going on?"

He had been worried about news of the photos leaking out, so he'd found an all-news channel on the radio shortly after leaving the ferry terminal in Port Townsend. There was no mention of the photos, but there was plenty of news of interest.

"Senator Morris Barton disappeared last night."

Danny caught her breath. "You mean he took off?"

"Not unless he did so without his car and without telling his wife. It's being treated as an abduction."

It only took Danny a second. "Taylor Smith."

"It sounds like one of his operations, doesn't it?"

"Yeah, it does. So what are you going to do?"

He sighed. "I guess I'm going to call him and see what he thinks he's doing."

♦

The eerily familiar baritone answered before the second ring.

"Taylor Smith?"

"Jason Reynolds, my favorite muckraker," Smith chuckled. "You have kept yourself busy since we last spoke, haven't you?"

"I do my best."

"Yes, you do. And while I know that you're more than capable of caring for yourself, I couldn't help but notice that the newest Goliath you've targeted is giving you a run for your money. So I decided the decent thing was to lend you a hand."

"Did you kidnap Morris Barton last night?"

"I borrowed him for a bit, yes. He's just insurance, mind you. He has not been harmed."

Jason couldn't believe he was having this conversation, now, sitting in the parking lot of a country store in rural Washington. "Insurance for what?"

"You, of course. As long as no harm comes to you, the Senator of sleaze will be released unharmed," Smith said.

"You're assuming they give a damn about him."

But his mind was working, going through possibilities and probabilities.

"Oh, I think they care. Some of them anyway—the ones that aren't sociopaths—he's family and that's what this whole thing has been about, isn't it? Family?"

In a twisted, deviant manner, Smith was probably right. This whole episode was about a family with too much power, fighting to protect themselves and that power. But he didn't have time to discuss it and he certainly didn't want to discuss it with Smith. He was only barely willing to talk to him.

"I've got to go," Jason told him. "Do what you're going to do. It doesn't change anything. You still had someone kill my dad."

"Of course. My help is offered unconditionally."

Jason ended the call.

As he started the car and pulled out on to the highway, he wondered just how the Sheriff and his people would react to the abduction of the family patriarch. After a few fruitless moments, he gave up. He had no idea. And it was out of his control.

♦♦♦♦♦

Sheriff Michael Barton arrived at the Bosque substation a little after 8:30 Monday morning. It was going to be an important day and he wanted to personally oversee every part of it. There was too much riding on this to allow a stupid mistake to screw things up. And a stupid mistake was more than possible. Though they worked hard and were as loyal as any soldiers anywhere, some of his deputies just weren't the brightest.

If they played their cards right today, the nightmare of the last few days would be over. There would be some whimpering afterwards, of course. There always was. Some big city bleeding hearts would squawk about civil rights or police brutality, or something for a little while. But they would fade away quickly as fresher news took over the headlines.

It was the way things like this worked.

Michael had heard about his father's disappearance last night. His mother had called him when she couldn't reach the Senator at the office or on his cell. He had calmed her down as much as he could and told her to call the State Police. They were charged with protecting government officials. Plus, they were there, in Olympia; he wasn't. They would determine whether foul play was involved and take it from there.

It worried him, of course, that his father was missing and possibly in danger, but he doubted it was connected to this mess in Dunham County. Reynolds was coming here; he didn't have time to go around kidnapping anybody. Morris was a wealthy, high-profile politician who had always refused bodyguards. Now he was paying the price.

Once things were settled here, Michael would probably head over to his parents' place in the city. In the meantime, his wife and sister had gone over to help.

The Sheriff glanced over the men crowded into the squad room. They were the best he had and the ones with the most to lose. A half-dozen were wearing the black jumpsuits of the Department's SWAT team.

He caught Jensen's eye. "Have everybody ready in fifteen minutes. We'll issue tactical orders then."

Jensen nodded and turned back to the men.

Sheriff Barton walked into his office—each station had one specifically for him—and settled in behind the desk.

The phone rang.

"Already?" he grumbled and picked up the receiver. "Yeah?"

"Sorry sir, but he insisted on speaking with you, personally," the deputy told him. "He says it's about the Senator."

That got his attention.

"Okay. Put it through."

A second later, the line clicked as the call was transferred.

"Sheriff Barton?" A smooth baritone asked. "Sheriff Michael Barton?"

"You're speaking to him. What do you know about my father?"

The Sheriff switched on his desk computer.

"Let's see, what do I know? How about: where he is and how you can get him back in one piece."

The Sheriff sat up. "What are you talking about?"

"It's time to play 'Let's Make a Deal'."

"If this is supposed to be some kind of joke..."

"Oh, I'm dead serious. I have your father, your dad, old man, the good Senator Morris Barton. He is alive, and in relatively good shape right now, but I can't promise he'll stay that way."

"Kidnapping is a serious crime, my friend."

"First, I'm not your friend. Second, so is murder. I would seriously reconsider doing any harm to Jason Reynolds or anyone else today, if you ever want to see your father again."

Sheriff Barton scowled. "Are you trying to blackmail me?"

"Of course not. I'm just telling you about the new rules. The first rule is: Jason Reynolds dies, your father dies. The second rule is: Don't forget the first rule. Remember, I'll be watching."

The phone line went dead.

Patrick Barton stepped into the waiting area outside the District Attorney's office in Genoa about twenty minutes before nine o'clock Monday morning, feeling like the known world was teetering on the edge of total collapse. Not only was there the issue of his brother, the Sheriff, and his blatant attempt to frame a nationally known journalist, but last night, someone had abducted his dad, Senator Barton. At this point, there was no evidence to connect the abduction to the Sheriff's office's problems. But the timing was much too coincidental.

Patrick's wife was an intelligent and perceptive woman who had always been completely supportive of him and his decisions, even when she disagreed with them. Families were always complicated, his maybe more than most. But he had been treading water as fast as he could for years now, and was growing tired.

Last night, after they'd learned of his father's abduction, she had embraced him, squeezing him hard in her strong arms and whispering in his ear how sorry she was. "Haven't you sacrificed enough for your family?"

That was it. Nothing else was said the rest of the evening. But it had been enough to keep him awake the rest of the night.

She was good like that.

Now, he paused in mid-step as two men in dark suits rose to their feet with his arrival.

"District Attorney Patrick Barton?" the oldest of the men asked. He looked to be in his late forties and stood with the confident aura of command.

"Yes," Patrick said, trying to look neither surprised nor intimidated. "I'm Patrick Barton."

"I'm Special Agent Bryant, FBI," he said, flashing official credentials at Patrick. "This is Special Agent Rodrigues. We'd like to ask you some questions."

Patrick hesitated less than a second. "Of course. Let's go back into my office."

"Lead the way."

Patrick waved at the clerk behind the reception window, who buzzed them through the sally port. "I assume this is about my father, Senator Barton. Has there been any progress?"

The agents exchanged a glance Patrick couldn't read. "We'd prefer to wait until we're in your office."

"Understood." Patrick wondered whether he should have bolted for the door when he first saw them and led them toward his office.

♦♦♦♦♦

Sheriff Barton thought about the situation for a full ten minutes before he made his decision. The Senator was his dad, after all, and he did love and admire him. The Sheriff wouldn't be anywhere near where he was in life if it hadn't been for his dad. And he wasn't just talking about the Barton name. His father had taught him how to be a man and how to be a lawman.

His father had also taught him that a man—above all—protected his family. Even if that meant dying, a man did whatever it took to make sure his family would be okay, physically and financially. Whatever it took.

That's what finally decided it. Michael Barton felt that if he'd been able to talk to Morris, his dad would tell him to go ahead and deal with the reporter. If it came down to it, the threat Reynolds posed to the Barton family was more important than one man's life, even that of the Barton patriarch.

That didn't mean he was going to just sit there while this asshole killed his dad.

Sheriff Barton punched the button for Sgt. Jensen's desk. "In my office. Bring Wilcox. There's been a change of plans."

♦♦♦♦♦

Almost as soon as Danny ended her call with Jason, her cell rang. It was so quick the phone was still in her hand. She thought Jason might be calling her back, but a glance at the display proved that wrong. It was Drew Parsons, from the FBI.

She accepted the call.

"Detective." Drew seemed to be shouting from the floor of a factory, while vast machinery clashed and pounded around him. "It's Special Agent Parsons from the FBI."

"I can barely hear you."

"I'm in a helicopter. We'll be at the airport outside Port Salish in fifteen minutes. You need to be there. I've already cleared it with the Sheriff. You're coming with us, but time is an issue. Get to the airport. Understand?"

"Understood. I'm leaving now."

Special Agent Parsons disconnected.

"Hold on, Jason. The cavalry is coming." She murmured, grabbed her purse, and headed out into the squad room.

♦

It was actually closer to twenty-five minutes before the navy blue FBI helicopter swooped low over the firs at the south end of the small airport and settled down in front of the little building that served as the terminal. The Ebey Island airport was for general aviation and medical emergencies only. There was no control tower and most of the time the terminal building was empty.

Danny stood by the San Juan County squad car she'd checked out, an overnight bag full of toiletries and her least dirty clothes dangling from her hand, as the helicopter's powerful turbine whined down to idle and the wash from the rotor whipped her hair around her face.

A door slid open on the side of the helicopter and a familiar man in suit and tie bent into a crouching run toward her. Danny met him just beyond the rotors' reach. They shook hands.

"Good to see you again," Drew said. "Sorry it's such short notice, but you guys didn't give us much time."

"We weren't given much to start with."

"So I gathered."

"You're going to move on the Bartons?"

He nodded. "But we have a problem. Reynolds seems to have turned his cell phone off; we can't reach him. We're hoping you might help us get on top of the situation."

Danny pulled a wisp of hair from her mouth. "Of course."

"Let's go then."

Danny followed him to the helicopter and climbed in.

Jason had turned off his phones, both his regular one and the burner they'd purchased in Aberdeen. He was playing it safe. Even though he was walking into a trap and knew it, he still did not trust the Bartons to play by the rules. It would be just like them to track his cell and ambush him on his way to an ambush.

He wasn't going to let that happen.

As it was, he'd seen no Dunham County cars as he drove, no sign of the Sheriff's Department at all along the highway. It was like they were all busy elsewhere.

Probably setting up the trap.

He pulled into Bosque from the north at 10:30, an hour and a half before the exchange was supposed to take place. It was all part of what passed for his strategy. All he had at this point was a general goal of getting Lisa and the Millers away from the Bartons first, before he turned anything over. But he needed to scout out the area of the exchange before it got hot.

He truly hoped a more inspired idea of how to get out of this alive would strike sometime before the actual exchange.

Jason pulled over to the curb across the street from the Millers' café and looked over at the restaurant. It was dark and empty. He wondered whether they'd even been allowed to lock up. Was the door standing unlocked right now? Open to every petty thief that passed by? Was the money still in the till? Dirty dishes still on the tables, the grills and fryers still burning?

He thought about going to check on the property, but talked himself out of it. He didn't need to be seen by anybody in town right now. Besides, someone had turned off the lights. Someone had taken care of it for them.

Jason pulled back out into the street and turned left at the next corner.

Thanks to the computer search they'd done last night, he knew exactly how to get to the Bosque Sheriff's station. It lay two blocks west and three blocks south of the Millers' café, in what appeared to be an older part of town. His guess was that the main road had run through here before the highway was built further north. Back then it had been the main drag.

It even had a park like a town square with plenty of benches, concrete walkways through the lawns, a playground for the kids, and a central fountain that was either broken or shut down for the winter. A copse of hemlock and red cedar towered over it all.

It was probably very nice when the weather was better. Now it was wet and deserted.

To the north of the park was Bosque City Hall, beside it the garages of the volunteer fire department. To the south, directly across the park from City Hall, stood the concrete and glass Bosque City Library. On the west side was the sheriff's substation, where he would be coming face to face with the Sheriff himself in a little over an hour. The east side was dominated by several tall brick buildings, housing businesses.

As Jason drove by, he tried to get a general idea of the station's layout.

The building itself was newer than most of the others around it and impeccably maintained. The red brick looked new. The windows were spotless despite the rain. It was set back from the street by a large parking lot, now filled with squad cars. There had to be a dozen or more, mostly standard sedans, but a couple of SUV's and at least one pickup.

"It looks like all hands on deck," Jason said to himself. It explained why he hadn't seen any sheriff's cars on the highway. They were all here.

Between the substation and the side street was an older cinder block building that housed a CPA office. It backed on to the sheriff's parking lot.

The nearest cover of any kind, other than the parked cars, seemed to be the playground equipment in the park across the street.

Jason had been hoping for inspiration. Instead, he drove on with nothing. If he went to the meeting—which he had to for the Millers' and Lisa's sakes—he would have to rely on his wits and instinct to survive. With as little sleep as he'd had, that wasn't reassuring.

That didn't mean he wasn't going to find some place to sit and watch the station for the next hour and see what struck him.

He drove off to try and find just such a place.

♦♦♦♦♦

"You should try and get some rest," Scott Barton gently told his grandmother. They were sitting in his grandparents' living room at the luxurious house they owned in Tumwater just outside Olympia. They stayed here when Senate duties kept his grandfather in Olympia.

His grandmother nodded numbly.

It had been a long night for everyone, but especially his grandmother. Morris Barton was the love of her life and now no one knew whether he was alive or lying in a ditch somewhere.

"Seriously, you're not doing anyone any good exhausting yourself," he insisted. "I will wake you if anything develops."

"You're probably right." She looked around as though just seeing her surroundings for the first time.

The Morris Barton home had been transformed over the past few hours from a well-to-do enclave to a mobile law enforcement headquarters. FBI technicians sat in front of several computer monitors set up on the dining room table, monitoring the Bartons' social media and email. Others checked and double-checked the equipment they had attached to the landline phone, waiting for a ransom call.

Two State Police detectives stood in a corner, talking with their FBI counterparts.

Uniformed police guarded every outside door.

"Honestly, Grandma," he told her. "Go upstairs and try to get some rest."

"He's right," Scott's mother said. "You should try to get some rest before you get sick. I'll come sit with you, if you want."

She relented and rose to her feet. Scott and his mother also stood, his mother moving over to take the older woman's arm.

"I'll come get you the minute we hear anything," Scott assured them.

Scott watched his mother and grandmother slowly climb the stairs to the second floor bedrooms until they were out of sight.

"I need a drink," he murmured to himself and made his way over to the bar. It was almost noon. And if these didn't qualify as extreme circumstances, he didn't know what did.

No one knew what was going on with the Senator, including Scott. After his grandmother had called the office last night, looking for her husband, he had immediately retraced Morris' route and come upon his car, unlocked, driver's door hanging open in the garage. He'd known then that foul play was involved. It was like a sign had been hung on the car "I've been kidnapped." He'd called the State Police.

He poured two fingers of scotch into a highball glass and swallowed a mouthful of the smoky warmth.

What had everybody scratching their heads about Morris' disappearance, from the police detectives to the FBI agents, was the lack of any kind of ransom demand. Morris had been taken something like sixteen hours ago and there still had been no word from the kidnappers.

If they wanted money or some sort of political concession they should have contacted someone by now.

So what if it wasn't about money or politics?

"Mr. Barton?"

He turned to find the two FBI agents immediately behind him. He looked down at the drink in his hand, back up to the agents. “It’s been a tough day.”

“We understand,” the senior agent said. Scott couldn’t remember his name. “It was a good move getting your mother to rest for a while. This may turn out to be a marathon.”

“Grandmother.” Scott corrected him. “But that’s what I was thinking.”

“While we’ve got you alone, you mind answering a few more questions?”

“Sure. Whatever you need.”

They moved over to the sitting area, Scott returning to the sofa he’d just been sharing with his grandmother, the FBI agents spreading into two armchairs facing him. For the first time, Scott noticed the thin manila envelope in the senior agent’s hand. The junior agent had a pen and notebook in his.

Scott took another swallow of the scotch. “You said you have some questions?”

“Sure,” the lead agent—Scott still couldn’t come up with his name—said. “It’s bothering us that there hasn’t been any contact from the Senator’s abductors.”

“That bothers me too.”

The agent nodded as though that was obvious. “Can you think of any reason the Senator might want to disappear on his own?”

“Absolutely not. On his own? You mean like run away? Start a new life somewhere?”

“Something like that. It wouldn’t be the first time a man felt the walls closing in and decided to start over somewhere else.”

“Senator Barton isn’t that type of man. He’s never run from a fight in his life,” Scott told them. “Besides, he doesn’t have anything to run from. There are no walls closing in.”

“Understand, we have to examine every possibility. We wouldn’t be doing a thorough job if we didn’t.”

“I understand. I just think you’re looking in the wrong place. The Senator is the personification of integrity.”

The senior agent nodded. His partner seemed to be just witnessing the conversation and taking notes. He could have been a stenographer.

"What about back in—," the agent checked with his partner.

"Dunham County."

"That's right, Dunham County. Was there anything in Dunham County he was worried about? You told us you'd both just returned from there yesterday."

"That's true, we did," Scott said. "But nothing happened that worried the Senator. It was pretty much a routine weekend. Just a chance to get out of town for a couple of days."

Scott swallowed another mouthful of scotch, resisted the sudden urge to go get a refill.

The agent opened the manila envelope, withdrew a single page of heavy paper and handed it to Scott. "This didn't worry the Senator?"

It was a photograph. It captured Scott's grandfather, Senator Barton, unclothed and in the process of doing something he shouldn't be doing with a teenaged girl. It had clearly been shot through the window of Hemlock Run.

Scott felt like he'd been dipped in ice water.

Thirty-five

Jason did not consider himself a martyr and never had. Despite what Lisa believed (and sometimes Danny), he did not rush into dangerous situations because he didn't care whether he lived or died—he certainly wanted to live—or because he liked the idea of sacrificing himself for a good cause. He didn't. He didn't like the idea of sacrificing himself at all.

He just couldn't bring himself to walk away from injustice without doing something about it. He just couldn't. It wasn't the way he was built. The idea of leaving a crime or abuse for someone else to correct burned at his soul.

It was often dangerous work. He trusted that his wit, his friends, and luck would bring him through unharmed.

It had so far.

Jason had found a spot where he could park the Jeep on the opposite side of the park, behind the cover of the hemlocks, but still see well enough through gaps in the foliage to keep track of the activity at the sheriff's station.

So far, there hadn't been much to see.

A little before 11:30, movement drew his attention and he raised the field glasses Danny kept in her glove box. Two deputies left the station and strode out toward the parked cars. One of them was definitely Wilcox. He'd recognize that physique anywhere. He wasn't sure about the second, smaller man, but thought he might have been the one who'd killed Peterson.

The deputies climbed into separate cars and pulled out of the parking lot in opposite directions, tires squealing.

"What was that all about?" Jason murmured.

He feared they'd been sent out to see if he was lurking nearby, but they went somewhere else. It was a relief, but a worry too. Now he didn't know where they would be, other than behind him somewhere.

More than anything else about this situation, he hated the feeling of being blind. It was always helpful to have other eyes on the situation. Another point of view to add to the decision-making process.

Truth was he wasn't all that confident of his own judgement at this point. He checked the automatic pistol Danny had forced him to take—upon pain of physical harm—again. It was loaded and cocked, the safety engaged.

A few minutes later, more activity drew his eyes back to the station. He watched through the field glasses as a stream of deputies emerged and trotted out to the parked cars. One-by-one the cars left the parking lot only to park at various places along the street. The deputies climbed out of their cars and streamed back to the station.

They were clearing the parking lot, depriving him of cover.

He was going to be a sitting duck out there. Jason Reynolds against the combined firepower of the entire Dunham County Sheriff's Department. No problem.

Jason even had an idea of what he was going to do. It was simple. He was going to go up to the station, and force them to trade Lisa and the Millers for the memory card, or the memory card and himself.

That was it.

That was his plan.

Even he thought it sucked, but he couldn't come up with anything better.

Now, if they just shot him right off, he was sunk. He was betting they wouldn't just shoot him like that in broad daylight. They'd at least make a show of trying to do things legally. He hoped to stretch that out long enough for the cavalry to come to the rescue.

Gradually, as the morning aged relentlessly toward noon, he began to notice a change in the neighborhood around the little park. What little traffic there was dried up, completely. It was like the streets had been closed; no cars entered or left the park area. No pedestrians moved along the sidewalks. No one darted into City Hall to pay their water bill. No one visited the library to turn in their overdue books. The bookkeeping agency, a small restaurant, the thrift store and every other business around the park received no new customers and sent none satisfied on their way.

It began to remind Jason of a western movie where the townspeople take cover indoors until the bad man and Marshal finished their shootout. He even thought he saw pale faces appearing at windows facing the sheriff's station. All the scene needed was a small child running out into the street, only to be snatched up by her bonneted mother and hurried back inside.

At ten minutes to noon, Jason decided there was no use delaying any longer. He started the car and pulled away from the curb.

♦♦♦♦♦

Deputy Sergeant Randy Jensen was the best marksman on the force. He had proven it on a weekly basis at their shooting range and had even done some competitions. While he hadn't always placed first, he'd always been one of the top two.

It was only logical that he be the department's primary sniper.

He'd set up his nest on the roof of the Schiller Building, at the southeast corner of the aptly named Barton Memorial Park. From here, he had an unobstructed view of the Sheriff's station and its parking lot, with a substantial height advantage.

Jensen laid a sandbag across the cornice at the edge of the roof, smashed it down, then pulled his rifle from its case. It was a Weatherby, Mark V, bolt action, chambered for .308. It was his baby. He could put five rounds in a quarter at a hundred yards with her. He could hit the bullseye at three hundred.

He would have no trouble blowing Jason Reynold's brains out with a single shot from here. No problem at all. The same for the mysterious friend the Sheriff thought Reynolds may have backing him up. It was Wilcox's job to flush that friend out.

Jensen checked that the magazine was full, levered a round into the chamber, and locked the bolt in place with the solid snick of oiled steel. Jensen then laid down behind the cornice, the rifle steadied by the sandbag, his eye to the telescopic site. He adjusted it a bit until the image was sharp and clear. Now it was just a matter of waiting until Reynolds showed himself.

Jensen had spent a great deal of time honing his skills on shooting ranges and in the woods. He considered himself a professional and he took professional precautions, including a laser range finder, a billed hat to protect his eyes from the sun and foam plugs to protect his ears from the decibel level of gunfire.

The foam plugs, his ear protection, were probably the reason he didn't hear anyone approach before the Taser leads made contact.

♦♦♦♦♦

Jason pulled into the Sheriff's station parking lot precisely at high noon. He stopped the car just inside the entrance, broadside to the station door, and switched the engine off. Two deputies were stationed outside the door as lookouts. One of them spoke into his shoulder mic, without ever taking his eyes from Jason. Both of them rested a hand on the butt of their sidearms.

Jason checked Danny's pistol in his coat pocket, and stepped out of the car. He left the driver's door open and the car between him and the station as he stepped up to the front fender.

"Good morning," he said to the two deputies. "Can Sheriff Barton come out and play?"

"Smartass," one of them muttered.

It was overcast and cool, but had not rained for a few hours. The asphalt of the lot was dried gray, except for a few cracks that continued to hold moisture, making dark zigzags across the lot. A touch of breeze stirred his hair.

At least he didn't have to worry about the sun in his eyes.

The station door swung open and a big, clean-shaven man in the sheriff's uniform and a genuine Stetson hat stepped out. He strode a few feet away from the door and stopped, hands on hips. Deputies filed out behind him, separating to form a line to either side. All looked terribly serious.

A voice in Jason's head asked whether he'd just stepped into a revival of West Side Story.

"Well, well. Jason Reynolds," Sheriff Barton said in a booming baritone. "We meet at last."

"Yeah. It's a pleasure, I'm sure."

The Sheriff laughed. "Will you listen to this guy?"

His deputies obediently laughed, though Jason couldn't see much humor in their faces. None of the hands moved an inch from their weapons. He also couldn't see Travis Wilcox anywhere. Neither he nor the other deputy who had left earlier had returned. Where were they?

He felt a peculiar itching between his shoulder blades.

"Where's Lisa Martin? The Millers? I want to see them. I want to make sure they're safe."

"Fair enough," the Sheriff said. "Bring out the prisoners."

One of the deputies disappeared inside, only to emerge a few moments later, leading a line of people walking with the peculiar shuffling gait of people in shackles. Their hands were handcuffed in front of them, the handcuffs linked by chain to shackles around their ankles. Tom Miller was in front, followed by his wife, with Lisa in the rear. There was no sign of Helen. They were still in street clothes. None of them looked like they'd slept recently.

Lisa looked particularly bad, with dark smudges under her eyes and her hair hanging in strings beside her face. She would not look up at Jason.

The deputies arranged them in a line just to the left of the Sheriff.

"Okay," he said. "Here are your friends. Where are my photographs?"

Jason held up the memory card from the camera with his left hand. He kept his right in his coat pocket, on Danny's gun. "Right here. Let them go and it's all yours."

"You don't seem to appreciate your situation, son. You're in no position to be making any demands."

"You going to shoot me down right here, unarmed, in broad daylight? In front of the whole world? "

"You're a fugitive from justice—a murderer—armed and dangerous. I have a duty to take you into custody. If you don't cooperate…no one will even question it."

As if on command, all the deputies drew their weapons and assumed shooting stances. Jason's pulse ramped up. He was facing a dozen or more guns. All it would take is one itchy trigger finger to end him.

"Wait! Just hold on!" Jason held both hands up, showing they were empty. "I'm not resisting. My hands are up. Just let Lisa and the Millers go. This doesn't involve them."

Danny's gun was still in his coat pocket, but he assumed that as soon as any deputy saw it, he would be dropped by a dozen hollow points. All he was doing now was trying to get the Millers and Lisa out of harm's way and buy some time.

"Jason Reynolds," the Sheriff said, raising one hand like a preacher haranguing his congregation. "You are under arrest for the murder of Gerald Peterson. Put your hands behind your head. Interlock your fingers."

The Sheriff dramatically dropped his arm, like signaling a charge.

The breeze sifted across the parking lot.

The Sheriff looked frustrated.

"Well?" He finally looked at the deputies to either side of him. "What are you waiting for? Go get him!"

The deputies advanced, slowly, their weapons never wavering.

"Take it easy, guys." Jason said, hands still up by his face.

"Shut up," the deputy farthest to his left ordered. Because of the car's position, he was actually the closest to Jason. "Walk slowly toward me, hands in the air."

Jason didn't so much as twitch. He could see the Sheriff watching the drama, while other deputies herded the prisoners back into the station. He thought he saw Lisa struggle a little, but it was hard to tell. She might have just stumbled in her shackles.

"Come out from behind the car!" the guy on the left shouted. "Do it now!"

Jason didn't move. He certainly wasn't going to make this any easier for them than it had to be.

"I will blow your fucking brains out!" this from another deputy directly in front of him.

Jason didn't know what to do. He didn't move. Where was the cavalry? Where were the FBI? They would come in handy right about now.

The deputy to his left took a step forward. "Come—"

He grunted and fell forward onto his face.

A sharp crack, like someone breaking kindling ripped the air. Thunder rumbled between the buildings behind him.

Everyone on the parking lot—including Jason—stared at the fallen man like they were trying to figure out what he was doing.

"Joey?" One of the deputies—the one directly in front of Jason—finally asked. He had noticed the blood rivulet across the asphalt.

Another piece of kindling snapped and another deputy, this time to Jason's far right, fell over.

"Sniper!" somebody yelled.

"Sniper!"

"Sniper!"

Everybody forgot about Jason and the photographs and the hostages. Their only interest was in finding cover. But there was no cover. They'd purposely removed all cover before Jason got there. It was an empty parking lot. Some deputies flattened out on the asphalt. Others scurried for the shelter of the CPA's office. Some went for the station door. Those closest sought to hide behind Jason's car.

Jason was no different. He ducked behind the open car door and tried to make himself as small as possible.

Taylor Smith.

Despite everything, Jason smiled.

A few of the deputies shot back at the sniper, but it was strictly to make themselves feel better. They had no chance of hitting anything. They didn't even know where he was.

Jason thought about slipping into the car and trying to get away, but decided against it. He would make himself an easy target for the trigger-happy deputies. More important, it would not solve the situation for the Millers and Lisa.

God only knew what was going on inside the station.

Movement behind him made him turn. One of the deputies had crawled around the tail of the car. He had his pistol leveled right at Jason.

"Call off your buddy," the deputy said.

"It isn't my buddy," Jason told him. "I don't know who it is."

"Bullshit. Call him off before I put a bullet through your head."

"Okay, okay," he told him. "Don't shoot. I'll need to get my phone out of my pocket."

The deputy's eyes narrowed. "Real slow. Got it?"

"Okay." Jason could see the gun trembling. It might have been fear; it could have been adrenaline. In the end, it didn't matter. The deputy was wound up, more than ready to pull his trigger. He just needed an excuse.

"It's in my right coat pocket," Jason told him.

"Real slow."

Jason inched his right hand down and into his coat pocket. His phone wasn't there, of course. Danny's pistol was. His fingers found it and closed around the grip.

Now what was he going to do? The barrel was pointed down.

The deputy's radio crackled. He used his left hand to key the shoulder mic. "It's Steiner. I've got Reynolds."

Jason turned the gun, just a little bit.

Another burst of static from the radio, then clearly enough that Jason understood it: "Kill that bastard. Right now."

Somewhere down the street, powerful engines roared. Jason glimpsed a huge black SUV barreling toward them.

The cavalry.

The deputy heard it too and glanced behind him.

Jason turned the gun in his coat pocket and pulled the trigger. He felt it kick, heard the explosion as it fired. The deputy jerked backward and his gun went off.

The world flashed dark and eerily quiet.

♦

Danny was in the lead SUV, along with Parsons and three other FBI agents. More agents were in three more SUV's behind the first and a couple of State Police cars followed them. It was the culmination of the most frustrating morning Danny had ever experienced.

After climbing into the helicopter in Port Salish, she'd ridden in mostly silence because, even with radios, the rotor noise was too much to communicate effectively. All she'd managed to learn was that the Bureau was taking the photos very seriously, as well as the kidnapping. They'd been suspicious of events in Dunham County for a while, but had lacked jurisdiction to do much of anything.

Now they intended to push their advantage as far as it would go.

They landed in an empty field several miles outside Bosque at 10:30. The three SUV's were parked along a road nearby. But instead of rolling out to stop the Bartons, they went into a meeting with a tactical commander. They gathered over a map of Bosque and discussed various ways of handling the situation.

Danny listened and watched the clock and did her best to not scream at them to just go in there and overwhelm them. They were the FBI, after all, and there were nearly two dozen of them. But they wanted to avoid a shootout.

"You know these guys as well as anyone," the tactical commander had even asked her at one point. "Do you think they will give up without a fight?"

Danny didn't have to think about it. "I think most of the leaders don't actually believe anyone will ever challenge them. If it's played right, you could have them before they actually realize it."

Parsons peered at her. "They're actually that arrogant?"

She shrugged. "They've been getting away with it for years. What would make them think anything's different now?"

That caused them to discuss things for another fifteen minutes. By then it was nearly 11:30 and they seemed no closer to actually doing anything. To make things worse, several State Police officers drove up and joined them. Now they had to be read in to the discussion and their suggestions considered.

Danny wanted to scream.

"You have to understand," Parsons finally told her. "It is very important that we do not end up in a firefight with the Sheriff's Department. The Federal Government is not popular in this part of the country. We don't want to do anything to rile up the local militia types."

"I can understand that," she told him. Barely. It was hard to understand how anyone could side with the Bartons, over the agencies that were trying to bring them to justice, but these were strange times. "Jason Reynolds is going to the station at noon today, by himself, to try and get the hostages released. He could be walking into a death trap and we're standing around flapping our gums."

"We're almost ready to go," he assured her. "We just want to be sure we do it right."

She had no choice but to accept it.

Parsons was true to his word and ten minutes later the order came to mount up. The agents and Danny strapped on Kevlar vests, checked their weapons—sidearms for everyone and either H and K MP5 submachine guns, or M-16's—and climbed into one of the SUV's. The engines started and the convoy headed into town.

It was fifteen minutes before noon.

The convoy passed through the countryside like a column of tanks. Any car they happened to overtake quickly swerved to the shoulder, out of the way. Even in town, they met no traffic holdups. Everyone had watched television. They knew that when a column of black SUV's comes rushing up to you, you didn't ask questions. You got out of the way.

They were well into town when the police radio crackled to life. "Shots fired! Shots fired! Officer down!"

"Step on it," Parsons said.

The driver stood on the accelerator.

Danny couldn't speak. Her throat was so tight it was hard to breath.

The convoy flew down the city streets, blowing through stop signs, fishtailing around corners and nearly running civilians off the road.

"Here we go, folks," Parsons finally said into his mic. "Let's make sure we all get to go home tonight."

The SUV arrived at the sheriff's station with a long slide on wet tires. All Danny could see was Jason on the ground by the open driver's door of her Jeep. A deputy laid sprawled on his back by the rear tire. More bodies lay strewn across the parking lot.

She threw the SUV's door open and was beside Jason in an instant. Around her, she could hear shouting in multiple voices. "FBI! FBI! Drop your weapons! Drop your weapons now!" All she saw was Jason, crouched on his knees, head to the ground, his hands over his face.

"Jason!" She crouched down beside him, one hand on his back. "Are you hurt?"

He flinched at her touch, made an effort to fight her.

"Jason!" She grabbed his wrists. "It's me, Danny!"

He collapsed against her. "I can't see. My eyes; my eyes."

Danny held him with one arm, tipped his head up with the other. Despite herself, she felt her stomach go cold.

Jason's eyes, the entire area from the tip of his nose up over his forehead, was stippled with powder burns.

"Medic!" she called out. "Need medical over here!"

Beside her, the deputy groaned and tried to sit up.

"Stay down." She t moved over, secured his gun. "You've been shot. Medics are on their way. Just sit tight."

She could see where the deputy had taken a round in his vest. It had probably saved his life. He'd walk away with broken ribs. Jason, however, could be blinded for life.

It only took a few minutes for the combined force of the FBI and State Police to secure the parking lot. The half dozen deputies still outside the station house took one look at the firepower and surrendered. They were seriously outgunned and knew it. Besides, the sniper was still out there; they welcomed the Federal agents as reinforcements.

Their "reinforcements", however, confiscated all their weapons and identification and gathered them on the curb behind the safety of the parked SUV's. Two State Troopers with M-16s stood guard over them.

Special Agent Parsons had the remaining agents gathered to either side of the sheriff's station door. He'd already sent others around the building, to watch for anyone trying to slip away out the back.

Parsons silently checked that everyone was ready. One-by-one, everyone indicated they were.

"This is the FBI!" he called through the broken glass of the door. "Everyone in the building needs to come out with their hands up!"

After a few moments a baritone voice replied. "This is Michael Barton, Sheriff of Dunham County. We've been attacked by a sniper. He's already shot two of my men."

"Medical assistance is on the way," Agent Parsons replied. "But they won't come in until we have the area secure. Come out with your hands up. We will protect you from any sniper."

Another few moments, while the Sheriff decided what to do.

"Okay, we're coming out," the Sheriff said. "Our arms are holstered."

"Walk slowly, hands out where we can see them."

One after the other the Sheriff and his remaining deputies stepped out of the station, hands in the air. Agents swept each off to the side, searched and disarmed them.

Parsons approached the Sheriff. "No one else is in the station?"

"Just some prisoners in the holding cell."

Parsons signaled the agents and two went in, weapons up to secure the building. A couple of minutes later, they returned, visibly relaxed. "It's clear."

"We need to go find that damned sniper," Sheriff Barton said.

"I'll send some people. Any idea where he was?"

"The shots seemed to come from that building." Sheriff Barton pointed to a brown, three story brick building a little more than a block away, beyond the park.

Parsons sent two agents to check the building out.

"It's chilly out here," Sheriff Barton said, one law enforcement brother to another. "Why don't we go inside where there's some heat."

Person agreed and they walked into the station. Though they could feel the relief of the deputies—the siege had been lifted and no one else had to die—it was a subdued gathering. Two of them had died today.

"You going to give my men their weapons back?" Sheriff Barton asked.

"Actually, no, not right now," Agent Parsons told him. "Where are the keys to the holding tank? I want to speak to your prisoners."

Sheriff Barton frowned. "On what grounds?"

Agent Parsons smiled. "Call it inter-agency cooperation."

The Sheriff pushed back his cowboy hat, made a show of wiping his forehead. "Look, I do appreciate you Federal boys riding to our rescue and all, but you have no reason to be poking your nose into Dunham County's business, do you? You're out of your jurisdiction."

"Actually, I'm not."

Two of Parson's agents moved up beside the Sheriff.

"Michael Barton, you are under arrest for suspicion of kidnapping Thomas Miller, Barbara Miller, Helen Miller, and Lisa Martin. You have the right to remain silent—"

One of the deputies started moving, ready to intervene, but a close-up of an FBI mp-5 changed his mind. The two agents handcuffed the stunned Sheriff's hands behind his back as Parsons read him his Miranda rights.

♦

Thirty minutes later the two agents Special Agent Parsons had sent to find the sniper's nest returned. On the roof of the building the Sheriff had pointed out, they had found another Dunham County Deputy Sheriff. His name was Randy Jensen and he had been hogtied with plastic zip cuffs. Duct tape sealed his mouth.

Near the edge of the roof, they had found a .308 Weatherby Mark V that had been recently fired and four empty shell casings.

Based on the evidence at hand, Agent Parsons arrested Randy Jensen on suspicion of two counts of murder for the deaths of his fellow deputies.

Jensen protested his innocence.

Over and over.

Shortly after 2:00 on a busy Monday afternoon Karen Hysop was working on the paperwork for the patients who had been through the emergency room. Mondays were always busy, but this one had been even busier than usual. Word was there'd been some kind of shootout up in Bosque.

The sound of the emergency room doors rumbling open made her look up, ready to ask her usual batch of triage questions.

What she saw made her rise to her feet.

An older man stumbled into the reception area, wearing only maroon boxer shorts and black dress shoes. His grey hair stood on end and whiskers dusted his cheeks and jaw. He looked confused, close to panic.

"Sir?" Karen hurried around her desk. "Are you alright?"

After a second, his eyes focused on her. "I'm Senator Morris Barton. Do you know where I am?"

Thirty-six

Jason didn't think he was dead. He was no expert and hadn't given it all that much thought—not compared with most philosophers or theologians—but he'd always imagined death as a bright, peaceful serenity. Possibly with a little dusting of knowledge unavailable to mere mortals. But the serenity was a given, a base-line measure, if you will.

He didn't think he was dead because he was in pain. Pain just wasn't allowed.

Jason groaned and opened his eyes. Only he couldn't open his eyes. He tried, but couldn't. Something was keeping his eyes closed. He managed to free his right hand from the layers of cloth that trapped it at his side and gently touched his eyes. They were covered with thick bandage.

"Good morning," Danny's voice sounded oddly muffled on his left side. "How do you feel?"

Jason considered the question. "Thirsty." His tongue felt thick and awkward.

"Okay." She took his left hand in hers, brought it to a straw. "This is water."

He drank. It was the nectar of the gods. He'd never had anything taste so wonderful before. He drank as much as he could, laid back against the pillow and ran his tongue over horribly chapped lips.

"I'm in the hospital?"

"Yeah. Your eyes were badly powder burned. You're also dehydrated and exhausted. The hospital is a good place for you right now."

"What's wrong with your voice?"

"Nothing's wrong with my voice. It's your ears," she told him. "The blast from the deputy's gun damaged your left ear drum, just like your eyes."

He let this sink in for a moment. "I've been shot?"

"No. He missed. He did put a nice hole through the driver's door of my Jeep though."

"Sorry."

"Better my Jeep than you."

Jason paused for a moment. "What about the guy I shot?"

"He was wearing a vest. He has a couple of broken ribs and a bruise the size of a softball. Otherwise he's fine."

"Good." He sighed. "How bad am I?"

"The doctor says you're going to be fine. The bandages are just to make sure you don't use your eyes for a couple of days."

"A couple of days."

"Yeah. He said there was no permanent damage. I guess the eyes are very good at healing themselves."

"Who knew, right?"

"Yeah, who knew?"

♦

"What about Lisa?" Jason asked. "And the Millers. Are they okay?"

"They're fine. Lisa spent a few hours here last night. I finally sent her to get some sleep." Danny paused. "She looked like hell, Jason."

He didn't doubt it. She'd been through hell. They might not even know the worst of it. Had she just spent the night in the Dunham County Jail? Or had she been put through even worse?

They were talking about the folks that empowered Wilcox, after all.

"Sheriff Barton is in FBI custody; so is Deputy Jensen. The rest of the deputies were sent home, suspended without pay, pending the investigation. The State Police are taking over law enforcement in Dunham County," Danny said.

"What about Wilcox?"

"He's gone. There's a bulletin out on him."

Jason didn't comment.

"Oh," Danny said. "You should see the front page of the paper. It's your story and a bunch of your photographs. The Bartons' goose is officially cooked."

"They printed the photos? How'd they do that without an X rating?"

"Creative cropping. They left just enough to know what's going on, without actually showing anything. Of course, the guys' faces are in perfect focus. There is no doubt whatsoever who they are. Just to make sure, they included official portraits. It's perfect."

Jason agreed. It was perfect, almost.

"What about Helen?" he asked.

Danny hesitated. "Nothing yet. They're still looking."

Damn. He no longer felt like celebrating.

♦♦♦♦♦

Becca Hawthorn was sixteen and beautiful in the fresh, innocent way some teenaged girls are beautiful. The principle of Genoa High School brought her in to the interview room they'd set up and introduced her to Special Agents Drew Parsons and Stephanie Galloway.

"I'll be right outside, if you need anything," the principle told Becca and closed the door behind her.

"Please, sit down," Stephanie told Becca, indicating the chair across the table. "Thank you for coming. This shouldn't take long."

Becca nodded, pulled out the chair, and sat. Her dark hair had been gathered at the nape of her neck in a simple pony.

Silver rings decorated each of her fingers, both thumbs, and her left nostril. "I don't even know why you want to talk to me."

"Have you ever heard of a place called Hemlock Run?"

Becca's face immediately went two shades paler, but she shook her head. "Never heard of it."

Stephanie scribbled something on the legal pad in front of her.

Parsons watched as Becca twisted the rings on her left hand, continuously, compulsively.

"You may have heard that we arrested the County Sheriff and several of his men the other day?"

"I heard something about it."

"We believe they are responsible for a bunch of crimes against the people of Dunham County. We want them to pay for those crimes. We want them to go to prison. But we need some help building our case. Will you help us?"

"Sure." Becca gave a noncommittal shrug. "I guess."

"Good. Thank you." Agent Calloway opened a manila file beside her legal pad, consulted it before returning to Becca. "Do you know a deputy named Travis Wilcox?"

"I've seen him around."

"Would you consider Deputy Wilcox a friend?"

She shook her head.

Stephanie changed tactics. "Okay, Becca, you're an intelligent young woman. I don't think I need to treat you like a child, so let's cut to the chase. We know what went on at Hemlock Run."

Becca didn't react.

Parsons merely sat there, listening. He did not make eye contact with the girl.

"We believe Deputy Wilcox forced teenaged girls to do things at Hemlock Run, things they wouldn't normally do," Stephanie continued.

Becca was blushing now, avoiding their gaze.

"What he did is a serious crime, a felony. We want to put Travis Wilcox in prison for a long, long time. He's a monster. He deserves it."

Becca twisted her rings, stared away from them.

"But we need help. We need evidence. We need witnesses to tell us exactly what he did."

The girl didn't respond.

"How did he make you do those things? What did he threaten you with?"

"I don't know what you're talking about. I'm not a whore."

Parsons and Stephanie exchanged a quick look. Parsons leaned back in his chair, relaxed, detached, unthreatening. He was barely paying attention. The interview was going exactly as they had hoped.

Stephanie leaned forward a bit, forearms on the table. "Look, Becca, we think we can fix it that Travis Wilcox spends the rest of his life in jail. The rest of his life. He'd never be able to abuse you or any other woman ever again. But in order for us to do that, we need his victims to tell us exactly what he did. It's evidence. It's the only way he's ever going to pay for what he did. It's the only way to make sure he stops."

Becca twisted her rings. Refused to look at the agents.

"Becca?"

"I'm not a whore."

"We know that. You didn't do this because you wanted to, or because you wanted money or drugs. You did this because Deputy Wilcox didn't leave you any other choice. What we don't know is how he did it. What did he have over you? What did he threaten you with?"

After a moment, softly. "Meth."

"Meth?" Stephanie repeated, trying to draw her out. "He threatened you with possession of meth?"

Becca nodded, still not looking at them. The rings went around and around her fingers.

"Do you use meth?" Stephanie asked.

"No. Never. I might have smoked pot a few times." Becca shrugged. "I've never touched anything like that."

"A lot of people have smoked pot," Stephanie said. "We don't care about pot."

"He said he'd arrest me for possession of meth, or maybe selling it," Becca said, her voice barely audible. "Forget college. Forget getting a decent job. If I didn't do what he wanted, he'd ruin my life, so I did." She wiped under her eye with the side of a finger. "Now you're going to ruin it instead."

"No, we're not," Parsons finally spoke. "You're a victim, Becca. You are the victim of a sexual predator. We don't punish victims. We punish criminals. Your name doesn't ever have to come up. I give you my word."

She finally looked at him, tears glittering in her eyes. "Really?"

"Absolutely. We're after Deputy Wilcox, not you. You're a minor; the court will protect your identity. You'll just be Jane Doe number 24, or something. Wilcox will go to jail for a very long time and you can get on with your life."

Stephanie pushed the legal pad and pen across the table. "Just write down exactly what happened."

Becca hesitated, then picked up the pen.

♦♦♦♦♦

Dr. Patel was of East Indian origin and had the lilting, clipped accent of his homeland that Jason had always thought musical. He introduced himself again to Jason that evening with his full name, then laughed and admitted almost no one could pronounce it without weeks of dedicated practice.

"Everyone just calls me Dr. Patel," he told Jason.

"That's easier to remember."

"Isn't it though? How are those eyes feeling?"

"They itch a little, but the pain is mostly gone."

"Good, that's a good sign," he said. "Let's take a look at them."

The doctor removed the bandages, then examined each of his eyes. "There is marked improvement," he said. "But I don't think we're there yet."

Jason closed his eyes again. It felt better when they were closed.

"I think I'm going to add a little steroid and another dose of antibiotic."

"Okay."

"And, since you don't live nearby, I think I'll keep you here one more night."

♦♦♦♦♦

Randy Jensen insisted he was not the person who'd shot and killed the two deputies in the parking lot of the Bosque Sheriff's station. He sat at a battered, government-issue gray metal table in an interrogation room attached to the County Jail. He wore an inmate's bright orange jumpsuit and had his left wrist handcuffed to a steel ring under the table.

FBI Agent Eric Gershon and State Police Lieutenant Greg Marlowe sat on the other side of the table, legal pads and file folders spread across the table in front of them.

"The problem here," Lt. Marlowe said, "is that the only fingerprints on the rifle are yours. The same is true for the shell casings in the magazine and the expended casings. There is no evidence anyone else fired that rifle."

"He was wearing gloves, for Christ's sake."

"Of course he was."

"Dumbshits!" Jensen made a strangled sound deep in his throat. "You think I hogtied myself too?"

Lt. Marlowe just shrugged. "Maybe a law-abiding citizen did a public service. Left you all neat and packaged for us. All you needed was a bow."

"He hit me with a Taser. I have the marks."

It was Agent Gershon's turn to smile. "Before or after you shot the deputies?"

Jensen dropped his head.

The cops across the table just smiled and waited.

"I want to make a deal."

♦♦♦♦♦

The next morning the doctor gave Jason sunglasses he was supposed to wear whenever his eyes were open. Either that, Dr. Patel told him, or the bandages for another day. He chose the shades.

At least with the sunglasses he could feed himself again. Which is what he was doing now, working his way through the scrambled eggs, pancakes and Jello the hospital had provided. It wasn't bad, as such things went. At least, he didn't need someone to feed him like a baby. And he had coffee.

He had sent Danny to get some rest and maybe a shower and decent meal. She had spent the entire night with him.

Fifteen minutes ago, a State Trooper had poked his head in the door and introduced himself as Bryan, with a "y". "I'm your security detail today. If you need anything just give me a shout."

Jason thanked him. "They think there's a serious threat?"

"They don't tell me too much," the trooper said. "But they think you have some enemies. There's a lot of media types around too. I'm not supposed to let anyone in who isn't on the list."

Jason had thanked him and returned to his breakfast.

Now someone tapped on the door. "You decent?"

"Barely." He looked up as Lisa stepped into the room. She was wearing jeans and a peach colored polo shirt under a blue raincoat, spotted with rain water.

A bruise on her cheek matched the patches under her eyes. She looked like she hadn't slept in days.

Lisa walked over and kissed him on the cheek, gave him a hug. "You look like a movie star with those things on."

"Yeah, I feel like one too." He looked up at her. "How are you?"

She smiled and pulled a chair next to the bed. "I'm okay."

Her eyes didn't quite support her words. Neither did her smile.

"Are your eyes going to be okay?" she asked.

He nodded. "In a day or two. They're supposed to cut me loose this afternoon."

"That's good."

He thought so too.

"What you did out there Monday," Lisa said, tucking her hair behind her right ear. "It was the bravest thing I've ever seen. You all alone standing up to all those cops. I thought they were going to kill you right there."

"I did too."

"What were you thinking?"

Jason sighed. "We'd told the FBI about the meeting. I was stalling, just hoping they would show up before things got too hairy."

"Helluva plan, Jason."

"It worked," he shrugged, looked up at her. "Did Wilcox…did he do anything to you?"

Lisa shook her head, maybe blushed a little, but her eyes darted to the window on the other side of the bed. "Nothing worse than I've gone through at a frat party."

Some pretty nasty things had happened at fraternity parties.

"You sure?"

"I don't want to talk about it. Please. I gave my statement to the State Police."

"Okay."

God. Wilcox had assaulted her.

He reached over and took her hand. There were bruises on her wrist too.

"I'm sorry. I'm so sorry."

She made herself smile. "I'm going to head back to Seattle tonight."

"Of course. You can't afford to miss any more class."

Lisa released his hand and quickly wiped her eyes.

"I expected Danny to be here," she said and moved to her feet, wandering over to inspect some of the bouquets he'd been given. "She wouldn't leave your side that first night."

"I sent her home to get some rest. I don't need to be babysat anymore."

She turned back to him. "Look, I know about you and Danny."

Jason started to say something, but she stopped him.

"It's okay. Really, it's okay. In a way, it's only natural. You make a great team and you've gone through hell together, twice."

"It just kind of happened," he told her. "Neither of us want to hurt you. That's the last thing we want."

"I know." Lisa said. "It's okay. She can give you something I never will."

"Lisa."

"No. She's a good woman and you're a good man. You deserve a chance to see if you can make it work."

"It doesn't mean we can't be friends, does it?"

"Don't be stupid." She smiled. "This isn't high school."

Lisa leaned over and they hugged.

♦♦♦♦♦

Scott Barton let himself into his condo, closed and locked the door behind him. For a few moments, he just stood there, staring blindly into space. But he finally trudged through the living room to the small bar in the corner. He threw the manila envelope he'd been carrying onto an end table and poured himself a generous serving of bourbon. It felt like a bourbon kind of day.

He swallowed a mouthful and winced at the smooth burn working its way to his stomach.

Today would be a good day to get drunk. He certainly deserved it, but he couldn't afford to let his self-pity get out of hand either. It didn't matter how you fell. What mattered was picking yourself up again.

And lord how he'd fallen.

His attorney had only bailed him out of jail this morning. The manila envelope contained a copy of the charges against him and other legal documents. None of which he wanted to look at right now. They would just serve to remind him of how thoroughly his political career had been destroyed.

It was all because of the damn videos from Hemlock Run. When the Feds had searched his office and apartment, they had seized his cell phones and computers. It wasn't a surprise. In fact, he'd expected it to happen sooner, or later. It's why he'd been so careful to make sure his face would never appear on any of those videos. They might know he was there. They might find evidence that he—at the Senator's request—had invited most of the guests to the lodge, and even that he had secretly filmed their exploits, again, at the Senator's request, but that was it. No one would have any proof that he'd participated in any of the festivities. He'd been smart about it.

But not smart enough.

Some of the girls had been under age when the videos had been taken and when he'd edited them down to their final, useful, versions. That had been his mistake.

He'd been charged with possession and manufacture of child pornography. And he was guilty as sin.

His attorney said there would probably be other charges once the investigation was finished. Extortion, almost certainly. Pandering prostitution, coercing prostitution, conspiracy charges were all possible. But it was the child pornography charges that destroyed everything.

The voters could and did forgive a great deal. The extortion charges, for instance, could be argued away as just politics. Dirty politics, but just politics. Everyone did it, he just happened to get caught.

Child pornography though, that was a different story. Voters wouldn't forgive a man for getting his rocks off with their teen daughters. Never. He wouldn't be able to win an election for dog catcher after that.

He'd be a sex offender.

He'd be lucky if he wasn't run out of town.

He swallowed the rest of the bourbon in his glass and poured himself some more. It wasn't even giving him a buzz.

♦♦♦♦♦

"Lisa stopped by today," Jason said.

Danny looked up from the clothing she was laying out on his bed. She'd washed and dried them so he'd at least have clean clothes when he was released.

"She didn't look very good."

"She had a rough day," Danny said. "A very rough day."

"Did you talk to her?"

"A little, while you were out that first night. She didn't say anything, but I think she was being treated here too."

Jason nodded.

"She figured out we were involved," Danny said. "Said it was pretty obvious if you saw us together, actually. She said it was okay with her."

"She told me the same thing."

Danny walked around the bed to sit beside him.

"Wilcox raped her, didn't he?" Jason said.

"She won't talk about it. But I'm pretty sure he did. She's acting like a rape victim."

"Why wouldn't she tell me?"

Danny sighed. "I don't know. She wouldn't tell me anything either. She probably just wants to forget about it. I can't even—" she shuddered.

Jason reached over, took her hand in his.

"We really need to get this bastard."

♦

Later that morning, Jason's cell phone rang again. It had been going off pretty regularly the entire time he'd been in the hospital, but Danny had fiercely and firmly screened those calls. Most had simply been friends and colleagues who'd wanted to wish him well. These she told he was recovering nicely, but was asleep. Most accepted this and went away.

Some had been more important, like questions from the FBI or State Police. And, of course, from the paper. Those she had let him take.

Danny looked at the display now and groaned.

"Who is it?"

"Miles again."

Jason sighed. "I'd better take it."

"Doesn't he understand the meaning of rest?"

"No, I genuinely don't think he does."

She made a face and handed the phone to him.

He accepted the call. "Good morning, Miles."

"Well you sound chipper. How are you feeling?"

"I feel fine. We're just waiting for the doctor to okay my discharge."

He briefly explained to his editor the diagnosis and prognosis of his eye injuries. Miles seemed to appreciate the seriousness.

"Listen," Miles said. "This story is blowing up again, going national. We're getting media and interview requests from all the news channels and a bunch of magazines."

Jason smiled. “You need another story.”

“Of course I need another story. I need a bunch of stories. The question is when will you be able to get me something?”

Jason laughed. “How about tomorrow by the end of business?”

Danny glared at him.

“Do you need someone to help? I could send a stenographer, or maybe Debbie.”

“I should be fine. I’ll give you a call if something comes up.”

“Only if you feel up to it. What about the interview requests?”

“Put them off until I get back, say Friday.”

“Okay, get better.”

Jason laughed and ended the call.

Danny looked at him. “Did he really just call you in the hospital to ask when he’d get the next story from you?”

“That’s just Miles’ way of saying he loves me.”

Wednesday, the office of the Dunham County District Attorney issued a press release announcing the immediate resignation of District Attorney Patrick Barton. The duties of District Attorney would be fulfilled by the current Assistant District Attorney Anthony Ross until such time as a new District Attorney could be elected.

No reason was given for the resignation. Rumors were circulating that he had agreed to testify against the rest of his family. The same rumors speculated that by doing so, his law license might only be suspended rather than revoked outright.

Also on Wednesday, Republican State Senator Bruce McKean of Kennewick, who had won his seat on a conservative “family values” platform, resigned in the wake of the Hemlock Run scandal. In a tearful press conference, he admitted he’d let down his family, his constituents, and the honor of the State

Government. His wife did not appear with him, nor did any other family members.

Shortly after Senator McKean's presser, local and regional news outlets received a press release from the office of Republican Representative Daniel O'Hara stating that he would not be seeking re-election when his current term expired. Though no reason was stated, Congressman O'Hara, a conservative Catholic from Longview, was also implicated in Hemlock Run.

Also on Wednesday, in further fallout from the Barton scandal, State Senate Democratic Leader William Congreave announced his decision to resign as leader of the Democratic caucus, effective immediately. He stated he did not want to become a distraction from the important business of the State Senate.

♦♦♦♦♦

Late Wednesday morning, Dr. Patel examined Jason again and decided he had improved enough to be released. He was given a prescription for eye drops and an oral antibiotic and the recommendation that he continue to wear the sunglasses until his eyes were comfortable in bright light.

It would probably be back to normal within a week, the doctor predicted. If not, he needed to follow up with a doctor in Seattle.

Jason told him he would.

So now he sat on the edge of his bed, wearing clean street clothes, and waited for the hospital staff to process his release orders. It seemed to take forever.

"What are we going to do with all these flowers?" Danny asked. "We'll need another car just to hold them all."

"I don't know," he told her. "Maybe the hospital can give them to patients who haven't gotten any. Minus the cards of course."

"That's a good idea. I'm going to ask if someone can do that." She disappeared out the door.

Jason smiled. The transformation she'd undergone just within the last day was amazing. The weight of worry and fear had been lifted from her shoulders and now she seemed to be walking a foot and a half above the ground.

While Danny was out of the room, Jason busied himself by collecting the note cards from the various bouquets of flowers spread throughout the room. Most were from colleagues at the paper, though one was from Andrea Meade, the San Juan County DA and another from the Millers. More interesting was one with no obvious name attached. Jason had to remove the card from the little envelope. The message read: *Happy you're on the mend. Watch out for Wilcox though. Nothing more dangerous than a psycho w/nothing to lose. Smith.*

"Look who I found," Danny said as she came back through the doorway. Drew Parsons, the FBI agent, followed, a bemused expression on his face.

The men shook hands.

"Sorry I haven't come by sooner, I've been kind of busy trying to unravel the rat's nest they've created out here."

Jason invited him to take a chair.

Danny sat on the bed beside him.

"So, where we stand," the agent said. "First of all, The Bureau of Indian Affairs law enforcement executed a search warrant on the Hemlock Run lodge. They found a supply of cocaine, pot, and all the alcohol you could ever want, just like your photographs showed. More important, they found a sophisticated network of surveillance cameras in each of the guest bedrooms."

Jason had had no idea.

Danny was shaking her head. "They just keep getting sleazier and sleazier, don't they?"

"Yeah," Parsons said. "We think they were organizing these sex and drug parties, then blackmailing the participants."

Jason nodded. "It figures."

Search warrants had been served at the homes and offices of Morris Barton, Scott Barton, and Sheriff Michael Barton, and several digital recordings were found that looked consistent with the lodge cameras. Just exactly who had been victimized and how, was still under investigation.

Sheriff Barton, Morris Barton, Randy Jensen and four other deputies were under arrest and lodged at the County Jail there in Genoa. Eventually they would be transferred to the federal facilities in Seattle, but right now, it was more convenient to keep them there.

"They didn't make bail?" Jason asked.

"We managed to convince the judge that because of their resources and their contempt for the law, they were flight risks."

Jason smiled. "Good for you. Keep them there forever."

"That's what we're shooting for."

"What about Travis Wilcox?" Jason asked, thinking of Smith's note.

"He's still out there somewhere," Parsons told them. "According to several people we talked to, Wilcox is an avid outdoorsman and some camping gear and weapons were missing from his home. We think he may have headed into the woods to wait out the search."

Jason sighed. That made a certain amount of sense. He could hide out in the woods without being discovered indefinitely, unless a hunter stumbled upon him.

"He was the worst of them all," Danny said. "We can't let him get away."

"We're not letting him get away. We have arrest warrants out and every agency in the region is looking for him. Sooner or later, he's going to need to come back to civilization. When he does, we'll be waiting."

They were doing everything they could and Danny knew it. "I just really wanted to see him in shackles."

"I know. I think a lot of women here do."

Danny shook her head. "What I want is to be the person who catches him. And him to resist arrest."

"I think a lot of women want that, too."

Jason reached over to take Danny's hand. She squeezed his. Hard.

"What about Helen? Helen Miller?" he asked. "Has anybody found her?"

"Not yet," Agent Parsons told him. "According to the girls we've talked to, she didn't travel with the rest of them, staying behind with Wilcox. She also was already at Hemlock Run when they arrived Friday evening."

Jason nodded. “We think Wilcox had been holding her prisoner there since Tuesday night.”

“Why?”

“We don’t know.”

“Maybe she was going to go public,” Danny suggested. “Maybe she was just trying to say ‘no’.”

“But we don’t know for certain.”

Parsons jotted something down in his notebook. “Anyway. State Police have been searching between Hemlock Run and here, but there are a lot of old logging roads. Wilcox could have stashed her in a cabin somewhere and it would take years to find her.”

Jason didn’t have to say what they were all thinking. He also may have shot her in the head and hidden her body. If so, they’d never find her. Not until some mushroom hunter stumbled across her bleached bones years from now.

“Any clue as to where Wilcox might be hiding out?” Jason asked. “I assume you searched his place, talked to his friends and family.”

“There was nothing that shouted ‘hey, look here!’ We’re still analyzing some things, but it’s a long shot,” Parsons said. “And his friends and family aren’t cooperating much at this point.”

Danny shook her head. “Surprise, surprise.”

“By the way,” Jason said, “thanks for riding in to save me the other day.”

“Glad we could get there in time. You were kind of pushing your luck out there.”

Danny speared him with a pointed look.

Jason didn’t respond. He knew.

“But I should be the one thanking you. We’d been stonewalled by the Bartons for years now; you broke the case wide open. Those photographs and spotting that Hemlock Run was on Indian land was the absolute key. I know a lot of experienced agents who would have missed that.”

“Thanks,” Jason shrugged. “It’s what I do.”

“It’s true.” Danny said. “It is what he does. It’s kind of spooky.”

"Have you ever thought about going into law enforcement?"

"Oh, no." Jason was shaking his head. "I don't like guns much."

Parsons laughed.

Thirty-seven

A little after 1:00 Wednesday afternoon Jason submitted to the inevitable and allowed a nurse's aide to push him in a wheelchair to the elevator and out the hospital's main entrance. He was perfectly able to walk out on his own, but it was hospital policy. Every discharged patient had to leave the hospital in a wheelchair.

Jason just sat back and enjoyed the ride.

Danny was waiting beside her Jeep at the curb, dressed in clean jeans and a dark blazer. The day was beautiful, clear skies and a warm sun that teased everyone with memories of summer. The last time he'd been outside, it had been gray and damp.

The hospital had purposely not alerted the media of his release, so there wasn't the crowd of shouting reporters he'd half expected.

"I think this is my stop," Jason said.

The aide giggled and stopped the wheelchair beside the Jeep.

Danny watched them with something like amusement on her face. "You guys seem to be enjoying yourselves."

Jason just smiled as he stood out of the wheelchair.

"Before you go, Mr. Reynolds," the aide asked. "Do you think I could get your autograph? You're the first real writer I've ever met."

"Sure," Jason smiled at Danny, who rolled her eyes and walked around the front of the Jeep to climb behind the wheel.

He scribbled his name on a scratch pad.

She thanked him profusely and turned back toward the hospital with the wheelchair.

Jason climbed into the Jeep beside Danny. "Any sign of him?"

"Not that I've noticed."

They had discussed the issue of Travis Wilcox for quite a while this morning. It wasn't just a matter of him managing to slip through the net the FBI had cast around the Sheriff's Department. That was bad enough. No woman was safe as long as he remained on the loose.

Jason, however, did not share the Feds' opinion that Wilcox had fled the area, or even that he was hiding out in the rain forest somewhere.

"Think about it," Jason told Danny. "Wilcox has been living in paradise. He's the ultimate alpha male, with a powerful family running protection for him. It's perfect. He's had no limits, certainly not since puberty. Whatever he wants he's taken and if anybody dares to resist, he hurts them, right?"

Danny nodded. "Pretty much."

"You couldn't design a better situation for a sociopathic sexual predator."

"But it's all gone now," Danny said. "There's no reason to stick around anymore."

"But that's just it. Where else can he go and be the alpha he was here?"

"Nowhere. Not like he's been here. No other place would let him get away with it for long. He'd either end up dead or in prison."

"Exactly."

Danny peered at him. "Where are you going with this?"

"What does a bully usually do when his power is taken away from him?"

"I don't know. Find different victims?"

"If there are others handy, sure. But if there aren't any, he doesn't suddenly become a well-adjusted member of society."

"Okay?"

"He escalates. In his mind he's been humiliated, disrespected, and he can't live with that idea. He will lash out against whoever he believes is responsible, as hard as he can."

"Like an abusive husband?"

"Exactly like that. Once his victim finally stands up to his abuse, he will attempt to regain his power. Sometimes, even if it means killing her and anyone he thinks helped her."

Danny paused to consider this. "So you think he's still here?"

"I think he's nearby," Jason said. "I think he's looking for revenge. And I think we're his targets."

Danny pulled away from the curb in front of the hospital and headed for the exit. Several other vehicles were moving in various parts of the hospital's lot, as well as fifty or sixty parked. Wilcox could hide within the mass of vehicles pretty easily, especially since neither he nor Danny knew exactly what he would be driving.

They had contacted Drew Parsons before leaving the hospital and got descriptions of the vehicles Wilcox might be driving. Parsons told them that Travis Wilcox had several vehicles registered with the State Motor Vehicles Division. He had a navy blue Ford F-250 4X4 pickup truck, a red Porsche 911, a Harley-Davidson soft tail, and a Kawasaki 250 dirt bike. When agents searched Wilcox's house, the Porsche and Harley-Davidson were the only vehicles still parked in the shop/garage.

So they were looking for a big blue pickup, or a little dirt bike, provided he didn't have something off the books.

It was better than nothing, but not much. Jason, for one, doubted a man like Wilcox would content himself with riding around in a stock pickup. He would have installed a lift kit, oversized tires, roll bars, maybe a custom paint job? It may bear little to no resemblance to the original truck.

Danny pulled out on to the street. No blue pickups seemed to be lurking nearby.

"So, we're heading straight home?" he asked.

"I promised the Millers we'd stop by before leaving town. After that, yeah, we're going to Port Salish before you can get yourself in any more trouble."

Jason nodded. That was the agreement they'd made. He would stay with Danny until she could be sure his eyes were fully healed. He would be able to write his stories just fine from there.

He wondered where Travis Wilcox was right now.

♦♦♦♦♦

Much to Jason's relief, a Washington State Police cruiser was parked at the curb right outside the Millers' *City Center Café* in Bosque. It meant the FBI was taking seriously the threat posed by Travis Wilcox. All along the drive from the hospital in Genoa, he and Danny had kept a wary eye on the vehicles around them. Would Wilcox try to attack them on a busy highway in broad daylight? Jason had no idea. He certainly wouldn't want to bet against it.

They'd only seen two blue Ford pickups during the drive, but both of them were heading in the opposite direction and neither had Wilcox behind the wheel. They hadn't seen a motorcycle at all. Not one.

Now Danny pulled into the curb behind the State Police car and switched off the engine.

Jason looked at the façade of the restaurant and sighed. "I'm not looking forward to this."

"Because of Helen?"

"Yeah, because of Helen. We haven't brought her home. We've failed. We don't even know if she's still alive, or not."

Danny reached over and took his hand in hers. "Like someone once said, no news is good news. Until they find her body, we have to assume she's still alive. And she's of more value to Wilcox alive, than dead."

Jason nodded. "We hope."

"They aren't going to blame you for anything. You brought down the Bartons. They think you're a hero."

"Okay. Let's go see the Millers."

The restaurant was quiet. It was almost 2:00 in the afternoon, and the midweek lunch was pretty much over. Only three booths were occupied. Two were older couples working on sandwiches and fries. The third was a uniformed State Trooper who sat a couple of booths from the entrance and studied them closely before returning to his paper.

Jason felt a little better. At least the Millers had competent protection.

"Jason!" Tom Miller stepped down the central aisle from the kitchen. "They let you go."

"Yeah, I was getting on the nurses' nerves."

"Please, sit down. Get you some coffee?"

"Coffee would be wonderful," Jason said and slid into the booth he'd come to prefer in the restaurant, where he could see the door. Danny slid in across the table from him.

Tom returned a moment later. He had two cups dangling from the fingers of his right hand. The rest of his right arm was still encased in a yellow fiberglass cast. He carried a coffee pot in his left.

"Let me help," Danny said and took the cups from Tom's fingers and set them upright on the table. Tom poured coffee into each cup then headed into the kitchen to get his wife.

"He seems almost giddy," Jason told Danny.

"I know. I wonder if something's happened we don't know about?"

Jason sipped his coffee. It was worlds better than the hospital's.

A few moments later, Tom returned to the table. Barbara was right behind him. Tom slid in the booth next to Jason, Barbara next to Danny.

"How are you feeling?" Barbara asked.

Jason was still wearing the sunglasses he'd been given. Dr. Patel's orders had been clear. He was to wear the glasses full time until at least Saturday. After a week, he could try going without.

"I'm okay," he told her. "They're still kind of itchy, but they're better than they were."

"Thank God for that."

Danny agreed with that sentiment. "Have you heard anything new about Helen?"

Barbara shook her head. "They're still looking for her, but they have a lot of ground to cover."

"It's like a needle in a haystack," Tom added.

Jason agreed. They were counting on luck now to find her. And that was a long shot.

"Do you think Travis still has her?" Barbara asked him.

"I think there's a good chance he does. He may see her as a bargaining chip if he's found."

"A hostage," Danny agreed. "Or he may just view her as his girlfriend."

"You don't think he'd hurt her?"

Jason hesitated, trying to be precise in his answer. "I don't think he has a reason to hurt her."

He glanced at Danny, who just smiled. Both knew there were probably as many reasons for Wilcox to kill Helen as there were to keep her alive. But they certainly weren't going to tell her parents that. Hope was the only thing they had. He wasn't about to take that away.

"It's good to see that they're taking your safety seriously." Jason indicated the Trooper sitting a few booths away.

"Oh, yes. There's been someone here every day," Barbara said. "We try to keep them from being bored too much."

Danny smiled. "They're used to being bored, believe me."

"And you haven't seen or heard from Travis Wilcox?" Jason asked.

Tom shook his head. "And we won't, not if he knows what's good for him. He needs to pray the Feds find him first."

Barbara turned her gaze to Jason. "Have you talked to Lisa?"

"She stopped by the hospital."

Tom grumbled something about coffee and left the table.

Barbara watched him go. "He's been through about as much as a man can stand. When his people are threatened, a man needs to defend them. Do something. Nothing is worse than being helpless and he's been helpless a lot lately."

"How's he doing?" Danny asked.

Barbara shrugged. "He's hanging on."

"It's tough," Jason agreed. "Hopefully, it's almost over."

"Hopefully."

Tom returned with the coffee pot and filled everyone's cup, then left again. Jason thanked him. So did Danny.

"Lisa didn't want to talk about what happened at the sheriff's station," Jason said.

"I don't blame her. Those aren't men; they're animals. She lived a nightmare."

Jason stared down into his coffee. It was official. They had brutalized Lisa. For some reason, it hadn't seemed real until just now. He had to fight the urge to call her. He had no idea what he'd say, what he could say, but he wanted to apologize. He wanted to disavow his gender.

He also knew that nothing he could say would ease Lisa's pain. Nothing could help her, but time and therapy. Her life had changed—she had changed—forever Sunday evening. Nothing would ever bring her old self back. From now on, she was a rape survivor.

Jason looked up and met Danny's eyes. They were blazing. It was the only way to describe the anger he saw there, fierce and dangerous, only barely held in check.

"Did he—?" Danny touched Barbara's forearm. "I mean were you—?"

"No. No, not like that." She patted Danny's hand. "I think I'm too old for them."

"Thank God for that."

Barbara smiled as Tom returned to the seat across from her.

An idea sprung into Jason's head, almost fully formed.

"What?" Danny frowned at him. "You've got that look again."

Jason ignored her and turned to the Millers. "Helen went out with Wilcox for quite a while before this all started, right?"

Both Millers nodded.

"For almost three years," Barbara added.

"Did they do much camping? Locally?"

"Well, sure," Tom said. "Everyone around here goes camping in the summer."

"Did Wilcox have a particular place he liked to camp? A favorite spot Helen might have mentioned?"

Barbara shook her head. "The State Troopers already asked us. If she ever mentioned it, we don't remember."

Jason sighed. It had been worth a shot.

"What about the local kids?" Danny asked.

"What about them?"

"What's their spot? Every town has a place the teenagers go to hold their parties. Their favorite party spot. Where is that around Bosque?"

Tom frowned. "We don't really run with that crowd."

"But it's a small town. People talk. Teenagers talk. You must have heard something."

Tom looked to his wife. She was thinking, trying to remember.

"Oh!" Barbara's eyes lit up. "What was the place they raided last summer? Willow something?"

She turned to Jason and Danny. "It was a big scandal. A bunch of kids got caught with alcohol, including the quarterback and halfback from the football team and the girl who ended up being valedictorian. It was all anyone could talk about for a while."

"And they all got off with a slap on the wrist," Tom said. "Community service, or something."

"What was the name of the place? Willow Grove? Willow Bar?"

"Willow Flats." Tom said. "It's just a gravel bar up the river a ways, not a developed campground. It's the only party place I'm aware of. But like I said, we're not exactly in the loop."

"But that helps," Jason told him. "More than you know."

Danny was peering at him, eyes narrowed. "You're supposed to be resting and recuperating."

"Just my eyes," he said. "Just my eyes."

♦

"You think he's going to be there?" Danny asked.

They were still sitting in the Millers' café, waiting for reinforcements. Jason had asked the Trooper on guard duty whether anyone had looked at Willow Flats, but he hadn't known. So they'd called Drew Parsons and told him. Parsons had never heard of the place, but seemed to see the same possibilities as Jason had.

"Stay where you are," Parsons told them. "I'm going to dig up some maps and put a team together. We'll come pick you up in thirty minutes."

So they drank coffee and waited. The Millers had a couple of new customers come in and were busy taking care of them.

"Yeah, I think he'll either be there or has been there," Jason told her. "Wilcox isn't a planner. He'd never needed to. When everything fell apart Monday, he didn't have an escape ready to go because it had never occurred to him that he'd ever need one. He was always number one; who would he need to escape from?"

"Okay. I can see that."

"So, when the Feds showed up, Wilcox knew he had to hide somewhere, but would have nothing ready to go. His usual refuges, Hemlock Run, his house, and his family's houses are all off limits, so where would he go?"

Danny smiled. "His favorite camping spot."

"His favorite camping spot," Jason said. "It's familiar, isolated, and this time of year it's probably deserted. What better spot for him to hide out?"

"It makes perfect sense," Danny said. "But we're still not going to be searching some gravel bar for a heavily armed fugitive, not with your eyes like that."

"I'm wearing sun glasses."

"Your eyes are still healing. Would Dr. Patel have let you out of the hospital if he knew you were going to be scrambling through the wilderness after a criminal?"

"I wouldn't have told him."

Danny's look said the discussion was over. Arguing was pointless. The case was closed. Nothing he could say would make any difference. "We're going to let the armed professionals do their job. They can tell us what they find when they're finished."

"Can we at least hang around nearby?"

"You expect me to believe you'd be content to just hang out nearby without getting involved?"

She had a point.

♦

Peter Zahrbock, of Zahrbock, Meyer, Straub, and Steinke, Attorneys at Law, was in his Seattle office Wednesday afternoon, working on a brief he needed to submit to the court by Friday. This was the third draft of the document and he thought it was getting close to what he wanted. The motion was to disallow a particular piece of evidence the State wanted to use against his client; he wanted it thrown out because the search that revealed it had been unconstitutional. To make that happen, he needed to marshal an impenetrable array of arguments backed by case law.

So he was mildly annoyed when his desk phone rang.

"Yes?" he answered, saving his work on the word processor as he spoke.

"Scott Barton's on line one. He insists he speak to you right away."

Peter eased back into his chair. Scott Barton had just been released on bail that morning. They had spoken briefly, just the basics: the conditions of his release, the charges, and the appointment next week to discuss the case in more detail. It was standard for a new client.

He wondered what could have happened since then to warrant an urgent phone call.

"Okay. Put him through."

Judy, their receptionist, hesitated. "Sir, he sounds drunk."

It figured. It wouldn't be the first time one of his clients tried to drown their problems in alcohol. It wouldn't be the last either, he was sure.

"Put him through."

The telephone clicked a couple of times and suddenly he was on an open line. "Mr. Barton?"

"Peter, I want you to do me a favor, okay? As my attorney."

He was definitely drunk.

"What do you want me to do?"

"Call up the DA and get him to drop those damn kiddie porn charges. They're destroying my career. No one will even answer my calls."

Especially when you're so drunk you can hardly talk, Peter thought. He didn't say that though. Counterproductive.

"Why should he? You have to give him a reason to drop them, Scott."

"Because they aren't kiddie porn. That's not why I had them. Everybody knows that."

"You went to law school, Scott; you know that. It doesn't matter why you had them."

"What if I gave him something better in exchange?"

"Such as?"

"Murder. Two murders, actually. I can tell them about two murders."

Peter perked up and drew a legal pad closer. "What murders? The U.S. Attorney will want to know some specifics before any discussion of plea agreements."

"Got a pen?"

"Go ahead."

"The first victim was Elizabeth Jensen in Renton a couple of years ago," Barton told him. "The second is Gerry Peterson. He was killed in Donald earlier this week."

"You know who the murderers are?"

"Oh, yeah. I know everything, but I want those charges to go away."

Peter scribbled the names on the pad and scratched a line under them. "I will talk to the U,S. Attorney. It will probably take a day or two to get an answer, but I will call you as soon as I get an answer."

Scott Barton thanked him and hung up.

Peter Zahrbock replaced the phone on its cradle and sat back in his chair, thinking about this new development. Barton was right. If he genuinely had evidence that would solve two open murder cases, the prosecution could very well agree to drop all the porn-related charges. Especially if Scott agreed to testify. And he would need to testify for any deal to be made. The problem would be that Scott could potentially be testifying against his family, including his father and grandfather. Peter didn't doubt that the young Barton would do it. He'd just feel better if Scott hadn't been intoxicated when he'd issued the order. Would he wake up sober tomorrow and change his mind? It was a distinct possibility.

Peter hesitated, then picked up the phone and dialed a number from memory. "Yes, I'd like to speak to Marcia Barton-Wilcox."

♦♦♦♦♦

Drew Parsons and more than a half-dozen FBI agents and State Troopers showed up just about when Parsons said they would. The Bureau was nothing, if not punctual. Jason and Danny told him what they'd learned about the party spot and what they'd expect to find there. Most important, in Jason's mind anyway, was the possibility Wilcox might be holding Helen there.

"You can't go in guns blazing," he told Parsons. "And you can't give Wilcox any reason to believe he has nothing to lose by killing her."

Parsons smiled. "We'll take that into consideration. Believe it or not, we do have some experience with hostage situations."

"Of course you do," Danny told him. "Jason's just not sure you understand Wilcox's psychology."

"He's a sociopathic sexual predator," Parsons said. "With nothing left to lose. But you know Wilcox better than I do and better than my people do. I appreciate any input either of you can give us."

Jason thanked him.

"So how would you handle this if you were me?" Parsons asked.

"Shock and awe, if you can. Overwhelm him before he has a chance to react," Jason told. "Especially if Helen is there with him. Otherwise, I think I would try to ambush him away from camp somewhere."

Danny agreed.

"That's pretty much what we were thinking," Parsons said and rose from the table. "Are you coming with?"

"No," Danny told him. "I promised the DA in Friday Harbor I'd bring her star witness back this afternoon. You have our cell numbers?"

Parsons promised to call them with the results of the search.

♦♦♦♦♦

Thirty minutes later, Jason and Danny were in Danny's Jeep, heading north out of Bosque. They'd said their goodbyes to the Millers, exchanged hugs, cell numbers, and promises to keep in touch. Now Jason sat in the passenger seat, both his and Danny's cells within easy reach as Danny drove. There had been no word from the FBI yet, but it was still early.

That's what Jason kept telling himself.

He had wanted to at least tag along. It drove him crazy to be sitting on the sidelines like this with no idea what was going on. He was a reporter. He was supposed to be at the center of the story, documenting what was happening. But Danny was having none of it, period.

It took every ounce of his self-control to resist calling Parsons for an update.

"You still upset?" Danny asked.

"I'm not upset."

"That's why you haven't said a word since we left the Millers?"

He shrugged. "Nothing much to say. Just waiting."

Jason held up his cell phone as a visual aid.

Danny sighed. "Be honest. Could you have just sat in the car while the raid happened?"

"Sure."

"What if Wilcox somehow escaped and you saw him?"

He shrugged.

"Which is why I don't want you anywhere near the operation," she said. "You're an exceptional reporter because you're willing to take risks, but there has to be a limit."

Jason nodded because it seemed the right thing to do.

"You're not trained for criminal apprehension, weapons, or hand-to-hand fighting. Plus, because of your eyes, you're not even at a hundred percent of the skills you do have."

She had a point there. If it came down to a physical confrontation with Wilcox, he would be toast, all but defenseless.

"Okay," he said. "You're right. But I don't have to like it."

Danny smiled. "Got to love a man who will admit when he's wrong."

They were passing through a heavily forested section of the highway. The hemlock and cedar grew so tall and the understory was so thick and so close to the road it seemed like driving through a shadowy green tunnel. What few houses they passed looked like they had been carved out of the forest yesterday and were valiantly fighting to prevent being retaken.

There was almost no other traffic on the road.

"We might not be able to get to Port Salish before the pharmacy closes," Danny said.

"I'll be okay. The hospital gave me a sample. It should be enough to get me through to tomorrow."

Another farmstead approached on their right, little more than a simple frame house with hundred-foot trees crowding all three sides and a simple gravel drive leading off the highway.

A lifted blue pickup with oversized tires sat on the drive, nose pointed toward the highway.

"Danny…" Jason felt his stomach muscles tighten.

"I see it."

To her credit, Danny didn't alter her speed or swerve even a little. They passed the truck at sixty-miles-an-hour, just like everyone else on Highway 10 had. Just like nothing was wrong. Jason wasn't sure, but he thought he saw one figure sitting in the cab, behind the steering wheel.

Jason twisted in his seat and looked behind them.

The blue truck had pulled out on to the highway.

"It could be a coincidence," Danny said.

"Sure."

But neither believed it. Especially when it became clear the truck was catching up to them and fast.

Thirty-eight

The area the locals called Willow Flats was an oval patch of bottom land in a bend of the Chumash River, surrounded by gravel bars on two sides. The modest height, relatively protected from winter floods, allowed the groves of willow that gave the Flats their name to thrive. Generations of youth in the Bosque area had made Willow Flats the preferred location for their illegal celebrations.

It was curious, considering the primary activity conducted at the area, that only one road led through the forest to the site, the only way in and out.

Tactically though, it was a defensive dream. A handful of armed men could hold off an army.

A tan nylon dome tent was set up in a small clearing among the willow about thirty yards ahead of Agent Drew Parsons and the rest of his team. The remains of a campfire darkened the ground in front of the tent. A blue and white cooler sat to one side and a fishing rod leaned against a stockpile of firewood.

Parsons could see no vehicle of any kind nearby and nothing moved in or near the tent. The campsite seemed to be deserted.

"How do you want to handle this?" Agent Victor Farias asked.

Parsons gazed at the tent for a few moments. Nothing moved except the breeze through the surrounding willows. If anyone was there, they were staying buttoned up in the tent, which made no sense. It wasn't like the nylon fabric offered any defense.

"I don't think he's here," Drew told the other agent. "I think Wilcox is off wherever his truck is."

Farias agreed.

"Cover me. I'm going to go take a look in the tent."

Farias ordered the other agents to watch their backs, then followed Parsons in a controlled advance across the gravel toward the campsite. Nothing moved. Nothing sounded that wasn't the breeze in the willow branches or the river working against gravel and rock. The tent looked abandoned.

Parsons still approached it as quietly and carefully as possible, his gun always trained on the nylon, ready for anything. Farias did the same with his M-16 about five feet to Parson's left.

Parsons caught Farias' eye, signaled that he was going around to the tent's entrance.

Farias nodded, raised his M-16 until he was sighting down the barrel at the tent. On full auto at this range, he could cut anyone in half in seconds.

Parsons edged around to the entrance of the tent.

It was zipped up tight.

The mosquito screen prevented him from seeing clearly inside the tent.

"This is the FBI!" he announced again. "Come out now with your hands in the air!"

Did something move inside? He couldn't be sure.

He stepped toward the door. Nothing happened. He took another step. A third brought him close enough to grab the zipper at the top of the tent door.

Farias had edged around to a position where he could see what Parsons was doing. Drew looked at him now. Farias nodded. Parsons jerked the zipper down and looked into the terrified eyes of a young woman. Her mouth was covered with duct tape and she wore only a tee and panties. Her hands were bound behind her back; her ankles zip tied

"Helen?" Parsons asked. "Helen Miller?"

She nodded.

"We need an ambulance here," Parsons said into his radio. "We've got the girl."

♦♦♦♦♦

The truck was gaining on them, and quickly.

"Danny…"

"I know," she said. "I'm going about as fast as I can."

Jason glanced over at the speedometer. She was at seventy-five now. On a narrow, winding, road she hadn't traveled much, seventy-five was about as fast as she dared go.

"I don't know that I can make it through any curves as it is."

Jason understood. "I'm calling the cavalry."

He glanced back at the pickup as he waited for Parsons to pick up the call. He seriously hoped the FBI agent hadn't shut his phone off for the operation at Willow Flats.

The truck was even closer—maybe four or five car lengths now—Jason could see the shape of the driver behind the wheel. Even more alarming, was the steel brush guard Wilcox had added to the front of the truck. Similar to what cop cars carried, it was designed to allow vehicles to hit obstacles without suffering crippling damage themselves.

"He's going to ram us," he told Danny.

"Reynolds?" Person answered his phone. "You're more impatient than my kids. I told you I'd let you know what we found when things were clear."

"Wilcox isn't there. He's on the highway right behind us, and he's gaining fast," Jason told him. "I think he's going to run us off the road."

"Where are you?"

"I don't know." Jason said. "On Highway 10, somewhere north of Bosque."

"Milepost twenty-one," Danny told him.

"We just passed milepost twenty-one, Highway 10."

“Hang tight. We’re on our way.”

The pickup was gaining on them quickly. He had to be doing over a hundred.

“Hurry,” Jason said.

“Helen was at the campsite,” Parsons said. “She’s okay.”

“Good. Now hurry.”

Jason ended the call.

“Grab my purse,” Danny told him.

It was on the floor beside his feet. He pulled it up on to his lap. “What do you need?”

“My backup gun! I don’t need it! You do!”

He grabbed the small pistol from the purse, dropped the purse back to the floor. “Parsons says they have Helen. She’s okay.”

“Wonderful.”

The pickup was close enough now he could clearly hear the roar of the big engine. Jason glanced at their speedometer. They were moving at just about eighty.

“Crap!” Danny hissed.

He looked up. Directly ahead of them, maybe a quarter mile away, the road bent to the left. A red SUV rounded the turn, heading south toward them. The people inside had no idea of the drama or danger headed toward them.

“Shit!” Danny said. ”We’re not going to make the turn.”

Jason agreed. They were going way too fast. But what choice did they have?

The SUV passed them, heading south, the driver’s eyes like cartoon saucers. Jason couldn’t blame him. His own were probably pretty much the same.

The bend in the highway was coming up very fast.

So was the pickup.

Jason couldn’t move.

“Brace yourself!” Danny yelled and stood on the brake.

He slammed against his shoulder restraints and both phones tumbled to the floor. He could feel the anti-lock system pumping the brakes.

The back window exploded and steel groaned as the pickup’s front end crushed the rear of the Jeep. Jason was thrown back against his seat, then against the restraints again. The Jeep seemed to crouch under the onslaught of the larger pickup, screaming like a wounded animal. More glass exploded, tinkled like tiny bells. Metal groaned. Ahead, the line of trees charged closer and closer. He could clearly see the fissures in the fibrous bark, drooping branches. The front fender of the Jeep kissed the bark on one trunk, stripping off a patch like peeling a scab, butted into another.

Then everything stopped.

Silence. Heavy, grave, ominous silence, broken only by the rattle of falling glass and a soft hiss of steam.

"You okay?" Danny asked.

"I'm fine." His hands were shaking. "You?"

"I'm pissed! I just bought this car!"

Danny removed her safety belt and pulled her pistol from the holster at her waist.

The sight of the pistol roused him like a slap across the face. There was no time for shock. Wilcox was still out there, behind them, his truck grafted on to the rear of Danny's Jeep.

Danny forced her door open and leapt out, her pistol trained on the pickup.

Jason's door was jammed shut. Danny was screaming at Wilcox. Jason tried to force it, but it wouldn't budge. He gave up, scrambled over the center console and through the driver's door. Danny was crouched by what remained of the pickup's front fender, both hands training her pistol on the cab of the pickup.

"Get your hands up!" she screamed at the cab. "Put your hands where I can see them!"

Jason could see nothing move in the cab.

He stepped up beside her, his pistol pointed at the truck's windshield.

"Is he dead?" he asked.

Two cars heading south had pulled over a short distance away, their hazards flashing.

Far to the south, Jason could just hear sirens. Probably Parsons and the FBI.

A man stepped out of the nearest car.

"Stay in your cars!" he yelled to him. "Call 911!"

The man quickly returned to his car.

Jason turned back to Danny. She'd moved a little further toward the rear of the pickup. Her pistol never strayed from the cab.

Jason could still see no movement in the pickup.

"What do we do?" he asked.

"Cover me," she said. "Shoot anything that moves."

Crap. Jason concentrated over the sights of the pistol.

Danny eased up to the pickup just behind the door handle.

The sirens were getting louder, but he had no idea how long before they would arrive.

"Wait for help," Jason told Danny.

She ignored him.

Shifting her pistol to her right hand, she reached out with her left for the door handle.

Oh, God, Jason thought. Wilcox could be right on the other side, just waiting for an easy shot. He shifted his position a little so he had an angle to shoot through the door if needed.

Danny nodded at him and flung the door open. "Do not move! Hands where I can see them!"

Almost in slow motion, Travis Wilcox fell sideways out of the truck onto the pavement. Blood covered the lower half of his face. The front of his tee shirt was soaked in it.

"Danny?"

Jason stepped to the side so he could see better around the truck door. "He dead?"

"He's breathing," Danny said. "Looks like the airbag broke his nose, knocked him out."

But her pistol never moved away from him and she kept her distance. She suspected he was playing possum. Or maybe it was her training kicking in. Better to err on the side of caution.

Jason stepped up beside her. He kept his pistol trained on Wilcox too, but he had relaxed a little. His peripheral vision caught the black SUV's appearing in the distance. The sirens were very loud now.

Danny muttered wordlessly.

"Back-up is here," he told her.

She didn't seem to hear him. He could now just make out what she was saying. "Just try something, bastard. Just try something."

Her eyes never left Wilcox.

"It's over," he told her. "We got him."

Thirty-nine

At 9:00 Thursday morning, on a day that promised to be dry and sunny, if not terribly warm, a spotless black Acura RDX pulled up to the front gate at the Redwood Estates Community. Joe Deroasch was working the gate and did not recognize the car. He was kind of a gear head and knew all the residents' cars. It also did not have the windshield decal that the owners' vehicles sported.

He left the barrier down and stepped up to the driver's window. "Can I help you?"

"I hope so," the man inside was middle-aged, with short dark hair and a dark goatee. He was wearing a striped polo shirt and sunglasses. "I'm supposed to meet Senator Morris Barton for a round of golf today at the Redwood Club. He said he'd call ahead."

"I'll check for you. Could I see some I.D.?"

"Sure." The man handed him a driver's license.

It was a Washington State motor vehicle license and identified the man as Trevor Sandford, with a Vashon Island address. The photograph was clearly of the man in the car.

"I'll be right back," Joe told him and returned to the guard house.

Joe picked up the clipboard with the computer-generated list of guest authorizations for the golf club. Trevor Sandford's name was right there, a guest of Senator Barton.

Joe returned to the car, gave the license back to the guest, and pushed the button that raised the barrier. "Have a good game."

"Thank you." Mr. Sanford smiled and shifted into drive. "I will."

♦♦♦♦♦

Thursday morning, a 911 call came into the Olympia call center from unit 647 of the Knightsbridge Condominiums, reporting a death. When police and EMS units arrived, they found Amalia Sanchez, the cleaning woman, nearly hysterical. She said she'd let herself into the condo as usual because the owner was always already at work by that time. She was immediately alerted because the unit was a mess. Her boss was normally remarkably neat. Instead, it looked like there had been a drinking party.

She directed the authorities into the master bath. There they discovered the body of Scott Barton in a tub full of cold bloody water. He had apparently cut his wrists. Preliminary time of death was estimated as sometime between 10:00 pm the night before and 2:00am that morning.

Mr. Barton, an attorney and Executive Assistant to State Senator Morris Barton, had recently found himself in legal trouble in connection with the Hemlock Run scandal in Dunham County. According to his attorney, he'd been taking his change of fortune hard.

By all appearances, Mr. Barton had committed suicide.

♦♦♦♦♦

Joseph Mullens, Director of Security for the Lundgren Corporation—but currently on unpaid leave while fighting charges of murder conspiracy—was not a good golfer, by anyone's standard. He carried a 15 handicap, largely because he'd never been able to correct his slice with any consistency. And he honestly didn't care. He had no interest in becoming a professional golfer. He didn't even like the game all that much. It was part of his job, like cocktail parties and board meetings. If you intended to succeed in business in this country—especially in the upper echelons of the corporate world—you needed to play golf.

So Joseph Mullens played golf, but had never been able to correct that slice.

He stood now on the fifth tee and watched with dismay as his shot headed straight down the middle of the fairway only to turn in that familiar, looping curve to the right. The ball landed on the right edge of the fairway and bounced into the trees.

Mullens groaned and returned the driver to his golf bag.

"Have you considered aiming forty-five degrees to the left when you tee off?" Roger asked.

His golfing buddies chuckled.

"Tried it once. But then I hit it straight as an arrow."

More laughter.

Five minutes later, Mullens parked his cart and entered the edge of the woods near where the ball had gone in. He knew the direction it had been moving and about how fast. The trouble was, if the ball had hit a tree trunk, it could have ricocheted almost anywhere.

A quick look proved his ball wasn't in an obvious location, so he began a bit of a grid search to try and find it, using his pitching wedge to move brush and shrubs aside as he looked.

"Looking for your ball?" a man's voice called out, deeper in the trees. "Think it's over here."

"Thanks," he replied and headed in that direction.

Within a few steps, he spotted a man in slacks and polo shirt standing on the bed of dead pine needles, looking down at a lone golf ball.

"Damn," Mullens said. "I might as well just take a penalty shot. I'll never get that back on the fairway."

"No. You probably won't make it back."

Something about the man's tone made Mullens look up.

The man had a handgun trained on him. A noise suppressor made the muzzle big and black and ugly.

"Hello, Director," Taylor Smith said. "You shouldn't have put that price on my head. You would have never seen me again."

Mullens stomach dropped through his groin. "Wait. Wait, we can work something out."

"I think not." Smith said and pulled the trigger twice.

Mullens crumpled to the pine needles.

Taylor Smith dropped the pistol beside Mullens' body. Nothing on or about it could ever be traced back to him. He strolled away through the trees to the fairway on the far side, climbed into his own cart and set off for the clubhouse.

Smith thought he might spend a little time on the driving range. He still had a bit of a slice himself and it just killed his game.

Acknowledgements

No one can conceive and execute a project the size of a novel completely on their own. The smart author, like a head of state, surrounds himself with a committee of trusted advisors. Someone who can tell him he's hip-deep in a swamp and might want to try a different route. In my case, I want to thank Stefanie Freele, Candace Callen, Cynthia Helen Beecher, Karen Helgeson and Dave Nyeland for their suggestions on early drafts of the novel. I also owe the members of our little critique/writers' group for much help with particular scenes: George, Mary, Candace, Mark I, Debbie, and Mark II.

I'd also like to thank the patient staffs of the Port Hole Café and Gold Beach Books for putting up with me as I put this together, sometimes with agonizing slowness.

And as always, my family, who have never doubted, even if they thought it pretty weird.

Thank you all.

About The Author

James Boyle is the author of four previous novels: *Ni'il: The Awakening, Ni'il: The War Within, Ni'il: Walking Turtle,* and *Deception Island*, as well as numerous short stories, essays and poems. He is a graduate of the University of Oregon and an organizer for the South Coast Writers Conference. He lives in Gold Beach on the Oregon coast where he is finishing his new novel.

www.ingramcontent.com/pod-product-compliance
Lightning Source LLC
Chambersburg PA
CBHW031943260626
47157CB00017B/2118
9780692830239

SHADOWS IN THE WATER

By Jo-Anne Tomlinson

SHADOWS IN THE WATER

First edition. June 28, 2021.

ISBN: 978-0473589141

Written by Jo-Anne Tomlinson.

For lovers of drama, murder and mayhem. Thank you.

1

INDI OPENED HER EYES. She was on her back. Soaking wet. The sky was blood red.

At first she felt nothing but biting cold, her body a numb slab of ghoulishly purple limbs. Then, pricking needles of pain stabbed at her brown skin. Slowly, as she forced herself into wakefulness, the needles became searing blades, broken glass. Jagged. Violent. Ripping and tearing at her.

Indi's first instinct was to survive. To breathe. She fought the tightening in her throat, retching until seawater spewed from her mouth. Her chest heaved, her desperate, sobbing breaths only intensifying the pain. She stifled her gasps, kept them shallow, but each rise and fall was excruciating.

Where was she? What happened? She searched her memories for answers but received only hollow silence in reply. Her thoughts were jumbled puzzle-pieces, a corner here, a familiar shape there, but mostly they formed a fragmented mess that only escalated her panic.

Indi needed to see. Then she could start putting the pieces together. She blinked, hoping to clear the haze, but the sky stayed red. She lifted her hands to her face, her fingers frozen and curled. She rubbed her eyes and soon the sky was blue, as it should be. Now it was her hands that were red. Deep red and dripping blood.

Indi screamed, but her fear and the cold smothered the sound. Instead, it escaped her lips as a murmur that turned to smoke in the air. Her hands fell to her sides, the ground soft and wet beneath her. Sand. She calmed herself and listened. She could hear waves breaking upon the shore. Indi turned her head and saw rows of shallow dunes dotted with pale yellow brush, bending in the winter wind. Memories slipped into place, and she whimpered with relief. She knew this beach. She came here almost every day during the summer. There was a parking lot just beyond those dunes. There would be people there, people who could help.

Indi had to try. She did not want to die. Not here. Not on this beach. She forced her brittle limbs to move until she was on all fours. The blood dripped from her head like a leaking tap, staining her ripped t-shirt and the soaking wet jeans she wore like a second skin. She staggered to her bare feet and began a slow, labored walk over the dunes.

It hurt. She was cold. And the blood wouldn't stop.

Why was there no one here? Why was there no one to help her?

The blood pooled in her eyes, and everything was red again.

"India?" a voice called. "India Peters? Oh, my god." A girl stopped in her tracks as she stared in horror, her dog's leash slipping from her loose grip. The golden retriever leapt clumsily over the dunes and lapped at Indi's fingers when it reached her.

The girl came closer and Indi glimpsed herself reflected in the girl's terrified eyes. Her face was bruised beyond recognition, her lips swollen and blue, and blood was spilling from a large, gruesome gash across her forehead.

"India," the girl muttered. "What happened?"

Indi parted her lips, taking a moment to recall the placement of tongue and teeth. "I don't remember." She swayed, her legs unable to stay steady a moment longer. She fell limply into the girl's arms, fading in and out of consciousness. "Do you know me? Please. Help me."

A COLLAPSED LUNG, BLUNT force trauma to the skull, and a wealth of bruises and scrapes. Indi's hospital chart might as well have read pretty fucked, but for the longest time, the doctors and her parents wouldn't talk about the larger issue. The brutal blow she had taken to the head had resulted in short-term memory loss. Indi's mind was a slate that had been scrubbed clean.

When she had first woken, Indi expected to be at home in her bed on the last Saturday morning she could remember. Cam was going to meet her at the park in the afternoon. They would lie in the long grass like always, saying stupid things that only they found funny, their fingers softly tracing upon each other's skin. Instead, she was in a stiff hospital gown with tubes stuffed in most of her orifices and, with every bleep of her heart monitor, she recalled the beach. The cold. The blood. At last she found the scream that had evaded her. It was ragged and raw. When her throat was hoarse and the screaming stopped, her parents tried to explain how it wasn't that Saturday anymore and hadn't been for weeks.

Indi could recall the basics. She knew her name was India Peters, that she was a senior at Army Bay High. She knew she could bake a red-velvet cake with her eyes closed and hated cross-country running. But it was what she didn't know that was of far more interest to her parents and to the police who visited with her daily. But as hard as she tried, the last few months of her life were a complete blank.

Why was she on that beach? What had she been doing the day before? Who had attacked her?

Those words, especially, tasted strange. Attacked her? Here? In Army Bay? She preferred the notion of some horrible accident to being savagely beaten and left to die. She was just ordinary India Peters. Pleasant, polite, but generally off the radar, just the way she liked it. The kind of girl that everyone remarked was pretty cool, in an unremarkable kind of way. Okay, so they might have whispered behind their hands that she was a bit weird, too. But, weird didn't get you killed. Right? Hate got you killed. Vehement loathing got you killed. Stumbling across a Columbian drug lord's poppy plantation got you killed and, memories or no memories, Indi was sure she hadn't done that. But all the denial in the world couldn't explain those rope marks. Even after two weeks they were there, clear as day. Deep braids of burnt, bruised skin circling her wrists.

The police were eager to share the theory they had jotted in their notebooks; a dark and unprecedented deed in Army Bay's history, sharing a page with their downtime doodles. Her attacker had bound and beaten her, then thrown her into the ocean to drown. But Indi had escaped and made her way to the surface before washing up on the shore. That information was all too much for Indi's fragile state, like a bowling ball resting on a thin sheet of glass. She did her best to stay strong and keep from shattering beneath the overwhelming weight of such a truth.

Someone had tried to murder her. Tried and failed.

When she had finally come home from the hospital, her father, Nathan Peters, had enveloped her in his thick, hairy arms. "My daughter's a fighter," he'd said.

Was she? That was one of the details her mind was holding hostage. The amnesia was unbearable, worse than the head injury and collapsed lung, worse than the bruises and rope marks. To be separated from her memories was the worst injury of all. Everything else would heal in time, but would she ever recover her lost moments? And, without them, was she even Indi any more, or was she someone else inhabiting her broken body? There was someone Indi remembered, though: a name the police had on loop. It infuriated Indi that she recalled this name so clearly, a name belonging to a person she despised. Someone as shallow as a rock pond and just as transparent.

They had asked, and kept on asking, if Indi knew where Brandy Hamilton was.

Why the hell would she know? Why the hell would she care? Brandy was a vapid uber-bitch, and if she had disappeared, Army Bay should be grateful. Was that a kind thing to think? Probably not, but even allowing for her memory loss, Indi couldn't recall a time when Brandy had been a decent person deserving of kindness.

The officer had scratched his head and rechecked his notes. "It says here that you and Brandy Hamilton were friends."

"Sure. When we were thirteen, maybe. But not since then." Indi hated having to explain that. It was a part of her life she wished she could forget. If only this amnesia could be more selective.

The officer addressed her parents instead, as if Indi were some toddler who didn't understand how the world worked. "I have statements that say your daughter and Brandy Hamilton were very close." He flicked Indi a glance. "Recently. I even have a witness who states they were seen together the day before the incident."

Her mother, Dawn, angled her body away from Indi, shielding her mouth to obscure her words. That would have been fine if Indi were deaf and needed to read lips, but that wasn't the case. She could hear everything.

"Officer," her mother started, "we think this has something to do with the short-term memory loss. You see, Brandy and India were close when they were younger, but they grew apart in junior high. Very recently they became friendly again. But Indi doesn't remember that."

Indi rolled her eyes. Friendly again? Hardly! And as for them growing apart, she meant Brandy had become an utter bitch. She didn't want to ride bikes along the beach anymore or scarf down ice-cream until they barfed. Suddenly Indi wasn't pretty enough, or thin enough. She didn't wear the right clothes or listen to the right music. Brandy made new friends. Rich, beautiful friends who liked everything she liked. If it had just been a clean break, then maybe Indi wouldn't have cared so much. But then she started hearing things whispered in class, private things she had only ever told Brandy. That her mom's parents were ashamed to have a mixed-race granddaughter, and that they had never even met Indi. That, in his youth, her dad had been a heavy drinker and had been arrested multiple times for assault. That Indi was scared of the dark and only stopped wetting her bed last summer. That her nipples were dark brown.

That was when Indi was officially done with the bitch and she'd never looked back. Then she'd met Cam and nothing else had mattered. Indi refused to believe that she and Brandy had somehow reunited.

Even so, Indi supposed Brandy's disappearance was a bizarre coincidence, and the Army Bay cops parroted the line used by the ridiculously attractive detectives on those murder-porn crime shows her mother loved so much: "We don't believe in coincidences."

But Indi had nothing to tell, nothing she was keeping secret, at least that she knew of, and although Indi was happy to see the back of them today when they were all out of questions, they'd been unable to answer the most crucial of hers. Who had hurt her?

They had no suspects. No leads. Her attacker was still out there. Somewhere.

Her father saw the cops to the door, leaving Indi and her mom alone in her room.

"Well, that was about as much fun as a fucking tumor," her mom sighed, tucking a wayward blonde curl behind her ear. "Are you okay?"

Indi shook out her pins-and-needles after sitting cross-legged for the entire latest round of polite interrogation.

"Yeah. I guess. My head doesn't hurt as much today, but I think that breakfast grapefruit is on its way up."

Her mom smiled. "I meant, with the questions."

"Oh." Indi wriggled her toes. "I just don't know what to tell them. I don't know what happened to Brandy or to me. They think I have something to do with Brandy going missing, don't they?"

"No," her mom said quickly. Too quickly. "I'm sure it's all just procedure."

That was another line she had borrowed from her crime dramas. A pity she wasn't half as good an actress as Mariska Hargitay. Of course they thought Indi had something to do with it, or, at least, knew something about it.

She stood from the bed, her mouth twitching nervously. "More flowers arrived for you today."

"Not from them again?" Indi dreaded the answer.

"I'm afraid so. It's an even bigger bouquet this time. There are some letters too and photos. Do you want me to bring them to you?"

"God no," Indi whined. "I hardly know those people. I thought you were going to tell them to stop."

Her mom put her hands on her hips and carefully selected her words. "We've talked about this, India. You have been friends with these kids for months, you've just forgotten about it. Seems rude to keep ignoring them when they are being so considerate."

"Mother," Indi said tersely, "in what universe would someone like me be so close to the top of the food chain? Those are apex predators up there. I mean, they're all part of Brandy's squad and I am, for want of a better word, not."

Her mom shook her head. "That isn't what I saw."

"I don't want to talk about this again. I will not play nice with strangers."

Her mom caught Indi glancing at her phone for the hundredth time. "Has she messaged you back yet?"

Indi frowned, shoving her phone under her pillow. "No. She must just be busy."

"I've tried to tell you, sweetheart, you and Cam don't talk anymore."

Indi wouldn't believe it. When the flowers first started arriving, she assumed they were pity offerings, but as the week went on more were delivered. The notes became personal; they mentioned things they couldn't possibly know unless she had told them. Then came the DMs that Indi left on 'read' for days while she tried to understand the photos on her social media. Photos of her and Brandy, of Sadie and Ben, of Rory and Avery, at the movies and football games. Indi didn't remember any of it. There was even a shot from that damned beach and, what the hell, was she wearing a bikini? That's how Indi knew this was a world gone mad. She unfriended them all. Set her accounts to private. Deleted the photos. They were not friends, no matter what supporting evidence they had.

Once she had processed that mind fuck, Indi messaged Cam, her actual best friend. But Cam wasn't replying and suddenly it was Indi left on 'read.'

Her mom had spent an entire evening trying to explain how India's life had changed the last few months, that she had made new friends and turned away from old ones. But by the time her mother had knocked back her fifth glass of pinot, Indi wasn't sure if she was talking about her or the star of some teen melodrama.

Her mom seemed to sense Indi's frustration. "It's okay. You'll get there. The doctors say things should start coming back in bits and pieces over the next few weeks."

Indi admired her mother's optimism, leaving out the part where they also said if she didn't start remembering things soon, the damage might be worse than first thought. Something to look forward to, Indi supposed. Either total recall or absolute brain implosion. The doctors had some good news though, and Indi immediately cheered up upon hearing it. She had healed enough to go back to school. That meant she could see Cam face to face and figure out why she had suddenly earned the cold shoulder. It might also be nice to have a conversation with someone other than her parents or the brave and clueless officers of the Army Bay Police Department.

"I'll find Cam tomorrow. I'm ready to get back to school." The words tasted like a vomit-flavored jawbreaker.

"There will be an officer monitoring you during school hours," her mom stated.

Indi's jaw dropped. "Really? So much for blending in."

"I'm sure he'll be very discreet," her mom hummed, "and honestly, you were never going to just blend back in, Indi. Everyone is talking about you.

Everyone wants to know what happened. Are you sure you want to go back? We can home school you." Indi had once caught her mom counting on her fingers to figure out the electricity bill. "Well, obviously we would hire someone," her mom said, recognizing Indi's lack of confidence.

"No, it's time," Indi declared.

The door creaked open and her dad popped his head inside. "I've got dinner ready. Everything okay up here?"

Indi gave a thumbs up and watched as her parents exchanged awkward smiles that seemed too formal for a couple married almost twenty years. He closed the door, leaving her mom staring blankly, lost in her thoughts.

Indi's mouth started moving before she had time to check her words. "It's weird. I used to want to stick my head in a toilet when you two would grope each other in the frozen food section. Now you barely even talk."

Her mom exhaled. "Some things take time. See you downstairs, yeah?" This was a topic she clearly had no intention of discussing, no matter how much pinot was on offer.

Indi's memory reached back far enough that she remembered when her parents started having problems. Her dad was the supervisor at a construction company and had several builds on the go. Her mom had given up selling Avon and got her real estate license. The older Indi grew, the less time they spent at home, throwing themselves into work and what they thought was the united goal of early retirement. In amongst the late nights and work trips, her parents acted like roommates rather than husband and wife. Passing each other at breakfast, trying to catch up over a late dinner, before falling into bed exhausted. Some days Indi couldn't remember if she saw them together at all, and somewhere between then and Indi washing up on the beach, her dad had moved out.

Her mom explained the details as soon as Indi woke up, not wanting her to find out some other way. Whatever had caused the separation didn't matter anymore. They had reconciled, and her dad was back home. He had even taken an indefinite leave from his sites so he could be with his family full time. But despite how happy they insisted they were, the house had turned dim and cold.

Her dad's barbecue guaranteed you a case of the meat sweats, Indi thought later as she pulled on a pair of loose-waisted pants and watched TV until she couldn't keep her eyes open any longer. As she shifted in and out of sleep, with one foot grounded and the other dancing between dreams, in her mind she saw something strange.

Two pairs of hands bound together with thick rope. The hands fought against their bindings, struggling in the murky dark until one pair, at last, was free. The hands drifted apart, one pair rising while the other disappeared altogether into the black void below.

The image haunted Indi throughout the night and she slept fitfully, a chilling cold gnawing at her, just like it had that morning on the beach.

2

IT HADN'T BEEN A PLEASANT night's sleep; it had barely passed for rest at all. More like a crappy eight hours, in the dark, that Indi had spent rolling around with her eyes closed.

Indi's mom had prepared a full-on breakfast, starting with a mango smoothie. Mangos made Indi giddy. She snatched it eagerly and slurped it down like a camel at an oasis.

"Eggs? Toast?" Indi queried the unexpected spread.

"The eggs are good," her dad chimed in. "You wouldn't even know the chickens were caged. They taste so free." He paused, waiting for Indi's usual reaction. "What, no lecture?"

Indi cocked an eyebrow. "Were you wanting one?"

Her parents exchanged glances. "You asked us to sign a petition to get the supermarket to sell only free-range eggs, before ... you know ... ," her mom said.

That sounded to Indi like a very un-Indi thing to do. Sure, she felt bad for the critters, but chicken guilt had never plagued her conscience, certainly not enough to organize a petition. "How progressive of me," Indi replied.

Her dad chuckled. "It was a little odd, probably Rory's idea. She was always protesting some cause when she was around here."

Indi rolled her eyes. "Of course. Probably down to Rory. Who's not even my friend."

Her mom slapped her dad's chest. "She doesn't like when we talk about those kids." Her dad clutched her hand before she could take it back and Indi wasn't sure where to look, or even if she should be in the room while her parents shared what seemed to be an intimate moment. Her parents had never shied away from gag-worthy PDAs, but that was before. Indi noticed how her mother now turned her petite body away from him, and how she avoided his eyes. In response, her dad seemed disappointed, slowly allowing her to slip free from his loosened grasp. When they appeared to remember Indi was in the room, they forced empty smiles.

Her dad sipped his coffee. "I'm sorry girl. I won't mention them again."

Her father used the word girl affectionately, an endearment like honey or sweetheart, strange to some but familiar in his Māori culture. Indi appreciated he was trying to get things back to normal, not dwelling on what had happened or giving a shit about who was sending her flowers and wanting to have a play-date. Indi's mom, on the other hand, seemed to push her toward them. Indi couldn't help wondering if her mother would rather she be friends with these kids because they were popular, just like her mom had been when she was in high school.

Her mother was probably the Brandy Hamilton of Army Bay High, circa 1996. She was short, blonde and mostly torso. She had been a gymnast and a dancer and, knocking forty, she was still in great shape. Most mornings she would swim out to the buoys. Well, that was before Indi's bloodied body had ruined that pastime. Not that she had said as much. She was too tactful to say so. But Indi had figured that was the reason for her mother's abrupt abandonment of her love of swimming.

Just like the typical boring small-town stereotype, the prom queen had married the prom king. Her dad had moved to Army Bay in their senior year to play basketball for the Mako's. In high school, he had been a tall, hulking athlete and things hadn't changed that much. He was still tall, of course, and had stayed in shape just like her mom. He had a thick shock of black, well-groomed hair and a manicured jaw of dark stubble that was becoming flecked with grey. Neither of her parent's families had approved of the relationship. The blonde, bubbly, head-cheerleader knocking boots with the rough, brown-skinned boy from out of town. But, luckily for Indi, her parents had given zero interest to what anyone else thought.

Physically, Indi mostly resembled her dad. Tall, with brown skin and dark features and far more body hair than was preferable, but she had her mother's mouth, meaning that she had full lips with a deep bow, and said fuck a lot.

"Fuck," she said on cue.

"Language," her dad groaned. He, on the other hand, did not curse at all.

Her mom shushed him. "I got you something," she continued, rummaging through an off-white cabinet and returning with a couple of items. She pushed them into Indi's hands. "To keep you safe."

Indi eyed the gifts. A Swiss Army knife. A key-chain bottle of mace. A rape alarm. "What. No gun?"

Her mom rolled her eyes. "I wish, but your dad said no."

"The state says no," her dad corrected.

"And you can keep them all in this!" she said excitedly, presenting Indi with a black fanny pack. "It's Nike."

Indi rolled her tongue over her teeth. "And you want me to wear that?"

"Why not? I've seen it on The Gram, all the kids wear them." Her mom shoved the anti-murder essentials into the pocket of the fanny pack and zipped it up. She offered it to Indi, who recoiled. Her mom frowned. "Do you want to leave the house or not?"

Indi sighed dejectedly and took the pack, clipping it around her waist. "I love it," she drawled.

Her dad walked to the window with his coffee cup and pulled back a corner of the curtain. "Doesn't look like there are any newspaper vans out there this morning. You might make it to the mailbox for a change."

Indi had already checked for them when she came downstairs. When this thing first broke, there were camera crews and journalists from all over the country camped outside like the new iPhone was being released. Then, as the weeks passed it dwindled to regional news, then local, and for the last couple of days, none at all. Indi guessed they were getting bored with the lack of updates and there were only so many ways you could flip the story of a not-dead teenager to keep it riveting.

"Are you sure you want to do this?" Her dad gave a guttural groan. "You don't have to."

Indi couldn't think of anything she wanted more. Freedom from the Peters' quarantine.

"Stick to the routine, right?" she said. "I used to walk to school all the time, plus it's a busy street. I'll be fine."

Her dad returned to the kitchen counter and stood close to her mom, putting a thick hand on her shoulder. She was more accepting this time, as if in desperate need of comfort.

"The minute something feels off, call the police," she instructed.

Indi looped on her backpack. "I'm in no hurry to get killed properly next time. Try not to worry." She donned her best empathetic smile, hoping it would give them some relief, but she could see it didn't. Nothing would. Indi made for the front door before they changed their minds about her going to school today.

As she whizzed through the foyer, almost tripping over the crocheted mat, she caught sight of herself in the large mirror above the hall table. The scar across her forehead was not as inconspicuous as the doctor had assured her it would be. The jagged line travelled from her right ear, angled through her eyebrow and ended at her hairline on the left. It was a ghastly purple color, making it even more noticeable against her brown skin. If she stuck a couple of bolts in her neck, she'd look like Frankenstein's monster in skinny jeans.

Not having had a haircut for months had solved one problem: her dreadful fringe had grown out and she could hide at least half of the mess with her dark-brown, loose waves. Now she was only partially terrifying to small children. In all honesty, it wasn't that bad considering what could have happened. Being dead would have been far more unattractive. Indi checked her mascara and eyeliner, thick as tar just the way she liked it, and a good layer of sunscreen because even someone who dodged death could still get melanoma.

She headed out the front door and began the short walk to school. It wasn't until this morning that she'd noticed how many other students walked the same way. Usually, they were all in motion, but today they were standing still. They weren't pointing exactly, but they might as well have been, and all eyes were on Indi as she walked by. The silence was dull and eerie. She could hear the pavement crunching beneath her red Chucks and the leaves rustling in the trees that lined the path.

Then someone shouted, "Hey, India. Did you kill Brandy?"

There were cackles afterward, but nothing remotely funny resonated with Indi. She almost choked on the fresh air. Is that what people thought?

She didn't turn around. She didn't want to know who said it. Instead, Indi kept her head down and stared at her feet, quickening her pace to put this street behind her.

ARMY BAY HIGH WAS PICTURESQUE, with its sprawling grounds and Spanish-inspired architecture. Who would have thought that it was also the epicenter of teenage hell?

It was comforting to see nothing much had changed in Indi's absence. The kids with cars loitered in the parking lot, chattering gibberish like boost gauge and 18-inch rims. Then there were the bus kids, their demographic split straight down the middle. At the front sat the more decent representatives of youth, those less likely to get pregnant before graduation or take part in smash 'n' grabs on Friday nights. At the back, your stereotypical teen-movie-loser types, usually the ringleaders of the smash 'n' grabs, who would probably grow up to become reformed motivational speakers. Then in the middle there were kids like Rory Zhang and her boyfriend, Avery Weiss. They were friends with Brandy, best friends, members of her Army Bay High squad, all with some enviable trait that had elevated them above the rest of the plebs. For example, Avery was the richest kid in school with the most on-point hair, while Rory was a track champion who leapt hurdles like it was her job. It always bemused Indi why such well-endowed individuals would choose to live content in the shadow of Brandy. They even allowed her to be at the forefront of their nauseating selfies, which Brandy would post and tag #SquadGoals.

What was Brandy's unique attribute? Well, she was beautiful, and not just the-most-beautiful-girl-in-a-small-town kind of beautiful. She was a head-turning, jaw-dropping, wet-dream-invoking stunner, with blonde hair down to there, tanned legs up to here, and all tear-drop tits and cinched waist in between. She was an uber-magnet and everyone else in the world was just a tiny pin, drawn toward her. Brandy could easily be a Real Housewife of Army Bay one day. Or could have been. Indi didn't enjoy struggling with which tense was appropriate.

As Rory stepped off the bus, Indi dashed behind a nearby tree. In her previous everyday life, Indi wouldn't have had to worry about Rory not seeing her. Indi doubted she even knew her name back then. But, apparently, now they were so close that Rory was coming over to her house and trying to convert the Peters family to free-rangers. Until Indi figured out what was going on, she didn't want to put herself in the path of social disaster. She had enough problems.

She watched Rory and Avery glide past hand in hand. Indi noticed Rory's t-shirt beneath her navy blazer. It had Brandy's picture plastered across the front with the words FIND BRANDY in bold print. Indi looked around the courtyard and soon saw the message in other forms. Posters, pamphlets and bumper stickers. Brandy's beautiful face was everywhere, and suddenly Indi felt sick to her stomach.

"Indi. Are you okay?"

Indi looked up, straight into the eyes of Ben Campbell who, to her knowledge, had never once looked at her, let alone given a hoot whether she was okay. He had tight waves of chocolate-brown hair, short around the sides but long enough on top that he always had to sweep it away from his gold-flecked, hazel eyes. His jawline was strong and square, his neck thick like his muscled body, and the thin, ribbed fabric of his blue shirt clung taut against his sculpted chest.

"Indi, are you okay?" he repeated.

She dragged her eyes away from his collarbone, unsure how her gaze had settled there. "Yeah. Why?" she blurted.

Ben chuckled uncomfortably. "You know, because ... everything."

Indi wasn't sure how to respond, so she just stood there, waiting for Ben to leave. She considered pretending to faint, but decided that would only up her freak status and give people more shit to gossip over.

Ben rolled his broad shoulders and hitched up the strap of his backpack. "Alright. I guess I'll go then. We'll talk later though?"

Indi furrowed her brow. "We will?"

Ben seemed just as confused as Indi. "Or not ... whatever you want. You know where to find me."

"I do?"

Ben put his hand on her shoulder, and Indi burrowed so deeply into the tree behind her she could practically taste the bark. "Ok. Bye," Indi spat. Anything to end this awkward exchange.

Ben gave a perplexed nod, then joined Rory and Avery in the courtyard, leaving Indi wondering if she were still at home in her bed, fast asleep, immersed in a dream entitled Wake Up India. There's Some Crazy Shit Going Down.

"India!" a girl cried out.

Indi was tiring of hearing her name as an exclamation. Before she knew what was happening, Paula Marshall had thrown her arms around her neck and was squealing frantically into Indi's hair. Paula was a mid-carder. She wasn't fabulous enough for Brandy's squad, but if there were a runner-up, Paula would be it. Her backstory didn't help her chances of ascension, however. No matter how well put-together Paula looked, with the right clothes and the right hair and the right backpack, most people knew her dad was in prison, and her brother sold drugs to half the Army Bay community. It was a fact Brandy liked to remind Paula of whenever she had the chance, just to keep her in check. White trash doesn't get to be prom queen. Although Brandy being out of the picture was sure to raise Paula's stock.

"Oh my gosh, are you alright, babe?" Paula asked. She began tweaking strands of Indi's dark hair, brushing it away from her eyes and tidying up her part line. "You are so brave to come back to school. Everyone is talking about how brave and amazing you are, aren't they guys?"

Paula gestured to half-a-dozen girls behind her, who responded with bright smiles and synchronized head nods. "Oh yeah," they replied in various tones. "So brave."

"My mom says you should have got some sort of award, you know, from the town or something. She says she's going to write a letter, or whatever," Paula added. Indi doubted Paula's mother had the grit to pull that bourbon bottle from her mouth, let alone write a letter. Paula turned her attention to Indi's purple hoodie and black skinny jeans. She winced. "Geez, India. Are you sure you're okay? You look like you're helping your dad clean out the garage." Paula laughed, and her crew laughed with her.

Indi did recall that she had once helped her dad move some things around in a very similar outfit. She feigned amusement with a sarcastic grin. "Should I look different?"

"I don't know," Paula replied. "You've been wearing your hair up lately, less hoodies, and definitely no fanny packs."

More fucking bikinis, Indi thought. She could only guess Paula was talking about the other Indi, the one she couldn't remember being. "Well, this is me so, if you've got boxes that need moving, call me."

Paula laughed uncomfortably, so her crew laughed uncomfortably with her. "Anyway," she said, "winter formal's coming up. I'm running for Frost Queen and I would love to have your vote. When I win," she paused and patted her chest, "if I win, I plan on including you in my acceptance speech. I just think it's so important for us to support each other right now, you know?" Paula squeezed Indi's hand. "Oh my gosh. You are so brave."

"So brave," her friends parroted.

"Probably going to be an easy sprint home with Brandy missing," Indi mentioned. "Who else is running?"

"Just Cody Gibbons, the asshole. I mean, why would a boy run for Frost Queen?"

Indi grinned to herself. If she knew Cody, it would be simply to piss Paula off. "One last thing," Indi muttered, moving close to Paula's ear while turning her back on her disciples. "Is Micah holding at all right now or ...?"

Paula scowled. "I have nothing to do with that shit. Okay?" She took a deep breath and reattached her smile. "Anyway, good luck. Vote Paula!"

With that, Paula bailed, and Indi tried to absorb everything she had heard without losing brain cells in the process. The most disappointing part of the conversation was Paula's reluctance to hook Indi up. Micah always changed his phone to avoid getting caught dealing and Indi couldn't remember the last time she'd got blazed. Literally. Could not remember.

Indi tried to center herself, push aside the chaos and focus on why she was at school today in the first place. Cam. Cam would make sense of this nonsense and everything would be right with the world. Or, at the very least, Cam might have some weed on her.

Indi knew precisely where to find Cam. Behind the gym in the smokers' circle. Indi headed there directly, enduring the piercing stares and whispers along the way.

About a dozen kids were congregated behind the gym, huddled in a circle strategically engineered to contain the wafting smoke. Cam's bright red hair stood out amongst the crowd and Indi wasted no time dragging her friend from the loop when she was only two passes away from the cigarette.

"What are you doing?" Cam snapped, her green eyes like daggers. Now she would have to wait for a full rotation before getting a puff. No savesies was a well-known rule within the smokers' circle.

Indi expected Cam's glare to vanish when she realized it was her, but it didn't. It stayed put. It actually got worse. Cam shook away Indi's hand as if she had cooties.

Indi gulped. "Hey, what's wrong?"

Cam mirrored the puzzled look Ben wore earlier. "What do you want, India?" Cam's snappy tone had caught the attention of the smokers, who were eavesdropping between passes. Indi turned her back on them to shield the discussion.

"I want my best friend, that's all. Not sure if you've heard, but I've had a pretty rough few weeks. You didn't visit or call me. Have I done something wrong?"

Cam's snarl only softened when she spotted the scar across Indi's forehead. "Right. Your memory. Your mom said that was a thing."

"You spoke to my mom, but you didn't speak to me?" Indi was growing impatient. "What's going on Cam? Everyone's acting weird. This morning someone asked me if I killed Brandy."

The name put a sour look on Cam's face. "Well, that's ridiculous." Indi sighed. Finally, someone said what she was thinking, and she knew it would be Cam. "Why would you kill your bestest bestie of all your besties, Brandy Hamilton? It's me you stabbed in the back."

Indi was so frustrated she could feel ugly, angry tears welling behind her dark eyes. "Cam, wait." She grabbed her hand before she could storm off. "I can't remember anything and I'm so scared." She laced their fingers. "Please, can we just talk, after school or something? Just tell me what I did so I know why you hate me."

Cam wrestled her fingers free. "I can't. Not now. Just go. Okay?" She returned to the circle.

This world was not one that Indi knew. It must have been a parallel universe where Indi was friends with people she loathed and enemies with those she adored.

As far as she remembered, after she and Brandy had ended their friendship, Indi had met Cameron in the carpark of Monster Burger. They were both blazed and split a combo with what little change they could combine from their pockets. They had been inseparable ever since. Cam had moved to Seradale for a semester when her dad got a job there. But when it didn't work out, and Cam moved back to Army Bay, Indi realized just how much she had missed her, and that her feelings were leaning toward something more than burn buddies. It had taken every ounce of her bravery to admit to Cam that she was in love with her, and when Cam responded with the softest kiss Indi could imagine, she was sure that the butterflies in her stomach were strong enough to fly her into orbit. Now Cam was turning her back on Indi and acting as if none of that had happened.

Surely they could come back from whatever it was Indi had done. If there was ever a time she needed Cam, it was now. Indi was doing all she could not to fall apart. She was afraid every day, but even more afraid to let anyone know that, and the line between coping and complete meltdown was as fine as a spider's thread and just as fragile. How could someone like Brandy have come between them? Indi cursed her name, and at that moment, her thoughts were cruel and vicious.

That bitch Brandy Hamilton should count her lucky hair extensions that she's already missing.

3

AT THIRD PERIOD INDI found herself on the other side of the courtyard. She figured the fastest route to her next class was through the garden and past the pavilion. A cluster of students were draped over the white lattice frame. But it wasn't until she was a few feet from them, far too close to discreetly run in the opposite direction, that Indi saw Ben was among them.

He bolted to his feet and smiled brightly, sweeping a hand over his perfect waves of hair. "You came."

Indi frowned. What unprecedented lousy luck. "Looks that way, doesn't it?"

"Indi!" Rory said, snaking her arms around Indi's waist. She had never been hugged so much in her life. "I was looking for you all morning," Rory grumbled. "I've been worried sick."

"It's true, she has been," Avery said, pulling Rory back down onto his knee. "She almost broke a sweat running laps around the school."

Rory grinned and slapped his chest. "Seriously. I wanted to find you straight away, but I didn't want to freak you out, not like stalker Ben here."

"Oh, I'm sorry if I was desperate to know if our friend was okay," Ben sighed.

Rory and Avery exchanged wide-eyed smirks.

"Oh, desperate, were we?" Rory giggled behind her hand.

Ben frowned, leaning on the wall of the pavilion. "Whatever, you know what I mean."

"It's so good to have you back, Indi," Rory continued. "It hasn't been the same without you."

"And Brandy," a voice said.

Indi hadn't noticed Elton sitting in the corner, though he was pretty hard to miss. He was tall and nicely shaped, with amazing black skin and a head of tight ebony curls. Plus, he could wear the hell out of a white V-neck shirt and drop crotch jeans. Indi had been madly in love with him between the ages of six and nine. That was until he called Meg Forester fat at her tenth birthday party. After that, Indi decided you didn't have to settle for mean if you wanted to love a hottie.

"Of course. Brandy," Rory snapped. She opened her blazer to show her FIND BRANDY shirt. "Any day now, she'll show up. I know it."

"Yeah. Show up dead maybe," Elton muttered. He was smoking discreetly, being far too cool to need the shelter of Cam and the circle.

Ben shot him a glare. "Watch your mouth, man, don't say shit like that."

"Come on. She's been missing for almost a month. Girl's definitely a corpse."

Ben charged forward, grabbing Elton by the collar of his shirt. "Are you going to shut your mouth, or do you need my fist in it?"

Elton rolled his eyes and gave Ben a sharp shove. "Please, Campbell. No need to put on a show for little India here."

Indi squirmed in her skin. These people weren't her friends. Never had been. They just happened to be in her same year. But they weren't acting like that was the case. They were acting like she was part of their circle. Rory hadn't taken her doe-eyes off her, and Avery was clasping her hands tightly just to get her fingers to stop trembling. Rory seemed genuinely concerned.

How was any of this possible? What life had Indi been living?

"Enough!" Rory insisted, shoving them apart. "You're going to scare the shit out of India. She's probably freaking out."

India nodded in agreement. "Yeah, this is weird. Thanks for the talk." She went to leave.

"Woah," Rory laughed. "You're not hanging with us?"

"I have to get to class," Indi replied. "I'm trying to stick to a routine. My rehab therapist says it could help." Indi clenched her teeth. She'd mentioned her therapist. Nice work.

"Right," Rory said. "You really can't remember anything then?"

Indi nodded. It seemed a popular question. "Not from the last few months."

"So, you don't remember the trip to the fair or the time Rory reversed into the ice cream truck?" Avery asked.

"Pretty inclusive of everything," Indi sighed.

"So, nothing about that night either?" Ben's eyes fixed on her, his brow furrowed.

Indi squirmed under his gaze. "No. Nothing."

Rory skipped to Indi's side, sheets of shiny hair streaming down her back. She had a cute little fringe that Indi didn't hate and eyes that were almost as black as her hair.

"You're going to party with us tonight," Rory announced. "Elton's having a get-together while his parents are away. It will give you a chance to get to know us. Again."

"No. I don't think that's a good idea," Indi said.

"What are you talking about? It's a great idea," she argued.

"Yeah, you should come." Elton exhaled a waft of smoke. "Unless you don't like fun?"

"I don't think your kind of fun and my kind of fun mesh," Indi snipped, not enjoying the patronizing tone of Elton's husky voice.

He smiled and took another drag of his cigarette. "Sounds like a challenge."

Rory tugged on Indi's arm to steal her attention. "Don't worry about these guys. They're just being assholes, as usual. I'll pick you up tonight, okay?"

Indi shook her head vehemently. "I don't think my parents will let me out."

"When has that ever stopped you?" Rory snorted.

Indi slipped her arm free of Rory's grasp and slowly inched away.

"Tonight then!" Rory called.

Indi waved over her shoulder, only half listening. All she wanted right now was to be as far away from that pavilion and those ridiculously attractive people as she could get.

Sanctuary should have come in the form of fourth-period algebra, but instead Miss Bates handed her a note and told her to report to the guidance office. Indi wasn't sure which was worse.

The counsellor, Miss Mathis, was always sickeningly cheery. Her office was a sky-blue demountable that sat away from the main school building. A droopy willow tree draped its branches over the door and a little carved sign in the blooming flower bed read Kindness Cottage. When Indi entered the room, Miss Mathis was sitting, stiff-backed, hands clasped in front of her on the desk. She was ordinarily bright-eyed and rosy-cheeked, but Indi figured that was before she had the victim of an attempted murder on her books. Miss Mathis looked anxious, her smile polite but wavering. She gestured to a chair, then quickly glanced to her left.

A tall, surly-looking man in a horrible brown suit was standing in the corner, and even his dark aviator glasses couldn't hide his piercing stare. Indi sat down and now it wasn't just Miss Mathis who was anxious.

"Welcome back, India," Miss Mathis said. "How are you finding your day so far?"

"Terrible, actually."

Miss Mathis gave an understanding nod. "I imagine it would be ... difficult."

Indi acknowledged the elephant in the room. "Who is this?"

"Detective Dean Braddock," the man answered. "I'm the lead detective just assigned to your case. Any problems today, India? Anything strange?"

"Just me," Indi replied.

"No one following you? Anyone tried to contact you?"

"Not that I'm aware of. Apart from my so-called friends, that is."

Braddock whipped off his aviators to reveal dark-blue eyes beneath whiskery grey brows. "You have to realize, India, that the person who attacked you is probably also the person who is responsible for Brandy's disappearance, and there is a good chance that one of your peers knows who it is. In fact, I'm almost positive that's the case. Someone at this school knows what happened. You need to be careful, and if anything seems out of the ordinary, no matter how insignificant, you need to let me know. I'll be close by, but I'll try to keep my presence as discreet as possible." He gave a farewell nod. "Stay safe."

He showed himself out, and before Indi could follow, Miss Mathis grabbed her hand.

"You're not the only one, you know, who had problems with Brandy."

Indi cocked a startled eyebrow. "What?"

"I'm just saying. I had students in here every other day who hated Brandy Hamilton. We all know she wasn't a nice person." Miss Mathis was fiddling with her beaded necklace. "Being mean was fun for her, so I can understand how someone might want to make her ... disappear."

What did that mean? Indi knitted her brows. "Okay then."

Miss Mathis donned a smile painted on as brightly as her red lips. "I hope they find Brandy, of course. We're all praying for her."

Indi was pretty positive that was a complete lie. She headed for the door before Miss Mathis could detain her again. She went straight to the bathroom, passing a couple of girls who couldn't get far enough away from her in the narrow doorway.

Indi had felt the polar opposites of social etiquette today. She was either everyone's favorite hugs-and-sympathy receptacle or it was like she had a nasty strain of chlamydia. Her best friend valued her spot in the smokers' circle more highly than their friendship, and kindness manifested itself as a pack of hot, lame, Riverdale understudies.

She splashed some water on her face, staring with bemusement at her sad reflection in the scum-streaked mirror, the hollow thrum of a dripping tap sounding like thunder in the silence. Indi splashed more water on her face, hoping to wash away her unseen woes. She closed her eyes, allowing the water to trickle down the bridge of her nose and fall onto the bow of her upper lip.

Indi exhaled and opened her eyes, then screamed when she caught sight of a pale figure reflected behind her, its face warped by the streaks. She gripped the basin so tightly that three of her purple-painted nails cracked, and she almost slid on the tiles as she spun around. What the filthy glass had hidden was a face of flawlessly fair skin and golden hair that fell in soft waves upon slender shoulders. Large blue eyes, framed by the longest, most delicate lashes in all creation, stared blankly, and Indi wanted to scream again, even louder, when the girl reached for her.

"Brandy!?" she gasped.

The outstretched hand swiftly slapped Indi hard across the face.

"You bitch. Where is my sister? What have you done with her, freak?"

Indi's cheek stung, and she nursed it against her shoulder. "Sister?" She looked at the girl again through watery eyes. "Sadie?"

Brandy had an identical twin, but only in the biological sense. Sadie Hamilton was nothing like her eight-minute-younger sibling; in fact, she did everything she could to be as unlike Brandy as possible. She dyed her hair black, wore dark colors to contrast with Brandy's love for soft pastels, and happily sported square-rimmed glasses while Brandy wore contact lenses. Sadie was also academically inclined, and there were rumors that Brandy's good grades resulted from signing her name to Sadie's beautifully written essays.

This wasn't that Sadie, though. She had transformed herself into an eerie copy of her sister. Indi was even reasonably sure that Sadie was wearing Brandy's daffodil-print ankle-socks. It was apparent that, regardless of their differing personalities, the bond between the sisters was unbreakable. Sadie was a member of the Squad, and by slapping Indi a second time, she confirmed whom she held responsible for Brandy's disappearance.

"I can't believe you're not locked up, that they're just letting you walk around, free as a bird."

"I don't know where she is," Indi snapped, shaking off the additional battering. "I'm free because I've done nothing wrong. I almost died for fuck's sake."

Sadie stormed forward, standing tall and intimidating, her eyes wild.

Indi didn't give an inch.

"I don't know why my sister gave you the time of day. She took you in, made you a part of something, and you're denying all of it." Sadie came closer still. "If I find out you had something to do with her disappearance, I will end you India."

The door of the bathroom swung open, and the inane banter of a gaggle of girls broke the palpable tension, although they abruptly fell silent when they came upon Indi and Sadie's showdown.

Sadie walked to the door, shoulder-barging Indi on the way.

"Oh my gosh, you're India Peters," one girl gushed.

"Yeah, yeah, I'm very brave. Excuse me," Indi growled, swiftly leaving the bathroom.

During fifth-period English, she chose not to pay attention, despite Mr. Green's idle threats of detention. The teacher could do no worse to her than what she had already endured. She nestled her head in her folded arms atop the desk and closed her eyes tightly to block out the stares, but still she found no refuge. Instead, images from her dreams beset her just as fiercely.

Those hands bound to hers, the dark that surrounded them, so black, so cold, so absolute. Indi prayed it was only a dream, only a figment of her imagination conjured up by a fractured mind, but she knew in her heart who that other pair of hands belonged to. Who else's could they be but Brandy's? The two of them tied together. The darkness that engulfed them was the seawater, blackened by night. Indi's eyes flashed open. It couldn't be real. It couldn't possibly have happened. Or could it? Had Brandy really been there with her? Had someone tried to kill them both?

Indi had had enough of this day. She stood from her desk and stormed straight from the room, blocking out Mr. Green's demands that she return. She charged through the halls, across the courtyard, until finally crossing the carpark and reaching the street. Before she could take a step off the curb, a grey sedan pulled up beside her, its window winding down.

Detective Braddock looked her over. "Going somewhere?"

"I don't feel well. I'm going home," Brandy replied sharply.

"Get in. I'll give you a ride."

Brandy shook her head. "I'll walk."

"I insist," Braddock said. He sipped at his Styrofoam coffee cup. "Get in."

Before today, Indi had never met Dean Braddock, never even heard of him. The only actual connection they had was Miss Mathis, and she was acting just as crazy as everyone else, not at all a reliable character reference.

Braddock was getting impatient. "I will not ask again, kid."

"I want to call my mom," she said, her voice wavering.

Braddock groaned. "Fine. Make it quick."

Indi pulled out her phone, quickly flicking her mother a text.

India: Dean Braddock. Know him????

Mom: Yes. Detective with Army Bay police. Didn't I tell you that? How's school?

Indi rolled her eyes. She didn't want to open that can of face-slapping worms. She walked around to the front passenger door and climbed in. This was the cleanest car Indi had ever seen. She almost slipped off the leather seats. "This thing new?"

"No. Just had it detailed."

"Special occasion?"

Braddock put his coffee cup in the holder. "It was dirty."

Indi noted that along with the Alpine Forest deodorizer that swung from the rear-view mirror, she could smell bleach. She recognized it straight away, as only yesterday she'd had to soak grape jelly from her white shirt after a midnight sandwich expedition went awry.

"So, anything happen after our talk?"

Indi said nothing about her dream. Until she knew what it meant, it was either the ravings of a crazy person or a flat-out confession.

"No. Nothing happened. Can you just take me home, please?"

Braddock nodded. He pulled the handbrake, and the car rolled forward, weaving through the student carpark. Then it stopped abruptly when Braddock plunged his foot on the brake and whipped off his aviators. "Goddamn Marshall kid!" He threw open the door and charged toward a parked, blue car with some random teen leaning in the window. "Hey!" he snapped.

The teen looked over his shoulder then swiftly back-pedaled, his arms raised in a protest of innocence. That's when Indi could get a look at the car's driver. She knew who it was straight away, like picking a perp from a line-up, and the person she was looking at knew all about that. Micah Marshall was that greasy, juvenile-delinquent kind of hot, with stringy brown hair always knotted in a man-bun and a thrashed denim jacket worn over a dark hoodie. He was never without a pair of black sunglasses hiding his eyes and a half-spent cigarette between his lips. He'd finished Army Bay High a couple of years ago and had done nothing since, which didn't explain why he was in the school carpark at two in the afternoon. Braddock wasn't in the mood for any bullshit. He snatched the teen's fist, forcing it open, then looked both shocked and disappointed to find it empty. So did Indi. It was no secret that Micah sold drugs. Nothing too hardcore. Uppers. Downers. A fair bit of weed. Pretty small-time shit. But that didn't make it any less embarrassing for Paula having him for a brother. She tried so hard to pass for class, but her family were all either in prison or on their way.

After a series of stern finger-waggles, Braddock ushered the teen back toward the school. He talked to Micah a moment longer and, going by Micah's expression, none of it was good. Micah jumped in his car, revved the engine and sped off down the street.

"Sorry about that," Braddock said when he returned.

"No problem," Indi sighed. "Is Micah in trouble?"

Braddock grunted. "Always." He started the car and hit the gas and, after weeks of waiting, thinking it was the one thing that would make it all better, Indi watched gratefully as Army Bay High grew distant in the side-view mirror.

4

WHEN HER HOUSE ON APPLEBY Drive came into view, Indi breathed a sigh of relief. Maybe now Braddock would stop talking. As soon as they pulled away from the school, he had asked questions, and Indi realized this would not be a simple ride home shared in silence. Braddock quizzed her on Brandy's friends, her parents, people she may have associated with outside of her Army Bay squad. Indi had spilt what she knew but then faked some period cramps halfway through the drive to get a little peace. It didn't last long.

"It's been six weeks," he said, to her dismay. "No ransom requests. No sightings. It's hard not to think the worst at this point." He took a sip from his cup. "You want to hear some theories?"

Indi's ears pricked up, and she looked at him sideways. Was he serious? "Shoot."

He leaned back, and his chair groaned in response. "I think someone snatched the two of you. Took you out to the beach. I think they beat the crap out of you both, then tied you up and threw you in the water to drown. And I think only one of you made it."

It was almost as if he had seen her dream. He was just missing the part where she and Brandy were tied together. Indi hooked on to his last words. Only one of you made it. She felt a pricking in her palm. She hadn't realized she was clenching her fists so tightly her nails were digging into her skin.

"You think she's dead?"

"I think she's been gone a long time," Braddock said. "Which brings me to my next theory. Maybe you two fought. She took you out to the beach. Maybe she beat the crap out of you, then tied you up and threw you in the water. Maybe right now she's hiding out cursing her damned luck that you survived and she didn't get away with murder." Braddock pulled into the driveway of the Peters' house and took his time applying the handbrake. "Or maybe it was the other way around. Huh?" Braddock's eyes were cold as steel. "Maybe you're the one who got away with murder."

Indi was shivering, the tiny hairs on the back of her neck standing on end. Should she tell him about her dream? Anything out of the ordinary, no matter how insignificant. That's what he had said. What about something that might not even be real? Brandy was taking up so much space in Indi's head nowadays. It shouldn't be a surprise she was hijacking her dreams as well. It's like when Indi watched Transformers six times in a row and then had sexy Megan Fox dreams for a week.

Indi couldn't tell him. Not until she knew more. Saying out loud that she believed Brandy was dead would only add fuel to Braddock's theories, which wasn't necessarily a good thing. Dude seemed hella intense.

"Well, this was fun." She gripped the door handle and pulled, but it didn't budge. She tugged again, harder at first, until she was rattling it angrily. Still, the door stayed shut.

"And you know what else, India?" Braddock continued. "I think whoever did this is still in Army Bay, watching and waiting, and if your memory is a loose end, that puts you in a hazardous situation."

"In that case, let's hope Army Bay's finest solve this mess sooner than later."

Braddock grinned. "Indeed. A suspect might be nice. A motive even better. Sure nothing interesting happened today?"

Indi glanced at her front door, hopeful that either of her parents would emerge when they heard the car in the driveway, but there was nothing.

"Doesn't look like anyone's home?" Braddock observed.

"Nooo. I'm sure someone's in there. Most likely, my big, strong Māori father," she warned.

"Have you got a key to let yourself in, on the off chance that your big, strong Māori father is indisposed? You know it's important that your kids always feel like they can come home, no matter what. Leave a key under the mat, that sort of thing. Teach them nothing is more important than family."

"Thanks for the inspiring message." Indi discreetly slid her hand into her fanny pack and felt the smooth case of the Swiss Army knife. Her heart was pounding. She had survived attempted murder. She could find the balls to shiv a cop with a corkscrew if she had to. "The door," she spat. "It won't open."

Braddock noticed her white-knuckled grip on the handle. "Kiddie locks. This is a police car, you know. Criminals tend to want to make a run for it." He climbed out, and Indi observed him as he moved around the bonnet and opened her door.

Indi released the knife and wasted no time jumping from the car while keeping Braddock at a distance. "Thanks for the ride," she murmured. She was lying.

"Anytime," Braddock replied, closing the door behind her. "Stay safe now."

Indi quickly scampered inside, then peeked through the curtains of the living room to see if Braddock was following her. He stayed parked for a few minutes, staring at the house and sipping at that Styrofoam cup.

Her mom came to an abrupt stop when she found Indi kneeling under the windowsill. "And what are we doing?"

"That Braddock guy is weird," Indi replied as she watched his car finally reverse and drive away.

"The police chief can't speak highly enough of him. He's sure if anyone can solve this case it's Detective Braddock," her mom stated. "Apparently, he's spent hours reading your files. He was supportive of you going back to school too, getting back into your normal routine."

Indi couldn't help feeling his motives were more of a bait-in-the-trap scenario than concern for her well-being. She turned from the window to see her mom standing there oddly, flashing those pearly white veneers. "What?"

"Don't be mad."

Indi expelled a loud moan, her shoulders slumping forward. "What have you done?"

She pointed up. "Rory is in your room."

"Mom! Why?"

"She literally arrived two seconds before you did. She came over when she heard you left school early, to check if you're okay. That's all. Gosh, Indi, she's so pretty and so smart. Just excellent breeding, you know."

Indi cocked an eyebrow. "Well, if I ever want to fulfil my dream of winning the Kentucky Derby, I'll be sure to throw a saddle on her."

"All I'm saying is you could do much worse than a friend like Rory." She turned her cheek and mumbled, "At least she doesn't reek of pot whenever she comes over."

"Really mom!"

Her mom inched toward her in a sort of submissive, pleading shuffle. She glanced upstairs. "You know, with Brandy missing, maybe you should think about running for Frost Queen. When I was campaigning in my senior year, I had all my popular friends host parties and network for votes. It's all part of it. Someone like Rory could get you the crown!"

"Cool. I'll wear it with my bikini," Indi groaned.

Seeing Rory right now wasn't something Indi wanted to do, but she would rather be where her mother wasn't. As she headed for the stairs, Indi noticed a stack of FIND BRANDY flyers amongst her mom's 'Open House' signs. Rory must have suckered her into joining the movement. Maybe she would be a good campaigner. Indi cringed, flushing the idea before it got comfortable.

She paused when she reached her door, tapping her fingers nervously against her legs. Rory was pretty-near perfect. Smart, athletic. Indi had heard she was working her ass off to get a scholarship to Franklin College, even though her wealthy banker father could no doubt pay the tuition himself. Indi had to admit it was kind of admirable that she didn't expect her money to do all the work for her.

Today's interaction with Rory was the only one she could ever remember having. Now she was here, in Indi's room, like it was the norm. Indi wished so badly that it was Cameron in there. She had looked so cute today. Indi had wanted to hold her, bury her face in that soft dip of skin where her neck met her shoulders, slide her hands beneath her shirt and caress those full curved hips that Cam hated so much. Instead, she was about to have a fantastically awkward encounter with Rory Zhang, her mom's preferred option for bestie.

Indi eased the door open and peeked inside. Rory sat on the edge of her bed, one leg on, one leg off, leaning back on her taut arms. An ensemble of black activewear clung to her lean, muscular frame, a long-sleeved crop top with little loops on the cuffs that hooked around her thumbs, and a shiny pair of tights with mesh panels down the sides.

Rory wriggled her fingers and scrunched up her tiny nose. "Hey girl, long time no see." She gestured to her clothes. "Excuse the Nike commercial. I've got training after this."

Indi couldn't look her in the eyes. She slipped in timidly and closed the door, almost as if this was Rory's room and she didn't want to intrude.

"Your mom said you got a ride home with that creepy detective. Braddock, right?" Rory sighed. "He's been at my house like a hundred times since all this happened. Wanting to know about you and Brandy. Ack, he's so annoying."

Indi kept her distance, choosing to slouch against her dresser on the other side of the room. "So what did you tell him?"

"About what?"

Indi tugged at the collar of her hoodie. Was it hot in here? "Like, what did you tell him about me and, um, Brandy?"

Rory sighed, changing position on the bed. Now she was lying on her side with her head propped up on her hand. Never in a million years would Indi have imagined Rory Zhang sprawled on her shabby, blue-gingham duvet.

"I told him the truth, of course. I'm not about to go lying to a cop. I might as well set my college applications on fire." She checked her short nails, shiny with a clear polish. "I mean, I didn't tell him about the fight. I didn't want him thinking it was a thing. It's not lying if you just don't talk about it, right?"

Indi shrugged. "Maybe it's withholding evidence or something like that."

Rory sighed. "Yeah, that's what I thought. But he seemed to know already. Some stupid dick-sacks at school running their mouths probably, wanting to feel in on it or something."

"Oh. Okay. I appreciate that. I guess. What fight was that again?"

Rory bit her lip. "Right," she drawled. "You don't remember. I didn't hear all of it. You guys were mostly done by the time I got there, but I heard you say something like ... how could you do this to me or why would you do this to me? Either way, you were pissed. Normally, you would get a ride home with her after school, but you came with Avery and me instead. We dropped you off and then, the rest ... well ... no one really knows, do they? Well, besides you and that little head of yours."

Indi tapped her temple. "The little head isn't cooperating at the moment." She put her bag on the floor and wandered to her window, resting on the sill. It was time to ask the question on all the kids' minds. "I know this is going to sound kind of douchey, but how the hell did we all end up being friends? I mean, last I can remember we didn't run in the same circles."

Rory adjusted position again, this time sitting cross-legged on the bed. "Okay. Yeah. That's a fair question." She exhaled loudly. "I suppose the best place to start is with Brandy. She was the one who brought you into the group. I mean, honestly, I didn't even know who you were. I'd seen you around school a few times, but I didn't know your name or anything like that. I was shook when Brandy told us you guys used to be tween besties. Full Twilight Zone realness."

Indi wasn't sure why those words had a little sting in them. A few months ago, she didn't give a shit whether or not Rory knew her name. Maybe because then it wasn't a stated fact, more of a bitter assumption. Having Rory sitting right there, flat-out telling her she was as invisible as she thought, was more of a kick in the balls than Indi thought it would be.

"I mean, I don't know the exact details of how, when, or why Team Brindia reunited, but, for whatever reason, after Brandy's birthday, it was on like Donkey Kong."

Indi refused to believe it was that simple. She probed deeper. "Really? That's it? Army Bay social structure as we know it gets shattered to its foundations, and society is cool with it?"

Rory cocked her head to the side. "What do you want me to say? That you were well below our pay grade, socially speaking? You were. You know it, and I know it. It had all the kids gagging, that's for sure. But bitch, you made Brandy happy, and when Brandy's happy, everybody's happy. You two were even hanging out solo. Not that I minded. Avery was always bitching that she took up too much of my time. It was nice having someone to share the Brandy drama load. I mean," her eyes darted left and right as if someone was listening, "Sadie didn't like it. Ben was kinda weird too, but he always is when it comes to Brandy. Dude needs to get a dog or something."

"He's not coping with Brandy missing?" Indi asked.

"Are any of us? I wake up ten times a night to check my phone in case she's messaged. I want to be there if she suddenly needs me, you know." Rory exhaled and rolled her shoulders. "That's why we need this party tonight. First big shindig since ... well ... you know."

"I think the cops refer to it as the incident, if that helps," Indi stated.

"Incident. Right." Rory licked her lips. "So, what are you wearing tonight? My only tip is to lose the fanny pack."

Indi was forgetting it was even there. She had no intention of going to this party tonight but, in news just to hand, she didn't feel like screaming that fact in Rory's face and kicking her to the curb. Rory was nice enough. She had answered all Indi's questions, was pretty chilled out, and funny too. That didn't make a difference to Indi's feelings about the party. She would still rather chew on electrical wire than go, but this conversation wasn't as cringey as she had expected. She decided to be polite.

"Hey, thanks for the invitation, but I'm not going to Elton's party."

For someone so smart, Rory didn't seem to understand the words coming out of Indi's mouth. She was smiling and electric shuffling across the room. "Yeah, you are. We're going to have so much fun. It's not going to make this mess go away, but a night off could be cool."

"Curfew," Indi spat. The epiphany was organic. "Can't be out after dark. Totes dangerous and all that. Damned authoritarian punishment."

Rory laughed when she reached the windowsill. She looked out, her eyes following the white pipe that ran down the side of the house. "Girl, like that's ever stopped us before. I'll be here at ten, and I'll bring peach schnapps."

Indi's head jerked. "You know I like peach schnapps?"

Rory shrugged. "Well, yeah. I'm your friend, aren't I?" She executed a perfect pirouette, as if Indi expected anything less, then glided from the room like a Lycra-clad swan.

"I'm not going to some stupid party," Indi mumbled to herself.

She noticed her closet out of the corner of her eye. *Especially Elton's party*, she thought. Still she eyed the closet. *I mean, there's a curfew, anyway.* Suddenly Indi's legs were steering her toward the white door, and she opened it before she could come up with a new excuse.

There were stacks of jeans, even some orange ones that still haunted her. She tucked those toward the back. She found a cute denim mini that she didn't completely hate. She would have to shave her legs though, which sounded exhausting. Black leggings underneath would solve that problem.

And she could pair those with an off-the-shoulder bodysuit that made her decolletage look crazy good. This could work.

"Not that I'm going," Indi muttered.

She pulled the hangers, trying to untangle the bodysuit's sleeves from some fishnet leggings she wore one Halloween. She tugged harder and when it came free, so did a load-bearing shoe box from the shelf above, causing an avalanche of retail regret. Indi couldn't help considering this to be karma for low-key wanting to go to some lame, cool party. She heaved the bags and boxes back onto the shelf one at a time, but paused at one package in particular. It was bright pink and had a pair of running shoes printed on the side. Indi snorted. There was no way she owned a pair of running shoes, especially pink ones. She hadn't changed that much. The box was light, much lighter than expected for its supposed contents. Indi popped off the lid and inside, all on its lonesome, was a phone she didn't recognize, an ancient Blackberry model at that. Indi handled it curiously, then clicked the on button. The screen flashed Low Battery. The message icon was blinking, and Indi clicked her way through the menu to reach the mailbox.

Brandy. Where are you? Are you okay? Please text me back. I love you.

Indi's stomach churned. "Oh god. It's her phone." She knew it wouldn't be Brandy's main phone, not this stone-age piece of shit. But it was definitely her burner. There were more messages, but before Indi could open them the battery died and the phone powered down. Indi puffed her cheeks. "Of course. Where do you get a charger for this?"

"India!" her dad called. "Do you want to watch some Deal Or No Deal before dinner?"

"Hell yeah," she yelled back. Indi put the phone in the box and stuffed it at the rear of the closet with those heinous orange jeans, before joining her dad downstairs.

5

DEAL OR NO DEAL WAS acceptable. Some girl with eighties' spiral curls took the banker's offer, which ended up being better than what was in the suitcase. Good for her.

Indi had flip-flopped about whether she would go out tonight about a hundred times. It wasn't the sneaking out part that had her worried, more the company. But she was so bored with being locked up in this house with her parents. Her parents were weird again tonight. They were using I feel statements across the table. Indi wished it wasn't so hard for them to be together. She was even a little bitter they couldn't just sort their shit out. She resented her mother sometimes. Her dad had taken time off work. He was home all day while her mom was still constantly on her mobile and hosting open houses almost every weekend. They were so busy unpacking each other's issues tonight that they barely spoke to Indi across the dinner table.

It helped her decide. If Cam wasn't interested, then why wouldn't Indi hang with people who actually wanted her around. She excused herself after eating only half of her pasta. "I'm going to do some homework and go to bed. See you in the morning," Indi called.

They smiled and nodded before returning to their exchange.

Indi went to her room and made a quick change into the skirt and bodysuit. She tried to fix her hair in a way that made her scar less Night of the Living Dead and layered her eyes thick with black liner. She thought she heard a rattle at the window and looked away from her mirror to where the winter wind whipped at her drapes. Indi knitted her brows. Had she left that window open? The gust receded and took the rattle with it. Probably a loose branch or something. She looked back at the mirror and tidied up the wing on her left eye. But she gasped and dropped the liner when the rattling returned, and this time it was louder. The moonlight cast shadows upon the walls and Indi suddenly felt the night closing in around her as the room seemed to darken. She could hear scratching right below the sill, nails clawing at the wood. Indi knew one thing for sure. There was no way she was going anywhere near that window. She charged purposefully for the door.

"Indi," a voice called softly.

She froze in her stride, unable to resist the urge to crane her neck and see what was there. Two arms flopped over the sill.

"Who's that?" Indi demanded.

"The tooth fairy. Who do you think it is? Hurry up will you? This drainpipe is chafing my thighs."

Indi reluctantly walked to the window. She looked down and saw Rory with her legs wrapped around the pipe.

"What is taking you so long? I told you to be ready at ten."

"I thought you would come to the door. I wasn't expecting you to arrive via drainpipe," Indi replied.

"You are completely missing the point of sneaking out. Come on. Avery is in the car."

"Okay," Indi groaned, even though her anxiety-ridden chest palpitations were telling her no.

Rory smiled and began shimmying down the drainpipe, her speed and prowess an indicator that this was not her first time. So much for Rory, the well-bred role model. Cam had never encouraged her to scale the side of the house like a Navy SEAL. Indi wanted to run downstairs right now and rub it in her mom's face. But the victory wasn't worth getting grounded.

Indi followed Rory, awkwardly at first, but quickly her body seemed to know exactly where to place her feet and which parts had the best grip. When Indi landed deftly on the grass below, she realized that this wasn't her first time, either.

AVERY WAS DRIVING A black SUV, and not particularly well. Maybe if he took his tongue out of Rory's liver for five seconds and watched the road, Indi wouldn't fear for her life in the back seat. She recalled seeing him get off the bus this morning.

"Why don't you drive to school?" Indi yelled over the music, struggling not to slip off the sunrise-orange leather seats.

Avery's grey eyes regarded her in the rear-view mirror. "I had a problem with a breathalyzer test at a checkpoint last summer."

"What was the problem with the test?"

"I failed it." Avery grinned. "Not allowed to drive."

Indi cocked an eyebrow. "But you're allowed to drive now?"

"Mom's away for business. Left this afternoon. What she doesn't know won't hurt me."

Rory looked over the headrest. "Don't worry, Indi. It's cool. Avery isn't drinking tonight."

"Someone has to make sure you get home safe," Avery said, burying his mouth in the curve of her neck.

Rory giggled. "Babe, watch the road."

"Yeah, let's not push my luck as far as dodging death goes, please," Indi added.

"You must feel like the luckiest girl in the world," Avery said, changing gears and pushing down on the accelerator. "Some people would kill for a second chance." His eyes found her again in the rear-view. "Don't waste it."

Avery was such a stereotype that it made Indi retch. Rich and handsome from an influential family. His mother was old money, which meant they had oil or stocks or whatever shit it took to get that title. Indi hadn't really bothered to investigate.

Avery pulled off the main road and down a long driveway, thickly lined with trees. The moon peeked through gaps in the clustered branches, speckling Indi's skin with dancing milky light. She could hear voices from the Georgian-style colonial house in the distance, even feel the loud music through those awful seats. Her stomach knotted tightly.

God, she hated parties. Why was she here again? Oh, that's right. Because she's a stupid basic bitch.

Dozens of cars littered the cul-de-sac. "I don't want to park too far away," grumbled Avery as he scanned for a spot. Suddenly he hit the brakes, flinging Indi forward before the seatbelt snapped her back. A teenage boy stumbled into the SUV's path, then slammed his fists on the bonnet when the bumper nudged him.

"Hey, fuck you man, don't touch my car!" Avery roared out the window.

"No, fuck you man. I'm walking here." He burst into laughter, his long hair hanging over his face. He banged the bonnet again. "I'm walking here."

"Motherfucker," Avery snarled. In an instant, he had thrown open his door and charged at the teen, grabbing him by his collar and shoving him to the ground.

Rory looked back at Indi with an absent calm. "Guess we're parking here then."

"Um, shouldn't we maybe help out there?" Indi asked, bemused.

"Oh no, it's fine. Avery's got it."

"That's not what I meant," Indi sighed. She stayed put in the car, peeking through the tinted windows and observing her schoolmates drinking, screwing and barfing their way around Elton's sweet digs. "It's nice where I am," she remarked. "I can party here."

Her door opened, and Rory was standing there frowning. "Come on. Get out."

They approached the house, Indi's anxiety escalating one unsteady footstep at a time. With her eyes on the ground, Indi didn't see Micah Marshall until she collided with him near the front steps.

"Hey," Micah grinned, thoughtfully exhaling his cigarette smoke in the opposite direction. "Welcome back India."

His eyes were usually as red as they were brown, but tonight they looked clear.

Indi's eyes lit up, and she wondered how much chitchat was polite before she asked if he was holding. "Thanks," she replied. "How have you been?"

"I've been better," he groaned. "Cops on my ass constantly. Need to lie low for a bit I think."

"So you're not here in a retail capacity then?" Indi asked with a half-smile.

Micah chuckled. "Sorry Indi. Not tonight. At least not open to the public." He tapped the backpack over his shoulder. "Just refilling a prescription for Richie Rich over there." He nodded toward Avery. "He pays double. I can't turn that away, regardless of the heat I'm getting from the cops. Someone needs to pay for Paula's stupid Frost Queen dress."

Indi cocked a curious eyebrow. "What drugs are you selling Avery?"

"Client confidentiality Indi. You know that. Let's just say I have him in my contacts as Doctor Sleep. He's a regular."

"Micah," Avery called, standing in the pale white glow of the SUV's headlights. He rolled his sleeves up his forearms and kicked one last time at the bonnet-thumper, who hobbled away defeated.

Micah replied to Avery with a knowing nod. "I'll catch you later, Indi. Take care."

Rory linked arms with Indi and watched as Micah joined Avery by the car, shaking his hand before sharing the contents of the backpack.

"What was that about?" Rory asked.

"I'm not sure," Indi replied.

Rory shrugged. "Okay, no more stalling. Let's show you off."

Indi expected the worst. Staring, whispering, maybe even a ballsy finger poke. She was almost disappointed when she received none. People were smiling and saying welcome back. Someone commented that her hair looked great and Indi didn't even contemplate telling them to get lost. Instead, she nodded politely, greeting them all with this strange, upward inflected hi she'd never used before. She tried to act normal, like this was all routine. Parties, sure, she remembered she did those. The only difference was these kids were drinking, there was no clown, and she wasn't nine years old.

Rory guided her through the house. They passed the living room and formal living. That's how you knew this place was fancy. Elton was in the ritzy games room, sitting on the pool table with a cigarette in hand. He looked bored, not making eye contact with the girl prattling at his ear while he sipped his drink.

Rory charged in, hands waving in the air like Kermit the Frog. Indi went another route. She tried to discreetly hide behind a wall of teens in the back and wait this thing out. Instead, she knocked over the rack of pool cues, which nudged a five-foot wooden giraffe, which then clumsily collided with an expensive-looking stained-glass lamp.

Indi closed her eyes, wishing it would all just go away by the time she opened them. Instead, she heard Elton's cackle and slow clap.

"Look who's here. Our resident victim. Do you destroy all your host's homes or am I special?"

Indi felt a fuck you surfacing, but Rory spoke first.

"He's just kidding," she said, linking arms with Indi. "Hey. Do you want a drink?"

"Sure. Why not."

Rory looked just as surprised as Indi at the answer. But if there were some magical cure for the circus that was her life, surely it would contain alcohol.

"I'll show you the bar," Ben said, appearing behind them. He smelled sweet and woodsy, and a sudden surge in the crowd pushed him into Indi. Her body fit perfectly in his muscled arms when he caught her.

Rory clicked her tongue. "Oh, snap."

Indi frowned and untangled herself from him. "You were saying about the bar?"

Ben swept back his hair. "Right. This way." He guided her through the games room, past Elton, who stared at her over the lip of his cup. He wasn't coy about it. His eyes bored straight through her, enough to get Indi's palpitations going again.

The music was a little quieter in the kitchen, where more teenagers were gathered around the island counter.

"So what'll it be?" he asked, gesturing to the assortment of beers, wines, spirits and mixers stacked precariously on the bench.

"Whatever works the fastest," Indi replied.

Ben exhaled. "I get it. But I wouldn't be a gentleman if I let you get wasted." He perused the offerings before settling on a bottle of peach schnapps.

"Great," Indi said. "Everyone knows about the peach schnapps."

"I can't take credit for it," Ben chuckled. "Rory told me to pick some up for you." He poured a splash into a red cup and handed it to Indi, then popped the cap of a beer for himself. "Let's toast to having you back. I ... I mean we ... were worried sick."

She nudged her cup to his bottle and took a sip. It was sickly sweet and what Indi imagined unicorn tears might taste like.

They swallowed their respective drinks and looked everywhere but at each other. Just when Indi thought she might have to throw herself onto a samurai sword to escape the unbearably awkward silence, Ben spoke. "You look nice tonight."

Indi winced. Where was a samurai sword when you needed it? She sipped her schnapps. "Yeah. I follow a lot of raccoon makeup tutorials. Sort of my brand."

Ben bit his lip to quieten his laugh. "It's good to see some things don't change. No one can make me laugh like you." Suddenly, his hand was cupping the side of her face, his thumb tracing her cheekbone. "Can we go somewhere private and talk?"

What fresh hell was this? Indi stared wide-eyed, unable to move, like a deer in the headlights. Ben moved closer. Was he going to kiss her?

A shrill voice, louder than the music, put a quick stop to whatever was about to happen. Indi slipped away from Ben's hand while he was distracted and knocked back the rest of her schnapps.

Ben frowned. "I know that voice. Not again." He walked toward the sound which was coming from the front door. Indi put her cup on the counter and followed at a safe distance.

"Is she here, Elton?" Sadie screamed. "Because I told you if she was here I wasn't coming."

Elton rolled his eyes. "I didn't invite you Sadie. I didn't invite anyone. It was an open invitation. Can you just relax?"

Indi still couldn't get over Sadie's transformation, with her blonde hair pinned back in beautiful, flaxen tangles and the plunging neckline of her red dress nearly reaching her navel. But why did she change herself? The Sadie that Indi remembered was happy. She was the only one of the bunch that Indi respected because she was the only one with a personality. Now she had assimilated Brandy, right down to her tantrums.

"So, are you going to tell her to leave or what?"

Indi could guess what Elton would say next. She prepared to find a backdoor exit so her eviction wouldn't be too humiliating.

"She's not leaving," Elton said sternly. "So do you need me to call you an Uber or what?"

Indi wasn't sure how many more shocked expressions her face could contort. This was some straight-up telenovela shit. She slowly backpedaled to the kitchen before Sadie's wrath was splattered all over this lovely wood paneling.

"India!" Sadie shrieked. "I see you."

Indi bowed her head. Shit.

"You got a Brandy pass when she was here, but now that she's not, you don't get to act like everything's normal."

"Oh, believe me, the last thing anything is right now is normal, Sadie," Indi snipped. "Especially you." Indi looked her up and down. "I mean, what the ...?" She looked at those around her, stifling their grins. "Right?" she asked.

Sadie gritted her teeth and charged, but Ben had forced his way through the rubberneckers and grabbed Sadie around the waist. "Okay Sadie. That's enough. I'll get you home."

"No!" Sadie argued. "She should be the one to go. It's my turn, goddamn it." The partygoers started whispering about Sadie. Indi felt a strange turn in the tide, as if the waves were flowing toward her instead of away.

Ben held Sadie firmly. "Calm down. You're embarrassing yourself. Come on." He dragged her away from the door, and when Elton shut it behind them the crowd erupted in applause.

Fucking nut job, Indi heard more than once. She's wearing her sister's skin like Buffalo Bill, joked another. None of those things were what Indi wanted to hear. She found them about as funny as when someone asked her in the street if she had killed Brandy. Indi regretted what she had said. She didn't mean to snap at Sadie like that. It was apparent she was suffering, and Indi had just made things worse.

"Well, she got put in her place," Avery remarked, sliding along the wall to stand beside Indi. "What's next? You going to run for Frost Queen? Take over the school?" Avery was swaying, the top few buttons of his white shirt undone, blood on his knuckles from the pedestrian he had pummeled outside. She could smell booze on his breath. So much for a sober driver.

"I've got no plans to take anything from anyone. Sadie can have Frost Queen if that's what she wants. It's not my thing."

Avery handed her a red cup, and the familiar sweetness of peach schnapps wafted to her nostrils. "Good to have you back Indi. We missed that spirit around here." Indi took the cup, and Avery lurched over her, watching as she lifted it to her lips.

"Babe, there you are!" Rory squealed. She ran at full pace and leapt into Avery's arms, wrapping her legs around his waist and kissing him passionately. Indi stood there for a moment, trying not to look, but couldn't avoid it when Avery took hold of Rory's ass and spun her around against the wall.

"Excuse me," she mumbled, shuffling away from them.

Whether it was the smoke or the loud music, the schnapps or Sadie's full Exorcist meltdown, Indi needed five minutes to herself right now. She tried each door-handle along the hall until, finally, one turned. Not caring where it went, Indi ducked inside.

6

THE GARAGE. THIS WOULD do just fine. A grungy old couch sat against the wall next to a scratched-up coffee table with an overflowing ashtray and empty coffee cups. Indi put her schnapps alongside them and fell onto the couch, throwing her legs over the rounded arm. At least the music was duller in here, though she could still clearly hear a chug chant.

Indi glanced around the room, looking at nothing in particular. The overhead lights cast a sepia glow, and she squinted to make out objects on the metal shelf across the room. There was a row of helmets, harnesses, and a pile of dusty shoes. She sat up, curious, her attention drawn to several neon-colored items at the very back of the shelf.

"I don't know what beef you had with my mom's lamp, but don't hurt Moldy. He's got nothing to do with this," Elton said, closing the door behind him.

Indi bolted upright, her brows knitted in confusion.

"The couch," Elton explained.

"Your couch has a name?"

"Doesn't yours?"

"No. But if it did, it wouldn't be something as explanatory as Moldy."

"Why not?" Elton grinned. "Usually that keeps nosey party guests away from it."

"I'm not nosey, I'm antisocial," Indi argued.

Elton glanced at her cup. "Didn't drink that, did you?"

Indi shook her head. "Not yet."

Elton picked up the cup and poured it into a pot plant by the door. "That's for the best. Girls have a habit of falling asleep after Avery fixes them a drink. It kills me that Rory hangs around with that piece of shit." He frowned. "But we've had this conversation before."

Indi tapped the side of her head. "Feels like the first time."

"Some things are worth forgetting. Avery's a bad dude."

Elton walked to the couch and sat down, closer than necessary. Indi responded by rocking to her feet and wandering toward the metal shelf.

"You hang with him though," she commented.

"Doesn't mean I like him. I invited Rory, but they're a package deal."

"I thought you told Sadie that it was an open invitation?"

Elton stretched his arms over the back of the couch. "You caught that, did you?"

He had this fantastic shape to his body where his toned chest tapered into his waist like an Olympic swimmer. She dragged her eyes away. "You like Rory then?"

"Sure. She helped me ace my English paper. If I don't get into a good college, my parents are going to lose their shit, so she's been tutoring me. I owe her big time. Plus, she's about the nicest person you'll ever meet." Elton raised an eyebrow as he watched Indi back away from him. "You're so jumpy. I guess everything is pretty weird, right? How far back do you remember?"

"I was still hanging out with Cameron Gibbons. I don't remember being this close to any of you," Indi admitted.

Elton laughed and scratched his neck. "Jesus. Why are you even here? We're like strangers to you. You must be freaking out." Elton surprisingly summed up exactly how Indi was feeling.

"Just trying to put the pieces together."

"Woah. Does that mean you thought you and Cameron were still a thing?" Indi nodded uncomfortably. "Wow, that sucks, man. Sorry. Probably for the best though, after that huge fight you had."

Indi jerked her head. "What fight?"

Elton shrugged. "I don't know exactly, just something I heard, not something you talked to me about." Elton lifted his pelvis to retrieve his cigarettes from his front pocket. His shirt inched up, and Indi glimpsed the sharply cut v-lines on his smooth, dark abdomen. "You didn't like me too much," he finished.

"Not much has changed then," Indi replied with cold disinterest.

Elton laughed and lit his cigarette. "Okay."

Talking to Elton wasn't terrible. Sure, he oozed arrogance and strutted around like he had ten pounds of swag in his pants. But every word sounded honest, like he was too cool to give a shit if you thought he was lying, so why would he bother? Indi saw it as an opportunity to get information that even creepy Detective Braddock was struggling to gather.

"Today in the pavilion, what you said about Brandy. You think she's dead then?"

Elton grimaced. "Of course she's dead. It's been what, almost a month. If she's alive, no one's asking for a ransom. The cops haven't found shit and who the hell in Army Bay would kidnap Brandy Hamilton? Everyone knows her."

"Maybe it wasn't someone from Army Bay?" Indi thought out loud.

Elton nodded, open to the idea. "Still. The odds aren't good."

"Did you like Brandy, Elton?"

"Yeah. I did like her when she was on her own. Problem with Brandy was she tried so hard to be everything to everyone that she left nothing of herself to show. What she needed to embrace was the simple truth that all people want to be assholes. You do what you think makes them happy, what you think will make them like you, but they just end up resenting you, anyway."

Indi understood that logic. "You're not like I remember from Meg Forester's tenth birthday."

Elton furrowed his brow. "Meg Forester?"

"You called her fat."

"Nooo. I wouldn't say something like that. I'm far too nice."

Indi grinned. "I was there. You said it while we were eating her cake."

"I remember the cake. I remember she was eating a lot of cake. I remember saying something about the amount of cake she was eating." Elton put his cigarette in the ashtray and stood up. "But I didn't call her fat." He moved nearer to Indi.

Indi took another step back. "Maybe I remember it wrong."

"Need to be careful of that, especially with your condition."

He was getting closer, and Indi was running out of room. Soon she felt the metal shelf prod her in the back and suddenly Elton was right in front of her with little more than a breath of space between them.

"If you can't trust your memories, how will you be able to tell what's real and what's not? Those memories locked away in that head of yours. They're nothing but trouble, India Peters." He exhaled. "Now, are you going to ask me any more questions, or is it my turn?"

Indi was shaking. "It's getting pretty late."

"You just got here."

"Pretty late in Norway," she mumbled.

She turned on her heels, her knee bumping into the shelf. She let out a pained grunt as the contents tumbled onto the ground. The helmets, the harnesses, the dusty shoes and, landing atop the pile, were the neon objects Indi couldn't make out from the couch. Close up she saw they were several lengths of brightly colored rope tied in bundles.

"You're just a one-woman bulldozer, aren't you?" Elton joked.

Images flashed through Indi's head. She saw the beach at night. The rain. The black sky. Between strikes of thunder, she saw her hands bound so tightly that her wrists bled. The color, she couldn't make out the color of the rope. The lightning was too bright, the night too dark. She grasped at her chest. She couldn't breathe.

"India," Elton took her by the shoulders, "are you okay?" Indi's eyes snapped open and she shoved him away as she staggered backward. Elton looked at the contents of the shelf scattered over the floor. "What? That stuff? It's my rock-climbing gear. Do you need to sit down?"

Elton reached for her again, but Indi recoiled. "I have to go."

She walked swiftly from the garage, doing her best not to run like a crazy person. Indi pushed through the clusters of swaying teenagers, finally making it outside and taking in a breath of air that didn't taste like cheap beer and body spray. Now she faced a fresh problem. Avery and Rory were her ride and going back to find them was the last thing she wanted to do.

"Indi!" Paula gushed, slapping a wet, drunken kiss on her cheek. Indi squirmed. "What are you doing out here? Do you need a ride?" she slurred.

"Don't worry. I'm sober driver," said a voice behind Paula. Indi didn't recognize the girl. At any other time of her life, that would have been enough to guarantee they had never met, but things were different now. For all Indi knew, they could have matching tattoos on their asses. When Indi didn't respond, the girl stared at her curiously. "Hi."

"Sorry. I'm India."

The girl nodded. "I'm Jenna."

Indi exhaled. It was refreshing to meet someone who didn't know her. "You don't go to Army Bay High, right?"

"No. A Catholic girls' school in Seradale. I just visit family out here on the weekends sometimes."

"Fancy," Indi said with an impressed grin.

Jenna rolled her eyes, seeming embarrassed. "I know, lame right? I wear a plaid skirt and tie, the whole cliché fantasy ensemble."

Indi laughed. "Do you have a pony and a cocaine addiction?"

"Oh my god, horses and coke are my life."

Indi liked this girl already. "So, how do you two know each other?" Indi asked, gesturing to Paula, who had passed out on Jenna's shoulder.

"We only met last week at some party." Jenna rattled her car keys. "I drew the short straw tonight." She glanced around the driveway. "Do you need a ride?"

Accepting a ride from a stranger was probably a bad idea, especially in her current situation. But Jenna didn't look like a murderer. Indi also wasn't looking forward to having to walk home. What she wouldn't give for the anti-murder fanny pack right now. "I've sort of been through some things lately. I probably shouldn't."

"I know who you are, India. I'm from Seradale, not outer space," Jenna laughed lightly. "Look, you know Paula, right? Paula can vouch for me. Can't you, Paula?" She gave her a shake, and Paula responded with a burp and something that sounded like a yes.

Indi looked back toward the house just in time to see Elton appear at the door, his hands gripping the frame above his head. "Okay, sure. I'm on Appleby," Indi said decisively.

Jenna nodded. "Cool. I'll drop you off first."

Indi helped carry Paula to her busted white sedan. They loaded her into the backseat, doing their best to keep Paula's dignity intact when her skin-tight minidress wound up like a roller blind. Indi hopped into the front, and quickly they were down and out of Elton's driveway.

"So, were you enjoying the party?" Jenna asked.

Indi frowned. Not at all. Ben had tried to kiss her. Avery apparently had tried to drug her. Sadie wanted to kill her and Elton, well, she was still trying to process what happened in that garage. But she was sure Jenna wouldn't want to know any of that. She settled on, "Oh yeah. It was a blast."

Jenna flipped her long silky blonde hair over her shoulder. Indi blinked. Either that peach schnapps was kicking in, or Jenna really looked like Brandy from this angle. Was that how things were going to be now? Every pretty blonde girl looking like Brandy, haunting Indi for eternity?

"Really?" Jenna said. "I thought it was horrible. I can't wait to get home and put on some elastic-waisted pants."

Indi sighed contently. "Binge-watching Ninja Warrior."

"Seeing the moment they disappoint their families and the thousands at home," Jenna chuckled.

Indi raised an eyebrow. "Yeah. I live for that."

Jenna fell quiet for a moment, stiffly adjusting her rear-view mirror and wiping something only she could see from her dash. "Yeah. Me too." She exhaled loudly. "You okay back there Paula?" Paula replied with a series of moans, growls, and gags. "I'm sure she's fine," Jenna said. "Hey. I don't suppose you smoke?" She reached into her jacket and pulled out a joint.

Indi sighed. "Are you my guardian angel or something?"

"I'll take that as a yes." Jenna turned off the main road and into the empty carpark of Food World, parking beneath a flickering light.

They climbed out and Indi checked on Paula in the back, who was snoring, fast asleep, with half her face in a drool puddle. Jenna climbed onto the bonnet, leaning against the windscreen and stretching out her legs. She lit the joint and took a long drag before handing it to Indi, who slid up next to her. Indi took a hit and closed her eyes, holding the smoke in her lungs as long as she could. When she exhaled, she felt every muscle in her body turn to soft butter, and suddenly her head didn't feel as heavy on her shoulders.

"When I was ten, I fell off a jungle gym," Indi started, gazing up at the bright night sky. "I broke my ankle, couldn't walk. So Brandy put me on her back and carried me for almost a mile to my house." She handed the joint to Jenna.

Jenna took a puff. "Sounds like a good friend."

"She was," Indi replied. "She was the best—the only friend I needed. Then one day she wasn't, and I felt like half of me was gone, you know? Like I'd been split down the middle. I missed her so much. But now we're friends again, and I don't understand."

"What's there to understand? You said you missed her. Isn't being friends again a good thing?" Jenna passed back to Indi.

"She became a different person. I couldn't believe how mean she was, especially toward me." Indi rolled the joint between her fingers. "I don't know why I thought I'd be immune. I clung to this idea that because we were close once, she wouldn't have the heart to treat me like she did everyone else. But she was just as mean, even a little more, since she knew everything about me." Indi took another drag, and her body tingled as if a thousand butterflies were dancing upon her skin. "I was fine with hating her. I really was. I almost preferred the simplicity of it. But now I can't stop thinking about her." She turned her head to look at Jenna. "And you know what else?"

"What?"

"I miss her all over again." Indi felt lighter with every word that drifted from her lips, and it had nothing to do with the weed. Elton was right when he had said that Brandy was everything to everyone. She had been cruel and spiteful, but when Indi's grandfather died, Brandy had hugged her non-stop inside a blanket fort while Indi cried for a week straight. Indi hadn't realized she missed Brandy until she lost the opportunity to do anything about it. "I can't stand to think of her out there in the water," Indi muttered.

Jenna turned. "Isn't she just missing though?"

Indi gulped and took a long drag before passing it back to Jenna. "I'm getting kind of tired. Would you mind dropping me off now?"

"Sure." Jenna smiled, inhaling one last time before stubbing out the smoldering tip of the joint and stuffing it back in her pocket.

When Indi returned to her seat, Paula was still sleeping soundly in the back.

"I meant to ask," Jenna started, pulling on her seatbelt. "Saw you at the party with some ripped hottie. In the kitchen. Is that your guy?"

Indi's mind was getting foggy. She pinched the bridge of her nose as she thought. "You mean Ben?" Indi shuddered. "Your guess is as good as mine. I don't know what that was about."

Jenna grinned mischievously. "You two looked pretty close."

It was giving Indi cramps just thinking about it. "He was acting like we were a thing, wasn't he?"

"You and Ben Campbell were not a thing," Paula spat from the backseat, wiping a stream of drool on the back of her arm. "I'll tell you that for free."

"Oh, hi Paula," Indi said.

Paula lunged forward and flopped her arms over Indi's chair, accidentally slapping her face with floppy fingers. "One. Ben was way too obsessed with Brandy to even look at anyone else. My cousin Trav, you know Trav, right? Well, he works at Ben's gym, and he said that girls would throw themselves at him on the daily, but Ben was like this iron monk, not interested in a single one of them. He only had eyes for Brandy, even though she was always screwing around on him, which is pathetic and so sweet." Paula paused and cupped her mouth, her eyes bulging. Indi and Jenna recoiled, bracing themselves for a barf explosion. But Paula swallowed whatever was trying to get out, which was slightly more disgusting. "And B," she continued, "you never hung with Ben. I barely saw you talk. It was you and Brandy, 24/7."

Indi regarded her curiously. "How do you know all this?"

Paula rolled her eyes. "Because I hated Brandy, so of course I was obsessed with her too. Duh?"

Indi turned to Jenna and nodded. "I kinda get that."

Paula swayed as her eyes grew heavy. "Vote Paula," she slurred before she passed out again.

Jenna curled her lips. "I think I better get her home now."

"Yeah. Good idea," Indi replied.

They bantered for the rest of the ride, and when Jenna pulled over outside Indi's house it surprised her how fast the time had gone. Jenna hadn't pressed her for details of the incident or gossip about Brandy. She had just listened without judgement, something that Indi had hoped Cam would do. Jenna had also had some pretty good weed.

Indi stepped out of the car and leaned in the window. "Thanks for the ride. It was nice meeting you. We should swap numbers." Jenna shuffled in her seat, and Indi immediately regretted asking. "Sorry. That was weird."

"No, no. It's cool. Give me your phone," Jenna said.

Indi handed it over, and Jenna quickly tapped in her name and number. "Text me. We should hang out."

Indi nodded and gave a wave from the curb as Jenna drove away with Paula still groaning in the back seat.

Indi scaled the drainpipe like a damned professional and tumbled through her bedroom window for a perfect dismount. She crept into bed and listened hard over her crinkling duvet for her father's snores. Her dad was at level three, a deep inverted honk, which meant he had been asleep for at least two hours. It looked as if she had got away with her excursion.

Indi had hoped that spending time with those people would make it easy to get rid of them. That they were incapable of being anything but awful and she would have proved herself right. Mostly, they hadn't let her down, but not all of them, and that had Indi worried.

She nuzzled into her duvet, exhaustion sweeping over her so quickly that she was asleep as soon as her head hit the pillow. Still, Brandy was present as ever in her mind. Until they found her, Indi would have no relief from her nightmares.

7

INDI TOOK A LITTLE longer to get ready for school the next morning. Her brain felt like a ball of mush rolling around in her aching head. She stared at herself in the mirror and traced the line of her scar. She looked tired. It didn't help that even after five passes of makeup remover wipes, there were still black smudges around her bloodshot eyes. She glowered at herself. "I look like a chimney sweep."

The doorbell rang, and Indi heard her mom's heels clapping along the hallway.

"Hey, India," she called. "It's for you."

Indi abandoned all hope of attractiveness and sunk into a fresh hoodie. She checked her phone ... eight a.m. Cam used to show up around this time so they could walk to school together. Indi held a hopeful breath as she left her room. At first she dawdled, but as the idea of Cam at the door gained momentum, she began to run down the stairs.

Indi frowned with disappointment. It was Ben standing in the doorway, his bag draped over one shoulder and a mango smoothie from Amped Juice Bar in his hand.

"Morning," he said with a soft smile. He held up the smoothie. "Thirsty?"

Her mom was still standing at the door, watching the scene unfold with great interest. Indi shot her a glare. "Thanks, Mom." Her mom smiled obliviously. It wasn't until Indi intensified her scowl that she picked up what Indi was putting down.

"Oh. Right. I'll go clean something that's somewhere else."

"Yes, please," Indi sighed.

"Great to see you again, Mrs. Peters," Ben chirped brightly. He took a step forward, and Indi quickly put herself between him and the doorway.

"What are you doing here?"

Ben shrugged. "I thought we could walk to school." He offered the smoothie. Indi's inner turmoil on whether to take it was far greater than it should have been. Taking the smoothie was an acceptance of Ben's company. Not taking it was dragging a delicious, innocent beverage into the crossfire. She took the smoothie.

"Fine. Let's go." Indi went to close the front door, but her mom peeked out from the living room.

"I don't see a fanny pack."

Indi rolled her eyes and said to Ben, "I'll be right back."

THEY DIDN'T SPEAK FOR the first five minutes, so Indi sprinkled the silence with slurps as her straw foraged the bottom of the cup for the last dregs of smoothie. She knew little about Ben Campbell, only what was public knowledge. He had a screw-up of an older brother named Jeff, who was a mechanic two towns over. Jeff got into deep shit in high school for pursuing Brandy when he was a senior and she was thirteen. Indi had always thought it odd that Brandy would date Ben after that mess. Anyway, it had pretty much destroyed Jeff's future. Being labelled a pedo was never helpful. Then there was Ben's father, who apparently beat the shit out of him if he ever dropped a football, worse if the Army Bay Makos lost a game.

"So about last night," Ben started. "I thought I should explain myself."

"Yeah. Probably," Indi replied.

"Don't get me wrong. I love Brandy. But it's not like we didn't have our issues."

Indi remembered Paula's words from last night. Was Ben just as aware as everyone else about Brandy's cheating? She stayed quiet. If he wasn't, Indi didn't want to be the one to tell him.

"I always felt a connection with you. We were getting really close before your attack, and I kind of thought we could build on that," Ben added. Indi felt his knuckles brush against her hand. Again, wise Paula's voice echoed in Indi's brain. She might not have been in their circle, but Paula was the finger on the pulse of Army Bay High. Nothing happened at that school without her knowing every detail, and Paula had said Ben and Indi were not a thing.

"I'm not looking to be involved with anyone right now, Ben."

Ben rolled his tongue in his cheek. "Is it Cameron?"

Indi stopped and nodded. "Yeah. I mean, she's not talking to me right now, and things have changed, I get that. But the way I remember it, we're still together. I need to figure that out before I even think about anyone else." Her eyes lingered on his collarbone and broad chest. "Even if they look like you."

Ben breathed out his nose, his shoulders drooping slightly. "I can wait, I suppose."

Indi was well aware that girls would kill to have Ben's hazel eyes look at them the way he was looking at her right now. But none of this felt right. If Paula was telling the truth, and Indi and Ben were not close, why would he be saying they were? How could he even think about building relationships when Brandy was still missing? Wasn't he utterly obsessed with her?

They started walking again, and Ben clicked his tongue loudly, which cut the fresh silence. "I also wanted to talk to you about Sadie."

"Let me guess. I can't sit with you at lunch because Sadie says so?"

"Nothing like that," Ben laughed lightly. "I tried to explain to her that this is none of your fault, whatever has happened to Brandy. That you're a victim too."

Indi welcomed those words. "You really think that? You don't think I'm involved?"

Ben shook his head vehemently. "Of course not. She loved you, and you loved her." He clutched his chest. "I believe that with my whole heart. Someone attacked you both. The cops just need to get off their asses and find her and whoever did this before someone else gets hurt." Indi would have hugged Ben right there. But she might not want to let go. Ben rolled his shoulders. "My point is Sadie wants to apologize."

Indi leaned forward. "Come again?"

"This has been tough for her. She overreacted."

Sadie's behavior so far hadn't endeared her to Indi. The two servings of slap in the bathroom were a particular highlight. But her twin sister was missing. Indi could forgive her for being a little unhinged lately.

"Hey, India," a voice called from across the street. She recognized the voice immediately. It was the same kid from yesterday, and she was reasonably sure she knew the theme of his incoming jibe. "Who are you going to kill next?"

"Hey, shut up!" Ben yelled.

Indi waved her hand with indifference. "Don't worry about it. He's just some douche-bag."

"It's cool. I'll take care of it," Ben replied. Indi looked up from her smoothie cup to find Ben was already sprinting across the street. He approached two boys a couple of years younger than them. Indi recognized them as the dickweeds who kick over the trash cans on collection day. Her dad had chased them away with a broom twice.

She watched as Ben spoke to them calmly, gesturing toward India and nodding his head sympathetically. All appeared fine, that was until Ben threw his bag off and punched one kid square in the face. The boy's friend raised his fist vengefully, but all it took was an aggressive lunge from Ben for the boy to shrink backward. He helped his friend to his feet, and the pair scurried away.

Ben returned. He straightened his bag and swept back a wave of hair, smiling at Indi as if the bizarre intercession was no big deal.

She stepped away from him. "Do you usually beat up people in the street?"

Ben chuckled, which was nice and creepy. "Some kids need to learn the hard way, I guess. He won't bother you anymore."

Indi noticed a droplet of blood on his white long-sleeved shirt. At first, her only thought was gross, but then suddenly she felt the dark close in around her again.

It was night. She was on the beach. Soaked wet by rain that fell in sheets. There was a flash of lightning and a chilling scream masked by the boom of thunder. Indi raised her arms in defense, but it was too late. A figure stood over her and smashed a rock against her head. Indi's blood sprayed her white shirt. The shirt she woke up in, that they had cut away in the emergency room. The shirt now inside a police evidence box with her name on it.

Indi's senses returned. She reached for the scar on her head.

"Yeah. That's a good one," Ben said, admiring it. "They uh, ever tell you how that happened?"

"It was a rock," Indi said blankly, as that puzzle piece slipped into place.

"Really? How do they know that?"

Indi exhaled. "Not them. Me." The vivid flashback lingered, and Indi even discreetly checked her fingers for blood. Her memories were returning. That was what she wanted, no matter how much they frightened her.

Ben adjusted the strap of his backpack. "Well, that's great, India. That's what everyone is waiting for, right? You to remember what happened?"

His eyes were probing, as if he was waiting for a concrete answer from her then and there. Ben had gone from the nice guy every girl swooned over to a tween-punching rageaholic in the space of ten minutes. Maybe she had told him too much.

He had been half right. People were waiting. But not for the same reasons she was. Indi wanted her old life back. This one was too manic and confusing. She wanted to know what she had done to deserve being hurt so brutally. She wanted to know for sure that it was Brandy she watched sink into the ocean. Everyone else just wanted fresh gossip for their walking group. And what did Ben want? He was still staring at her, but Indi would not give him an answer. Not until she could draw out more guiding memories, like a needle drawing blood.

WHEN THEY REACHED SCHOOL, Ben stalled at the front gate.

"So I'll see you later? We'll catch up at the pavilion?"

Indi gave a non-committal nod. Ben reluctantly turned his back on her and crossed the parking lot. Indi went in the opposite direction. She entered the math building and walked down the main hall until Cody Gibbons forced her to a stop.

If Army Bay High was a bowl of Neapolitan ice-cream, Indi decided Brandy Incorporated would be the heavily favored chocolate. Paula and friends the middle of the road, but still highly sought, vanilla. Last, there would be the often-discarded strawberry. The last resort. Delicious because hey, it's still ice cream, but just not as popular as the other two. The strawberry at Army Bay High was Cody, and he ruled the drama and band brigade with a moisturized iron fist.

Indi wasn't sure what to expect. She and Cody had never had issues. You could even go as far as to say they were friends. But Indi wasn't sure if all that had changed during the months she couldn't remember. Cody and Cam were brother and sister, and siblings tended to side with each other. She was curious to know where Cody stood.

Cody was fussing over placing a poster. A girl that Indi recognized as first chair flutist, Ava, was on one side. On the other stood Sam, break out star of last year's school production of Chicago.

"Left. Left. No! Right!" Cody yelled, gripping his fiery red hair at the roots.

Indi glanced at the poster. Cody Gibbons is your Frost Queen! His hair was slick with silver gel, his lips and eyes painted blue. He was posed regally on a prop throne the drama club had used for King Lear, complete with a scepter and glittering crown.

"There, that's it!" Cody squealed, clapping excitedly. Ava and Sam marked the spot, then taped the poster to the wall. Cody rested his hand on his chest. "I look fabulous. There's nothing else to say."

"I don't know," Indi interrupted. "You could have contoured. But we can't all have my bone structure."

Cody's face was blank at first, and Indi worried she had made the wrong move. Slowly, a smile curled onto his lips. He opened his arms and rushed to wrap them around Indi. She closed her eyes, savoring every second.

"I should have called," he said into her hair. "I'm sorry."

"Don't be. This more than makes up for it." She squeezed him, glad that not everything had changed. He still smelled like old lady perfume: gerberas or some shit.

Just when Indi felt some semblance of getting her old life back, Cody pulled away. "I'm not supposed to be talking to you."

Indi frowned. "Cam?"

"Not just Cam. Christa."

Indi knitted her brows in confusion. "What about Christa?"

Cody noticed Ava and Sam eavesdropping. He hissed and shooed them away before turning back to Indi. "How could you be friends with Brandy after what she did to Christa? I could deal with any boring, basic bitch drama you and Cam might have had. But choosing to associate with that walking jizz-receptacle? Sorry, Sis. That's a deal-breaker."

Shit. Indi hadn't even considered how Christa would factor into all this. No wonder Cam was so mad at her. "I'm still trying to figure this out, but I want to make things right. I need Cam to talk to me for starters." Indi hoped her eyes were pleading enough. She was going for sad puppy, but it could come off as blobfish.

Cody pondered through half-shut eyes. He pointed at his poster. "I have your vote, right? Paula Marshall has cornered the skank market, but I'm still in it if the hockey team turns out to the booths." Indi cocked an eyebrow, and Cody grinned wickedly. "That's a tale for after dark."

Technically, Indi hadn't promised Paula her vote. If that's all it took for Cody's help, it was a small price to pay. She nodded. "I'm on board. Cody 2020."

He clapped and held out his hand. Sam magically appeared and placed a sticker version of the poster on Cody's palm. Cody slapped it on Indi's chest. "Keep an eye out for my text, bitch. I got you."

The bell rang out, and Indi groaned. "Shit. I'm late." She stole another hug from Cody before barreling down the hall.

"Is that a fanny pack?" she heard him call after her. "Good god."

Indi slid to a stop outside her classroom.

Math.

Numbers + Mr. Friedberg's neck beard = Sad India.

8

AFTER JABBING AT HER calculator like she knew what she was doing, Indi decided she had no clue what X was, and that algebra was stupid. She leaned back in her chair and huffed out a heavy breath. Paula's disciples huddled in the corner, locked in what appeared to be an intense conversation. Then Indi noticed something missing. Paula.

"Hey," Indi whispered. The girls turned in unison. "Where's Paula?"

They looked at each other as if deciding who would speak on their behalf. The tallest, Amy, was selected.

"We don't know. We've been messaging all morning, and she's not replying."

"Have you tried her house?" Indi asked.

Amy frowned. "Why would we have her home number? To swap recipes with her mom?"

The others laughed. Indi was pleased she could ease their worry with her sensible question. Typically, when someone wasn't at school there were a hundred logical explanations. But that was logic Indi trusted before someone tried to murder her and before Brandy went missing, before Army Bay felt a little less safe. Paula was right in the middle of her Frost Queen campaign, and Indi couldn't rationalize her taking a day off.

"I saw her at Elton's party last night," Indi said. "She was wasted. Maybe she's home with a hangover."

Amy rolled her eyes. "Paula went to a spin class with violent diarrhea because Taylor Swift's neighbor's cousin's niece was going to be there. She can handle a hangover."

Indi winced. "Oh my god, she did?"

"Yeah." Amy yawned. "She just plugged her asshole."

"Amy!" gasped a girl named Heather.

Indi tried to scrub that detail from her brain. "Are you guys worried?"

"She's probably fine," Heather said. Amy had apparently lost her speaking privileges. "What's the worst that could happen in Army Bay?"

Indi cocked an insinuating eyebrow.

"Oh. Right," Heather said.

This morning's smoothie gurgled in Indi's stomach. Was she overthinking this? Paula was just at home with her phone turned off. Probably with her head in the toilet. Or ... she was on the beach, in the cold, bleeding to death. Fuck. Indi had to stop telling herself this was no big deal. A girl was missing, and she could have been one of the last people to see her. Well, her and that girl Jenna. What was her last name again? Had she even said? Indi tried to remember her face. Blonde hair. Fair skin. Blue eyes. Or were they brown? She kind of looked like Brandy, didn't she? It was dark. Indi wasn't paying that much attention. She didn't know she might have to provide a description later. No, they were blue. Definitely blue. Indi needed every detail. Jenna could know something. Or worse. Wait. She had her number! She could just ask her.

Indi grabbed her phone and swiped through her contacts until Jenna popped up. Okay. This had to be smooth. She wanted the message to be casual, but with a hint of urgency. Somewhere between How are you? and What have you done with the body?

Indi settled on...

Hey. This is India from last night. Did Paula get home safe? She's not at school.

Indi's finger hovered over Send.

Was this the right thing to do? Maybe she should just give Jenna's number to Braddock. Let him deal with the questioning rather than getting herself involved. She wasn't sure her reputation could survive another missing girl, and what if she was wrong? The school day was almost over, and apart from the Paulettes, no one seemed concerned that Paula wasn't here. Surely her parents would have called, and surely there would be police all over the school asking questions.

The shrill of the bell startled her. Indi clutched her chest before her heart exploded. She looked at her phone and slowly deleted the message one letter at a time. Indi had to keep her cool. She needed facts ... Nah, fuck it. She re-entered the deleted letters and hit Send. She waited, watching the

Paulettes flitter out of the room. Then her phone beeped. If Jenna was a killer, at least she was prompt.

Message undelivered. No such number.

Indi's stomach knotted. That wasn't good. Not only could Jenna be the most wanted person in Army Bay, but she'd also left Indi a false number, which was kind of rude. She thought they'd got on pretty great. Indi chided herself. What are you doing? Time to find creepy Braddock.

INDI WONDERED HOW MANY troubled teenagers had died from boredom in this horrible wooden chair. She yawned as she waited outside Kindness Cottage. It had been a while. Indi secretly hoped it had something to do with Paula. Sick or missing, she would take either at this point.

Miss Mathis opened her door, already fidgeting nervously at the very sight of Indi. "Yes, India. How can I help you?"

"I need to talk to Detective Braddock." Indi was whispering behind her hand. She didn't want anyone else within ear-shot to hear such gossip-inspiring banter.

Miss Mathis was even more uneasy now. "Oh, dear. Of course. Come in."

Indi slipped through the small gap in the door, and Miss Mathis ushered her to a more comfortable chair with a cushioned seat. She rifled through her desk until she found Braddock's card, then dialed the number so slowly that Indi felt compelled to leap over the desk and do it herself. Miss Mathis shoved the phone at Indi when it started ringing.

"Braddock."

"Yeah. Hi. It's India. I was wondering. Have you heard anything about Paula Marshall?"

"Hello, India. Paula Marshall? What about her?"

"I don't know." What had Indi done? This felt stupid. But she had gone too far now to turn back. "Has anyone reported her missing or something like that?"

He paused. "No. No missing person reports."

Indi was almost disappointed. "Are you sure?"

"Only matters of interest today are a stolen Ford Fiesta and some graffiti on the Town Hall. Now, what exactly is going on, India?"

Miss Mathis snapped her fingers to draw Indi's attention. "What are you saying about Paula?" she whispered roughly.

Indi put her hand over the mouthpiece. "She's not at school. I think she might be missing, like Brandy."

Indi tried to talk to Braddock again, but Miss Mathis was more urgent with her gestures now, shaking her head firmly. "You need to hang up the phone, dear, I think you're mistaken."

Indi had passed the point of no return. She went all in. "Look, Braddock. I think another girl is missing. I have a name and ..."

"India!" Miss Mathis snapped. Indi didn't know the guidance counsellor's voice could reach that octave. "Paula was sent home not long after showing up at school this morning. She smelt like a brewery and left a vomit trail across the quad. I put her in her mother's car myself."

Indi gulped. "But. She's not answering messages."

"Judging by how displeased her mother was, I don't imagine she'll be answering any messages for a long time. Let alone running for Frost Queen."

Indi suddenly felt very, very stupid.

"India?" Braddock coughed over the phone. "You have a name?"

Indi couldn't summon a single syllable. She stuttered for a bit until Miss Mathis took the phone from her.

"Detective Braddock? I apologize sir. I think India has got a little confused. No. Paula Marshall is not missing, just at home sick. I can personally account for her. Yes."

India wanted to crawl under the desk and disappear. She hadn't even thought to ask Miss Mathis if she knew anything about Paula, just took the Paulettes on their word. Indi had almost turned in a perfectly nice girl. Jenna did rudely give Indi a fake number, but that wasn't the point. Ghosting Indi and killing Paula were two very different things.

"Alrighty, Detective Braddock. Talk again soon. Bye, bye now." Miss Mathis hung up the phone. "Do you need to lie down, dear?"

"I'm so sorry," Indi finally pushed the words out. "I don't know what came over me."

"I'm going to hold your hand. Is that okay with you, India?" Miss Mathis asked. India rolled her eyes and gave half a nod. Miss Mathis gripped her hand. "If I were in your position, the last thing I would do is hunt down the one responsible for the horrible deed done to you. But I guess you think that will give you closure. Yes? Just like you think that if you find Brandy, you will get answers for both of you. Then you will both have closure. Yes?"

"That's the general idea. I guess."

Miss Mathis rubbed Indi's hand, and one of her long pink nails snagged against her skin, not cutting deep, just enough to leave a bright red scratch. "I admire your intentions, India. But Brandy has no secrets to tell, no clues to help you. Brandy Hamilton is gone. We should say our goodbyes and wish her well. The sooner you do that; the easier your life will be."

Indi snatched back her hand. "Why would you say that? Aren't you supposed to be counselling or something?"

Miss Mathis smiled and put Braddock's card back in her desk drawer. "Do you know what Brandy told me once when she was sitting in that very chair? She told me you and Cameron were a pair of dirty lesbos." The candor startled Indi, and the words stabbed at her heart. "The thing is, I hadn't mentioned you or Cameron. The conversation was about something completely different, although just as profane. Brandy liked to shock me with her escapades. You and Cameron just happened to be walking by my window at the time. Brandy took pleasure in being cruel. Don't forget that. Some things, some people, are best left dead."

The last bell of the day rang, and Miss Mathis sighed contently. "Finally! Are you alright to get home, dear?"

Indi stumbled up from her seat, weary and fearful after their exchange. "Yeah. Fine." She shuffled from the room quickly as she could. Brandy's disappearance had drawn something dark out of Miss Mathis. Something Indi hadn't seen in her before. She often presented as an insufferable do-gooder, but things weren't always as they seemed. Every time they were together, Indi got the feeling Miss Mathis wanted her to open up, maybe to confess something. Or possibly she was testing Indi's receptiveness to reveal something herself. Whatever it was, if Indi never saw Miss Mathis again it would be too soon.

Indi hustled through the quad and out toward the front gate. Her dad was picking her up today, and Indi couldn't wait to see him. She needed to be close to someone she trusted. Nothing to hide and nothing to gain. Someone to assure her she wasn't crazy, and that everything was going to be alright. When she caught sight of her dad smiling at her from his car, she was confident he was the one to do just that.

Suddenly, something caught Indi's ankle. Her knee buckled, and she fell forward, but a pair of hands snatched her before she could go face-first into the ground. Avery had caught her. He jerked her upright, his hands clutching her waist far tighter than was necessary—his thumb worming its way under her shirt and kneading the skin below her breast.

"Saved your life," he said. "Can't have many more left."

Rory slapped his shoulder. "Ave, shut up."

Even with Rory standing right there, Avery hadn't removed his hands yet. It took Indi's glare and a forceful shove to pry them off her body. Avery grinned, and Indi turned away in disgust, but the view to her left wasn't much better. She stared off with Sadie, who was still wearing Brandy's face. Indi had to stop thinking that. It was Sadie's face too, as it always had been. Brandy had just seemed to dominate the rights to it.

"Sorry, did I trip you?" Sadie asked. She smelled like pears and violets. It triggered something in Indi that made her miss Brandy terribly at that moment. "Is this part of your condition? You just blank out from time to time?"

Indi sighed. "Is the plan just to assault me whenever we cross paths?"

A grin tugged at the corner of Sadie's mouth. "Oh honey, if I wanted to hurt you, that emo mug of yours would know all about it."

"Ah, ah, ah!" Ben chirped, wedging himself between the pair. "She comes in peace. There is nothing but rainbows and cuddly puppy feelings here. Sadie wants to call a truce."

Indi noted that Sadie's sour expression hinted otherwise. Then she spoke. "I'm sorry. Okay? I miss my sister, and I put that on you. Last time I saw Brandy, you were losing your shit at her right where we're standing. You can't blame me for thinking you were involved."

"I don't know anything about that."

"Well, you're the only one. The entire school saw it. Next day, you're Laura Palmer with a pulse on the beach and Brandy's ... gone. I shouldn't have slapped you in the bathroom." She paused. "Twice. Plus, Rory won't shut the fuck up."

Rory raised her hand. "Guilty as charged."

Indi could remember the old Sadie, the one that wore Brandy's shadow. She barely spoke louder than a whisper. Now here she was throwing fucks around like they were on a reality show. But this is how Indi remembered Brandy to be; loud, obnoxious, and regrettably, cooler than most people could ever hope for in their entire uncool lives. For Sadie, this change in appearance and personality wasn't just a makeover. It was a takeover.

Sadie's stiff posture eased. She brushed her waves of blonde hair away from her face. "Do they think you'll ever get your memory back?"

Indi shrugged. "Maybe. Maybe not. They say it'll take time. More time that passes, more likely the maybe not."

"And you really think Brandy is still alive?"

"I hope she is."

Sadie smiled. A full, genuine smile that cracked through the layers of overpriced foundation and gooey lip gloss. Indi's guilt panged in her chest. She did hope Brandy was alive, but the bloody flashes in her head said otherwise.

Sadie looked over Indi's shoulder. "Jason Momoa is waving at you."

"Who?"

Rory laughed into her hand. "That's what we call your dad."

Indi turned and saw that her dad had left the car and was at the gate, spinning his arms like windmills to get her attention. First, how super embarrassing. Second, Jason Momoa? There was no measurement system for the copious amounts of disgust clogging her throat.

"Well, come on. Let's not be rude." Sadie linked arms with India and walked her toward the car. This was not a mutual stroll. Sadie was literally dragging Indi through the quad.

Her dad froze when he saw Sadie. His eyes dark and wide like a solar eclipse, his mouth agape.

"Dad," Indi said. She slapped his arm when he didn't respond. "Dad! Stop staring."

Sadie giggled. "I don't mind."

"I'm sorry," he mumbled, clearing his throat. "You just look ..."

"Like Brandy. Obviously, Dad," Indi groaned. "They're twins."

"Right." He dragged his eyes away from Sadie. "We need to go. Your mother is waiting. You know how she can get." He walked briskly to the driver's side and started the engine before he had even closed his door.

Indi frowned and farewelled her ... friends. She climbed into the car and scowled at her father. "You're acting nice and weird."

Sadie leaned in her window, and the scent of pears and violets was intoxicating. "Bye, Indi. Bye, Mr. Peters."

Sadie had barely taken a step from the curb before her dad hit the gas and sped away.

9

INDI SPUN IN HER SEAT and looked back to make sure they hadn't hit Sadie. That would be the icing on this shit cake.

"Geez, Dad. What was that?"

He shuffled in his seat, fidgeted with the dials on the dash and turned the heat up. "It's too bizarre how similar they look. Like seeing a ghost. I don't remember them looking much alike at all, but now, wow!" He shook his head solemnly. "Poor Brandy"

"Really? I thought you didn't like her. Too snobby. A troublemaker. Isn't that what you used to say?"

Her dad grumbled. "When you were thirteen-year-olds, and just because I might have said those things doesn't mean I can't feel sorry for a missing girl."

Indi felt sweat beading at her temple. She reached for the dial to turn down the heat, but her dad knocked her hand away. For a brief moment, their skin touched. His was cold. She had never stopped to think how something like this had affected her parents. Her parents had watched Brandy grow alongside their own daughter. Brandy had been there for sleepovers, birthday parties, days spent at the beach. The Peters had even joined the Hamiltons on their boat for a weekend. Her mom had spent the entire trip puking over the side. Even if Indi and Brandy's friendship had ended, that had nothing to do with her dad. He would be a monster if he were unaffected by Brandy's disappearance. So it made sense that seeing Sadie, now that she had remade herself in Brandy's image, would be upsetting.

Indi kicked off her shoes. If she had to sit in this sauna on wheels, she needed to get some layers off before she combusted. She struggled to digest today's platter of bizarre happenings. The days were just getting stranger and stranger.

Halfway through the drive, Indi's phone beeped. She retrieved it from her fanny pack, an item she was finding quite useful. It was a message from Cody.

Merry Christmas. See you at 6.

Holy shit. Did that mean Cam had agreed to see her? Indi shoved the phone in her pack, then gripped the edges of the car seat. She wanted to wind down the windows and scream her lungs out. But her dad was obviously going through some stuff. So, instead, she dug her nails into the foam and ground her teeth in silent elation.

When they reached home, her dad pulled the car into the driveway and clicked off the engine. "It just reminded me how close we came to losing you," he said at random, as if the thought had been tormenting him the entire drive.

Indi chewed her lip when she saw his eyes glass over. She lightly pinched his arm. "Dad. Don't. I'm fine. See?" She wriggled her fingers and bare toes.

He chuckled and sniffed away a tear before it had the chance to fall. Then his face turned somber. "I don't think you should hang around with those kids anymore, girl. They're no good. I worry about your safety. I wouldn't be surprised if one of them knows what happened that night, perhaps even did it?"

The thought intrigued Indi. But how could they live with themselves? Why would they welcome Indi into their circle with open arms? Turning their backs on her would have been less work. Plus, teenagers can't be sociopaths. That was just nonsense they put in movies. That thought crumbled in seconds when Indi remembered what a messed up world she lived in. Most teenagers were actually narcissistic, lunatic time-bombs packed full of hormones, anti-depressants and Red Bull. Indi indulged in the possibility. Who among them would hurt her or Brandy?

Ben? No way, he was in love with Brandy, but then, love can make you crazy.

Sadie? Didn't make sense; everyone knew she worshipped her sister. Maybe that was the problem.

Rory? Impossible. Indi was sure a vegan diet suppressed those kinds of violent tendencies, but even if she hadn't just made that up this instant, Rory wasn't capable of harming anyone, not without good reason. But what if there was a good reason?

Avery? Gah, utter slimebag, but was being a piece of shit enough to make him a suspect? Perhaps Avery could have had something to do with this whole thing. He was undoubtedly grabby. Maybe he grabbed Brandy that night and things got out of control? He seemed frighteningly familiar with her own body today. Had he touched Indi before? India didn't know what was more gross--the chance he was maybe a killer, or that sexual assault was a daily indulgence for him.

Then came Elton. Intriguing, brazen Elton. Couldn't be. He had admitted that he liked Brandy and, on the Most Likely to Be a Psycho list that India had just invented in her head, he was at the very bottom. Even not-missing-Paula and bitchy Cody were above him.

Now those two, they hated Brandy; it was never something they denied. But could the shallow desire to wear her crown be enough to hurt someone? And even with her gone, neither had ascended the Army Bay High throne. Brandy was getting more attention now than when she walked the halls. And what would be their reason for attacking Indi?

What soured Indi most on the idea of the Squad's involvement was that, one day, she might remember everything. She might remember precisely who wanted to kill her and exactly what happened to Brandy. She would know their name. She would know their face. They would have nowhere to hide, and Indi would show them no mercy. She had received none. That was a big gamble for one of these kids to take. Knowing that at any moment India Peters could remember everything. She felt as if tiny icicles were stabbing at her skin, even though the car was still ridiculously hot.

What if they knew that Indi remembering was just a matter of time? She suddenly realized that it wasn't just her attacker who was in trouble if that day came. Whoever hurt her would need that night to remain a mystery that would never be solved. Next time they wouldn't make the same mistake.

Indi had almost forgotten her dad was waiting for an answer. He glowered at her. "India. Do you understand what I'm telling you? Those kids are trouble."

"You know I'm getting some mixed messages here." Indi frowned.

"That's your mother. I don't know what she's thinking, but she's always wanted you to be one of those types. Make-up and parties and proms, like she didn't get enough of that when we were kids. I think she was making one of those TikToks the other day."

Indi wasn't sure if her dad wanted her to respond or if he just needed to vent. It was an odd choice. Smack-talking your wife in front of your daughter and suddenly contradicting everything the doctors had been looping for the last few weeks. Seeing those kids had obviously flipped him out, Sadie in particular. Indi could relate. Brandy 2.0 was freaking her out, too.

She balled her fists awkwardly against her knees. "I don't want to lie to you, so I can't tell you what you want to hear."

In an instant, the patience and empathy drained from his face. "You don't want to lie? That might have helped six weeks ago. Do you know what your mother and I have gone through? It killed us to see you like that. We were barely hanging on by a thread as it was, and your mother couldn't take care of you alone. I had to come home. Do you know how hard that all was?"

Indi felt the air sucked from her lungs. What was she supposed to say to that? Once again, was she supposed to say anything at all? Was this just an info dump of stuff he had been carrying on those massive shoulders since Indi inconveniently washed up on the beach? But why did everything in his word-vomit seem to make it Indi's fault? What about the fact that someone had tried to murder her and almost succeeded? Perhaps that motherfucker deserved some blame too.

She wanted to scream at him, curse in English and Māori, maybe even a little Hebrew she had overheard at Cody's bar mitzvah a few years back. But even with her dad being a prize dick, she couldn't. What would be the point? Freak out and get grounded. She might as well be in quarantine all over again. Tell him what he wanted to hear. Indi needed freedom right now, not a fight, regardless of how cathartic it would have been. Her submission might even get her some sympathy.

"Fine. I get it. I won't see them again," she muttered.

Immediately her dad slumped in his chair, with weight seeming to melt from his shoulders. There was silence for a moment before his tense face softened and he smiled, bringing out the dimples in his jaw. "I'm sorry. I shouldn't have snapped like that. It all came out wrong. You know we love you girl. I love you." He clasped her hand in his, and it all but disappeared. "I would do anything to keep our family safe."

All Indi could do was nod and force a smile that she hoped brought out her own dimples. When he pinched her cheek, as he used to when she was little, she knew she had succeeded. Now was the time to fish for some perks. "I was thinking of doing some baking and maybe heading over to Cameron's place."

"Right. Cameron." He scratched the back of his head. "How's that going?"

"Not great," Indi replied. "But I'm known for being persistent."

"If that's what you want, then go get it." He softly tapped her leg, which signaled the end of daddy/daughter time. "Maybe bake some extras that I can take to work tomorrow."

"Oh. You're going back?" Before his meltdown minutes ago, he had been a pretty great quarantine buddy. They had binge-watched Supernatural and played Cluedo religiously before her mom pointed out that a murder mystery game was probably inappropriate. So, they'd played Mouse Trap instead. It had been pretty cool.

"Well, with you better now and back at school, your mom and I thought it might be time."

Indi highly doubted her mom had much to do with the decision, but she wasn't going to be a bitch about it. They'd had a good run. Someone had to pay the bills and keep flour and red food-coloring in the pantry. "Do you have some big builds going on?" She didn't really care about the answer.

"We do, we're finishing up the new apartments on Willoughby."

That sounded vaguely familiar, like from before Indi's memory blank-out. She nodded politely. "So it's cool if I go to Cam's place then?"

"Sure," he replied. "I'll drop you."

After dumping her backpack on the stairs and cranking up The Weeknd, Indi headed straight for the kitchen, covering her mother's impeccably spotless counters in a hurricane of flour and red food coloring. It was the most normal Indi had felt in a long time. The waft of vanilla and the roar of the mixer. It was all science and measurements. You got out what you put in. Indi liked the simplicity of baking. She also liked the fluffy red-velvet goodness.

She started rehearsing in her head what she would say to Cam. First, she wanted to know what she had done and, second, what she had to do to move past it. Part of Indi's dedication to everyday life was getting back to the last day she could remember. That day was making out in the long grass with Cam.

Somewhere between the soft kisses and Indi washing up on the beach, everything had changed, and Indi was desperate to know why.

An hour passed and Indi had baked and iced a dozen perfect cupcakes and arranged them on a tray. She contemplated spelling out Cameron's name, but decided against it. Indi changed out of her flour-smeared hoodie and jeans, relying once again on the off-the-shoulder bodysuit. Indi lingered in front of the bathroom mirror, deciding whether to pin back her thick brown waves of hair. If she did, it would draw more attention to her scar, and Indi wasn't sure if she was ready for that. As a compromise, Indi tied the back but left the front loose, overdosing on hairspray to keep it all in place. Even when she had finished, she felt like she could do more. As if one little tweak would solve everything and she and Cam would be together again. Indi glanced around the bathroom counter, waiting for that special ingredient to scream out to her. She opened the cabinet drawer and instead heard the clank of her cherry-blossom body spray as it rolled from the back. Okay. Maybe that was it. When Indi gripped the pink can, her hand brushed the sharp edge of a glass bottle tucked away next to it.

"What are we, twelve again?" Brandy laughed. "Body spray?" She reached into her bag and pulled out a square perfume bottle. It was decorated with gold filigree and had a little red tassel tied around the neck. She held it out elegantly between her fingers like a hand model on the home shopping network. "This honey, is what big girls wear."

When Brandy spritzed the perfume on Indi's neck, the scent of pears and violets overwhelmed her. It filled her head and sent the blood racing in her veins. She realized quickly it was just how Brandy smelled. Indi stared at Brandy's reflection in the mirror. How perfectly her hair sat on her shoulders, lustrous and golden and not a strand out of place. How blue her eyes were, the kind of big blue eyes you only remember seeing on Disney princesses. Her skin was fair, but ever so slightly tanned and every time she moved, Indi could smell those pears and violets.

"I can't wear this. It's your perfume," Indi protested.

"And it's done me wonders," Brandy giggled. "Trust me. Cameron will love it." She dabbed an extra few drops behind Indi's ears. "There. Perfect."

Indi smiled. "Thanks. I've never really been great with this stuff."

Brandy pulled open the cabinet drawer and dropped the perfume inside before sliding it shut. "Well, that's what friends are for, isn't it? Come on. I'll give you a ride."

"India, who are you talking to up there?" her dad called before arriving at the bathroom door.

Brandy grinned. "Good afternoon, Mr. Peters."

"India!"

Indi snapped from her daydream. She was still in the bathroom, her hand on the perfume bottle in the drawer, but Brandy was gone, and her dad stood in the doorway looking confused.

"India. I've been calling out to you. Are you ready to go?"

She slammed the drawer shut. "Yeah. Sorry. I'm ready."

Indi swung past the kitchen and grabbed the cupcake tray. Once they were in the car, she refused to negotiate about the heater situation, demanding her dad turn it down so the icing wouldn't melt. He was talking the entire drive, but Indi didn't hear a word of it. Her mind looped through that moment in the bathroom. It was the first time she had remembered her and Brandy being together and, of all places, in her own house. She smiled. It was like when they were kids before high school ruined them. Indi had wondered how she would feel about being friends with Brandy again. If she could put the past behind them and bury her anger. Could it be the same? The answer was yes, wonderfully the same. She lurched forward when her dad hit the brake.

"Do you need me to pick you up?"

"Maybe. I'll text you." Indi climbed out, being extra careful not to lose the tray. She approached the door and took a deep breath, then balanced the tray in one hand to ring the doorbell.

10

INDI DIDN'T HAVE TO wait long before Cam answered the door. She stood, silent, for the longest time, indifferent in the doorway. Was Indi supposed to speak first? Is this where she apologized for whatever it was she had done? Did she look stupid holding this tray of cupcakes?

Cam snarled. "What are you doing here?"

Indi grit her teeth, momentarily forgetting how to speak. Cody. That evil bitch.

Cam furrowed her brow. "I thought I made it clear at school ..."

"Oh yeah, there was a definite get lost vibe." Indi laughed awkwardly and wanted to crawl under the closest rock when Cam didn't laugh back. "Cupcakes?" She winced.

Cody descended the staircase and laughed into his hand when he spied Indi. "Oh, snap. That's right."

Cam craned her neck and scowled. "You knew about this?"

"I work hard for my constituents," Cody replied unashamedly. He gestured to the living room. "Teatime?"

Cam rolled her eyes. "Come in, I guess."

Indi bowed for some reason before gawkily slipping inside. As she passed by, her arm just barely brushed against Cam, enough to feel her warmth and the tiny hairs on her elbow. Indi's blood raced. She followed Cody into the living room and placed her cupcakes on the coffee table. Cody had already sprawled himself over the chaise section of the grey modular couch. He tapped the cushion beside him, beckoning for Indi to sit.

Cam slunk into the room, her arms crossed tightly against her chest. She was mad. Indi could tell because whenever Cam was pissed, her skin turned so red you couldn't see her freckles. She sat as far away as she could on the opposite end of the couch.

Indi couldn't help noticing Cody's outfit. He had traded his loudly printed polo and burgundy chinos for a shapeless beige shirt and matching drawstring trousers. Not that Indi was one to judge. The universe frequently brought her fashion sense into question. But Cody was a higher being in that respect, so should know better. "And what are we wearing?" she asked.

Cody shuddered. "I know. I got a part-time job at the hospital. My parents refuse to cash in my college fund for a Birkin bag, so it's up to me now."

"Wow. The hospital?"

"Don't be too impressed," Cody sighed. "I mostly give people pudding. Anyway," he held Indi's hand, "tell me what happened."

"What part?"

"All the parts."

Indi sunk into the old couch, which remembered her perfectly, molding to her body like it would when she and Cam binged Netflix. Cam would eat Frutti Corn and wriggle her red-polish-splashed toes. Indi would count Cam's freckles starting at her brow, but always lost count when she got to her mouth.

"The last thing I remember before waking up in the hospital was the day Cam and I planned to go to the park." She glanced at Cam, but nervously kept her eyes lowered. "Do you remember? You wanted to talk to me about something."

Cam and Cody exchanged looks.

"You don't remember what we talked about?" Cam asked.

Indi shook her head. "Care to fill in the gaps?"

Cam spoke before Cody could. "Brandy had invited you to some lame party, and you wanted to go. I was meeting with you to end things."

Indi narrowed her eyes. "What? You broke up with me over that? What party?"

Cam shrugged. "Probably the same kind of stupid party you went to last night. Yeah. I heard about it. All anyone can talk about is you and Ben tongue fucking in the kitchen."

A breath caught in Indi's throat. "That isn't what happened."

"I heard you broke Elton's mom's antique lamp," Cody stated.

"Oh. That happened," Indi replied. "But the tongue fucking. Definitely not." She paused, trying to find the logic in Cam's disclosure. "Was that a good enough reason to break up with me, Cam?"

"Yes," she snipped.

Indi continued. "Why would Brandy have asked me to a party in the first place? What happened for us to even be on speaking terms?"

"All I know is that Brandy called, and you answered."

That wasn't good enough. Indi needed more. Her frustration at the lack of an explanation for Brindia overshadowed her disbelief in Cam's pathetic breakup reasoning. Oh no. Did she just think the word, Brindia?

Cody squeezed Indi's hand to remind her he was there. "So, what after that? The beach?"

Indi gulped. "The beach."

"What about the police? Do they know anything?"

"No suspects. No clues. Seawater is good at washing away evidence. They think Brandy might have been kidnapped, but they're not sure."

"Or she could be dead," Cody mused.

"They don't know anything for sure," Indi repeated. She could see the cogs turning in Cody's head.

"Well, I mean, it's obvious what really happened. It was Brandy. She tried to kill you, and now she's in hiding."

"Not the first time I've heard that theory," Indi said. "But I can't think of a single reason Brandy would want to kill me."

"Ben Campbell," Cody said matter-of-factly. "You two were screwing around, right?"

Indi immediately checked for Cam's reaction. She was even ruddier now with her nostrils flared. "What is with this Ben garbage? None of it is true!" she defended.

"That's a new one," Cam chimed in. "Been going around today along with the kitchen tongue fuck."

Indi searched Cam's eyes for an ounce of common sense. "Do you really think I would screw around with someone's boyfriend? Especially Brandy's? Especially Brandy's, who happens to be Ben? Sure, he's hot, but you know I've never been into jock types. It's the muscular calves. Too veiny."

Cam gulped, tightening her arms across her chest. "Sometimes, people hide things, Indi. Even people you trust."

The room was spinning. This Ben rumor was getting out of hand and driving a bigger wedge between her and Cameron. Indi wanted to continue her passionate denial, but the wall Cam had put up was thick and threaded with barbed wire. Every word out of Indi's mouth was only making it worse. Imagine what would happen if Indi spoke what she was really thinking: that there was more to this than Cameron was letting on. That her coldness was only pushing Indi closer to Brandy Inc. That if she had ever loved Indi, she would try harder to fix things.

As those thoughts floated dangerously near the surface, Cam spoke and the tremble in her voice almost broke Indi's heart. "And we've not even mentioned what this all did to Christa."

Cody folded at the sound of that name, just as he had in the hall. His emerald eyes drifted to the mantle and the family portrait that hung above. Cody and Cam were front and center, with their red-haired mother and blond father standing behind, but at his mother's side was a third Gibbs child, with Cam's freckles, Cody's broad smile, and older than them both. She wore white lace like some Celtic maiden, her bright red hair draped over her shoulders in curls. Indi couldn't remember a time since then that Christa Gibbs had looked so happy.

She had been a year ahead of them at school and pretty popular for a drama kid, but she had unknowingly earned the ire of Brandy Hamilton, who was just a budding bitch back then. Brandy had her vagina set on some hot senior who asked Christa to the prom instead. The story still comes up sometimes, like some urban-legend-warning to any girl looking to screw with Brandy. Wherever Christa's name appeared, whether it was on production posters, bulletin board announcements, activity sign-ups, Brandy would scribble it out and write Lava Crotch instead. Brandy spread rumors that Christa was sleeping with guys from other towns and spreading herpes, or the red plague, as she called it. She would Photoshop Christa's head onto porn stars and Snapchat the pics to any phone that had a signal. Even after Christa and the guy broke up and she moved schools, Brandy would still taunt her on social media. A reminder of who the queen of Army Bay was. Not long after, Christa slit her wrists. Her dad found her, got her to a hospital before she bled out. She'd been a patient at the Joyness Clinic in Seradale ever since.

"She's coming home soon, you know," Cody said. The flourish in his voice disappeared, now somber and low. "We're having a dinner party. You should come."

Cam threw her arms up in protest. "Can you quit with the invites Cody? Jesus Christ."

Indi picked up her courage and joined Cam on her side of the couch. She leaned in close but was mindful of the space Cam demanded. "Can I talk to you, please? In private?"

Cody's ears pricked, and his nosiness infuriated Cam. She nodded and led Indi into the dining room, seemingly just to annoy him. Indi didn't care what the reason was.

Cam sat on the table, her feet dangling, her pale skin showing through the tears in her jeans. Indi struggled not to move between her thick thighs, take her by her round hips, tangle her fingers in the fuzzy red hair at Cam's nape. No. It wasn't the time for that, even though it was what Indi wanted most in the world right now.

"I want to fix this," Indi said softly. "I want things to be like they were."

"Well, they can't be," Cam snapped coldly.

Indi dropped her chin. "Why? Because of Brandy? Because of something I can't remember? That doesn't seem fair Cameron." Suddenly Cam's eyes glassed over and pooled with tears. Indi's heart cracked. "No, don't cry! I didn't mean to upset you."

Cam bit her lip angrily and hooked her hands under Indi's ears. "Why can't you just remember! Don't you know that would make everything easier? How many things it would fix just like that?"

Indi leaned into her touch and closed her eyes. "You don't think I want that too? It's happening, you know, little flashes."

Cam sniffed away her threatening tears. "Really? It is?"

"When I'm with the Squad. I see things. I see ..."

Abruptly, Cam's hands abandoned her, tucked coldly against her sides. "Are we really talking about them? Again?"

It left Indi dazed when Cam withdrew her touch. "What? I'm trying to tell you."

"I don't want to hear any more about that pack of slags and assholes. Okay? One of them probably did this to you in the first place." She sniffed.

"Probably Elton. He's too quiet and secretive. He's got murderer written all over him."

Indi took a deep breath, trying to keep her cool. She was getting close. She didn't want to frighten Cam away now. "What reason would Elton have to hurt me?"

Cam growled. "Stop looking for a motive, India. Teenagers are latent psychopaths. You probably snagged the last snickers from the vending machine once, and he's been obsessing over it ever since. That's how this shit happens."

Indi shook her head. "I don't think ..."

"Can you hear yourself defending them?" Cam spat.

"Would you let me finish one sentence, Cameron!"

They heard a shuffle in the alcove and turned to see Cody freeze in place like they were playing a game of statues. He flinched. "Don't mind me."

"Cody. Get lost!" Cam cursed.

"Enough, Cam. She's trying to make this right with you. Can you not be a bitch for like, a fifth of a second?"

Cam gripped the edges of the table, her chest heaving with frustrated breaths. She locked eyes with Indi, and Indi wasn't sure if she was going to kiss her or hit her. That was becoming a regular thing lately.

"Come to dinner when Christa gets back," Cam said, her voice strained. "I just need some time to think stuff through. Okay?"

Indi nodded immediately. "Yes. Totally. I haven't seen Christa forever. I'll be there. Just text me the details."

"Cody can text," Cam replied. "I deleted your number."

Okay. One last nail in the coffin just when Indi thought she was about to claw her way out. She silenced the voice in her head that questioned why she was still here. Why she was still fighting for someone who clearly didn't want her. It wasn't the first time she had heard that voice during their relationship.

Indi swallowed. "Fine. I'll wait for Cody to text."

Cam leapt off the table and breezed past Indi before heading upstairs.

Cody wandered over and nudged Indi's shoulder. "I don't know what to tell you. My mother was probably huffing asbestos while she was pregnant with that one."

"No. It's fine," Indi said, forcing her lips to curl upward. "I've hurt her, and she's making me work to get her back. That's what happens in relationships, right?"

Cody gave a comforting smile. "Not the good ones."

"Well, she's your sister."

"Hey," he growled. "Only by blood." They laughed, and it helped Indi drop at least a few ounces of disappointment at how this visit had turned out. "Did you want to hang around and wait for your ride? We can watch Tiger King?"

"It's okay," Indi sighed. "I think I'm going to walk."

Cody's stare was questioning. "Is that safe?"

"The mood I'm in, no killer would want to mess with me."

Indi showed herself out, dragging her feet down the paved walkway. When she reached the footpath, she turned and looked up at Cam's bedroom window, just in time to see the curtain hurriedly close. Indi had only suffered a few days worse than this one. The last one was when she washed up on a beach.

She decided it was probably best to text her dad for pick up. He had asked her to, and Indi didn't make a habit of letting him down. Just as she reached for her phone, it beeped in her pocket. Indi checked the message.

Rory: Grabbing some food. Want to come?

Indi checked the time. She could eat. She was out anyway.

Indi: Sure. I'll wait at the corner of Painter Way.

Rory: Cool. Be there in 5

AVERY'S BLACK SUV PULLED up by the curb. The tinted window wound down dramatically, and Rory exploded into sight.

"Hi! Hop in."

Indi smiled, and she didn't have to force it. That was becoming easier the more Cam pushed her away. At least Rory was happy to see her. Indi climbed into the back seat. No Ben or Sadie. That was a relief. She wasn't in the right mood to confront Ben about the rumors, and she'd likely puke if Sadie brought up Jason Momoa.

"Hey," Avery greeted from the front, his eyes not shifting from his phone.

Indi glowered. This guy, on the other hand, she didn't trust. The wrapping might have been irresistible, but the inside was rotten.

"Hi," she replied anyway. Indi had learnt that Avery and Rory were a package deal and as much as she tried to deny it, Rory was growing on her.

"So, change of plans," Rory sighed. "Everyone's got together online and organized a march for Brandy. It's going to start at Cooper's Park and finish at the Town Hall." She flashed her FIND BRANDY shirt. "Hopefully this will get the cops off their asses to do something."

"Okay." Indi took time to process. "I guess we're marching then."

Rory turned around in her chair to face Indi, and hugged the headrest. "I knew you wouldn't mind, and you know when this was being planned I thought to myself, yes, it's important we draw attention to Brandy's disappearance and demand the police work harder. But we forgot about somebody." Rory pulled out a brand-new t-shirt from behind her back and whipped it open.

Indi's eyes bulged. "Oh, no." The shirt had Indi's picture printed on the front with the words JUSTICE FOR INDIA. The worst part? Rory had used the photo of India in a bikini. It just seemed all kinds of inappropriate. Brandy's shirt had an airbrushed glam shot while Indi's had lopsided boobs. No one else might have been able to see it. But she did. Indi cringed. "I thought I deleted that photo."

Rory laughed. "Girl, nothing is ever deleted from the Internet. Come on now." She inspected the shirt. "You look amazing. Anyway. I think Army Bay has got so caught up in Brandy that everyone forgets what happened to you and that there is some psycho out there." She tossed the shirt to Indi.

Indi frowned. "Is it weird me wearing my own shirt?"

Rory looked to Avery for input, and when he was silent, she slapped his arm to break his swipe-up trance.

"It'll look dope," he mumbled.

"Put it on!" Rory squealed.

Indi's fingers flirted with the idea of lifting off her sweater but, for the first time, Avery's eyes abandoned his phone and found Indi in the rear-view mirror. Gross sleaze. Instead, Indi pulled the shirt on over her hoodie and smiled wryly at his reflection.

Avery grinned and put his phone away, then took hold of the steering wheel and hit the gas.

11

COOPER'S PARK WAS WHERE Indi used to go with Cam. It had a kids' playground with slides and swings and a giant, terrifying, climbing frame that seemed like a lawsuit waiting to happen. Beyond a row of picnic tables and charcoal grills was a patch of long grass threaded with pastel-purple flowers.

Indi stared at the grass as it swayed in the frostbitten breeze, imagining the flowers tangling with Cam's red hair.

"India!" Rory giggled, wrapping her arms around her. "Where do you go when you get like that?"

"Nowhere," Indi replied. She didn't want to share too much with Rory, at least for now. Whenever she got close to someone, they abandoned her.

About thirty teenagers were gathered at the park, making a nuisance of themselves by scaling the slide and hanging upside down on the swings. Indi scrutinized them. They didn't seem to be doing much marching, and there was a lot of beer for a non-stationery event.

Indi frowned. "Are you sure this is a march? It kind of just looks like a sit-in."

"Sure it is!" Rory said. "Look, they're all wearing shirts."

"Gah!" Indi cringed and covered her eyes when she saw her lopsided boobs on the lacrosse team's chests. "Oh, god. Set it on fire."

Rory dragged Indi's hands away from her face and smoothed out her wild waves of brown hair. "This march is for you. Enjoy it."

Indi thought on her words. I don't think that's how marches work. God bless her, though. She was always perky. Fifteen minutes passed, then another thirty, and soon they had been waiting an hour for the march to get started.

"I hate to be that guy," Indi said reluctantly. "But it's going to be dark soon." Her dad hadn't texted yet, but he would any minute.

Rory's optimism was slipping as she scanned the crowd, which had grown in numbers but dwindled in motivation. Even Avery had switched camps. Indi saw him talking to a girl who had wandered past with friends. She didn't look older than fifteen. Then someone turned on a speaker, and a chorus of ripping beer tabs welcomed the dusk.

"So, I guess they were just organizing a party."

"It's the thought that counts," Indi said, patting Rory's back supportively. "They're all wearing shirts."

Rory smiled. "You're right. They are. That's something, isn't it?"

"Oh, for sure."

Rory exhaled, but then immediately sucked the air back in and jumped at Indi as if someone had prodded her with a hot poker. "I forgot to tell you! I have a big meet tomorrow in Seradale. Everyone's going. You have to come!"

Indi squirmed. "I don't know. This week has been pretty rough. I kind of just want to crawl into bed and sleep for 72 hours straight. Maybe do a little ugly crying into my pillow. That sort of thing."

"You can do that anytime. Just come watch me run first," Rory joked.

How could Indi say no? A track meet. Sure. She could do that. She was going to parties and non-marching marches. Why not this too? If nothing else, it would mean more opportunities to be around the Squad and hopefully open more of the locked doors in her mind. Cam wanted Indi to remember, which just made Indi want it more.

"Okay, sure."

Rory clapped her hands and hugged Indi tightly. "We will pick you up in the morning. Speaking of which, we should get going. If I'm not marching, I have to get to bed early. Got trophies to snatch." She looked for Avery but he had disappeared, Indi noticed. So had the girl. Rory shrugged. "He must have taken off with some of the guys. Uber I guess?"

Indi nodded. It wasn't her place to word vomit all the things she had been told about Avery or offer any of her own opinions. It might have been selfish, but Indi was enjoying Rory too much to risk upsetting her like she had a habit of doing with everyone else. They shared an Uber home, then swapped grumpy cat memes until Rory declared earnestly at one a.m. that she had to get some sleep.

THE NEXT MORNING, INDI'S mom paced the foyer. Her nails were almost chewed down to the beds. "Are you sure this is a good idea? You've only just started back at school. Now road trips?" She had been on repeat for the last hour.

Indi leaned against the wall, slurping the last dregs of her mango smoothie, waiting for her mom to take a breath so she could get a word in.

"I mean, don't get me wrong, I want you to have fun. I want things to go back to normal, and god knows I want you to write your own story." Indi rolled her eyes as discreetly as she could. Where did she hear that? "But there is still a psycho on the loose." She whispered this through clenched teeth as if said psycho was listening. She gripped the balustrade. "I'm hyperventilating. Oh my god, the room is spinning."

Indi discarded her smoothie cup and dragged herself to her mom's side. She stroked her back with around seventy-percent effort. "I'm just going to a track meet in Seradale. It's no big deal."

She nodded. "I know. I know. Do you have your supplies?"

Indi patted her fanny pack. "Never leave home without it." A horn beeped from outside, and Indi sighed with relief. "I'll be back tonight. I'll text you."

Her mom turned her face and waved Indi away, which meant she was crying.

Two cars were parked in the driveway: Avery's black SUV and a sleek twilight-blue BMW. Indi was oblivious when it came to cars, but even a dumbass knew what that little logo on the hood meant. Sadie was in the back of the SUV with her window down, her eyes hidden behind a pair of black kitten sunglasses, with a bright red lollipop in her mouth. Beside her sat Ben, and he leaned over, trying to get Indi's attention.

"There's room in here if you like?" he called.

Rory nodded eagerly in agreement. "Or you can ride with Elton."

Elton sat alone in his BMW and, when he heard the suggestion, he gave a subtle nod. "Doesn't bother me."

As much as Elton made her nervous, a forty-minute drive wedged between Sadie and Ben sounded like a nightmare. "I'll go with Elton." Ben looked disappointed.

"Whatever," Sadie drawled, winding up the window.

Indi approached the passenger door and Elton leaned over to push it open. "Sorry about the mess, I'm an animal."

It wasn't that bad. Some empty energy drink cans and a few burger wrappers. No worse than what was under Indi's bed. She eased into the leather seat, unclipping her fanny pack and tossing it into the back.

Elton grinned. "Make yourself at home." His black hair was thick with product that made it shine brighter than the surface of the sun. It looked a fraction shorter than she remembered, and the corkscrew curls at the end had vanished. Had he cut them off? Maybe curls were too soft for the look he was going for, more cutesy cherub than a rebel without a cause. He grasped the gear stick and looked Indi over with a sideways glance. "You look nice," he said.

Indi cocked an eyebrow. "Am I supposed to swoon at that?"

"No. I was just commenting. Your hair is back, and I like that t-shirt. Geez."

Indi was wearing a stonewashed shirt printed with a big pair of pink lips and the name of her favorite indie band, Shelter. "You like them?"

"I went to see them last year when they played Duke Stadium."

"Huh. Cam and I went to that concert, too. It was great."

"I mean, they were okay. I think their sound has changed a lot with Trent on backup vocals. Not sure how I feel about it, but I'll give their new album a shot. I think it comes out in August."

Indi suddenly felt relaxed. A typical conversation about music. "It's June."

"Right. June." Elton smirked. "She likes Shelter. She better not like baseball, or I might start thinking she's alright."

Indi shook her head firmly. "Hate baseball. Most boring game on the planet. I would rather wash my eyeballs with bleach than watch that shit."

Elton started his car. "Well, thank god for that then. Otherwise, I would have had to take you to a game. Maybe dinner afterward, then who knows. Dodged a bullet, huh?"

Indi snorted her amusement under her breath and watched the muscles in Elton's forearms tense as he changed gears. He reversed and waited for Avery's SUV to pass so they could follow.

"See you soon!" Rory called excitedly as they drove ahead.

"She's a lot," Indi stated.

"Always has been," Elton replied. "It's all a cover, though. You must see that." He steered his car through the maze of suburbia before following Avery onto the highway. "It's blindingly obvious."

Indi furrowed her brow. "It is?"

"Sure. Her boyfriend is a douchebag, her parents are overbearing assholes, and her friends are a bunch of narcissistic sociopaths."

"I wouldn't say you're a sociopath," Indi said wryly.

"Anyway," Elton grinned, "you two seem to get along, which is great. She could do with a reasonably normal friend."

"Wow. Reasonably normal. You're making me blush. Did we not used to get along?"

"You hung with Brandy, mostly. Didn't have much interest in anyone else before ..."

Indi knew what he was going to say. "Before the beach?" she prompted.

Elton changed gears, his BMW tearing down the open road. "Yeah. How's that memory coming along?"

"I saw Brandy." The words slipped from Indi's mouth before she could stop them, and Elton looked taken aback. "I mean, in my mind, I saw her. She was in my bathroom, helping me get ready for a date with Cam."

Elton shook his head. "I don't know what you did to Brandy, but somehow you turned the Wicked Witch of the West into Dorothy. There was a time she was actually nice to people. Well. Other people. She was trying. You know, she used to spit some serious shit about you and Cam."

Indi remembered what Miss Mathis had said, the insults that had been slung at her and Cam for no good reason. "I know. It doesn't bother me. What people think is none of my business."

"Do you remember anything else?" Elton probed. Indi spied a tremble in his throat. "Anything about the night you were attacked?"

His company may have been annoyingly enjoyable at the moment, but Indi was in no hurry to share more details of her recovered memories with Elton. Especially being underwater and tied to someone she believed was Brandy. That could be dangerous information if revealed to the wrong person.

"Not yet," she replied, becoming more and more skilled at this little lie stuff by the day. "But if I'm getting some memories back, hopefully, the rest will follow."

Elton pushed down on the accelerator as Avery weaved around cars ahead of them. "Fingers crossed."

Soon the exit sign for Seradale grew clear in the distance. The town was bigger than Army Bay. More stores in the mall and twenty-four-hour burger joints. It was also home to the Seradale Sabretooths of Seradale High. They had a better football team, a better hockey team—a better almost everything. However, her dad liked to brag that the Army Bay Makos had beaten the Sabretooths at the buzzer when he played basketball back in high school. That was a while ago, and now the new athletic superstar was Rory Zhang. Not even Seradale had a faster sprinter. Their track coach had cheekily called her parents, trying to entice her to switch schools, but Rory would never leave Avery.

"Should be there soon," Elton stated, turning off the highway and heading toward the towering egg-shaped stadium.

Indi nodded and lunged into the backseat to grab her pack. The bright pink shoes on the floor stood out like, well, bright pink shoes. She recognized them immediately. They matched the box in Indi's closet hiding Brandy's burner phone.

"I wouldn't pick you for a pink trainers guy. We're learning more about each other every minute."

"They belong to Rory," Elton snickered. "She probably left them in here last time I gave her a ride."

"Give her a ride often, do you?" Indi enquired.

"She tutors me. I told you that," Elton said quickly. "I sometimes pick her up from training and drop her home afterward."

Rory's shoes. Why would Brandy's burner phone be in Rory's shoebox? Indi cleared her throat. "I thought maybe they might be Brandy's shoes."

Elton laughed louder than Indi had heard before. He even tried to soften the sound by biting down on his fist. "Brandy? Run? No. She wasn't a fan of physical exertion." He corrected himself. "Well, only if it was horizontal."

Indi couldn't curb her curiosity. "Speaking from experience?"

"No." He exhaled, regarding Indi with a sober gaze. "We were just friends." He stared longer at her than Indi thought he would, so much so that she was the first to turn away under the weight of his eyes. "We're here."

Elton swerved into a carpark and turned off the engine. His knuckles inadvertently brushed over Indi's thigh as he pulled up the handbrake. The caress was so light, Indi wondered why she had even noticed it, or why that spot was tingling now. He leaned back in his seat. "Shall we?"

His meaning didn't register with her at first, but soon she saw Rory across the way, waving her down and pointing toward the entrance to the stadium. Indi was out of that car quicker than you could say, What the fuck was that?

12

GOD DAMN. RORY WAS in good shape. She stood at the start line in a red crop top and matching pair of tiny shorts, shaking out her long, sinewy limbs. Her stomach was taut, her thighs thick and fibrous, the muscles well defined through her arms and shoulders. Indi took a slurp of her raspberry slushie, then noticed Elton chuckling from two seats over, his crossed ankles resting on the row in front.

"Perv much? Did you leave your trench coat and super thin moustache at home?"

Indi cocked an eyebrow. "Whatever do you mean?"

"I can see your lady boner from here." Elton glanced at Rory. "Didn't think she was your type."

"I can look at a girl in a purely platonic way, thank you very much. You see, to me girls are like cheese. Just because I'm attracted to Gouda doesn't mean I want to bang Havarti. Even though they're all cheese. Get it?"

Elton shook his head, bemused. "Remind me never to eat the cheese in your fridge. So is Cameron Gibbons your Gouda?"

Indi exhaled and swirled the ice around the bottom of her cup. "I thought she was. I'm beginning to wonder. Even before the beach, she never felt all in. Just sort of a toe in the pool, testing the water. When we were alone it was as if nothing else existed, but as soon as we were out in the world ..." Indi trailed off. What was she doing? Had this slushie frozen her brain cells? This was not a conversation she wanted to be having with Elton.

"Sucks being the one who cares most," Elton replied, lacing his fingers and stretching his arms above his head. "That's who usually gets hurt first."

Suddenly the start gun blasted. Rory burst from her block with gritted teeth, her arms pumping ferociously.

Elton sprung to his feet. "Yeah, Rory. Go!"

Further down the bleachers, Indi spied Ben and Sadie sitting side by side. Their eyes were locked intently on each other, their expressions cold and sober––far too severe for a Saturday afternoon track meet––and neither of them seemed even mildly interested in the race. Ben glanced over his shoulder, catching Indi in her prying stare. Indi looked away sharply, but he had already noticed. She gulped, anxiety stewing in her belly. It was hard for her not to think she was the topic of conversation. Indi turned back to the race just in time to see Rory lunge for the finish line, her black ponytail whipping against the air as an official clicked his flashing camera.

"Yes!" Elton howled with rapturous applause. "All day, Rory! All day!"

Rory's smile was strung from ear to ear. Her face glowed bright red, and her arms reached triumphantly for the sky as they announced the result over the loudspeaker.

"In the girls 200-metre sprint, first place goes to Rory Zhang, Number 47, Army Bay High School."

Indi couldn't help it. She began clapping too. Say what you will about Rory's perpetual perkiness and the over-familiarity that made Indi slightly uncomfortable. The kid was a workhorse. This was the third race she had run and won today. Sometimes, Indi was out of breath after a vigorous shampoo session.

Rory faced the bleachers and beamed that big, bright smile. Elton cheered louder, even Sadie and Ben took a breath from their guarded discussion to applaud. But Rory was looking for someone else. The jubilation drained from her face and Indi could only assume it was because she didn't see Avery celebrating alongside them. She abandoned her search when an official called her off the track to take photos.

Avery was here a minute ago. Indi hadn't even seen him leave. She nosily scanned the stadium, and it didn't take her long to spot him tucked away in the shadows of the tunnel that led to the locker rooms, his arms stretched against the concrete wall, a willowy raven-haired girl giggling at his every word. Now and then he would twist her hair around his finger or draw circles with his thumb on her upper arm. Indi squirmed and went to speak, but Elton got there first.

"What a sack of shit." He was glaring at Avery, his hand curling into a fist. "Why even bother coming? Surprised she's his type. She's conscious."

Indi grumbled. "You act all pissed, but it's not like you do anything about it. You're still friends with him."

"I'm friends with Rory," Elton said tersely. "I told you that. I was friends with Brandy too. Once upon a time I was good friends with Ben as well, and, as for Sadie, well shit, I don't know who Sadie is anymore. The other person I can't figure out is you." He slid across the seats that separated them and suddenly Indi found they were in close confines, his knee gently nudging hers. "First, you were nothing. Then you were something. And now, you're everything. Victim. Murderer. Hero. Liar. Innocent. Guilty. Tell me, India Peters, how does it feel to have an entire town obsessed with you?"

Indi shoved him away and stifled the urge to spit in his face. "I take it back. You're as much of an asshole as Avery. You just hide it better." She stood and turned her back, then craned her neck and scowled. "And I was never nothing."

Indi abandoned the bleachers and ignored Ben's call as she descended the stairs. She headed toward the locker rooms in the opposite tunnel to where Avery was man-whoring. Rory had gone to change after the podium photos. Indi decided enough was enough. If no one else was going to say something to her, then she would.

Indi found Rory seated on a bench amongst the rows of lockers, running a roller over her quad muscles. Her face lit up as soon as she saw Indi. It was nice feeling wanted. This Havarti was growing on her. "You were amazing," Indi said, taking a seat.

"I know, right!" she gushed. "That was my best 200 meters yet by almost a second. I just have the relay to go, and then I'm all done."

Indi thought hard about what she was going to say next. Tactfulness was never her strong suit; in fact, if you were ever looking for Indi's foot, check her mouth first. Indi flip-flopped for a moment, questioning if this was any of her business. Avery and Rory had been functioning this way for a long time, and Rory was too smart not to see what was happening. Indi couldn't be the first to say something. She u-turned again. No. Rory's supposed friends were unfeeling assholes, too wrapped up in their hedonistic bullshit to care about her toxic relationship. It was blatantly clear that Rory was the only sane and decent one amongst this rabble. She deserved better.

"Rory," Indi stuttered, rubbing the back of her neck. "Why are you with Avery?"

Rory jerked at the question. "Why wouldn't I be? He's hot. He's rich. He loves me. Tell me one girl who wouldn't kill for all that."

Indi had hoped for an answer that wasn't so inadequate. "You must have heard the rumors, Rory."

"And they're just that. Rumors," Rory snapped. She threw the roller into her bag, and for the first time Indi saw her facade crack. "Just because one jealous whore went crying to the police doesn't prove anything. It's all lies, made up to ruin him and us. I've been with Avery for almost three years. He's never forced me to do anything."

"Micah Marshall said ..."

Now Rory was on her feet. "Micah Marshall? Paula's brother? You're going to believe that loser? Like anyone cares about him or his trash family?"

Indi was wrong. Rory had heard this all before. Maybe not directly, but she was smart. You see things. You hear things. You put things together. Rory had rehearsed these responses. It didn't seem worth it now, Indi making Rory so mad for nothing. As much as it sickened Indi to her stomach, this wasn't a secret. Indi backed off before she made things worse.

"I'm sorry. I shouldn't have said anything."

"No shit," Rory spat. "Who do you think you are?"

Indi stood and retreated slowly with her head bowed. This method was effective against rabid dogs, and right now, Rory's demeanor wasn't so different.

"I obviously made a mistake. You're happy. I get it."

Rory's bottom lip trembled, and before you could say bipolar, she burst into tears and crumbled into a ball on the bench. Indi stood silent and still, not sure whether to stay or run. "I know he cheats," Rory sobbed, her head tucked between her knees, "but I have a plan, can't you understand that? We're going to go to the same college, we're going to graduate, we're going to get married and have two kids, and it's going to be perfect. We just need to get out of high school." Her face slowly emerged, her tears mingling with sweat. "I didn't get the scholarship. It went to some other girl. It was supposed to be mine! I had the grades. I had the track results. How did I not get it? My parents can't afford to pay for an ivy league college. I needed that ride."

Indi was taken aback. "I thought ..."

"Well, you thought wrong," Rory snapped. "My dad made some bad investments last year. We're lucky that we can keep our house. But Avery's mom, she knows some people. She might be able to get me a special admission or something."

"And that's all worth it?" Indi asked. "That's worth letting some asshole degrade you?"

Rory took a deep breath. She forcefully scraped away her tears with the back of her hand in a manner that seemed almost chastened. "For a perfect life? Yes. It's worth it. Now if you don't mind. I've got to get ready for the relay."

"Yeah. Of course." Indi left quickly. She had never pitied anyone as much as she did Rory at that moment, pitied her for desperately wanting the most basic bitch lifestyle at the expense of her dignity and morality.

Indi shut the locker room door and stared down the tunnel. She could see the stadium in the distance, the sunlight unable to reach the end of the narrow corridor. The fluorescent bulbs flickered overhead, and Indi's strides echoed in her ears. At first it was only the rhythmic thud of her own footsteps, but then another set of steps joined in, only just out of sync. Heavier and hollower. Indi thought nothing at first. Someone else in the tunnel of a stadium didn't warrant concern. Unless perhaps you were India Peters, who had almost been murdered a few weeks ago. She turned her head barely, hoping to glimpse whoever it was in the corner of her eye—a shadow cast along the wall, but it was too indeterminate to recognize. Indi quickened, and her heart pounded in response when the follower matched her pace.

"Fuck this," Indi muttered. She spun on her heels, ready to confront the jackass trying to scare her, but before she could set eyes on them Indi was grabbed by the shoulders and shoved face-first against the tunnel. She struggled, pushing against their weight, but her attacker was stronger, driving her harder into the wall. With each brutal thump, her vision blurred and her balance wavered. Then two hands snaked around her throat and squeezed.

Soon the shadows crept in. Indi felt the icy wind on her face. Saltwater through her hair. Sand on her lips. She fell so slowly, almost not at all, the sea cradling her as if she were its long-lost child. It pulled her deeper. She was lost in the dark. She felt alone. But she wasn't. Her fingers were entwined with someone else's, desperately clinging to each other in the black water. Indi opened her red eyes. It was Brandy, but her eyes were closed, her skin stark white and threaded with purple veins. The rope that bound their wrists loosened. As the seawater filled Indi's lungs and her life drained away, their fingers unraveled, and Brandy was lost in the shadows. No. This wasn't how it was going to end. Not as long as there was a sliver of fight left within her. With a last surge of strength, Indi kicked toward the surface.

Indi fought the urge to slip into darkness. She reached for her fanny pack, her useless hands fumbling for something, anything. Indi retrieved the mace and pushed it into her attacker's face, then sprayed. There was a furious roar. Her attacker stumbled, releasing her throat. Indi tried to focus and clear the haze, but the last thing she remembered before everything turned black was a fist striking her face.

"INDIA! CAN YOU HEAR me!" The voice was dull in her ears, like thuds on a drum. "India!" Her eyes flickered open, her vision distant and foggy, but slowly Elton's face came through. He hovered over her, his hand cupping the side of her head. Her wits returned, and Indi lunged forward, driving her fist hard against his chin before kicking away across the tunnel.

"Get away from me!" She coughed and gagged, gasping for air and touching the tender skin around her neck.

Elton raised his arms in innocence, his face wracked with concern. "No, Indi," he pleaded. "I'm trying to help."

Indi fought to get her breath back, her vision still veiled like steam on a window. "I was attacked," her voice rasped in her throat. "Where did they go?"

"I don't know. I came down to look for you and found you like this. They must have heard me coming and taken off." He kept his distance. "We need to get you to the hospital."

The words flowed from her mouth without hesitation. "No. I need to go to the beach. Now."

Elton gave a stunned shake of his head. "What are you talking about? You need a doctor or the police. Why the hell would you want to go back there?"

Indi swallowed the lingering pain in her throat. "Please. Take me to the beach, Elton."

13

INDI WOULDN'T LET ELTON carry her to the car or even hold her steady. Instead, he walked a step behind, lunging to catch her any time she wavered. It was annoying, and kind. Before they hit the highway, Elton texted the others to say they were heading back early. The trees along the road sped past them, a swirl of greens that entranced Indi's frantic thoughts. Brandy was dead. She knew that for sure now, felt it in her bones. She stared blankly out the window, silent the entire drive.

The road to Breakers Beach was narrow and winding, weaving through dense bushlands and down sloping hills. Elton seemed to know the way like the back of his hand, not missing a single turnoff or hidden bend.

When they reached the carpark on the cliff, it was empty. Grey clouds rolled across the late-afternoon sky, hinting at rain, the gloom sucking the golden hue from the sand below. Indi stepped out of Elton's car, already feeling stronger. The gravel crunched beneath her sneakers and her body jerked in response. That sound, she knew it. Loud and grating. She remembered it from that morning, the last time she had been here. It was the footsteps of the paramedics at either end of the stretcher delivering her to the waiting ambulance.

"You okay?" Elton asked. He shivered slightly in the cold. Not surprising. He was only wearing a thin shirt that clung tighter to his chest with every gust of the westerly wind.

Indi couldn't feel the cold. Almost as if her body had grown accustomed to it. "Don't you have a jacket or something?" she asked.

Elton popped open the trunk and rummaged through a mess of climbing gear and car tools. He fished out a black jersey and pulled it over his head, destroying his molded hair and flattening it over his brow. Indi grinned. She appreciated how lame he looked, even if it was only because of a mild hair mishap. He was more real, like a doll you could play with, not just keep in the box because you didn't want to get it dirty. Indi glimpsed his smooth-skinned abdomen as he threaded his arms through the sleeves. God, she wished she could be normal. Just a normal girl at a normal beach with a normal guy. But no. That wasn't her life. Her life was blood and secrets and heartache.

From here Indi could see the dark dunes dressed in bowing reeds. Fear crept in under her skin. What lay beyond those dunes was not something Indi was sure she wanted to see. She was quite happy to leave it there undisturbed for the rest of her days and never set eyes on it again. But those thoughts just reaffirmed why she needed to see it. Someone had tried to kill her. Again. In the last place she expected. Had they followed her to Seradale? How long had they been waiting for an opportunity like that? Then there was the possibility that her attacker was alongside her. That she was invited to the track meet for that very purpose. She had upset Rory minutes beforehand. Ben and Sadie had seen her go into the tunnel, and Avery could have easily seen her too from across the field. But it was Elton who found her. Right? She looked him over suspiciously. His jaw was bruising where she had hit him, but he didn't seem bothered by it. She looked at his hands and his toned forearms. They were strong, strong enough to squeeze the life out of someone if they wanted to. No. She remembered spraying the mace; she'd heard someone cry out in pain. Elton's only wound came from Indi's right hook. Whoever it was, this was the day that Indi had been dreading, that gave her nightmares when she was wide awake. Her memories held the key to the attacker's identity and, for that, she needed to die. Indi was as adamant now as that morning she washed up on the beach. She didn't want to die, and she didn't want to be afraid every day she was alive. She had to find out who was responsible for trying to steal that choice from her.

"Why are we here?" Elton asked.

"This is where it happened. This is where my memory was lost. Maybe it's where I'll find it."

Elton was unconvinced. "Are you sure?"

There was only one answer. "Yes."

Indi crossed the carpark, counting down the seconds before her foot left gravel and touched the soft sand. Her boots sank, and every step became more difficult as they climbed the rolling dunes. Indi heard the sea, long before her eyes caught sight of the dark water. She could still taste the salt and feel the grains of sand between her fingers. Suddenly, she couldn't breathe. The beach, the sand, the crashing waves and the slippery shore. It was all too much. The world was caving in around her, smothering her, drowning her.

Elton took hold of her waist when she staggered backward. "This is crazy. Let's go back to the car. We shouldn't be here," he insisted.

Indi steadied herself, forcing her rubbery legs to straighten. "It was further up," she said blankly. "There."

Indi nuzzled into the collar of her jacket as the wind struck her face. She carried on down the beach and soon found the spot that haunted her dreams. There was nothing here now, no sign of what had happened. Indi wasn't sure what she was expecting. The shape of her body still hollowed in the sand? A trail of blood leading toward the dunes? But it was just another patch of beach now, and with the police cordons removed it was open once again to the public. Children could build sandcastles here, in the same place where Indi had bled for hours. The thought made her queasy.

What was she expecting to find that the police had not? Then it came to her, something strange and unusual. The idea swelled in her mind. Indi dropped to her knees and lay on the sand flat on her back, just like that morning.

Elton's wide eyes conveyed his shock. "What the hell are you doing?"

Indi rested her hands at her sides. "Something crazy." She took a long breath, then exhaled and closed her eyes. She saw the rope and the rock. The pitch black of the deep ocean, and the figure in the dark she knew for sure was Brandy. She already had these pieces. She needed something more, something new. Indi closed her eyes tighter, straining every muscle, hoping to force some sort of memory into fruition. She needed to remember before the water; before the rock; before the rope. Something. Anything. "Anything!" she screamed at the slate-grey sky.

Fractured shadows took form in her mind, melding together and manifesting into a large, crooked oak tree on the edge of a cliff. A landscape unfolded around it, emerging piece by piece like a watercolor painting. She bolted upright. "The drinking tree."

Elton shrugged. "What about it?"

Indi held out her hand and Elton yanked her to her feet. "I remember the drinking tree. I was there that night." She winced in confusion. "Why do I remember the drinking tree? I've never been there."

Elton gave a sympathetic half-smile, and Indi took that to mean she had been there, with them of course, in the days she couldn't remember. He pointed down the beach. "It's that way."

Step by step the grand old oak grew larger in the distance. It had a dozen twisted branches unfurled like open arms, each strong enough to hold two horny teenagers and a box of vodka-cranberry mixers. It was out of sight from the main road and carpark, near the edge of a grassy cliff that dropped two-hundred feet into the ocean. The youth of Army Bay had claimed this patch of beach in the name of underage drinking and pre-marital sex. Judging by the empty bottles and condom wrappers scattered about the trunk, both were still happening in earnest.

"We haven't been here for a while," Elton said. "Brandy liked it here. She liked to watch the waves."

Indi rummaged through the nests of rocks near the trunk, hoping some random stone she kicked over would reveal a clue. With each clang, with each jagged edge, Indi couldn't help revisiting a memory she wished she could give back--her head bashed with a rock just like these. She tried to make it go away but, as horrible as it was, it ignited a blank page.

Indi was here that night, at the tree. There was yelling and sobbing and a scream that turned her blood cold. It was Brandy. She couldn't see her face, couldn't hear her speak, but Indi knew in her shivering bones that it was her.

"We were both here at this tree," Indi muttered. "We were together on that night. She's dead, Elton, drowned. I remember that much. She didn't make it to the surface, but I did." Indi's eyes welled with tears. "They tried to murder us both."

Elton approached warily, offering his arm, and Indi took it. Her head fell on his chest, and she sobbed, harder and louder than she had since her first waking scream in the hospital. He said nothing and didn't hold her too tightly, just enough to reassure her he was there. At this moment, it was everything that Indi wanted. Even so, she wondered why it wasn't Cam.

Suddenly, there was a commotion from the beach below, a voice screaming into the wind. Indi wiped her tears and stepped away from Elton before he got too comfortable with her in his arms. He walked to the cliff edge and peered down.

"Looks like someone walking their dog sees something on the rocks." He strained his eyes to see the misshapen lump the woman on the beach was pointing at. A jogger joined her on the shore, followed by a couple of fishermen further down. Soon, the jogger was sprinting across the sand. "We need some help. Call the police," he yelled.

Elton staggered backward. "India, let's go back to the car."

"What is that?" Indi sniffed through the last of her tears. "What do they see?" She took a step forward, but Elton was quick to cut her off.

"Don't look." It was plain on Elton's face what he had seen. She peeled his fingers from her arm.

"No. I need to see." She ran from the cliff, scaling the steep slope, her feet moving faster than she could control. She snagged her arm on a thorny brush, scraped her nails against the rock face, but she felt none of it, and when her feet touched the sand, she ran.

The fishermen had waded out to the rocks and were pulling in the sodden mass. Indi hit the shoreline just as the smell hit the air. She gagged and covered her mouth.

"Oh no dear, you shouldn't see this," the woman with the dog warned, her yappy beagle snapping impatiently at her ankles.

Elton soon arrived and gently touched Indi on the shoulder. "India..." Indi was deaf to them both, her watery gaze fixed on the body. She made out the dip of a woman's waist with her shoulders slumped, her face masked by webs of matted blonde hair, and her pale blue skin marbled with veins. Indi turned away when she could no longer stomach what weeks in the ocean had done to the rest of Brandy Hamilton. Elton took her back to the car. She wasn't really walking, her feet were just flipping and flopping enough to resemble it. Elton bundled her in before climbing into the driver's seat. He fidgeted in his back pocket for his phone.

"I can't believe this," he stammered. "She was right there, just waiting to be found. How long do you think she's been there?"

Indi said nothing. That could have been her. She could have ended up just the same, dead on a rock and discovered by some woman and her dog. Elton found his phone and Indi heard him talking. His voice was muffled in her ears, just tones with no meaning. She was still processing what she had seen and coming to terms with the truth. Brandy was dead and had been for a long time. Army Bay had been looking for a ghost. Brandy had no secrets to tell, nothing to offer Indi's search for answers. She was just a body—a body; when Indi repeated that in her mind, she felt sick.

"Police are on their way. They want us to wait here," Elton said, tossing his phone on the dashboard. "They want to question you."

Indi stirred from her thoughts. "Why?"

Elton tried to be polite. "Half the town thinks you knew something about Brandy's disappearance and now you're there when her body is found. They're probably suspicious." He narrowed his accusing eyes. "I mean, you wanted to come here, like you really, really wanted to come here."

Indi furrowed her brow. "What is that supposed to mean?"

"Forget I said that. I'm just acting weird. This is insane." He slumped in his seat and dragged his fingers through his hair. On the cuff of his black sweater was a streak of crimson, a dried mess that had ran up the arm and was embedded in the fibers.

"What's that?" Indi already knew. She had seen enough of her own to recognize it.

Elton inspected the mark. "I don't know." He studied the sweater. "Wait. Is this even mine?"

"It was in your trunk," Indi stated.

"Yeah. I guess. I don't think it's mine, though." He scratched the red substance, and it flaked away, staining his fingertips. He rubbed it with his thumb and immediately looked up, wide-eyed.

"That's blood. You have blood on your sweater."

"I told you, it's not mine." He shook his head vehemently. "No. I've got nothing to do with this. I had no beef with Brandy. I don't know where this thing came from, I swear."

Indi fumbled with the door handle. Elton heard the rattle and lunged across her, holding the door shut. "Where do you think you're going?"

Indi gulped. "Let me out of the car, Elton."

"I didn't do anything to Brandy." His eyes were piercing, oblivious to all else around him, with Indi's face reflected in the flecks of brown.

"If that's her blood, I doubt anyone will believe you."

Elton pulled off the sweater and tossed it in the back seat. "Someone's trying to set me up."

Indi, wrestled the door open at last. "Fine. You tell the police that. I'm walking back to town."

Elton hung out the window as Indi crossed the parking lot. "They told us to stay here."

"They know where to find me," Indi called over her shoulder.

Deep inside, Indi struggled to believe that Elton would have killed Brandy, and if that was her blood on the sweater maybe he was right. Perhaps the real killer was trying to pin it on him. But Indi couldn't take any risks, not when her life was at stake.

The image of Brandy's body flashed behind her eyes and Indi wept. She remembered her smile and her laugh. That she sang terribly and couldn't snap her fingers. That she broke her heart, but Indi never stopped loving her. Indi's tears of grief mingled with relief. Brandy Hamilton was found.

14

INDI WAS BARELY TWENTY minutes from the beach when Braddock's car pulled alongside her. He wound down the window and slid his aviators to the tip of his nose. His first question was the last one she had expected to hear. "Are you okay?"

Indi shrugged, digging her trembling hands into her pockets. "Not really, but what's new?"

Braddock exhaled loudly. His car door creaked open, and he stood over Indi, tall and willowy. "We need to get a statement. I've already called your parents. They're meeting us at the station."

She nodded and walked toward the front seat. But Braddock stopped her, opening the back door instead. His eyes were stern, and he tipped his chin to the waiting seat. There was more of a formal police/suspect vibe to this encounter with Braddock, no longer the sympathetic escort. Indi didn't argue. This day would have come eventually, and she would never escape suspicion. They would want to know why she had survived when Brandy hadn't.

The old crinkled leather squelched as Indi slid into the car. She pulled on her seatbelt, her twitching fingers struggling to find the latch, and when they finally did the click seemed to thunder in her ears.

Braddock shut the door, then climbed into the front seat and started the engine. He adjusted the rear-view mirror to catch Indi's eyes. "Don't be scared. It's just routine."

Indi nodded again. It was the most she could muster as a response right now. She kept seeing flashes of that bloated figure on the beach, that was Brandy Hamilton, interspersed with recollections of the girl she used to be. Brandy, loved and despised, desired and dreaded. She was something to everyone she met, which is more than you could say for most people, those who go through life invisible or inconspicuous, pretty much the way Indi thought of herself. What was Brandy now, though? How would she be remembered? As they found her? Never. Very few would see her that way, and they should thank their lucky stars for that. Indi wished she could stop seeing it for just two seconds. But even fewer would remember her fondly. They didn't need to see what washed up on the beach. They had their unique Brandy nightmares to remind them. But Indi had other memories, fresh and new, of Brandy showing her kindness and friendship. It was impossible; these two people could not be the same. The jigsaw pieces were coming together, but there was still a giant hole right at the center. Brandy's body was only a part of the puzzle. To finish it, Indi would have to know why they had returned to each other, and who had wanted them both dead.

The drive to Army Bay Police Station was quick, the way back always was. Braddock guided Indi inside, past the chatter of the reception area, through a gauntlet of stares and whispers. Her parents waited at a table in a beige room, both jumping to their feet when Indi entered, their chairs skidding loudly against the linoleum. Her dad grabbed her and pulled her tight against his chest while her mother laced their fingers together.

"It's all right girl. You've done nothing wrong." He glared at Braddock as he walked inside and closed the door behind him. "I'll take care of this."

Braddock ignored the statement and crossed to a window that looked out into the bullpen. He pulled a string to lower the blinds, but just before they slid shut Indi caught a glimpse of cops leading Elton into another room, his hands cuffed behind his back.

She gasped. "Have you arrested Elton Riggs?"

Braddock took a seat across from them and dropped a thick file on the table. "I can't talk about that." He gestured for them to sit. "I'd like to ask India a few questions if that's alright with you, Mr. and Mrs. Peters?"

Indi's dad held her tighter as he became more defensive. He growled. "Depends what you're asking."

"That's not how it works," Braddock replied.

Her mom's eyes were glassy, her skin red and puffy as if she had been crying. "Maybe we should call our lawyer, Nathan?"

"You're more than welcome to do so." Braddock's voice never changed pitch, calm and monotone. "But that will not alter the questions I'll be asking. India is not under arrest." He paused. "Not right now, anyway."

The Peters sat down, India smack dab in the middle. She'd almost lost the feeling in her fingers from her mom's vice-like grip, while her dad had her shoulder pincered protectively in his hand.

"As soon as I start hearing things I don't like, this is over. We're leaving," her dad stated. "Like you just said, she's not under arrest."

"Fair enough." Braddock flipped open the file. There were two black and white photos on top. A yearbook photo of a goth-like India from a couple of years back, sporting a black home-dyed mullet and an emo sneer. The second was a photo taken at the ER showing Indi bloody and bruised. To be honest, she wasn't sure which image was worse.

Braddock exhaled long, pensive breaths before he spoke. "Why were you at the beach today, India?"

She had to decide pretty quickly if she was planning on lying, telling the truth, or mixing the two into a sticky paste. If caught in a lie, Indi might as well brace herself for handcuffs and a jail cell. But if she told the truth, she should probably mention that she was almost strangled to death in Seradale a few hours ago. Something that might worry her parents a smidge and get her ass put under house arrest for her own safety. If Indi wanted to play detective, and possibly do a better job than the actual cops, any kind of prison was the last place she wanted to be. Sticky paste it was.

"I was at the Seradale track meet with some friends."

"What friends?" Braddock picked up a pen.

"Rory Zhang. Elton Riggs. Sadie Hamilton. Avery Weiss. Ben Campbell." It felt weird saying those full names out loud, let alone stating they were friends. "Rory was competing."

Braddock scribbled some notes. "Anything happen in Seradale?"

"No," she replied with indifference, though her mind repeatedly shocked her with images of hands closed around her neck. Her throat suddenly felt scratchy and dry. "But while I was there, I remembered something. Something about Brandy."

Braddock looked up from his notes. "Are you saying your memory is returning?"

"Not all of it." Indi felt the need to spit that out before everyone got too excited. "Just pieces. I remember Brandy being at my house once, and I remember ..." She didn't want to gulp. That felt like something a guilty person would do, but her throat was so dry. "Can I have some water?"

Braddock narrowed his eyes and pushed down the button of a speaker box on the table. "Can I get a water jug in here please?"

"Sure thing," a man's voice crackled back.

Braddock smiled. "Should be here in a second. Carry on. What else do you remember?"

"I wasn't sure at first if I imagined it, but it feels too real and then when I saw her, I knew. I remember Brandy and me underwater together, sinking together. Our hands tied together. I could feel myself drifting, no ... fading ... no," there was only one word that truly embodied what Indi meant, " ... dying," she muttered. "I just had this urge to fight, to survive, so I started pulling and tugging, trying to get my hands free from the rope." Her mother was whimpering, her fingers tightening around Indi's. Her dad was silent, stoic, but his welling eyes conveyed his struggle. "The rope came free, but the water was dark, and I couldn't see straight. I couldn't save Brandy." Indi paused, holding back her tears. "I couldn't save my friend."

The door opened and a man walked in, placing a water jug and a stack of tumblers on the table before leaving. Braddock poured three glasses, not needing one for himself. "Take a moment," he said. "Have a drink."

Indi couldn't keep her hand steady, and the water sloshed about as she lifted the cup to her lips. It tasted like nothing. She could barely feel it go down her throat, and it didn't quench her thirst. Her thoughts left her for a moment and her mind went blank. It was quiet and hollow, almost as if she were inside a bubble suspended high in the air, looking down on everything and everyone, distant and alone.

Suddenly Brandy was beside her. She rested her head on Indi's shoulder, smelling like pears and violets. The TV glowed in the darkness, casting a pale blue hue across their faces as they sat cross-legged on the floor.

"Geez, Patrick Swayze was beautiful," Indi sighed. "They just don't make them like that anymore." Her eyes widened, and she planted several quick slaps on Brandy's thigh. "Here it comes. Here it comes. He's about to work the shit out of this clay."

"Please. Demi is the star of this pottery barn porn. Did you know Demi was my first girl crush?"

"Crush? How lame. Vigorous masturbation stories only please."

Brandy was grinning at her phone, her fingers flittering across the keypad.

Indi rolled her eyes. "The dick pics can wait. Patrick demands your attention."

"Okay, okay," Brandy giggled. "I'm going to live-tweet it." Her eyes rolled back in her head as music flowed from the screen. "Oh my god, I love this song. What is this again?"

"Unchained Melody," Indi answered immediately.

Brandy's tongue peeked out the corner of her mouth as she typed. Looking for someone to handle me like Demi handles a vase. #90sMovieNight #UnchainedMelody. She hit Send, and her phone went ballistic with likes. Indi heard the ding of a DM, followed by Brandy giggling while she replied.

"So, who are you in love with this week? A Patrick or a Demi?"

Brandy gasped and tossed her phone on the bed. She entwined her arms with Indi's and lazily scratched at her chipped black nail polish. "I'm not in love. But I am in like."

It got to the part when Patrick lifted Demi onto his hips. Brandy and Indi swooned in unison.

"Well, details? Height? Hair color? Eyes? Blue or brown?"

"Sometimes they're both," Brandy sighed blissfully. "I don't know. Maybe it could go somewhere, I guess." Her phone beeped again, and her smile slipped away. "Ben. He wants to talk. I told him I needed a break."

Indi grabbed a handful of popcorn. "Well, maybe don't bang him again for old time's sake and then he'll stop DM'ing you."

Brandy pouted. "But he's packing a nuke down there. It's a W.V.D."

"Don't you dare say it!" Indi warned.

"Weapon of vagina destruction," Brandy blurted, and the laugh that followed was a raucous blend of snorts and honks.

Indi shook her head. "I'm embarrassed to be your friend. He needs to chill out."

Brandy leaned over Indi to grab some popcorn. "It's not his fault. He has a constant erection, so has a limited blood supply to his brain. That's science."

Unchained Melody hit the chorus, the high note ramping up before musically decimating anything with eardrums.

Brandy clutched at her heart. "I love this song. This is my song now."

"Yours and Demi's song," Indi corrected.

Brandy grabbed her wine flute filled with chocolate milk. Indi did the same, and they clinked glasses as the TV faded to black.

"India." Braddock's voice resounded until Indi's bubble popped. "Are you ready to talk some more?"

"There isn't more," she stuttered. "I just needed to go to the beach after that. I thought maybe if I was there, I would remember. Then a woman screamed, and before I knew it they were dragging Brandy's body from the water."

"What about the memories that are returning to you? Do you remember how you got to the beach that night, or if anyone was with you?" Braddock asked.

"No."

"Do you remember Elton Riggs being with you?"

Indi's eyes flickered. "Elton? No. Why?"

Braddock scribbled some notes. "We are waiting on Brandy's autopsy, but the attending officers have reported her hands were still bound with nylon rope." He gestured to Indi's wrists. "The same kind we think caused your scars. The kind of rope used in rock climbing. Does Elton Riggs rock climb?"

Indi shivered, and shrugged. "Maybe. I don't know. I barely know the guy."

"You were with him, though, this afternoon? He drove you to the beach from Seradale, didn't he? He was with you when the body was found?"

Indi felt her parents' eyes boring into her. "Yes. I was with him. But I don't know him very well."

"So which is it?" Braddock asked pointedly. "Barely know or don't know very well?"

Indi blinked her eyes tightly. "What?"

"We found a sweater in Elton's car. It has some bloodstains on it. We're having them tested. Did you see that sweater when you were in Elton's car?"

"Sweater?" Indi suddenly felt dizzy, and her stomach churned. Did he do it? Her answer to this question could seal Elton's fate. Was Indi that sure? She fought with herself. "No," she lied.

"It was right there. Are you saying you didn't see it? Who do you think the blood belongs to? Could it be Brandy's blood?"

Indi gripped the edge of the table. "I don't feel very well. Can we stop, please?"

Braddock's voice was as icy as his stare. "Do you think Elton killed Brandy?"

Indi could taste vomit in the back of her throat. The beige room spun around her. All she wanted to do was curl up tight on the floor. "Dad. Mom. I don't feel good."

Braddock scanned another set of notes. "Are you in a relationship with Ben Campbell? Wasn't he Brandy's boyfriend?"

"No," Indi snapped.

"No, he wasn't Brandy's boyfriend?"

"No, I'm not in a relationship with him," Indi corrected sharply.

"That's not what Ben Campbell says. I also have statements you were seen being intimate, at a party recently. Is that true?"

Indi stammered, unable to find the words she needed to defend herself.

"Seems like a good reason to want Brandy out of the picture. Getting her boyfriend all to yourself." Braddock pushed relentlessly. "How did you feel about Brandy? Did you really try to save her or did you let her go? Did you push her down, perhaps?"

"That's enough!" her dad boomed, stomping to his feet and slamming his fist on the table. "Can't you see she's a wreck?"

Braddock leaned back in his chair, his stern face unflinching, his tone steady. "Please calm down, Mr. Peters. I'm just trying to get answers. Brandy Hamilton deserves justice, doesn't she? How would you feel if it were India's body in the morgue right now?"

Her mom exploded into hard sobs. "It almost was! Maybe instead of accusing India, you do your fucking job and find out who really did this. My daughter is a victim too. I've heard enough. Nathan, let's go. Let's take Indi home."

Indi felt her mom's arms envelop her and help her to her feet.

Her dad nodded. "As you said, she's not under arrest. We can go."

Braddock tapped his pen on the table. "Of course. We will have more questions when the autopsy results are back."

Her dad snarled. "You can call my lawyer."

They hurried Indi out, back through the reception area that was now deathly silent, through the double doors and straight into the flashing lights of dozens of waiting cameras.

"India, can you tell us what it felt like seeing Brandy's body?"

"India, was Brandy badly decomposed?"

"India, how does it feel knowing Brandy's murderer is still out there? Are you afraid you might be in danger?"

"Don't listen, girl. Don't listen." Her dad shielded her, held her tight, pushed the aggressive reporters aside and put Indi into the back seat of the car. Her mom snuggled up beside her, stroking Indi's hair while her dad fought his way to the driver's door. "Leave her alone, you vultures!" He yelled as he climbed in. "She's just a kid."

He started the engine and stepped on the gas, causing several reporters to leap out of the way if they wanted to keep their legs. Her parents were bickering the entire drive, blaming each other for allowing Braddock's questioning. For not getting the lawyer in there straight away. For not being more attentive parents in the first place. Then there were other mentions Indi only half heard. Mutterings about their marriage, about mistakes and lies.

"Now is not the time!" her dad snapped, and her mom fell reluctantly quiet.

Soon they were home, parked in the driveway, but things were different now. Brandy's body had breathed new life into a waning story. A missing person case was now a murder. They even had a suspect. Elton. Indi's memories were returning at speed. At this rate she might remember everything at any time; she could confirm the police's suspicions, she could tell them if it was Elton; or it could be someone completely different. Someone out there right now, waiting for the opportune moment to finish what they started and keep Indi silent. Her mind went back to Braddock's words, his warning to her dad. What if it was India in the morgue right now? But it wasn't. She was here, alive and well, bent but not broken. She was a fighter. A survivor. And even if she was still learning the truth, she had made an unspoken pact with Brandy that night in the water. She might not have been able to save her body, but she could save her spirit, her memory. Braddock was a king-sized asshole, but he was right about one thing--Brandy deserved justice. Indi sniffed back the last of her tears. India would be the one to see that her friend got it.

15

FOR NOW, INDI WAS NOT a suspect in the murder of Brandy Hamilton, and as of a couple of hours ago, neither was Elton Riggs. The rope around Brandy's wrists could have come from a thousand supply stores. It was the kind Elton used, but dozens of other climbers used it too, and there was nothing that connected this specific rope to him. The police had tested the blood on the sweater he swore wasn't his. Army Bay, hungry for equal parts drama and justice, was shocked when the police released a statement: it wasn't Brandy's blood; it wasn't India's either, or even Elton's. They didn't know whose it was, and now that sweater sat in a box in the evidence room.

The town had lost its mind since Brandy's body was found. It was all the news channels talked about, and not just local. Indi had even seen Brandy's face on the BBC late one night. She was the disgustingly morbid content this world thirsted for. Young, beautiful and dead. The reporters were back on Indi's doorstep, the news vans littering the street. The police assigned a squad car to watch the house, and they were handy for getting rid of the press, but they also made it impossible for Indi to leave unnoticed, either by the front door or drainpipe. Indi was naïve to think finding Brandy or her body would get things back to normal; it had only amped up the crazy.

Indi pulled on her backpack. After the mace had saved her life, her anti-murder kit had dwindled to the Swiss Army knife and the rape alarm. She retired the fanny pack, slipping the items into the front pockets of her jeans. Indi may have doubted her mom's gifts at first, but after what happened in Seradale, she never would again.

Ben didn't come by the house that morning as Indi thought he might. She was disappointed. That perfect jawline had kept her awake all night. Indi had been looking forward to breaking it. Gossiping teenagers were one thing, but Braddock confirmed Ben was telling people he and Indi were in a relationship. It wasn't true. She wouldn't do that, and now it was being used against her as a motive.

Indi tore down the street, her eyes fixed ahead. The little shits across the road didn't say anything to her today, likely fearful of repercussions from Ben. But he wasn't the one to be afraid of. Not right now, anyway. Indi crossed the carpark, ignoring the blaring honk from the school bus as she walked in front of it. Ben stood at the gate talking to Rory, his bag looped over one shoulder. As Indi approached he smiled, and when she was close enough Indi punched him, just as she wanted to, hard on his jaw.

Rory's eyes bulged and she gasped, "Oh my god. India. What are you doing?"

Ben's head reeled from the impact and he staggered. He nursed his jaw, but before he could speak, Indi pointed her finger in his face.

"Why are you telling the police there is something between us? Do you know how that sounds?"

Ben grunted. "No. But why don't you tell me?"

"It sounds like we are hiding something. Like Brandy was in the way. It gives us a motive, you idiot."

Ben winced as he wiggled his jaw. "I guess it does. So what?"

"So what?" Indi felt anger bubbling beneath her skin. "I didn't kill Brandy, that's what. And I may not remember a few things, but I know for goddamn certain that nothing is going on between you and me. Now I don't know why you're saying this shit, but if you don't shut the fuck up, I will make you regret it."

Ben grinned. "Geez, Indi. I wouldn't let the cops hear you talk like that. Sounds very suspicious."

Rory slapped Ben hard against the chest. "What is wrong with you, Campbell?" She linked arms with Indi and led her away from him toward the pavilion.

Indi went with her stiffly. She remembered their conversation in the Seradale locker room and wasn't sure where they now stood. Rory sat on a bench and pulled Indi down beside her. Her eyes were dark, wide, and on the verge of tears, but Indi found it hard to muster sympathy today. There was so much pain and sorrow eating away at her she was beginning to feel nothing at all.

"I can't imagine what you're going through," Rory started. "Finding Brandy like that, then having the cops interrogate you. And that stupid fight we had in Seradale. Indi, I'm so sorry. I didn't mean to say those things. Life is not supposed to be this way. We should be having fun and going to parties and being dumb kids, right? That's the job description. Where does it say that Brandy has to die, and the world implodes?" She held her head in her hands. "The police questioned me last night. They wanted to know things about Avery too. He's not at school today. He lost his phone in Seradale and won't leave the house. I'm freaking out. I just don't think I can handle this anymore. My parents are talking about moving." She looked up at Indi through her fingers. "What do we do now?"

Indi stood up and shrugged. "I'm going to algebra. You can do whatever you want."

She left Rory with a gaping mouth and stunned expression. Indi just couldn't do it today, couldn't be calm and accommodating to other's feelings. She didn't care that Rory was sorry, or where Avery was, and she wished she had hit Ben harder. She stormed the halls, running a gauntlet of stares. No one said a word to her. Maybe because her resting bitch face was dialed way up, or perhaps they were just scared if they got in her way they might end up like Brandy.

Indi paused when she passed the spot Cody had been hanging his Frost Queen propaganda. His poster was gone, replaced with a bigger and bolder version starring Sadie Hamilton. Indi noticed the crumpled remnants of Cody's sign sitting next to a trash can. Of course, Sadie was running for Frost Queen. Brandy had won the last two years, even though juniors never won. Sadie was Brandy now. So it made sense Sadie would try to go undefeated.

"Bitch, right?" Paula said with venom as she arrived at Indi's shoulder. She glared at the poster. "You know, I thought I had it this year. Cody was never going to win. No matter how many hand jobs he gave the hockey team and, believe me, there was a long line. I'd be surprised if he can still hold a pen. With Brandy out of the way, it should have been me. Now Sadie will probably get the sympathy vote." She whispered, "Know any killers looking for a victim?"

Indi narrowed her eyes at Paula. She felt her fingers curl into a fist that turned heavy as lead.

"Paula!" Micah yelled as he walked at pace toward her.

Paula rolled her eyes, doing a quick sweep of the hall to see who was watching. "Keep your voice down, idiot. I don't want people to think we know each other. I can't afford to lose votes because of your stoner ass."

"Shut up," Micah groaned. "Where's Avery Weiss?"

"How should I know?" Paula replied. She gestured to Indi. "Ask her. They're friends."

"No, we're not," Indi corrected. "And I don't know either. His girlfriend said he isn't here today."

Micah gritted his teeth. "Asshole is dodging me."

"Isn't he your best customer?" Indi reminded.

Micah gave a sarcastic grin. "Well, my best customer hasn't paid his tab, and now I've got the guy I buy from breathing down my neck. These people don't screw around. If there's no money soon, someone's going to get hurt." Micah surveyed the hall one last time. "If you see Weiss, don't tell him I was looking for him. I want it to be a surprise."

"Just another drama-free day at Army Bay High," Paula sighed as Micah walked away. She eyed Indi critically. "I heard you thought I was dead?"

Indi was growing accustomed to word getting around fast in this town. "Thanks for proving me wrong," she replied.

Paula turned her attention to Sadie's poster and stood calmly for about two seconds before grabbing a corner and ripping it off the wall. The loiterers in the hall gasped, whipped out their phones and recording.

"Well, I'm not giving up without a fight. I've been number two for long enough. This is my last year. Time to leave my mark." Paula tore the poster down the middle and let the halves fall to the floor. She ground her heel into what remained of Sadie's face for good measure, then strolled down the hall.

Indi avoided people, especially Rory and Ben, for the rest of the day. She went to her classes, sat in the back and tried to pretend that the world wasn't an infinite loop of hate and violence that chewed you up and spat you out. By last period she was exhausted.

Cody walked into the science room, and his eyes found Indi immediately by the window. She hoped he wouldn't come over, but he did, making himself comfortable on the steel stool.

"I'm not great company today," Indi mumbled.

"No shit, I'm sure." He nudged her shoulder. "I'm sorry. If that helps." It didn't, but Indi appreciated the gesture. Then Cody gasped. "Oh my gosh, look. Mathis."

Indi followed the line of his pointed finger, out the window and toward the courtyard, and saw Miss Mathis crying. She carried a box in her hands packed full of books, knickknacks, and framed certificates. Braddock walked behind her, a firm grip on her elbow as he guided her toward the carpark.

"You know what I heard?" Cody chirped, shuffling his stool closer to Indi. "The cops got an anonymous tip, so they raided her office. They found letters she had written to Brandy, death threats. Pages and pages of them, talking about all the ways Miss Mathis wanted to kill her. There were pictures of Brandy with her eyes scratched out or cut up into little bitty pieces. Can you believe it? I always thought Miss Mathis was nice. Who knew?"

Indi watched them reach Braddock's car, and Miss Mathis clutched her beaded necklace as she hunched into the backseat. Miss Mathis had said some pretty inappropriate things, but Indi could not believe she would hurt someone.

Cody slapped her arm as he thought of something, and Indi glared with annoyance. "She confiscated my selfie stick last week when I accidentally pointed it into the locker room after the football game." He grinned. "Time to get it back. At least we know she won't be in her office."

"We?" Indi questioned.

"You need a friend right now, and I need a lookout. Sisters helping sisters."

Indi didn't want to do it. She didn't want to do anything. But even beneath the layers of lethargy and cynicism, the hope of reconciling with Cam still motivated her. Cody was the key to that lock.

"Fine. I'll be the lookout. Just don't take too long. I want to go home and dive face-first into a tub of Chunky Monkey."

Science class was business as usual until Cody refused to vivisect a mouse. Then it became an ethics discussion which carried them through the remaining hour. As the students filtered through the halls toward the front gates, Indi and Cody hung around a while longer until the school was empty. They crossed the silent courtyard to Kindness Cottage and paused beside the droopy willow near the door.

"Okay, back in two ticks," Cody said as he darted into the building.

Indi tapped her foot impatiently. The school was abandoned, apart from the caretaker, who glared at Indi suspiciously as he passed by pulling a wheelie bin. Indi forced a smile and waved. What was taking so long? She groaned, spun on her heels, and stormed inside.

Cody wasn't even in Mathis' office yet. He was clinging hard against the wall, peering around the corner.

"What the fuck Cody?" Indi snapped.

Cody put his finger to his lips and dragged Indi back behind the wall with more strength than she gave him credit for having. "Shhhhhhh!" he hissed. "You're not going to believe this." He swapped places with Indi and nudged her to look around the corner.

Fine. Anything to get this moving. The Chunky Monkey was waiting. Indi inched her head along the wall and looked through the window. She watched as a couple writhed in Mathis' office, their bodies entangled. The girl sat on the desk, her legs knotted around the boy's waist, her blonde hair thrashing as he thrust. The boy gripped her hips, pulling her roughly against him, and when he threw back his head and released a deep, guttural growl, Indi saw it was Ben. He lifted the girl to his mouth, kissing her passionately. He took a fist full of her blonde hair and jerked her back. Sadie!

Indi's heart was pounding. She knew she should look away but couldn't as the pair continued to grind against each other. It wasn't until Cody yanked her back that she even took a breath.

"How twisted is that!" Cody squealed into his hand. "Banging your murdered girlfriend's twin in the guidance counsellor's office!" He gripped his hair by the roots. "Why am I not live streaming this!"

Indi tried to make some sense of the chaos in her head. She grabbed Cody by the collar and dragged him outside Kindness Cottage.

"What are you doing!" Cody moaned. "I wanted to see what his jizz-face looked like!"

"Just go home Cody," Indi said, her tiredness showing through her weary tone. "It's none of our business." Indi checked her phone. "I've got to get home before my parents put out a missing person report. You're still going to give me the details about Christa's dinner?"

Cody nodded, disappointed at not seeing the end of the Kindness Cottage porno. "I'll text you."

Indi nodded and walked away before breaking into a jog, hoping to get home before her parents lost their shit. As she pushed off the concrete, adding Rory's pumping arm technique to improve her form, Indi not only had Brandy's body haunting her thoughts. Now Ben dicking Sadie would be stuck in her head too.

Indi fell through the doorway and braced herself for her dad's lecture. But there was nothing. Instead, she heard the white noise of the TV in the living room and her mom humming, oblivious, as she burnt dinner in the kitchen. Indi's dad greeted her, smiling as if seeing her for the first time. Indi knew he was just happy she had made it through the day.

"Is that her? Is she home?" Her mom called. She came running from the kitchen, wiping her hands on a washcloth. "How was your day?"

All this interest was claustrophobic. "It was fine. Same old same old."

Her parents exchanged looks. Then her mom took the lead. "Justine Hamilton called today. The family is having a private service for Brandy tomorrow night at their house. They would like us to go."

"Okay," Indi said, scratching the back of her head. "I guess that's something we should do."

"Are you sure, girl?" he asked. "I told your mom, we don't have to go."

Indi's mom frowned. "And I told your dad that we absolutely should go. We need to pay our respects to the family. We've known Brandy for years."

"Or you just want to leave some cards on the coffee table for her rich friends," he muttered tersely.

Indi's mom said nothing, just stared daggers at him while a fist formed around the washcloth. "Why don't you go upstairs and wash up for dinner, Indi? It'll be ready in five minutes."

That was a good idea. Indi had enough on her plate right now. A parental unit domestic would sink her when she was just barely staying afloat. She climbed the stairs two at a time and closed the door behind her as she retreated to her room. Indi stretched her arms and yawned, shucking her backpack. Then she walked to a wall, slid down until she was sitting on the floor, and burst into tears.

16

INDI STOOD IN FRONT of her mirror for the longest time, wondering if it was appropriate to wear denim to a funeral service. She went with a long black cardigan instead, layered over a swing dress with a dark floral print, and uber-black tights. No makeup today. She wanted her face bare. Indi didn't even care that with her hair pulled back tightly into a braided bun, her scar stood out prominently on her brow. When she had pushed the last hairpin into place, her phone dinged.

It was Elton. They hadn't spoken since she had left him at Breakers Beach.

Elton: Are you going tonight?

India: Yeah. You?

Elton: Wasn't invited. Not charged, but like that matters. I don't care what people think. Well. Maybe one person. Do you think I did it?

India: No. But I'm not the one to ask. Half the town thinks I did it too.

Elton: They will start saying we did it together soon.

India: Probably.

Elton: Someone's messing with me though. The sweater. The rope. I'm being set up.

India: Who would set you up for murder?

Elton: I haven't figured that out yet. You need to take care of yourself. You haven't told anyone about what happened in Seradale have you? Otherwise it would be all over the news.

India: No. I'd just have more eyes on me. My parents would freak the fuck out. I'm remembering and I need some breathing room.

Elton: This is dangerous shit Indi. Brandy's killer is out there and you're the only one who knows who it is. Don't get too brave.

"India!" her dad called from downstairs. "We're leaving."

India: I have to go.

Elton: Watch your back.

India: You too. TTYL.

Indi headed downstairs and met her parents at the door. Her dad tugged uncomfortably at his collar. He had squeezed his broad body into a tight-fitting black suit and hated every minute of it. Her mom was living her best Morticia Addams fantasy, draped in a slinky black gown that hugged every curve and finished in a short train behind her.

Her dad ran his thumb lightly over Indi's scar. "You look beautiful, girl."

"Come on. We don't want to be late!" her mom chirped, grabbing her purse from the hall table.

They left the house and climbed into her dad's shiny posh truck. It was nearing dusk when they reversed away from their Appleby Drive home, and night had arrived by the time he turned the last sloping bend into Oceanview Lane. The Hamiltons lived in a lavish, columned mansion that sat high on the cliffs overlooking the beach. They pulled into the long weaving driveway, silent and pitch black beneath a vast canopy of trees. But slowly, a faint light grew brighter in the distance until its majesty was unmistakable—a white, traditional neoclassical house with large bold columns and rows of perfectly symmetrical windows. Beyond the tall iron fence, sphere-shaped topiaries lined the brightly lit brownstone driveway, and a bevy of expensive cars circled an ornate cherub fountain. Her dad parked and switched off the engine while her mom hung her head out the window.

"Are we late?" her mom asked. God, Indi hoped not. The last thing she wanted was to walk into a packed room of people staring. They left the car and her mom looped arms with her. "Don't worry. Everything will be fine."

A butler, dressed to the nines complete with bowtie and tails, held open the door and ushered them into the marble-floored foyer. The room was packed with black-clad mourners, most with a glass of champagne in one hand and a tissue in the other. Just as Indi had dreaded, they all paused to watch her walk in.

Suddenly the guests parted like the Red Sea, giving way to Justine Hamilton standing, statuesque, at the foot of the grand curved staircase. She looked like Indi imagined Brandy might have in twenty years'. The thought sent a shiver down Indi's spine, knowing that Brandy would never get that chance now. Justine's black satin dress clung like a second skin without showing any actual skin at all, long-sleeved, high-necked and hemmed at her ankles. Her lips were red, her eyes were blue, and her skin was powder white, but more stunning than any of that was her sadness which radiated from her in waves.

"India," Justine's voice was husky and dry, "I'm so glad you could make it." She glided over, her long willowy arms reaching out. They embraced before Justine's eyes found her parents, standing behind Indi. She smiled warmly. "It's so good to see you again. It's been too long. Please, have some champagne. I'd like to speak to Indi for a moment if that's okay?"

Her dad nodded, but her mom was too busy visually price tagging every object in the room. He nudged her gently and she bolted to attention.

"Sorry, Justine. It's just your house is even more beautiful than I remember." She looked either side of her. "Is August not here?"

Indi saw Justine's lips quiver before she spoke. Indi remembered August was often absent, but surely he would have turned out for his daughter's service.

"Important business, unfortunately. Couldn't be avoided. He will be here for the funeral, of course." Now her body quivered as well, and she was quick to put a tissue to her eye. If she started crying, Indi did not know how she'd react. She just hoped her mom didn't whip out her business card and make this any more awful.

"Come on dear," her dad said, saving the day. "Let's get a drink from the bar."

As Indi watched their backs leave, she caught sight of Rory, Ben and Avery in the living room. Ben dropped his chin and sipped at his drink. Rory took a step forward, and for a moment Indi thought she might come over. But Rory changed her mind, shrinking back and returning to the conversation. As for Avery, Indi didn't have time to see his face at all, but she recognized that perfect blond coif. He turned with drink in hand and disappeared into an adjoining room. Indi was curious to know if Micah Marshall had caught up with him yet.

Then Indi felt long slender fingers on her arm, having momentarily forgotten that Justine was standing there.

"Follow me, would you?" She led Indi to the stairs.

Shit. At the very least Indi had hoped this unwanted conversation would take place here, with a roomful of witnesses close by. Secondary locations were famously to be avoided. She paused, and Justine craned her long neck when she felt Indi's resistance.

"Is everything alright?"

Indi gulped. "We're going upstairs?"

Justine nodded calmly, her serene smile unnerving. "Yes. There's something I want to show you." She tugged on Indi's hand, but Indi planted her feet. "Please." There was a refined pleading to her tone. "It would mean a lot to me."

Every smidge of common sense told Indi not to go up that ridiculously elaborate staircase. She didn't want to be alone with Justine. Was she going to cry? Would she have questions about Brandy? The anxiety of not knowing what she wanted had Indi's stomach gurgling the burrito from lunch. One thing was certain. Whatever was going to happen up there was going to be super weird.

Indi feigned a smile and followed Justine upstairs. When she was about halfway and already short of breath, she looked down at her parents sipping champagne from tall glasses, their warm gazes being less than helpful. When they reached the landing, Justine ushered her to the left and into a long hallway lined with large photo prints. Indi remembered these. Infant twin girls, fair and pretty with tufts of blonde hair. It was like a timeline, the girls ageing with every step Indi took. Where they were once indistinguishable, with equal screen time, suddenly one girl seemed to take the forefront. Maybe not deliberately, more so because it was in her nature. She was a little taller, a little stronger, her hair was bouncier and her eyes a shade bluer. The other girl drifted further into the background until, eventually, the photos became single portraits. It didn't take a rocket scientist to know that this dominant twin was Brandy, someone so desperate for the limelight that not even her identical twin sister could get in a picture with her. Indi's eyes lingered on the last shot of them together. It was maybe only a couple of years ago. By then Sadie had dyed her hair black, ditched her contacts for glasses and her ballet slippers for army boots. She was drastically different from the girl Indi saw getting railed on a desk the other day.

Justine came to an abrupt stop outside door number nine. A photo board was tacked to the wood, dozens of pictures decorated with cutesy stickers and ribbons. Indi spied her own face amongst them. She and Brandy at the arcade, another at the pavilion, and one with the whole gang together--Brandy, Sadie, Rory, Avery, Ben, Elton, and India. They had their arms around each other; they were smiling and laughing. Even though Indi knew herself clear as day, she barely recognized that version of her. There was nothing different physically. She still rocked a messy bun and distressed denim, but she looked so happy. Where was her apathetic smirk? Did she smile this much with Cam? Why was that such a hard thing to remember?

Justine took a deep breath and tightened her long, ringed fingers around Indi's hand. She pushed open the door, giving way to a massive room with a fluffy, pink circular rug atop plush white carpet. To the left there were glass doors dressed in gossamer curtains that looked out over a private balcony. The entire wall to the right consisted of a series of bifold doors, which fronted Brandy's closet. There was a vintage French-style vanity in the corner, flooded with makeup, lotions and perfumes, next to a floor-to-ceiling mirror.

"I've not touched a thing since she went missing," Justine said. Indi had hoped this would be as far as they would go, but Justine proceeded with her tour, walking Indi across the room and sitting her on the four-poster bed. Indi hated every moment of this, regardless of how soft the duvet was.

"I know you and Brandy had a history," Justine started. "But this horrible thing that happened has connected you now. That's a bond that will stay with you forever." She rearranged the piles of pillows that adorned the bed. "The police tell me you tried to save my Brandy. I want to thank you for that. I'm not naïve enough to think my daughter was completely innocent. I was your age once. I know what girls like Brandy are capable of." Her voice trembled. "But she was still my child, and no one should have to see their child that way, should have to bury their child that way. Whoever hurt her like that is pure evil. If more people were like you, maybe my sweet girl would be here now."

Indi tried to clear the anxious lump in her throat. "People loved Brandy. Her friends downstairs ..."

Justine scoffed. "Were they friends? Brandy seemed to hate them as much as she loved them. They were always fighting one minute, unbreakable the next. The friends, the boys, the drama, I couldn't keep up and, to be honest, I didn't care. That is what teenagers do. Every drama is the end of the world. I just didn't know that my time with her would be cut so short. I thought I had time to be better. To make up for the trips away and the missed calls. How could I have known?"

Indi felt for Justine, and it had been a while since she'd felt anything like this. Justine's agony was right there behind her eyes, desperate to break free and consume her lithe frame. But she held it back with an enviable strength.

"Now that Brandy's gone, I don't want this room to sit here frozen in time like a tomb. I thought you might like to look around and take something to remind you of her. Something to keep you connected."

The hairs stood up on Indi's arms. "Mrs. Hamilton, I don't think I should."

"You made Brandy so happy lately. She smiled at me in the mornings. We weren't screaming and fighting every damned day. That was your doing. I won't take no for an answer. Here, how about I start?"

Justine opened Brandy's bedside drawer, digging around briefly before retrieving a heart-shaped pendant strung with a gold chain. She turned it over in her palm to reveal an inscription. No Ends. Just Beginnings.

"Brandy loved this phrase," Justine said. "People can say what they like about her, but she was an eternal optimist. Lemon into lemonade, that sort of thing. When her father bought this for her birthday, Brandy didn't take it off for a year. I think this would be perfect for you India. The night my Brandy was murdered could have been your end too, but look at how strong you have become. This is your beginning." Justine fastened the necklace behind Indi's neck. "There. Perfect."

Without warning, Justine's arms swept around Indi and squeezed tight. Indi was stiff for a moment, as she always was when another human being wanted intimate contact, but slowly she relaxed and hugged Justine back ever so lightly.

Justine smiled. "I'll leave you to it. See you downstairs."

When she left, Indi sat still and silent for a minute, rubbing the pendant between her fingers, feeling the grooves of the engraving. Maybe Justine was right. Perhaps this was Indi's beginning. She tucked the necklace beneath her collar, then turned her attention back to the room, taking in the luxury and privilege. She imagined Brandy seated at the vanity, brushing her hair or pouring over the contents of her closet, deciding what to wear. Then a thought crept in. That is probably what outsiders imagined Brandy's life was like. That her very existence revolved around clothes and boys and makeup, that she had no character or depth beyond that. But that wasn't true. Brandy was more than the label they had stuck on her. She deserved answers; they both did. Answers that might be somewhere in this room that India had been left in, conveniently alone.

She sucked in a breath and rocked to her feet. The closet seemed like a good place to start. She pulled back the bifold doors and was confronted with rows of clothes, shoes and bags organized into colors and seasons. Geez. Where to start. Indi strolled along the racks, her fingers brushing the soft fabrics. One jacket stood out from the rest, tucked away right at the back amongst the winter coats. It was stiff, with a starched collar and it was a shade of forest green that didn't seem to fit with Brandy's color wheel. More than that, it was polyester. Indi pulled it from the rack. It looked to be Brandy's size and was fitted at the waist with several school badges on the lapel--Head Girl, Sports Captain, Chess Honors--and emblazoned on the chest pocket was a coat of arms containing a scroll, a dove and hands in prayer, with 'St. Margaret's Academy' beneath. Was Brandy switching schools? Indi dug through the pockets and checked the tags. Nothing. She closed the closet and walked to Brandy's desk. She opened a drawer cluttered with papers and scented pens. On top was an opened envelope, the letter inside peeking out just enough for Indi to see the Franklin College crest. It was the best college in the state. If you managed to get yourself accepted you could pretty much guarantee a successful adulthood with the right house and the right car and the right family. Happiness wasn't such a sure thing, but success and happiness were good companions.

Indi slid out the letter and unfolded it carefully. She jerked with shock. Brandy had been accepted to attend after graduation, on a full athletic scholarship, for track. Indi didn't need her memory back to know that was impossible. Brandy was many things, but superstar athlete was sure as hell not one of them. She returned the letter, being sure not to add any new creases. Then she caught sight of a black cord near the back of the drawer. She tugged it loose of the paper and saw it had a plug at one end, a port at the other. A phone charger with Blackberry printed in white. Shit. In all the chaos of living, Indi had forgotten about the burner phone in the pink shoebox. This had to be its charger. Why else would it be here? Technically, it wasn't even stealing. Justine had said she could take something. Probably not what she had in mind, but there were no hard rules in this deal. Indi snatched the charger and tucked it into her purse.

"What are you doing in here?" came a shrewish voice at the door. Indi spun on her heels to find Sadie glaring venomously. "Who let you in?"

Sadie looked different again. Like a hybrid version of her goth self and the Brandy she was trying to be. Her hair was still blonde, but she wore her glasses, and she had ditched the pastels for heavy black layers. However, that could just have been a mourning thing.

Indi raised her arms defensively. "Your mom brought me up here. She said I could look around."

Sadie rolled her eyes. "Might have been nice to ask me first." She crossed the room and sat down at the vanity, taking off her glasses and putting them in the drawer. Indi watched in silence as Sadie popped in her contacts and touched up her highlight, all the while showing great familiarity with her surroundings.

"Wait. Is this Brandy's room or yours?"

Sadie looked over her shoulder. "Can't it be both? Sometimes I feel like being Sadie, and sometimes I feel like being her." She flicked her eyes at a framed photo of Brandy on the vanity. "The best part is, I get a choice now."

Her tone was callous and she wore a sneer, even though Indi was sure they had called a truce recently. Jason Momoa and all that. Indi had never enjoyed having her chain yanked and had no patience for Sadie's games.

"I saw you and Ben in Mathis' office," Indi spat. "How long has that been going on?"

Sadie smiled coyly. "I don't know. A while. Now that she's gone, I get to play with Brandy's things."

"Is that why you changed yourself? To get Ben?"

Sadie rose from the vanity and laughed. "See, that's what none of you understand. I didn't change myself. This has always been me, but no one could see that. Now they can."

"Because Brandy's not here?" Indi asked.

Sadie shrugged, choosing not to answer. "How are those memories of yours coming along? Any closer to finding out who the Army Bay murderer is?"

"Not yet. But things are getting clearer every day." She regarded Sadie suspiciously.

"That's great news," Sadie replied. She took some perfume from the vanity and spritzed it over her shoulders. The scent of pears and violets filled the air. "I'm really interested to see how this thing is going to end."

Indi had heard enough. She inched toward the door. "I'll leave you alone."

"Have you heard I'm running for Frost Queen?" Sadie called just as Indi was halfway out.

Indi exhaled. "Yes. I heard."

"I thought I would wear Brandy's dress from last year. The red strapless with the sequins. Do you remember?"

"No, I don't," Indi replied, monotone.

"I might need to get it taken in. I'm a little more cinched at the waist than Brandy, but that shouldn't be a hassle. Maybe you and I should go together?"

Indi cocked an eyebrow. "What do you mean, together?"

"Silly Indi," Sadie giggled. "As a couple. Duh."

Indi had been right to be reticent about coming upstairs. Things had got weird. She shook her head, bemused. "I'm not interested in dating you, Sadie."

Sadie folded her arms crossly. "Did you miss the part where I said I get to play with Brandy's things?"

Indi's breath hitched in her throat. She tried to stay calm, fight the urge to run across the room and deliver the right hook she was becoming proficient with. Indi repeated facts in her head to keep her calm. Sadie's sister was dead. She was in mourning. Mourning does crazy things to people. "Good luck with Frost Queen, Sadie. Bye."

Indi left the room before Sadie crossed any more lines, even breaking into a light jog to clear the ridiculously long hallway. She reached the landing and looked down at the guests, who stared at her again over the top of their champagne flutes. Her parents were among them, and it looked like crab cakes were being served. Indi made a beeline down the stairs and through the dense gathering, arriving at her father's shoulder.

"How did it go?" he asked.

"Oh, super weird. Thanks for asking." Indi widened her begging eyes at her mom's glass, hoping she might budge.

"Fine." She frowned, handing over her champagne. "But only because it's a special occasion."

"I'll keep that in mind," Indi replied, knocking back the bubbly drink in one gulp.

"You missed the speech. I think the guy who spoke is a judge," her mom said.

Her dad was still tugging at his collar, and his itchy cufflinks added to his discomfort. "When can we go?"

"When everyone else goes," her mom groaned. "I don't want to be the first to leave. That's rude."

"I'm with Dad. I want to go now," Indi stated. This entire experience had left a foul smell on her skin that needed to be scrubbed away asap.

"Fine," her mom grumbled. "Let me just introduce myself to those out-of-towners, and then we can leave. Okay?" Indi and her dad nodded in unison as her mom donned a bright smile and insinuated herself into the conversations of strangers.

"So what did you talk to Justine about?" her dad asked as they waited.

Indi shuddered. "You don't want to know. I'm not sure how many more awkward conversations I can have today. If someone asks me when I got my first period, that would pretty much be the icing on the cake."

"Don't worry. I won't ask." His voice trailed off when he caught sight of the oversized wreath in the living room encircling a photo of Brandy. "It still scares me. That could have been you."

Indi gripped Nathan's hand, and a half-smile eased onto his face. She wouldn't let that happen. She couldn't save Brandy, but she would sure as hell save herself from the crooked secrets emerging from the dark crevices of this town. Sadie was right about one thing. It would be interesting to see how this would end.

17

INDI'S DAD NODDED AT the cops in the squad car across the street as he pulled into the driveway. Her mom had her stilettos off before she even got to the front door, tossing them in the living room before disappearing into the kitchen. Indi headed straight for the stairs, eager to see if this charger would bring Brandy's burner to life.

"You're going to bed?" her dad asked as he closed the front door.

Indi turned. "That was the plan. Did you want me to do something?"

"Oh, no," he sighed. "I was just thinking of watching some TV if you were interested."

He posed it as a casual request, but Indi felt it was more like he needed her company. The charger was burning a hole in her bag, figuratively, of course. The more she thought about it, the more she found her feet were drifting up the stairs and away from him.

"Raincheck?" she replied, looking at him through half-closed eyes. "I'm really worn out after the service."

The disappointment in his voice tugged at Indi's guilt. "Of course. You've been through so much this week. I'll see you in the morning."

Indi felt like shit, but there was no getting around the fact that if she didn't get to her room right now and charge that phone, her head would explode.

Indi jogged up the stairs. She entered her room, closed her door and was chill for about two seconds before dashing to her closet. She fumbled around with the boxes on the shelf, but it didn't take long to spot the box for the pink running shoes. The phone sat inside so innocently, and Indi's heart raced with anticipation as she pulled the charger from her purse and compared the ports. With a breath held tight in her chest, Indi brought the two together and, like Cinderella's glass slipper, this was a match. She plugged the charger into a wall socket and slowly the bars lit up. This thing was dead flat. It would take a few minutes just to get a decent enough charge to turn it on. Indi paced the room, her eyes not shifting from those flickering neon-green bars. Just when she thought she might pop a blood vessel, the light went solid. She scrambled onto the floor and mashed her fingers against the power button. The Blackberry buzzed to life. Indi wasted no time in pulling up the text messages. They were all from the same number but there was no name saved. Indi scanned the dates. They started a month before Brandy was killed and the last message was received the day Indi washed up.

Brandy. Where are you? Are you okay? Please text me back. I love you.

Indi read through the previous messages, but the longer she scrolled, the more emotional whiplash she had to trawl through. That, and a good chunk of hardcore sexting. It didn't help that descriptive sex acts made Indi cringe. She deduced it was a guy, judging by the constant talk of his gigantic cock with the pictures to prove it, and if she had to read one more time how amazing he felt inside her, Indi thought she'd puke. But while they were describing how tight Brandy was in one conversation, they were arguing and calling it quits in another. Sometimes it was him. That things were getting too complicated, and it had to stop. Then other times it was Brandy, stating she was growing bored with him and keen to move on to someone less dramatic. But within a couple of days, they were back to screwing, if the follow-up messages were anything to go by. Then toward the end came the I love yous. He said it first. She said it back later, and when he asked her to prove it, Brandy sent a pic of her snatch. Indi squirmed and poked her tongue out, wishing there had been a NSFW warning.

Well, it was apparent she was seeing someone. But who was this guy? Not Ben. Why would she need a burner phone for her often-boyfriend? Maybe she was screwing around with Avery behind Rory's back? No. This guy said such sweet things, and there was always concern and kindness, even when they were fighting. Indi was pretty sure Avery didn't have an empathetic bone in his body. What about Elton? The photos may have been blurry, but Indi was confident, from color-matching alone, that it was not Elton's dick she was looking at unless he had a super-specific case of vitiligo.

Indi read the number over and over, hoping it would be familiar, but her mind was blank. Her thumb hovered over the dial button, even pressed down on it ever so lightly. Should she just call it? Would he even pick up? What would she do if he did? Indi's thumb itched more than she could stand.

She hit dial and put the phone to her ear. It rang for the longest time and, with every ring, Indi's heart thumped against her ribs. She stayed on the line for a while, when most others would have hung up by now, and just when she thought it would ring forever, there was a click and the call ended. No voice message. Just another dead end. She opened the chat box and, though it seemed pointless, she strung together a text born from her frustration.

New phone. Who dis?

Indi clicked her tongue as she tossed the phone on the carpet and let out a long, exhausted sigh. Even though Indi was determined to find out what happened on her own, this was definitely something she had to give to the police. Whoever was at the end of this phone could have killed Brandy.

Indi grabbed her own phone, checking Facebook and Instagram in a zombified state. Rory had uploaded a few photos from the service, which felt kind of inappropriate. Indi was glad she'd missed it. Rory had her arms looped around Avery's neck. Indi got a good look at his face, which she hadn't seen up close at the Hamilton's house. She strained her eyes and changed angles to be sure it wasn't a busted pixel or something like that. It wasn't. Avery's eyes were bright red and bloodshot and the surrounding skin badly swollen. It was an odd sort of wound, an allergic reaction maybe? Indi tried to convince herself of a dozen explanations, avoiding the one at the forefront of her mind, as if it were too preposterous to be true. Indi had seen that kind of reaction on reality cop shows, on bail jumpers who got sprayed with mace.

Was it Avery in the tunnel at Seradale? He had been avoiding school and dodged Indi at the service. He knew she would see his eyes. Shit. She had to know for sure. Suddenly, her phone beeped in her hand and she almost pissed herself. It was an Insta DM from Rory. Indi groaned. She was too tired and freaked out for any new bullshit.

Rory: Hey what are you up to?

India: About to go to sleep. What's up?

Rory: You should come down. The cops are gone.

India: Down where?

Rory: Down the pipe. I have to tell you something.

Indi wiped her hazy eyes and crawled over to the window. She looked out onto the street and, sure enough, the cop car was gone. They usually changed shifts around now. She peered down into her yard. It was quiet out. The grass looked damp with mist below the moon, veiled by black clouds. Just as she was about to turn away, a shadow moved amongst the trees, and a figure dressed in dark clothes waved a hand. Her phone buzzed again.

Rory: It's me. Are you coming down? I need to tell you something. It's about Brandy. Please.

Information about Brandy. That's all Indi wanted nowadays, but whether she was willing to climb down a pipe and walk into the darkness for it, that was another matter.

India: Why don't you come up?

There was a long pause, and suddenly the hairs on the back of Indi's neck stood on end. She looked out the window again. Rory still lingered in the shadows.

Rory: Okay. Open your window.

Indi did just that. She put her phone on her desk and lifted the pane, then watched Rory cross the lawn and climb the pipe. With each gain, Indi grew wearier. Her stomach churned with discomfort; there was a chilled gnawing deep in her bones. Indi couldn't see Rory's face. Her hoodie masked it, and she couldn't quite make out her body beneath the baggy clothes.

"Give me a hand," Rory coughed, her voice faint.

Indi leaned over the sill and reached out. Suddenly her breath was ripped from her throat as Rory grabbed her with a vice-like grip and pulled hard, trying to drag her from the window. Indi planted her feet and pushed against the wall to keep her balance, but Rory did not relent. With her arm wrapped around the drainpipe, she pulled harder with more strength than Indi expected. Indi was losing the struggle. Her feet were sliding on the carpet, her arm aching as it fought to keep her from falling.

"Let go!" Indi yelled. "Rory, what are you doing!" She felt stupid. This wasn't Rory. It was someone else, someone who wanted to pull her out that window and break her body on the concrete patio below. Indi fought harder, trying to shake away her attacker's grip. She looked desperately around and spied her purse on the carpet, the smooth red case of the Swiss Army knife teasing her, just out of reach. To grab the knife she would have to take her hand off the wall, the only thing that was keeping her from being dragged out the window. In a split second she decided it was worth the risk. Indi lunged for the knife. She flicked through the tools in panic and the corkscrew popped out. That would do. Indi plunged the metal spiral into her attacker's forearm, so deep it became wedged in the flesh. Blood spurted from the wound and Indi slipped free when her attacker tried to grab at the knife. Then the stranger slid down the drainpipe with the corkscrew still in their arm and sprinted away into the night.

Indi fell to the ground and scurried across the carpet, backing up against her bed. She tried to slow her breathing, tried to calm herself. What should she do now? She needed to tell her parents and call the police. That was the logical thing to do. Or maybe she was drawing Brandy's murderer into the light. She could expose this bastard, get justice for her and Brandy. Do what the Army Bay PD was sucking pretty hard at right now. Twice the murderer had risked it all to keep Indi silent, and they were getting desperate. If Indi brought in more cops she could lose her chance to end this once and for all.

When Indi could breathe again, she grabbed her phone and messaged the only person who understood what she was going through, and who she trusted to keep his mouth shut. Elton.

India: Hey. I need a ride somewhere. Can you come and get me?

Elton: Sure. I guess. Where are we going?

India: Avery's house.

AVERY'S PLACE MADE the Hamilton's house look like a squatter's shack. It wasn't as classical, built from rigid, cold materials like steel and glass, with lawns and trees sacrificed for rock gardens and abstract sculptures. When Elton pulled into the driveway every light in the house was on and loud music was blaring through the open door. Indi looked around for other cars or loitering teenagers, thinking perhaps they had interrupted a party, but she and Elton were the only ones here.

"Why would the door be open at two in the morning?" Indi asked, her stomach already in knots. Elton didn't answer. Instead, he climbed wearily from the driver's seat and paced slowly toward the door. Indi tried to follow.

"No. Stay here."

She shook her head. "This was my idea. I'm not sitting in the car. I can handle whatever is happening in there."

Elton gave a frustrated grunt. "Can you at least stay behind me?"

"No. But I'll let you walk beside me. How's that?"

Elton didn't have a choice. They walked into the house together and immediately Indi's shoes cracked on shattered glass scattered across the tile floor.

"Careful," she said, tiptoeing around the mess. "It's slippery."

Elton put his hands on her waist as she stepped over the glass. Indi wasn't sure that was necessary, but she also didn't feel obliged to tell him to stop.

Inside the music was so loud that Indi couldn't hear her footsteps or Elton talking beside her. They followed the synth melody up the patterned concrete stairs and along an open walkway that overlooked the minimalist living areas. The music was louder still as they approached an open door, a dull, blinking light spilling into the hallway. This didn't feel right. The hairs on the back of her neck stood on end. Indi gulped, forcing her feet to continue onward even though a part of her wanted to turn and run. They came to the door and Elton touched her shoulder.

"Wait," he breathed in her ear. "Are you sure we should go in there?"

Indi shook her head. "No," she mouthed. Then she turned from him and entered the room. A standing lamp lay knocked over near the bed. Its loose copper-wire bulb strobed soft light. As it stuttered on and off, Indi saw Avery's body in sporadic flashes. First, she saw he was naked and face down on his bed. Then she noted his wrists were bound to his ankles, stringing him up and stretching his bluing limbs. Last, she saw the pool of vomit on the mattress and the thick foam still oozing from his gaping mouth.

Indi stumbled backward and Elton caught her.

"We have to go, Indi. We can't get caught here with a dead body," Elton muttered.

Indi couldn't move, her feet frozen in place. A moment ago she had wanted to run, but that now felt impossible. Elton had to drag her out of the room, but not before Indi forced herself to endure a last glimpse. The bulb flickered and Indi looked at Avery's forearms. There was no corkscrew wound.

Elton guided Indi through the hall and down the stairs. "Don't touch the railing," he instructed. When they were near the door Elton scooped her into his arms and ran to his car. He buckled her into the front seat before speeding away from the house.

Indi sat, silent, with her forehead pressed to the window, the image of Avery's body burning behind her eyes.

18

"INDIA. WAKE UP." GENTLE fingers tucked her hair behind her ear.

Indi wasn't asleep; she had been awake for hours. She'd heard her parents get out of bed and start moving around the house. Listened to the rubbish truck arrive at dawn and the ladies' walking group saunter by thirty minutes later. She was exhausted beyond measure, but Avery's face wouldn't let her sleep.

Indi's eyes flickered open and found her mother hovering over her with the color drained from her face. Her mom shivered, noticing the open window and the curtain billowing in the brisk morning breeze.

"Did you leave this open all night?" She crossed the room and pulled it shut. Her eyes found India's phone on the desk. "Look at all these messages and missed calls. You don't know what's happened, do you."

Indi rubbed her eyes, only half-listening, but she knew exactly what her mother was talking about. She couldn't say that though, not without giving everything away and earning herself another hour in a beige room with Braddock.

"What missed calls?"

Her mom struggled to find the words. She paced back and forth before the window. "It's Avery Weiss. They found him this morning." She swallowed the lump in her throat. "Murdered."

"Oh my god," Indi croaked, as his contorted limbs flashed in her mind.

Her mom crossed her arms to stop herself from trembling. "I know. Can you believe it? It's all over the news. Rory found him in his house. His parents are away. How horrible for them, having to come home to this."

Indi swung her legs over the edge of the bed and rested her heavy head in her hands. "Can you hand me my phone?" Her mom passed it to her and Indi tried to open the DMs that had come from Rory last night. The messages had been deleted. Even Rory's account was gone. Indi searched for her profile with no results. She swiped through her feed, and already it was flooded with Avery tribute posts.

"Maybe you should call her," her mom suggested.

That wasn't a good idea. Not only had Indi been less than sympathetic about Rory's woes during their last conversation, but she also wasn't confident she could lie about what she knew. Avery had been murdered. This went way beyond polite nods and fake smiles.

"Maybe later," Indi replied. "I'm not feeling the best. Can I stay home from school today?"

"Of course. Do you want me to make you some soup?"

Indi shook her head. "No. I'm just going to take a shower and go back to bed. Is Dad home?"

The question seemed to irritate her mom. "No. He had to work. I called to let him know about Avery. I don't think he knew him though."

After her mom had left the room, Indi stretched out her arms, still trying to forget Avery's eyes rolled back in his head, that flickering bulb revealing the scene one flash at a time. Indi wasn't sad. That struck her first, not something she would admit out loud, especially if she didn't want to be a suspect. Indi felt for his parents, losing their only son so young, and there was no doubt Rory would be a mess. But now wasn't the time to say heartless things like, she's better off without him. Sometimes the best thing to do is shut up and let people feel any way they chose.

Indi's eyes drifted to her window. She could still feel the hand tight around her wrist, pulling her down. She'd thought it was Avery. After seeing the pictures from the service, knowing he had been in Seradale and that he would have access to Rory's Instagram, Indi had convinced herself that he was her attacker, even that he had killed Brandy. But everything was different now. Indi knew she had stabbed the person in her window, but of all the obscene things done to Avery's body, there was no stab wound on his arm.

Indi faced the terrifying fact that it may have very well been Avery who strangled her in Seradale, but that someone entirely different had attacked her last night. Then, of course, there was the fresh horror to further complicate Indi's life. Who'd killed Avery?

Indi stood, her legs aching from climbing up and down that drainpipe last night. She crossed the room to grab some clothes then stumbled when she tripped on the charger cord. Shit. That's right. The burner phone. She picked it up and scanned through the messages she had already read, including the random text she sent last night. New phone. Who dis? Then her heart froze in her chest and ice-water flooded her veins. Next to the text in faded grey italics were the words Seen 5.16 am.

Seen by whom?

IT WAS THE LONGEST, hottest shower Indi had ever taken. She stood motionless under the water, letting it stream over her face and body, hoping to take some of this frightening cold away. But it wouldn't budge. The cold clung to her bones. She imagined everyone at school would be losing their shit right now. Brandy and Avery were a big deal. One of them murdered was cataclysmic on its own, but both of them? Armageddon. After half an hour Indi didn't even notice when the water turned cold. But as her fingers pruned up and her skin turned blue, her mind transported her to the beach, that horrible fucking beach, and reminded her of how things could have ended. She turned off the water, stepped into a towel, then dragged herself to her room. Her phone was ringing when she got there, and she didn't hesitate to pick it up when she saw Elton's name flashing on the screen.

"Hey."

"Hey." Elton exhaled. "Are you okay?"

"No. Have you spoken to Rory yet?"

"No. She's been at the station all day. I bet she's a wreck. What do I say when I see her? I can't get last night out of my head."

Indi was relieved to know she wasn't the only one. "Me too." She paused. "Did we do the right thing, not calling the police?"

Elton's silence seemed to last forever. "If we had stayed we would both be in jail cells this morning. They already think I might have something to do with Brandy's death. They find me next to a dead body and they're going to care less about evidence and more about having someone to blame. And what about you? Can you handle being accused of murder again? I mean, Indi, how much more of this can you take?"

The short answer was, not a lot. Shattered glass was the best way Indi could describe the effect of all this confusion. Nothing was simple or straightforward. It was all jagged and sharp, a collection of images reflected on broken shards. But she couldn't let herself become fragmented as well. She had to hold her shit together if she was going to see the end of all of this.

"You're right. The police would think we had something to do with Avery too. Why else would we be there?" Even though Indi said the words out loud, she still wasn't able to absorb them completely. She changed the subject. "Are you at school?"

"Yeah," Elton replied. "The police are talking to students. Paula is with them right now."

"Paula? Why Paula?"

"They're looking for Micah. The word is Avery overdosed on pills, the kind that got Micah picked up for selling a couple of months ago. Sleeping pills or something."

"He didn't kill himself," Indi said. "Not the way we saw him." She remembered Micah's outburst in the hall, how furious he was at Avery and the threats that followed. Could Micah have done this?

"No," Elton agreed. "It wasn't suicide. Do you still think he was the one who attacked you in Seradale?"

Indi dragged fingers through her wet hair. "Yes. No. I'm not sure. I sprayed mace at whoever it was. How else can you explain Avery's face?"

"But no stab wounds," Elton added.

Indi's chin dropped. "No. There must be someone else."

"Shit," Elton grunted. There was a commotion in the background, and Elton's voice grew faint. "I have to go. I'll talk to you later." The call ended.

Indi spent the day trying to catch up on schoolwork, which seemed like the biggest waste of time in the world. What good would end-of-year exams be if she were dead by next week?

Her mom was out at showings all afternoon. Apparently, another murdered teen wasn't a good enough reason to put off house hunters. Indi lounged on the couch double-fisting popcorn into her mouth. Her phone beeped in her pocket and she checked the message.

Cody: Dinner. Tomorrow night. 7 pm. Did you hear they found Avery strung up like a thanksgiving turkey?

Indi cringed and tossed her phone away. Cody came out with some messed up shit. Right. Christa's dinner. Indi found it hard to keep track of everything these days, and as for Cameron, she was time-sharing with Elton in Indi's thoughts.

At around six o'clock Indi's dad arrived home. She looked over her shoulder when he came into the lounge. "You were working late tonight." She winced. "Did I sound like mom then?"

He ruffled her hair and collapsed beside her, hoisting his feet in heavy work boots onto the coffee table. "There's nothing wrong with sounding like mom. Is she home?" He balled his fist around some popcorn.

Indi shook her head. "She's showing a house. Said to have leftover meatloaf for dinner."

"Not really that hungry," he replied.

Indi grinned. "At least not for meatloaf."

He chuckled before his lips withered into a straight line. "I heard about that boy. This is getting out of control. Did you go to school?"

"No. Been upstairs all day."

He exhaled. "I think it's a good idea if you spend more time at home. Army Bay has become a dangerous place."

"You're sounding like Braddock," Indi moaned.

"Maybe that's not a bad thing. That man has been much more amenable since I threatened to sue him for harassment. You're not involved with any of this, and I won't have him accusing you anymore. You're a victim here, just like the others. The only difference is that I am the luckiest father in the world to still have you here with me." He scooped up Indi's hand, which looked tiny within his grasp. "You are the best thing in my life and I won't lose you. So do your father a favor, will you? Stay home!"

"Sure," Indi inhaled, "after tomorrow night."

He suddenly looked exhausted. He flopped onto the couch and groaned. "What's happening tomorrow night?"

"I've been invited to Cameron's for dinner. Christa is back home."

He angled away from her but Indi pawed at him to turn back. "Please Dad! After that I promise I won't take a single step out that front door without your permission." That was a small misdirection. She would leave the house by drainpipe.

Her dad's reluctance persisted. "What do you think Braddock would say?"

"Oh, you're listening to Braddock now?" Indi teased.

He glared and pinched her hand. "I see what you're doing."

"Everything has been going so fast, like an out-of-control carousel that won't let me off. I have about this much hope left that Cam will change that." Indi allowed the tiniest breath of space between her thumb and finger. "Come on," she whined, "be a pal."

He furrowed his heavy brow and scratched pensively at the stubble on his chin. "Fine. Go. But I will drop you off, and I will pick you up. Deal?"

"Yes! Deal!"

"Now, what's the homework situation?" he asked.

Indi scrunched up her nose. "Negative."

Her dad pointed toward the stairs. "How about you ride that carousel of emotion toward your textbooks."

"Okay, okay," Indi smirked, planting a peck on his cheek and heading upstairs. The cold twilight wind struck Indi when she opened her bedroom door. She was sure the window had been closed when she left. Indi crossed the room and pushed down the pane.

"Don't freak out," a voice whispered from behind her.

Indi spun on her heels, backing up against the window, and she almost screamed, but the sound shrunk in her throat when she saw Rory sitting on the bed.

"Quiet!" Rory insisted.

"Rory!" Indi's voice was a shrill whisper. "I almost shit my pants. How did you get in here?"

"How do you think?" Rory muttered. "Up the pipe."

Indi gripped her hair by the roots. "I'm over that pipe. I'm going full lumberjack on its ass tomorrow, I swear to god. The cops didn't see you?"

Rory frowned. "This is the Army Bay Police we're talking about, right? It's a donut sudoku party in that squad car. They didn't even notice me." Dark circles enclosed her eyes, her drooping frame dressed in black leggings and an oversized sweater, her black hair knotted into pigtail buns. The vitality and perpetual peppiness Indi had grown accustomed to had vanished. This was Rory, weakened by sorrow.

Indi composed herself quickly. This was the moment she had been dreading, face to face with Rory, knowing the truth. She and Elton had found Avery's body first. The plan was to let Rory do all the talking. That way, Indi stood a better chance of not screwing up.

Rory patted the space beside her, and Indi sat down. "Sorry if I scared you."

"Scared is pretty much how I identify these days," Indi mumbled.

Rory leaned her head on Indi's shoulder. "You're not going to say anything about Avery?"

"What do you want me to say?"

Rory shrugged. "Just don't say anything I don't want to hear, even if it's true."

"Okay."

"Whoever did this to Avery, it was so ... intimate. It's someone who knew things about him, about us. They put him on display. They wanted him humiliated. Exposed."

"Exposed for what?"

Rory sniffed and rolled her eyes. "Are you giving me some pity sympathy or deliberately forgetting what you said in the Seradale locker room? The sleeping pills. Whoever did this wanted to get everyone talking, and they succeeded. The cops wouldn't stop asking if Avery had ever forced himself on me, or if I had ever blacked out when I was with him. That's all people are going to remember about him now. That he was some kind of gross sex offender."

Indi remembered Rory's request. Don't say anything she didn't want to hear, even if it were true. She spat out something vague and generic instead. "Do they have any suspects?"

"Me," Rory sighed. "You. Micah. No one. I have an alibi, of course, home all night. Our security cameras prove that, so the hours they kept me at the station were a complete waste of time."

"Yeah. I heard the cops were questioning Micah."

Rory nodded. "I think he did it. He's trash. He could have forced those pills down Avery's throat. He was at the station for a while. I could hear Paula bawling in the waiting room. Anyone would think it was someone she loved that died. But that's Paula, so desperate for attention, to be somebody.

Somebody like us." She grazed Indi's forearm with her knuckle. "But they'll never be like us. None of them."

Indi squirmed beneath her skin that suddenly felt tight and stretched too thin. Every word that she forced past her lips was fake, and Rory's every reply was apathetic. This wasn't friendship or support; it was an empty, soulless exchange that had Indi questioning if they were even human.

"I guess that means Micah killed Brandy, and that he tried to kill you too." The words flowed with ease from Rory's lips. The confidence startled Indi. "Now if the police would just do their jobs and lock him up, we can put this all behind us and get on with it." A smile slid onto her face. "I got a call from Franklin today. They've offered me the scholarship. There were problems with the previous recipient."

"Well yeah, because Brandy died." Indi couldn't stop the words from falling out.

Rory jerked. "You know about that?"

That wasn't the response Indi had expected. "You know about that?"

Rory turned away, suddenly disinterested. "You must have told me."

Indi grabbed her arm. "I haven't even spoken to you since I found out. Why didn't you say in Seradale that you knew Brandy was the recipient? We both know there is no way she could have got an athletic scholarship. She must have lied on her application or something. You had to be pissed at her?"

Rory peeled Indi's fingers from her arm and smiled. "Brandy was my best friend. I would never be mad at her. Maybe you should lie down, Indi. You're getting pretty worked up."

Indi furrowed her brow, tucking her hands under her arms. "No, I'm not."

"Looks like it from where I'm standing. You sound straight up, bat shit crazy." She narrowed her eyes. "You didn't like Avery, did you?"

No, she didn't. She also didn't like where Rory's abrupt change of attitude was going, almost as much as she didn't like being called crazy when she was probably the sanest person in Army Bay right now. She deserved an award for such a feat. Indi cocked an eyebrow. "What does that have to do with anything?"

"So you admit it then? And you've made it pretty clear that you bought into this bullshit being spread about him?"

Indi exhaled a deep breath and with it her last threads of patience. "Look. You've been through a lot. This isn't the time to unpack all of that. Why don't I get my dad to give you a ride home or something?"

Rory sneered. "Don't patronize me India."

Who was acting crazy now? Indi glanced at the door. Nathan was still downstairs watching TV. Maybe it was time for reinforcements. But then Rory slid in front of the door, and Indi's heart thumped loud in her ears.

"Avery took care of me. He always had my back. He was there for me when no one else was. He loved me so much."

"That's great Rory," Indi muttered.

"He did love me!" she snapped. "And I loved him. Our love was deeper and truer than the rest of these fake assholes. Ben and Brandy? Please. She cheated on him like it was a competitive sport. I should know. I had to cover for her every time she went out to catch some dick. Sadie and Elton? She's too busy being in love with Ben because she's a masochist, and Elton's dick is apparently made of gold and too good to stick in anyone or anything. Avery and I were real, and he never hurt me. That's how I knew I was special. Because he did that shit to those whores and not to me."

Indi's body jerked. "What did you say?"

Rory buried her face in her hands. "Nothing. I said nothing. Just ... just shut up and stop confusing me."

"Come on Rory. Let's call your parents. You're not yourself right now." Indi moved forward, slowly reaching out to her.

"Don't touch me," Rory hissed.

"It's okay," Indi said softly. "I'm not going to hurt you."

"I said don't!" Rory shoved Indi's shoulders and pounced, pushing her to the ground. She was crying now, her face red with anguish. She pinned Indi's hands to the floor. "This is all your fault!" Suddenly, her bloodshot eyes drifted from Indi's face and found Brandy's burner phone charging at the wall socket. Rory shivered. "You still have it. So you know?"

The door flew open and her dad charged in. He hooked Rory under the arms and dragged her off Indi.

"What the hell is going on in here!" His voice was thunder. "India, are you okay?"

Indi climbed to her feet. "I'm fine. It's alright, Dad, she's just upset."

"No. That's not good enough," he growled. "Not after what you've been through." He pinched Rory's arm in his hand and when she struggled he gripped harder. "Come on. I'm taking you to the cops across the street. They can deal with you."

There was no room for compromise. He dragged Rory from the room, her sorrowful eyes being the last thing Indi saw before the door slammed shut.

19

FIRST THING NEXT MORNING Indi's dad got in a contractor to reposition the drainpipe. If that wasn't bad enough he had bars installed on Indi's window, though they were the fancy wrought-iron baroque type that didn't make it look so much like a cage.

Indi crossed her arms. "It wasn't my fault. I didn't invite her; she just showed up."

"Well now, no one else can just show up," her dad said sternly. "That girl is crazy. I don't want you seeing her again."

"She's in mourning dad. She's freaking out. She found her boyfriend overdosed in a full BDSM nightmare. She's allowed to lose her shit."

"Not like that. Not at you. Those kids. They're poison Indi, and there's someone out there right now who wants to draw them all out of this town's wounds." Indi smirked, but he did not allow her to shrug away his concern. "When did the world become this way? When did children stop being children? It's just sex and drugs and drink, and now you're killing each other." His chest sunk. "This is some damned place we live in."

Indi touched his arm and felt him shivering. "Dad. I'm sorry. I didn't mean to upset you."

He entwined their fingers tightly and exhaled. "Do you really need to go out tonight?"

"Yes," Indi spoke as firmly as possible. "I really do. You know how much seeing Cam tonight means to me. Especially now. You can drop me off. There'll be cops stationed at the house. I'll be completely fine. Who is going to hurt me at Cam's house?"

Indi was relieved when her mom tapped on the door and poked her head into the room. "You two hiding up here or what?"

"I'm just getting ready to head over to Cam's place."

Indi read her mother's feigned smile. "Right. Cameron. How's she been through all of this?" Her voice trailed off. "Not here, that's for sure."

Indi frowned, bewildered that even with two of the elites dead and another dragged out of here screaming in the middle of the night, her mom would still prefer they be the kind of people Indi associated with.

Her mom turned her attention to her dad. "Just you and I then. Did you want to order in some Thai? Watch a movie?"

He scratched the back of his head. "I have some paperwork to look at." Indi's mom scowled, and he spun his reply. "But that can wait. Of course, it can. Thai sounds great."

She nodded but didn't smile. Indi couldn't tell whether or not she was pleased, but either way she slipped away from the room and her dad followed. Indi prayed he wouldn't want to talk anymore, knowing that she couldn't give him what he wanted to hear. The lying was becoming exhausting. If anything good had come from last night's events, it was receiving Rory's permission to lie, as long as it gave her fleeting moments of peace. That was all Indi wanted for anyone mixed up in this insane mess. Peace. She must have had an angel on her shoulder because her dad didn't speak another word, closing the door behind him.

The best part about getting ready to see Cameron? The lack of needing to get adequately prepared. Well, maybe that wasn't the best part, but it was a close second. She hoped the best part would comprise dark corners, sweet kisses and hard grinding. A long-sleeved black bodysuit, off the shoulder of course, distressed jeans showing both knees and a good chunk of thigh, topped off with a cropped leather jacket because this was a dinner function, after all. Indi dug around her dresser, tossing aside hoop earrings and chunky necklaces until she pincered a blush-pink scrunchie in her fingers. Cam had its twin, and even though it seemed stupid, if Cam were wearing hers too, that would be a sign. A sign of what? Who knew? Maybe that she wanted to be friends again. Maybe they could start hanging out. Maybe they could ditch the foreplay and get straight to the grinding. Indi didn't want to get her hopes up but her body was ready for the latter. She pulled the scrunchie over her ponytail and tugged her hair taut. She expelled a deep breath that rose hotly through her like steam.

"Fingers crossed no one dies tonight," she said to her reflection. When Indi reached the door, she could hear the car rumbling in the driveway. "Bye, see you tonight," she called over her shoulder. She walked down the cobbled path and when she looked up from her feet it surprised her to find her dad wasn't filling the driver's seat with his massive shoulders. Instead, her mom waved and gave half a smile, her eyes darting every which way like a tiny blonde bird, keeping an eye out for predators.

Indi climbed into the passenger seat and pulled on her seat belt. "Hey. I thought dad was ..."

"Change of plans." She scanned her eyes over Indi. "No bag? You're not taking your supplies?"

"You mean my anti-murder kit?" Indi was reminded that only the rape alarm remained. When all this was over she would have to thank her mom. Twice now, those items had saved her. "I won't need it at Cam's house. I'm safe there."

"Fine. Okay." Her mom shrugged. "To Cameron's house then." She reversed out of the driveway and paused, waiting for the parked police car to start its engine and follow. When they were practically sitting on her bumper, she slipped the car into drive and sped to their destination.

"So, about last night," her mom started.

"You don't need to rip into me too. Dad did an amazing job. I promise you. Still not sure why it's my fault, but who am I to make sense of this?"

Her mom cleared her throat. "No, I mean before that. Your dad. What time did he get home? Do you remember?"

Indi furrowed her brow. "I dunno. Like six? Why?"

Her mom's full red lips contorted into a giant painted smile while her eyes kept their uncertainty. "No reason. My open house went late last night, and I couldn't remember if I'd asked him to pick up my dry cleaning."

"Well, he didn't come home with any, if that makes a difference," Indi drawled. What kind of conversation was this? It prompted a question within her, though. "You've been working a lot lately. Weird considering you used to bust dad's balls when he worked late."

Her mom turned a corner and Indi immediately recognized the towering oak on the berm, its wide roots cracking the footpath. Cam's house was only a couple of streets away.

"I'm rushed off my feet," she replied. In her agonizing excitement, Indi had almost forgotten what she had asked. "Folks want to sell up and move on."

"Gee, I wonder why," Indi said. "Beautiful beaches. Excellent schools. Lots of murders."

"Oh enough, India," she groaned. "The rate I'm flipping these places we'll have your first year of college paid for."

Indi slumped in her seat. College. Great. If she stayed alive that long.

At last, they pulled into Cam's street, and her mom maneuvered up the bumpy driveway. She scowled. "They should really get this fixed. It would lift the price up if they ever wanted to sell."

Indi clambered out of the car as quick as she could then leaned in the window. "Oh, did you want me to give them a card or something?" She watched a genuine smile swallow her mom's feigned one as she reached inside her jacket, but Indi was quick to wave her away. "No? Okay, then. Bye," she hummed.

Indi ran toward the door before her mom could growl at her, but she heard a faint fuck you whispered on the wind as her mother drove away. She passed a car in the driveway, if it could even be described as a car. More of an itsy-bitsy mauve cube with windows and wheels. The license plate read CODYSQT. Oh. That explained it.

As she knocked on the door, she craned her neck to see if the police car had arrived. It pulled up on cue, with two of Army Bay's finest in attendance, with sharp buzzcuts and crisp shirts, ready to protect and serve. Indi told herself that the anxiety bubbling in her stomach was nerves about seeing Cameron, but she knew that was only a half-truth. She was a fool not to have brought the alarm.

She wobbled her arms and legs as if being limber would make this any easier, then applied two more hard, sharp knocks on the door. She could hear shuffling, not steps, slow and unenthusiastic, and when the door opened Christa stood there in a crumpled white robe, her sunset-red hair in a loose, low ponytail. She looked different without makeup, younger, even shorter, if that were possible. She was still gorgeous though, if a little skinny, and when Indi glanced at her feet she noticed a pair of fluffy crocodile-head slippers staring back at her.

"Cute," Indi chuckled awkwardly, gesturing to the slippers.

Christa tipped her head to the side and took in Indi's every feature for a good long while, scanning her like some cyborg collecting information. "India," she said at last.

Indi didn't want to patronize her. Who knew what kind of baggage Christa was carrying. She had been in a mental health clinic, for Christ's sake. "Yeah, Christa, it's me, India. How are you?"

Christa narrowed her eyes. "Hungry." Indi jumped in her boots when Christa yelled over her shoulder, "Cameron, your girlfriend is here."

There was groaning from the stairs and the clack of heeled shoes on the wood. "She's not my girlfriend Christa. How many times do I have to tell you that." Cameron appeared, and it was like the moon rose and set all at once. She had layered a long sleeve shirt with a floral crop top because she hated showing her arms and would never in a million years let her stomach hang out. She wore tight stonewash jeans that hugged her full hips and thick thighs, and black stiletto boots that took her from 5'4 to 5'5. Indi ripped her eyes away from Cam's body long enough to check her hair. No scrunchie. Indi swallowed her disappointment so it didn't manifest itself as hysterical, ugly crying.

"You look really nice," Indi forced herself to say.

Cameron strolled across the entryway. She crossed her arms at first, but slowly they parted and fell to her sides. Her eyes lifted from the floor and found their way to Indi's gaze, and the tiniest of smiles crept into the corner of her mouth. "You look okay too. Come in."

Christa held the door open and as soon as Indi crossed the threshold she slammed it shut. "Guess I better get ready."

"I told you hours ago Christa," Cam groaned as her older sister ran up the stairs. "She always takes a little while to adjust when she comes home. It's the reduced meds, mom says."

Indi waved away her explanation. "No, it's totally fine."

They stood there fidgeting like gawky teenagers on a first date, no remnant of the horny bi-girls they had been not long ago. "Do you want to go into the living room? Dinner should be ready soon." Cam guided her toward the large white room, then almost spun on her heels. "Oh. Don't worry, we'll find somewhere else." She glared at Cody, who lay sprawled on the couch.

The TV blared in the background even though his attention was strictly on his phone.

"Don't be a bitch," Cody sighed, his fingers tapping with urgency. "Come on, sit down. There's tea to spill."

There would be no escaping Cody's teatime. Far too much had happened, and Indi didn't doubt that he knew every single detail.

"Where to start?" Cody gushed, never taking his eyes from his phone. "Is it true you have a restraining order against Rory Zhang? I heard she broke into your house last night and went full Jack Torrance on you. Have you seen The Shining? Oh em gee, I love The Shining."

"What? No!" Indi was still processing the last few words of his sentence. "It wasn't like that. She's going through shit."

"Oh, don't even get me started on that. There is far too much to unpack, but if you're interested in my opinion," whether or not Indi was, she knew she was about to hear it, "I think Avery knew the gig was up and offed himself. It was just a matter of time before a bunch of underage high school juniors formed a line around the block and showed the police on a doll where Avery dicked them."

Cam rolled her eyes. "If he killed himself, how did he tie his legs and arms behind his back, genius?"

For the first time since Indi arrived, Cody put his phone down. He tapped his finger against his chin. "Suicide pact then. Someone helped him do it." Cody clapped. "Duh. Rory. She found him, right? Convenient much? She was probably happy to lend a hand, not wanting to go down with the sinking ship and all that, bailing before everyone found out what a great Bill Cosby impersonation Avery did." Cody chuckled to himself.

"Smidge on the disrespectful side, isn't it? He has been murdered, you know," Indi said.

"Pfffft, screw that guy," Cody heckled. "He was a spoiled asshole who got away with heinous shit because he was living his best-privileged life. What a cliché."

"So he deserved to die the way he did then? What about Brandy? Her too?" Indi felt both Cody and Cam's eyes boring through her, but neither of them was the first to answer.

Christa glided down the stairs in a stark-white swing dress over fishnet stockings and cute ankle boots, her hair draping over her shoulders in fine red sheets.

"Really?" she asked, seeming more disappointed than surprised. "Maybe it's been easy to forget what she did to me because you haven't had to see my face for months, out of sight, out of mind, right? But I have to look at me every day. Is it sad Brandy died? Sure, why not. But am I sad Brandy died? What do you think?"

Indi was slowly and regrettably concluding that she was living in a town of full-fledged psychopaths. Her dad was right. This place was poison.

"Dinner!" Fern Gibbs leaned against the door frame, wiping her freckled hands on a tea towel. "It's good to see you again, Indi." Indi smiled, and before she could debate whether a hug was appropriate, Fern had already crossed the room and wrapped Indi up in her arms. Cam's mother was the type of person who was easy to be around. Someone you could watch TV with and not feel obliged to talk to during the commercials. It seemed like a large opinion to have about your friend's mother, but Indi had spent more time in this house than hers last school holidays and quietly preferred Fern's company to her mom's.

"You cut your hair," Indi remarked, taking in Fern's curly red bob.

Fern ruffled her new fringe. "Felt like a change. You still like fettucine?"

"Yes. Kept that information," Indi said. "Smells great."

"Well, come on then." Fern's smile shifted to a glare. "Cody, don't bring that thing to the table. That goes for all of you. No phones."

When she turned away Cody muttered something bitchy that he would never say to her face. He left his phone on the couch and walked to Christa, taking her hand. She was turning in circles, her eyes drifting around the room as if it were her first time here. Cody laced their fingers. "Come on, sis. Hungry?"

Her eyes focused on him and she smiled. "Starving."

Indi watched them walk to the dining room. Christa was a different person when she came home from the Joyness Clinic, and Indi hated that she didn't know how to act around her. Was she supposed to pretend all that bullshit hadn't happened, or was it raw emotion out in the open for everyone to see and discuss? Either way, she felt like an asshole for not being there for Christa, and even more so for defending Brandy in the Gibb's own living room. Suddenly, Indi smelled coconut and felt Cam's arm brush against hers. Whether Cam meant to do it didn't matter. It had Indi's heart thumping either way.

"Probably best we don't talk about any of that stuff tonight."

"Stuff?" Indi snorted. "You mean all the murders?"

Cam grinned. "Yeah those. I don't want Christa to get upset. Her weekends at home are supposed to be chill, you know."

"Sure. I get it."

"Come on then. Let's eat."

Cam's hand lingered behind as she headed for the dining room and Indi felt the familiar soft scratch of velvet against her fingers. She glanced down, and around Cam's wrist was a pink scrunchie. Fuck. Yes!

The Gibbs had a dining room that always felt like it was Christmas. Walls painted pine green with gold accents and cream wainscot panels, mahogany chairs upholstered in Santa-suit red and poinsettia on display regardless of the season. Warren Gibbs sat at the head of the table and seemed less enthusiastic about Indi's presence, watching her dubiously as she took a seat next to Cam.

"How are you, India?" He had already looked away before she could answer.

"Fine. Yeah. Good," Indi replied, shuffling into her seat.

Warren grumbled something in the ballpark of that's nice, then turned to Fern and said, "Pass the garlic bread please dear?"

Fern tried to be polite for the both of them, chuckling as if Warren's dismissiveness was an inside joke. She didn't have to. He had been weird ever since the first time he saw her and Cam kissing in their pool. Indi never really liked him anyway, so dull and distant.

The fettucine was as terrific as expected, but not nearly as amazing as Cam's eyes were tonight. No circles of black eyeliner like usual, so Indi could make out her wispy ginger lashes that framed swirling green pools. She felt a nudge under the table, ignoring it at first. Probably just someone stretching. Then it happened again, this time softer, and it didn't end at her foot. Instead, the caress rolled around her ankle and inched up her calf. Indi turned to Cam beside her with an enquiring gaze. Cam said nothing, just gave a half-smile that contorted her freckles. Indi discreetly peeked under the tablecloth and saw Cam had somehow magically kicked off her boot and was indeed playing footsie. This was a good thing. Right? It had to be.

"Do you want to see my art?" Christa asked abruptly, dropping her fork loudly onto her plate.

Indi cleared her throat. "Yeah. I'd love to."

Christa stood and went to the nearby glass cabinet, plucking a block of stone about a foot long from the shelf. She placed it roughly on the table and Indi caught Fern wincing, probably concerned about the wood getting scuffed. On closer inspection Indi made out the curves and crevices carved into the grey stone. It reminded her of rolling waves, which some might find calming. Unfortunately, anything involving the beach had become a trigger for Indi.

"It's beautiful," she lied, fighting away the flashes of Brandy's blue skin.

"Christa's counsellor recommended stone carving to express how she was feeling," Fern stated. "I think she has a flair for it."

"I sell them on my Etsy," Christa said matter-of-factly. "They're eighty-five dollars. Do you want one?"

Indi didn't think it was necessary to comment they were overpriced. "I'll ask my mom," she said instead. "She might want to buy a bunch for house showings."

Christa seemed pleased with that response. "I'll text you a link." She returned the statue to the cabinet before going back to twirling pasta around her fork.

"I'm full," was the next sentence yelled across the table. It was Cam this time. "Can Indi and I go up to my room?" Indi's leg twitched, and she tried not to gulp too loudly. Fern nodded while Warren bowed his head and kept his eyes on his plate. Cam stood up. "Great dinner, Mom." She looked at Indi. "You coming?"

"Yes," Indi spat, knocking her knee on the table as she stood up.

Cody reclined in his seat and grinned slyly as they passed him. "Have fun, whores."

"Cody!" Fern exclaimed. "You can clear the table and do the dishes by hand. What is wrong with you? This is your home, not The Ricki Lake Show."

Cody frowned. "Who is Ricki Lake?"

Indi didn't stick around for any more of their conversation. In all honesty, right now, she couldn't care less. All she knew was that following Cam up the stairs, and watching her hips sway, was a religious experience. She didn't want to read too much into this. Cam had made her feelings truly clear. She probably just wanted more details on Rory and the craziness that had unfolded last night, or to exchange morbid gossip about Avery. They reached the landing and crossed the hall into her room. Cam closed the door behind them, and, before Indi could say a word, she found herself pushed hard against the wall with her bottom lip tight between Cam's teeth. Indi felt her body melt into the wood panels as Cam cupped her face, her tongue teasingly sliding in and out of her mouth. Indi's hands found their way beneath Cam's shirt, trailing a finger down her spine and drawing circles on the small of her back. Oh. Right. This was what heaven felt like.

When Cam pulled back, Indi struggled to recall how breathing worked. In. Out. In. Out.

"Well, that was nice," Indi stuttered.

"Maybe you should stay the night," Cam suggested. She tilted her head to the side, her half-smile sending Indi's blood racing.

"Really?" Indi suddenly remembered the sobering truth that she was not living an everyday, teenage life right now. "I can't ... my parents, the cops. I'm sort of in witness protection." Cam tried to stifle it at first, but soon the laughter burst from her puffed cheeks. Indi laughed too. "Yeah. It sucks." She pulled Cam against her, their chests heaving in unison. "You don't know how much I want to stay. Can we try again another time?" She felt Cam's hand on her hip, pushing away. "I mean, we don't have to stop this, though," Indi said quickly, a subtle pleading in her tone.

Cam walked away, and Indi was suddenly cold, as if the sun had set and stolen all the warmth in the world. "I just don't know how much longer I'll be in Army Bay," Cam said. "Dad told us today that we're moving back to Seradale."

Where Indi's heart had been thudding furiously for the past five minutes, now it was dead still. "Like moving, moving? For good?"

"He wants the family to be closer to Christa, and Army Bay just isn't as safe a place as it used to be."

Indi gulped. "No shit. When?"

"Soon."

"So what was this? A goodbye make-out session? A pity pash?"

"So what if it is? I thought that's what you wanted?"

Cam's words were like a cold shower. "Yeah, it was what I wanted, so it's really shitty for you to tongue bang me when you're about to move towns, Cameron."

"Whatever. You should be grateful I want to tongue bang you at all, after everything that's happened." Cam threw her arms up in the air. "You know what? Forget it. We would never work again. Not after you made up with that bitch who destroyed my sister."

"Like you're so innocent?" Indi snapped. "At least I didn't bang some douchebag soccer player over the summer. Camp counsellors boning in bushes. So pathetically basic."

The color drained from Cam's face. Her eyes widened. "What did you say?"

"You heard me. Camp is dumb," Indi snapped.

Cam frowned. "Not that. You remember ... what I did?"

The neurons in Indi's brains sparked like fireworks. "Holy shit. I do remember." She shrieked excitedly. "I remember that!" But soon the euphoria slipped away. "You cheated on me. That's why we broke up. That was the fight everyone saw. I remember."

Cam shook her head firmly. "How many times do we need to go over this India? Just because we dry hump sometimes during study breaks doesn't make us Ellen and Portia. I'm not like Cody, okay? I don't want to be out, living loud. You and me, it was never a serious thing."

Indi tried to breathe through the slicing pain in her heart. "It was for me. You're all I've wanted since I woke up on that beach. Doesn't that mean anything to you?"

"You hated me for three months Indi. You started over, and so did I. You might not remember that, but I do. We were different things to each other and, if I regret anything, it's crossing that line and losing my friend. I can't be what you want." Cam exhaled. "I don't want to be what you want."

Indi hated that Cam made sense. She thought nothing would hurt more than her broken body did when she washed up, but this was worse. It was bottomless, throbbing pain, hands cracking open her lungs and squeezing her heart. There was no blood and no bruises, but Indi could still feel the scars forming on her skin.

"Then I regret it too because I can't look at you in any other way." She exhaled. "I'm going to head out." It was the only thing she could think of to avoid bursting into tears and running away. She spun on her heels and pulled open the door, but a swatch of green from Cam's closet caught her eye. She recognized it straight away, the crisp blazer with its familiar emblem that Indi had seen somewhere else recently.

Cam followed her stare. "What. My uniform? Mom bought it yesterday."

"St. Margaret's?" Indi asked.

Cam cocked an eyebrow. "Yeah. You know it?"

"Not by choice." She gave Cam a last glance over her shoulder. "Bye."

Indi left quietly, avoiding the living room where the Gibb family had gathered to watch TV, and she was careful not to let the front door click too loudly when she slipped out. She talked the cops parked outside into taking her home and employed the same stealthy maneuvers to get into her own house unseen. She wasn't in the mood for her mom's condescending sympathy or her dad's coddling. She just wanted her bed, her pillow and a starless sky to stare at blindly while she cried herself to sleep.

20

INDI STIRRED AS HER phone vibrated in her pocket. Her eyes flickered open to the moonlight streaming through the iron bars on her window, painting flower shadows on the pale wall. Her door was open a crack, her boots neatly on the floor side by side, her duvet draped over her fully dressed body. Her parents had come in to check on her, most likely. Indi was grateful that slumber had saved her a conversation with either of them. The phone vibrated again, reminding Indi of what had woken her. She fumbled in her jeans before wrestling the phone free and awkwardly dragging it up to her ear.

"Hello."

"India," Elton's voice was low. "It's happened again. She's dead."

Indi shut her eyes tight, then sprung them open, hoping that would shake the haze of sleep. "Sadie?"

"No." His breathing was all Indi heard for what felt like forever. "Rory. Someone killed Rory."

Indi wasn't sure why her first guess had been Sadie. Maybe that was who she secretly wished it to be. It didn't seem real for it to be Rory. Unlike Brandy and Avery, who had as many enemies as they did friends, Rory was one of the good guys. She was dealing with the usual teenage bullshit that brought out the asshole in her sometimes, but even then it was in micro doses. Elton said someone had killed her, but Indi couldn't help but wonder if she might have taken matters into her own hands. Her boyfriend had just died horribly and, with the pain that girl had swelling inside of her, it wouldn't surprise Indi in the slightest if that sadness had swallowed her up and forced her into a frightening choice.

"Are you sure? I mean that it was her? That it was murder?" Indi thought she heard him sob.

"I need you," he said.

Indi checked the time on her phone. It was just after one a.m. "I can't sneak out. My parents have got me on lockdown."

"I think you could if you wanted to. I'll meet you down the street. Fifteen minutes."

"Wait. What?" The call ended before Indi could get a response.

She clenched her jaw and slammed her phone on the bed. Rory. Shit. She and Elton were close, so Indi could understand why he was so distraught. When Indi had needed Elton to be there for her he was, without question. Now he was asking for her to do the same for him. No. Things were getting insane; there was no way she was going to disobey her parents and sneak out to meet him. How could she, anyway? Maybe through the window in the internal garage? Indi's dad hadn't got around to fixing the sensor light in the backyard, and if she was quiet enough she could probably get across the lawn and jump the neighbor's fence unnoticed. But would anything she did make a difference? The Squad was nearing its end. Once upon a time Indi would have never included herself in their numbers, but shit was way different now. Cam had confirmed everything Indi had struggled to convince herself wasn't true. Indi and Brandy had reunited. Indi and Cam were over. Kids were dead. The world was a sick, evil place.

Indi rolled onto her side and pulled her duvet up to her neck. Common sense dictated that she not go running around in the middle of the night when her classmates were dropping like flies. But Elton never asked for much. He had been there in the tunnel, and on the beach, and had the only semblance of sanity when everyone else was losing their mind. He was one of the few people who had never asked if she killed Brandy. Indi rolled her tongue over her teeth. Fuck it.

She crawled out of bed, swapped her leather jacket for a plain black hoodie and stuffed her phone back in her pocket. She could hear her dad snoring as she crept past her parents' bedroom. She peered over the railing, looking for a flash of light from the TV downstairs that might suggest someone was awake. But it was dark down there, making Indi's decision to sneak out easier. She might have hesitated if her dad was on the couch or her mom was stress-eating by the pantry. She tiptoed down the stairs, wincing with every bellowing creak. Indi released a tightly held breath when she reached the bottom, then hurried to the garage. The stiff window took a good thump to open, and when Indi's ass caught on the frame she felt like Winnie the Pooh stuck in the honey pot. She quietly shimmied herself free before landing with an ungraceful thud on the cold grass. A quick dash across the lawn saw her find the shadows of the neighbor's trees that hung over their yard, pissing her dad when they shed their leaves every fall. The fence was easy to scale, even for someone with Indi's crap athleticism. She swung one leg over, then the other, and soon she was completely out of sight of her parents' bedroom window and the cops parked outside her house.

Elton's BMW sat partly illuminated in the sallow glow of the streetlights, framed by the pitch-black night. When Indi emerged from the shadows his brown eyes found her quickly. He leaned over to the passenger door and pushed it open, and Indi burnt the last of her speed, diving into the front seat. She accidentally kicked a couple of beer cans on the floor and noticed the emo ballad wafting from the speakers. She heard a crunch and turned to see Elton crushing another can and wiping his lips on the back of his hand. He tossed the can into the back seat.

Indi had never seen him look so tired. Without their usual coating of product, his curly waves sat frizzy and unkempt, the luminescence of his dark skin lost beneath a fine layer of tears, and his eyes, puffy and red, conveyed a sadness that had Indi unnerved. He looked beautiful, as strange as that sounded, more beautiful than she had ever seen him. Indi shrugged off the urge to kiss him and silently admonished herself for being a pathetic rebound cliché. Her heart was as messed up as her head.

"Thanks for coming," he said. The six-pack on his lap had dwindled to three. He jerked one loose, pulled the tab, then took a long swig. Indi watched his throat throb with each gulp. "I just can't deal. What could Rory possibly have done to deserve this?"

Elton's words mirrored exactly what Indi had been pondering herself. "What happened?" she asked.

Elton took off the handbrake and slipped the car into drive. "We're going to find that out right now."

"How?" Indi chuckled lightly, but knew that he wasn't joking.

"They found her body on the track at school, so that's where I'm going. I want to see what this son of a bitch did to her."

Indi gripped his hand on top of the gear stick. "That's not a good idea. That shit will stay with you, Elton. You don't want to see it." Brandy's shriveled hands and nibbled fingertips seared Indi's mind. She blinked the image away. "We can just sit for a while and talk, maybe?"

Elton bit his lip, his eyes glassing over. "No. I need to see." He stepped on the gas and the car screeched along the street, shifting between patches of streetlight and darkness. Indi scowled her disapproval at the racket. If she got caught in Elton's car in the middle of the night surrounded by empty beer cans, she could kiss goodbye to any idea of freedom during her remaining teenage years.

He pulled a hard left, thankfully avoiding her street and the cops outside her house. His face was set with purpose. His eyes fixed on the road. The veins in his forearm tensed every time he roughly threw the car into gear, and his knuckles flexed as he squeezed the steering wheel.

"This is my fault," he muttered, pushing down on the gas pedal.

"Of course it isn't," Indi said firmly. "There is a psychopath on the loose, and that has nothing to do with you."

"I dropped her off at the track," Elton said through gritted teeth. "She wanted to train and needed a ride, so I dropped her off and then I left. I should have stayed. Why didn't I stay?"

"You couldn't know what would happen," Indi said. "There is no reason for any of this. You can't blame yourself."

"Well I do," he snapped. He buried his foot on the gas pedal. The car was moving so fast that it was barely touching the ground. Indi felt as if she were flying, her stomach churning with a nervous flutter, like being flipped upside down in a roller coaster. She gripped the door and leaned back into her seat, hoping the seat belt would stop her from going through the windshield if they crashed. Indi didn't want to die like that, death being a subject that was prominent in her thoughts of late.

When Army Bay High came into view, Indi expelled a sigh of relief. The flashing LED sign read: Our thoughts and prayers are with the family of Avery Weiss. Rest in Peace. It was cruelly obscene that this message would need to be updated in the morning.

Indi could make out flashing red and blue lights at the back of the school where the field and racetrack were. Elton immediately hit the brakes, slowing the car to a quiet roll. A dozen squad cars were scattered in the carpark, and an ambulance was stationed on the grass. Officers with flashlights stalked the grounds while paramedics and men in dull, grey suits came in and out of a blue tent erected by the stands.

Elton's lip trembled when he caught sight of that tent. "She's in there, isn't she?"

Indi didn't answer. She had no idea how recently this had all happened, but it seemed Rory's body was still there. "I think we should go. We could get in a lot of trouble if they find us here."

Suddenly the flaps of the tent snapped open. A stretcher emerged, a paramedic at each end, and carefully they steered it toward the ambulance. Beneath a stark white sheet, Indi could make out every haunting detail of Rory's body. Her head, her shoulders, the tips of her feet. She was growing numb to the sight of death. It was a constant in her life now.

The officers dismantled the tent and the cars dispersed one by one.

"Come on," Elton said, his eyes following the ambulance as it pulled out of the field.

"Come where?" Indi asked, startled. It wasn't really a question. She hoped her shock would help Elton realize what a terrible idea it was to leave the car and enter a crime scene.

"They might have missed something," he continued. "Stay here if you want then."

Before tonight, it had been Indi fearlessly throwing herself at anything that might help her remember, anything that might expose the killer lurking in Army Bay. But the memories of Cam's betrayal and the callousness of her words had dampened the fire inside Indi, and there was a suffocating sense of helplessness as the number of bodies started to stack up. Indi was no closer to discovering who was responsible. Suspects were being re-classed as victims at a terrifying pace. Now was not the time for her to feel sorry for herself. Not if she wanted to avoid the grim fate of a blue tent and a white sheet.

"Wait," she said, her voice catching like a hiccup. Elton paused and looked back at her. "I'm coming."

He nodded and climbed out, then walked to her side and opened her door. The morning wind was bracing and left tiny prickles of cold on Indi's skin. It was an unsettling cold, the kind you felt in your bones, that numbed your ears, so everything sounded like echoes in a bottomless cave. They crossed the carpark and approached the spot where the tent had stood. Indi was relieved to see there was no blood. The thought had crossed her mind, and she wasn't sure if she could stomach the idea of Rory dying in a gruesome, slasher film way.

Elton dropped to one knee and strained his eyes, scanning the ground. "What happened to her?" he mumbled. He spoke to the wind. "What did they do to you, Rory?"

Indi looked too, but they had scrubbed the area clean. Soon, kids would run the 200 meters here again. Her eyes swept over the field and glimpsed the long-jump pit before taking in the empty stands and the hundreds of seats.

"God, this is boring," Brandy sighed. She lifted her long legs and rested her feet on the row of seats in front, causing her cute, pink tennis skirt to rise even higher up her thighs. She nudged her rose-tinted glasses to the edge of her nose and stared at the racetrack. "If I wasn't desperate to go to this concert tonight, I'd have bailed ages ago."

Indi knocked her shoulder. "Don't be like that. Maybe try to pretend you're a supportive friend."

"Hey, I do!" Brandy whined, taking exception. Then she grinned. "To her face. How long have we been here?"

"Like, half an hour," Indi replied. She angled Rory's phone to make sure she wasn't missing a thing, even zoomed in when Rory was on the far side of the track.

Brandy peered over at the screen and rolled her eyes. "She is so extra about this stuff. What's she going to do, just watch herself run?"

"It's so she can analyze her form," Indi stated. "It's actually a good idea."

Brandy inched closer to Indi's cheek with her eyes crossed and her tongue poked out. Indi ignored her at first, but eventually caved when Brandy blew a raspberry at her ear.

"Gross," she half laughed, half groaned, while wiping Brandy's spritz of saliva on the shoulder of her jacket. "You're a child, do you know that?" Before Brandy could answer, Indi's attention switched to a broad silhouette crossing the field, a backpack flung over one shoulder, brown waves of hair swept back by a barely there breeze. "Ben's coming."

"Yeah, I invited him to the concert." Brandy pushed up her glasses and turned her head, no doubt trying to avoid Indi's glare and imminent freak-out.

"I thought you two were over," Indi snapped. "You know, on account of him being a complete psycho."

"It's not as easy as that," Brandy sighed. "We've got history, plus he's ridiculously hot. Not as hot as Elton, but I'm not getting anywhere with his frigid ass. His loss."

Indi exhaled and drooped her shoulders, shaking her head with disapproval. "I thought you were seeing someone else anyway?"

"I'm always seeing someone else," Brandy giggled. "It's my brand."

"I thought this someone else was different, though. I think you used the word special?"

Brandy blushed, an unusual color for her. She slapped Indi's leg as Ben came closer. "Shut-up. I'll tell you more later."

Indi glanced at the screen and saw that Rory had completed the track. Now she was sitting with legs splayed on the terracotta-colored concrete stretching out her calves. Indi hit Stop on the camera and tucked it into her bag.

"Hey," Ben said, standing over them. He cupped the side of Brandy's face and kissed her. "You look beautiful."

Brandy tugged on his thin maroon shirt. "Thanks. Are you looking forward to tonight?"

"Yeah, for sure," Ben replied. "We waiting on Rory?"

Brandy nodded and raised her arms. Ben lifted her in the air and kissed her, his hands sweeping under the curve of her backside.

Indi cringed. "That'll be enough soft-core porn for the afternoon."

Brandy laughed and pecked affectionately at Indi's cheek. "I'll pick you up in an hour."

"Cool. I'll meet you at the door."

"Nah, it's okay. Take your time. I'll come in and wait."

"Okay. Whatever." Indi slipped past Brandy and Ben as they continued to dry hump each other in the stands.

"See you soon, bestie," Brandy called when she came up for air.

Indi waved a hand behind her as she headed down to the racetrack to return Rory's phone.

INDI GASPED, HER LEGS quivering like the reeds on Breakers Beach. The memory sunk in, the seams of its edges blending into the puzzle until it was whole. Was there a chance? She stared harder at the stands, at the spot where she and Brandy had sat in her memory. Indi ambled at first, skeptical of the possibility she could be right. But her pace quickened as the idea gained momentum in her mind until, eventually, Indi was running. She didn't believe it at first, accustomed to life not giving a shit about her and refusing to help. She even rubbed her eyes like a kid on Christmas morning to be sure it was real. Rory's phone was propped up on the seat and still recording.

"What is it? Did you find something?" Elton jogged up the stairs to stand behind Indi, looking over her shoulder. "Is that? ... she didn't. ... of course she did. Rory always recorded her runs." Indi felt his heated breaths on her neck, and he stood close enough that his muscular chest pressed against her back. "Do you think it might have recorded the killer?" Elton asked.

Indi was shivering but couldn't be sure of the cause. Rory's murder, the wintry morning air, the sweet, musky smell of Elton's skin. She eyed the phone as if it were a ticking bomb. "Only one way to find out."

Indi swallowed her nerves. She picked it up and slowly turned the screen, reluctant to see whatever the camera had captured. She hit Stop, then swiped back through the recording until she was at the beginning. It started with Rory up close, lining up her phone to get the best aspect of her run. She wore her hair slicked back tight and had little heart-shaped studs in her ears. Something was missing from Rory's turned down eyes with none of her brightness shining through and, with every random twitch of her bottom lip, Indi thought she might burst into tears.

When Rory had set the camera she jogged down the stairs, showing her baggy grey sweats and pink trainers. She ran one loop, then another, and two more after that. Apart from Rory, the track was empty and silent, no company but a half-moon in a bleak sky.

Indi's heart thumped hard against her ribs, anxiety swelling in her gut. It was the waiting that was terrifying—watching Rory go through her simple routine, living her normality and knowing that at any moment someone would appear and rip that away from her. Then Rory's pace slowed to a jog, then to a walk. Her gaze shifted toward the tunnel where the blue tent had been erected earlier. She was yelling something the phone couldn't capture, her voice muffled by the distance. She crossed the track and Indi noted Rory was smiling politely, like you would if a kind-looking stranger asked you for directions. She walked out of shot and she never came back. Indi swiped through the timestamps, then paused when a security guard wandered into view, rhythmically tapping his torch on his thigh while his mouth percussed a drum solo. Then he froze, his torch falling to the ground, and the next few seconds showed him frantically wrestling his walkie talkie from the clip on his belt and yelling at someone on the other end to call the police. The squad cars arrived not long after that.

"Did the killer know she was recording?" Elton said, a woeful timbre to his voice.

"How could they? Only we know she does that. Unless they had been watching her, maybe saw her put the phone up here?"

Elton leaned over her shoulder and started swiping the phone himself, holding Indi by the waist with his other hand for a reason that eluded her. She didn't stop him though.

"There's no one coming or going," he said in frustration. Then he stopped and pincered his fingers on the screen to zoom in. "Look, is that a car? Parked by the fence."

Indi strained her eyes. "Yeah. An old sedan. Grey." Her breath caught in her throat.

"That's gotta be the guy's car," Elton said firmly. "We have to take this to the police. They could run the plates or whatever bullshit they do."

A cog turned in Indi's mind, and her shoulders sagged when some uninvited truths clicked into place. She looked at her hands holding the phone and Elton's finger skimming the screen. "We can't," she snapped.

He furrowed his brow. "What do you mean? We have to. This is Rory we're talking about."

"Elton, who's at the top of the Army Bay PD's suspect list right now? They think you and me are involved and the fact that we're still alive while everyone else is getting picked off isn't helping. And now what? We show up with a phone covered in our fingerprints and tell them we found it at a crime scene we shouldn't have been at? We might as well tell them about Avery's house while we're at it."

Elton exhaled deeply and rubbed the back of his neck. "So what do we do then?"

Indi turned to face him. "We get out of here and don't tell them shit. They need someone to pin this on, and they're going to stop caring if we're innocent soon, and even if they believe us, they can't protect us. Brandy, Avery and Rory are proof of that. We need to protect ourselves."

He crossed his arms. "So you believe it wasn't me then?"

She studied his face. His eyes were dark, almost black, and they stared with unflinching intensity. "I believe you. What about me? Do you think I killed them?"

His fingertips trailed down her arm, his knuckles brushing over her fingers. "No. I don't." A weight lifted from her shoulders and a smile blossomed on her mouth. It was nice hearing someone say that. He narrowed his eyes. "Sadie. Ben."

"You mean Roid Rage and the Uber Bitch?" Her face twitched just thinking about them. "If they're not behind all this, then they're probably next." She shivered against a whip of cold air. "Let's get out of here. Don't murderers like to return to the scene of the crime?"

Elton chuckled. It was the first time his lips had turned upward since Indi had caught sight of him beneath the glow of the streetlights. "You've been watching too much SVU," he said.

"Our lives are SVU."

"Come on. I'll take you home. At least I'll get to watch your terrible vault over the fence again."

She gritted her teeth and slapped his chest, partly for effect but also as an excuse to touch him. "Hey," she said, her tone softening. "I'm really sorry about Rory."

He nodded and gave half a smile, his chin dipping, then he turned and jogged down the stairs.

Indi subtly looked at the phone one last time, swiping back to the car parked by the fence and zooming in. She didn't want to say anything to Elton, knowing he would drive immediately to the police station and throw accusations around. It was information she would keep to herself, at least for now, until she knew what to do with it. Indi knew precisely who the car belonged to. It was Detective Braddock's.

21

INDI SAT AT THE BREAKFAST bar, rolling a chorizo sausage around her plate with a fork. It was Saturday morning, and her dad always made a big breakfast before he headed out to play rugby in the afternoon. Sausage, bacon, eggs and hash browns. Pretty much everything cardiac doctors recommended you don't eat. Usually, it was a highlight at the end of the week for Indi. There was nothing as satisfying as binging Netflix for a couple of hours with a grease moustache and a loaded belly. But she wasn't feeling it today, for obvious reasons. Her dad had even gone out first thing and brought her back a mango smoothie from Amped. He watched her flick the straw unenthusiastically.

"Okay. What's wrong? I'm pretty sure you not knocking back that smoothie is a sign of the apocalypse."

Indi frowned at him, hoping that she was adequately conveying what a stupid question that was. He immediately retracted.

"Sorry. I don't know why I even asked that. That poor girl."

"You mean the one you put bars on my window to protect me from?" Indi snipped.

Nathan barreled his chest defensively. "How could I have known something like that would have happened? That's a rough thing to say, girl."

Indi would not apologize. She didn't blame Nathan directly for Rory's death, but her thoughts dwelled on how much pain Rory was in when she had last seen her. Avery's death had crushed her, in body and in spirit, and had sent her spiraling down into her sadness. Indi wasn't mad at Rory for attacking her that night. She understood that grief made people do messed up stuff sometimes. But if Nathan hadn't freaked out and called the cops maybe Rory would have calmed down and found just a scrap of peace. If she had been made welcome in the Peters' house, perhaps a darkened racetrack wouldn't have been the only place that comforted her. It was all hypothetical, probably just wishful fantasies. She might be dead anyway. Still, Indi felt bitter that her father had added to Rory's misery when he kicked her out that night.

As if on cue the morning news update rolled onto the TV. Promising Student-Athlete Strangled to Death at Local High School.

Rory's death would hit Army Bay hard. A weird thing to say, considering she wasn't the only dead kid in town. The sobering difference was that people had liked Rory. She was kind, smart, funny, and cute as a button. With Brandy now a favorite of murder porn enthusiasts, and Avery becoming the poster boy for white privilege, Indi continued to struggle with why someone like Rory had latched on to them. Maybe it was as basic as marrying Avery and his money and living out an idyllic, boring life with a six-car garage and a live-in-nanny, who he would no doubt screw one day. As for Brandy, well, she was gravity, plain and simple, pulling you in whether or not you liked it. Indi had been one of those people, staring at the sun even though it stung. Did that make her a bad person, wanting to be close to something that shone so brightly? And, apparently, Indi had run straight back, even after being burned. Tiny sparks of memory were igniting, but the reason behind her reunion with Brandy was still lost in the fragmented corners of her mind.

With each flashback Indi's conviction wavered, and she wondered what she wanted to know more. Who had tried to kill her? Or why she had forgiven Brandy? Her thoughts drifted to a pair of blue eyes locked with fear and blonde hair weaving through the black water. A knock at the door startled her, and she scraped her fork loudly against the plate.

"You alright?" her dad asked. Indi spared him a fleeting glance, but said nothing.

Her mom skipped down the stairs, her head tilted to the side while she put on some dangly earrings. There was a second knock, and her mom looked at the door then at her dad and Indi, motionless in the kitchen.

She frowned. "No one get up, I'll get it."

She marched to the door and pulled it open. Indi overheard polite banter before the door shut and her mom staggered into the room, struggling with the weight of a large box in her hands.

Her dad abandoned his plate and went to help her, picking it up himself. "Woah," he grunted. "What's this?"

"It's addressed to Indi," her mom said, inspecting the label.

His eyes narrowed suspiciously. "Were you expecting something? Maybe we should get the cops outside to look at this."

Indi quietly agreed. She had never watched the movie Seven, but thanks to the Internet, she was very familiar with the What's in the Box scenario.

Her mom found another label on the back. "It says it's from Christa Gibbs."

Indi dragged herself from her seat and wandered over to the pair of them without the slightest sense of urgency. Her dad placed the box on the floor and Indi dropped onto her knees, pulling off the strips of masking tape until the lid sprung open. She waded through the pool of environmentally unfriendly peanuts until she felt something rock solid and thankfully not oozing. It was heavy, and when she had it in both hands, she yanked it free.

"Christa's carving," Indi said matter-of-factly. "She makes them in therapy." Indi peeked deeper into the box. "Looks like there's a few more in here." A note was amongst them.

Dear, India. For your mom. See my PayPal below.

Indi awkwardly grit her teeth. "Oh. Right. I told her you might buy some for your house dressings."

Her mom snatched the letter; her eyes bulging when she saw the price. "Really? For some wavy rocks?"

"It's fine," her dad said, taking the note from her hand. He winked at Indi. "I'll pay for them." Indi ignored his attempt at groveling.

Her mom sighed. "I guess I can use them. I have some open houses this weekend. You know maybe I could put little price tags on, make some money on them."

"Whatever," Indi said, groaning as she stood from her knees. "I'm going to my room."

"You're not coming to watch my game?" her dad asked with hopeful eyes. "I thought we could get some hotdogs afterward, maybe catch a movie."

Right. That was something she used to do. "No thanks," Indi replied coldly.

"Oh, there was this too," her mom said. She pulled a crumpled brown package from her blazer pocket and handed it over. "There're no stamps or anything; someone must have just put it on the doorstep."

"That one is definitely going to the police for checking," her dad said sternly.

Indi wasn't as concerned as she had been about the box. This package was far less head-sized, though it could probably fit a small foot. This is where her mind was going nowadays. For India. From Elton, was scrawled across the front. Indi clutched it to her chest. "It's fine. It's from a friend. I'll see you guys later."

She walked past them, crossing the foyer to the stairs and using the balustrade to tow herself up a step at a time. Indi already had the package torn open by the time she reached her room. She closed the bedroom door behind her and pulled out a small mobile phone that looked like a burner. She clicked the home button and the screen lit up, showing that it was fully charged with a text message waiting. Indi wasted no time reading it.

Hey. It's Elton. Thought it would be a good idea to use burners. Like you said the cops are watching us so if we're going full Sherlock Holmes probs best not to leave any tracks. Can I c u tonight? 1 a.m.? I'll pick u up same place. Please continue to b terrible at fence jumping. I need something to look forward to.

The goofy smile swept over her face before she could stop it. Cam was all she had wanted for the longest time, but her bitchery had made it easy to allow someone else to fill that vacant space. She tried to text back something creative and intriguing, but instead, she typed Okay. See you then. And hit Send. After muttering into her pillow for around twelve minutes, lamenting over what a lame-o she was, Indi drew the curtains over her barred window and buried herself beneath her covers. If she was going to be sneaking out, defying her parents and risking her life at one in the morning, she could probably use a nap.

WHEN INDI'S MOM CAME to check on her at nine, she pretended she was only just getting ready for bed. Her mother had got all four of the stone statues into houses she was showing and was raving about what a good person she was for aiding Christa's therapy. She kissed Indi's cheek, sang I love you, then pottered off to her bedroom. Her dad didn't come in at all.

Indi lay fully dressed under her duvet, staring blankly at the ceiling with the burner phone clasped in her hand. All she could think about was one a.m. and seeing Elton again. He was taking up valuable real estate in her head. The phone vibrated at 12:45. Indi's movements played out in super slow-mo, creeping from her room, slinking down the stairs, worming through the garage. She weaved in and out of the slants of moonlight and reached for the window. Locked. Okay. She looked closer at the latches; they just needed to be unhinged. But no. She scowled when she saw brand-new deadbolts had been installed.

"Fuck," Indi hissed under her breath. When did her dad have deadbolts put in? There was no other way out. The doors were all locked. The garage door would be far too loud. She looked at the sheet of grubby glass that stood between her and freedom. Then she remembered last summer when a single pebble flung up from the lawnmower had shattered the window completely. It was thin and cheap, and her dad had replaced it with something similarly thin and cheap. Indi knew that because her mom had bitched all week that she had wanted double-glazed and frosted. After the initial disappointment that she wasn't talking about donuts, Indi had decided that adult problems were totally mundane.

Was she actually going to do this? Indi grabbed an oil rag from her dad's tool bench and wrapped it around her elbow. Then she clenched her jaw, closed her eyes and shoved her elbow through the glass. It shattered almost silently, no worse than dropping a handful of pins on the floor. She used the rag to clear the tiny shards from the frame, then climbed through. When she fell out the other side, she stood up with a few scratches on her shoulders and arms, but apart from that it was a clean getaway. Indi had to admit she was getting good at this. She hunched over and scurried across the lawn, and this time when she reached the fence she gracefully swept a leg over and landed with a spin. She saw Elton smile in his car across the street. Who knew he could be this damned charming?

He pulled a crawling U-turn, so she didn't have to cross the street. That was chivalry from a teenage boy. Indi climbed in and noticed the lack of empty beer cans. "No binge drinking then?"

"Only Monday through Thursday," he replied.

Indi laughed. "So where we headed?"

"Maybe the field near Swanson Street. It's right beside a creek that's kind of nice. You know the one?"

Indi knew precisely where he meant. It was the same park where her dad played rugby on Saturdays, but that wasn't what caught her attention. "Are we parking?"

Elton gulped, suddenly nervous. "No, of course not. I just thought we could talk more about stuff. Shit, it does sound like parking, doesn't it?"

"I'm kidding," Indi said in the fakest giggle she could conjure. She wasn't kidding.

"I've found out some stuff about Rory. It might help us figure things out."

Indi wiped the smile from her face and gave herself an inner slap. She had to stop being such a horny idiot and focus. Elton was here to swap information. Period. Whatever she was feeling wasn't even slightly on his radar. "Yeah," she said. "Field sounds good."

Elton drove a short way across town, avoiding as many intersections and main roads as he could on the off chance that they crossed the path of a patrolling squad car. There was a curfew after all. They pulled up at the field, the car's headlights brightly probing the green turf. As soon as Elton clicked them off darkness blanketed them, but in the distance Indi made out a hazy yellow glow over the public restrooms, sallow and clouded by a swarm of moths.

She wriggled to get comfortable, angling herself toward Elton. "So, what're the details?"

"I spoke to Rory's mom yesterday. She invited me over. Rory had some of my textbooks in her room and she wanted to give them back." Elton's voice drifted off. "They're burying her next week." Indi's throat felt dry as she tried to think of something to say, but Elton carried on, not missing a beat. "She was talking about Franklin University. You know Franklin, right? Well, it's where Rory applied to. She was going for their athletic scholarship, and she should have been a shoo-in, right? Star student, star athlete, ticks the diversity card, home run, yeah. Well, guess what?"

"She didn't get in," Indi finished.

Elton cocked an eyebrow. "Yeah. Did you already know?"

"She told me in Seradale. You know, the day someone practiced the Heimlich on my neck."

"She told you?" Elton didn't seem willing to believe. "Why would she tell you and not me?"

Indi shrugged. "She just blurted it out. She was mad though. I was giving her shit about Avery, and she blew up."

Elton nodded, slowly coming around. "Okay. Well, did you know Brandy got the scholarship? Rory's mom found her bawling in her room a couple of nights before you got ... before Brandy disappeared. Apparently Brandy was bragging about it. Can you believe that shit?"

Indi appreciated how Elton always tried to avoid mentioning what had happened to her. It wasn't necessary though. She recalled the night at Brandy's house and the letter she had found in her room. A few weeks ago she would have been wary of sharing information, too fearful of squandering any insurance policies she might unwittingly have, or attracting the attention of her attacker. But not with Elton. She trusted him. The idea tasted strange in her mouth.

"I know. I found the acceptance letter in Brandy's room," Indi revealed. "Full athletic scholarship. In track."

Elton's jaw gaped. "Brandy never ran a day in her life. She still had to sit an entry exam though, right? How did she pass?"

All Indi had to do was raise a knowing eyebrow and Elton figured the rest out himself.

"Sadie? She took the exam?" He slumped in his seat. "No way."

"I saw something else while I was in her room that didn't make sense. It was a blazer for St. Margaret's girls' school in Seradale. I've seen a few of them lately. Can you think of why she would have one?"

Elton thought for a moment but came back with a shrug. "I don't know anyone who goes there, and it doesn't make sense for Brandy to transfer when the year's almost over."

"Maybe she knew someone who goes there," Indi speculated.

"Seradale's not that far away. I mean, maybe she did." He gripped his hair by the roots. "Damn, this is frustrating. We need to talk to Ben and Sadie."

Indi shook her head firmly. "Have you forgotten that they could be the ones behind all this?"

"Why would Sadie kill her sister? Why would Ben kill his girlfriend? They both loved her."

Indi snorted mockingly. "They also love each other lately. I saw them in Miss Mathis' office." Indi squirmed, and Elton leaned in, hanging on her next words. "They were having sex."

Elton blushed. "Oh. That's messed up. Doesn't make them killers though."

"You obviously don't watch the True Crime channel. Ever heard of a crime of passion?"

"Okay fine. But why Avery?" He exhaled. "Why Rory?"

Rory. She was the game-changer. She didn't deserve to be in the same basket as the others. "Wait," Indi muttered, knitting her eyebrows. "We keep saying Rory had no enemies, why she doesn't fit with Brandy and Avery. What about me? Where do I fit in all of this?"

Elton leaned sideways into the headrest, his gaze warm, his half-smile empathetic. "I've been thinking about that too. I don't know. I didn't really know you that well before all of this."

It was an epiphany that Indi couldn't believe had taken her this long to realize. Maybe she hadn't pissed someone. What if, instead, she knew something she wasn't supposed to? What if they all did? It was the only thing that made sense, the only way she and the others could be connected that didn't come down to a shared enemy. Indi had always maintained she wasn't significant enough to murder, she was just an awkward bi stoner trying to make it through high school. Her mind had a second of reprieve. Stoner. What she wouldn't give for a joint right now. Not likely. As well as still being a person of interest in Avery's murder, Micah was currently in juvenile detention, and Indi wasn't interested in expanding her circle of drug dealer friends to score.

"Have you spoken to Paula lately?" Indi asked, segueing to Micah's younger sister.

"Only what I've seen on Insta and Snapchat. It's pretty messed up." Elton lifted his pelvis and fumbled his phone out of his pocket, and Indi savored a glimpse of dark, smooth skin. He opened Instagram and showed her Paula's profile. Rows and rows of photoshopped pictures of Brandy, some with her eyes scratched out, most scribbled with You deserved it bitch. Her most recent post was a shot of her and Micah smiling, sitting on a dune at Breakers Beach, with the hashtag #MicahIsInnocent. Considering Paula had done her best to distance herself from her brother's criminal activity, it gave Indi some hope in the human race that she was there for him when he needed it most.

"Brandy and Paula never got on," Elton said. "Always competing to be supreme bitch leader of Army Bay High. But when they found all those pills around Avery and traced them back to Micah, Paula lost it. Something went down before Brandy died though. I don't know what, and to be honest, at the time I didn't care. Probably just more schoolgirl bullshit. Still, Paula was pissed."

"I TWEETED THAT MONTHS ago, it's not my fault someone screenshotted it," Brandy groaned.

Indi leaned against the bathroom stall while Brandy fidgeted loudly inside. "Why don't you just talk to Paula, then? Is it worth all this drama?"

The toilet flushed, and the door flew open, and Brandy handed Indi the smoldering roach.

Indi frowned. "Gee, thanks for saving me some."

Brandy laughed and blew a waft of smoke in Indi's face. "Suck that in." She stumbled to the cloudy mirror and began fixing her hair, which was unnecessary.

Indi put the roach to her lips and inhaled, the embers singeing her fingertips. She winced and tossed what remained in the toilet bowl. "I'm staying neutral," Indi said, holding the smoke in her lungs. "I don't want Micah to get pissed at me. He gives me a discount because Paula thinks I'm cute."

Brandy retrieved a stick of red lipstick from her bag and carefully painted her plump lips. "You think I want that either? We all buy our shit from Micah."

"Then say sorry," Indi insisted. "I thought you were trying to be a better person. That was the deal, remember. That's why you need me?"

Brandy smacked her lips together and smiled at Indi in the mirror. "I need you because you're the only decent person in this whole town." She turned and leaned on the edge of the basin. "But I'm a shit person, India. I've done some seriously heinous things. You think one apology is going to scrub all that away?"

Indi finally exhaled, and her body melted like ice-cream on hot pavement. "Well, this would be a good start."

Brandy stumbled forward and wrapped her arms around Indi's shoulders. "I fucking love you."

Indi sighed and hugged her back. "I love you too. Now let's go before that beefy security guard comes back whose been following us around the mall since we got here."

"SHE TWEETED PAULA WAS white trash," Indi said absently, stirring from the memory. They were returning to her now in quick succession. "Posted some pictures of her house on Baker Street and an article on her dad getting arrested for those burglaries a few years back."

"I remember that," Elton said. He screwed up his face. "Who cares?"

Indi shook her head at Elton's obliviousness. "You don't know shit about teenage girls do you?"

"Most of them aren't worth knowing," he replied. He stared at Indi, his hand reaching out and curling her hair behind her ear. The motion shifted her fringe, exposing the deep, white scar across her forehead. Indi dropped her chin and tried to turn away, but Elton cupped her face and brought her eyes back to him. "I'm glad I'm getting to know you better now. Not the greatest time and place," he chuckled lightly. "But my timing has always been bad."

"I don't know," Indi hummed, leaning into his hand. "It feels pretty perfect to me."

Elton moved tentatively, and when he was close enough his tongue slid along his bottom lip just before he kissed her. His hand moved to her nape, and he held her with a tender confidence that sent Indi's blood racing. She kissed him harder, but he slowed her, pulling away only enough for breath to pass between them.

"Weren't we supposed to be investigating?" he whispered.

Indi forgot how talking worked for a second. "Huh?"

Elton laughed lightly, his lips brushing against hers. “Did you want to go and talk to Ben or Sadie?”

The names were sobering. “Right. Those two.” They fell away from each other and slumped in their respective chairs, but his salty taste lingered on Indi’s lips. “Can we start with Ben? Sadie scares the shit out of me, to be honest.”

“Sure. I’ll text him.” Elton grabbed his phone and began typing a message.

Indi scanned the field for nothing in particular, twiddling her thumbs while they waited for Ben to reply. Her eyes found the pallid light that flickered above the restroom, strange and eerie amongst its pitch-black surroundings. At first she thought it was just her eyes getting tired, that the chaos of life was making her see things. She blinked hard, then opened her eyes again. A dark silhouette stood by the restroom, only half its body within reach of the light, the rest obscured by the shadows. It didn’t move, not even when Indi was sure it could see her watching. It just watched back.

She shivered. “Elton. Do you see that?” His eyes were fixed on his phone. Indi nudged his chin with her finger, pointing him in the figure’s direction. “Do you see that?”

He turned, and the color drained from his face. “What is that? Is it a person?”

Indi felt as if her heart was going to pound right out of her chest. “I’m not really interested in sticking around to find out. Can we get out of here?”

Elton already had the keys turned in the ignition. The engine roared. He slung his arm over the passenger seat and swiveled his head, spinning the wheel frantically to reverse. Still the figure didn’t move. Elton sped through the carpark, his car’s axle slamming with a thud on the curb as the tires screeched through a hard turn. Still the figure didn’t move.

Elton’s phone beeped. “Check that. It could be Ben.”

Indi’s hands were shaking. She picked up the phone from the center console and opened the message. “It’s him.” She exhaled. “He’s at his dad’s beach house. He wants us to come over.”

Elton read her distress. “We don’t have to go.”

Indi shook her head. “I just want this to be over. It all started at that beach. Maybe we can finish it there.”

22

ELTON MANEUVERED THE tight bends in silence, his eyes set intently on the road while driving a little faster than Indi would have liked. It was still dark, the sort of inky blue between midnight and dawn. Even with the headlights on high beam they could barely see a few feet of road in front of them. The road markers zipped by almost hypnotically, vanishing beneath the hood as if the car was gobbling them up.

On the opposite side of Breakers Beach stood several houses, abandoned in the winter. As the road turned to gravel and Elton steered them closer, Indi saw only one house had lights on, with Ben's car sitting in its driveway. The house was rustic and minimal, a change from the modern predominance of boring glass boxes that overlooked the water. Sandy shoes sat by the door, and a swing seat on the porch creaked with each timid wisp of the breeze. Through the windows, with their frilly lace curtains, Indi saw a figure pacing. She had never wanted it to be Ben so much in her life. The figure turned when it heard the car rolling over the gravel. The door opened, and in the glow of an overhead light Indi saw Ben's face. She breathed a sigh of relief.

Elton stepped out and waved. Ben waved back and beckoned for them to come. Elton walked behind the car and popped the boot. Indi could hear him fumbling through the contents, banging and clanging, but the boot slammed shut soon enough and he was quickly at her door. He pulled it open and took her by the hands, lifting her to her feet.

"You're shaking," he said.

"I'm fine."

"Don't be scared." Elton lifted his shirt above the waistband of his jeans, the moonlight glinting upon the steel crowbar tucked into his belt. "No matter what happens in there, I'm not letting you get hurt again on this beach."

Indi rolled onto her tiptoes and kissed his cheek. "I'm getting surprisingly good at dodging death. Maybe I should be looking after you."

Indi reached into her pocket and retrieved her rape alarm, the last piece of her trusty anti-murder kit. "Here. It'll save your life one day. I guarantee it."

Elton eyed the item curiously as Indi slipped it into his pocket. "I didn't know we were at the gift exchange point of our relationship." He grinned and leaned down, pressing his forehead against hers.

"Jesus Christ, when did this happen?" Ben hollered from the door. "You coming in or what?" he called as he retreated back inside.

Elton gripped her hand and together they walked to the beach house, the worn stairs groaning as they arrived at the door. Ben lay sprawled on a couch, draped with a fuzzy tartan blanket. His feet rested on a nearby coffee table, the old wood barely visible beneath a scattering of crushed beer cans. A speaker was propped up amongst the mess, belting angry emo tunes. Indi glanced at the walls, their collection of generic beach prints mingled with family photos. Ben, his catalogue-model parents, and Jeff, the screw-up older brother.

"So, did I miss something?" Ben asked, knocking back another beer. "When did you two become a thing?" He offered Elton a can, and even though Indi hoped he would refuse it, Elton took the beer and pulled the tab.

"What does it matter, Campbell?"

Ben laughed and hung his arm over the back of the couch. "Just making conversation. You texted me, remember?" He took another swig and eyed Indi from head to toe. "Didn't mention she would be coming."

Indi squirmed under his gaze, crossing her arms and standing half behind Elton as if he were a shield.

"Does it matter that she's here?"

"Yeah. Kind of. I'm not sure we can trust her."

Their voices were hard and terse. Restrained for now, but Indi visualized their interaction as a long, lit fuse creeping at a snail's pace toward a barrel of gunpowder. Indi wasn't sure she wanted to be here when it all went boom.

"Of course we can trust her. She's a victim of all this too."

"But she knows who did it. She could end all this right now if she wanted to."

"She has a fucking name," Indi snapped, scorning the both of them. "And if I knew who did it, don't you think I would have said something by now? I can't remember, Ben."

He slurped at his can. "How convenient for you."

"All right, Campbell, enough," Elton growled. He put the beer on the coffee table without having taken a sip, and Indi was silently grateful. The last things they needed in this powder keg were two drunk alpha males. "What do you know? Are you hiding something?"

Ben rolled his tongue over his front teeth. "Nope. Not a thing. What about you, Riggs?"

"I've got nothing to do with any of this. I just don't want anyone else to get hurt, even an asshole like you. Not after what happened to Rory."

At last, there was empathy in Ben's eyes. He rubbed his stubbled chin, and that's when Indi noticed how unlike himself he appeared. His hair was shaggy, the darkness around his eyes hinting that he hadn't slept well for some time, and his gruff, patchy facial hair the telltale sign that he just didn't care anymore.

"I heard they're going to name the gym after her," he grunted. "They should burn the whole place down."

"What about Sadie?" Indi interjected. "Have you talked to her? Do you think she could know something? Maybe even be involved?" Indi didn't want to mention what she had seen in Miss Mathis' office. Informing Ben that she had watched him banging Sadie like a drum would not help anyone right now.

"Sadie?" Ben burst into laughter. "She's scared of her own shadow, and she loved Brandy. Do you honestly think Sadie is strong enough to string Avery up like that and strangle Rory to death? Sadie Hamilton?"

"She's not been that Sadie lately, not since Brandy disappeared," Indi remarked.

"How did you know Avery was strung up? That Rory was strangled?" Elton questioned.

"Oh screw you, Riggs. Don't try this entrapment bullshit. It's all over the news." Ben finished the last dregs of beer, crushed the can and tossed it with the others. He looked at Indi. "It wasn't Sadie, okay. She's too weak."

"Then we're back to you," Elton countered.

Ben rose to his feet, his solid frame not lost beneath a loose sweater and baggy jeans. It was odd not seeing him in a form-fitting tee and his football jacket, the uniform of the high-school-jock stereotype. Indi glanced back at the family photos, paying attention to one in particular. Jeff Campbell standing over a barbeque, tongs in hand, with his family seated at a picnic table in the background. He was wearing the same sweater Ben was wearing now, same color, same knit fabric, a fabric she had seen before. The blood-smeared sweater from Elton's car, the one that had made her accuse him of being a killer.

"Is that Jeff's?" she asked, pointing at the sweater. Judging by Ben's puzzled look, it couldn't have been a more random question.

"I don't know. Maybe. There's a bunch of clothes around here. I just threw on whatever I could find."

"Does Jeff have others like that?" Indi pressed.

"What the hell kind of questions are these? Jesus. If you two are the crack team who are going to tear this thing wide open, then a shitload more people are going to die while we wait."

Indi leaned into Elton's ear. "It's the same style of sweater as the one from your trunk. The one with the blood on the sleeve."

Elton thought for a moment, then took a closer look. He narrowed his eyes at Ben. "Where is Jeff lately? Didn't he get into trouble with Brandy?"

"Who didn't," Ben replied. "I don't know where Jeff is. I haven't seen him for almost a year."

"What would you say if I told you that a sweater just like the one you're wearing was in my car and covered with blood?"

Ben reached into his cooler and snagged another beer. He pulled the tab. "I'd say it sounds like you need to do some laundry," he laughed.

Indi rolled her eyes. "This isn't getting us anywhere. He's not confessing, and he's not dead. Those are the two things we came up here to check out."

"I'm going to outlive both of you," Ben said snidely. "And I'm going to track down that son of a bitch who killed Avery and Rory and rip out their throat."

"And Brandy," Indi amended. Ben shot her a bewildered sneer. "You forgot Brandy."

He shrugged with frustration. "Yes and Brandy, of course. What is your damage, India? I knew Brandy should never have fallen back in with you. You've been nothing but trouble. Look at the shit that's happened since that ginger cheated on you and you came crawling back to Brandy because you didn't want to hide in a bathroom stall to eat your lunch." He covered his mouth. "Oops. Spoiler," he squeaked mockingly. "Or did you not remember that part? That Cameron Gibbons cheated on you. I mean geez, what's the point of scraping the bottom of the barrel if it's not even faithful?"

Elton gritted his teeth and lunged forward, but Indi hooked his elbow before he could make ground. "Leave him," she grumbled. "He's drunk, which takes him from a fifty percent piece of shit to the full hundred. Let's just go. It's not him."

Elton stewed a little longer, his fists clenched. "See you later, Campbell. If you live that long." He turned to the door, gripping Indi's hand as she followed.

Indi couldn't help but twist her neck to get one last word in. "And it wasn't spoilers, by the way. I'm getting some memories back, and I remember what happened between Cam and me. It's just a matter of time before I remember everything. Hopefully, I can end this before anyone else, even you, gets hurt."

Ben stumbled, his thumb sliding around the lip of the can. "Really? You're remembering?"

She nodded, regarding him suspiciously. "Things about Cam, Brandy, everybody."

He sculled back the beer without taking a breath, then crushed the can between his palms like a compactor and tossed it behind his head. "Well. I guess it's time to come clean then."

Ben bolted to his feet and lunged at India. She gasped and stumbled backward, and Elton was quick to intercept Ben's sloppy attack. Elton shoved him, then pulled the crowbar from his waist and held it over Ben's head.

"What the hell are you doing, Campbell?"

Ben shrunk when he saw the weapon. "I wasn't going to do anything. I just want to talk to her."

"Really? That's not what it looked like." Elton's chest heaved with a nervous breath. Indi touched his hand to calm him, sensing he had the will to smash in Ben's face at any minute.

"Riggs, you know me. I've got nothing to do with this." He glared at Indi. "How do you know it wasn't her? What if she's just turning you against us to save her own ass? Pretending to like you to get you on her side."

Indi cocked her head. "Is that what you were doing, Ben? Why you were being so nice, crushing on me like a little bitch? Why? Did you want me on your side?" Her accusing stare drifted to his arms, the sleeve of his sweater rolling back to his elbow, her eyes centering on the strangely shaped wound on his forearm. The corkscrew.

"Elton." Indi gulped. "His arm." She took in Ben's face. "Did you attack me at my window?"

Suddenly, the lights turned off and the room plummeted into darkness.

Indi's heart clenched. "What's happening?"

"It's probably the fuses," Ben groaned. He went to take a step, but Elton rattled the crowbar, keeping him still. Ben raised his arms. "Riggs. Come on, man."

Elton shook his head. "I can't trust you, Campbell. Not until I get some answers." Elton tugged his belt free. "Hold out your hands."

"Are you serious?"

Elton bound Ben's wrists, looping the belt until it was tight. "Sit your ass on that couch and don't move."

Ben dropped onto the cushion, shaking his head. "What? Is this about my arm? I stabbed myself with a wheel jack when I was changing a tire. Jesus. How about you cut the crap and let me fix the fuses. Or do you like standing in the dark?"

Indi and Elton strained to make out the whites of each other's eyes. Just as Indi was about to speak, a raucous medley of bleeping sirens and honking horns rang out through the breathy silence. Elton rushed to the door and pulled back the lace curtain.

"What is it?" Indi gulped.

"My car alarm," he replied. He opened the door and took a step onto the porch, his eyes scanning the dark for movement, his hand tightening around the crowbar.

Indi felt a brisk wind at her back, sending a ripple of goosebumps across her skin. She shivered, craning her neck. "Is there a back door or something?"

The song playing through the speaker faded to its end, and a shiver ran down Indi's spine when a familiar piano melody blossomed in the silence.

Ben frowned at the speaker as the first verse unfolded. "What is this?"

"Unchained Melody," Indi answered immediately.

Ben squirmed, his grunts escalating with each thrash against his bindings. "Please untie me. Do you really think a blacked-out beach house in the middle of nowhere is a good place to be right now?" Indi flinched and glanced at Elton, who remained on the porch. "What, India? You need to check in with him first? When have you ever asked anyone's permission?" He exhaled. "Look, you want details. I'll give them to you. Just let me loose."

Indi crept toward him, their eyes locked in a game of who would give in first. They both wanted something. The question was, how much would they risk to get it? Indi reached out, and Ben's grin gleamed, even in the dark. Then Indi's eyes were drawn to a shadowed figure standing behind him, staring at her with cold, angry eyes. A black balaclava masked its face, its clothes dark, plain and unmemorable. Indi backed away.

"No, wait," Ben pleaded, oblivious to what Indi could see. "Please. Where are you going?" He thrashed at his bindings. "Come back here, you fucking bitch!"

The bridge of Unchained Melody had just ended over the speaker. The chorus was ramping up. The rhapsodic tenor tones soared, and when it peaked at the spot that had always moved Brandy to tears, the figure raised a thick, grey object and brought it down hard across the top of Ben's head. Blood sprayed Indi's face in a grotesquely perfect slant, soaking her eyes in a horribly familiar red haze. Her body jerked beyond her control, her breath lodging in her throat. She gasped for air, unable to drag her eyes away from the assault.

The first hit had stupefied Ben. He swayed, his eyes rolling back in his head, but he was still alive. The figure hit him again, over and over, every bash leaving a new dent until his head caved in altogether and Indi watched as an oozing clump of skull and hair slid down what remained of Ben's face. His legs shook, his feet twitched, and his arms still seemed to fight his bindings, even though pieces of brain tissue were falling into his lap.

Indi couldn't move, frozen in fear and horror. When the figure had finished its ghastly attack, and there was no more skull to crush, they dropped the object, and it rolled slowly across the floor, coming to a stop at the toe of Indi's boot. Blood had seeped into its every crevice, clumps of hair imbedded in pale pink brain smeared across its surface, but the wave pattern was unmistakable—Christa's carving.

The figure stepped around Ben, moving toward Indi, and at last she could release the scream that had been building inside her.

Elton spun around, and in the few seconds he had to comprehend what he was seeing, he swung the crowbar blindly and yelled. "India! Run!"

Her muscles spasmed and she could move again. Indi backpedaled toward the door, joining Elton outside, then grabbed the handle and slammed it shut. She planted her feet and held the knob tight, just as she felt a brute pull on the other side. Through the curtain, Indi could see the figure tugging the handle, fighting against her grip. Elton grabbed the handle too with his one free hand, holding the crowbar high over his head with the other.

The figure withdrew, bowing out of the contest. Indi and Elton watched breathlessly as the figure moved silently through the house, disappearing as Unchained Melody ended.

"What was that!" Elton exclaimed.

Indi grabbed his hand, dragging him toward the car. "Come on. We have to get out of here."

"Was that the same thing we saw at the field?" Elton shrieked.

She pinched his arm forcefully. "Elton. We have to go. Now. Okay?"

He nodded frantically, the crowbar trembling in his hand. He found his keys in his pocket and turned off the alarm, then they climbed in, slammed the doors and locked them. Elton got the car started, and soon they were rolling over the gravel, speeding toward the long road to Army Bay.

In the distance Indi saw another car skidding away in the opposite direction. A grey sedan.

"Where are we going?" Elton gulped, wiping his sweating brow on the sleeve of his shirt.

"The police station," Indi replied without hesitation. "It's time to come clean."

23

THE POLICE SEPARATED Indi and Elton immediately. They took Indi to a bathroom, let her shower and wash away the blood. It mingled with the steaming hot water, channeling over the curves of her body before running off her toes and spinning red around the drain. Could that wound on Ben's arm really have come from the corkscrew? Were the marks on Avery's face a result of the mace? And if all that were true, why had they tried to kill her? Indi had no proof, just her assumptions, but she didn't want her dead body to prove her right. They were both gone now. Did that mean she was safe?

A female officer with a friendly smile gave Indi some ill-fitting sweatpants and a Minnie Mouse sweater from lost and found. All she needed was an oversized pink bow in her hair and she was ready for the teacups. Indi didn't really want to know the story behind abandoned police station clothing, but it really couldn't be any worse than the tale she was starring in at the moment. She could only hope there had been fewer skull fragments involved.

They seated her in Braddock's office rather than an interrogation room. Framed plaques and medals hung from the walls, a declaration to the world of what a fine, upstanding police officer Dean Braddock was, that his honor and chivalry were a shining light in a gloomy world. Bullshit. Indi had just watched him crack open a teenage boy's head like a piñata.

The desk's wooden surface was worn with deep gouges and flaking varnish, practically bare aside from a single photo in a plain black frame. It was of Braddock as a young man with a cute blonde toddler bundled in his arms. They were happy, laughing beneath a towering oak that had a tire swing hanging from its branches—a family man. Of course. They all were. Indi had seen a million Netflix documentaries just like this. Their family values and normality were the mask they wore to hide what sick weirdos they were, or something like that. When Indi exposed him to the world, she imagined he would get his own documentary or miniseries, maybe even a six-episode special. Her character would probably get whitewashed, played by some Disney channel alumni trying to break into more serious roles.

His office had a large window that looked over the bullpen through narrow plastic blinds that were slightly open. The station was bedlam, with uniformed and plain-clothed cops tripping over each other to field calls and dealing with the media pounding at the doors. They were up to four dead kids now. Indi had overheard a couple of officers lingering by the window, saying a mob of worried parents were on Mayor Stein's lawn right now, demanding he do something to keep their children safe. God, if only her parents were there waving signs in the air. At least then they wouldn't be staring at her through the blinds as they sat in the waiting room, their expressions flip-flopping between empathic relief and seething rage. She almost felt safer being in this office alone with Braddock, a murderer, than out there with them.

A barrier of cops protected the doors of the station from rioting moms and reporters armed with cell phones. They cleared a path through the chaos and Indi watched the Gibbons arrive in single file through a flurry of flashing cameras. Fern was first, shielding her eyes from the flares of light. She looked up from the floor long enough to see Indi's parents, and they exchanged polite smiles. Cody and Cam were next, their demeanors at opposites as usual. Cody was practically beaming, waving while comically yelling no comment. On the other hand, there was no physical way Cam could get her chin any deeper against her chest or cross her arms any tighter, and the way her red hair fell over her distraught eyes twinged Indi's heart.

Christa arrived, sheltered in Warren's arms. He kept her close with one hand, the other he used to bat away the cameras while Christa burrowed into him. The police would have found Christa's carving by Ben's body, so it was obvious they would bring her in. Could it have been Christa? Really? To be honest, Indi couldn't tell if the figure had been a man or a woman. She wouldn't have been confident about suspecting Braddock if she hadn't seen his car again. But if the cops were looking for someone to blame, Christa had motives. Her hatred of Brandy was the stuff of legends. Brandy had tormented her into a nervous breakdown. She may as well have helped Christa pack her bags for the Joyness Clinic. But what did Avery, Ben and Rory have to do with all that? They didn't help create those pictures of

Christa, but they liked them on social media. Was that just as bad, being guilty by association? Indi couldn't think of any other reason Christa would want them dead too. And what about herself? India. Had falling back in with Brandy earned her a share of Christa's vengeance? Cam hadn't held back her disgust at the reunion. Indi would be deluding herself if she considered anything different. No. Braddock. It had to be Braddock. Indi had seen his car twice now in the same vicinity as a dead teenager.

Indi heard the door begin to open, and she was grateful she'd have someone else in here besides her frantic thoughts. She had been sitting a while now, thinking of what exactly she would say to Braddock when he walked in. Should she be more passive and play it calm? Wait to see how he reacts? Or instead, should she take a flying leap off the desk and stab him in the neck with the number-two pencil she found in the drawer? Decisions. Decisions. Either way, Indi was ready for this, ready for it to end. Was she scared? Well, she hadn't pissed herself yet, but that didn't mean she wasn't petrified. He wouldn't do anything here though, surely, not in a station filled with cops. Not if he didn't want all his co-workers to unload their state-issued guns into him. Not if he ever wanted to see that blonde kid by the tire swing again.

Indi could have told the police it was Braddock, right after she told them where to find Ben's body. But she needed this. To confront him face to face. She needed to know what she had done to deserve death, what any of them had done.

She curled her lips; the door seemed to open slower than realistically possible, as if it were a 500-pound slab of rock. Indi saw a hand on the frame and, at last, a face peeked inside. It wasn't Braddock.

"I'm Detective Shelley," the woman greeted. She shut the door behind her and walked over in her fitted grey suit, the sensible heels of her shoes clapping on the wooden floor. She sat down and pulled a pen and notepad out of the breast pocket of her jacket. "Are you ready to make your statement?"

Indi waited, peering curiously around her toward the door. Shelley noticed and glanced over her shoulder, then back at Indi.

"Are you expecting someone?" she asked, her thin lips barely moving when she spoke.

Indi gulped. "I thought Detective Braddock would interview me."

Shelley narrowed her eyes and leaned back in her chair. "Why would you think that?"

"It's always been him, that's all." Indi couldn't read Shelley's tone, but she was definitely giving off don't screw with me vibes.

Shelley flipped open her notebook. "Braddock is on leave. I'll be taking over your case for now."

No. What? This wasn't how things were supposed to happen. "Where is he?" Indi blurted, abandoning any semblance of chill.

"Not that it's any of your business," Shelley sighed, "but he's been visiting some family up north for the last week. Don't worry. I'll pass all the information on to him when he gets back, if that's what you're worried about."

Way to be a shit detective, Indi thought. That wasn't even remotely what she was worried about. How could it be Braddock if he wasn't here? She dug through the recesses of her mind, tossing out garbage as if she were looking for a lost earring at the bottom of a dumpster. It was his car, right? A grey sedan. Was it his license plate? Indi chided herself. Shut up, idiot. Like you even paid attention to what his license plate is. She berated herself. Did you actually see Braddock? Indi watched through the blinds as they led the Gibbons to an interrogation room. They had Christa. Her carving was the murder weapon. Why wouldn't it be her?

"Miss Peters," Shelley coughed. "Are you okay? Did you want to speak to a counsellor?"

Indi didn't need to voice her feelings, hear them played back loud and tinged with sobbing. Instead, her emotions were painted in a single color. Red. It was the color of her blood, the color of her anger, the color of her fear, and she didn't need thick blood in her eyes anymore to see the world through that crimson haze. The view was constant, normal, and it scared Indi that it might never change, that she might always be this angry and afraid.

The door burst open and Indi's mom tumbled in, almost tripping on her ridiculous stilettos, but her dad caught her before she could fall. She didn't pay him even a passing, grateful glance. "So whose idea was it to question a child without her parents?" she snapped, flinging her handbag over her shoulder like a nunchuck.

Shelley kept her back to the Peters while she rolled her eyes, but Indi saw it and smirked. "Mrs. Peters," Shelley said, pushing against the desk as she stood. "You and Mr. Peters were welcome to view the interview by video in another room. We wanted to speak to India without the negative influence your presence might cause."

Her mom's eyes widened, and her nostrils flared. "Who the fuck do you think you are?"

Shelley put her hands on her hips. "Watch your language, Mrs. Peters, or I will have you escorted off the premises."

"Oh, I'd like to see you try, Low Ponytail," she sassed.

"Alright, Dawn, for Christ's sake!" Indi's dad took his wife by the arm and held her back. "Look. We would prefer to be in here with our daughter. She might come across as a stone-cold hard-ass, but she's suffered more than we will ever understand, and I don't want her to be alone anymore."

Fuck, Indi loved her father. His words were a gut punch. She didn't think she wanted him here at all, and then he had to go and say something like that.

"I want them to stay," Indi said with urgency. "Please."

Shelley tapped her foot. "Fine. Can we just get started?"

Her dad pulled up two chairs on either side of Indi, and he and her mom sat down. Her father gripped Indi's left hand, her mother took the right, and a wave of ease and contentment washed over Indi's skin. For a fleeting moment, things weren't as red as usual.

"So, tell me everything," said Shelley.

The words toppled out of Indi's mouth faster than she could categorize them. If the killer wasn't Braddock, it could be anyone, and after watching Ben murdered horrifically in front of her, Indi would not take any more chances with her life. She told Shelley what had happened in the Seradale tunnel, and about the hoodied stranger who tried to pull her out the window.

She didn't want Elton to get into trouble. During the drive back to town they hadn't talked about collaborating their stories, and Indi didn't want to place him somewhere he wasn't meant to be. So, she left out their visit to Rory's crime scene, deciding that she would anonymously return Rory's phone in the next couple of days instead. While she was at it, it was probably time to turn in Brandy's sexting phone too. She finished with every detail of the thing that murdered Ben, and that she thought she saw a grey sedan leaving the beach. Indi didn't mention Braddock, though. Not now, when she doubted her suspicions.

Two hours had passed, and by the end Indi's throat was hoarse. She nervously eyed her parents for their reactions. Her dad's upper lip was twitching like a dog weighing up whether or not to bite. Her mom, too, had turned a little sour, her grip loosening around Indi's hand. She had lied, after all, not told them about the attacks and snuck out in the middle of the night. Indi knew their sympathies would only go so far, but she was getting used to living with consequences.

"Well," Shelley began, flipping her notebook closed. "Thank you, India. That is all extremely helpful to our investigation. We are questioning several suspects. I'm sure you saw Christa and Cody Gibbons earlier."

"Cody?" Indi almost choked. If it was hard to believe Christa was capable of murder, then it was downright ludicrous to suspect Cody. "You think Cody did this?"

"We found a lot of questionable material on his cellphone. He's been posting some inappropriate content on forums, comments about the victims. He also had access to the murder weapon. Speaking of which, Mrs. Peters, I've heard reports that you have several similar statues in vacant houses around town?"

Indi's mom froze. "Yes, I bought them from Christa. I was trying to help," she stuttered, on the verge of tears. "Oh my god, I'm not a suspect, am I?"

Indi frowned. "No. But I still am, right? That's what this is about."

Shelley forced a toothy smile that rippled her cheeks. "Just trying to get all the details, India. What about Paula Marshall? Do you know her?"

Indi nodded, but said nothing. If she didn't speak, she couldn't put her foot in her mouth.

"Paula has also expressed the desire to inflict violence on Brandy Hamilton and her group of friends. Her brother Micah was also in possession of the same prescription medication that Avery Weiss overdosed on. Could they be involved?"

"I thought Micah was locked up in juvenile detention," Indi said.

"He was incarcerated at the time of Rory Zhang's and Ben Campbell's deaths. That is true. However, Paula was not. Could she have committed the murders single-handed?"

The question was pointed. "I don't know," Indi snapped defensively.

Shelley leaned on the desk, the intensity of her stare unwavering. "Did you know Elton Riggs is a keen rock climber?"

Indi knew where this was going. It was old news. The cops had already spun this angle with Elton. She tried not to look pleased with herself for being a step ahead of Shelley, who she liked less and less by the minute.

"Yes. I know that."

"And do you know the ropes that made the scars on your wrists and the type of ropes found on Brandy are the same kind he uses, that we found in his garage?"

Indi nodded.

"And did you know that Rory Zhang was strangled to death with that same kind of climbing rope?"

That was something Indi wasn't privy to. She shuddered and felt tears well behind her eyes when she imagined how terrified Rory must have been that night. Indi held the tears back. The police had already said the rope was common, sold at hundreds of stores online. This meant nothing.

"Unfortunately, we couldn't collect any incriminating evidence from your wounds, and Brandy's body had been in the water too long. Any DNA on those ropes was washed away. Shelley reached into her briefcase, retrieving a file and tossing it on the table. It had Elton's picture on the cover, "However, the rope around Rory's neck had DNA, and that DNA belongs to Elton Riggs."

Shelley's voice went dull in Indi's ears, as if she were hearing her underwater. "No. That's impossible. He would never have killed Rory, and I was there when Ben was murdered. Elton was right beside me."

"That reminds me," Shelley said, and it irritated Indi that Shelley didn't respond to her protestations. Instead, she sifted through the file and clicked her tongue when she found the appropriate slip of paper. "That sweater found in Elton's trunk, the one we had tested and couldn't match to anyone, even Elton. Well, they ran tests in the morgue during Ben's autopsy, and guess what? It's Ben's blood."

Indi dropped her head into her hands, resting her elbows on the desk. "What does that mean?"

Shelley sighed. "I don't know, but I'm sure it won't take long to figure out."

"That sweater belongs to Ben's brother, Jeff," Indi muttered absently. "He said so himself."

"Oh, really?" Shelley returned to her notebook and scribbled something down. "The plot thickens." She noticed Indi floundering and, for once, relaxed her scowl. "I'm going to be honest with you India. I don't think you had anything to do with these murders. I think you're a victim, just like the rest of them."

Indi looked up at Shelley through laced fingers. "Thanks."

Shelley grimaced. "I didn't always think that. My first hunch was that you were faking all this amnesia stuff, using it as an alibi because you were the one who killed Brandy." Her dad went to stand, but Shelley held out a firm hand to halt him. "But then I read Braddock's case files. He is so adamant you're innocent. He made me believe it too. He's a good guy to have in your corner." Nathan hesitated then sat back down just as Shelley stood up. "You can take her home. I have no more questions. Detective Braddock is back next week. I'll update him. He will probably want to talk to you himself."

Indi's mom put her arm around her and squeezed tight. "Come on, baby, let's go home."

Indi dragged herself to her feet, and if her dad had not been guiding her, she probably wouldn't have been able to walk at all. She was exhausted, mentally and physically. It couldn't be Elton. It couldn't. When they reached the door, Indi turned back to Shelley in desperation.

"Sadie Hamilton. What about her?"

Shelley looked up from returning the files to her briefcase. "Sadie Hamilton has no motive for any of these murders. But, as it's procedure, we have already spoken to her. She has an alibi for every murder—home with her parents. I'm sorry if this isn't what you want to hear, India, and maybe we're wrong about Elton. We have other suspects, but the case against him is getting stronger. Unless we get some concrete evidence that it's not him, it doesn't look good."

Indi's dad urged her to turn around and say no more. "Let's get out of here girl."

Indi didn't walk out of the room, her parents herded her. She had no purpose, no direction. She didn't care if she went home or if she stayed in this police station for the rest of her life. What did any of it matter anymore? A part of her wished it was Christa or Cody or Paula or Jeff, as long as it wasn't Elton. She didn't know these feelings had taken root inside her and grown into heart-shaped leaves on a vine that weaved through her ribs. She was even willing to throw Sadie under the bus. Home with her parents? What a dull yet full-proof alibi. If that's all that was needed to uncheck the murderer box next to Sadie's name in Shelley's little notebook, then Indi would just have to find one for Elton too or, of course, find the killer herself. Fucking alibis. Then Indi froze in her tracks so abruptly that her parents stumbled on either side of her.

"Honey, what's wrong?" her mom asked.

Indi had thought it couldn't be Braddock because he was visiting family up north. He wasn't in town, therefore couldn't make a lasagna out of Ben's head. Or is that just what he wanted people to think? Maybe that was his grey sedan. Maybe Indi was right all along.

"Fucking alibis," she muttered, a smile spreading across her dry lips.

Her parents exchanged confused glances before encouraging Indi to keep walking.

24

"YOU KNOW, WHEN I FOUND that broken window, I thought someone had kidnapped you," her dad growled. He paced the living room, rubbing the back of his neck red raw. "And thanks for that, by the way. Now I'm going to have to replace it with that double-glazed frosted stuff your mother wants."

Indi sat silently on the couch, her eyes set to the floor. The less said the better, but her silence just seemed to infuriate him further.

He stared at her. "Are you not going to say anything?" He crouched, gripped her shoulders, and forced her to look at him. "India. You could be dead. Don't you understand that?"

"Nathan. Enough," her mom interrupted from the doorway. "You've been yelling at her for long enough. She gets it."

"Does she?" he said tersely. "I used to think she got it, but apparently I was a damned fool because she's been sneaking out of the house all week to drive around with some boy and almost get murdered."

Indi turned her head, fighting to avoid his scolding gaze.

"Well, she gets it now. Don't you, India?" her mom prompted.

"Yes. I get it," India mumbled. Whatever it took to get her out of this room.

Her dad stood and dug his knuckles into his hips. "I wish I could believe you girl. You're grounded. No one comes in, and you never go out. Not until this killer is caught, tried and convicted."

Now India was looking at him. "That could take forever!" she protested.

"Well, you better get comfy then. Time to switch to home school. Guess I'll be your date for the prom."

Indi stood, seething, her jaw clenched. "I wouldn't go to the prom with you if you were the last guy at home school." She gripped her hair by the roots and shrieked. "You can't just keep me locked up here. I'll go insane."

"It's not up for negotiation," he declared.

"What if she comes to work with me?" her mom suggested. "That way at least she's not under house arrest. I'll have a cop follow me while I'm doing viewings this afternoon."

Indi's mouth shifted from a scowl to a pout in an instant. "Yes. Please. Watching people blindly take on massive amounts of debt is better than having to stay here all day."

Her dad turned to her mom and shook his head despairingly. "Really? You're not going to back me on this?"

Indi realized she had inadvertently wedged herself in the middle of their disagreement. She didn't like to take sides, but she was obviously rooting for her mom.

"I agree with you, Nathan. Grounded. Yes. But I don't see the harm in Indi stretching her legs and getting some fresh air if you or I are supervising. She can come to house showings with me later this afternoon and then to the site with you tomorrow."

Indi changed her mind. Nosing around in people's houses and napping in the guest room was one thing, but the construction site was utterly lame. No Wi-Fi, and mandatory hard hats. Unfortunately, it seemed as if her dad was warming to the idea.

He exhaled roughly and held out his hand. "Give me your phone."

Indi cocked an eyebrow. "What?"

"You heard me. Give me your phone." He drawled every syllable.

Indi reached into her back pocket and slipped out her cell, then slapped it bitterly onto his palm.

He closed his hands around it swiftly, as if it would fly away given half the chance. "Fine then. You can go to work with your mom today and then come with me tomorrow. At least we'll always have eyes on you."

Her mom smiled proudly, pleased that she had won the argument. "I'm leaving in fifteen minutes." She looked over Indi's police-issue outfit. "Did you want to change, or ...?"

"I'll change," Indi replied quickly. She scratched at her stomach where the Minnie Mouse sweater was itching. "Can clothes have bed bugs?"

Her mom cringed. "That's probably just fleas, dear. Maybe you should shower too."

"Shit," Indi groaned, clambering to her feet.

"Can you at least pretend that you know I don't like it when you swear Indi?" her dad sighed.

"I'm sorry, I'm sorry!" she said. "My brain isn't functioning properly at the moment." Brain. Every time she heard that word, it transported her to the beach house and the bowl of strawberry pudding on top of Ben's neck that used to be his head.

Indi left the lounge, and her mom presented her cheek as she passed by, hinting for a thank you peck. Indi obliged. Having to spend time at the work site was a small price to pay for semi-freedom. She threw the sweats into the trash and turned the shower temperature to scalding. There was a sting at first. There always was, but slowly her reddened skin grew accustomed to the heat, and she could barely feel it anymore. That was the way of most things nowadays. It hurt; she got used to it; it didn't hurt as much. Death was the new normal, waking her in the night or waiting bright and early the next morning. Avery's funeral was next week. Rory's the week after. Indi had never had so many burials in her calendar.

She rewashed her hair, vigorously scrubbed under her nails and exfoliated her face until the tube was empty and her skin felt paper thin. She could still feel it though, all that blood and tissue clinging to her, wet and warm. When she was clean and numb, and her fingers had become prunes, she turned off the shower and swaddled herself in a towel before heading to her closet. Jeans, she decided, can't go wrong with jeans. She glanced out her barred windows and noted the overcast sky and the slight breeze through the trees. It seemed like it might be a good layering day, so she pulled on a long sleeve with a plain black tee over the top. She tried to wrestle her hairdryer free from a cluster of appliances: clippers, a straightener, a curler, all with their cords tangled like the tails on a rat king. Her elbow slammed against the closet frame and she winced, sucking her teeth. Brandy's burner phone tumbled from a shelf and onto the floor, followed by Rory's and then Elton's.

"Fuck," she muttered before biting her tongue when she recalled her dad's disdain for her potty mouth. She had forgotten all about these incredibly incriminating phones she was hiding from the police. She was lucky her parents hadn't found them yet. They'd probably think she was an escort or a drug dealer. Either would be easier to admit to than the truth. Rory's phone had a bar of charge left, and after Indi had closed the recording the password protection had taken over. Indi was still unsure how she was going to get rid of it. Giving it to the police was the straightforward answer, but that would place her and Elton at Rory's murder scene. With Elton in mind, Indi checked the burner phone he had sent her. No messages. She didn't know what had happened to him at the police station; if he was still there or sent home. The morning news update about the Army Bay murder spree didn't mention anyone charged, so they mustn't have had as much concrete evidence as Detective Low Ponytail was making out. Even with what had transpired in the last few days, even with everything that Shelley had said, and with Indi having worn through the last scrap of her parents' trust, her plans were unchanged. She had to prove Elton was innocent, and she had to stop the killings and get her life back.

Indi shoved Rory and Elton's phones back in her closet and covered them with dirty laundry. She lingered over Brandy's phone though, having almost forgotten all about it. The last message she had sent was still on the screen, sitting on Seen from whoever was at the other end. It came as no surprise that there'd been no reply. Brandy was dead. They either didn't want to get involved or were just plain freaked out. With no names or faces in the pictures, it went without saying that this brief fling was on the down-low. This should all go to the police, Indi contemplated.

"India, let's go!" her mom called from downstairs.

For now, Indi shoved it back in the closet with the others and jogged to meet her mother.

INDI HAD NEVER BEEN to this side of Army Bay. It was a little more rural, probably the farthest you could get from the beach while still being in town. There were long stretches of green acreage, no suburban clusters of doppelganger mini-mansions. It was all older-style farmhouses with picket fences and wide porches, shingle roofs and attic bay windows. The serene quiet was all-consuming, with just the rhythmic bump of the car tires over the uneven road ringing in Indi's ears. She was almost sure she could hear the sunlight gleaming as it strained through a sky of grey clouds.

"Where are we?" she asked.

"Really, India? You've lived in this town how long now?" Her mom clicked her tongue. "This is Mistley. It's got that rural enchantment that will make you feel a million miles away but is only a 25-minute commute from downtown Army Bay. There's a bus service that drops children at a fantastic range of nearby quality schooling, and the historic Mistley Community Hall hosts a farmers market every Sunday."

Indi rolled her eyes. "Oh my god."

Her mom winked. "I know, pretty good, right? That's in the listing." She lifted her chin and looked up ahead. "We're coming up to the house now. People should start arriving in about half an hour. I'll get you to hand out flyers at the door."

"Yeah, sure," Indi replied, her tone laced with boredom. She leaned back and glanced at the rear-view mirror, catching sight of the unmarked police car following closely. "Do they have to hand out flyers too?"

She pursed her lips. "Maybe I could have them greet people. Promote what a safe community this is to live in."

Indi almost choked. "Yeah. Shame about all the murdered teenagers within a 25-minute commute."

"Don't mention any of that," her mom said sharply, waggling her finger while keeping her eyes on the road. "I have some out-of-town buyers coming to view this house."

"Believe me, mom, they know. Everybody knows."

Her mom chuckled. "Shhh. Ignorance is bliss." She gripped the wheel, the sun catching the diamonds in her wedding band.

Indi's thoughts drifted. "So did you sort that thing out with dad? The dry cleaning?" She saw her mother's throat tighten.

"Yep. All sorted," she said, her jaw clenched.

"So you guys are okay, then?" Indi pressed.

Her mom's smile was as fake as her magenta acrylics. "Yes. Of course."

If she was trying to ease Indi's mind, she was doing a terrible job. "We've just never really talked about it. I still can't believe you guys separated."

"Well, we have been a little distracted India. Do we really need to talk about this now?"

Indi shrugged. "I just thought it was something well-adjusted families did. Dr. Phil is pretty adamant about that."

"Well, Dr. Phil has never met a family like ours then," she said with a smirk.

"Mother. He helped a psychic time-traveler impregnated by bigfoot gain closure with her Martian birth mother. I think he can find his way around an everyday separation."

Her mom gave her a side-eye glance. "I thought you had seen enough over the last couple of years to know where it came from. Dad was hardly ever home. My business was taking off. It just became harder than it should be."

"And now?" Indi was nervous to hear the answer.

"You are the most important person in our lives. Sometimes you have to put things aside and focus on what matters. Your dad and I decided that, while you were lying in that hospital bed covered in bruises and stuffed full of tubes." Her blue eyes with their curled black lashes shifted back to the road. "Does that answer your question?"

It was a more straightforward and safer explanation than Indi had expected. No crying with mascara running down her cheeks, screaming what a jerk he was, and that she was done with men. As always, Indi wished she could remember, but this struck a more personal chord. It wasn't horror and pain, or life and death. It was learning that, for a time, the two people she loved most didn't want each other and it selfishly pleased her that almost dying on a beach had reunited them. A part of her was content for that to be the end. They were back together now. They could work it out. But Indi saw every day how different they were. If only her amnesia was contagious, and they could forget what had hurt them as well. The more Indi's memories returned, the more she missed the peace of not knowing. As her mom said, ignorance was bliss.

"Yeah, that answers it," she replied, at last, her head slumping on her shoulder.

The long road stretched before them. They approached a midnight-blue, two-story house with a driveway that circled an old well surrounded by a bed of pansies. In the front yard stood a giant oak tree and, as they whizzed by, Indi was sure she saw a tire swing swaying from its branches. She craned her neck but couldn't quite see, so instead whipped off her seatbelt and turned herself completely, propping herself up on her knees and peering over the headrest.

"Indi, sit down!" her mom hissed, slapping her backside. "I don't want those cops to give me a ticket."

For a moment, Indi couldn't hear her. All she was concerned with was that oak tree and that tire swing and being sure her eyes weren't deceiving her. Indi played a matching game in her head. The same tree, the same wildflowers around the trunk, the same tire, the same barren green farmland in the distance. It was the place in the photo on Braddock's desk.

"India. Turn around. Now." Her mother's voice had lost all patience.

Indi swiveled onto her butt and pulled her seat belt back on. "So where's this house you're selling?" she swallowed, trying to sound calm.

"Right here," her mom replied, pulling down on the steering wheel and turning into a long, cobbled driveway.

No way. She couldn't possibly be this lucky. The house that could be Braddock's was only two doors down.

"Fuck," her mom groaned, pulling up the handbrake. She scanned the dozen or so people congregating at the door and checking their watches. "What time is it?" She glared at the broken digital clock in her dash that always blinked 00.00. She would get it fixed one of these days.

"I would love to help, but dad has taken away my phone, so I have lost my connection with the world and the way it works."

Her mom grumbled and frantically ransacked her purse for her own phone. "Fuck!" she shrieked. "I was supposed to be here twenty minutes ago. Quick commute, my ass." She turned to Indi. "I haven't checked over the upstairs. The last thing I need is some good, god-fearing family finding a giant dildo in the guest bath or something. Can you go make sure everything's okay while I get them all to sign in and show them downstairs?"

Indi heard that as permission to be somewhere else. "Dildos. Got it."

Her mom gave a sigh of relief, slapped a hand on either side of Indi's face and planted a red lipstick stain on her forehead. "You're the best. Wish me luck." She took a deep breath, closed her eyes, and pulled an imaginary string from her hairline to her belly button. Then she threw open the door and bounded out. "Hello everybody, so happy that you could all make it. Excuse my lateness. I had to take my Labrador to the vet. Poor old thing, had her forever, and she can barely see or hear these days. Breaks my heart. Loves to curl up at my feet when it rains, terrified of lightning and thunder, but god bless her, so am I. Can't imagine what I'd do if I ever had to be without her."

There was a subtle tremble in her voice, and it came through stronger in crucial parts of her story. It went without saying that they had never owned a dog, but the potential buyers who flocked around her with sympathetic pouts and a chorus of aaaaaws didn't know that. Indi nodded her approval. She was good.

When they filed inside, Indi climbed out just as the tailing police car pulled into the driveway. The window wound down, and a clean-shaven man with a thick neck and a buzzcut poked his head out.

"Are you alright there, Miss Peters?"

Indi saluted loosely, then immediately regretted such a dweeb move. "I'm fine. Just going to help Mom with the open home." Why was she still talking? She tried to stop, but instead, she said, "Dildos."

The officer furrowed his brow, and his partner stifled a laugh in his fist.

"Okay then," the officer drawled awkwardly, winding up his window to end the conversation.

It wasn't quite as she had planned it, but whatever worked. Indi spun on her heels and casually strolled into the house. She walked inside, wiped her feet on the red and gold Turkish rug, and breezed past her mom as she was demonstrating how the underfloor heating worked. Indi bypassed the stairs, continuing down the short hall and into the kitchen, her eyes widening on the back door that led into the yard. When she was outside she was grateful to see there were no high walls dividing the properties. She was famously terrible at fences. Instead, it was just a few thin rows of waist-high wire strung between posts. She scissor-legged the first wire fence, then dodged a flock of charging chickens in the second yard before skipping that fence too. When she landed, she could see the enormous oak beyond the roof of the midnight-blue house. When they had driven past, there was no car in the driveway. Specifically, there was no grey sedan. Indi crossed the lawn to the back door, the soft bed of grass squelching beneath her boots. She climbed the stairs to the back porch and looked through the windows. There was no movement inside, no sound either. She curled her lips tight and knocked.

Indi waited for what seemed the longest time and, when no one came, the second phase of her unplanned plan took shape in her head.

Indi turned the knob. Locked. Was she really going to have to break the window if she wanted to get inside? She was an old pro at this point, just ask the garage window, but this was a detective's house. Was this really who she had become? She looked around the porch, hoping a solution would jump out at her.

It's important for your children always to feel like they can come home, Braddock had said to her, the first day they had met. Always leave a key under the mat, that sort of thing.

Indi's gaze fell upon the rubber welcome mat at the foot of the door. No way she could be that lucky, right? She crouched and peeked underneath, then smiled when she spied the door key. She was on her feet with the key in the lock before you could say breaking and entering. Indi let the door open with its own momentum, sliding over some gross floral linoleum, which gave way to a country-style kitchen decorated with fake fruit and gingham curtains.

Indi continued to pour over the pros and cons of this mess she had got herself into. She could turn around right now, go back to the house showing, and let the police figure this whole thing out. Or she could count to three and drag her cowardly ass over this threshold. One. Two. Three. Indi stepped onto the lino, making her choice.

The house remained silent, just the birds chirping whimsically in that big oak, their songs seeping through the old wooden boards. Indi passed a dining room with two chairs, a living room with a small couch and a worn leather recliner. She immediately noticed there was no TV, which only fueled her suspicions that Braddock was a serial killer.

Across from the living room there looked to be an office through an alcove beside the stairs. As Indi walked by she glanced up, half expecting to see some axe-wielding asshole in a hockey mask standing there, because this was her messed up life after all. But there was no one, and she exhaled, continuing into the office space.

Indi skimmed through papers on his desk. Some case files she wasn't interested in, notes that meant nothing to her. Her ego was almost a little affronted that her files weren't front and center. Not to brag, but she was a pretty big deal at this point. She leaned down and yanked open a large, heavy drawer at the bottom of the desk with an audible grunt. Indi read the labels on the thick manilla folders inside: Complainant 1, Andrews; Complainant 2, Simpson; names she didn't recognize, and that went all the way to Complainant 11. As Indi sorted through them, she came across a file with a name she knew. Avery Weiss. She opened it without hesitation and sprawled the contents over the desk. Drug possession. Drunk driving. Indi gulped. Sexual assault. The complainants were his victims, girls he had wooed with his money and capped-white smile, then plied with drugs and booze until he could do whatever he wanted with them.

Indi looked over the dates. Some statements were recent, but most were months before Avery died. That meant Braddock had been building a case against him for a while. Indi spied a yellow envelope amongst the papers, the scribbled writing catching her eye. Brandy Hamilton. Indi shook the envelope loose and slowly peeled back the tab, inching out the first of a dozen printed photographs. She gasped into her hand and threw the envelope away, but not before one photo slipped free, floating down to the desk like a leaf from a tree. Indi immediately recognized the garish orange leather seats from the back of Avery's SUV. Then her eyes welled with tears. She also recognized Brandy sleeping across those seats, vomit dripping from the corner of her mouth into a pool on the carpeted floor. She had no shirt on, her tennis skirt knotted around her waist, her legs were limp and splayed. The other photos were worse.

Indi felt woozy, a retch building in the back of her throat, the hot putrid taste of sick burning behind her tongue. She fell forward, her palms flat on the desk. Indi breathed, in and out, in and out, trying to calm herself. She planted her legs to keep herself steady, but none of it was helping. How could he do that to her? How could he get away with it? Her gaze drifted to a photo frame on Braddock's desk. It matched the one in his office exactly. The tree, the field, the tire swing. No. Wait. It was different. Braddock was older. The blonde girl was older, too. Indi squinted, her vision blurring. Was that Brandy in his arms?

Suddenly, car tires rolling over the gravel broke the silence. Indi ducked down, fighting to regain her wits. She peeked over the windowsill and saw a grey sedan pulling into the driveway. She dropped onto all fours before she could see who was driving.

Get it together. Indi chided herself. They'll convict you and Elton both if you don't get your ass out of here.

Indi forced her muscles into motion. She gathered up the files and shoved them back where she had found them, then scurried across the smooth office floor, down the hall and into the kitchen. She heard the car door shut and footsteps crunching upon the gravel toward the front porch. She stumbled but caught herself on the breakfast counter, using it to keep steady as she staggered the rest of the way to the back door. Indi grabbed the handle with both hands and swung around, holding her breath and using every ounce of control she had to quieten the click when it closed.

She dropped to the ground when she heard the front door open. Indi crept across the porch and down the stairs, but when she had almost reached the fence, she bit her tongue and turned back. The key was still in the door.

She gritted her teeth and scampered back, staying low to the ground, up the stairs and onto the porch. She could hear movement inside, the hollow thump of flat shoes and the puckered pop of the fridge opening. Indi couldn't wait for them to leave the kitchen. She couldn't risk they wouldn't come to the back door and discover her. Indi reached for the key and turned it so slowly she could see the tendons in her hand flexing. She closed her eyes, praying to whoever might give a shit for the lock not to click loudly. She managed a full rotation before the key stopped without even the slightest sound. Indi gently loosened the key and returned it to its spot beneath the mat. She scampered once again down the stairs and across the lawn, climbing fences and outrunning chickens until she was back in the yard of the house her mom was showing.

When Indi felt she had made a clean escape, when she was safe, at least for now, she keeled over, bracing her hands on her knees, and puked her guts out.

25

INDI SAT IN SILENCE for the drive home, her arm leaning on the window, her eyes lost in the world's blur as it flashed by. On the other hand, Indi's mom hadn't stopped talking. The open house was a success. She had three offers on the Mistley property, as well as two valuation requests for some cliff houses near Breakers Beach. She was none the wiser that Indi hadn't gone upstairs on a dildo hunt and had successfully completed her first break-in. As productive days went, this one was pretty stellar. It was a shame that Indi had more horrid images to add to her growing collection.

She'd thought the sight of Brandy, bloated and rotting on the beach, was the worst she would ever have to see her. That was until Indi found those photos. She knew Avery was a bastard. She'd heard all the rumors. But nothing could have prepared her for that, seeing a girl stripped of her choice and dignity. Indi could feel the vomit at the back of her throat again. She swallowed. Her mom would be pissed if she puked in her car.

Searching Braddock's house had dug up more questions than answers. Had Brandy gone to the police about Avery? Indi hadn't seen her name on the list of complainants, but that didn't mean she hadn't told Braddock about it. Then there was the photo in the frame and the fact that Brandy and Braddock were far closer than Indi knew. She had never met him before the murders started. If they were that familiar, surely he and Indi would have crossed paths at some point, and wouldn't his relationship with Brandy be a talking point as the lead detective working on her murder case? Was Brandy the little girl in the other photo? Indi breathed deeply to stop herself passing out. When they were home, and her mom pulled into the driveway, she had never been so happy to see the bars on her window.

Indi's dad had made a boil-up for dinner. Fatty sausages, pork bones, doughboys and boiled potatoes, all the good stuff. Which meant her mom would have a microwave Weight Watchers' risotto tonight. But her dad hadn't made it for her mom. It was for Indi, and binge eating her woes didn't seem like the worst idea right now. She served herself a giant portion and drowned the lot in tomato sauce. Indi's mom ate in the family room with one eye on Sixteen and Pregnant reruns and the other on the paperwork from the open house. Indi and her dad sat across from each other at the breakfast bench. They didn't talk, just slurped at the pork bones and exchanged quick nods if they caught each other's gaze. Indi was grateful. She really didn't have words for what she was feeling. It was all raw emotion that she wanted gone, ripped out of her if necessary. Even her body couldn't physically take it anymore. Even now, she was a single horrifying flashback away from passing out or regurgitating these doughboys.

Finally, when Indi had reached the bottom of her plate, and her fork scratched at the mandala pattern smeared with sauce, her dad cleared his throat and spoke.

"Bright and early tomorrow, yeah, girl? I've got a dozen concrete trucks showing up in the morning."

Right. The construction site. Indi nodded. She didn't care anymore. There was an old, lumpy couch in his office trailer. She would lie down, curl into a ball fetus style, and find a way to exist in this disgusting world.

"I'm going to get some sleep then," she mumbled. Indi stood, lifting her plate, but her dad was quick to take it from her.

"I've got it. You get some sleep."

Indi glanced into the family room when she heard her mom laugh at the TV. "Are you and mom okay?"

Her dad stacked the plates and turned to the dishwasher. "We're fine. You don't need to worry about any of that. The important thing is that we're a family again. Okay?"

Indi folded her arms and nodded. He cupped the back of her head and pulled her into his barreled chest, his lips pressed against her forehead.

"I love you girl," he said, his voice peppered with a genuine ache.

"I love you too," Indi breathed into his shirt. He let her go, and she walked backward through the kitchen, a half-smile breaking the surface of her exhaustion. "See you in the morning."

INDI'S DAD WASN'T KIDDING. When the dawn's ochre sun lurched over the horizon, she threw on some leggings and an oversized sweatshirt, then climbed into his posh truck. Indi fished his glasses out of the glove box and put them on, trying to sneak in another thirty minutes of sleep while she could. She woke when they hit the uneven road of the construction site and, even with her seatbelt on, she was catapulted into the air, banging her head on the roof.

She cradled her head in her hands. "I take it we're here then?"

Her dad nodded, gazing proudly over the vast quarry stocked with cranes, diggers and towers of scaffolding. "Home, sweet home."

Indi couldn't help but notice the irony in his words, that his dedication to his work had put his actual home in jeopardy.

He pointed to the far side of the site. "Concrete trucks are here, right on time. I'll drop you in the office. Hey, maybe you can order in some coffees and pastries for the crew? The number for Devlin's is in my desk drawer."

Indi wiped the dried drool from the corners of her mouth and waved apathetically. "Yeah. Sure. Whatever you want Dad." With that, he hit the brakes, and Indi lunged forward, the seat belt snapping her back. "Oh my god Dad, are you the worst driver in the world or what?"

He pulled down her sunglasses. "I'll take an apple Danish."

Indi groaned and pushed open the door, almost falling when she misplaced her foot on the step. She stumbled out instead, then threw her weight into the heavy door to get it closed. The truck roared off, leaving her standing in a cloud of grey dust. Indi coughed and spat out the grit, then lazily turned and headed into her dad's trailer.

The drawn curtains darkened the room, and Indi sighed contently, removing the glasses. There was the paisley couch with its familiar lumps and mysterious stains, seeming to call her name, like a siren with terrible personal hygiene. Indi collapsed and tucked her legs in, pulling her long hoodie over her knees and down to her ankles to form a cozy, purple cocoon. Just five more minutes and then she would call Devlin's.

A digger groaned loudly outside the trailer, followed by the relentless pounding of a jackhammer into solid rock. Indi bolted upright and wiped the sleep from her eyes. "Apple Danish," she exclaimed. Her tiredness lingered, and she staggered across the small space to the window and peeked out the curtains. She spied her dad in his hardhat, pointing indiscriminately at some blueprints while his crew scratched their heads. She still had time. Indi dashed to his desk and rummaged through the drawer for Devlin's number. "Aha!" she boasted, celebrating over a scrap of paper with the scribbled digits.

She slammed the drawer shut but paused when she heard a strange rustling from inside. Indi opened it again, reaffirming that there was nothing inside apart from paper, certainly nothing that could make that puzzling sound. She slammed it again and again and heard the sound every time, something scraping, then coming to an abrupt stop. Indi opened the drawer once more and emptied the paper. She knocked on the wooden bottom. Her head jerked, puzzled, when it made a hollow sound. Indi pushed on the corners, and the panel popped out of place, revealing a false bottom. She stared at the ancient Blackberry burner-phone hidden inside.

She didn't want to acknowledge that it was the same make and model as Brandy's burner. That would raise questions, and Indi was tired of questions. She picked up the phone casually, trying to convince herself that she didn't care, explaining to no one as she ran a thumb over the buttons that there was a perfectly innocent explanation of why her dad had it. She hadn't meant to wake the screen. Or maybe she had. Unlike Brandy's it was password protected. Indi half-heartedly punched in a few numbers. They all came back incorrect. What did it matter, though? This was just a work phone. Probably nothing but contractor numbers and an old-school snakes game knowing him.

Suddenly, the door flew open and her dad stepped in, tossing his hard hat onto the couch. Indi froze, clasping her hands around the phone and shoving it behind her back.

He ruffled his dark hair and scanned the room for her. "Ah. There you are. Did you place the order?"

Indi bumped the drawer closed with her hip. She gulped. "Yeah. They're running late. Might take an hour."

He frowned, surprised. "That's out of the ordinary. Nothing we can do about it, I guess." He looked around. "What are you doing?"

"Nothing," Indi said quickly. Too quickly. There was no reason to freak out.

"Okay." He peered at her. "You seem a little jumpy."

Indi forced her lips into a smile. "Nope. Totally fine."

He nodded and shrugged. "If you say so. Look, I'm going to be out here with these idiots all morning. Don't suppose you can amuse yourself for a while? I think I have a Top Gun DVD somewhere you can watch on my laptop."

"Oh great," Indi replied, holding that smile firmly in place. "Val Kilmer in his prime. Can't wait."

Her dad laughed. "Yeah, it's the best. My laptop is in my bag in the truck. I'll talk to you later, girl. Let me know when the pastries arrive."

He headed back outside, and when she was sure there was some distance between them, Indi stuffed the phone in the pouch of her hoodie and headed for the truck. She found his bag and pulled out his laptop, then took the phone and buried it at the bottom beneath some receipts. If Indi was going to convince herself this meant nothing, the Blackberry needed to find its way to Appleby Drive. She zipped up the bag and returned to the trailer and placed the order with Devlin's, then curled up on the couch and watched Top Gun multiple times for the rest of the day. Indi did everything she could to avoid thinking about the phone, while dreading that she was right.

Right before Goose was about to eject, a Facebook notification popped up on the laptop screen. Indi didn't even know her dad had Facebook. She didn't know a lot of things. The mayor was about to go live. Indi clicked the link. Her fragile psyche couldn't handle watching Goose die one more time.

Mayor Stein was tall and lean, with a face like a haunted tree. He had a kind voice though, talked expressively with his hands and somehow was still polling very well, considering Army Bay was the home of a serial killer at large.

"Good people of Army Bay," he started. "Our beloved town has suffered. We are broken people at the mercy of a psychopath. Rest assured that the fine men and women of our police force are doing everything they can to bring this murderer to justice. And trust me when I say that I am exhausting every single resource I have to make Army Bay safe again." He curled his lips in reflection. "Good people. Now is not the time for us to hide in our homes and endure this pain alone. It is time for us to come together as a community, to cry on each other's shoulders. To embrace those that you consider strangers and make them friends. It is time to celebrate the lives of the wonderful young people taken from us too soon. That is why this Friday, at the town hall, I ask that every single one of you comes together to remember and pay your respects to the memories of Brandy Hamilton, Avery Weiss, Rory Zhang and Benjamin Campbell. We can get through this, Army Bay. Together. There will be tea and coffee and light refreshments."

The stream ended, and Indi decided that was enough for the day. She closed the laptop and lay back down on the couch, falling into a trance as the jackhammer continued to pound outside the window.

At around four p.m. her dad appeared again, his clothes coated in a fine layer of dust, his skin darker and ruddy from the overcast sun.

"I think we'll call it a day," he announced. "How about you?"

Indi looked up at him and nodded. "Sure. If that's what you want."

He pursed his lips. "Are you sure you're okay, girl? You don't seem yourself."

Indi stood up and tucked the laptop under her arm. "Just feeling a little sick, I guess. I'm looking forward to getting home."

"Me too." He smiled and beeped her nose, but Indi turned ever so slightly and faked an itch on her cheek. She didn't want him to touch her right now.

He farewelled his crew, and he and Indi climbed into the truck and headed home. It was dark by the time they reached Appleby Drive. The outside lights gave the house a warm, welcoming glow. They climbed out, and he slung his bag over his shoulder. When they got inside, the whole place smelled like sugar cookies, and her mom ran into the foyer, proudly displaying a tray of baking.

"Guess who closed on the Mistley house," she sang.

Her dad leaned forward and kissed her cheek, and for the first time in a while her mom appeared not to mind. She even plucked a cookie from the tray and snapped it in half in his mouth, taking the other half for herself. They watched each other chew, giggling like lovesick teenagers.

"That's great news," he said, kissing her crumb-spotted lips. "Congratulations babe."

"You know, I thought when all this blows over, maybe we can take a trip. Maybe a cruise." She smiled at Indi, who stood silently at the door. "What do you say, India? All-you-can-eat shrimp. Salsa classes. Fucking shuffleboard."

Her dad frowned and grabbed another cookie. "Language."

"Sounds great," Indi replied absently. "I don't feel very well." She clutched her stomach for emphasis. "I'm going upstairs for a bit."

Her parents exchanged perplexed looks.

"You don't want any cookies?"

Indi shook her head. "Raincheck, Mom." She walked by them and retreated to her room. The closet stared at her with a mocking arrogance. It knew what it was hiding. It knew what she wanted. After reminding herself that closets didn't know shit, Indi marched across the room and opened the door, rifling through her dirty laundry until she found Brandy's burner. It was the same as the one in her dad's hidden drawer, but she knew that already. She collapsed onto her bed and reacquainted herself with the messages and, reluctantly, the pictures. Swipe after swipe of Brandy's tits and some guy's hard dick. Was it the same color as his skin? Weren't dicks darker than the rest of the body? Was that a thing?

Indi slammed the phone on her bed. Why was she even thinking about this? She tried to picture Brandy's bloated body or Ben's pulverized skull; anything was better than trying to guess what color her dad's dick was. What she wouldn't give for Micah to be out of juvenile detention. She could do with some weed about now.

She heard footsteps coming up the stairs, easily recognizable as her dad's steel-capped boots. They lingered outside her door, and Indi buried the phone under her duvet in case he came in. But he didn't. He walked past into his bedroom. Indi even heard the thud as his bag dropped on the bed. Indi sat up and stared at the phone. She couldn't stay like this, always wondering if this ridiculous idea could be real. She had to know before she imploded. Indi hit dial, then walked to her door with the phone to her ear. It rang. Indi waited, first to see if she could hear the burner in his bag ringing, maybe to see if he would answer, that she would hear him talking from the room next door, confirming that it was him sexting a seventeen-year-old dead girl. Indi closed her eyes and exhaled a suffocating breath. There was silence from her parents' bedroom. The notion she was wrong took root quickly. She could breathe again.

Suddenly the phone in her hand beeped, and the text message icon flicked onto the screen.

Who is this?

Indi's heart pounded. She panicked. She needed to get rid of this thing. Who cared if it was evidence. The window. She would throw it as far as she could and just be done with it. Then the phone started ringing. The volume was at max. Indi had never bothered to check that before. She yanked at the bars on her window, but they wouldn't budge. She tried to slip her fingers through the narrow slits, but her hand wouldn't fit and all the while, this phone wouldn't stop ringing!

Then Indi's door flew open, and her dad stood in the doorway, the burner from his bag against his ear. His shoulders slumped, he hung his head, and when he clicked End the phone in Indi's hand fell silent.

Her bottom lip quivered, her eyes glassed over. "No," she sobbed.

"I can explain." His voice was less than a whisper.

"Were you screwing her, Dad?" Indi's sobs hardened, the sadness slowly being devoured by rage.

He glanced over his shoulder toward the stairs. "Keep it down, girl. Your mother might hear."

"Were you fucking her?" Indi screamed.

Her dad charged into the room, slamming the door behind him. He stormed toward Indi with a ferocity in his eyes she had never seen before, soulless, bottomless, desperate. He grabbed Indi by the shoulders and shook her, soft at first but firmer as his anger escalated.

"It wasn't like that. Stop using that language. I am so fucking sick and tired of you and your mother using that fucking language!" He shook her harder, pressing her against the bars of the window.

"She was seventeen, Dad. She was my friend. How could you?"

"It was her!" He protested. "You saw the way she acted, the things she said. She made me, India!"

Indi shook her head vehemently, tears streaming down her cheeks. "Let me go. Now."

"I'll let you go when you calm down," he snapped. "It was a mistake girl. A stupid mistake, but no one has to know. Brandy's dead now and once we get rid of these phones ..."

"What's going on in here?" Indi's mom stood in the doorway, the breaking moonlight catching her pale skin. "Nathan. Let go of her."

He froze as if seeing his hands upon Indi for the first time. He snatched them away and stared at them like they were some foreign instruments. "Dawn. Don't. She doesn't need to know."

Indi's blood turned to ice in her veins. "Mom. You knew?"

Her mom kept her poise. Chin up, shoulders back. Elegant as always. "Brandy disappeared. It hurt less with her gone."

"I don't know you. Either of you. What the hell is going on." Indi shoved her father out of her way and stumbled toward the door, her legs numb beneath her. She confronted her mother. "Did you kill her? So no one would find out?"

Her mom rolled her eyes. "Don't be ridiculous, India. Do you really think we could kill Brandy?"

"I don't know what to think!" Indi laughed hysterically, throwing her arms in the air. "So tell me, Mom, what am I supposed to do now? Just hang around the house with you and dad knowing the whole time that he was banging my best friend? Is that how life works now?"

"What would you prefer? That your dad go to prison? Is that what you want?" her mom questioned tersely. "Because if it is, go ahead. But I'll tell you right now, India, if this gets out, it will destroy our family. I will be humiliated, and the town will label your father a sex offender. Could you live with yourself?"

"Maybe," Indi cackled, dragging her fingers roughly down her cheeks. "Maybe repressing messed up shit runs in the family." Indi tried to push past, but her mom held her ground. Indi gritted her teeth and stared daggers at her mother. "Move."

"No," her mom said defiantly. "We need to talk about this."

"I don't want to talk. I'm sick of talking. Now, I said. Move."

Her mom planted her feet. Indi had never felt so much merciless anger. It pumped blood hot and fast through her veins. It caused her heart to boom like a freight train in her ears and filled her with the urge to mow down anyone who stood in her way. Indi ploughed hard into her, knocking her off her feet. Then she ran, faster than she knew she could, fast enough to outrun anyone who tried to stop her.

"India! Wait!" her mom screamed from the ground.

But Indi blocked her out. She didn't want to hear her mother's voice, her dad's either. She just wanted to hear her heart, feel the wind thrashing against her face. She skidded to a stop at the police car parked on the street, pounding both fists on the bonnet and startling the cops inside. They climbed out, regarding Indi warily.

"Do you need some help, Miss Peters?" said Buzzcut.

"You should stay inside, Miss. It's dangerous out here at night," added his partner.

Indi burst out laughing, crowing so hard her throat grew sore. "It's no better in there, boys." She ran at Buzzcut at full speed before leaping onto him and hooking her legs around his waist. Before he knew what was happening, she had his head in her hands, and Indi pulled him roughly onto her lips. It was over quickly, and when she moved away, his eyes were wide with shock.

"Catch me if you can," she teased. She slid down his tall frame, and soon she was running again, screaming into the night and spinning in the street. Sensor lights flicked on, a house at a time, and nosey neighbors stood glued to their windows watching India Peters publicly lose her mind.

"I'm not going to wait anymore," she yelled. "If you want to kill me, then do it already!"

Suddenly, after a screech of car tires and flash of headlights, Indi's body was thrown in the air. She landed on the car's bonnet with an obscene thud before rolling over the grill and onto the road.

Indi lay there, unmoving, voices around her loud but muffled.

"I didn't see her," a woman called. "What was she doing in the middle of the road?"

"This is Car 17," said Buzzcut. "I need an ambulance at 16 Appleby Drive right now. Over."

Then there was one last voice Indi heard in her ear before everything turned dark.

"India. It's Braddock. Can you hear me, India? Hang on. Hang on."

26

IN HER DREAM, INDI leaned against the kitchen counter, gnawing her nails down to the quick. She watched as Ted Crumby, a self-employed father of four, eyed up the warped wall.

"It's all in the approach," she muttered between chews. "Come on, you son-of-a-bitch. Run."

Ted rolled his shoulders and expelled five sharp breaths, as if he were in a birthday-candle-blowing race. That was probably a thing in Japan. Then he leaned into his running pose, a deep lunge accompanied by pumping arms.

"Here we go. Time to make Tammy-Lee, Sandra-Lynn, little Jimmy and Ted Junior proud," Indi said as the camera flicked to his family cheering in the stands.

With one desperate burst of speed, Ted pushed hard off his planted foot, digging into the padded floor, his face working its way through every ugly expression imaginable. He ran at the warped wall; he jumped; he reached ... he fell.

"Boo, you suck Ted," Indi groaned. A timer beeped, and she clapped her hands excitedly, grabbing the remote and turning off the TV. When she'd fumbled her hands into the oven gloves with all the finesse of a T-Rex, she opened the oven door and inhaled the red-velvet goodness within. Indi picked up the cake tin, placed it precisely on the counter and tossed the gloves over her head like a bride's bouquet. With surgeon's hands, she tapped the baking tin and released the clip, and when it slid away, the red velvet cake sat perfectly. No cracks. No sinkholes. Flawless.

"Nailed it," Indi grinned. "Now let's get some buttercream on this bad boy."

Suddenly her phone rang, and she was quick to hit silent before it woke up her parents. It was two in the morning after all. Unidentified number. Seemed like a good reason for an instant reject. Still, curiosity got the best of her, and Indi answered. At least if it was a Nigerian scam, she could have a laugh while she iced her cake.

"Hello," she chirped.

"India," said a weeping woman's voice on the other end.

Indi put the phone closer to her ear and knitted her brows. "Yeah. Who is this?"

"Brandy."

She snorted. "Hilarious. Who is this?"

"No, India, it's me. I swear to god."

It sounded like her, though Indi had hardly ever heard her cry, so couldn't be entirely sure. "Say I believe you. What do you want, Brandy?" speaking her name in a mocking tone.

"I need your help. I don't have anyone else I can call." Her voice shivered. "Something's happened. I can't remember." She sniffed. "I don't know where my clothes are. Please help me."

Indi gulped. "Are you serious? How do I know this isn't a prank?"

"When you got your first period, I doubled you on my bike to the emergency room because we thought you were bleeding to death."

"You knowing that doesn't make this any less of a trap."

"India. I am begging you. Please. Help me."

Indi knew what her bruised ego wanted to do. Sign off with a fuck you and hang up. Instead, she rummaged through the bowl where her mom kept her car keys. "Where are you?"

Indi didn't drive often; she preferred the leisurely passenger life. But when the situation called for it, sure, she could drive a stick. Not well, but well enough. She turned the key in the ignition, hit the gas and headed for Breakers Beach.

Before she knew it, Indi was in the carpark with her high beams on. She couldn't remember how she had got here. Her thoughts were too overwhelmed with why Brandy asked her, of all people, for help. The cloudless night was murky black, and an icy wind rolled in with the waves. Indi could hear the constant rush of the ocean breaking on the shore, swells tumbling and colliding like furious whispers competing in her ears.

Indi checked her phone, then glanced across the carpark. She frowned, asking herself on repeat why she was doing this. Indi climbed out and pulled her jacket tightly around her, digging her hands into her armpits for warmth. She crossed the gravel carpark and lumbered over the low dunes before her feet hit the soft, compacted sand on the shore. She made out a woman's silhouette near the water, her knees drawn into her chest, the waves lapping at her toes. The woman shivered, rocking back and forth in the sand, and as Indi got closer, she could hear crying and chattering teeth.

She whipped off her jacket, suddenly, not feeling the cold. "Brandy. What happened?" Indi draped the coat over Brandy's bare chest, regretting not bringing extra clothes to cover the rest of her.

Brandy looked up. Her mascara streaked across her cheeks. Her lipstick smeared around her mouth. "I don't remember. But something bad, India. Something really bad."

Indi curled her lips with discomfort, noting the bruises around Brandy's wrists and thighs. "Come on. Let's get you home."

Brandy gripped Indi's hand. "No. I can't go home. I don't want my dad to see me like this."

"Okay. My house then."

"Really?"

"Yeah. Really. Come on."

Indi helped Brandy to her feet and held her waist as they walked along the shoreline toward the car. She found some old picnic blankets in her mom's boot and wrapped them around Brandy's waist before buckling her into the front seat. The drive back was silent, but now and then Brandy would burst into tears. When they arrived at the Peters' home, Indi took her straight upstairs and put her into a hot shower.

"Don't go," Brandy asked as she went to leave.

So Indi sat on the toilet seat with her back to the shower curtain, listening to the water spin down the drain. She offered Brandy clean pajamas and then her bed. Indi set up the trundler bed beside her.

"Do you want to talk about it?" Indi asked, struggling to find the thin mattress's sweet spot.

"No," Brandy replied. She rolled onto her side and hung her arm off the bed, wriggling her fingers. Indi saw them, long and slender. She reached out with her own, and they skimmed their fingertips against each other. "I didn't think you would come."

"I wasn't the one who cancelled us," Indi said, a subtle snideness in her tone. "Where are all your friends tonight?"

"What friends?" Brandy snickered. "They aren't real. People surround me, and none of them exist."

"Sounds nice. They can't hurt you if they don't exist."

"Yeah. I heard about Cameron Gibbons. Sorry."

Indi exhaled. "Nothing to be sorry about."

Brandy rolled onto her back but left her arm to dangle over the side. She yawned. "Indi."

Indi closed her heavy eyelids. "Yeah."

"Thank you."

"Yeah."

INDI'S EYES FLICKERED open, and she immediately shielded them from a stark white light. It took her a moment to focus. The stiff blanket had her pinned to the bed, and when she jerked her hands to get free, a cluster of wires that were apparently attached to her thrashed in the air. Then she heard the heart monitor, and she let out a long, guttural groan. "No way. Not again."

The last time this happened, Indi had woken up to find her mom beside her. She looked over, curious to see if her mother had the balls to be sitting in that chair. She didn't. Instead, Braddock was there, his chin rested on his steepled fingers, and Indi wondered how long he had been watching her sleep.

"This is becoming a habit," he said with a smirk.

"No shit," Indi replied. She propped herself up on her elbows, discreetly peering around the room.

"They're not here. Your parents. If that's who you're looking for. Mayor Stein was going to ask you to be a guest speaker at the town memorial. But after all this," Braddock said, sweeping his hand over Indi's busted body in the hospital bed, "he begged your parents to speak instead. Before the good people of Army Bay rioted in the streets."

Indi wanted to laugh out loud. The nerve. Her father paying respects to the murdered teenage girl he was exchanging nudes with. She realized Braddock was staring at her as if trying to decipher her expression. The bitter, furious part of Indi that despised her dad for what he had done wanted to tell Braddock everything. But her mom's words clung to the edges of her heart, no matter how much Indi wished they would let go. She didn't want to destroy her family. Not now. Not yet.

Instead, Indi tried to sit up, then winced in pain, her ribs and shoulder aching. "Broken?"

"Just badly bruised," Braddock said. "Happens sometimes when you get hit by a car."

She lay back down. "I heard your voice before I blacked out. What were you doing there?"

"I've been away visiting family. Just got back into town. Detective Shelley caught me up on your last interview. Thought I would follow up. I arrived just in time to see some poor soccer mom in hysterics and an Indi-shaped dent in the bonnet of her people mover."

"Oh god," Indi moaned. "Can you imagine? Surviving a serial murderer only to be killed by a suburban tractor."

Braddock chuckled. "You're funny. Smart too. But your breaking-and-entering skills could use some work."

Indi froze and tried to keep her eyeballs from exploding in their sockets. She stammered, but Braddock waved away whatever attempt at deflection she was about to make.

"I'm a police detective, India. You don't think I have security cameras at my house?"

She frowned. Of course he did. "Am I in trouble?"

"Probably, but not from me. I don't see any point in making your life more difficult. It's not like you took anything, right?"

"No. Nothing." It was nice not having to lie for once.

He nodded. "Then there's nothing to talk about, unless there is something you want to talk about."

In reality, it was a conversation Indi never wanted to have. Something she wished she could forget. But it needed to be said. "The photos."

"Right. The photos. You don't remember then that you are the one who gave them to me?"

Indi's stomach churned. "I am?"

"They were evidence against Avery Weiss. Some of the first pieces of evidence I had. Then someone mailed his cell phone to me anonymously. Dozens more pictures on that thing. It helped me identify a few local girls willing to make statements." Braddock sighed. "Of course, then the bastard had to go and get murdered. Much too kind a punishment in my opinion for the type of scum he was."

Indi vaguely recalled Elton mentioning Avery's cell phone going missing in Seradale. Was it Elton who had taken it? Maybe to get evidence on Avery or use the photos to convince Rory he was a monster. With the reason for the pictures explained, Indi nervously asked her second question.

"I saw a photo on the desk in the house. It was like the one at the station. That's how I knew where you lived."

"Nice work," Braddock commended. "Maybe you should have my job."

Indi smirked, but it hurt her jaw, so she went limp in the face like a blobfish instead. "I saw Brandy in those pictures. Why didn't you say you knew her?"

Braddock furrowed his brow. "Brandy? It's not Brandy in those pictures. That's my daughter, Jenna. I guess you could have mistaken her for Brandy. They look a little similar, I suppose. Blonde hair, same height."

Indi thought hard, rolling the name over in her head. "And she goes to Army Bay High?"

"No. She lives with her mother in Seradale. Goes to St. Margaret's. It's a Catholic girls' school."

Indi remembered the blazer in Brandy's closet. "She wouldn't be head girl, would she?"

Braddock beamed, smiling proudly. "Actually, yes, she is. How did you know that?"

"Lucky guess."

Indi had been in the throes of a panic attack when she had seen that photo on his desk. Even now, she couldn't remember exactly who it was in Braddock's arms. Jenna from Seradale. Jenna. No. Wait. Not sober driver Jenna, from Elton's party? That was forever ago.

"Where is Jenna now?" Indi continued. She stifled her trembling hands, not wanting to give away that she was questioning Braddock. He seemed none the wiser.

"Probably back in Seradale for school. But she might come down for the weekend, usually does. My ex-wife wants her to buy her own car rather than us buy her one, so until that happens I let her borrow mine whenever she visits. It'll take her a while to save. She works part-time at some clinic in Seradale. Happiness? Gleeness ...?"

"Joyness," Indi corrected.

Braddock snapped his fingers. "That's the one. Joyness." The alarm on his watch beeped, and he clicked his tongue. "Damn it. Mayor Stein wants me to give a speech at this memorial tonight. Haven't even had a chance to write something down. Guess I'm winging it." He stood from his chair and gave Indi's forearm a sturdy wiggle. "Don't worry, India. Now that I'm back on the case, I'll catch whoever did this in no time. I promise you that."

He adjusted his jacket, then made for the door.

"Hey, Braddock," Indi called to his back.

He craned his neck. "Yes, Ma'am."

"Elton Riggs. Is he in jail?"

Braddock grumbled under his breath. "Not enough evidence to keep that one, I'm afraid. His lawyer is arguing it's a frame-up job, that the rope with his prints was planted and nothing places him at the scenes. He was released this morning. But there's more than one way to skin a cat."

Brandy nodded politely but absorbed none of what he said, apart from that Elton was out of jail. Memories flashed behind her eyes as the puzzle pieces merged and took shape. It was becoming more clear. The white was the clouds. The blue was the sky. The green was the grass. But where did Jenna Braddock fit?

Indi couldn't just accuse her right there to her father, based on purely circumstantial coincidences. As far as she knew, Jenna didn't know Brandy or any of them. She had said that herself at Elton's party, where his climbing ropes had sat openly in the garage. Jenna barely knew Paula, either. Paula, who could have put her in touch with Micah, who had the drugs that killed Avery. Then there was her connection to the Joyness Clinic, where Christa had been a patient, where she had carved statues like the one used to murder Ben. But why?

The idea that her parents had killed Brandy was still fresh in her mind. They were liars, but did that make them murderers? Or was Indi pushing the blame onto this girl she didn't know because it was easier than facing the truth?

There was one last piece that could solve the entire puzzle. Sadie. Indi just had to get to her first. She ripped the tubes from her skin and forced herself to sit up, even though it hurt like a bitch. She glanced around the hospital room, searching for a way to get out of there. Her eyes found the untouched dinner on the tray beside her. An idea bloomed in her mind, and she pushed the assistance button, then lay back down.

A nurse wandered in and gave Indi's chart a brief once-over. "Everything alright, dear?"

Indi flicked her head toward the tray. "I don't suppose I could get extra pudding?"

"Well, we don't normally do that," the nurse started.

"Come on, just this once?" Indi pleaded. "I've had a pretty rough day."

The nurse's stern demeanor softened, and she smiled sympathetically. "Of course you have. I'll get the orderly to bring one up to you right away."

Indi watched the nurse leave and make a call from the nurse's station. Within a few minutes, Cody arrived in his shapeless beige uniform, pudding in hand.

He pulled back the curtain and frowned dramatically when he saw Indi. "This is for you? If I'd known that I would have put drain cleaner in it."

"Not really the climate to be throwing around death threats," Indi replied. She urged him to come closer, and he did so, but not without an exaggerated eye roll.

"I need your car and your pants," Indi whispered.

"Not the first time I've heard that."

She nudged his shoulder. "I'm serious. I need to get out of here."

"Why would I help you? I get why the cops might suspect me, but Christa? You couldn't even lie and say it wasn't her you saw. After everything she's been through."

"I don't think it was either of you. Not anymore," Indi said.

Cody cocked his head to one side. "Thanks."

"Look, if you help me get out of here, I will prove that you and Christa are innocent. I promise."

Cody pondered for longer than Indi would have liked, but eventually he sighed and nodded and slipped out of his drawstring trousers and shirt, leaving him in boxer briefs and a white long-sleeved top. It surprised Indi how unaffected he was at being pant-less. When she had dressed in his clothes, Cody tossed his car keys.

"Level Two. Space 69. Hey-yo."

"Thank you!" she quietly exclaimed.

"Just prove my sister didn't do this, okay?"

Indi nodded and peered out the curtain. When the coast was clear, she dashed through the ward with her head bowed and straight into the elevator. Even without the immaturely hilarious space number, Indi would have found Cody's car relatively quickly. It was the only one that looked like a tampon box with wheels. She climbed in, turned the key and the engine sputtered into a whoosh, kind of what she imagined a panda fart might sound like. Indi practically pushed the gas pedal through the floor, but the car only gently puttered in response. If she hadn't desperately needed to commandeer this vehicle to save lives, she would have set it on fire just to put it out of its misery.

27

INDI PULLED THE CAR into Elton's driveway. Her last memory of his house was the night of the party, with a light on in every window, music pounding so hard you could feel it reverberate through your shoes, and the unmistakable scent of vomit and regret wafting through the air.

Now, cloaked in darkness and silence, it felt more like a mausoleum. Indi parked Cody's car and crossed the cobbled courtyard to Elton's front door. She knocked and waited, then buzzed and waited a little longer. Indi heard footsteps approaching from inside, and she held her breath when the door creaked open. Elton kept to the shadows as he warily answered, but as soon as he set eyes on Indi he was on the doorstep with his arms encircling her waist, lifting her to his lips.

He stole the breath she was holding, and Indi melted into him, her hands searching out the smooth skin at his nape.

Elton withdrew his lips first, and Indi felt his heart thumping through his chest.

She winced. "This would be so romantic if my ribs weren't cracked."

Elton bit his lip and took a cautious step back, which was the opposite of what Indi wanted, regardless of the pain. "Shit. I'm sorry," he mumbled. "I was just so worried. Where have you been? I've been calling you."

"My dad took my phone," she explained, fighting to resist sinking into his soft lips again. "And I kind of got hit by a car."

Elton jerked. "What? That was you? How?"

Indi shrugged, her eyes fixated on his mouth as he spoke. "Just lucky, I guess."

Elton then noticed the bruises along her jawline, tracing them carefully with his knuckles. "It's never easy with you, is it?" Indi dropped her chin, but he tilted it back up. "I wouldn't want it any other way." He left a light kiss on her lips. "I thought you might be at that thing at the town hall. That's where my parents are, where half the town is, anyway."

"I just bailed from the hospital. I think I know who is behind the murders."

Elton frowned. "Oh, so this is just a business call?"

Indi knocked him in the side, and he winced. "I'm serious. I think we can draw her out."

"Her? Who?" Elton cocked an eyebrow.

"Jenna Braddock." She watched the cogs turn behind his eyes. "Detective Braddock's daughter."

"Get out of here!" Elton spat. "Why her?"

"I'll explain in the car, but right now, we have to find Sadie. I think she could be in danger. Do you know where she is?"

"Yeah, of course," Elton said nonchalantly. "The winter formal got cancelled for safety reasons, so Sadie crowned herself Frost Queen. She's having a party at her house right now."

"That's a good thing, right? No way Jenna would go after her there with so many witnesses," Indi said, her voice inflecting optimistically.

"Sure. Let's go with that," Elton replied.

She frowned and grabbed his hand, and Elton had a second to close the door before Indi was dragging him toward Cody's matchbox car.

"Oh shit," Elton laughed behind his hand. "What is that?"

"I had to borrow Cody's car."

"I'm not being seen in that."

"Okay. Where's your car?" Indi sighed.

"The cops impounded it as evidence."

Indi shook her head snidely and opened the passenger door. "Well then, after you."

The defeated droop in Elton's shoulders signaled the loss of his dignity. He climbed in the car, his knees practically against his chest, his head brushing the roof. Indi stifled her laugh as she closed the door, sealing him in.

She took her seat behind the wheel and hit the gas, the car plodding along a little slower with the added weight of Elton and his degradation.

"So, she was at my party?" he asked, wriggling for what legroom he could find.

"She was with Paula. She gave me a ride home after ..."

"After you ghosted me in the garage," Elton finished.

"Stop living in the past," Indi said. "The point is, she was there and if I could get into that garage easily, that means she could have as well. She could have taken your climbing ropes to set you up for these murders."

Elton nodded. "Okay. Fine. But why? I mean the others aside, do you know her? If she killed them, she must have been the one who attacked you."

Indi didn't have answers for that; she was piecing this together as she went and knew how ridiculous it must have sounded. She may have had thoughts about how, but the whys evaded her. If it was Jenna, then why didn't she take her opportunity to finish what she had started after Elton's party? She and Indi were alone. Then she wouldn't have to risk being discovered.

"That part I'm a little less sure about." Indi exhaled. "Maybe Sadie can fill in these blanks. Come on car, move!" Indi rocked back and forth impatiently, as if that would make the car go faster.

"Don't waste your energy," Elton said, tucking in his elbows to keep them from knocking against the door. "A microwave has more power than this thing. It would honestly be quicker if we just kicked holes in the floor and Flintstoned this shit."

"No. Cody is doing me a solid. I'm returning this car to him in one piece." Indi turned down Sadie's street. She veered to the left and clipped a parked car before she had time to straighten up. Cody's wing mirror snapped off with a thwack and Indi watched in the rearview as it bounced away behind them. "Whoops."

Indi maneuvered up the driveway as it snaked steeply through dense trees. She heard the party before she saw it, thumping dance music that was dull at first, but as soon as they broke the tree line, each synth chord and drum machine beat was crystal clear. The guests had abandoned any kind of parking etiquette, leaving the cars looking like an askew Tetris game. Indi did her best to slot in Cody's car before she climbed out and went to Elton's aid, having to unfold him from his seat.

They approached the party, and it wasn't until Indi was bombarded with side-eye stares from girls in bodycon minidresses that she remembered she was wearing a hospital orderly's uniform. Meanwhile, Elton was receiving high fives and secret handshakes galore from a bevvy of Shawn Mendes lookalikes. Indi knew how she must have looked walking beside this Nubian prince. She hadn't even brushed her hair when she left the hospital. Before she could over analyze their stares and perhaps lay a bitch out, Elton laced his fingers with hers, pulling her close to his side. He kissed her, not casually on the cheek or tenderly on the forehead; hard on the mouth and lingering, with parted lips.

"You ready to do this?" he asked.

Indi liked Elton kissing her in the open like that. She smiled when she noticed the stunned gawks of the minidress collective. She could get used to this. Not the status or the envy or sticking it to everyone who considered her weird and unworthy of an identity. She could get used to being with someone like herself, someone who didn't give a shit what anyone else thought.

They let themselves in and immediately became immersed in a sea of gyrating teens wielding red paper cups, spilling cheap beer all over Justine Hamilton's Italian marble floors.

Elton flagged down some guy in a muscle tee. "Hey, man. Seen Sadie?"

"Upstairs," Muscle Tee replied, bumping fists with Elton before the crowd swallowed him.

"Come on then," Indi said firmly. She marched purposefully, the long staircase giving her time to scan the crowd for any sign of Jenna, whose face she couldn't clearly recall. It seemed keeping an eye out for someone who looked like Brandy would be the best way to recognize her. They reached the landing and walked down the hall. Indi had to rattle Elton's hand, keeping him focused as he became distracted by the Hamilton twins' portraits. She passed by Brandy's room, curious to see the rooms further down. Elton, however, stopped in his tracks outside her door.

"This one right?"

Indi knitted her brows. "You know which one is Brandy's room?" She didn't like it when he paused.

"I mean. Yeah. I guess."

"So you've been in her room before?"

He exhaled. "It's not like that, Indi. Geez. I'm on your side, remember? Aren't we here to save Sadie?"

A single loud click alerted Indi to the fact they were not alone.

"I'm not the one who needs saving. Sorry to disappoint you." Sadie stood at the end of the hall, her body draped in Brandy's red-sequinned gown, a gun firmly in her hand and pointed straight at Indi. "I knew you'd come. It was just a matter of time." She jerked the gun. "So I made sure I was ready."

Indi shook her head. "Sadie. No. It's not us. We're here to help you."

"Shut the fuck up," Sadie groaned. Her eyes drifted to Indi's neck and widened when she caught sight of Brandy's pendant. Sadie wound the chain around her wrist and ripped it from Indi's throat. "How dare you!" She flicked her head toward Brandy's room. "Both of you. In there. Now." She grew impatient when they didn't move. "Or I can shoot you both dead right here. I'll say it was self-defense. Everyone knows you're both suspects in these murders. Your choice."

Stalling. That was a thing, right? Maybe once they got inside the room, they could talk, and Indi could calm her down. She took a step forward.

"Don't," Elton muttered. "She'll kill us either way."

"She's scared," Indi said quickly. "We just need to talk to her." Indi felt his reluctance, but he followed her regardless.

They entered Brandy's darkened room and Sadie waggled the gun at the bed. Indi and Elton sat down with their hands raised. Indi felt dizzy, as if the hectic dash from the hospital to here had finally caught up with her. Her aching shoulder and ribs were a reminder that she was still recovering from a car accident. The swaying room, as if Indi were on the Hamilton's boat again, was surely a sign of a concussion. Indi's hazy view drifted to Sadie. She had to tell herself that it wasn't Brandy standing before her, the resemblance as disorienting as ever.

"I have to admit. I was expecting more. You murdered the others with such flair. So what was your plan, then? What were you going to do to me?"

"Sadie, we aren't here to kill you. You have to believe us."

"Us?" Sadie glared at Elton. "How long have you been in on this with her? You don't even like her."

"That was never true," he said defensively. "And besides, things are different now."

Sadie eyed Indi sourly. "You could do so much better. You could have had Brandy if you wanted. You could have had me too, and I'm even more beautiful than she ever was. People can see that now. You can only appreciate the other stars when the brightest one dies. I mean, I'm the fucking Frost Queen."

Sadie wavered, and Indi could smell alcohol on her breath. She pleaded. "Sadie. I think I know who's behind this. I just don't know why. Do you know Jenna Braddock?"

Sadie screwed up her face. "Who the hell is Jenna Braddock?"

"She's the police detective's daughter. She had access to everything found at the murders. She was trying to set Elton up to take the fall. She's picking off the group one at a time, and it only makes sense that she will come after one of us next. She could even be here now."

Sadie smirked. "Sorry, didn't invite a Jenna Braddock. Didn't invite you either." She straightened her arm and pushed the gun barrel closer to Indi's head. "This was supposed to be my special night, and here you are, ruining everything like you always do."

Indi gulped. "But Jenna ..."

"Enough with this make-believe bullshit!" Sadie screamed, her eyes welling with tears. "You did this. You murdered Avery. You murdered Rory. You murdered Ben. I told them you would remember. But they wouldn't listen. Ben thought he could get you on side, so did Rory. I knew it wouldn't work. Only Avery had the balls to do what needed to be done. If he had just finished you in that tunnel, this would have been over ages ago, but by the time Ben finally agreed with us, it was too late. How they could not kill a pathetic little bitch like you I'll never understand." She pushed the barrel to Indi's forehead. "I guess I'll have to finish you myself."

Indi's heart pounded in her chest, sweat beading at her temple and trailing along her jaw. "What are you saying? If you think I killed them, does that mean you think I killed Brandy too?"

"Of course not, you dumb cunt." Sadie leaned in close. "We killed Brandy."

Elton lunged for the gun, his hands clasping the barrel. Sadie struggled against his grip and then time stopped. A loud bang pierced the air, ringing in Indi's ears. Blood pooled at Elton's stomach, seeping through his shirt. His wide eyes glassed over and he stared speechlessly at Indi.

Indi screamed. "Elton! No!"

He stumbled, pressing his hand to the wound. His lips trembled, the warm hue of his skin fading like autumn leaves. He fell, and Indi caught him, lowering him to the ground as gently as she could. Her hand brushed against his pocket, where she felt a familiar square-shaped object.

Sadie was breathless, her chest heaving, but she was smiling too. "Like I said. Self-defense. You two came in here to murder me, just like the others. It was you or me." She cocked the gun. "I always choose me."

Indi yanked the rape alarm free from Elton's pocket. She pulled the tab and held it out toward Sadie. The high-pitched screech had Sadie grasping at her ears as she staggered backward. Indi fought her way to her feet as Elton bled out on the floor. She had to get out of here; she had to get help. Sadie looked up, and with nothing else to defend herself with, Indi threw the alarm square at Sadie's head.

Sadie squinted and rubbed her reddening brow. "That hurt, you bitch."

Indi vaulted over the bed just as another gunshot rang out.

"You're not leaving this room alive," Sadie threatened. "If you give up now, I'll make it quick. Right between the eyes."

Indi backed up on the other side of the bed, her breaths hard and fast. Then she noticed Brandy's closet was slightly open, and from the floor, Indi saw two feet tucked away in the corner. Slowly, the door opened, and a figure stepped into the shadows.

"Who the fuck are you?" Sadie yelled.

Indi had no time to react. The figure looked down at her, then lifted its boot and kicked her hard in the face. Indi swayed, her senses lost, her mind spinning in frantic circles before she fell flat on the floor. The figure moved toward Sadie. Indi could hear Sadie cursing, and there was a struggle followed by a loud thud. She saw the gun drop to the floor and then watched in a daze as the figure dragged Sadie from the room.

Indi's eyes grew heavy as the world continued to spiral around her. Then she blacked out.

28

FOR THE LONGEST TIME, there had been a wall thick with brick and bone separating Indi from the things she needed to know. It had been so bottomless and endless and hopeless, but now, just when the devouring despair threatened her will the most, the wall was cracking, like veins of memory rippling over its surface and making it weak. Now, she could see.

The group had been acting weird those last couple of days. Indi wondered if they had found out she had given those photos to the police. Avery had sent them to Brandy and thanked her for a great night. The sick bastard. He must have thought she would just keep her mouth shut. Brandy wouldn't want Ben to find out, or the school to gossip about what a slut she was. He might have been right, too. But that was before Indi rescued Brandy from the beach and before Cam Gibbons had broken Indi's heart. In the dark, their sadness had led them back to each other. Their bond had strengthened. Brandy needed the group less and less, and Indi loved feeling needed again. So, no. Brandy would not keep her mouth shut. Avery was going to pay for this. Now that Indi was here, she would make sure of that.

She lay back on her bed with her phone in the air and typed out a message.

India: Have you seen them today?

Brandy: No. You?

India: No. Something feels off. It's too quiet.

Brandy: Maybe we shouldn't have said anything.

India: No. Avery can't get away with that shit. It's over. You did the right thing. What about Sadie? Has she spoken to them?

Brandy: No. She wants to go to a movie tonight. Cheer me up. We haven't done that forever.

India: Sounds fun. Text me after.

Brandy: Okay. Love you. Bye.

India: Love you too.

Indi tossed aside her phone and had just got comfortable when her mom called up the stairs.

"Indi. Rory's here."

Indi bolted up. She slowly left her room, her stomach knotting with each step as she descended the stairs. Rory was in the doorway, a bright pink box in her hands.

"Hey," Indi greeted.

Rory's face was somber. "Can we talk?"

INDI WOULDN'T BELIEVE it. She scrolled through the messages and turned in disgust at the pictures. "You're fucking lying."

Rory shook her head. "No. I'm not. It's been going on for weeks now. She meets your dad at work. They screw in that trailer." Rory pulled out her phone. "She sent me this."

Rory hit play on a video. It was blurry and zoomed in, making it almost impossible to make sense of. Then, for a split second, everything was clear. Brandy lay on the paisley couch in her dad's office, smiling at the phone in her hand. A shirtless man heaved on top of her, grunting as the couch knocked against the wall. He turned his head, searching for Brandy's lips, then recoiled when he saw the phone.

"What are you doing? Turn that thing off," he yelled.

Brandy laughed and hit Stop.

It was true. It was him.

Indi's lip quivered beyond her control, and tears came harder and heavier than she knew possible.

Rory stroked her back. "I didn't want to tell you. I know this hurts. But I didn't have a choice. You had to know the type of person Brandy is."

"Why would she do this to me?" Indi sobbed. She couldn't breathe.

"She can't help herself," Rory replied. "She only cares about what makes her feel good. The rest of us are just in the crossfire, just casualties of her need to have anything and everything she wants, no matter who gets hurt. I wouldn't be surprised if the only reason she reconnected with you in the first place was to get close to your dad. She always talked about him, how she was sure he had a thing for her when you guys were growing up."

Indi gritted her teeth and clenched her fists. Not again. They would not hurt her again. She had given her heart and soul to these people who just treated her like shit. She had sacrificed her own identity to make them feel better about themselves. And what did she get in return? Cameron cheating on her with some dumb boy and Brandy pretending to be her friend while she screwed her dad.

"I'll kill her," Indi muttered. "I'll fucking kill her."

"It's okay," Rory said, brushing the tear-soaked hair from Indi's face. "We're going to meet Brandy tonight. All of us. We need to tell her how we're feeling. Like an intervention. There's more going on than you know."

Indi gulped. "Will Avery be there?"

Rory nodded silently.

"She won't come," Indi stammered. "Not if he's there."

"Right now, you're the person she trusts most in this world." Rory exhaled. "She will come if you convince her it's safe. That we just want things to go back to the way they were. Just best friends hanging out like we used to. Can you do that? Will you help us save Brandy?" Rory gently lifted Indi's chin and met her eyes. "We need you, India."

Indi sniffed back her tears, shivering breaths causing her body to tremble. In that moment, she couldn't see past her anger. Her senses were devolving into a thick, black tar, blinding her to reason, and any lingering sympathies or second thoughts were being swallowed one by one.

She found her voice, though it was hollow and distant in her ears, almost as if it wasn't her voice at all and somehow, that made it easier to speak. "I'll do it."

THE SUN SET, AND IT felt like the last precious memories of autumn went with it. The days were getting longer and darker, and the cold of winter was setting in. The beach was empty when the group arrived in Avery's SUV. Avery sat in front with Rory holding his hand atop the gear stick. Brandy curled up in Ben's arms, nuzzling into his dark sweater while she scrolled through her phone. Sadie sat next to her and Indi was at the back, in the second row of seats.

Brandy didn't seem to have a care in the world. She laughed and made jokes, asked why they were going to the beach instead of the movies, kissed Ben long and deep.

When Avery had parked, the group piled out of the car. The sound of crashing waves carried on the biting air, and the dapples of moonlight led them across the dunes toward the drinking tree. They came to a stop at the trunk and Brandy climbed. Ben grabbed her arm, pulling her back down.

"Wait," he said. "We have to talk."

The others gathered around her, Indi amongst them. They exchanged knowing looks, their breaths rising and falling like the waves beneath the cliff.

Brandy cocked an eyebrow. She looked beautiful tonight, like always—her blonde hair a perfect tangle down her back, her flawless porcelain skin rivalling the moon.

"What is it?" she asked.

"We know, Brandy. We know everything," Avery said as Rory tucked in under his arm. "You sent those photos to the police. Are you trying to destroy me?"

Brandy gulped and turned to Indi, but Indi didn't respond. All she could see was Brandy's smug grin as her dad thrust inside her.

"I know about the whore in Seradale," Ben added, his jaw clenched. "As well as every other guy in town. How long did you think I would let you humiliate me?"

"I know you lied to get my scholarship," Rory said. "And that you're trying to send Avery to jail. Why couldn't you just shut up? Do you have to ruin everyone's life?"

Brandy was shaking. She put her back to the tree and looked at Sadie. "What about you? Got something to share?" She spat a nervous laugh.

"It's time to choose me," Sadie muttered.

The group walked forward, circling her like a pack of wolves. Then Sadie raised her hand and slapped Brandy hard across the face. Brandy's eyes were wide with shock as she nursed her mouth, blood pooling at her lip.

"What is wrong with you?" Brandy yelled. She went to break free of the circle, but Avery grabbed her, throwing her back against the tree. Next was Rory, who slapped the opposite side of Brandy's face.

Brandy whimpered. "I'm sorry, okay. I get it. What do you want me to do?" She looked desperately at India once more. "Indi. Please. Make them stop this."

"You've been sleeping with my dad," India said absently. "This whole time." Before she could speak, Indi slapped her as well, and Brandy collapsed onto her knees. Indi looked down at her coldly. "Come on. Let's go."

"Go? But we're just getting started," Ben said with a smile.

Avery rolled his shoulders and lurched over Brandy. He grabbed her by the collar of her shirt, turning her face to the light. "You couldn't just enjoy it like the rest of them?" He drew back his fist and struck Brandy's face.

Indi gasped and lunged forward, pulling at Avery's wrist. "What are you doing?"

Ben shoved Indi back. "You know why we came here. We've had enough. She needs to be taught a lesson."

"I didn't agree to this," Indi shouted. "Let her go. Now."

The others exchanged looks, and just as they had closed in on Brandy, suddenly it was Indi in their sights.

"I told you she wouldn't go along with it," Sadie groaned.

"Well," Avery sighed. "Looks like it's both of them then. Everyone okay with that?"

The others nodded, and suddenly Indi felt Ben's hand around her throat. He pulled a rock from the base of the tree and raised it over her head. It was the last thing Indi saw before the sky turned red. She could feel the dirt beneath her body and the blood streaming over her face. She could hear Brandy screaming.

"Bitch bit me," Ben yelled. "Get rid of this sweater."

After what felt like forever, Indi's body lifted from the ground. A rope tightened around her wrists. Her were fingers laced with someone else's. She could hear Brandy crying. Then they were falling. Then floating. Then sinking. It was freezing and so hopelessly dark in the shadowed waters.

The cold stabbed at Indi and forced her to open her eyes. When she did, she found Brandy. Their wrists lashed tightly together. Brandy's eyes were closed.

Indi fought against the rope. The fibers tore at her skin, but she felt nothing, just the need to breathe. The ropes fell away, and Indi reached for Brandy, but she was gone, asleep and sinking deeper into the darkness.

INDI GASPED DESPERATELY for precious breath when she woke, as if bursting from the water all over again. Where was she? Oh my god! Brandy's room. Sadie! Elton! Was he alive or dead? She tried to sit up, but the crowd that had gathered tried to lie her back down.

"We've called an ambulance and the police," someone said. "You shouldn't move."

Indi pushed them away and fought to her feet. "Tell them to go to the beach," she murmured.

Indi hugged the walls to stay upright, demanding that her body hold out just a while longer. She made it to the stairs, grasping the railing and dragging herself to the bottom. She missed the last couple of steps and stumbled to the ground. But again, Indi would not stay down. She found her feet and made for the door. Her eyes focused on Cody's car, and she used the last shred of strength in her legs to fall into the driver's seat. She knew precisely where Brandy ... no ... Sadie would be.

This would end where it began.

Indi's senses returned to her slowly, and when she pulled into the carpark at Breakers Beach, she could at least walk alone without falling over. The sand tried to slow her every step, but Indi wouldn't allow it. She stomped through the dunes, refusing to let them drag her down. Not until she finished this. She tumbled over the last dune and saw a figure standing in the shallows.

"Jenna! Stop!" Indi screamed.

The moonlight caught Jenna's face as she looked up from the water. The thrashing at her ankles stopped, and silence replaced the frantic splashing. When Jenna straightened upright, the water stilled and Indi gasped into her hand when Sadie's lifeless body bobbed to the surface.

Jenna waded toward the shore, her arms raised innocently in the air. "It's over now," she said, her voice soft and calm. "You'll be safe. Everyone will. Safe from those horrible people."

Indi couldn't move. She felt as if the sand was swallowing her and pulling her down, but it wasn't. Maybe she just wished it was. She couldn't drag her eyes away from Sadie's motionless body as it floated out to sea, cradled by the gentle waves.

Jenna stepped onto the shore, her sopping wet boots sloshing with each step. "Someone had to punish them. But nothing more has to happen after tonight. We can just go home and forget about all of this."

Indi gulped. "Until you decide to tie up a loose end and come looking for me?"

"I was never going to hurt you. That was never the plan. I know you had nothing to do with what they did to Brandy."

Indi's strength dwindled, and she couldn't hold back the tears any longer. She sobbed and dropped to her knees. "But I did. I just didn't know it would go that far and I couldn't stop them. I was so mad. I couldn't think straight. But I helped them bring her out here that night. I knew we were going to hurt her. I just didn't know how far it would go."

Jenna ran a hand over her long blonde hair, sweeping it from her face. "No. That can't be right. They left you to drown, just like her."

"When I tried to stop it, they turned on me." A blood splatter flashed in Indi's mind. "Ben hit me with a rock, and when I passed out they must have tied me to Brandy. I woke up when we were in the water, and I got loose. But I couldn't save her."

"Why would you tell me this?" Jenna asked through gritted teeth. "I killed them. All of them and didn't think twice about it. What makes you think I would show you any mercy? Why not lie and live?"

Indi shrugged weakly. "I don't want to lie anymore." She locked eyes with Jenna. "And I'm not sure I want to live anymore either."

Jenna came closer and stood over Indi for a moment, taking a strand of Indi's dark hair between her fingers. "Why were you mad at her ... at Brandy? Why did you help them?"

The words tasted like rotten food in her mouth. "She was having an affair. With my father."

Jenna bit her lip and turned away, leaving the wind to catch Indi's hair. "No, she wasn't. She wouldn't."

"She was. She did," Indi muttered.

Suddenly, Jenna dropped to her knees and forced Indi's chin up from her chest. "You're lying."

When the clouds shifted, the moonlight struck Jenna's face again, and Indi could see that one of her eyes was blue while the other was brown.

"Huh." Indi gave a weak smile. "You're her Demi."

Jenna's eyes welled with tears. "She told you that? Then you must know you're lying. We were in love." Jenna's voice trailed off. "She never said what Avery did to her. I found out by accident when I saw the photos on my father's desk. Then she died. The first thing I did was string that bastard up. It was only supposed to be him, but then he was so desperate to save his own life that he told me everything. I must have shoved the pills down his throat before he got to you." Jenna struggled with Indi's words. "No. We were in love. She wouldn't do that to me."

Indi exhaled. "I don't know why Brandy did the things she did. Those little secrets were hers to keep. I don't understand how she could love someone with one hand and then stab them straight through the heart with the other. She was something different to everyone, beautiful and magical, and fucking cruel. Avery and Ben and Sadie and Rory, they deserved to be punished for what they did to her. Me too. I deserve to be punished. But no amount of death and blood and revenge is going to bring back the Brandy that you loved."

Jenna's face turned hard, her eyes seemingly rolling over to solid black like a shark when it smells blood in the water. "I know it won't bring her back." Her lip quivered. "But it still makes me feel better to know you're all dead too."

Suddenly, her frozen hands were squeezing around Indi's throat. Indi gripped Jenna's wrists, digging her thumbs into the soft skin, pitting all her strength into fighting herself free. Jenna bore down, squeezing tighter. She stared at Indi unblinking, seemingly taking extra care to keep her head up so she could see the fear in Indi's eyes.

At that moment, all Indi wanted in the world, even more than surviving, was never to have to endure Jenna's chilling gaze ever again. Indi moved her hands from Jenna's wrists to her face, clawing her fingers along Jenna's cheeks until her thumbs found the curved dips of her eye sockets. Indi pressed hard, feeling them sink into Jenna's skull. She was unmoved by Jenna's escalating screams, unfazed by how her eyes were firm at first but were slowly softening. Just when Indi thought they might burst, Jenna released her throat and buried her face in her hands.

Indi gasped for air, filling her lungs as quickly as she could while crawling to her feet. She went to run, but Jenna reached out, ripping her ankle out from beneath her, and Indi fell hard onto the wet sand that hit her like a punch in the face. Jenna stood slowly, blood trailing from the corners of her red eyes. She held tight to Indi's ankle, turning her and dragging her toward the water.

Indi screamed and dug her fingernails into the sand, clawing to gain back ground. She kicked, thrashing her free foot at whatever it could reach, striking Jenna in the shin and at the knee. Jenna grimaced but did not release her, and inch by inch they neared the water until Indi could hear the splashes of Jenna wading into the waves. The broken shells in the shallows scraped against Indi's stomach and soon her head was underwater as Jenna dragged her deeper. Indi screamed again, the sound turning to hollow gurgles. As the current lifted her, Indi bent her body and thrust herself upward to break the surface. She coughed and spat salty water, then sucked in all the air she could before she sank again. With her eyes open beneath the waterline, she could see Jenna was hip-deep now. Indi kicked again, the current giving her momentum. She fought to free her other foot from Jenna's grasp, thrashing as she imagined Sadie had. But slowly the fight in her dwindled. Whether it was the spirit of vengeance burning inside her or only the basic instinct to kill or be killed, Jenna was stronger.

Indi felt her muscles loosen, her limbs fall limp, the water fill her lungs. Jenna let go of Indi's ankle, grabbing her head instead and holding her down. It was just as dark beneath the water as Indi remembered, the moon casting fleeting shadows through the endless void. She closed her eyes, and Brandy's face appeared before her, her blonde hair drifting in shimmering sheets around her oval face, her skin pale as the moon that had watched her die, the water catching the tears that streamed from her blue eyes. She was so beautiful, so magical, so cruel. She moved closer and her lips curved into a smile, then she kissed Indi softly in a blissful moment that felt like it lasted an eternity. When Indi opened her eyes, Brandy was gone, but her kiss lingered, leaving behind a final breath that demanded she fight.

With all she had left, Indi burst from the water and wrapped her arms around Jenna's neck. Her mouth found Jenna's ear, and she bit down until her teeth clenched, and she could feel the thin tissue in her mouth. It took a second for Jenna to realize half of her ear was missing, as though she was scared to touch the ratty, bleeding stub. Indi spat the scrap of the ear into the water, then brought her fist up hard into Jenna's chin. Jenna staggered, her eyes finding Indi just as she landed another punch. Blood erupted from Jenna's mouth. Her red eyes lost their focus, staring blankly at the shore.

Slowly, Jenna waded toward the sand, lost and disoriented. Indi followed, her jaw clenched, her eyes fixed on the back of Jenna's head. The blood tasted warm in her mouth, the sound of bones cracking a harmony in her ears, and all she could think about was finding the biggest rock she could and smashing Jenna's head in.

When the water was at her ankles, Jenna fell onto the sand, a second spew of blood spraying the shoreline. She lay there, barely conscious, cupping the side of her face where her ear used to be, her nose and jaw slightly askew, her breaths little more than gurgles in her throat.

Indi emerged from the water, passing Jenna with indifference as she scanned the area nearby. She smiled when she caught sight of a fist-shaped rock amongst the brush. Indi picked it up, caressing its smooth surface and admiring how perfectly it fit in her hand. She returned to Jenna, who hadn't moved, and straddled her chest.

"Please," Jenna sputtered, her body jerking beneath Indi's weight, "I don't want to die."

Indi shrugged and raised the rock high over her head. "You can't always get what you want."

"India!" Elton's voice rung out over the dunes as he ran, his hand clutching the bandaged wound at his waist. "Don't do it India."

Indi hesitated, her eyes glassing over. She looked at Jenna; her face was masked with blood, just as Indi's had been that morning, the morning that changed everything. The morning that showed her the fathomless evil that dwelled within people. What made her different from any of them? She was just as guilty. Why shouldn't she let go and embrace what she was? A murderer.

"You don't know what I did, Elton," Indi yelled, her salty tears becoming one with the seawater.

"I don't care what you did," he said, arriving at the shore. "I just care what you do now." He came closer, and Indi felt his touch upon her trembling hands. "Don't let it end like this."

Indi's anger stoked hot in her belly as the last few months flashed before her in blinding color. She let out a blood-curdling scream and clenched her hands tighter around the rock before plunging it toward Jenna's head. The rock impacted with a hollow thud and lodged in the sand just beside her missing ear.

Elton lifted Indi into his arms, holding her head to his chest as she sobbed. They fell to the ground together, and he cleared away the sheet of soaking wet hair that clung to her face. Through her tears, she heard the shrill of police sirens, and streaks of blue and red lights chased away the darkness.

She could remember the basics. Her name was India Peters. She was a senior at Army Bay High. She could bake a red velvet cake with her eyes closed and hated cross-country running. She loved and helped kill her best friend, Brandy Hamilton, who was something to everyone and, tonight, Brandy Hamilton saved her life.

EPILOGUE

THE ARRIVAL OF SPRING was breathing warmth into the air and chasing away the chill of winter. Indi weaved through the headstones and stopped at a slab of white marble crowned with a weeping angel, the soil below lost beneath dozens of garlands and bouquets.

Here lies Brandy Beatrice Hamilton. Sleep peacefully, beautiful girl.

Indi knelt beside the grave and placed a pot planted with deep purple violets. The leaves rustled overhead and a breeze brushed over Indi's skin, gentle as a friend's touch. She kissed her fingertips and pressed them to the etching.

"I miss you," she whispered. She climbed to her feet and the trees quieted, but Indi felt them watching as she left the cemetery and made her way to the coffee shop on the main strip.

She spied Braddock alone at a table, already with two empty cups stacked beside him. He stood when Indi walked in and called to the waitress, "One hot chocolate. Extra foam."

Indi smiled and sat across from him. "Hey, Dean. How are you?"

Braddock sat down. "Good. Better. Somewhere around there. You?"

Indi shrugged. "Same."

"Did you visit Brandy again this morning?"

"There are always so many new flowers there," Indi replied. "I bet she loves people still making a fuss over her. Have you seen Jenna lately?"

Braddock cleared his throat and shuffled in his seat. "I drove out to the Joyness Clinic yesterday. They let us walk in the garden, which was nice. Normally I only get to see her through a glass screen."

The waitress placed a hot chocolate on the table, and Indi inhaled the wafting cocoa steam. "That's great Dean. Really great."

Braddock grinned over this third coffee cup. "You're sweet considering Jenna almost killed you."

"I know why she did what she did. She loved Brandy, like the rest of us. I just wish I'd got to know the Jenna I met at Elton's party. We probably had a lot in common." Indi blew on her hot cocoa, hesitant to take the first sip. "Does she ever talk about that stuff?"

"Sure, when she talks at all. She doesn't deny any of it, takes every ounce of blame. She says she didn't want to hurt you, but things had gone too far to turn back." Braddock exhaled. "I didn't even know that she and Brandy were seeing each other. I guess she thought her mother and I wouldn't understand. I can't help feeling like I failed her because of that."

Indi shook her head. "That's not why she killed them, Dean. It had nothing to do with you. She was heartbroken. Teenagers do messed up shit when they're heartbroken." Finally, Indi dared to sip her hot chocolate. She winced, still too hot.

Braddock's grin wilted. "I'll never see my daughter outside of that place for the rest of my life."

The beach materialized in Indi's mind and she saw herself holding the rock over Jenna's head. "At least you don't have to visit her at the cemetery, although I wouldn't mind the company."

Braddock nodded. "Thank you for letting her live."

The words sent a shiver down Indi's spine. No one should ever have to thank her for acting remotely human. "The streets are a lot quieter," she coughed. "All the news crews have gone home. Maybe things will finally start getting back to normal around here."

"It's nice." Braddock scratched his head. "All this talk about me. How are things with you?"

"Getting easier. Mom and I had a proper conversation this morning. I spoke to dad on the phone the other night. He's doing fine, living with my grandparents in Trenton like a loser, but he'll get back on his feet. He always does."

"This tragedy has taken its toll on everyone in Army Bay," said Braddock. "But it's almost summer. That beach will be crawling with happy holidaymakers and laughing kids, and soon people will start forgetting."

Indi took another sip of hot chocolate. "Lucky them." Her phone beeped in her bag, and she checked the text.

Elton: Outside when you're ready.

Indi glanced out the window and saw Elton's car.

"How are things going with that?" Braddock asked.

Indi sighed. "Just friends, for now. My whole life I've been letting someone else be everything to me. Brandy, then Cameron. I never put myself before them, felt like shit whenever I let them down, but ignored the fact they were letting me down every day." She looked at Elton, and their eyes met. He smiled and waved. "I just want to know I can be on my own before I let someone in again."

"That sounds like a wise thing to do," Braddock replied. "Don't let me hold you up. I probably should do some work, anyway. I'm sure there's graffiti somewhere that needs to be reported."

Indi knocked back her hot chocolate and exhaled loudly. "Same time next week?"

Braddock's smile returned. "I'd like that."

Indi stood and left the café, the jingle of the doorbell bidding her farewell. Elton opened her door like always, and Indi slid herself into the leather seat.

"Hey," he said, a grin tugging at the corner of his mouth. "You look nice." Indi frowned, and he raised his arms defensively. "Friends can tell each other they look nice, you know. Just because your mind's in the gutter."

Indi laughed. "Fine. You look nice as well. Thanks for giving me a ride home."

"Always. Who knows when one of these rides home could end with a kiss goodbye. I'm not missing out on that chance."

Elton started the engine and gripped the gear stick, and Indi covered his hand with hers. "Thank you for understanding. I just hope you're still around when I've got my head straight."

"I think a guy should always wait for the girl he's willing to take a bullet for," Elton replied, nodding at his abdomen. "It's just polite."

Elton stepped on the gas and drove toward Appleby Drive. They didn't say much to each other; they didn't need to, and it was wonderful having someone to be silent with. If not for Elton and Braddock, Indi wasn't sure she would have survived these last few weeks. She woke screaming most nights and did her best not to cry in the street when those memories surfaced. Her relationship with her mom was a work in progress at best, but her mother was always there when the nightmares were at their worst, holding Indi like she used to before their world fell apart. Indi wasn't sure if she could ever forgive her father, who had moved out and left town before the case of Brandy Hamilton had officially been closed. The relationship between her dad and Brandy was Indi's last secret. Even after everything that had happened, she still couldn't bring herself to tell Braddock and utterly ruin what remained of her family. Indi often wondered if Jenna would tell him herself. But, after dozens of hot chocolates, not a word. Yet.

The song playing on the radio gave way to a news report, and Indi turned up the volume when she recognized a name.

"The search has been resumed for the body of Sadie Hamilton, which has not been recovered since she was murdered by Jenna Braddock, daughter of police detective Dean Braddock, at Breakers Beach last winter. Boats returned unsuccessful again this afternoon with many Army Bay residents likening the situation to that of her sister, Brandy Hamilton, whose body took weeks to wash up on our once peaceful shoreline. We can only hope that her body is found soon so that our beloved town can lay Sadie, and the horrors of the Army Bay murders, to rest."

Elton flicked off the radio and grumbled. "This thing is never going to end. Even if they find Sadie, some new nightmare will show up. That's how things work in this town." Indi shivered, and Elton was quick to grasp her hand. "I'm sorry. That was a dumb thing to say."

"No. It's fine." Indi smiled through her unease. "After what I've been through, anything else would be a fucking tea party."

Elton parked on the street beside Indi's house. "I'll pick you up for school tomorrow?"

Indi thought for a moment, then exhaled. "I think I want to walk. You know. Routine."

Elton grinned. "I'll see you at school then."

She waved as he drove away, and she shook off the lingering dread that Sadie's name left in her bones. The police hadn't found her that night and, even though the Squad had been exposed for murdering Brandy, and Jenna had been found guilty of her bloody revenge, the puzzle wouldn't be complete until Sadie was buried.

Indi turned and saw her mom at the door. "I've made some popcorn," she called. "Thought we could watch My Sweet Sixteenth?"

"Sure," Indi replied. "Sounds fun."

Her mom's face broke out in a relieved smile. "Great. Can you clear the mail on your way in?"

Indi nodded and flipped open the letterbox, sorting absently through the stack of flyers and generically labelled letters. An envelope at the bottom caught her attention. For India, it read, scribbled by hand. Her heart stopped long enough for her blood to turn cold and her breath to disintegrate to nothing. Indi shivered as she opened the envelope, her trembling fingers seeking its contents. She pulled out the thin string of gold, the heart-shaped pendant resting in the center of her palm. No Ends. Just Beginnings.

Indi spun on her heels, her eyes searching either end of the quiet street.

"India," her mom called. "Come on. Popcorn's getting cold."

Indi found her breath again, forced her heart to beat, and demanded her body stop shaking.

"Coming," she replied, turning her back on Appleby Drive as the sun set over Army Bay.

THE END

ABOUT THE AUTHOR

Jo-Anne Tomlinson was born and bred in the mystical land of New Zealand. No, she wasn't in Lord of the Rings; no, she doesn't know that guy, Steve; yes, she has seen a kiwi and they are both powerful and majestic.

As well as writing, Jo is an inventor, currently designing a sophisticated robot that will spit out a completed manuscript based on a very vague synopsis. Unfortunately, as she hasn't even mastered the TV remote, progress is slow.

When not writing or reading, you'll find her at the netball courts, playing video games, watching terrible movies or eavesdropping on people who argue in malls.

Lastly, she doesn't mind if you call her Jo.

www.ingramcontent.com/pod-product-compliance
Lightning Source LLC
Chambersburg PA
CBHW032031240626
47154CB00003B/867

9780473589141